Praise for Daddy's Girls

'The bonkbuster is back – but hipper, sexier and more intelligent. Debut author Tasmina Perry scores a winner with this dazzling tale of London paparazzi darlings The Balcon Sisters . . . *Daddy's Girls* is the perfect beach read; a sexy guilty pleasure you devour like a caramel Magnum . . . A brilliant antidote to all those girl-seeks-boy-and-shoes chick lit books, this is glittering escapism that gives you a peek into the fabulous lives of the rich and powerful' *Glamour*

'*Daddy's Girls* is the hottest holiday accessory this season. Slick, glossy and gloriously bitchy it's about sibling rivalry and the super-glam Balcon girls – but which one killed Daddy? The bonkbuster is back' *Elle*

'Amid all the romping and camp one-liners, there are tart observations about race, class and family dynamics, too. The perfect beach read' *Marie Claire*

'This glam and glitz, power and corruption romp of a book celebrates the genre of the great big beach read with no holds barred' *Good Housekeeping*

'Is your holiday incomplete without a glamorous, suspend-disbelief read? Then grab this . . . The spirit of The OC bottled in a book' *Cosmopolitan*

'A sizzling summer read brimming with style, sex and sibling rivalry . . . A pacy bonkbuster that you won't be able to put down until its explosive climax is revealed' *Closer*

KT-556-582

TASMINA PERRY

Daddy's Girls

HARPER

Harper
An imprint of HarperCollins*Publishers*
77–85 Fulham Palace Road,
Hammersmith, London W6 8JB

www.harpercollins.co.uk

This paperback edition 2007
2

First published in Great Britain by
HarperCollins 2006

A catalogue record for this book is
available from the British Library

ISBN-13: 978-0-00-722890-4
ISBN-10 0-00-722890-2

Set in Meridien by Palimpsest Book Production Limited,
Grangemouth, Stirlingshire

Printed and bound in Great Britain by
Clays Ltd, St Ives plc

Acknowledgements

Thanks go to my mum, dad, Farrah, Digs and Dan for enduring eighteen months of book talk and still managing to be unfailingly enthusiastic and supportive even when they were probably bored stiff of hearing about it. To Belinda Jones and Marie O'Riordan for giving a complete novice a break into journalism. Big thanks also to Louise Chunn, Polly Williams, Johnny Aldred, PB, Dog, Will Storr, Adrian Broadway, legal eagle John Kelly and Steven Wright for police procedure – any mistakes are mine. Matthew Williamson for Venetia's address, Katerine in Megeve, Deborah Joseph for the house and the adventures during the Cannes film festival and to Basil Charles in Mustique who knew everything there was to know about the island.

To St Thomas's hospital and my lovely midwife team for looking after me when I had a bad pregnancy and a book to write. To the fantastic team at HarperCollins for believing in *Daddy's Girls* and working so hard on it, particularly Wayne Brookes, editor extraordinaire, for his impeccable judgement, support and for making the whole process a great deal of fun. And of course to my agent Sheila Crowley, Naomi Leon, Linda Shaughnessy and Teresa Nicholls at AP Watt.

Lots of love goes to my son, Finlay, the world's cutest alarm clock, and finally my husband and hero John, a much better writer than I am, who parked his own dreams of penning a novel so I could pursue mine. He read and edited the whole manuscript and made countless suggestions to make it so much better. Thanks for everything – this one's for you honey.

To John

PROLOGUE

Christmas Day – the present
He was late. The tick-tock of the ornate grandfather clock reminded them how late. The Balcon sisters were never kept waiting for anything. They glanced independently at their watches – Cartier, Rolex, Patek Phillipe – wondering if their visitor was ever going to show. The four girls all had better things to be doing with their time. Their father was dead, there was a funeral to arrange and they had lives – busy, glamorous lives.

Cate Balcon stared out of the French windows of Huntsford Castle, watching as shadows fell into the dark study, snow settling on the sills. Outside, she saw two orbs of light moving up the long gravel drive.

'I think he's here.'

A few moments later, the heavy oak door to the drawing room creaked open, and David Loftus, a slim, wiry man, with eyes slightly too close together, walked in.

'Mr Loftus,' said Cate, rising to shake his hand. It was cold and dry, with the yellow-stained fingertips of a smoker. 'This is David Loftus, the friend of Daddy's,' she said to the other women. 'Mr Loftus is a writer. Just moved into the

3

village, I believe. Please, David, take a seat.'

Ignoring her, Loftus moved to the huge open fire, rubbing his hands. 'Stinking weather out there,' he said, motioning his head towards the window. 'The car could hardly get down the drive. Do you know there's about a dozen photographers by the gates?'

Venetia Balcon nodded. 'For some reason the press seems to think our father's death constitutes news.'

'And you're surprised by that?' replied Loftus with a sarcastic look. 'You're celebrities. Every hack in the land wants to be in this room today.'

His smile was crooked as he took in the grandeur of the room. The ancient Welsh slate fireplace, the walls lined with leather-bound books. His eyes moved up to the ceiling, all veined like a vintage cheese under the paintwork. Cracked under the magnificent surface. He smiled sourly: just like the Balcon family.

'Well, now you're here, what do you want?' snapped Serena Balcon, who was feeling particularly impatient. Even for an actress, she'd had quite enough drama for one Christmas. She was the one who had found her father's body in the castle's moat the morning after the Christmas Eve party, mouth gaping open, skin frozen and spidered with purple veins. She shuddered at the memory as David Loftus watched her.

She was just as gorgeous in the flesh as on the screen, he thought. In fact, all four of Lord Oswald Balcon's daughters were exactly as he'd imagined them to be. Blonde and beautiful, privilege clinging to them like expensive scent. And that haughty way they carried themselves: they thought they were so special. But now he was the one with the trump card and he was going to savour every sweet minute of it.

Without being asked, he poured himself a Scotch from a

4

Murano glass decanter on the table and swirled it around the tumbler. As a barrister, Camilla Balcon recognized his technique. She'd used it in the courtroom a hundred times before: make your audience wait. Make them nervous.

'I suppose the police have been round?' Loftus asked, taking a swig of his drink.

'And why is it any of your business?' asked Camilla, her voice prickling with hostility.

'Oswald was my friend,' Loftus said. The whisky glistened on his upper lip.

'Oswald was our father,' replied Camilla firmly.

Loftus walked to the window, Huntsford's grounds now just a series of shapes and shadows in the dark.

'Accidental death? Is that what they're saying?'

The girls looked at each other, unsure of how much to tell him. 'Exactly,' Cate said finally, staring into the fire. 'He fell from the ramparts. He was watching the fireworks.'

'Fell?' said David, lifting one dark bushy eyebrow into a heavy arch.

Camilla flashed him a look. 'And you are implying . . .'

Loftus cut Camilla short. 'You do *know* that a lot of people wanted your father dead?'

'He could be a bit difficult,' responded Cate tartly. 'But it's hardly the same thing as being wanted dead.'

'Difficult? Is that what you call it?' he asked, tossing back the last of the whisky.

'Your father was despised by half the people who knew him. No, I don't think your father fell from the rooftop. I believe he was pushed. Deliberately.' He paused. 'I think your father was murdered.'

The fire was spitting and crackling in the background as the sisters looked at him, not daring to speak.

'And I think that one of Daddy's little girls killed him.'

PART ONE

1

Ten months earlier

The Honourable Serena Balcon lay back on the top deck of the Egyptian sailboat, *La Mamounia*, wriggled out of her pink Dior hot pants, and congratulated herself with a lazy swig of a Mojito. *What a good decision*, she thought smugly, looking up to watch the white sails of the boat fan out like two huge butterfly wings. Back home in London's Chelsea, she hadn't been sure whether to accept fashion designer Roman LeFey's offer of a two-day cruise from Edfu to Luxor. As she received more than one hundred social invitations in the average week, she politely declined everything except the most public and most exclusive – or the odd charitable gesture. But this trip was looking very promising indeed. Only thirty of Roman's most fabulous friends had been invited to the strictly A-list jaunt and, not only had Serena been invited, she'd been assigned *La Mamounia*'s Cleopatra Suite, a spacious, exotic cabin at the stern where you could open the shutters and enjoy the receding view from a claw-foot bath. She fished around for a phrase to describe the scene's subtle grandeur. She smiled. It was *appropriate*.

'How incredible is this?' said Tom Archer, Serena's boyfriend, leaning over the boat's railing to get a 360-degree view. One of Britain's most successful, not to mention fabulously handsome actors, the backdrop of the Nile suited him to a T.

'Yes, you look very Agatha Christie, darling,' said Serena with a hint of sarcasm, peering up from under the wide brim of her sunhat. 'But don't lean so far out. There could be piranhas or anything in that filthy water and I'm not jumping in to get you.'

Tom had conditioned himself not to listen to Serena's sniping. Instead he carried on looking at a water buffalo grazing on the opposite bank, next to which an old woman was doing her washing in the tobacco-coloured waters. 'Look at it,' he smiled, 'it still looks so biblical. I keep thinking we're going to see Moses sitting on the bank.'

Serena glanced up casually. 'I thought he was dead.'

'Who?'

'Moses.'

Tom rolled his eyes and Serena caught the gesture. 'I saw that,' she said sourly.

He turned to face her. 'What?'

'You just rolled your eyes at me as if I was stupid.'

'Well, you were being stupid. Of course Moses is dead.'

'I was joking,' she snapped, hiding her face with a copy of Italian *Vogue*. 'But yes, you're right. It is rather special.'

Tom gave his girlfriend a wry smile, predicting the answer to his next question. 'In that case, are you coming with me to Karnak after lunch? Biggest group of temples in the world, apparently. Roman was asking who was up for it. Doubt there'll be a good turn out from this lot, though,' he said, motioning towards the mezzanine deck where the rest of Roman's guests were draining the bar.

'Don't be daft, darling. What do you want to go there

for?' asked Serena, dropping her magazine onto her bronzed knees. 'It will be riddled with flies and tourists. And anyway,' she sighed dramatically, 'I'm too busy thinking about where we can have my birthday party. I mean – nowhere in London has a capacity of a thousand. It's bloody ridiculous.'

'A thousand people,' said Tom, eyebrows raised. 'Do we have that many friends?'

'You don't, no.'

Tom tutted.

'You *don't* have that many friends though, do you?' she glared. 'Then again, you don't seem to like meeting people. You haven't stopped complaining since you arrived and you haven't made the slightest effort to talk to anyone, which is so rude because I could have invited dozens of friends in your place.'

'Maybe you should have.'

'Well, in future I will.'

'Go on then.'

They glared at each other.

'Look, just stop complaining and go and get me another drink from that turbanned chappie,' said Serena finally. 'I want Cristal. I'm parched.'

Tom strode over and snatched the magazine out of Serena's hands. He brought his face down so she could see him under the brim of her hat. 'Well there he is,' he spat, pointing at a dark-skinned man with a tray of drinks. 'Get off your backside and go ask him yourself.'

Serena Balcon and Tom Archer's relationship was in the stage that most therapists refer to as terminal. Held together by familiarity and convenience, even the most innocent conversation quickly became a nettle patch of hostile banter. For Serena, the hostility was brought on by festering disappointment. Tom Archer had started off as a novelty

11

boyfriend; he was cute and uncomplicated, and the complete opposite of the long procession of Serena's former boyfriends – ex-Etonians, Hugh Grant-alikes and floppy-haired trust-fund banker boys. At first, it didn't matter that Tom didn't have *pedigree* – his mother worked in a factory, his father was a gardener: not a hint of good breeding anywhere in that family tree. But he was hot, the sexiest British film star since Jude Law, and he had increased Serena's celebrity stock immeasurably.

Before she had met him on the set of a tiny British indie movie five years ago, Serena had been just a posh blonde who dabbled in modelling and importing pashminas. She was famous in the society pages for being one of the fabulous Balcon girls, but who wanted to be stuck in *Tatler* forever? She wanted a bigger stage, and at Tom's side she got it. The media loved them – the unlikely but classy combination of Tom, the British-born movie star, and Serena, the sexy daughter of a baron, was potent and irresistible. Her impeccable sense of style wasn't lost on the fashion press either. Within weeks of their party debut as a couple, she was US *Vogue*'s 'Girl of the Month' and within the year they were a huge Tom & Serena franchise that was like a golden VIP pass into the world of fame.

Five years later, it wasn't enough. Yes, her family were titled, but much to Serena's annoyance, the Balcons weren't a grand English family like the Marlboroughs, the Wellingtons or the Balfours. Serena wanted a home to rival Blenheim, she wanted the tiny ducal crown on her headed notepaper and the state wedding with an engagement ring in the colours of her national flag, just like the one that Prince Rainier had once presented to Grace Kelly. And the fact that her bloody sister Venetia had managed to marry into semi-royalty tormented her even more. Put simply, Serena wanted more than Tom could give her.

12

She stretched out her long aristocratic legs on her sun-lounger and turned to look at Tom fuming at the rail on the far side of the deck. She smirked. It wasn't all bad. There was no denying he was gorgeous. That square jaw, the cobalt blue eyes framed by jet black lashes, the mussed-up crop of dark hair and that incredible body peeking out from his open white Turnball & Asser shirt. Tom's good looks could blend into any social situation. In a pub, he exuded a handsome-boy-next-door ordinariness. At a country house dinner with her father, Tom's fine English features took on a rather noble, *Brideshead Revisited* quality. And put him on an LA film set and he glowed with that indefinable X-factor that agents the world over wished they could bottle.

Maybe he wasn't so bad . . .

'Sorry for being a bit cranky,' she said softly, curving her pillow-soft lips into a pout. 'Come here . . .'

Despite himself, Tom could not resist the sight of her stretched out suggestively in her Missoni string bikini. He moved sulkily to the sun-lounger. She straddled him, pulling off her bikini top and pressing her naked breasts against his chest. Tom groaned as she tightened her thighs against his.

'How about we go back in the cabin and make up properly . . . ?' she purred in his ear.

'Oh Serena,' he said, struggling between two emotions – lust and anger.

'Serena, Tom. Here you are, you lovebirds!' Roman LeFey's singsong voice pierced the silence. The biggest French designer since Yves Saint Laurent, he was a tall, black man with skin the colour of cocoa, his large belly hidden by a dark green kaftan. 'What are you doing on the top deck in the mid-day sun? Mad cats and the English, hey?'

'Mad cats exactly, Roman,' said Tom, slightly abashed as

Serena swung her feet onto the deck and slipped a tanned foot into a Manolo Blahnik flip-flop, tying up her bikini top without the slightest hint of embarrassment.

'Roman, darling,' she purred, kissing him on both cheeks. 'I was just persuading Tom to be a bit more sociable.'

'Looks like it,' smiled Roman playfully. 'Now lunch is about to be served, so stop hiding yourself and come downstairs,' he said, leading them both towards the spiral stairs which snaked down to the boat's mezzanine area.

'Oh, I can't go down in this tiny thing,' moaned Serena. 'I must go and change.'

She tip-toed across the top deck and slipped into her cabin, the welcome whirl of the ceiling fan cooling her skin and her mood. She threw open the wooden shutters of her closet and began flipping through a rack of chiffon, linen and silk clothes, thinking how exhausting it was to be known for your taste. An ill-considered outfit at even the most casual of gatherings – well, she shuddered to think about it.

Deciding on a tiny white Marni sundress, she stripped naked and pulled the thin fabric up over her long, lean, tanned body, accessorizing with a huge quartz ring and a copper bangle pushed high up her bronzed arm. She scooped her long layered honey-blonde hair up into a top-knot, patted her face with a towel and dabbed her cheekbones with a light, rose-coloured blush that accentuated her big aqua-marine eyes. At twenty-six she knew she was at the peak of her physical beauty: understated, stylish, stunning. Very Julie-Christie-on-holiday, she thought, looking at her reflection in the glass.

She fixed a pair of Ray-Ban Aviators over the bridge of her nose and walked to the mezzanine deck, taking slow, deliberate steps so that her entrance would be fully noted. She paused for a minute, taking in the scene. A crowd of people were drinking flutes of champagne and nibbling at

14

canapés. The air smelt of cumin; a small band in fezzes played traditional Egyptian music by the bar. She moved through the crowd, away from where Tom was talking to a laughing crowd, and grabbed a martini.

'What do you think of the dahabeah?' asked Roman who had appeared by her side and taken her hand.

'The what?'

'My baby!' he laughed. 'A dahabeah is an Egyptian sail-boat.'

'It's amazing,' she said, giving him a playful kiss on the cheek and leaving a ring of pale pink gloss on his skin. 'And I love our suite.'

'I thought you'd like the Cleopatra Suite,' he smiled knowingly, picking up a fig from an overloaded plate. 'I should be in the studio finishing off the collection for Milan,' he added, 'but I can't help being naughty.'

'You're so decadent, darling. That's why I love you,' sighed Serena generously, then instantly became businesslike. 'Now tell me who's here,' she said, craning her long neck to survey the crowd. 'I haven't really been introduced to anyone yet.'

'Well, let's do that now,' he whispered conspiratorially. 'Who would you like to meet?'

She scanned the deck, looking for familiar faces or inter-esting people with whom to network. Someone had told her Leo DiCaprio was coming but she couldn't see him anywhere. Roman could be so random with his invitations, she thought. She spotted a photographer from US *Vogue*, a media mogul's daughter, a Victoria's Secret model. Perhaps it wasn't as AAA-List as she'd been led to believe.

'I don't really recognize anyone,' she smiled, trying to hide her disappointment.

Roman stepped up onto a little platform and looked across the deck, lifting a podgy little finger to identify his guests.

'On this trip, I wanted to invite friends who would appreciate Egypt,' said Roman seriously.

Serena smiled, trying to look grateful.

Roman went through his guests one by one, giving a potted history on each. The Russian princess, the gay interior designer, New York's top session hairdresser, a society florist and a three-Michelin-starred chef from Barcelona. In the centre was Michael Sarkis, the billionaire hotelier. 'Here with the girlfriend,' whispered Roman.

Her interest was waning.

'Now there is Rachel Barnaby,' said Roman, clapping his hands together and pointing to a luscious-looking girl by the bar. 'She's going to be huge. Did you read the cover story in this month's *Vogue*?'

Serena smiled. Of course she had. The dazzling Welsh girl with her long raven hair, alabaster skin and pillowy lips had been touted as the next big thing. Huge talent. Beyond glamorous. Her jaw stiffened just thinking about it.

'Well, everybody's the next big thing in *Vogue*, aren't they,' she replied archly. 'So many people don't quite make it though, do they?'

Roman tapped her on the bottom. 'Don't be unkind,' he smiled. 'You have nothing to fear. She hasn't even got a proper publicist yet – I had to ring her mother to invite her on the cruise.'

Serena smiled broadly. Of course she had nothing to worry about from a pretty, bland teenager. So Rachel Barnaby had snagged a *Vogue* cover. Someone must have dropped out. Serena, on the other hand, had the front-row seat at the shows, the two-million-pound cosmetics contract. And OK, so she hadn't quite scooped a big Hollywood role yet, but those kinky, overweight Hollywood producers preferred malleable trailer-park trash to someone with genuine class and manners. And anyway, she was Serena Balcon. Every

16

move she and Tom made – the holiday frolic, the Ivy supper, the last-minute dash to Harrods for Christmas presents – all made front-page news. Beat that, you Welsh oik, she thought smugly.

Recovering her poise, Serena decided that Michael Sarkis was the best of numerous evils on *La Mamounia*. She didn't know much about him, other than that he was born in Beirut – of an American mum and a Lebanese father, so she had once read – and raised in the Bronx. One of the world's most successful hoteliers, he was a real rags-to-riches entrepreneur who had made a great deal of money peddling gaudy holidays to super-rich Arabs. His hotels were hallmarked by casinos in the lobby, shark tanks in the gardens and gold leaf everywhere; vulgar little places that Serena wouldn't be seen dead in. But still . . . he was filthy rich and he was talking to Rachel Barnaby.

She walked over to where Michael was standing by a long table piled high with Egyptian delicacies. There were tiny honey-glazed baklava, twists of pistachio-infused pastries, piles of white peaches and bowls of flat bread cut into rough chunks. It looked like the Last Supper.

'I hope you're hungry,' smiled Serena, popping a plump, dark-green olive into her mouth and unleashing her most dazzling smile on Michael.

'I hope you're thirsty,' he replied, picking up a bottle of wine and pouring Serena a glass. 'I'm Michael.'

'Serena. Pleased to meet you.'

Michael put out a tanned hand to shake hers. As he gripped her fingers, she noticed what extraordinarily sexy hands they were. Big and tanned with an artisan's squareness about them, the fingertips were smooth and manicured – and the chunky expensive gold watch on his wrist didn't hurt either.

Michael seemed to notice Serena's interest and allowed himself a smile. 'Do you like the wine?' he asked.

'The wine?' repeated Serena. 'Gorgeous. Pétrus, the forty-seven, I think?'

Michael twisted the bottle to read its label. 'You know your stuff.'

'Well, the forty-seven was one of the best vintages of the century for the vineyard. It's even better than the seventy, I think. Really rather wonderful.' She turned to face Rachel Barnaby. 'What do you think? The forty-seven or the seventy?' she asked.

Rachel flushed. 'I can only just about tell the difference between red and white, let alone anything else,' she laughed politely.

'How sweet,' smiled Serena, flashing her a patronizing look. 'Still, you're an actress, not a sommelier.'

Rachel Barnaby suddenly needed the ladies' room and Serena watched her go.

'Nice girl,' said Michael.

'Very sweet and *simple*,' smiled Serena.

Michael looked her up and down with a deep penetrating stare that unnerved her. Slowly running one finger up and down the stem of his glass, he gave her a slow, flirtatious smile. 'So, how are you such an expert on wine?' he asked, taking a sip of his drink.

'My father's a wine buff,' said Serena, unconsciously tracing her lip with her finger.

'Lord Balcon?' asked Michael, lifting a bushy black eyebrow into a scruffy arch.

'That's right, do you know him?'

'Not really,' replied Michael, his brow furrowing. 'He's on the committee of a club in London that just turned me down.'

Serena watched a dark cloud cross his face and realized

instantly that Michael Sarkis was a man not used to being turned down for anything. 'Which one? White's? Annabel's?'

'Hamilton's, actually.'

She picked up a canapé and laughed out loud. 'What do you want to go there for? Full of stiffs my father knows from school. I had you down as a Bungalow 8 or Billionaire kind of guy.'

'I have my own clubs, too,' he smiled, 'but sometimes you want to try something new.'

He moved nearer to her and rested his hand on her hip. It was a sudden and intimate gesture that sparked a jolt of desire through her. Unsettled, she struggled to rationalize it. Wasn't he too old? It was hard to place an age on the dark-haired man. He could be forty, maybe even fifty. She'd hardly call him good looking: the hooked nose was too long, the dark eyes narrow and beady, his head too small for his body; but like so many older, more powerful men she had met through her father, he oozed an arrogant, almost danger-ous allure that was definitely sexy.

'Where are you going after the cruise?' he asked in a way that suggested an imminent offer.

'It's not as hectic as usual,' she smiled coyly, trying to leave herself open. 'Got to do some press for *To Catch a Thief* but, other than that, the world is my oyster.'

'Oh, I heard you were doing that remake.' He smiled appreciatively. 'The Grace Kelly role, of course.'

'Of course,' smiled Serena, flattered that he knew about her work. 'And David Clooney as Roby the handsome jewel thief. It's a great cast.'

'Where are the junkets?'

'Oh, it's tedious. London, New York, LA,' she said, show-ing a fashionable lack of interest at being flown privately all around the world and having half the world's press fawn at her feet.

19

'When you're in LA, give me a ring so we can hook up. Where do you live?'

Serena flushed slightly and pushed a stray tendril of hair behind her ear. 'Actually I live in London at the moment. But I'm thinking of getting a couple of other places: go bicoastal. In the meantime I'm staying at The Viceroy.'

She looked up at his face, which lay somewhere between disappointment and puzzlement.

'What's the matter?'

He smiled. 'It's nothing.'

'No, what?' she repeated almost petulantly.

'I just wondered why you still live in London.'

'What's wrong with that? I live just off Cheyne Walk.'

His look bordered on bemusement. 'I thought a woman like you would be thinking bigger.'

Her brow fell into a sharp crease. 'I don't quite understand.'

Michael paused. His head was bowed and he was smiling to himself, as if in an internal dialogue he was telling a joke.

'I was at dinner last week in LA. My friend Lawrence owns Clerc, the jeweller's. Do you know them?'

She nodded. They had lent her a pair of yellow diamond drop earrings for last year's Oscars.

'They're looking for a "face", a spokesperson, whatever you want to call it. They're talking about the obvious names: Julia, Gwyneth, Catherine. Someone mentioned you and, having met you now, I would say you'd be the perfect choice.' He stroked her cheek lightly. 'You are incredibly beautiful.'

Serena looked away.

'But . . . your name was dismissed for not having – ah, shall we say – international appeal.'

Her mouth immediately curled into a wounded, pained expression. 'For your information I have a lot of visibility

20

in the States,' she retorted, straightening her back. '*Vanity Fair* are desperate to do a profile. I'd hardly say that was parochial.'

Michael spread his hands in a gesture of appeasement. 'My mistake, I just thought you'd like to know.'

'Well, thank you for your opinion,' said Serena frostily. 'Now, I think I'd better go and see Roman.' She turned away, suddenly consumed with a fury about Tom's irrational obsession: to stay living in London. And how dare she be overlooked for a major advertising campaign? She was a huge star. She had breeding – didn't the Americans love all that 'lady of the manor' stuff?

A dark flicker of insecurity exploded in her consciousness.

Serena moved purposefully through the crowd, her mind already working on meetings with agents, real-estate buyers and publicists, her ambition to conquer Hollywood completely refuelled.

2

Three thousand miles away, a 747 touched down on the Heathrow tarmac, wobbling from side to side, its wheels screeching to the ground and forcing business-class passenger and nervous flyer Cate Balcon to reach out and squeeze the hand of her grateful neighbour.

'Sorry,' she smiled at the old man in a Harris tweed jacket, aware that it was the first contact she'd had with him during the entire trip. The man, who had recognized her from Richard Kay's page in the *Daily Mail* as soon as he'd boarded, gave her fingers a little squeeze back. 'Crosswinds,' he smiled kindly, 'nothing to worry about.'

Mildly embarrassed, Cate was on her feet as soon as the engines wound down. That's the beauty of business class, she thought, slipping her Jimmy Choos back on: the quick getaway. She grabbed her leather holdall from the overhead compartment, peered through the window at the grey, drizzling London day and politely pushed her way to the front of the queue, looking at her watch anxiously. She hated the overnight red-eye flights from New York in the working week; they brought her back into London just too late to slip home for a quick sleep, yet too early to blow out the day's work altogether. Still, she thought as she darted for the arrivals hall, if her PA had booked a car and it was waiting for her, she might just get back for the twelve noon production meeting.

'Cate Balcon?' asked a young, tanned driver as Cate charged through the automatic doors.

'Yes. Let's be quick,' replied Cate officiously, handing him her black wheelie case and tying back her long, thick hair with a tortoiseshell clip as she went. 'Alliance Magazines, just off Aldwych.'

As Cate settled back into the leather seats of the black Mercedes, the scenery slipping from airport to suburbs to city, she tried to make some use of the time. The New York shows had been particularly good this season, she thought, opening her notebook to look at her scribblings from the front row. The fashion crowd might coo over the Paris leg of the collections for the spectacular fashion theatrics of Dior and McQueen, but Cate loved New York for its elegant, wearable clothes, and for the ideas it gave her for the magazine. They could do an Edith Wharton-flavoured story spinning off the tweed at Ralph Lauren, a safari shoot based on the linen and leather she had seen at Michael Kors and a Great Gatsby-style feature based on the jewelled coloured tea-dresses at Zac Posen.

She pulled out her Mont Blanc pen and started jotting down more ideas, completely unaware that her handsome driver kept glancing in his rear-view mirror at the striking woman with the red-gold hair on his back seat. Cate was oblivious, immersed as always in her work. She told herself that she worked twice as hard as everybody else because everybody expected Cate Balcon 'the baron's daughter' to be twice as idle.

Although it was true that Alliance Magazines recruited its staff from a shallow gene pool – it was an industry joke that you had to be posh and pretty to get past their human resources department – Cate's appointment to editor of *Class*, the company's upmarket fashion and lifestyle flagship publication, had still fired a vicious whispering campaign in the media industry. The tattlers were outraged. Sure, they argued, there was the odd minor aristocrat at Alliance: the social editor on *Verve* was a countess and there was a viscount's daughter in *Rive*'s fashion cupboard, but no one seriously expected them to become editors. The rumour mill had gone into overdrive. How had Cate become editor at the tender age of thirty-one? Whom had she slept with? What strings had Daddy pulled? It added insult to injury that the photogenic Cate Balcon was famous. British editors weren't supposed to become celebrities – only Anna Wintour had the right to that crown. Cate Balcon simply didn't deserve it, said the gossipmongers. But then anyone who had ever worked with her knew differently.

'Morning Sadie,' she smiled at her curly-haired PA who was sorting through a big lever-arch file outside her office. She glanced around the room at the young attractive women on the phone, rummaging through rails of fabulous clothes or typing away at computers; all noticeably more absorbed in their work the moment Cate arrived.

'Afternoon, Cate,' smiled Sadie, looking up at the clock. 'I think Nicole's taken the liberty of taking the twelve o'clock meeting on your behalf.'

The two women rolled their eyes at each other. 'Typical,' said Cate quietly. 'Better do me a big favour and make me a strong cup of coffee.'

'Cate! You're back,' called Lucy Cavendish from the other end of the office. Lucy was *Class*'s senior fashion editor and the nearest thing Cate had to a friend in the office. The six-foot black girl strode over wearing a thigh-skimming miniskirt and over-the-knee Versace boots, looking every inch one of the supermodels she styled.

'You'll never guess,' gushed Lucy. 'François Nars has said yes to us doing a shoot at his house on Bora-Bora. If you tell me I can't go, I will die.'

'Before we arrange the funeral, let's check the budget with Ciara and we'll take it from there,' said Cate, smiling, as she walked into her office.

Lucy followed her in to catch up on the Fashion Week gossip. 'Did you go to the Zac Posen party? Sorry I missed it but I had to make yesterday's flight.'

'Yes, I went and yes, it was fun,' Cate replied, smiling at the memory.

Lucy gave Cate a mischievous grin. 'I detect gossip, chief . . . So who did you meet? What was he like?'

She motioned Lucy into her office, a corner space on the eighth floor, just high enough to have views over the London Eye and the river. Lucy sat down and Cate flopped into her toffee-coloured leather chair behind her desk, quickly beginning to open the huge pile of mail that had accumulated in her absence. She casually tossed each item in front of Lucy as they spoke. Acres of press releases, stiff white party invitations and parcels of gifts from grateful advertisers and retailers. A Jimmy Choo bag and a white designer scarf, a stiff cardboard bag full of beauty products that Cate doubted would even fit through the bathroom door in her tiny Notting Hill mews house. She pushed the bag towards Lucy. 'Need any of these?'

'I don't need products, I want gossip,' said Lucy. 'Come on, spill.'

Knowing she was not going to get away with distracting her friend, Cate relented with a smile.

'The party was excellent. In this huge, amazing loft in the Meatpacking district. And they gave a great goody-bag, you'll

25

be delighted to hear. A hundred-dollar voucher for some underwear and a bottle of perfume. I've got it in my bag somewhere if you want it.'

Lucy flew a dismissive hand across her face. 'Goody-bags, schmoody-bags! Catherine Balcon, you met a guy, didn't you? Praise Jesus, tell me you've found someone, even if he does live in Manhattan.'

Only Lucy could get away with being so brazen and cheeky. A wide smile spread across Cate's face, her ripe cheeks rounding out like two Cox's apples as she conceded defeat. It was so long since she had met anybody decent. Serena's perma-tanned playboy friends held no interest for her, while straight, single men in London's media world were as rare as hen's teeth. She'd had sex with two men in the last two years and not had a proper relationship in – well, too long. She didn't need a shrink to tell her she had intimacy problems, and the longer it went on, the harder it became. Serena was forever telling Cate that she made herself seem as available as Fort Knox. She was certainly right, except New York had been a bit more productive.

'He was a photographer called Tim. He was nice. He won't ring.' Cate shook her head. 'Satisfied?'

'No. Not satisfied. Getting any personal detail out of you is like drilling for deep-sea oil! If I had met a gorgeous New York hunk, I'd . . .'

Lucy's fantasies ground to a halt as a willowy, size zero blonde in a cream Chloé trouser suit waltzed into the office and sat proprietorially on the arm of the sofa, crossing her legs and dangling a Manolo off her foot. 'So how was New York?' asked Nicole Valentine, her voice hard and nasal.

Cate looked up at her deputy editor, annoyed that she had interrupted a rare moment of confession.

'Hi Nicole, it was fine,' she said. 'Look, Nicole, we're talking . . .'

Nicole ignored Cate and turned her attention to Lucy. 'The fashion cupboard is a tip,' she barked. 'And why have we got racks of clothes in the meeting room? I need it cleaned, Lucy. Like, yesterday.'

Lucy flashed a look at Cate and left. Cate turned to her deputy. 'Nicole. There is no need to talk to a senior member – any member – of staff like that.'

Nicole raised a perfectly threaded eyebrow at her boss. 'As you wish,' she replied defiantly. 'However, we have more important things to worry about.'

'Is that why you started the meeting without me?'

Nicole paused dramatically, playing smugly with the five-carat Asscher-cut engagement ring on her finger. 'I started the meeting because we need to start getting things done. I spoke to Jennifer's publicist last night and it looks like the April cover isn't going to happen.'

Cate felt panic starting to flutter around her body. 'What do you mean, isn't going to happen? We've done the shoot. We've designed the cover. It looks great,' she started, then rubbed her forehead. 'Bloody hell. We go to press in a week. What went wrong?'

'We said we'd give picture approval and when we sent the images over to her publicist – well, they don't like the shoot.' Nicole pursed her lips into a self-satisfied smile that said, 'So, what are you going to do about that?'

Cate looked at Nicole and thought – not for the first time – how much the New Yorker unsettled her. Everything about her deputy, from the platinum-blonde highlights to her Manolo Blahnik heels was hard. Cate was a tough but fair boss: she gave respect and courtesy and received it in the same way from a grateful staff that, she was sure, had been enjoying life on the magazine since Cate became editor a year ago. But her relationship with Nicole was awkward and competitive and she regretted the day she'd hired her from *W* magazine in New York. Nicole was cold, efficient and ambitious, and it was that ambition that scared her, knowing how often it went hand in hand with deceit and disloyalty.

Sadie popped her curls round the door. She was holding a steaming china mug. 'For my jet-lagged editor,' she said, placing it on a flower-shaped coaster on the desk. 'And William Walton has called three times this morning. He said could you pop up to see him as soon as you've settled in?'

In the six months since Walton's appointment to the board of Alliance Magazines from a large advertising and marketing agency in Chicago, Cate had had very little to do with him. As his background wasn't editorial, he showed no interest in *Class*, apart from the sales figures at the end of every month and any free tickets for the opera, Formula One or art-gallery openings that the features department could throw his way.

'Really?' said Cate, feeling a flutter of alarm. 'What does he want?'

She caught the look on Nicole's face, which was one of someone who'd just been given an early birthday present.

'I don't know,' said Sadie with a sympathetic look, 'but his secretary is starting to call every five minutes.'

All alone in the lift, Cate stared at the buttons and wondered what to say to Walton. Despite the sinking feeling in her stomach, she knew she should feel confident: if the reaction she'd got in New York was anything to go by, both the readers and advertisers were finally getting it. She'd spent twelve months redesigning the magazine, and had by sheer strength of will changed *Class* from a dated, pompous society magazine to a glossy fashionable read for smart, successful women. The catwalk shows had been a wonderful vindication; a raft of prestige advertisers who so far had only ever appeared in *Vogue* in the UK had suggested that *Class* would be added to their advertising schedule in the fall. That should please Mr William Walton, thought Cate, as the bell pinged for the top floor.

She walked through the double doors and down the cream corridors lined with giant-sized magazine covers, until she reached an unsmiling redhead behind a computer.

'Is he busy?'

'Go straight in,' replied the woman, not looking up from her computer screen.

William Walton's office was unlike anything else Cate had seen in the Alliance building. Interior-designed at great expense, it was decked out in walnut wood and shades of taupe instead of the usual Formica and magnolia walls that everybody else had to put up with. The man himself was sitting behind a wraparound leather-top desk. His self-possessed presence filled the room. Powerfully built, with wiry black hair, Walton's expensive bespoke clothes masked the fact that he had got to the top the hard way. The very hard way. When, twenty years ago, the young William had beaten thousands to win a scholarship to Yale, he had assumed it would pave the way to privilege. He was mistaken. The doors to American society's elite were still very much closed to a boy from the southside of Chicago and, instead of spending his summers making contacts in Connecticut country clubs, he was forced to fight his way through the mailrooms of Grey's and Ogilvy & Mather to achieve the status he craved. But he had made it. Power and privilege, he'd learned, were things to be won by hard work and cunning, not born or bought into. All of which explained precisely why William Walton was looking at Cate Balcon with such distaste.

'I wanted to see you as soon as you got in,' began Walton. 'I hear we have a few problems.' Walton paused, his dark, feral eyes sizing her up. He'd seen her before, of course, and read about her in the society pages she seemed to monopolize along with her sisters. But alone and face to face for the first time, Walton was impressed despite himself. She might not be a patch on that actress sister of hers, but Cate Balcon was still a knockout. The firm, slightly sulky rosebud mouth, the wavy, dark-golden hair flowing over that elegant neck. And then there was the curvy body, no doubt considered plump by the stick-thin Zone-dieted women he'd dated in Chicago, but when he imagined it naked and wet under his shower, her plump lips round his cock, swallowing him whole . . . He stopped himself and shifted in his seat, motioning her to sit in one of the hard black leather chairs in front of him.

'As you know, Cate, magazines are a business,' he began. She nodded hesitantly. 'Of course. I had lots of compliments in New York about how we've really improved the magazine. The advertising is looking very promising.'

William didn't seem to notice what she was saying as he flicked through an issue of *Class* with what looked suspiciously like disdain.

'Magazines are a business,' he repeated. 'And I was brought into Alliance to improve that business. They are not simply entertainment, they are a commodity, and to be honest with you, Cate, I don't think the numbers *Class* is selling at the moment really warrants the investment.'

Cate immediately realized that this was not going to be a friendly, 'How were the New York shows?' catch-up. She needed to do some firefighting.

'With respect, we're showing a definite turnaround in circulation,' she said as calmly as she could. 'If anything, William, since I arrived at Alliance, we've improved the *Class* business by at least fifteen per cent. We've stopped the circulation rot and improved advertising volume and yield.'

'I wouldn't call a hundred thousand sales a month show-stopping business,' interrupted Walton tartly, throwing the magazine down on the desk.

'Well, it's not the *News of the World*, no. But it's better than both *Tatler* and *Harper's*,' said Cate.

Walton steepled his fingers in front of his mouth and regarded her coolly. Cate Balcon was clearly no pushover. But then neither was he.

'I suspect, however, that the magazines you mention all have a cover for their April issue.'

The hairs on Cate's neck began to tingle. She could practically see Nicole Valentine's smile as she whispered into Walton's ear. She squeezed her nails into her palm and decided that she'd fire Nicole this afternoon and hang the consequences.

Cate took a deep breath. 'So someone's told you about Jennifer. I just heard about that this morning, too. It's not ideal, but it happens. I've actually got something in reserve,' she said, her cheeks flushing lightly at the deliberate lie. But Walton wasn't watching. He'd got up from his seat and had turned his back on her to stare at the London skyline, absently rolling a golf ball around in his palm.

'I am not interested in the micromanagement of your magazine, Cate,' he replied flatly. 'A picture of my grandmother could go on the cover if you could guarantee me sales. What I am interested in is revenue. I think *Class* should be a more mass-market, more profitable magazine. I don't want to be outselling *Tatler*, I want to be outselling *Glamour*.' He turned back towards Cate and banged the golf ball onto the desk. 'I want to be outselling *everyone*.'

Cate was used to being bullied by her father – she'd put up with bullying then and would put up with it now.

'A fine ambition, of course,' she said evenly, carefully smoothing down her skirt. God, she was shaking, she

31

thought, looking at her hands. She hated confrontation and tried to imagine what her sister Camilla would do in her shoes.

'But you'll be aware that *Class* magazine is not published on a mass-market model. We are advertising rather than circulation driven, and I think you'll need a massive repositioning of the product to change that.'

He looked at her, smiling cruelly. 'Exactly, Cate, exactly. So you'll understand completely what I'm about to say.'

The bile was beginning to rise in Cate's throat and she was finding it impossible to open her mouth to speak. 'Which is what?' she finally croaked.

Walton wasn't to be hurried. He'd pictured scenes like this every time he'd been humiliated by a toffee-nosed Ivy-Leaguer in college, and he always enjoyed every second of revenge when it came. He walked around his huge desk, perched on the corner and looked down at Cate.

'The Honourable Catherine Balcon,' he said with a superior smirk, and Cate shivered, sensing that the fatal blow was about to be delivered. 'While it's obviously wonderful to have someone of your high profile editing one of our titles, I have to wonder what it really brings to the party. If *Class* is going to be more populist, more popular, I need someone at the helm more in touch with the Great British Public. Not someone whose daddy owns a castle.'

'What a ridiculous thing to say,' retorted Cate angrily. 'My background has nothing to do with whether I can be a good, commercial editor or not. And anyway, if you got to know your employees better, you'd find out that I'm not the out-of-touch aristocrat you clearly think I am!'

Walton took in the long curvy legs hiding under the navy wool pencil skirt and actually began to regret the missed opportunity of getting to know Cate Balcon better. 'You're just not my person for the job, Cate,' he said coldly. He stood up and briskly walked back to his seat. 'I have immediate plans for *Class* magazine,' he continued, already starting to flick through his mobile-phone menu for the number of his lunch date. 'And I'm afraid that you're not going to be part of them.'

Cate stared at him, her head starting to feel dizzy. It had all happened so fast. 'What are you talking about?'

'In plain Queen's English, Miss Balcon, you're fired. With immediate effect.'

Cate felt paralysed. She was unable to move from her chair.

'On what grounds? That my DNA is wrong?'

Walton didn't seem to hear. His attention had already wandered to something on his computer screen.

'Fine,' said Cate in a quiet, controlled voice, rising unsteadily and moving towards the door with dignity. 'You will, of course, be hearing from my solicitors.'

William Walton glanced up and took one last look at the long legs exiting his office. 'Get them to call my secretary.'

3

Karnak was spectacular. Even though Tom had wanted a siesta after the enormous lunch and huge amounts of booze he'd had on *La Mamounia*, he was glad he'd made the effort to join the very small group of guests visiting the temple complex on the outskirts of Luxor. He wandered through the huge sandstone pillars, the long shadows dancing between the tall shapes stretching into a cornflower blue sky. He smiled to himself. Celebrity had a habit of making you feel so tall, so special, but here he felt like an inconsequential speck. He could stay here all afternoon, he thought. The last thing he wanted was to get back to Serena, even though it had irked him over lunch to see her talking to that slimy Yanky letch.

Serena. The first two years of their relationship had been wonderful. Tom had thought her cranky, dramatic ways were perversely adorable. Having had little contact with the upper classes before he'd met her, he assumed that's how they were: self-obsessed and spoilt. He'd never once considered it might just be Serena's personality. But now he was convinced that she had ice water running through her veins. While he understood it – the Balcon family were clearly seriously dysfunctional, irritation rather than affection was the over-whelming emotion he felt for her. He had even started fancying the barmaid at the Pig & Piper back in the Cotswolds village where he kept a house. He liked her wonky teeth, her fleshy breasts and the pink blushing cheeks when she served him his pint. Above all, he liked her warmth.

Then the Sheffield lad in Tom caught himself. *Was he mad?* He lived with Serena Balcon! One of *People* magazine's Fifty Most Beautiful People, or so he had read at the airport newsagent. They were right, of course: she was stunning. From the moment he'd seen her on her trailer step reading a script, her feet bare on the ground, her fair hair blowing gently in the breeze, he had thought she was the most fabu-lous-looking creature he had ever seen. He would never tire of looking at Serena, but he was sick to death of listening to her – those plummy tones, the inane babble. Tom had struggled through a tough comprehensive, to university, to RADA, clawing his way up, desperate to improve himself, so he couldn't quite believe he was living with a woman whose idea of current affairs were the party pages in *Vanity Fair*.

He flicked at a fly buzzing around his face. *So why couldn't he leave her?*

The thought had crossed his mind a hundred times. But when he really imagined life without her, he was caught between a sense of sheer relief and horrible insecurity. What would happen to Tom without Serena? They were as insepa-rable as Siamese twins. He shuddered despite the heat.

'Tom Archer! Come and join the group, you naughty thing.'

Jolene Schwartz was a brazen, heavily tanned fifty-some-thing Texan who had married well and divorced better. She came sashaying towards him, twirling a frilly white parasol above her like a deep-fried Dolly Parton.

'Just coming,' called Tom, getting to his feet. 'Are we leaving?'

'We were supposed to meet at the Great Hall twenty minutes ago to head back to the boat.' She wagged her finger at him at the same time as fixing him with a flirtatious smile. 'I'm going to have to put you over my knee.'

Unconsciously, Tom found himself looking at Jolene's legs and her unnaturally smooth knees – an obvious product of the latest surgery craze that was sweeping New York. He tore his gaze away and gave a weak, cracked smile.

'I'd better get a move on then, hadn't I?'

They walked as quickly as the hot sun would allow to the entrance, where a black Range Rover was waiting for them. Tom wedged himself into the cream leather back seat between Jolene and Roman's boyfriend, Patric, a handsome, grey-haired, softly spoken architect from Provence.

'So, who are you going to introduce me to on the boat?' said Jolene playfully to Patric as the car began to weave through traffic towards the docks. 'I haven't worked out who's single yet.'

'What about Frédéric?' suggested Patric playfully.

She spluttered, 'But he's queer!' She looked at Patric's mock-crushed expression and quickly corrected herself. 'Sorry, sorry. I love gay men. I just don't want to date one.'

'What about Michael Sarkis?' asked Tom. 'I'm sure he's not gay.'

Jolene looked at him and giggled. 'Now honey, that's where I draw the line. In New York they call him the cat burglar. Always after other people's pussy,' she giggled with a smoker's rasp. 'I don't know anyone he hasn't screwed.'

Patric shifted uncomfortably in his chair as Jolene smiled at him.

'No, what I want is someone like this one,' she said, squeezing the top of Tom's knee.

Catching Tom's frozen expression, Patric tried to change the subject. 'Did you enjoy Karnak, Tom?' he asked. 'It's sometimes good to get away from that boat, yes?'

'Yes, the *Mamounia* was getting a little busy,' said Tom diplomatically.

'I know,' replied Patric sympathetically, 'I'm the less social one in our partnership, too. Roman, he loves to throw parties even when he should be working. But me . . .' He trailed off.

'Sounds a lot like our household,' smiled Tom, trying to edge away from Jolene's thigh.

'How is life with you and Lady Serena?' chimed in Jolene, keen not to be left out of the conversation.

'She's not a lady.'

'So I've heard.'

Tom smiled thinly. 'No, I mean that in England a baron's daughter has the title "The Honourable". A lady is like a duke or earl's daughter or something.'

'Lady or not, she's so beautiful,' said Patric approvingly. 'I know Roman can't stop giving her clothes. She wears everything so incredibly. I think she may be becoming the ambassador for the line this year.'

'More clothes,' laughed Tom, looking out of the window at the chaotic traffic. 'Our house can't stand any more clothes! I mean, did you know she has nearly a thousand pairs of shoes! They have their own room where they sit on these little carousels. Why does anyone need shoe carousels?'

'If you were a woman, you'd know,' laughed Jolene, touching his arm lightly.

'This is life with the beautiful,' shrugged Patric. 'Wonderful, but high-maintenance.'

Tom laughed to himself. Patric didn't know the half of it. Serena was broke and it was he who was supporting her jet-set lifestyle. She had got though a small trust fund left to her by her mother years ago and there was little obvious income from the Balcon family trust. Old money? *No* money was more like it, if you listened to the rumours about Oswald's financial difficulties. And while Serena still earned something in the region of two million pounds a year in advertising contracts and film roles, her expenditure was enormous: the Cheyne Walk townhouse, the six-thousand-pound-a-year John Frieda highlights, the agent and publicist's fees, the Dior couture clothes, the weekly manicures, pedicures and facials – the list was endless and her tastes were expensive. 'Keeping up with the Jemimas,' she called it. So it was left to Tom to mop up the bills for the Necker Island holidays, the Hermès bags, the San Lorenzo suppers and the brand new Aston Martin. Having been brought up in a house where everyone knew the price of a loaf of bread, and not knowing whether his movie career would last another three or thirty years, the level of spending was making him nervous. It was a high-maintenance lifestyle indeed – for both of them.

As they arrived at the dock, the sun was much lower in the sky, smudging the blue with purple and apricot, and criss-crossing the walnut decking of *La Mamounia* with long grey shadows. As Tom walked up the gangplank into the bowels of the boat, he could immediately see Serena through the crowd. For a moment he stopped to watch her. Her head tipped back laughing, the blonde hair spilling down her back, one strap of her sundress falling off her shoulder leaving it round and bare like a scoop of ice cream. He began to smile, then noticed that Serena's hand was on Michael's shoulder, while the playboy's fingers were reaching like a predator's to touch her arm. Tom's stomach tightened. The mixed feelings he'd been having all afternoon – regret, pity, sadness – all crystallized into one clear emotion. He grabbed a large gin from a passing steward and drank it in one gulp, striding over to where Serena and Michael stood laughing.

As Tom approached, Michael walked away towards the bar.

'Where've you been?' demanded Serena immediately.

'I've been to Karnak with Patric and Jolene. Not that you would have noticed since you've been glued to that play-boy since I left.'

'Oh, was it fascinating in the desert, professor?' taunted Serena sarcastically, her words slightly slurred. 'You must tell me all about it.' Her eyes looked glassy and her voice had the edge of aggression that came with cocaine.

'Let's go to the cabin,' he said, struggling to control his voice, 'I need to change.'

'And why would I want to come and watch that?' said Serena mockingly. 'Anyway, I'm talking to Michael, and he's getting us drinks.' They both looked over to the bar where Michael was collecting two flutes of kir royale.

'Come on, we're going,' said Tom, grabbing her arm to pull her away. The drink and heat had hit him and his touch was a little too heavy.

'Get off me,' Serena yelped, pulling her arm away and rubbing her bare skin. 'I'm talking to Michael. He's invited us to stay at his boutique hotel in the Valley of the Kings after the cruise. At least he has some manners.'

Tom brought his face close to hers. 'We're not going to any more sodding hotels,' he hissed, 'particularly not his. You know I've got a meeting in London on Wednesday. I'm not missing it on account of him.'

Serena's eyes blazed defiantly. 'Well, I want to go.'

Tom laughed cruelly. 'Oh, I bet you do.'

'What do you mean by that?'

'You want to fuck him, don't you?'

'What did you say?' spat Serena incredulously.

'You. Want. To. Fuck. Him,' said Tom, his voice turned hard and emotionless.

Serena gasped, her face contorting into disgust. 'You are revolting,' she said quietly, her voice a malevolent whisper. 'You can take the boy out of the gutter . . .'

Tom felt his heart pound so fiercely he thought it would explode. Never before had she seemed so snobbish, so shallow, so ugly.

At that moment Michael appeared by her side, sipping the kir. 'Have you told Tom about coming to my hotel?' he asked, as if it was a little secret between them.

Tom looked him up and down, taking in the white shirt with the black tufts of hair creeping over the collar, the sweating narrow face, the veins bulbously protruding from the side of his forehead. What can she see in him? he thought for a moment, then became angered by the very notion.

'OK, let's go,' said Tom, taking Serena's arm again. Serena was outraged now and shrugged him off, edging closer to Michael. Tom bridled as he watched Michael's fingertips brush against the side of her thigh.

'So you'll both come for a couple of days?' said Michael, misunderstanding. 'It'll be fun.'

'I wasn't talking to you,' said Tom, his head now spinning.

Michael placed a hand on Tom's shoulder in a placatory gesture. 'Come on, it's a very beautiful place, and I know you will love the Presidential Suite.'

'Get off me. We're going to our cabin,' snapped Tom, reaching for Serena's arm again.

Michael stood back as Tom and Serena's eyes locked. 'Fine,' said Tom finally, dropping his hand, 'you go where you want.'

'I think she wants to stay here,' said Michael, interrupting the moment between them.

'I don't give a fuck what you think,' said Tom, turning towards Michael, his voice full of anger.

'I think you'd better come with me,' said Michael, turning to lead Serena away to the bar.

Before he knew what he was doing, Tom turned and landed a stinging punch on the side of Michael's face.

Michael stumbled back onto the deck, his glass smashing. Serena screamed. Instantly, a crowd gathered around them, mouths agape. The band had stopped playing and an embarrassed mutter rang around the crowd. Roman LeFey pushed his way through the crowd and crouched down to help Michael from the deck. He turned to look at Tom, his eyes full of disappointment.

'I'm sorry,' whispered Tom, rubbing his sore knuckles. 'I'm sorry.'

'I think you'd better go,' said Roman softly.

Tom looked at Serena desperately, but she refused to meet his gaze.

Feeling more alone than he had ever felt in his life, he turned and walked to the back of the boat. Grasping the rail and hoisting himself up, he looked back for Serena once more. Then he jumped into the waters of the Nile.

4

Camilla Balcon felt the enormous rush of orgasm wash over her and bit her lip to muffle her moans of desire. Even so, the sound of sexual climax still filled the room as Nat Montague thrust deep inside her one last time, shouting out with pleasure as he collapsed onto his girlfriend's naked breast.

'Will you please be quiet,' hissed Camilla, pushing him away until his cock slid gently from inside her. She had felt a real illicit thrill when Nat had grabbed her on the four-poster bed as she had shown him around her old room in the east wing of Huntsford Castle, but now Camilla was annoyed that she'd allowed him to seduce her. It was the only time she ever lost her poise. Nat wasn't to be so easily brushed off, however, lowering his head to seek out her hard, round, raisin-like nipple with his tongue.

'Scared someone will hear us?' he teased, kissing his way down her long slender body.

Nathaniel Montague, one of London's most eligible bachelors, had bedded half the models and society girls in the capital, but Camilla Balcon was something else. Her honey-blonde hair, usually held up in a prim ballerina bun, was now spread wantonly across the pillow, surrounding an angular but striking face still flushed from her pleasure. He loved her contradictions, the way Camilla was outwardly a severe, upright career woman but in bed was bold, hungry and passionate. Many times he had met her after work in Lincoln's Inn, just to seduce her in the close confines of her legal chambers, tearing off her starched suit and taking her across her wide desk, papers and files flying. He felt his groin stir at the thought and reached for Camilla again, a sly grin on his face, but Camilla slapped his hand away.

'No, Nat. We're supposed to be downstairs for dinner in ten minutes and I want to take a bath,' she said, her lily-white buttocks perched on the end of the bed, ready to leave. 'Do you want to use the shower room next door?'

Nat wrapped his chunky rugby player's arm around her waist and pulled her back. 'Why don't we just go down reeking of sex?' he whispered into her ear. She pulled away and threw a white fluffy robe at his head.

'Go down smelling of sex?' She laughed harshly at the suggestion. 'Daddy would just *love* that!'

'I thought you didn't care what he thought,' said Nat, his ardour finally cooled.

'I don't, but you know how the slightest thing can set him off.'

Sighing, Nat bounced off the bed, pulled on the robe and made for the door, rubbing himself against Camilla's naked body as he passed her. 'You'll be begging me for it later, baby, you know you will,' he smirked.

As Nat's footsteps faded away down the polished wood of the hallway, Camilla walked over to the claw-foot bath and slid one leg into the water that had now gone cool. The bathroom was dark, lit only by two candles that sent an eerie shadow of her naked body dancing up the rich red paintwork.

I thought you didn't care what he thought?

She sunk down into the tepid water and soaped her skin vigorously, irritated by Nat's observation. If Nat was so right about her ambivalent feelings towards her father, why was she here? She was almost thirty, a strong, intelligent, independent woman, old and wise enough to recognize that she despised her father's company. Unlike her sisters Venetia and Cate, who seemed to feel obliged to visit Huntsford no matter how bad Daddy's behaviour became, Camilla Balcon was ambitious, ruthless, tough – that's how she'd been described in a recent *Legal Week* article – and, as one of the most feared young barristers in London, the word 'sentimental' didn't even enter into her vocabulary. As far as Camilla was concerned, the only positive thing her father had given her was a desire to get away from his crumbling castle and the drive to succeed in spite of what he had done to her – to all the girls – when they'd lived under this godforsaken roof.

So what did bring her back? And why was she feeling so on edge? Of course, deep down, Camilla knew the reason; she had spent years suppressing it, pushing it down into a corner of her mind where it couldn't do her any harm. But here, where the memories were still so fresh . . . Suddenly a rush of dark images filled Camilla's head and she squeezed her eyes tight, not allowing herself to think of the one thing that pulled her back to Huntsford. She rubbed soap into her face, blew the bubbles from her nose and submerged her head under the water before she could think about it any further.

Downstairs in Huntsford's Great Hall, Lord Oswald Balcon, tenth baron of Huntsford, paced around irritably, glancing at his watch in the vain hope that there might be time to take one of the classic cars parked outside the house for a quick spin. Driving hell-for-leather through his Sussex estate, hood down on the car, the precision engine muffled by the wind in his ears was the only time he really felt happy these days. Certainly bombing through the grounds at top speed was far preferable to the pointless socializing he was about to subject himself to that evening.

For years Oswald had been the Great Entertainer, throwing open his doors for huge Christmas balls or shooting weekends – kings, dukes and celebrities had all visited Huntsford during those glittering decades. But of late playing host had been far more inconvenient than enjoyable for Oswald, not to mention expensive. His friend Philip Watchorn in particular had impeccable and gluttonous taste in wine, and Oswald knew that by Sunday his reserves of Dom Pérignon, Châteauneuf du Pape '58 and vintage Rothschild would be gone.

He caught sight of himself in the long looking glass above the fire and allowed himself a smile. He was sixty-five but looked fifty. Still a handsome man, he thought, adjusting the collar of his Ede and Ravenscroft dinner shirt. His tall frame was still strong and wiry from years of competitive polo, his eyebrows were thick and grey but distinguished, framing bright blue eyes that, in his glory days, had frozen enemies and melted admirers.

Thoughts of the old days reminded Oswald of the profile piece the *Telegraph* had run on him last month and he frowned, swilling his Scotch around in its tumbler. What Oswald had thought was going to be a glowing piece about his life in politics had turned into a hatchet job describing him as 'the robber baron who frittered away the family fortune on harebrained schemes, gluttony and excess.' He had briefly considered legal action before he realized he really didn't want certain details of his life being dredged up in court. But what had annoyed him more was the way the piece had dwelt so much on his daughters. He could still remember one particularly galling sentence: 'Queens of the scene, the Balcon Girls are Huntsford's crown jewels and saviours of the Balcon legacy.'

It was a raw nerve for Oswald. He still hadn't pinpointed the exact moment when his daughters had become a national obsession. There had always been some interest in the Balcon family, of course. His wife Margaret had been a beautiful model and a sixties' icon – an aristocratic foil to Twiggy's East End quirks. Wealthier than Jean Shrimpton and David Bailey, better-looking than John Paul and Talitha Getty, Oswald and Maggie Balcon had been society's power couple. But Maggie's death, shortly after Serena's birth, had dulled some of the Balcon glamour. It wasn't until Serena's career took off that the media began to take an interest again, especially when they realized that Serena was one of four beautiful, successful sisters.

As if those ungrateful wenches had done anything except spend his money.

The whoop of a helicopter's blades snapped Oswald from his thoughts and he peered out through the long windows to see Philip Watchorn's ink-black helicopter settling on the lawns. Typical of Watchorn to arrive in such a vulgar fashion, he thought. He'd better not scratch my cars with his damn rotors. Flash bloody Jew.

'Philip. Jennifer. So glad you could make it.' Oswald embraced Watchorn at the door and gave Philip's wife the benefit of his broadest smile. A fellow *homme du monde* during the sixties and seventies, Oswald had met Philip Watchorn on their first day at work at a city stockbroker's. The two men had been close friends throughout those heady years, cutting a swathe through the miniskirts of the 'swinging' nightclub scene before Oswald inherited his title and Philip disappeared to become one of the most formidable corporate raiders of the eighties.

'We've brought Elizabeth with us for the evening, hope you don't mind,' said Philip as a short redhead in a velvet suit bustled through the door. Oswald groaned inwardly. The Watchorns had a terrible habit of bringing Jennifer's younger sister with them to social occasions, apparently under some deluded matchmaking pretext. It wasn't that he resented the sentiment; after Margaret had passed away, he had been more than open to the possibility of marrying again, but in his mind there were two types of women that circled in the top flight of society – beautiful, well-off girls of one's own station whom one could marry and who might well be useful in terms of money or land. And then there were the cheap, gold-digging sluts who wanted to marry you and take you for every penny. Elizabeth was very much in the latter category. Just like Philip's wife, Jennifer, in fact: a former air-hostess turned society wife. *Cheap whores, the pair of them.*

'Dear Elizabeth, how wonderful to see you again,' gushed Oswald, taking the woman's brown leather suitcase and handing it to Collins the butler.

'You ladies go and settle in. Collins will show you where you're sleeping and I'll see you for a drink in a minute.'

Philip put an arm around Oswald's shoulders and led him towards the drawing room. 'So, tell me. Who's up this weekend?'

'Charlesworth, Portia, Venetia, Jonathon. Camilla and her chap Nathaniel Montague. I think you know his father? Eleven, including myself and Catherine,' said Oswald, as Collins appeared at their side with a silver tray bearing two generous Scotches.

'Eleven? Not like you, Oz. What happened to "the more the merrier"?'

The more the merrier! Did Watchorn think he was *made* of money? Besides, Oswald was keen to keep numbers down after the *Telegraph* piece. He didn't want people accepting his hospitality and sniggering at him behind their dessert spoons.

'Just a select group tonight, old boy,' said Oswald, slapping Philip on the back a little too hard. 'Speaking of which, where the bloody hell are my children . . . ?'

Venetia Balcon pulled up outside Huntsford Castle in her BMW four-by-four. She was in a very bad mood. Her husband Jonathon hadn't said one word since she'd scraped the car's wing mirror against a stationary truck twenty miles back, and she knew better than to force conversation when he was in this frame of mind. Cate had been no help either, sitting sullenly in the back seat for the entire ninety-mile journey. And they were late. Venetia hated being late for anything, especially one of her father's soirées – she knew she'd get blamed for their tardiness, even though she'd sacrificed having an eyebrow wax and an Alpha Beta peel to be early.

Walking into the family dwelling only served to depress her further. To most eyes, Huntsford would be an incredible place to call home. From the outside it was a rambling, honey-coloured stone wedding-cake of a building, with romantic castellated turrets, long mullioned glass windows and a vast oak front door approached by a sweeping arc of gravel drive. On either side of the building sprawled hundreds of acres of grounds, from woodland studded with foxgloves to open fields of lush grass – but inside the castle it was a different story. Despite the Old Masters that lined the panelled walls, and the hand-painted frescoes and chandeliers that decorated the ceilings, Huntsford just made Venetia shudder. As one of the country's most successful interior designers, she saw the house as gloomy and tired and getting more faded by the visit. The once-lustrous walnut panels were cracked and mottled like old leather, the plasterwork was crumbling, the French crystal chandeliers hung unpolished and dull. Huntsford had become a shabby shadow of the immaculate palace it had once been. Venetia, whose career had been built on the sympathetic renovation of old family houses, had made countless offers to redesign her beloved home but, so far, her father was resistant to any modification of the place, apparently content to let it slip quietly into decay.

As she stood looking around the room, Oswald appeared at her side and placed a chilly hand on her shoulder. Venetia flinched at his touch, turning away to disguise her discomfort. 'So you've finally decided to make it,' he said tartly.

'Sorry we're late,' she said, pushing her hair behind her ears. 'Jonathon didn't finish till six. Then we had to pick Cate up from home. The traffic was terrible.'

'It would have helped if she hadn't almost crashed the car on the way over,' muttered Jonathon.

Oswald immediately sided with his son-in-law. 'Yes, Jonathon, that can't have helped, can it?'

The chilling disapproval of a childhood scolding flashed before Venetia.

'And what's wrong with Catherine?' Oswald said tartly, pointing to his other daughter who was taking the bags out of the car boot. 'Face as long as a racehorse's. Tell her to perk up, can't you? I need her to entertain Jennifer Watchorn and her ghastly sister with some London tittle-tattle. Perhaps that magazine job of hers is actually good for something.'

'Oh actually, Daddy,' Venetia said quickly, 'Cate has had a rather horrid day at work today, so if you could keep away from shop talk . . . ?' She caught a whiff of his breath and immediately regretted her words. Her father was obviously in a belligerent mood and whisky always roused the devil on his shoulder. She certainly didn't want to give him any more ammunition. She was just about to turn back to her father when her attention was caught by a shimmering blonde coming down the stairs. 'Camilla!' cried Venetia and Cate together as they both ran up the stairs to hug her.

Oswald stood watching them, his anger building. *Saviours of the Balcon legacy indeed!* He snorted into his whisky. Look at them! Venetia: airhead, a silly puppy desperate for attention. Cate, uptight and unsmiling, always on that bloody mobile phone of hers, as if women's bloody magazines were high finance or some such, while Camilla was defiant, truculent . . .

With the exception of Serena – whose beauty and A-list celebrity secretly delighted him – he was increasingly disappointed in his girls. Every time they came down it was the same: clinging together like monkeys, gossiping and giggling in the corner without a thought for their father who had raised them with pain and sacrifice. Oswald took another pull of his whisky and looked across the room to where Jonathon and Nat were greeting the final guests, Oswald's old friends Nicholas and Portia Charlesworth. At least Venetia and Camilla had had some success in attracting the right partner, conceded Oswald. Montague was from an established family – new money, of course, but he seemed solid enough – and Jonathon – von Bismarck, well, he was definitely cut from the right cloth. Of course he had recognized the ruthless City player as a scoundrel from the first. He had heard wild rumours about Jonathon: his exotic sexual preferences, the endless stream of discreet and not-so-discreet affairs. But Jonathon came from a long line of Austrian aristocracy, and that made him a useful addition to the Balcon line – whatever his extra-curricular activities.

Collins the butler clanged a gong and dinner was served in the Red Drawing Room. Rich scarlet curtains framed high

French windows, the walls, hung with a rose-pink damask, blushed apricot in the candlelight, while the enormous marble mantelpiece was lined with photos of Oswald posing with various dignitaries: Thatcher, Reagan, Amin. A sharp observer might have noticed the lack of family portraits beyond the dark, disapproving faces of Balcon ancestors staring down from the gilt-framed portraits high on the walls.

Oswald took his place at the head of the table and surveyed the room, while animated conversations about politics, parties and business bounced around.

What was Watchorn going on about now? thought Oswald, catching the end of a story. Philip was telling Nicholas about his recent stay at Chequers. Although he nodded and feigned interest – *Chequers! How marvellous!* – Oswald was silently bristling at his friend's growing proximity to the Cabinet. It wasn't so long ago that Oswald had been the one with the high-flying political connections and tales of the corridors of power. As a proud peer of the realm, Oswald had taken his Lords' duties very seriously, making the journey to London to sit three times a week in the upper chamber. But that was before New bloody Labour culled over eighty per cent of Britain's hereditary peers in Parliament in one fell swoop. It was the end of the twentieth century and the end of Oswald's life as he knew it. Now Oswald's days were empty, occasionally dropping by the Balcon Galleries in Mayfair, which had been thriving for years with very little input from him. He had also written a well-received book about the Viceroy George Curzon and his time in India. But that wasn't real work.

'Been over to St Bart's today,' said Philip, turning to face Oswald.

'Fabulous!' gushed Venetia. 'We wanted to go there for New Year, didn't we Jonathon? The hotels get terribly booked up, though.'

Philip raised an eyebrow. 'The hospital,' he said.

Oswald looked over. 'Trouble?'

'No, no. Not me. Haven't you heard about Jimmy?'

'Jimmy Jameson?' He shook his head. Although Jimmy had been part of the crowd in the sixties and seventies when a big group of them would frequent Annabel's and various other Mayfair watering holes, Oswald had been deliberately poor at maintaining the friendship. He frankly did not want to get his nose too dirty. Jameson had been the business partner of Alistair Craigdale, another friend of the group, who had sensationally disappeared in the seventies after shooting his wife's lover dead. 'The Craigdale Killer Case' was how the tabloids had luridly referred to it. Oswald had taken the scandal as a prompt to leave that life of gambling and carousing behind – in public at least – and while Philip, Nicholas and a handful of other useful friends had remained in his circle, the likes of Jimmy Jameson had been axed from his life.

'It's awful,' said Jennifer, her voice slurring slightly from an enthusiastic intake of wine. 'Cancer,' she whispered.

'Bloody broke my heart to see him,' said Philip, wiping his mouth with a crested napkin. 'You know what a big lad he was, Oswald? Mustn't be more than nine stone now. Doctors say visitors are keeping his spirits up. Apparently a lot of the old crowd have popped down this week. I'm sure he'd love to see you.'

'Of course, of course,' replied Oswald, having absolutely no intention of making the trip to London. 'Anything for an old friend.'

Across the table, Cate was dying a slow death of her own. *Why am I here?* she asked herself as she answered another mind-less demand for celebrity gossip from Jennifer and Elizabeth. The truth was, Cate had been so desperate to see a friendly face after her confrontation with William Walton that the threat of her father's disapproval had seemed a small price to pay. Now, as she looked at his frowning face, she wasn't so sure.

At the best of times, Cate had a real love-hate relationship with Huntsford. Her earliest memories were fond: her mother reading them stories, the smell of a warm apple crumble, Camilla on a tricycle being chased by their nanny through the hall. But those later memories – well . . . Cate was well practised in sweeping them under the carpet. But they had a nasty way of tripping you up.

'So, Catherine, what's this fracas at work that Venetia's been telling me about?' said Oswald, cutting through Cate's thoughts. 'Horrid was the word, I believe.' He rolled the word off his tongue mockingly.

Cate shot Venetia a look. She had hoped to get to Huntsford early in order to tell her father about her dismissal, but now there was nothing for it but a public announcement of her unemployment. She took a deep breath and stared at her plate.

'Actually I was fired this afternoon,' she said quietly. 'Apparently for being too posh.'

Nicholas Charlesworth, a card-carrying member of the upper classes, pro-hunt and pro-class division, spluttered with outrage. 'How utterly ridiculous,' he cried. 'I hope you're seeking legal advice, Catherine.'

Camilla looked over at Cate in shock. 'Oh Catie. I'm so sorry – I had no idea. I know an excellent employment lawyer if you need one.'

Cate shook her head. 'As much as I am furious, I don't think it would be sensible to take it to an industrial tribunal. You know how it works, blotting your copybook in the industry.'

Philip Watchorn gave Cate a good-natured smile. 'Take it

from an old man, Cate,' he said. 'If you get through your working life without ever being fired, you're doing something wrong. I'd been dismissed –' he began counting on his stout fingers silently – 'four times before I was your age. Then I thought, bugger the corporations, I'll do it my own way.' He spread his hands as if to say, 'I rest my case.'

Oswald's face, however, seemed set in granite. 'Thirty years old, with no job and no man. Things aren't looking too good, are they?' he smiled thinly.

Cate met his eye for the first time. 'Actually, it's thirty-two, soon to find a better job, and waiting for the right man,' replied Cate with as much dignity as she could muster.

'That's one way of looking at it,' said her father, his laughter strained with cruelty.

Feeling her eyes well up, Cate rose from the table. 'I think I've had enough,' she said politely, moving quickly for the door. 'I hope you'll all excuse me.'

'Oh Catie, don't . . .' said Camilla.

'Cate, please . . .' echoed Venetia, watching her leave the room.

'Let her go,' mumbled Oswald with a casual wave of the hand.

Camilla began to rise to follow her sister, but froze at the sound of her father's palm banging the tabletop. 'What did I just say?'

Camilla and Oswald's eyes locked.

Nicholas Charlesworth looked around the room and began quickly talking about the fishing. 'Think it'll be a good year, Oswald?'

'Always a good year in these waters,' replied Oswald, his eyes still on Camilla.

'Thought we'd return the hospitality next month if you're up for it,' continued Nicholas. 'Got tickets for *Così Fan Tutte* at the ROH.'

Concerned about Cate, but keen to diffuse the tension, Venetia seized her opportunity to change the subject. 'Speaking of opera,' she began tentatively, clearing her throat, 'Did I tell you, Daddy, I'm in the middle of a commission for Maria Dante?'

Nicholas Charlesworth noticeably perked up and Philip Watchorn whistled.

'The singer? Not exactly Pavarotti, is she?' said Oswald moodily.

Philip playfully chided his friend, hitting him with the end of the napkin. 'Don't be so uncharitable, Oswald. Maria Dante is as good as Callas. Better looking, too. What's she like, Venetia? Feisty young bird, I should imagine.'

'Quite. You should hear her speaking to the builders.'

'Where's the property?' asked Jennifer. She was always eager to collect information for her social database.

'Three-storey stucco in Onslow Square. Needless to say she wants a very theatrical look for the house. All blood-reds and purples. Awful. I'm sure she wants Dracula's castle.'

'That's the wops for you,' said Oswald.

'Actually,' said Venetia, turning to Philip, 'she was thinking of arranging a musical event for sometime before she flies to the Verona festival in July. She would perform, of course, possibly get some friends of hers on the bill – Lesley Garrett, maybe even Dame Kiri – and the proceeds would go to charity.'

'What about a venue?' asked Philip, quickly grasping that such an event would be a wonderfully original occasion to invite clients to. 'She'll be lucky to get a slot at the Barbican or Royal Festival at this late stage, won't she?'

Venetia took a deep breath, her hands shaking slightly under the table. She knew Huntsford would be perfect as a venue, but she was also aware of her father's distaste of commercial ventures. 'I actually suggested Huntsford to her,' said Venetia, avoiding her father's eyes. 'It's so beautiful here in early summer, and the proximity to London is perfect.' She paused. 'It would be a hotter ticket than Glyndebourne.'

Oswald leaned forward in his chair. 'Under no circumstances am I allowing anything like that to occur at Huntsford,' he said, glaring at his daughter. 'Unlike your bloody sisters, who can't seem to keep out of the newspapers, I value the privacy of this family.'

'We could do it for the Royal Marsden,' chimed Jennifer Watchorn, always eager to join a charitable committee.

'Balls to charity,' boomed Oswald, 'it will ruin the lawns. There'll be bloody Japs everywhere with their sushi picnics. Christ, I suppose you intend making the orchard a car park?'

'Give it some thought, Oz,' said Philip, taking a cigar from the wooden casket Collins was passing round. 'I thought you were supposed to be a patron of the arts,' he said teasingly.

'Yes, well. Not at the bloody expense of my property,' he said, pouring a glass of port.

Just then there was the sound of raised voices from the hallway followed by a loud crash. 'What the hell?' Oswald quickly strode to the far end of the room and pulled the doors open. Sprawled on the floor, dressed in a pair of white jeans and a green kaftan, was Serena, half buried under a suit of armour. She looked up at her father with a chastened expression, her huge aquamarine eyes pinched and rimmed with red. Then she burst out laughing.

'Serena, what the hell's going on?' boomed Oswald as the rest of the guests gathered behind him in the doorway.

Serena slowly picked herself up, trying vainly to regain her poise, staggering against the heavy oak doorway like a music-hall drunk.

'Hello, everybody,' she slurred, waving a half-empty champagne bottle. 'Guess what? I'm home.'

5

Ten-year-old Cate Balcon clutched the tow-rope anxiously and threw a nervous smile to her sisters who were standing on the jetty behind her. Her bent legs wobbled as she bobbed in the chilly water, waiting for the engine to growl to life. She squinted, the glare of the Côte d'Azur sun bouncing off the sea as she looked to her father sitting in the boat in front of her. She hadn't wanted to water-ski. She wasn't a strong swimmer, so the open sea scared her, but if there was one thing that frightened her more, it was her father.

'Are you ready?' he shouted, turning from the wheel to salute her as the hum of the motor grew louder and louder. She nodded, her knees shaking as the boat roared away. Concentrate. Straighten legs. Pull up. A breeze slapped against her navy blue swimsuit as she stood shakily on the water. They were going fast now. Waves splashed onto her legs and the pine trees that flanked the shore blurred into the granite rock of the Cap Ferrat coastline behind them. But she was up; she was water-skiing.

Cate glanced at the jetty to smile proudly towards her sisters. Suddenly her right knee buckled. Too fast. Too fast, Daddy. She screamed out, but the growl of the motor swallowed it up. Her small body flipped over, her face smacking the water as she was pulled violently forward. Stop, Daddy, please, stop, but the boat carried on *faster and faster. She gripped tighter onto the rope, determined not to let go, but her body sank lower and lower into the sea and water rushed into her eyes. Help me. Please, she croaked between gasps for air. Finally the engine fell quiet. The boat turned in a horse-shoe around her, the rope falling slack, and then there he was, her father. Cate coughed violently, spewing up curves of salty water. A tanned, hairy hand came over the side of the boat, but its grip was hard and angry, leaving deep red welts on her shoulder.*

'You can never do anything right, can you?'

A gentle knock on the bedroom door woke Cate up from her sleep.

'Can I come in?'

Cate rubbed her eyes as Venetia came into her room, a tiny space in the castle turret that was still decked out in chintz and lilac from when she called Huntsford home. Her sister perched on the eiderdown and Cate had a rush of *déjà vu*. It was a familiar scene with the Balcon girls – one sister creeping in to comfort another in the night, or sneaking away to the rickety old boathouse down by the lake to escape the shouting, the mocking, the disapproval. The boat-house had been the only port in their storm; Venetia, as the eldest sister, would take it upon herself to bring out rations of sweets and fizzy drinks and comfort to whoever was bear-ing the brunt of their father's anger. Although Oswald deliberately sent them to different boarding schools to quash the bond, their closeness had survived into adulthood, and the Balcon girls still turned to each other in times of trou-ble – they were the only ones who really understood.

'You're crying.'

'In my sleep, I think,' said Cate, wiping the dampness from her cheek.

She felt a wave of guilt and sat bolt upright against her pillow.

'Anyway, forget me. How's Serena?' she said quickly. Cate had run to the top of the stairs when she'd heard the commotion, but had left Venetia to deal with putting her drunk, emotional youngest sister to bed. 'I'm so sorry I left you to it.'

'Don't worry about it,' smiled Venetia, handing her sister a mug of cocoa. 'She was flat out as soon as you left her. Glamorously slumped out, of course.'

'Slumped?' said Cate raising an eyebrow. 'Sloshed, more like it. She must have had a skinful. I've never seen her drunk before, let alone like that.'

'Well, I'm not surprised. Apparently she drank half the bar on the flight over from Egypt.'

'It's so sad, isn't it? Her and Tom. I just never saw it coming. They'll get back together, don't you think?'

Venetia shrugged. 'You have to leave people to it.'

She noticed Cate's red-rimmed eyes and put her hand on her shoulder. She knew that, for Cate, losing her job was equal to losing a lover.

'You've got to learn how to ignore Daddy, you know. He was being an idiot tonight.'

Cate shrugged. 'I've spent over thirty years trying to do precisely that, but he does seem to have a gift for making people feel as shitty as possible.'

'Good job Collins put four shots of whisky in your cocoa, then. You'll feel better after that.' She walked over to the windowsill and lit a candle perched on top of it. 'You'll get another fabulous job, no problem.'

Cate shook her head. 'No. All the big jobs at *Elle*, *Vogue* and *Harper's* have all been filled recently. And anyway – I really want an editorship. At this stage in my career I don't think it's time to start going *down* the job ladder.'

She tailed off and leaned back to sink into the plump pillows, feeling small and childlike. She looked up, and for

59

a second in the dim, amber candlelight, Venetia looked like someone else.

'You look like Mum,' Cate said quietly.

'Don't be silly. You can't remember.'

'I can. Sometimes I think I can.'

Cate had been seven when their mother had died of a brain haemorrhage, just months after the birth of Serena. One minute she had been sunbathing in the garden of their Cadogan Gardens home, with Cate running around barefoot and happy, the next minute she had a headache and, before they knew it, she was gone. It was the beginning of the end of their carefree childhoods as the four girls came under Oswald's unbending control. Brought up by their nanny, Mrs Williams, and the shadow of a tyrant.

Venetia was right, though, thought Cate; she had only the foggiest memories of Margaret Balcon, just the vague smell of perfume, the feel of a soft sweater, and the odd detail of her face, the fullness of her lips as she tucked Cate in at night and kissed her. They were memories that came back at the most random of times, and tonight as Venetia leaned over her to put the coffee cup on the floor, their mother reached out across the years. Not for the first time, Cate wondered what life would have been like if their mother had still been around.

Feeling suddenly very tired, she pulled the eiderdown up to her chin. 'Can we talk about this tomorrow?'

Venetia nodded and left the room.

Although the castle walls were three feet thick, Cate could hear the howling of a winter wind outside quite clearly. She lay back in the half light, trying to clear her head, but here in her teenage bedroom that was too hard. Despite wanting to forget about the job and her embarrassment at dinner, her thoughts kept drifting back to another time, another misery, another dinner when her father had humiliated her in front of his society crowd. On that occasion fourteen years ago, Cate had been home from Wycombe Abbey school for the weekend, to break the news that she had missed out on a place at Oxford.

'See? I've produced a tribe of thickies,' Oswald had mocked her in front of one of his selected audiences, this time down for a weekend of shooting. 'And to think, I actually thought Catherine might have a brain. Well, at least my other three girls are lookers.'

Talk about the last straw. Over the years since her mother's death, Cate had somehow slipped between the cracks and become an insignificance in her father's eyes. Not the eldest like Venetia, not the cleverest like Camilla, not the most beautiful like Serena. At that moment, Cate knew she had to strike out on her own. That weekend was the last time she returned to Huntsford for six and a half years. Daddy could no longer hurt her if she didn't see him, she reasoned.

From then on, Cate spent her weekends at school or with friends. Easters were spent studying art in Florence, summers backpacking around Morocco, Egypt, Spain. She didn't go to Oxford, or her second-choice university, Bristol. Instead she enrolled to study literature at Brown University in Rhode Island, the liberal, Ivy-League institution that encouraged creativity and self-expression. The east coast elite, who thought royalty had graced the campus, loved her – Cate had dated an Astor, a Vanderbilt and a Rockefeller, spending holidays in the Hamptons, in Aspen and Palm Beach. She spent every penny of the small trust fund her mother had left her on tuition fees and a Madison Avenue wardrobe, but had gained bags of confidence, connections and self-belief in return. She took internships at *Vanity Fair* and the *New Yorker*, and emerged back in Britain six years later stronger, leaner, more accomplished, and with a set of John

Barrett russet-blonde highlights that meant, from that moment on, Cate Balcon would always be described as a looker too.

She wiped her eyes and blew her nose on a clump of Kleenex she had stuffed under the pillow. OK, she told herself sternly, enough self-pity for one evening. She picked up a tatty copy of *Madame Bovary* from the little bookshelf by the bed, but still she couldn't concentrate.

It was bad enough she'd been sacked, but from what she'd learnt from her PA Sadie that afternoon, she'd also been outmanoeuvred. Sadie had been asked to book Nicole Valentine a Eurostar ticket to Paris – for the shows – two weeks earlier. Someone knew that Cate wasn't going to be around to take her front-row seat . . .

Cate couldn't stop thinking about Philip Watchorn's words at dinner.

I'd been fired four times by the time I was your age. Then I thought, bugger them. I'll do it my own way.

Still wrapped in the eiderdown, she leaned out of the bed to drag her big Mulberry bag onto the mattress. Inside was a black plastic folder filled with notes, photographs from fashion shoots, and rough magazine layouts. She flipped it open and pulled out a mocked-up cover which featured a beautiful image of Serena lying in a hammock. The elegant masthead read 'Sand'. She smiled. This was her labour of love. It had been eighteen months ago, at Alliance Magazines' summer drinks party, that she'd been approached by the then managing director with an idea. Cecil Bradley, William Walton's predecessor, could not have been more different from the boardroom shark. A cuddly, affable man of sixty, Bradley had been impressed by Cate's quiet ascent through the ranks of the company, her experience in New York and her reputation as a creative editorial force. He'd cornered her over a Pimms in the hot August sunshine and asked her to come up with a concept to expand their existing women's magazine division. The project wasn't allowed to interfere with work, he'd warned her with a wink, but there was a board meeting in October and, if she could get a proposal ready by then, he would see if he could move it into development.

Cate was ecstatic. This was her dream. For two months she spent night after night poring over UK and international magazines, looking for the gap in the market, tearing out images that captured her imagination, listing names of photographers she knew would work for her. And celebrities who, through Serena, she knew would agree to appear. From market research commissioned for *Class*, she knew that travel and style were big growth areas in the upmarket magazine sector. *Sand* would create a delicious lifestyle for cash-rich, time-poor couples to embrace. Less fashion than *Vogue*, more lifestyle than *Condé Nast Traveller*, *Sand* would be crammed with exotic holidays, fashionable shopping breaks, fantastic clothes and dreamy interiors, all with a dash of class and glamour from a bygone age.

The thought of all that sunshine was making Cate feel cold. She plugged in a tiny electric fan heater in the corner of the room, which chugged out a little stream of warm air. She lit another candle for more light, drained her boozy cocoa, and spread all the images over the bedspread, stroking the dummy layouts that her art-editor friend, Carol Shelley, had designed in return for a Chanel bag. They were beautiful, graphic, impressive. And such a waste.

Cate thought back to when she'd been told, two weeks before the October deadline, that there had been a management buyout of the company. Cecil Bradley and the older members of the executive were paid off into retirement, and in came the hotshot marketing and money men like Walton. An email went round to say that all launch activity was to be temporarily halted in favour of 'rationalizing and restructuring' the company.

Cate had been gutted. She'd briefly thought about taking *Sand* to another company, but then she'd been offered the *Class* editorship and she'd consigned her precious dummy to a box file under her bed. This afternoon she'd rescued it and made a list of which companies – Emap, Condé Nast, Time Warner – she might take it to. But still thinking about Philip Watchorn's words: why couldn't she try and launch it by herself? Jann Wenner had started *Rolling Stone* from his kitchen, likewise Tyler Brulé and his style magazine *Wallpaper*. It was certainly a more competitive climate these days, and the odds never favoured the little guy, but why couldn't she give it a try?

She felt a tingling in her tummy. An enthusiastic planner, Cate pulled out a blank sheet of paper and, eyes straining in the dim light, started writing a 'to do' list: meetings to arrange, paper costs to research, advertising directors to talk to – not to mention the thorny issue of financial backing. She knew there was no point turning to her father. After forty-five minutes she was exhausted. She walked over to the windowsill to blow out the candles and stumbled back to her cosy canopy bed in the pitch black, feeling her way in the dark. It was something she was going to have to get used to.

6

The kitchen at Huntsford was the warmest room in the castle. Buried in its west wing, heat spewing out of the claret Aga and always smelling of freshly baked pies, it was a cosy sanctuary that everyone was drawn to. As a child and well into her teens, Serena would spend hours there, sitting at the big farmhouse table and stuffing her face with warm muffins when she should have been revising, or practising the piano, or tidying her room. Mrs Collins the cook should have sent her away or reported her to Oswald, but she was always such entertaining company, gossiping about school or making fun of her father, she didn't have the heart. It was no surprise to the Huntsford staff that Serena had relied on her good looks and charm to make her way in life.

'Here you are!' Cate stood at the doorway in bare feet, holding a mug of coffee, and smiled to herself at the familiar scene. Dressed in an old pair of corduroy trousers and a tiny white cotton vest that stretched just far enough over her pert breasts, Serena had her feet curled up on the oak bench and was picking at a banana muffin, looking rather sorry for herself. She looked beautiful now rather than merely pretty, as she had done in her youth, thought Cate, but it still could have been a snapshot from ten, fifteen years ago.

'Muffin?' Serena's voice was feeble and wobbly, her wide mouth downturned and sombre as she held out a conker-coloured cake in Cate's direction. 'Mrs Collins made me a batch but I can't eat a thing. I just feel sick to my stomach.'

'Hungover, perhaps?' asked Cate with a smile. 'Bananas, a diet coke and a brisk walk always do the trick for me.'

Serena looked at her incredulously. 'What do you mean, "hungover"? I am sick with *misery*. In case you weren't paying any attention last night, my relationship has unravelled.'

Cate was used to treading on eggshells around her sister – the slightest thing could easily set off a diva hissy fit, and it was clear that today she had to be extra careful. She went over to give her sister a hug; she felt thin and delicate in Cate's arms. Her hair, pulled back into a ponytail, smelt fresh, but the red eyes from last night's performance remained.

'I still think we should take that walk. How about it?'

'I have to wait for my PA to come over,' sighed Serena. 'I've got nothing suitable to wear, unless you call a kaftan suitable for a bloody miserable February.'

'Well, borrow something of mine,' said Cate.

Serena let out a snort. 'I'm a *size eight*.'

They turned their heads as Venetia strolled into the kitchen, wearing a pair of Katharine Hepburn trousers and a slim-fitting olive cashmere polo neck, with a stack of newspapers under her arm and a frown on her face.

'You'd better take a look at this.' She threw the papers onto the tabletop and they spread out in a fan. Serena's name was on every front page.

'What the hell?' Serena's face went deathly pale as she saw images of Tom jumping off Roman's dahabeah splashed across the front page of every tabloid.

'Tom In The Drink – Serena Splits', read one. 'Nile Nookie Sends Serena Spare', screamed another.

'The papers were going to find out sooner or later,' said Venetia, trying to strike a positive tone.

'This is precisely what I pay a publicist thousands of pounds a month to keep out,' hissed Serena as she frantically rifled through the papers. 'I am going to fire her arse as soon as I get back to London.'

She stopped dead in her tracks as she read the first spread in the *Sun*. It carried a picture of a heavy-breasted girl in a bikini pouting next to a superimposed shot of Tom.

'Archer tried to pick me up.' As she read out the words, Serena's voice began to wobble. She spun round to face Cate, stabbing the newspaper with her finger so hard it made a hole.

'Just who the fuck is this tart? Who?' she screamed, finally bursting into tears.

'Come on Sin,' Cate offered, using her youngest sister's oldest nickname. 'She's just some nobody after a fast buck,' she continued, putting her arm around her sister's heaving shoulders.

Serena looked up suddenly, stopping the tears as quickly as they had started. She looked at Cate hopefully. 'This isn't true though, is it? Tom would never cheat on me, would he?'

Cate looked over Serena's shoulder to read the story, while passing her sister a mug of tea. 'I'm sure it's just some silly barmaid in his local pub,' replied Cate reassuringly. 'She probably mistook Tom giving her a tip for a come-on. It's amazing how people's memory can change once they've had a big Fleet Street cheque waved in front of their nose.'

Outside the big mullioned window they could hear the clip-clop of horses' hooves in the kitchen yard. Cate unbolted the big oak kitchen door to see Camilla climbing off a big bay mare. She was dressed in a pair of cream jodhpurs and fitted navy hunting jacket.

'If there's coffee on the go, I'll kill for it,' she called to Cate. She took off her riding hat, her blonde hair tumbling onto her shoulders.

'Watch your step,' Cate whispered as she approached the door, 'Serena's about to kill someone herself. Her story's broken in the papers.'

'What's the matter?' Camilla strode purposefully into the kitchen where Serena now had her head in her palms. She looked up as her sister entered.

'Camilla. Thank God. There must be something legal we can do about this,' she moaned.

'But it's true, darling,' interrupted Cate delicately. 'You and Tom *have* split up.'

Serena rounded on her sister crossly.

'Thank you for the recap.'

Camilla was speedily running her finger over the text in professional mode.

'We can potentially get an injunction to stop other things appearing – but we'll be lucky to catch the *News of the World* coming out tomorrow.'

'Anyway,' said Venetia, curling a lock of hair around her finger, 'it's not entirely negative. I think you come out of it quite well,' she said, pointing to the *Mirror*'s lead story, head-lined, 'Fairy Tale Over'.

'What fairy tale?' spat Serena, flinging newspapers across the room. 'Beauty and the Bloody Beast? How can you possibly think I have come out of this "quite well"? *Quite well* is a multimillion-dollar divorce settlement, not tabloid humiliation.'

Having managed twenty-six years of Serena's tantrums Venetia knew the best thing was to quash it as soon as possible. 'Come on, let's all go and get some fresh air,' she said firmly, clapping her hands and herding them outside like a party of nursery-school children. 'This will be old news by next week.'

Reluctantly Serena pulled on a pair of gumboots, grabbed Mrs Collins' old multicoloured poncho from the back of the chair and slung it over her shoulders as they walked out into the grounds. The castle faded slowly from view as they walked further and further, the windows of the house glowing like a pumpkin against the dark drabness of the morning. From a distance Huntsford looked particularly grand, neo-Gothic with striking castellations, and the dramatic hills rising in the background cradled Huntsford like an emerald womb. Oswald had made some impressive renovations to the property since he inherited it; re-excavating the moat and adding a cricket pitch, a maze, a stunning light-filled orangery – and even a nuclear bunker in the eighties when everyone was feeling particularly jumpy about the Russkies. Even though it was looking a little ragged round the edges – the moat where Oswald used to take a daily swim was now full of moss, leaves and lichen – it still looked stunning at this time of day.

Serena was in no mood to sit back and enjoy the landscape. Her emotions were running riot. Anger. Hurt. And weaker forces she could hardly let herself admit – embarrassment and fear. It didn't make sense, she thought, furiously stomping through the damp grass. Why would Tom be interested in some fat country girl, when he had her? She was sure Tom wouldn't have been unfaithful, no matter what the papers said, but she was disappointed that she hadn't found him waiting at the house when she'd returned from Egypt. After he'd finally been fished out of the Nile, Tom and Serena had had a prickly conversation about 'spending some time apart'. Tom was going to take the first flight out of Cairo, while Serena had gratefully accepted Michael's offer of his Gulfstream.

As there'd been no hordes of paparazzi waiting for her at Northolt, the RAF base in West London used by many celebrities to land their private planes, Serena had supposed that their bust-up had gone undetected by the media. She'd been relieved. On home soil she was sure she and Tom could work things out amicably, make a few choice appearances at the Ivy, smiling and holding hands to dispel any rumours, and take things from there.

But so far there had been nothing. No tearful appearances from Tom, no midnight phone calls, no expensive 'forgive me' Paula Pryke flower arrangements. Not even a text message to see how she was coping. *The selfish bastard.*

Having never suffered the indignity of being dumped before now, she couldn't understand how their relationship had unravelled so fast, much less why Tom would want to end it so suddenly. What scared her most was what else it might be the end of – the best beds by the pool at the Eden Roc, the best table at the Cipriani, the invites to the couture shows, yacht parties, the Oscars. She felt nauseous thinking about it.

'The worst thing,' said Serena, getting suddenly aggravated and spinning round to face her sisters, 'the very worst thing is that I'm in New York in a few weeks. *Vanity Fair* is hosting a party to celebrate my new film while I'm doing the East Coast junket. How can I turn up alone? I mean, Graydon isn't even single any more.'

Cate and Venetia looked at each other cynically, looping an arm each through Serena's as they walked along the long, dew-sodden grass as it sloped down towards the lake and the boathouse.

'Come on, Sin, you are beautiful, talented, funny,' said Cate, pulling her along.

'Every man in the world would give his right arm to be at that party and find you single,' added Venetia. 'You're fabulous.'

A weak smile pulled at Serena's lips. 'It's true, isn't it?'

Camilla smiled to herself. Such confidence in a crisis.

'And that's assuming you'll even be single in a fortnight,' she added, joining in the family motivation session. 'Are you sure this isn't just a tiff? What makes you think the relationship's actually finished?'

Serena sighed dramatically. 'The only way he could make this more final is if he hands me a bloody P45. He said he wants to take some "time out", and he hasn't even had the decency to call me.'

'So why don't you call him?' asked Cate. 'By the sound of it, you've hardly talked this through.'

'No. Why should *I* be the one to ring *him*?' Serena said tartly. 'He was the one that behaved like a disgusting hooligan and then has the cheek to say we should take a break, as if I was the one in the wrong. He can keep that stupid fat country tart and see where that gets him.'

'But if you don't give him a ring, it's going to be stalemate,' said Cate pragmatically.

They had now reached the edge of the water. Serena looked out over the gleaming lake and began biting one tiny manicured fingernail. She looked sideways at Cate in a way that made Cate instantly on guard. She had a sixth sense when she was about to be manipulated by Serena.

'*You* could always call him . . .' Serena said slowly. 'You two always got on. He'll speak to you.'

Cate smiled and shook her head. 'Oh no you don't. Don't try this one.'

'Oh, *please*. I'll do anything if you just do me this one favour.'

Venetia and Camilla exchanged smirks while Cate kept shaking her head.

'Please, Catey. You never do *anything* for me,' replied Serena sulkily, but seeing Cate's face, she softened and changed tack.

'*Please*. You can have that white Chanel couture coat I know you love. It probably won't fit you, but you can have it anyway.'

Knowing it was futile to resist, Cate gave Serena a hug. 'I'll see what I can do, but I'm not making any promises.'

The moment was broken by a shrill ringing. 'My phone,' squealed Serena, pulling it out of her pocket. 'You answer it,' she said, thrusting it at Venetia. 'If it's Tom, tell him . . . tell him I've run away.'

Venetia refused to take it, so Serena angrily snapped it open, stalking off up the lakeside path towards the boathouse. 'Yes?'

It was Janey Norris, Serena's PA, who quickly and officiously ran through the arrangements for Serena's day as if she was describing the D-Day landings. The ETA of Serena's suitcases at Huntsford, the time of a meeting with her publicist, an emergency summit with her agent. 'Your shrink and life-coach are both on holiday until next Friday,' revealed Janey as Serena took exasperated breaths, 'but I've arranged for a private masseur to come to your house on Tuesday for a hot-stone treatment, relaxing cranial therapy and four wave Hawaiian massage.'

'Very good,' nodded Serena. 'And messages?' she asked hopefully.

'Forty-seven since this morning,' reported Janey. 'None from Tom, but somebody called Michael Sarkis was insistent he speak to you.'

Serena exhaled and snapped the phone shut, her conversation with Janey immediately terminated.

'Has Tom called?' asked Cate expectantly, trotting to catch up with Serena.

'No,' snapped her sister, 'but I have to make a call, if you'll excuse me.'

'Who to?' pushed Cate.

'Why are you so interested?'

'Who to?' asked Cate again, her journalistic instincts sensing intrigue.

'Michael, if you must know.'

Cate looked up, bemused. 'Which Michael? Caine? Stipe? Angelo?' she said with a smile.

'Michael Sarkis, actually,' said her sister a little smugly. 'His GV brought me back from Egypt.'

'Michael Sarkis the hotel guy?' Cate lifted an eyebrow.

'What's that look for?' Serena stomped away towards the boathouse as Venetia caught up with Cate.

'What's wrong now?' asked Venetia, linking arms with her sister. 'It's so sad. She looks in so much pain.'

'Pain?' smiled Camilla cynically. 'Fear, more like. She needs Tom and she knows it.'

'You say that,' said Cate with a frown, 'but she's just off for some secret chat with Michael Sarkis.'

Camilla looked worried. 'She doesn't want to get involved with the likes of him. He's semi-criminal from what I've heard. Rumours of arms dealing and all sorts.'

All three girls looked at each other. 'You know what she's like.'

They did.

Serena had reached the boathouse – a small half-timbered structure on the far side of the Huntsford Lake. She opened the door with a creak, pushed a cobweb away with her hand and looked around tentatively, scared of mice or spiders. It was eerily quiet inside, but the soft eggshell paint of the interior and the tattered padded wicker chairs overlooking the water gave it a sense of calm.

She brushed some dust off the window seat and sat down, dialling the number that Janey had given her. Her fingernails stabbed at the buttons of the mobile – she was angry at Cate's reaction to the name Michael Sarkis. Totally competitive, Serena assumed everyone was that way and, as much as she loved them, she was convinced her sisters didn't want her to shin any higher up the greasy social pole.

She stared out at the lake, shimmering dark silver in front of her as the phone rang out. Her thoughts drifted to Tom and how she wanted to hurt him for making her feel so foolish, so humiliated.

The voice was male and businesslike but immediately softened when Serena announced herself.

'Serena. How are you, my darling?' he purred playfully. 'I saw the pictures in *Le Monde*. I have no idea how they got pictures on *La Mamounia*. There must have been a long-lens photographer at the dock.'

Secretly pleased that her story had gone international, Serena still adopted a wounded tone. 'It's fine,' she sighed, in a voice that indicated things were far from fine. 'But thank you so much for the lift to London. I can't tell you what a relief it was to just disappear after everything that happened. Not that I can actually return home. I've had to come to my father's place.'

'I know,' said Michael firmly, 'which is why I'm calling. I know you must have a hundred places you can escape to from the paparazzi, but I think my villa in Mustique would be perfect. It's very, very private.'

Serena's heart fluttered. She'd heard he had one of the most impressive houses on the island – bigger than Tommy Hilfiger's, prettier than Princess Margaret's old villa . . .

'Does that sound any good?'

Serena paused, trying not to sound too excited. 'It sounds lovely.'

'That's good. I want to offer it to you for as long as you need. Go, take a friend, relax, have a few spa treatments. You might even enjoy it.'

'Are you sure?' she breathed flirtatiously.

'Of course I'm sure. It will be a pleasure. My secretary will call you tomorrow with further arrangements. Ciao, Serena.'

The line went dead with a click and Serena flopped back on the cushions. Thinking of Tom, her mouth tightened into a sour scowl and then, a second later, broke into a broad, victorious smile. She ran out of the boathouse, as fast as her gumboots would take her, skipping playfully as she approached her sisters.

'Right then,' she announced, pulling her arms tightly around her poncho as she felt her hangover kicking in. 'Who fancies going to Mustique?'

7

Venetia and Jonathon von Bismarck's Kensington Park Gardens home was the sort of huge Palladian villa that passers-by would look at, wondering who lived there. But inside the premises, its owners looked totally unaware of their good fortune. The mood was quiet, oppressive, the uncomfortable silence only disturbed by the rustling of Jonathon's *Financial Times*. Taking delicate sips of the freshly pressed apple juice that their Polish housekeeper Christina had made, Venetia looked at her husband with both sadness and resentment. She was used to the man of the household being a cold and detached entity. As a little girl, days would go by when the only contact she would have with Daddy was when she crept into his study for a stilted goodnight, hoping against hope that he'd shout at her for some infringement of his arbitrary rules. At least it was attention. But now she was living with another man, once again in the same house, but so far apart they might as well have been living in different cities. And they say you end up marrying your father, thought Venetia.

'When do we have to leave then?' said Jonathon finally, folding his paper closed.

'If you're going to come, you should at least come with

good grace,' said his wife, pouring a cup of dark Colombian coffee from the cafetiere.

Jonathon looked up sharply. One of London's most successful hedge-fund managers, he wasn't used to being told what to do. Fully dressed for work in his Kilgour navy suit, his gold cufflinks winking from under the long jacket sleeves, he looked at his wife in her expensive cream silk dressing gown and snorted irritably.

'I object because you don't even seem to be trying to get ready,' he responded tartly. 'You know I'm in a hurry this morning. I've got back-to-back meetings all afternoon and, frankly, I have better things to be doing than sitting here with you.'

Venetia went behind his chair to wrap her arms around him, kissing the back of his neck gently. 'Don't be like that, darling,' she said softly. 'We don't have to be there until ten and, really, it shouldn't take long.'

He shook her off and pushed his chair back noisily across the terracotta floor, snatching up his mobile phone from the table.

'Are you sure I have to go?' he asked coldly, one ear fixed to his mobile. 'How about I get Gavin to drop you off on the way to my office?'

Venetia felt the familiar rush of hot tears prickling behind her eyes. She was feeling terribly vulnerable these days, and the slightest criticism or offhandedness from Jonathon seemed to set her off.

'You have to come. I need you,' she whispered.

'You need me?' The corners of his mouth turned upwards slightly. Jonathon craved control and he was enjoying this minute of power over his wife. 'Very well. Fine. Well, hurry up, get dressed then.'

She watched him stalk into the drawing room. When he had disappeared, she rested her forehead on her arms. She didn't know why she was so upset. She was used to the cold, frosty interchanges between them, his long absences from the house, the lack of support, the total disregard for her feelings. It wasn't so much that the honeymoon period was over after eighteen months of marriage: if she was honest it had never really begun. She had never felt that bond, that excitement, the closeness she had shared with Luke Bainbridge, her photographer boyfriend of five years, who had left her abruptly shortly before she met Jonathon. After Luke had slipped out of her life like a shadow, she had felt desperate for someone to protect and look after her. And in the pit of despair and loneliness, Jonathon had come along, introduced to her by Oswald, of all people. And he had sort of fitted the bill. He was handsome, almost beautiful, she admitted, thinking of his fine-boned features and the blond hair curling over his shirt collar. But he was no companion. She might be married, but these days she felt more fragile, more isolated than ever.

She padded down the hallway in her pink leather slippers, past the huge arrangements of pale magnolia verbena roses and up the long flight of stairs into her bedroom. She walked through into the en-suite wet-room and, standing in front of the long mirror next to the shower, let the gown slide off her milky shoulders. She stared at the reflection of herself and ran her fingers across her neck. Not too crepey, she mused, tracing her fingertips up her cheek and into her short, champagne-blonde hair. Her skin was very smooth for a thirty-seven-year-old, she thought: not too many lines, wrinkles or traces of Botox, unlike the frozen faces of half the ladies who lunched around Knightsbridge.

She was doing OK, still attractive. Not that Venetia minded getting older. Always old for her years compared to most, as a result of being the mother-figure in her family, she almost welcomed being forty. It was like a reassuring plateau. She reached down to stroke the smooth curves of her bare belly. If only they had a family, her life would be exactly as she would want it to be. A baby would surely soften Jonathon's uncompromising mood swings and give them a much-needed bond. But, despite twelve months of trying and an adorable pale lilac nursery waiting at the top of their house, there was still no patter of tiny feet. She was hardly a spring chicken any more, but she knew plenty of friends who'd got pregnant in their late thirties without too much trouble, so it was time to consider fertility problems. She'd long given up hope that they would be one big, noisy family driving down to Huntsford, kids and dogs cluttering up the four-by-four. But surely one child wasn't too much to ask?

Freshly showered, she walked over to the bed, where she had already laid an outfit on the crisp Frette linens. Old habits die hard, she smiled as she dressed, thinking back to her days as a fashion assistant at *Vogue*, when she'd spent her whole time in the fashion cupboard ironing and hanging up the beautiful designer clothes. She'd turned her sharp, creative eye from fashion to interior design over a decade ago, but she still got a thrill from picking fabrics, shirts and shoes and mixing them all together to delicious effect.

'Are you ready yet?' Jonathon's voice boomed from the bottom of the staircase. 'Gavin's here.'

Venetia slipped on her thick cashmere overcoat, grabbed her python clutch bag and ran down to where Jonathon was already sitting in the back seat of a slate-grey Jaguar.

'Let's go,' muttered Jonathon to Gavin his driver. 'Take Knightsbridge, it'll be quicker.'

His pale, slightly hairy hand was resting on the cream leather seat, his little gold signet ring glinting in the sun; Venetia took hold of it to squeeze it. He reached over to her cheek and stroked it with his index finger. 'Sorry, darling, I apologize.' His gesture startled her. After almost two years of marriage she still could not get used to his hot and cold emotions. They'd squabble and, just when he knew he'd pushed her too far, he'd throw her a morsel of affection and reel her back in again. She was sure it was some management technique he'd learned at one of his fancy business schools. She turned her head to look out of the window, lest Jonathon see the tears in her eyes.

The journey to the offices of Doctor Vivienne Rhys-Jones, the finest gynaecologist in Europe, took less than half an hour. The building was the usual white stucco-fronted mews, and through the wide red door there was a sombre, formal atmosphere more like a library than a doctor's surgery. Venetia stepped inside with a sense of dread. She was sure it was all going to be terrible news.

'Mr and Mrs von Bismarck, good morning,' said a pretty blonde pony-tailed girl sitting at the front desk. 'If you'd like to go upstairs to Dr Rhys-Jones.'

The couple made their way up the wide staircase to the first floor, where they were greeted with a faint smile by a short, grey-haired lady behind a large desk. 'Venetia, isn't it? And this must be your husband.'

'Jonathon,' he replied brusquely, stretching out his hand.

'I've been sent your notes by Dr Patrick,' said Vivienne slowly, peering intently and owl-like at a sheaf of papers before her. 'But we might as well start from the beginning.'

As the doctor stared quizzically at the couple, one eyebrow raised slightly above the rim of her glasses, Venetia decided she liked this woman's confident approach. Dr Rhys-Jones was the second fertility specialist she had consulted. The first, Dr Ebel, had been far too trigger-happy with his IVF suggestions for Venetia's liking. Jonathon meanwhile had been offended by Ebel's suggestions that the infertility might be his fault. How dare he make him take a sperm-count test, in that revolting little cubicle with its grubby porn magazines? Jonathon could have told him about the von Bismarck family tradition of producing a line of healthy male heirs, though perhaps less readily about Suzie Betts, his former secretary . . . How could she have been so stupid? All he had wanted was to feel her stilettos striding up and down his back in a Mayfair hotel once or twice a week. But the little slut had got pregnant. It had cost Suzie an abortion and Jonathon fifty thousand pounds in hush money.

Venetia took a deep breath and began recalling their history of trying for a baby, trying to overcome her embarrassment at telling her such personal, intimate details. The number of times they had sex per week, the family history of fertility, her menstrual cycle, which under the stress of not being able to conceive, had faded away to almost nothing in the past three months.

'It's your menstrual cycle I'm most worried about,' said Dr Rhys-Jones, tapping the file gently with the back of a pencil. 'Especially as you say you've become irritable, hormonal, and been suffering from insomnia . . .'

'Women, eh?' said Jonathon, who was ignored.

'I know you're looking for answers on how you can conceive, Mrs von Bismarck, but for the minute I'm interested in the why not.'

'It's not me,' blurted out Jonathon, suddenly riled. 'There's nothing wrong with my sperm count.'

'So it seems,' said Dr Rhys-Jones, thumbing down the notes.

'What do you think it could be?' asked Venetia anxiously.

The doctor smiled thinly and pulled the glasses from her nose. 'Infertility in women, as Dr Ebel might have told you, can be a result of lots of things. Hereditary factors, viral infections, many things. I want to take some blood tests, measure your hormone levels. I don't think we should rule out the possibility that you're going through a premature menopause.'

Venetia felt her guts twist. 'The menopause? That hasn't been mentioned as a possibility before.'

Dr Rhys-Jones looked at her kindly. 'It often isn't. Some practitioners, usually men, I might add, tend not to consider premature menopause as a potential cause of infertility, but about two per cent of women do have the menopause before the age of forty, so it must be considered. Some even have it pre-puberty,' she added, as if to suggest, 'Look, it could be worse.'

Venetia felt her hands tremble as a flood of emotion built up inside her. 'And if it is . . . what about children?'

'A high-resolution ultrasound scan can show if you have eggs left. But you have to prepare yourself: you could have only a few months left in which to try and conceive. If you don't have any eggs left, then a natural conception is, of course, impossible. The standard IVF process, as I'm sure you know, requires your egg and your husband's sperm, so we can also rule that out. There is the option of egg donation,' she continued slowly.

Jonathon let out a cynical snort. 'Someone else's eggs? Surely not, Venetia?'

Both women turned to look at him. 'It depends on how much you want children, Mr von Bismarck.'

Outside the surgery, Jonathon and Venetia stood on the street, a sharp wind pinching their cheeks. Jonathon motioned to Gavin to let him into the car.

'What are we going to do?' asked Venetia, looking to her husband for answers.

He looked at her contemptuously. 'You know people are

expecting us to have children. What am I supposed to tell them? My wife is incompetent?'

Venetia glared at him – for once her upset was overtaken by her fury. '*Incompetent*?' she snarled. 'I'm not one of your *staff*.'

'I assume you knew this before we got married,' replied Jonathon coldly, one foot already in the car. 'You've been forcing me to come to these ridiculous sessions, making me feel that this problem has been something to do with me.'

Venetia felt punch-drunk – so stunned, she could barely get her words out. 'Are you still going to the office?' she whispered.

He got in the car. 'I should have been there two hours ago. Do you want Gavin to drop you at the house?'

She bit hard on the inside of her lip. She was not going to cry in front of him. 'So you're really going . . . ?' she repeated.

'Let's not start this again.'

'But we have things to talk about.'

Jonathon turned to face her, his face impassive and cruel.

'Talk about what? Egg donation? I'm not having some tart's eggs transplanted into my wife in the name of children. We have the family to think about,' he said, struggling to control his voice.

'This is our family, Jonathon.'

'The family line.'

Venetia shook her head angrily. 'Jesus, Jonathon you sound like a bloody Nazi.'

'It's just how I feel. Now, are you getting in the car?'

She pulled her coat collar further up around her neck and shook her head.

'Please, Venetia. Get a grip.' Jonathon slammed the car door and the smoked electric window purred down. 'And don't forget we've got William and Beatrice coming round for drinks tonight. Can you please make sure you're in a better mood?'

As the car pulled away, Venetia stood very still, quietly letting the tears roll down her face.

8

Cornwall Chambers was housed in an austere, imposing Georgian building on Lincoln's Inn Fields, a prim London square that reeked of establishment values and dour respectability. However, inside, in the office of Charles McDonald, QC, there was a party atmosphere. Grey-haired men in Savile Row suits were smiling broadly and chinking glasses, a rare break in the usual sobriety of one of the best commercial practices in London.

Charles McDonald tapped his crystal tumbler of tonic water with the back of a silver teaspoon and cleared his throat.

'I don't need to tell you what a productive month these chambers have had,' he said to his colleagues in his rich Edinburgh drawl. 'So productive that I felt it would be rude not to finish it off with drinks, even though I'll only be joining you with a mixer.'

Light laughter rang politely around the room. Barristers, particularly heads of chambers, were not known for their sense of humour, so any levity always raised a disproportionate amount of laughter.

'Gerry and David,' he nodded over to a round man with

a florid face and to a smaller, thinner man in moon-shaped glasses by his side, 'a fantastic win in the Petersham libel case. Look out for a page three interview with Gerry in next week's *Lawyer*.'

More laughs as Charles once again raised his glass. 'Can I also take this opportunity to congratulate Cornwall Chambers' resident celebrity, Miss Camilla Balcon. A wonderful victory in the Kendall versus Simon case. I frankly thought it was unwinnable. Congratulations, Camilla.'

All the men in the room turned towards the attractive blonde woman in the corner, always grateful for an opportunity to look at her. Camilla Balcon nodded politely, smoothing down the skirt of her bespoke Gieves & Hawkes suit to look even more presentable for her audience.

As she sipped at her flute of champagne, she wondered whether this acknowledgement might finally trigger a more heavyweight and prestigious caseload. She was getting impatient to reach the top of the legal tree. For any other twenty-nine-year-old woman at the bar, Camilla Balcon's career trajectory would have been termed stratospheric. Balliol College, Oxford, top five in her year at Bar school and a tenancy in one of London's most elite chambers. In the last twelve months alone she had been junior counsel for the chambers' top silks in three major fraud cases. She had a growing reputation as an astute and brutal cross-examiner in her own right, and consequently was topping six figures in yearly fees. Not bad for someone regularly dismissed as posh totty.

But still, it was not quite good enough for Camilla, whose entire life had been spent plotting her next conquest, her next brilliant achievement. It was her legacy as the third child in a high-achieving family. You either gave up before you'd even started, or you worked your damnedest to outshine them all. And Camilla wanted to shine.

She turned to look at her colleagues and reflected that

they might just be the reason her career was going more slowly than she would like. While her commercial chambers had a fantastic reputation, with so much ego and talent in one building it was hard enough to get noticed, let alone scramble up the ladder. So while Charles McDonald might throw her the odd compliment during a Friday night's drinks, she felt sure it was simply to pacify the chambers' only female tenant.

A tall, gangly, but good-looking man bounded over with a bottle of Moët. 'I see somebody's glass needs a refill,' said Matt Hornby, one of chambers' senior clerks with a blush. 'Charles has splashed out on the good stuff so we might as well quaff it.'

'Just because it's free, doesn't mean we have to drink it all,' said Camilla, holding out her glass with a coquettish smile. Aware that Matt, a twenty-five-year-old East Ender, had been hopelessly in love with her since she started at Cornwall Chambers, she didn't want to encourage him, but he had a kind, handsome face, peppered with freckles, and she found it rather cute that he considered champagne such a treat.

'Saw you in those *Evening Standard* party pages last night,' continued Matt, drinking the Moët in nervous gulps. 'So what are you up to this weekend that could possibly be more glamorous than tonight's soirée?'

She laughed and sipped her champagne. 'Lots of invitations to things – not looking forward to any of them. In fact, in about two hours I should be at a Charles and Nigella's dinner party. The food will be fantastic, but nothing sounds better right now than being tucked up in bed with a video and a Chinese.'

'Why don't you take me along and let me be the judge of what's the best night out?'

She smiled, unable to stop herself. 'Where to?' she purred, 'Charles and Nigella's or back to mine?'

'Oy, you little minx. Are you flirting with me?'

She slapped him on the arm and put her glass on the table. 'Absolutely not. And anyway, I think Nat might freak if I turned up with you as Friday night entertainment.'

Matt tried to smile at the mention of Nathaniel Montague, whom he'd only met twice but regularly saw gurning in the *Daily Mail* diary pages.

'You have a point,' laughed Matt, filling his flute to the rim and stuffing his mouth with a handful of Japanese rice crackers. 'He scares the bejesus out of me.'

As Matt disappeared to 'find some more snacks', Camilla felt a tall presence at her shoulder. 'Are you staying around for a little while or are you dashing off?' asked Charles McDonald, in a manner that wasn't so much a question as a request.

'I haven't got to be anywhere until about eight p.m. Why?'

He gently put his hand on her shoulder, steering her towards the door conspiratorially. 'Shall we go somewhere quieter?' he said, 'I need to talk to you about something you might find interesting.'

Camilla felt her stomach flutter as they went down the staircase to her office on the second floor. This had to be the talk about improving her workload, she thought. Charles stopped Camilla at the door and picked up her Armani coat from the hat stand.

'I think we should get out of here,' he said, holding up her coat. 'This is fairly confidential. Walls have ears, and all that.'

The Pen and Wig, tucked away in a side street behind Lincoln's Inn Fields, was the perfect barrister's watering hole. Dark and Dickensian, its stools were upholstered in faded red velvet, while caricatures of corpulent judges sat holding court around the bar. It was busy, full of lawyers killing time before they returned to wives and children in Victorian villas in Wandsworth Common. Not exactly the ideal place for a private chat, thought Camilla, as Charles fetched her a gin and tonic from the bar. Still, if he was about to increase her caseload, or move her to the more prestigious upper-floor offices, it was probably best if he did so out of the earshot of the other tenants.

'Thank you so much for your acknowledgement of my work earlier,' she said, impatient as always to cut to the chase. 'Hopefully you'll see that I'm ready to move up to lead counsel soon.'

Charles paused, putting his orange juice down carefully. 'Actually, it wasn't chambers I wanted to talk to you about,' he began, fixing Camilla with his gaze and leaving a dramatic pause. It was a technique Camilla had seen him use to devastating effect in court when he was about to annihilate someone under cross-examination.

'Camilla, you're almost certainly the most ambitious law student I have ever interviewed for pupillage,' said Charles. 'And, believe me, we've had a lot of gung-ho lawyers through the doors of Cornwall Chambers.'

'Isn't everyone super-ambitious when they're twenty-two and trying to get into good chambers?' she smiled, relieved that she hadn't been brought here for a dressing-down.

'I suppose. But I always found it strange with you, with your background. We've had a lot of public school- and Oxbridge-educated barristers in this chambers, but I've always been suspicious of taking on the truly privileged ones.' Charles whispered the word 'privileged'. 'Lazy bastards, a lot of them.' He stopped.

'Which is why I was hesitant to take you on, Camilla.'

Beginning to wonder where this conversation was going,

Camilla began swirling the ice cubes at the bottom of her glass around and around.

'Do you remember when I took you out for lunch in your first week?' asked Charles.

Camilla remembered it well. It was to Wilton's in Belgravia. She was the only woman in the restaurant and she ate pheasant when she knew she should have ordered the fish. It was the first time she had felt small, scared and a little out of her depth. Rather like now, in fact.

'Do you remember that Michael Heseltine was sitting in the next booth and you became terribly excited?' said Charles.

Camilla smiled. 'I think I even said hello.'

'I think you might have been a little drunk, actually. Don't worry,' he chuckled, lifting his orange juice. 'Lunchtime drinking never agreed with me, either. But I remember thinking at the time, why is this girl so excited about meeting Heseltine when she must have met dozens of high-ranking political sorts through her family? I think your father was a Lords' frontbencher at the time, wasn't he? You had a fierce look in your eye and you told me that Heseltine had once said the president of the Oxford Union was the first step to becoming prime minister. And that's the reason why you went for it, and won it.'

'Actually, I think he said it was a chore that had to be suffered,' remembered Camilla, thinking back to the months of Machiavellian plotting required to secure the prestigious Oxford office, and then the weekly attendance at one fatuous debate after another.

'And anyway,' she continued, 'it didn't quite work out that way for him, did it? So much for the Oxford Union plan.'

'He didn't do so badly,' said Charles, his voice serious, 'he got deputy prime minister. And I think you, Camilla, could do just as well.'

Camilla stopped and looked at Charles intently.

'Politics? But what about the law?'

'Ach, do you really want to be a QC?' said Charles dismissively. 'Would that be the end of a satisfying career for you?'

Camilla knew she had to tread carefully. But the truth was, the law didn't put the fire in Camilla's belly. Yes, she was good at it. She had the discipline and the intelligent, incisive mind to reach the very top of the profession, and once she knew she was good at something, she didn't stop until she was the very best she could be. But Camilla wanted more, much more.

'It's something I have thought about,' she replied truthfully. 'But I've still got my work here and I'm not even thirty.'

'Don't even begin to bring age into it,' chuckled Charles. 'Did you know I ran about, gosh, thirty years ago now?'

She shook her head. 'I assumed the law was your life.'

'Many barristers are frustrated or failed politicians,' laughed Charles. 'I'm one of the failed ones.'

'So what happened? You'd have been excellent.'

'I was twenty-eight, twenty-nine when I ran for parliament. I won a Tory nomination OK, but they made me fight some unwinnable seat in South Wales that had been held by a Merthyr Tydfil teacher for twenty years. I didn't have a chance with my Edinburgh accent.' He started shaking his head at the memory.

'I can't imagine you gave up that easily, though,' said Camilla, leaning forward, fascinated and excited at the same time.

Charles shrugged. 'Well, I did. I was making good money in fees, my name was being mentioned as a future silk, and that's nice when you're married with a couple of kiddies with a big fat mortgage to pay. Truth is,' he said slowly, 'it gets too tempting to stay put in the law. Who wants to trade a five-hundred-thousand-pound salary for fifty thousand as an MP? I didn't. And maybe now I regret it.'

Camilla looked at the sad expression on Charles's craggy face and wondered how it was possible for a successful man to have such a huge, unfulfilled ambition. And suddenly she felt a desperation, a desire to reach that pinnacle Charles had so regretted turning away from.

'Isn't your wife chairwoman of a Conservative Association somewhere?' asked Camilla.

'Esher,' he replied. 'Do you know Jack Cavendish?'

She nodded again. 'Well, my father knows him. Tory MP for Esher, right?'

'Yes, but who knows for how much longer?' Charles responded softly. 'A whisper has started that Jack is going to stand down at the next election, which could be as soon as May next year.'

'Is Esher a safe seat?'

'Not by a long shot. His majority has been whittled down to a couple of thousand. But if he does stand down, the party will be inundated with CVs. It's a wonderful seat for somebody. Wealthy, close to London . . .'

Camilla could barely contain her excitement at where this conversation was going. 'What sort of candidate is the party looking for?' she asked, trying to keep her cool.

'Someone capable of winning a campaign. Someone like yourself, Camilla.'

'How do you know I'm a Conservative?'

'Oh dear,' laughed Charles, suddenly embarrassed. 'I assumed like father, like daughter.'

Truth was, Camilla was political without having any particularly strong party affiliation. Some of her opinions swung to the right, others were squarely towards the left.

But in her mind, politics wasn't about policies, and there

was very little between the three major parties now anyway. To her, politics was about power. It was the thought of the respect and authority that turned her on. The glamour of her heels clicking down the corridors of Westminster, the credibility she would get when compared to Cate and her fancy magazines or Venetia with her over-decorated society houses. More importantly, to the outside world she would no longer just be a satellite in Serena's stardust-sprinkled universe.

'I voted Tory in the last election,' she replied, without adding, 'only just.'

'Then you have everything you need to win a campaign,' nodded Charles, pulling a leather cigar holder from out of his top pocket. 'Do you mind?'

Camilla shook her head. One of her first memories was the heavy smell of cigar smoke and damp tweed; she was used to its sticky, woody aroma.

'You have political nous; you have determination. And you have profile. Never discount the importance of celebrity,' he smiled. 'Look at Boris Johnson and Glenda Jackson. And surely your father could canvass some support for you.'

Camilla doubted that. Her father wanted more than anything to get back into the Lords in one of the elected seats, but had been defeated in the last two by-elections. She wondered how he'd take to the news of Camilla running for the Commons. Not well, she suspected.

'Are you sure I'm not a bit young?'

'No. The party needs an injection of youth and fresh, modern ideals. It needs to modernize – completely – in the way New Labour did in the nineties, and that process has already begun.'

'You're sure I'm eligible?'

'You're the daughter of a baron. It's fine.'

She paused, more confused than she thought she would

be. 'If I do decide it's something I want to do, and if Jack Cavendish announces his retirement, what do I do next?'

'I assume you're not on Central Office's approved candidates' list?'

She shook her head.

'Well, that's step one.'

'It's obviously something I need to think about carefully,' she replied, running her thumbnail up and down the grain of the table. Then she looked up into Charles's knowing eyes. 'But I don't suppose there's any harm in looking into it, is there?' she grinned.

'I'll smoke to that,' replied Charles, inhaling his big fat brown Cohiba and blowing a perfect smoke ring into the air as a fat-faced barrister behind them started coughing. And Camilla began to smile.

9

Michael Sarkis's Mustique villa, La Esperanza, was the complete opposite of the gaudy deluxe hotels for which he was famous. Perched at the tip of a lush headland jutting out into the hazy turquoise waters of the Caribbean, it was a huge, Balinese-style mansion with a jade green infinity pool, ornate koi carp pond full of lilies and an enormous sweep of terrace overlooking the sea.

'I can't believe we've been here two days already,' sighed Serena, nibbling on a lobster salad as she swung in an enormous blue cotton hammock on the terrace, eyes gazing upwards at the palm trees.

'It's the Cotton House cocktail party this evening,' said Venetia, looking over the top of her Valentino sunglasses. 'Shall we wander down for a few martinis? Or are you still officially in hiding?'

Serena put down her salad bowl and plumped the soft linen pillow under her head. 'Darling, the whole point of coming to Mustique is to avoid tourists rather than actively seek them out,' she said. 'I'm sure you understand and you know I appreciate you being so supportive.'

'Oh, and I appreciate being here. Whatever you want to

do,' laughed Venetia, taking a swig of mineral water. 'The villa is lovely enough on its own.'

'Can you believe Cate refused to come?' said Serena. 'That ungrateful sod. Not that you were second choice or anything,' she added quickly.

'She's not ungrateful,' said Venetia with a wry smile. 'But you know she always feels guilty about having fun. Actually, I think she is really busy this time. I spoke to her this morning because I thought she might be a bit depressed and she said she was working on some magazine idea she wants to try and launch.'

'Well that's typical, isn't it?' sniffed Serena. 'While she's unemployed she should be doing something useful like going to see Tom for me, rather than pretending she's Donald Trump. She is so impossibly selfish.'

Venetia smiled to herself. Cate's heart was as big as Serena's ego, but she knew it was fruitless to say anything. Tired from their morning's ride – they had picked up two gorgeous chestnut horses from the Mustique Equestrian Centre that morning to take for a canter along L'Ansecoy Beach – she lay back and opened a historical biography, pulling her sunglasses down deep onto the bridge of her nose to avoid the sun glaring back up from the page. She tried to stop herself smiling, feeling like a naughty schoolgirl. Jonathon had been furious when she'd announced she was off to Mustique. It was a spur-of-the-moment decision after she'd got the first results of her hormone tests. Her mind instantly had become too full of things she did not want to think about. A failing marriage. Failing ovaries. Failure. She had to escape.

A steward in a pristine white uniform appeared with a frosted pitcher of fruit punch and a plate of brilliant-white coconut slices. Obediently, he placed a glass of punch in Serena's outstretched hand.

'I also have a fax for you,' said the handsome steward, handing Serena a rolled sheet of cream paper on another silver platter.

'A fax?' asked Venetia, craning her neck over. 'What is it? Don't say the press have tracked you down here already. I don't feel prepared for my paparazzi close-up.'

'Oh,' said Serena after a moment, scanning the scratchy black words.

'What's the matter?'

'Michael says he's flying into Esperanza this evening. He would like to join us for dinner.' She shot a puzzled expression in Venetia's direction, which slowly began to pull into a smile.

'It's an awfully long way to come from New York, isn't it?' she said as her mouth continued to curl up.

'And a bit weird just barging in?' said Venetia, taking a bite of coconut. She paused, the penny dropping. 'Or did you know he was coming?'

She raised an eyebrow at her sister who sat, sphinx-like, saying nothing and everything all at once. Venetia was irritated, despite herself. It was typical of Serena to drag her all the way to the Caribbean just to while away the time until someone more interesting came along. Serena had always been the high priestess of manipulation.

'Well, Michael didn't specifically say he was coming,' said Serena, looking her sister confidently in the eye. 'But it's hardly barging in. It is his place, after all, and he's entitled to pop by whenever he likes.' She bit a crisp crescent out of the coconut and smirked like the cat who'd got the cream.

'Two thousand miles for supper is hardly popping by.' Venetia stopped and eyed her sister suspiciously. 'You fancy him, don't you? I feel so stupid for not thinking of it sooner.'

'Oh, for God's sake,' said Serena dismissively, lying back

in the hammock and closing her eyes. 'This isn't school, you know! And in case you've forgotten, I am in the middle of a desperately painful break-up. Getting involved with someone else, even someone with a villa like Michael's, is really not on my agenda.'

Venetia looked at her sister lying half naked in the Caribbean sun and doubted that was the case.

The runway at Mustique Airport was too short for Michael's Gulfstream to land so, like all the other thousands of visitors that arrived on the island, he came by tiny charter jet, being picked up by one of the villa's staff in a Mercedes. By the time he found the girls, standing on the terrace sipping early evening cocktails, he was relaxed and playful.

'Hello girls,' he beamed, scooping them both up in a huge hug and kissing them both on the cheek. 'How are you enjoying yourselves?'

Venetia moved back, her good breeding a little overwhelmed by this stocky man. He was certainly more attractive than she was expecting, and he was definitely the sort of man whose presence took up more space than his body. Michael's gaze was intense, his clothes – a pair of linen slacks, navy polo shirt and tan Tods loafers – oozed a casual power and, despite her reserve and the gun-running rumours, Venetia found herself gushing. 'Oh, it's wonderful here,' she said, enthusing about the interiors, the space and the beautiful peachy light on this soft, early spring evening.

'This is a nice surprise,' said Serena, turning on her bare foot to walk back to the thatched casita by the infinity pool. Michael smiled and looked her up and down, his eyes pausing at her firm round breasts that were barely restrained by a tiny white bikini top.

'Well, I was in Barbados on business and it's not so far – a hop down to the Grenadines. I thought you might appreciate some more company – it's quiet out in Mustique before Easter.'

'Quiet?' smiled Serena flirtatiously. 'Exclusive. Just how I like it.'

Michael stepped closer to her, his fingertips brushing hers, and she felt her nipples tighten in an instant.

'I'll just change and then we'll meet for dinner in, say, half an hour? We'll set the table in the pagoda.' He pointed in the direction of a hexagonal-shaped outbuilding on the headland. 'It's beautiful up there. Why don't you ladies go to your villas to freshen up for the evening and I'll meet you there?'

Serena's villa was beautiful and her wardrobe even better. She clicked on some lazy Latin jazz with the CD remote and fingered through the vast collection of couture she had brought for the week's stay, all neatly stored away by her personal butler. Her long fingers danced across a sheer kaftan shot through with metallic thread, silk headscarves in a rainbow of colours, tailored cream trousers, fine chiffon shirts and tiny printed sundresses with handfuls of copper and turquoise necklaces hanging from the rattan handles of the wardrobes. After some deliberation, she slipped on a tiny pair of cream Valentino hot pants, cut so short that the curve of her bronzed lower buttocks peeped out on parade. Not wanting to look too sexy – it was only dinner and she knew Venetia would disapprove of anything too revealing, she teamed it with a thin vest in the finest navy cashmere. She pouted in the full-length mirror, wondering whether it was too Maine rather than Mustique, and quickly made it less preppy with a turquoise bangle, hoop earrings and a long gold Garrard chain. She slipped on some flip-flops, applied a slick of translucent coral gloss to her lips and turned off the stereo. With a final squirt of perfume, a signature scent that she had made especially for her at great expense by

Jean Patou, she was ready. She fastened a huge magnolia bloom behind her ear and, realizing she had been over an hour getting ready, made her way to the pagoda.

Michael and Venetia were already at the table drinking a fruit punch and chatting. It was a small and intimate space, the rough-hewn table seeming to float in a sea of blackness with only two small oil lamps and the vast smudge of stars for light. She watched Michael laughing as he poured wine into a ruby-coloured tumbler for Venetia and felt a sudden stab of jealousy. *The second her back was turned and Venetia goes muscling in on the host*, as if she had something to prove just because she had failing bloody ovaries.

She caught herself and realized that somewhere between the Nile and this moment on the terrace in Mustique, Michael had become incredibly attractive. Especially for a billionaire.

'Now this is what I call a restaurant,' said Serena, placing herself at the head of the table directly opposite Michael and letting the thin strap of her top slide off her shoulder.

'Ah, Serena! Late, but great,' said Michael, smiling wolfishly.

Serena smiled coquettishly as Michael beckoned over two stewards carrying huge silver platters. 'I was just saying to Venetia that she has exquisite taste. I could use it in some of my hotels. We must set up a meeting next time I am in London.'

Serena smiled weakly. 'But of course,' she purred, flashing her sister a secret warning. 'Anyway, what are we eating?'

'I asked the chef for something simple tonight,' smiled Michael. 'I hope you ladies don't mind.' He clicked his fingers and the stewards pulled off the silver cloches to reveal plates of red snapper, thick wedges of sweet potatoes dipped in a spicy sauce and a huge bowl of green beans. The three sat eating quietly, each enjoying the food against the sound of waves and the gentle wind. Venetia looked up

100

and noticed Michael looking up at them both, smiling broadly.

'Hey, why the grin?' she asked.

'I'm laughing at the purity of the English genes,' he said. 'I look at you two and I see one thousand years of Anglo-Saxon pureness.'

'Actually we have some Spanish blood sneaking in there somewhere back in the sixteenth century,' said Serena. 'Persecuted Catholics infiltrated the family. So we're not that pure.'

'Well, I would hope not.' Michael's remark was playful and loaded.

They all smiled and turned back to the food, the snapper crumbling into tender shards, the beans squeaky fresh.

'So. How's business?' said Venetia to Michael, wiping her lips with a napkin.

'Very good. The travel industry has been hit badly in the last few years, but at the luxury end where the Sarkis Group operates we have been largely unaffected,' said Michael coolly.

'Actually, I must talk to your other sister, the editor,' he added. 'I want to publish a travel magazine to send to all our customers and put in all our hotel rooms. I want it to be the best – stylish, sophisticated.'

'It's funny you should say that,' said Venetia. 'Cate's in the process of launching her own magazine. Maybe the two of you should meet.'

'That sounds interesting. And I'll certainly enjoy meeting another Balcon girl.'

He threw Serena another long, lingering look. She held it this time, spurred on by Michael's interest in Cate and Venetia. Venetia did not miss the look and, feeling jet-lagged and a bit drunk after a bottle of good Merlot, decided it was time to withdraw to her villa. She knew where leaving Serena alone and half dressed with a renowned playboy could lead but, with her eyelids drooping, she wasn't in the mood to care.

'I must get to bed. Goodnight both of you,' Venetia said.

Michael got up to kiss her on the cheek, while Serena sat quietly in her chair, glad to be rid of her.

When Venetia had walked off into the dark, there was a sudden knowing silence between Serena and Michael.

'I can't eat or drink another thing,' said Serena finally, hooking her fingers over her waistband to expose a slim band of flesh.

'Well, shall we go for a walk then?' smiled Michael. 'I don't think I can stay awake if we stay here.'

Serena nodded and they walked down the stone stairway at the side of the terrace, onto another level of Esperanza where there was a large Jacuzzi and gazebo made from walnut and thick curtains of white voile. The only light was a creamy moon bursting out of a black sky and four blazing torches at each tip of the pool that crackled softly.

Serena walked over to the promenade that looked out to sea, the wind picking up and sending the creamy silver reflection of the moon waving over the black surface of the sea.

She turned around to see Michael behind her. He had undone a couple more buttons on his shirt; a thatch of jet-black hair peeked over the fabric.

'I hope I'm not disturbing you?'

'Feel free. A great silence is worth sharing. Just listen – there's nothing!'

'Just a little sound of the sea.'

Michael rested his powerful hands on the stone wall beside Serena and looked up into the star-freckled sky.

'I hope you didn't mind me coming,' he said. 'I was actually in Palm Beach, which we both know isn't exactly round the corner . . .' He looked towards her and smiled, a hint of danger curling at the corners of his mouth.

'It's your house. It's not for me to say when you can come to stay.'

'Let's just say I wasn't in the area. Are you glad I'm here?'

'Of course,' Serena laughed nervously, still a little unsure where this encounter was going.

'It's just good to be with someone who is going through the same thing,' said Michael.

'The same thing? What do you mean?'

'Well, things with Marlena, my girlfriend – I think you met her in Egypt – they aren't too great.'

Serena touched his shoulder gently. 'Oh, I'm so sorry. I had no idea.'

He laughed, dipping his chin. 'We argue all the time. And she spends like crazy. Half a million dollars on couture. Two million at JAR. I'm a generous guy but I don't like to feel exploited.'

'So are you leaving her?'

'It's been talked about.' He stopped and bent his head to smell the magnolia blossom in Serena's hair, gently stroking a strand from her face.

'Relationships take a long time to end after they are over,' he said softly.

Serena suddenly moved away from him, overwhelmed by the rush of emotions that having Michael so close brought on. She walked a little way down the terrace and sat on one of the day beds by the pool, making invisible swirls on the terracotta tiles with her toes.

As Michael moved next to her, a uniformed steward appeared from under the thatched casita and gave them two flutes of Krug before disappearing without a word.

'How are things with Tom?' asked Michael, sipping his drink.

Serena shook her head, long strands of blonde hair flicking over her shoulders. 'I haven't come here to talk about Tom.'

Michael put down his glass and slid across the white mattress, his right arm snaking around Serena's waist.

She gasped softly, unsure of taking the next step, but wanting more of his touch.

'You know why I'm here?' he whispered into her ear.

She turned to face him. 'Yes,' she breathed, letting him push her down. Sinking back onto the bed, she let Michael caress her neck, lips and stomach, her pubic muscles tightening suddenly as he lifted the tiny cashmere top up over her head in one swift movement.

She was lying on her back now, naked except for her hot pants. Michael took her half-full flute of champagne and poured it over her breasts, his mouth descending to lick the glistening liquid off each rose-coloured nipple. She gasped as his tongue lapped, his teasing getting harder and harder. Taking the signal, his lips brushed down her flat stomach while her hands unzipped and scooped off the hot pants. For a moment, Michael lifted his head to inspect her body. They locked eyes, both blazing with desire as Michael quickly removed his clothes. Naked now, he moved between her legs, parting her thighs with firm hands, his tongue snaking down, swirling across her narrow strip of pubic hair before delving deep inside her. Serena let out a long moan. 'Oh yes, don't stop.'

Just as she was about to buckle with pleasure, his mouth returned to her nipples while he held his rock-hard cock in his hand and gently but insistently circled her clitoris. Suddenly he pulled back, flipped her over and, pushing her buttocks up into the air, he entered her from behind. His hands scooped under her, his fingers teasing her clitoris as he pumped his thick cock into her. Serena groaned and panted in pure ecstasy as waves of pleasure washed over her, finally collapsing on the white mattress.

They turned to face each other, Michael wiping the beads of sweat off Serena's face. She lay back, breathing deeply, letting the warm night breeze blow over her naked body and releasing a huge sigh of pleasure as she realized she'd just had the best sex of her life.

10

Even though it was February, the English countryside could not have looked more lovely. Cate had her foot to the floor of her silver Mini Cooper, Stevie Wonder blaring from the CD player as she sailed through the heart of Dorset, taking her eyes off the road occasionally to admire the view. Past ringing church steeples and old ladies scurrying to worship, past green-black hedgerows and ochre fields made all the more vivid by the sharp winter sun. It was a perfect morning for a drive, she thought, turning a corner and finally glimpsing a line of silver shimmering on the horizon – the sea. If only she wasn't in such a lousy mood. The drive might be nice, but the last thing she wanted to do on a Sunday morning was come two hundred miles out of London on a mercy mission. But Cate, as always, was concerned for Serena. She couldn't believe she'd gone swanning off to Michael's compound in Mustique, despite Cate's pleas to think it through. Serena had always been an impulsive and bloody-minded child and, as an adult, she was just the same. Yet, despite her gung-ho screw-Tom attitude, Cate knew that, underneath, Serena was hurting – and she hated to see her sisters suffer. The only way to avoid a no-good rebound relationship

106

between Serena and that slime-ball playboy Michael was to track Tom down and convince him to give their relationship another go. Cate wound down the window, a blast of salty coastal air lifting her mood, and squeezed her foot down on the pedal even harder.

Petersham House hovered into view on a broad bluff, a low-rise stone building with two plump gable ends and a chimney billowing smoke. It belonged to Dorothy Whetton, the aging sister of Tom's agent, who lived in Fulham and let the house out in the summer. Tom had his own Cotswold house – a sprawling manor he had bought the previous summer – but it was currently minus a heating system and undergoing major architectural surgery. So Dotty Dorothy had come to the rescue and given Tom the keys to this cute bolt-hole, along with the assurance that his residence at Petersham House would remain a secret from the hungry paparazzi.

'Ooh, very *Wuthering Heights*,' said Cate, as Tom opened the door in jeans and a frayed T-shirt, his bare feet on the black slate floor.

'What, me or the house?' replied Tom, chomping on a piece of toast.

She stepped inside and a warm smokiness embraced her.

'Hope you've not had brunch,' said Tom, licking butter from his fingers. 'You're just in time for a fry-up.'

Cate followed him across the flagstone hall into a small wooden kitchen where a tin kettle was whistling on top of an Aga.

'Brunch? Better make that lunch,' said Cate, checking her watch. Tom shrugged with a grin and began turning a pan of sizzling sausages. 'Bit of a surprise this, Cate,' he said, throwing some bacon and sliced tomatoes into a copper-bottomed pan. 'Got the shock of my life when you called last night. Thought I'd be *persona non grata* and all that.'

She took a proffered cup of tea and wrapped her fingers around the mug. 'Yes, it's a long way to come, I know,' she said hesitantly, unsure how to bring up the subject of Serena. 'Fabulous place, though. Does anyone know you're here?'

Tom shook his head happily. 'There's about ten paparazzi stationed outside my place in Gloucestershire, even one in a helicopter circling over the house, but the only gawking you get around here is from the seagulls. Bless Dorothy Whetton. She's even stocked the kitchen up for about a month, so I don't need to leave the house too often. After those pictures of me leaping off Roman's damn boat and that barmaid in my local pub with her mad fantasies about an affair, I think I need to keep a fairly low profile.'

Cate noticed that his cheeks were flushing slightly. 'So the barmaid was lying?' she probed, thinking back to the tabloid kiss-and-tell.

'Yes. It was a lie,' Tom repeated softly, deliberately. 'Anyway,' he continued more happily, 'I'm definitely enjoying the splendid isolation.' He pointed to an untidy heap of paper and a titanium laptop sitting on the kitchen counter –

'I'm writing a script about Donald Campbell – you know, the nineteen-fifties land-speed record guy? I'm really excited about it: it's one of those stories that's got the lot. Cars, romance, tragedy, handsome men in flying goggles.'

'Sounds great. I'm sold,' smiled Cate, pleased to see his boyish enthusiasm returning.

'If it gets the green light I wouldn't mind playing Campbell myself.'

'The handsome man in the flying goggles?'

They laughed, both glad for a brief respite from the awkwardness between them.

Tom moved the pan off the heat and turned towards her. 'Look, Cate, why are you here?' His expression was sad.

'Well, a peace mission I suppose . . .'

'Ah, Mr Kissinger. I didn't recognize you without the glasses,' said Tom, moving over to the toaster as it popped.

Cate forced a smile. 'You know why I'm here, Tom – Serena. She says you've been avoiding her calls for the last week. She's going spare.'

She looked at him imploringly, but he just grunted and turned back to the Aga, feeling embarrassed and a little guilty. He really liked Cate. In fact he'd often wished that his girl-friend could be a little more like her older sister, to have the same heart and humility. It was just like her to be here on a peace mission and he hated to disappoint her.

'Cate, I . . . it's complicated . . .'

'Come on, Tom,' said Cate, 'you can't just turn your back on five years with somebody. How are you going to sort all this out if you won't even speak to her?'

'Sort out what?' he snapped, turning to face Cate, and for the first time she noticed the dark hollows under his eyes. 'What exactly is there to sort out? A one-sided rela-tionship that was going nowhere? Some sort of fairy-tale ending?' Tom trailed off and gazed down at his plate intently. 'Look, you shouldn't have come all this way,' he said. 'It's good of you, but . . .'

There was a long pause as Tom rubbed at a grease-spot on the worktop, then he looked up and fixed Cate with his movie-star eyes.

'Do you know why I jumped off that boat?' he asked.

'Ridiculously wankered on margaritas?' offered Cate with a twisted smile.

'Actually, yes.' He smiled briefly, then turned to the window, staring out at the long lawn that swept down to the cliffs. 'I've not been unfaithful, Cate. I've just been miserable. For months

– years, maybe. When I jumped, it was like I was liberating myself from my life and the way I was living it. Of course I care about Serena,' he added. 'She's beautiful, yes. And at one point, we really used to have fun.' He trailed off wistfully as he remembered snapshots of better times. 'But that London life is such shallow shit. The same crowd going to the same old boring parties. And she got so taken in by it all. Sometimes I just wished she was a bit more grounded. Like you.'

There was a long tantalizing moment that passed between them, then Cate moved a step backward to stop herself thinking a forbidden thought. Tom looked at her a moment longer, then shrugged.

'Well, Serena loves the scene, and if I stay with her it'll just be really difficult to get rid of all that stuff from my life.'

Cate had known for years that Tom had had a drink problem in his early twenties when he was doing the fringe theatre circuit and mixing with a troubled, boozy crowd. She knew as well that he was drinking again now and that there'd be countless dinner parties where they quaffed wine and finished with port, but Cate had no idea how hard it was for him to keep his drinking under control.

'Just give her a ring,' Cate offered, forgetting momentarily that Serena was in Mustique.

Tom turned back to the stove and irritably stabbed a sausage. There was a quiver of anger when he spoke. 'And say what? "Sorry, darling, been a bit of a mix-up. I'll be home in a couple of hours"?'

Cate blinked at him.

'So that's it?' she asked.

He shrugged and pushed the abandoned breakfast away. 'I'll talk to her when I'm ready, Cate. I just think it's better to have a bit of distance sometimes, you know? I don't want to get talked into a situation I don't want to be in. Do you know what I mean? She's very good at that.'

They both laughed, knowing how difficult, charming and manipulative Serena could be.

Tom led Cate through a sun-filled conservatory and out into the garden. The gulls squawked around their heads and in the distance the sounds of the waves crashed up on the rocks. Cate watched him walk ahead, ambling towards the cliff edge, which sloped down to the beach, kicking a pebble along the grass with his shoe. Trust Serena, she thought. To have a movie star who made a mean fry-up, then blow the relationship royally. Cate wondered whether to tell him about Michael, but she didn't want to make it sound like blackmail.

'Anyway, Miss Balcon,' said Tom, picking up the stone to throw it over the cliff. 'What's happening in your life? Editor of *Vogue* yet? Any sexy suitors on the horizon I should know about? I will, of course, have to vet them ruthlessly. Serena never tired of telling me you have terrible taste in men.'

'The answer to that is no and no. My love life, as you probably know, has been nonexistent for aeons. I did meet someone in New York, a photographer. But he hasn't called.'

Tom laughed.

'And the other thing you obviously don't know,' continued Cate, 'I got fired last week.'

'Oh shit. I'm sorry.'

'Yeah. I'm livid.'

Tom threw her a lopsided smile. 'No wonder. And what are you going to do in the meantime?' he asked, flinging another rock towards the sea. 'You can come and be my script assistant, if you like. There's plenty of room in this old place for another London refugee.'

For a second Cate hoped he was serious. It might be nice just giving it all up and moving out here with the gulls and the waves. If she was honest, she hadn't told anybody about her plan to launch a magazine because she was afraid that people would laugh at her lofty – and possibly unrealistic – ambitions. But the longer she kept it a secret, the longer it would take to get anything off the ground.

'I was going to freelance. But . . .' She looked at Tom's open, honest face and she knew she could trust him with her plans. '. . . I developed a dummy magazine last year which I was going to present to the company. That didn't happen and I still have the dummy, so I was thinking –'

'You're going to publish it yourself?'

She grimaced. 'Well, possibly.'

'Let's go back into the house.'

Tom led Cate into the study, a snug space with just enough room for a desk and a big leather-backed chair. He picked up his big black Smythson diary and flipped it open.

'I think you should phone a friend of mine,' he mumbled, scribbling down a phone number on a pink Post-it note. 'Do you know Nick Douglas?'

Cate shook her head, looking at the number as he passed it over. 'I know the name,' she fibbed.

'I've known Nick since school. He's a really good friend of mine. You'll like him. He's been publisher of some sports magazine in America for a couple of years and he's just come back wanting to do the same as you, to publish his own stuff. I've no idea how far he's got raising finance or even if he's got an idea for a magazine, but it won't hurt to talk to him.'

'OK, thanks. I'll do that this week,' she said, putting the number in her bag. She knew she needed to work with a publisher to get her idea off the ground, but had already started making phone calls to contacts she knew. She was seeing Cecil Bradley on Tuesday to see if she could get him involved in some way. The old man had more than enough time on his hands. With a bit of luck, she wouldn't need Tom's charity.

'In fact, let's give him a ring now.' Tom pulled his silver mobile out of his jeans pocket, flipped open its lid and started dialling.

'No – you don't have to. I'll call him –'

Tom held up a finger. 'He only lives in Highgate and you're still in Notting Hill, right?' he whispered, walking out into the hall. 'Bloody crap reception around here. Can only get a signal in certain parts of the house.'

He disappeared and Cate perched on the edge of Tom's desk, leafing through the property section of the *Sunday Times*, occasionally hearing the sound of laughing and banter.

Tom popped his head back into the room. 'You free next Sunday?'

She nodded.

'Is meeting in Highgate good for you?'

She nodded again. 'Don't make it too late,' she whispered.

Tom winked at her. 'Cinderella will be in bed by midnight.'

11

Of the many fashionable and exclusive restaurants in London, San Paulo was – right now – the most exclusive and the most fashionable. Oswald usually detested these fly-by-night destination eateries, feeling much more at home in one of the private clubs that peppered the SW1 district in tiny pockets of old-school exclusivity. Still, it was good for crumpet, he thought, looking around at the lunchtime crowd, a throng of well-groomed Euro-Sloanes en route to a Mandarin Oriental spa treatment or a Neville hair appointment. There were bankers' wives, Russian wives, footballers' wives: the whole place smelt of husbands' money, he reflected with disapproval, looking at the Jimmy Choo carrier bags and Hermès Birkins that lined the floor around the tables.

'The doctor's, eh? What's wrong with you this time, Venetia?' Oswald asked his eldest daughter, snapping his fingers to attract the attention of a waiter.

'Not sure yet,' said Venetia, keeping her head down. This was only her second day back in London after returning from Mustique, but she'd spent the entire time worrying about her test results. This morning the doctor had told her nothing, only taken more blood 'for further investigation'. But however anxious Venetia was, she certainly didn't want to suggest to Daddy that something was wrong.

'It's always something with you, isn't it?' Oswald paused and looked at her shrewdly, 'Not women's things, is it? It's about time you and Jonathon started dropping a few sprogs.'

Venetia began studying the San Paulo wine list intently. 'As I say, we're not sure what the problem is,' she replied stoically, her heart racing.

'Well, it's about time one of you gave this family an heir. Still, at least we know you *can* have children, don't we?' he leered, fixing Venetia with a cruel smile.

The memory she had been deliberately suppressing for weeks now came flooding back with a force that was frightening. She'd been seventeen years old. She'd had a summer fling with a boy in the village that ended three months later in a Marie Stopes clinic in London. Her father had insisted on literally dragging her to the door. It was not her age he had objected to, but the father. 'Do you want a retarded ape for a child?' he had taunted her. 'Well, not under my roof!' She wondered if the abortion had had anything to do with her infertility now, but she couldn't mention it to Dr Rhys-Jones, not with Jonathon's disapproving face watching her every move.

Her painful thoughts were brought to a halt as a voluptuous dark-haired woman approached the table. In her late thirties, Maria Dante wore heavy make-up over her handsome features, her curvy body wrapped in a sharply tailored corset dress and jacket.

'Hi Maria,' smiled Venetia, trying to regain her composure. 'Good to see you again.'

Maria Dante nodded graciously and allowed the waiter to pull back her chair for her to sit down.

'How were rehearsals?' asked Oswald, stretching over to kiss her powdered cheek.

'Going well,' replied the singer, in an accent that was a cocktail of Italian and American. 'The opening night is on the twenty-third, so you can see for yourself how well. That is, if you would still like to come?'

Venetia looked at the two of them, puzzled by the familiarity between her father and the singer.

'Oh, have you two met?' she asked.

'Only on the telephone,' laughed Maria, looking at Oswald appreciatively. He had surpassed her expectations.

Oswald took a sip of wine, and smiled smugly at his daughter.

'After you mentioned the possibility of a musical evening at Huntsford, I took the liberty of phoning Miss Dante.' He looked over at her like an antiques dealer sizing up his latest sideboard. 'We were surprised that we had so many friends in common, weren't we, Maria?'

The singer giggled girlishly. 'Oh, too many people.'

Venetia smiled weakly. She had set up the lunch as a business meeting to introduce them, in the hope that Maria might charm Oswald into holding the event at Huntsford. Now she felt as if she were gate-crashing a first date.

'Let's cut to the chase so we can get on with a civilized lunch,' said Oswald, swilling his wine around the glass. 'I'm up for the event in principle. But if we are going to stage it at Huntsford, I want it done properly. Something on a grand scale. Something elegant. Something spectacular. I mean, bloody hell! anybody with access to the bloody Internet goes down to Glyndebourne these days. I'm not having that. Don't want it to be like a ruddy singsong in someone's back garden. The Balcon family have a reputation to protect.'

He paused to rub his stomach, which hung over the waistband of his trousers.

'I completely agree that it should be exclusive,' interrupted

Venetia, 'which is why I think we should be looking at two hundred and fifty pounds a ticket. That way at least fifty per cent of the ticket price can go to charity.'

Oswald put his glass down and sighed.

'I thought I made it clear about charity,' said Oswald, correcting the hard tone of his voice when he saw the startled expression on Maria's face.

'You should be the first one to know how much everything costs these days,' he said to Venetia. 'God only knows, you spend enough of Jonathon's money.'

She bridled.

'Anyway, we have Maria's fee to take into consideration,' he continued, glugging more Pinot.

'Fee?' said Venetia, shifting in her chair. 'I thought . . .' She tried unsuccessfully to catch Maria's gaze. 'But what about the charity?'

'My daughter.' He began talking to Maria as if Venetia wasn't present. 'She always wants to help everyone. She wants to save the world!'

He laughed, then turned back to Venetia. 'Darling, the commercial reality is that these things are expensive. Don't you think all these so-called charity concerts are lining somebody's pocket? What's the point on skimping on our evening of music just so we can send some loose change to some cripples? I for one won't pretend it's some grand humanitarian effort. It's hypocritical nonsense.'

Venetia was surprised to see that Maria was nodding as Oswald spoke, since the singer had been quite excited about the proceeds going to the National Children's Home when they had spoken about it the previous week.

'Now Maria.' He placed a hand on Maria's knee that she allowed to linger. 'It all begins with you, my darling. What dates did you come up with?'

She burrowed for her diary, not bothering to look at

Venetia. 'I have a couple of shows in Verona in the second week of July. I was rather looking at the first week of June.'

'Splendid!' said Oswald, reaching for the bottle of wine. 'Now then, Venetia, do you think Serena would compere it? You do know my daughter Serena Balcon?' boasted Oswald to Maria. 'Such a beautiful girl.'

Venetia rolled her eyes. The way he paraded his preferences for his youngest daughter never failed to rile the other sisters.

'And couldn't we get Camilla to rustle up all those legal bores she knows?' he continued. 'There's huge corporate possibilities with all this,' he added in a stage whisper to Maria.

Oswald was clearly on a roll now, enjoying being centre stage. 'Charlesworth's quite connected in the classical world. And bloody Watchorn can put his money where his mouth is and drum up some of his Cabinet friends he's always banging on about. I wonder if the PM would be around about then?'

He carried on with his plans happily, draining his glass and clicking his fingers irritably for service, but Venetia sat silently, with her hands in her lap, feeling totally wretched, realizing that her brilliant plans for a glorious evening at Huntsford had been well and truly hijacked.

12

It was 9.30 p.m. and Nick Douglas had still not arrived. The Flask pub on the edge of Highgate's tiny green had been cranked up to full Sunday-night volume, the air full of loud laughter, weekend gossip and the smell of beer and cigarettes. Cate had been lucky to find a seat in the corner where she sipped a glass of white wine and pretended to read a leaflet advertising yoga classes. She glanced at the Cartier Tank watch on her wrist and considered going home. She usually gave up waiting for people at half an hour, and if any of her other publishing contacts had shown the slightest interest in joining her fledgling company she'd have given up long ago and slunk back to her flat to watch *Midsomer Murders*. As it was, Cate was feeling very alone. The three publishers that she had approached had told her that they were unhappy in their jobs. The thing was, none of them were that unhappy that they wanted to take a risk with Cate. Even Cecil Bradley, while supportive of Cate's ambition, had declined to come out of retirement. There was frankly only one person left: Nick Douglas. And even he couldn't be bothered to turn up.

'Cate Balcon?'

She looked up to see a tall, slim man wearing jeans and

a long, grey wool coat. His light brown hair was cropped, his hazel eyes were intense and his wide, full-lipped mouth was unsmiling. Nick Douglas had the sort of broody handsomeness and the lean skier's build that usually made Cate drool. But without a word of apology or even a smile, Nick Douglas looked like the typical arrogant public schoolboy nightmare of her teenage years.

'Nick? I was just about to go.' She couldn't stop the words coming out spitefully.

'We said half past nine.'

'It was nine, actually,' said Cate, her smile thin and fixed. She took a deep breath. She didn't want this to get off to a bad start. Nick certainly didn't look particularly enamoured by his first impressions either.

'Can I get you a drink?' she said, trying to thaw the atmosphere.

'No, no, I'll get them,' said Nick. 'They know me here. White wine, is it?'

'No more wine,' said Cate, shaking her head, aware that she was feeling a little light-headed after drinking two large glasses of Chardonnay in quick succession. 'Just a Diet Coke, please. Ice and lemon.'

'A Diet Coke girl.' He smiled and swaggered off. Cate felt her dislike of Nick Douglas increase. As he headed to the bar, Cate noticed that he had instantly attracted the attention of a pretty blonde barmaid. Maybe she had agreed to the meeting too hastily. He might be a friend of Tom's, but Cate didn't know Nick Douglas from Adam and now, here she was, half drunk in a London pub, about to show this cocky upstart her precious magazine dummy. How did she know that this Nick Douglas wasn't going to steal all her ideas and then drop her like a hot potato?

By the time she had drained the remnants of her wine, Nick had brought the drinks, pulled his coat off and squeezed into the tiny space beside her, the warm leg of his jeans pressing against hers.

'This is a bit odd, isn't it?' he smiled for the first time.

'How do you mean?'

'Feels like a blind date.'

Cate laughed nervously. 'Well, it certainly felt as if I'd been stood up.'

He took a sip of his Guinness, leaving a frothy white-foam moustache on his top lip. 'Sorry about that. I did know it was nine o'clock.' He grinned. 'I was just watching, well, the end of *Midsomer Murders*, actually.'

Cate snorted quietly, clinking her glass of Coke against his dark pint glass sarcastically. 'Thank you. Glad to see you just couldn't wait to meet me.'

Nick bristled. He knew he'd been out of order arriving late, but he was the one doing her the favour, wasn't he? He was only here because Tom had asked him to be. He was sure that Cate was going to be the career-bitch twin of her sister Serena, all blonde highlights and blue-blooded attitude. He'd witnessed his old schoolmate Tom being henpecked by Serena for years. He had no intention of falling into a similar pattern, but without any of the bedtime benefits.

'Tom says you've been in America. Why did you leave?' asked Cate.

Nick looked at her. He could see no reason to try and impress this over-privileged princess, so he just shrugged and told her the truth. 'Same reason as most people who leave a ridiculously well-paid job in New York for unemployment in London.'

Cate smiled at him. 'Fired?'

'Got it in one.'

'Well, you and me both,' she smiled with a hint of embarrassment.

121

Nick softened, looking at her wide smiling mouth. Her trying-to-hide-it nervousness was actually quite endearing, he thought. Shame she was such a pompous cow.

Nick took a big gulp of Guinness and continued. 'The funny thing is, it's terrible being fired and all that, but I'm sort of glad. I was bored shitless, but I could have carried on for another ten years, with my nice West Village apartment and summer weekends in the Hamptons. It was nice. Really nice. But when things are too nice, you don't take any chances.' When he grinned at Cate, faint little creases crinkled around the corners of his eyes.

'So, how far have you got with your publishing company?' asked Cate, feeling as if she was interviewing him.

'Is that what Tom told you? I had a publishing company?' Nick laughed, draining his pint glass. 'It's less a company, more of an idea. You see, I've got great contacts in the ad world and I know some people in the City who might be interested in backing a media venture, but I don't think I've quite got the product to present to them yet. When you're a start-up company, the first product has got to be absolutely right, and I don't think that *Your Parrot* magazine is going to set the City on fire.'

'Your idea is for a bird magazine?' said Cate, her heart sinking.

'Parrots.'

'Well, the pet market is huge,' she acknowledged, not wanting to mock his idea.

Nick started laughing – a deep, loud laugh. 'No, I'm not doing a bloody parrot magazine. That was a joke.'

It was Cate's turn to feel riled. How dare he make her feel stupid when she was only trying to be kind? She bowed her head to stop him seeing her cheeks burn red and began to rummage around in her bag, trying to find her mobile to call a taxi. She'd had enough of this. Nick Douglas was obvi- –

ously not the charmer Tom had described. Unable to find the phone, she pulled out a thin portfolio she had put together, full of layouts and mood boards, and put it on the table.

'Is this it?' asked Nick, craning his neck over to the side of the table.

Before Cate could stop him, Nick was reaching for the black leather portfolio. She shot out her hand and put it on top of his.

'I wasn't giving you that,' she snapped pulling it back.

'Then why are we here?' He looked up at the angry, determined line of her mouth, which he found, against his better judgement, quite cute.

'Hey, don't look so worried,' laughed Nick more softly, putting his palms up in surrender. 'I'm not the KGB! If you're worried about me pinching your idea, which of course I won't, I am quite happy to sign a NDA.'

'A what?'

'Non-disclosure agreement. Not that they are worth the paper they are written on, but I'm happy to sign one.'

Cate took a deep breath and looked into Nick's intense eyes. 'OK,' she said, pushing the folder across to him. 'I trust you,' she added, not very convincingly. Nick returned her gaze, then nodded.

He opened the folder and sat patiently and methodically working his way through the layouts, spreading them out onto the battered wood of the pub table as Cate launched into a passionate description of her vision and her belief that there was a real niche in the market.

He carried on flipping the pages, occasionally glancing up at Cate. She was sitting under a wall-lamp, the light spilling down on her face. She looked as if she was glowing in happiness.

'I love this,' said Nick at last, 'I'm genuinely impressed.

It's so fresh. Makes all those dull travel magazines look so bloody boring and personality-free. And the fashion is gorgeous,' he said, pointing at a picture of Serena astride an elephant, a late-evening Indian sun shining on her skin. 'It makes the fashion mags look so po-faced.'

'Well, that is a Mario Testino shot,' shrugged Cate, trying not to burst with pride. 'He makes people look so exotic and luscious.'

'Even so, this is brilliant, Cate. I know the advertisers will just love it. It's glamorous, it's escapist, it's new. And there's certainly nothing on the shelves like it.'

He shut the file, which closed with a whispering thud.

'So?' Cate had gathered he liked it, but wasn't sure whether he thought of it as a business opportunity.

'It's exactly what I, sorry, *we*, need,' he continued carefully. 'From a business point of view, it would be madness for a small start-up publishing company to launch a mainstream women's magazine like *Marie Claire* or *InStyle*. Our pockets just wouldn't be deep enough to compete. And if we did try, the big publishing companies like Alliance would just try and destroy us with their muscle at the news-stand. But this,' he clinked his empty pint of Guinness against Cate's glass, 'this is brilliant. A travel and fashion magazine is niche enough for us to build a thriving business under everyone else's radar. But it's also commercial enough that I think we could easily shift fifty thousand a month. And we'd get good advertising too.'

Cate was tingling all over. 'So what does that all mean?' she asked.

'It means it could work.'

She felt her tummy leap with excitement. 'That's fantastic. So what's the next step?'

'The first thing we need is a business plan to take to potential backers. I'll do the figures and draw up a publishing strategy. You need to prepare a really slick presentation of what you've just shown me. All this is great editorial stuff, but we've got to demonstrate a gap in the market so I need all the facts, figures and circulation figures of any competitors we can think of.'

Ideas started to bounce between them like a Wimbledon tennis rally.

'I'll get a list of all celebrities, publicists and photographers we can get on board.'

'And I'll get in touch with my ad contacts. If we could just get Armani, British Airways, Chanel – any of the major advertisers – on board before we go to the City, that would be fantastic.'

Cate furiously scribbled down everything into her little black Moleskin notebook. When she looked up, she saw him smiling at her.

'What's so funny?'

'You. Like a little beaver.'

In all the excitement and planning, she had almost forgotten that Nick Douglas was the most smug, cocky man she had met in ages.

'Well, Mr Douglas, if you think I'm so funny, forgive me for spoiling your little cabaret show. I have to be going.'

Nick looked around and, noticing that the pub was emptying out quickly, slipped his arm into the scarlet silk lining of his coat. 'I've got to be off, too. The girlfriend gets nervous if I'm out too late with other ladies,' he teased, sensing she was a little cross. 'If it's all to her honourable's approval, does that mean the pair of us are in business?'

He flashed her a smile that would have been heart-meltingly sexy if it hadn't been coming from such an arrogant face.

Against her better judgement, Cate extended her hand and gave him something resembling a smile. She was angry all right, but something about tonight's planning had made her prickle with excitement. If it was a choice between him or her magazine – well, she was just going to have to take her chances.

She put out her hand. 'Nick Douglas, I think you just might have a deal.'

13

Serena was so bored she could hardly keep her eyes open. Although she usually loved talking about herself, she was sick to death of repeating the same glib sound bites about her 'work' on *To Catch a Thief*. Since she'd got back from Mustique two weeks ago, there had been three draining days of interviews in London and hundreds of phone interviews with all sorts of Japanese and European publications. Boring questions from people who could hardly speak a word of English. Now she had another two days of press and television interviews in New York, and if she had to trot out one more tired, clichéd line about, 'What attracted me to the movie', she swore she'd commit hari-kari with the heel of her Jimmy Choo.

'Final question, please,' said Clara the publicist, popping her red-bobbed head into the Four Seasons Suite overlooking Central Park where Serena was enduring her final interview of the day.

Thank Christ, thought Serena, forcing one final smile for the journalist from *Time Out New York*. She took a dainty sip of Badoit mineral water and crossed her legs, smoothing down the sharp crease of the Gucci slacks with her fingers. 'Fire away.'

The journalist shifted in his chair. Clara had warned him that all questions related to Serena and Tom Archer's recent break-up were strictly off the agenda, but with minutes of the interview to go, he had to give it a shot.

'So then,' he began, pushing his Dictaphone a little further in front of Serena, 'you and your sisters are big stars in England. Do you think you can be as successful in New York?'

Serena tossed a sheaf of hair over her shoulder. This was the sort of question she enjoyed. 'Well, of course I'm rather well known in London,' she smiled, trying to sound modest. 'And because of that my sisters have some degree of popularity . . .'

Having warmed her up, the journalist decided to change tack.

'You went on a cruise on Roman LeFey's boat. Did you enjoy it?'

Serena's eyes instantly narrowed.

'Yes, Roman is a very good friend of mine and we often travel together.' She instantly knew where this was going and she wasn't going to let this sallow hack get any sensational headline out of her.

'Egypt is a beautiful country. I had a wonderful time,' she said obliquely.

'And I understand Roman introduced you to the billionaire hotelier Michael Sarkis?'

Serena gave up, a cloud of disapproval evident on her face. 'I'm here to talk about the movie,' she snapped, so ferociously that even the thick-skinned writer drew back in shock.

'Of course,' he stammered, 'I just thought one quote about . . .'

Serena picked up the telephone beside her. 'Clara, darling, we need you in here one moment.'

Clara bustled back into the room, her clipboard held tightly against her chest and a fixed smile on her face. She was one of the best publicists in the business and could get rid of unwanted attention in an instant. Serena pointed at the journalist haughtily. 'Personal questions, darling,' she said, shivering with distaste.

Clara beamed at the journalist and thrust a press pack into his hands. 'I think that's it for today. Any other information you might need should be in there. Goodbye!'

The journalist looked at her, deflated, pushed the papers into his bag and scurried out of the door, leaving the two women alone in the grandeur of the suite. 'How was that? Not too awful?' asked Clara kindly, topping up Serena's mineral water.

Serena flopped back into the luscious feather down of the sofa, resting one stiletto boot heel on the coffee table, rubbing her toes through the leather.

'I'm bloody exhausted,' she pouted. 'Journalists. They're such a headache. Speaking of which, those lilies are making me feel sick,' she said, flapping a hand at an enormous vase of trumpet flowers. 'Can you move them and then get me some aspirin? I've got to leave this room before I get cabin fever.'

Clara was both professional and experienced, and over the years had dealt with more divas than she cared to remember. She merely smiled sweetly and phoned the concierge. 'Aspirin's on the way,' she replied, busily tidying up the coffee cups as Serena tutted from the sofa.

'You do remember,' added Clara gently, 'that the cast and crew screening of *To Catch a Thief* begins at eight p.m.?'

Serena flashed her a look of undisguised boredom. She had no intention of sitting in the dark with the third assistant director and the costume mistress. And besides, she had much bigger fish than *To Catch a Thief* to fry.

'I'm afraid I won't be able to make that, darling,' she replied airily, lighting up a cigarette.

'I have a very busy evening tonight and I want to be fresh for tomorrow. By the way,' she continued casually, 'can you make sure we have San Pellegrino instead of Badoit in the room tomorrow? Badoit is just a tad too salty.'

Upstairs in the Four Seasons' presidential suite, Serena took a shower then paced around the room nervously. She walked over to the suite's dining area, that jutted out fifty-one floors above Madison Avenue, making you feel as if you were floating in space over the pulsating heart of Manhattan. Perching on the edge of the dining table, she looked out at the panorama of New York spread out in front of her. Central Park had become a thick black gulf in the growing dark while yellow taxis darted around it like hornets. She took another drag of her cigarette. New York. She looked at it twinkling in front of her like a golden opportunity made physical, and shivered. Never before had she felt quite so exhilarated, yet quite so apprehensive. In London she had been the queen of the social scene; it was safe and cosy. But here, in front of the Manhattan skyline, London just seemed insignificant.

Serena didn't want to be London's hottest star; she wanted to be the world's hottest star. And that was why she was about to meet Stephen Feldman in the Four Seasons' bar. Feldman was chairman of Feldman Artist Management, one of the hottest, most ruthless and best-connected artist managers in America. Bicoastal, bisexual and brilliant, even a two-bit waitress was one Feldman strategy away from being a Hollywood superstar. And now he wanted to meet Serena Balcon. She glanced at her watch, then looked at herself reflected in the darkening window. She looked good, and if she played her cards right, New York – America – would soon be hers.

* * *

'Two words. Grace Kelly,' said Stephen Feldman in his camp New York drawl. 'In fact, you're gonna be bigger than Kelly. Sure, she was classy, but she was the daughter of a bum. Serena Balcon is the genuine article. I just know we're gonna do something very special together.' Stephen downed his glass of claret and waved the bar's wine waiter over for a refill. Serena sat back in her banquette and basked. She was loving the attention that Feldman was lavishing on her, eyeing her up like a trainer inspecting a prized stallion.

'That said, honey, you've got a lotta problems,' he said picking a speck of dust from his camel Brioni cashmere jacket.

Serena looked at him, startled. 'Problems?' she spluttered, almost spilling her cocktail. 'You've just been telling me how wonderful I am!'

'Sweetie, just hear me out,' he said, pursing his lips. 'If we're going to get you up there with Julia, Catherine and Gwyneth, we're gonna have to make some changes, which starts with getting a proper support system around you. I can't believe you haven't already got a manager!' he said incredulously. 'Honey, even waitresses in LA have a manager.'

'I have an agent in LA and London and a publicist in London and it's worked for me so far,' she replied, trying to contain her annoyance. If Feldman didn't have such a fearsome reputation, if he hadn't worked wonders with the careers of Hollywood legends like David Sanders and Michael Montgomery, she would have been long gone.

'It's worked in London, honey. You're playing with the big boys now,' smiled Feldman, running his hand through his highlighted blond hair. 'Plus, you don't have Tom Archer by your side any more. Sure, he was cute, he was going places – he's even got Oscar buzz around him now, but he's gone. Now you have to get noticed by yourself.' Feldman started stroking his chin, thinking up an angle. 'Hooking you up with Hollywood royalty wouldn't hurt. Look how Zeta-Jones skyrocketed after she met Douglas. Or what about the real thing? Hey, why not have a discreet affair with Prince William? You must know him, right?'

They ordered another round of drinks and Feldman took her through his plan. It was both dizzyingly exciting about the future and brutally critical of her past. Serena, he pointed out brusquely, had spent the last five years working on her celebrity not her career. Did she think Julia Roberts or Tom Cruise had made it without a carefully considered strategy? Yes, Feldman had watched some of Serena's tapes, he said, but they had been mediocre movies with mediocre performances. However, there was some good news. Within five minutes of meeting her, Feldman said, he had known that Serena Balcon could be a good actress and, more importantly, a big, big star. She had a fabulous voice; a little plummy, sure, but rich and sexy, and there was charisma and expression in every little gesture she made. And her physical beauty was awesome.

'So we're going to get you to some acting classes,' he told her bluntly. 'I know a great woman, Ellen Barber, worked at Lee Strasberg for years, now she does a lot of stuff for me.'

Serena squirmed, caught between anger and embarrassment and still thinking about this so-called 'Oscar buzz' around Tom. Where did that come from? Not that poky little arthouse film that had had blink-and-you-miss-it distribution, surely?

'Acting lessons? At this stage?'

Feldman just raised his eyebrows and looked at her. Serena met his gaze for a moment, then just nodded. Pleased, Feldman carried on with his vision. She would sign up with Greg Bloomberg, former whizz kid at the huge talent agency

CAA, who had recently formed the SPK super-agency with some other talent from William Morris and CAA out in LA. He wanted her to be personally looked after by one of the top publicists, not one of their underlings – Pat Kingsley in LA, Lesley Dart or Muffy Beagle in New York. Most importantly, she would have to move to LA.

'LA,' she stuttered, instantly balking. She cast her mind back to several years earlier, shortly after she had been expelled from St Mary's school, when she had flown out to LA to 'make it'. It had been the only time she had met serious opposition from her father and the only time she had failed at anything. Six months, hundreds of auditions, and a bit-part in a mobile phone commercial later, she had returned to Britain with the stale taste of America's West Coast in her mouth.

'But I hate LA,' she said, 'the whole city is one big car park!'

Stephen laughed. He had been right about Serena: the girl was a diva already. 'Sure, and that's why I spend half my time in New York.'

'Well, why couldn't I then?' asked Serena, pulling her best little-girl face.

Feldman thought for a moment. 'I guess you could. Liv Tyler, Uma, Julianne Moore, lots of the big girls are based here. You'd still have to go out regularly to build up your profile on the West Coast, but I guess you could do it. The main thing is that you gotta forget about London and come to where the action is, baby!'

'Well then,' said Serena, lifting her flute, 'I guess we're in business.'

'Damn straight!' replied Stephen, clinking his glass against hers. 'By the time we've finished, you're not going to be just an actress, you're going to be an international business brand – clothing lines, perfumes, real estate.

J-Lo's gonna shit when she sees you coming. We're gonna be rich, baby, real rich!'

As she left the hotel and stood by the steps waiting for Michael Sarkis's car, Serena looked into her compact mirror. She was pleased with the reflection. Her cream Stella McCartney trouser suit, left tantalizingly bare under the jacket, was the right side of casual but with enough chic to impress the Upper East Side ladies she was about to meet.

'Just a low-key supper,' Michael had said, insisting she come and meet some of his friends. Serena had been cautious, but flattered by the invitation. Since their passionate night in Mustique, Serena and Michael had been on as many dates as his hectic schedule would allow. There had been a night in Michael's Mayfair apartment when he had been over in London on business, a dinner at the Voltaire in Paris when she had been doing the European junket and then there had been the weekend in New York. They had stayed in, eaten Chinese from little white cartons, and had had great sex in every room of Michael's Fifth Avenue duplex; in the Jacuzzi, on the Philippe Starck coffee table, over the white leather couch. She'd been left exhilarated but uneasy. She had no idea whether their relationship was just fabulous, frenzied sex or whether they were edging towards something more. This invitation to meet Michael's friends suggested it might just be the latter. And, to her surprise, she found herself hoping that might be the case.

'Serena, baby. You look good enough to eat.' She stepped into the back of the black Lincoln in which Michael was waiting, sinking into the deep leather seat. He motioned to his driver to close the privacy window. As the glass hissed upwards he slipped a hand under her jacket, brushing his thumb across her nipple.

'Remind me who these friends are again?' she mumbled softly, running her hands inside his cashmere overcoat. 'Couldn't we just turn around and go back up to my suite?'

'Later, baby, there're some people who want to meet you,' smiled Michael.

Serena sat bolt upright in the black leather. 'What do you mean, want to meet me?'

'Relax. It's just that word about us is getting around, darling,' he laughed gently. 'Apparently Liz Smith wrote a diary piece about us yesterday. I didn't see it.'

Serena was shocked, but not surprised. On the one hand, it was surely good news that the big gossip columnists were writing about her, but on the other hand, she had only wanted word to get out about her and Michael after she was sure about their relationship. Tom was fading from her mind so swiftly that she sometimes had to ask herself if she had really spent five years of her life with him. But, as they pulled up to the dignified townhouse on East Seventieth Street, she wondered whether she really wanted to go public with Michael.

'Michael, sweetheart. So good to see you!' A platinum blonde in her mid-forties stepped forward as Serena and Michael entered the chandelier-lit drawing room. Harriet Fletch, ex-wife of millionaire restaurateur Daniel Fletch, was dressed in a powder-grey Tuleh chiffon dress with enormous diamond earrings drooping from her lobes. She smiled wanly at Serena, her eyes showing both curiosity and distaste.

Low-key supper, my foot, thought Serena, glancing quickly around the room. It was a cavernous space for Manhattan – all marble and oak panelling with gilt fittings and framed oil paintings. All rather vulgar, Serena judged absently, before her attention was distracted by a handsome Hispanic waiter in black tails who was presenting a platter of caviar blinis to other prototype blondes, all dressed in identical expensive designer clothes and jewellery and all with that same hungry, ruthless look in their eyes.

Thank goodness I wore the trouser suit, she thought as another gorgeous waiter handed her a glass of Krug. Whatever happened to the dress code for supper being a pair of Seven jeans, some heels and a pretty little Diane von Furstenberg top? That was how it worked in Chelsea, after all.

'So this is Serena Balcon, I've heard so much about you. Welcome to my home,' said Harriet, extending a thin, bony hand. 'I loved seeing your sister's place in *Vogue* the other day. Venetia is such a talented interior designer. I can't wait until she opens her little store over here.'

Serena smiled graciously, but bristled underneath. She certainly didn't need reminding of that little embarrassment; she was still smarting from Venetia's appearance in her favourite magazine. Serena had reassured herself that Venetia's Kensington home had been the star of the feature, but still, *Vogue* was her turf, and she didn't like her sisters muscling in.

'And how lovely to see you here with Michael,' continued Harriet, stroking Michael's cheek. 'One of my favourite men in the world.'

The truth was, Harriet Fletch was far from delighted to see Serena at Michael's side. On Monday, when she had heard the delicious rumour at Frederic Fekkai's salon that Michael and his two-bit model girlfriend had split up, she wasted no time organizing one of her legendary soirées. Ever since her divorce from Daniel Fletch, Harriet had been on the lookout for husband number four, and Michael Sarkis more than filled her long list of requirements. Fabulously wealthy, incredibly sexy and with all those wonderful spa hotels all over the world, she need never spend another penny at the Bergdorf salon again! So she was seething as she read over her citron pressé and wheat-free pancakes that Michael had been seen squiring this wealthy English girl. But seeing Serena in the flesh, Harriet felt she was not defeated quite yet. OK, Serena was good-looking, but that aloof expression, the pompous Princess Diana accent, this Balcon girl was the ice queen incarnate, and Harriet knew from the Upper East Side gossip mill that Michael liked his women exotic, malleable and extremely adventurous in bed. This frosty frigid Brit wouldn't last two minutes.

Harriet had of course made very sure that Serena was separated from Michael at dinner, placing her amongst people she had been sure would dislike her. Courtney Katz, Harriet's best friend and ruthless social conspirator, and Gary Becker, plastic surgeon to the stars, who was sure to be turned off by Serena's fleshy, natural look. However, Harriet had not reckoned on Serena's social resilience; as a battle-hardened veteran of her father's soirées, she could squeeze sparkling conversation from a shy Trappist monk. By the time the diners had reached their pistachio soufflés, Serena had steered the chat onto safe dinner party territory: whether the Hamptons were over as the summer weekend destination of choice. Serena let the conversation float over her head and glanced over at Michael, sandwiched between Harriet and an elegant woman in her sixties at the other end of the table. He tipped his head towards her and smiled. She gave him a slow wink back, unaware that Harriet was watching her every move.

'Anyone who wants to take coffee in the study, feel free,' announced Harriet suddenly, determined to interrupt this moment of intimacy.

'Shall we?' asked Gary Becker, the plastic surgeon sitting to Serena's left, pulling out her chair. He was keen to spend more time with the English beauty: she was the first woman he had seen in years who had no need for cosmetic enhancement. She was like a precious gem to his artistic eyes, a perfect orchid to a botanist. The guests filed through the double doors of the dining room into the 'study'. The huge room was crammed with oversized leather sofas and lamps with shades the size of space hoppers; these cast a warm yellow light around the room and onto the walls of neatly lined books.

Keen to shake off Gary, Serena strolled over and ran a finger down the spines of the books. Not quite the Huntsford collection, she thought smugly: more likely put together by an interior designer who had brought in the leather-bound science tomes, the heavy books of art and architecture, even the row of orange and white Penguin classics. Every one of them looked suspiciously unloved and unread. She took a black filter coffee from one of the ever-present gorgeous waiters and wandered through another door, finding herself in another spacious room, this time filled with English and French antiques. Who ever said New York properties were small? thought Serena.

Realizing that the coffee had wiped away her plum lip-gloss, she went to look for the bathroom to freshen up. As all the waiters were attending to the guests with silver coffee pots, she dismissed the idea of asking for directions and drifted upstairs, following the curve of the thick mahogany banister to the second floor. The wide corridors were lined with framed black-and-white photographs and smelt of Tiger lilies, but there was no sign of a bathroom. As she was turning to go back down, Serena distinctly heard a voice say her name. It had come from a room at the end of the corridor; she edged towards the sound of the voices. Through the tiny crack of the open door, she could see a huge mirror surrounded by light bulbs, and just caught the reflection of Harriet Fletch and Courtney Katz reapplying their heavy make-up.

'I don't see how she can make a living as a model,' said Harriet cattily, rubbing a smudge of colour into her lips. 'Rather big, isn't she? Must be one hundred twenty pounds at least. She certainly shouldn't be wearing that white pant suit.'

'Seemed a little dull, too,' said Serena's dinner companion. 'Lovely skin, though.'

Serena felt the hairs on the back of her neck prickle. *Big? Dull?* She had never been called big or dull in her life.

'I mean what is she, other than Tom Archer's ex?' asked Harriet, her hard voice muffled by the door.

'An actress, I think. Can't tell you anything she's been in, though,' said Courtney pointedly.

Serena's jaw tightened with anger as she heard the two women dismiss her clothes, her career, her family. Only one second ago she'd been saying how fabulous Venetia's house was: now Harriet Fletch was dismissing it as 'stuffy'. Quivering with rage, she had to put a finger on the rim of her coffee cup to stop it rattling.

'Thing about these upper-class Brits is that they still think they're something special,' continued Harriet. 'The Empire is over, honey – it's the twenty-first century! And most of those so-called grand families have so little money these days. I mean, that woman who writes Harry Potter. I hear she earns more than the queen these days.'

'I don't know what you were so worried about,' laughed Courtney, snapping her compact shut. 'I pumped as much information out of her at dinner as I could. She's going back to England tomorrow. She's only here to do some publicity.'

'Is that so?' said Harriet, the glee purring out from between her thin coral lips. 'Well, I think I'll give Michael a ring on Monday. Maybe invite him over for a more private supper.'

Hearing the women move from the dresser, Serena darted

into another room, waiting until she could hear the sound of their heels clacking on the parquet of the ground floor. She took a deep breath to compose herself. How dare those hideous women talk about her like that? Who exactly did they think they were? If they could trace their lineage back fifty years to some jumped-up soup millionaire, they thought they were social royalty. They were anachronisms, vultures; women who could trap a man into marriage and then pick his carcass clean before moving on to the next poor sap. After a few more moments burning with righteous anger, Serena composed herself and slipped back down the stairs to rejoin the party, studiously ignoring Harriet Fletch who was scolding a waiter for putting a hot coffee-pot directly onto the top of an antique writing desk.

'There you are, darling,' said Michael, appearing at her side and slipping a hand around her waist. 'Are you enjoying yourself?' he purred, brushing his warm lips across the top of her ear.

'What a nice evening,' she whispered, planting a lingering kiss on Michael's cheek in direct eyeshot of Harriet.

'Well, everyone loves you,' he drawled, leading her through French windows onto a terrace that had a view of Central Park. Michael pulled Serena to him and cupped her face in his hands.

'How much are you enjoying it?' he whispered, kissing the top of the nose. 'A lot or enough?'

'Enough? What do you mean?' asked Serena.

Michael paused, a dangerous smile on his lips.

'Enough to move here? To spend more time with me?'

Serena thought back to her conversation with Stephen Feldman and a flash of excitement lurched in her stomach.

'Oh, I think I'll take Manhattan,' she laughed, gently gripping his fingertips between hers.

'Well then, move in with me,' said Michael softly. 'I know

it's soon for you, but I just want to see you all the time. I don't want to have to grab a dinner or a night with you when I'm rushing around on business. I want you to be here.'

She turned away from him, stalling for a moment to think. She desperately wanted to live in New York, but surely it was too early to jump into anything?

Her eyes moved from the skyline of New York back inside the house, where the drawing room glowed amber in the dark. Standing at the French windows was the silhouette of Harriet Fletch staring out onto the terrace, her hand on her hip, watching them intently.

Serena smiled over at her triumphantly before moving her head towards Michael to nuzzle his ear.

'Move in with you?' she whispered playfully, still looking at Harriet over his shoulder with unflinching eyes. 'It would give me the greatest pleasure.'

14

'The problem you face is this,' said David Goldman, sticking his fork into his medium-rare steak and trying to make himself heard over the Coq D'Argent lunchtime crowd. 'You're trying to raise money for magazine publishing, one of the highest-risk businesses of all, and investors are frightened of it.' Goldman paused to chew his beef and looked at Cate and Nick sitting nervously across the table from him. 'And they're frightened for a good reason. Did you know that out of four hundred and fifty-three new consumer magazine launches last year, three hundred and seventy of them have already folded? Not good odds, is it?'

Cate took a sip of her wine and sized up her lunch guest. A slick, mid-thirties corporate broker with a Meribel tan and an immaculately tailored Gieves & Hawkes suit, David Goldman oozed confidence. It was just a shame none of that confidence seemed directed at their magazine project.

'All that may be true,' said Cate, glancing to Nick for support, 'but the magazines that do succeed can make a lot of money. We have a great product, years of experience, a strong management team –'

David wiped his lips with a linen napkin, the corners of

his mouth turning into a smile. 'Cate, you don't have to convince me about how good your proposition is. Your track record speaks for itself. As for young Nick here –' he hit his friend on the arm playfully with his napkin – 'I've known him since our first day at university together, so I know that, even though he can act like a buffoon, he can also make anything work if he puts his mind to it.'

Nick Douglas managed a weak smile. Trapped in his badly fitting suit, drinking wine he knew he could not afford should David not offer to pick up the bill, Nick had felt uncomfortable since lunch had begun and his friend's harsh assessment of the business's prospects hadn't helped. 'Thanks for the vote of confidence,' he mumbled, poking dispiritedly at his *moules-frites*, 'But seriously, do you think we can raise enough cash to do this thing or are we wasting our time? We have to launch in June or we'll miss all the summer trade – not great for a travel and style mag. The only other option is to leave it for another nine months, by which point I'll be jobless and bankrupt.'

David Goldman let his eyes wander across the restaurant to a curvy blonde in a tight short skirt wiggling across the room. 'Well, the other problem you face, of course,' he said, turning reluctantly back to look at Nick, 'is the amount of money you want to raise. How much is it again?' he asked, flipping through the pristine business plan that Nick had placed in front of him. He nodded and pursed his lips. 'One point five million quid?' There was something about the way he said it that made it seem an insignificant amount of money.

'What's wrong with that?' asked Nick anxiously. 'Too much? Not enough?'

David put his glass of wine down on the business plan cover sheet, leaving a claret-coloured mark. 'Difficult amount, that's all. A bit too much money for most individual investors, a bit too small for the venture capital companies. They usually deal in investments well over five mil. Even then, they don't like start-up companies.'

Nick and Cate looked deflated. Since their first meeting a little over a week ago, they'd worked fifteen hours a day creating a convincing business plan. Now they were sitting in one of the City's hottest power-broking dens, multimillion deals bouncing off the walls around them, and it was beginning to sound as if it had all been a waste of time.

'Is there any good news?' asked Nick grimly, his large hazel eyes searching his friend's.

David slowly gave something that resembled a smirk.

'Look, if it wasn't you two sitting opposite me, I'd turn this gig down right now. It just wouldn't be worth my while when frankly I think it's got a fifty-fifty chance – at most – of raising the cash. But . . .' He looked over at Cate and flashed her a brilliant row of straight white teeth. '. . . there is something quite sexy about investing in a glossy magazine.' He laughed, his gaze still fixed on Cate. 'It's certainly a damn sight more glamorous than putting your money into widgets; although widgets are a much better investment in my opinion. However,' he continued, running a finger up and down the stem of his glass, 'I reckon that's how you get your investors. By appealing to their vanity.'

He picked up the business plan and thrust it into a calf-skin leather briefcase sitting on the seat beside him, snapping it shut with a click.

'I tell you what, I'll sound out a few of the VC firms for you – see if any of them are interested in a small media project, but I think your best bet is to get a handful of high-net-worth individuals to chuck in some cash. All you're asking is for two hundred thousand pounds each to say they own a slice of a fancy magazine, and that's a day at the races for some of these guys. Maybe you could even chuck in a dinner-date with your sister, Cate?' He looked again at Cate in her fitted Alberta Ferretti black silk dress and corrected himself. 'Actually, forget Serena, chuck in a dinner-date with you.'

Cate laughed politely, carefully moving her foot away from David's, which seemed to have slipped next to hers under the table.

'So we're looking for investors with a few quid and a bit of time on their hands,' said Nick. 'Blokes like Cate's old man, for example?'

David perked up, his financial radar sensing a kill. 'That's a point, Cate – your dad and some of his mates might want a punt at this. It would really help me get the ball rolling with other investors if I say we have some initial investment, particularly from high-profile investors.'

Cate felt some colour drain quickly from her face. 'I don't know about that,' she stammered.

'Come on, Cate, give old Daddy a ring,' chided Nick. 'Why not call him now? I'm going to call Tom to see if he'll chuck in a few quid.'

'Our family doesn't have money coming out of its eyeballs, you know,' she replied firmly. 'And I don't think he'd take it too seriously anyway. I'll speak to Daddy if we have to, but . . .'

After only a week in Cate's company, Nick had come to recognize her resistance when the name Oswald Balcon was mentioned. He flashed David a look.

'OK, OK,' said David, checking his watch. 'If money from your family is not an option, do we have any other source of initial investment? Can you two bring any money to the table, for instance? Can we get a mortgage on any property?'

Nick laughed again. 'Like I'm rolling in money. I've been unemployed since Christmas.'

Cate said nothing, suddenly feeling very sick. The last thing she wanted to see was her adorable Notting Hill mews house, the beautiful haven into which she'd ploughed every last penny she'd earned, slapped with a fat mortgage.

'Well, you'd better find something quick,' said David, draining off the wine in his glass and running his tongue over his lips. 'Investors are going to want to see something from you two other than good looks and a good idea.' He clicked his fingers to summon the bill and turned his attention back to the blonde in the miniskirt. The meeting, it seemed, was over.

'That didn't go too well, did it?' said Cate, pulling up the collar on her cream cashmere coat as a cold northeasterly wind slapped against her cheeks. She stuck her hand out to hail a black cab.

'Well, it could have been worse,' replied Nick, climbing into the taxi behind her. 'Anyway, where are we going? Your house?'

She smiled. 'My house? You mean our office.' She laughed, thinking of the cramped top floor of her house, tucked away in the eaves, that had become their makeshift studio, the floor strewn with magazines, the walls papered with pictures and ideas.

'Oh yes, the office,' laughed Nick, giving the driver the address and sinking back in the seat as they rumbled down the street. The laughter was soon replaced by a gloomy silence, however.

'Well, I don't see how you can possibly think that went well,' said Cate after a while, looking out of the window at City workers scurrying through the drizzle. 'Basically he said we've got to find a dozen billionaire gamblers or we might as well forget it.'

'Yes, well, don't underestimate the sort of people that

146

man knows,' said Nick. 'Believe me, he knows everyone. How else do you think he got to be head of corporate broking at the age of thirty-five? Anyway,' he added, 'he certainly seemed to like you.'

Cate blushed furiously and pretended to stare out of the window.

'Don't be silly,' she said.

'Oh, I've seen David Goldman's slick seduction moves before and he definitely fancies you,' teased Nick, poking her in the ribs and trying to get a reaction. 'Some people consider him something of a catch, you know. Although as his halls-of-residence roommate for twelve long months, I can tell you that his personal hygiene is terrible.'

Now Cate twisted herself around to face him and slapped the back of his hand playfully.

'Will you stop it?' she said, her voice flushed with embarrassment. 'And anyway – you shouldn't even be suggesting such impropriety. It's not professional.'

They both began to laugh, the tension of the meeting finally broken. Nick ran a hand through his short tousled hair as he watched fat droplets of rain bounce off the steamed-up window. His voice turned more serious once again.

'There are a lot of rich private investors out there, but the real problem is raising that initial finance. I agree with David that we're more likely to get the ball rolling if we can put in some personal funds. I can seriously only scrape together about twenty grand, max.'

'And I am really, really nervous about mortgaging my house any more,' admitted Cate, 'especially with all those statistics about three in four ventures failing. It seems so scary.'

For a second she wondered if they really were doing the right thing. Wouldn't it be easier to take the dummy to Jonathan Newhouse, European chairman of Condé Nast, to see if he was interested? At least they would have the financial muscle required to launch a magazine, plus they'd be able to see the potential of *Sand*.

'Ah, don't go wobbly on me now, Cate,' smiled Nick, as if reading her thoughts. 'What about your sister's husband? Doesn't he have a hedge fund or something? He must be rolling in his own cash – or at least other people's?'

'Not that I completely understand what a hedge fund is, but I've already sounded Venetia out. Apparently his company doesn't deal in investments like this. It's all about very high risk, very high return with him, and apparently a start-up magazine doesn't quite qualify.'

Nick nodded slowly. 'OK . . .'

Cate looked at him pleadingly.

'Nick, I want to try and do this myself. To you it might look like I have a cushy life, but it's hard when you've spent your life being made to feel grateful for everything.'

It was the nearest thing to personal detail he had got out of her in the whole time he'd known her.

'And no, I don't want to ask my father for the money either,' she said gently. 'Even if he did have lots of cash sloshing about for investments, he's not the easiest of men to deal with.'

Nick watched her, trying to work out what she wasn't telling him.

'You two don't really get on, do you?' he said quietly, guessing her emotions.

She shook her head. 'It's not really that,' she said. 'He's just a bit unpredictable. I couldn't tell you how he'd react if I asked him to be an investor. On the one hand, ever since I was a little girl he's been, "Catherine, you must do better! You must achieve!"' She mocked his pompous accent. 'And yes, now here I am trying to do something, so you never know . . .'

148

'But on the other hand?' asked Nick.

'On the other hand he can shout me down, make me cry and make me feel absolutely crap. Believe me, he has an incredible capacity to do that to people, no matter how confident you feel. He can destroy you in a minute,' she said, clicking her fingers.

Nick put a friendly hand on top of hers and gave her a reassuring smile. 'You've always struck me as a person who's afraid of no one . . .'

She smiled at him and suddenly feeling empowered, reached into her pocket for her mobile. She drummed her fingers on it for a moment, thinking of the conversation, his tone of voice, the things he would say. She put the phone into her handbag and turned back to the window.

'Let's see how David gets along and then maybe I'll call him,' she said. But somehow, the thought of asking Daddy suddenly made the idea of mortgaging her house seem much less scary.

15

'I could have bought half the shop!' laughed Camilla, stepping onto the Belgravia pavement from the front door of Christian Louboutin.

'You almost did,' smiled Venetia, looking at her sister struggling with four large bags.

'Well, it is my birthday,' smiled Camilla, feeling slightly guilty at her splurge. Still, her American Express Black card, given out only to very special customers, could more than cope with a couple of thousand pounds spent on shoes. The girls took one last look at the beautiful high-heeled pumps laid out like precious jewels in the window and started the slow amble through Belgravia. 'I've made a lunch reservation for one-thirty at San Lorenzo,' said Venetia, turning up the collar on her Fendi jacket. 'What do you want to do until then? Harvey Nicks? We could even go back to mine for a coffee?'

Camilla shook her head.

'Oh, sorry, Van. I'd have loved to have stayed out a bit longer but Nat wants me back at the flat for twelve-thirty. He says it's a surprise.'

'Has he got you anything for your birthday yet?' asked Venetia, slipping an arm through her sister's.

'Not yet,' replied Camilla, 'but I assume that's my surprise.'

Thirty. Ever since she was a teenager, Camilla had been dreading slipping into old age. Except now that the big three-oh had arrived, it didn't really feel like that at all. Being thirty definitely suited her – and where she was heading. Parliament. She got goose-bumps and butterflies just thinking about it.

'It's twelve already. Does that mean we've got to say goodbye?' asked Venetia in mock horror.

Camilla nodded. 'I'm afraid so. Thank you for my birthday shop, and my lovely, lovely present,' she smiled, holding up a cream Jo Malone bag festooned with black ribbons. 'I think I'd better jump in a cab before I collapse under the weight of my shopping.'

Venetia was sad to see her sister go. Although they lived within a few miles of each other, Camilla worked such long hours she was lucky to see her twice a month.

The sisters embraced and a taxi pulled to the kerb to pick up the beautiful blonde girl with the armfuls of shopping. 'Glebe Place,' she said before sliding back into the seat. She watched the expensive stuccoed streets of Belgravia slip by and wondered what her big surprise could be.

One of the most beautiful apartments on one of London's most prestigious streets, everybody who had seen Camilla's fabulous four-bedroomed duplex flat assumed the interiors were the product of Venetia Balcon's renowned design talents. In fact, Camilla had taken great delight in turning down Venetia's offer to revamp the place when she had bought it, and, ever the control freak, had instead set about doing the work herself. She'd chosen every carpet, fabric and curtain, supervising every major structural improvement and even making innovative suggestions to Tom Barrett, the architect, who had been so impressed by her design savvy that he'd nearly offered her a job.

Camilla clearly had a hidden gift because the apartment was stunning. The walls were chalky white and lined with Diane Arbus prints. The carpets were so thick and soft that they were like a sheet of sheared mink, and the Far Eastern feel of the furniture, in shades of dark teak and cherry, somehow worked alongside the very modern pink neon heart 'art piece' and the big stack of photography books on the huge Perspex coffee table. French windows book-ended the apartment, with the back doors stretching out onto a balcony littered with terracotta boxes of flowers and hedgerow. Only a stack of legal files bound in red twine on the big walnut desk hinted that the house belonged to a barrister and not a designer.

Camilla walked into the reception room to find Nat Montague standing in the middle of the cream carpet, a grey cashmere jumper straining over wide shoulders, a crop of nutmeg hair falling mischievously onto his face. She noticed that his navy-blue eyes were sparkling and that he was standing next to a pile of tan leather suitcases.

'You're five minutes early,' he smiled, picking up one of the cases.

Camilla trotted over to her boyfriend and kissed him urgently. 'Oh Nat, I hate waiting for surprises,' she pouted. 'Tell me what it is! What's with all the luggage?'

'Your surprise,' said Nat, wrapping his arms around her shoulders and kissing her bottom lip gently. He slid his warm hand down the back of her jeans to stroke the base of her spine and the top of her buttocks.

She pulled away, giggling. 'Nat . . .'

He shrugged, disappointed. He would have liked nothing better right now than to peel her clothes off, take her up to the emperor-sized bed and make love to her all afternoon. But, glancing over to the big antique clock on the fireplace, he realized there was not even time for a quickie on the Perspex coffee table.

'Put your shoes and coat back on,' he smirked mysteriously. 'We're off out.'

Camilla looked puzzled. There was a very cautious part of her that really didn't like surprises. 'But Cate is coming round at three . . .'

'I've cancelled her,' said Nat with a smug look.

Camilla glanced at her desk, piled high with case files and yellow legal notepads and felt a rush of panic. 'And I've got to do some work . . .'

She looked at the irritation on Nat's face and gave a weak, worried smile. 'OK, OK, let's go.'

It was only when Nat's grey Aston Martin turned up the Heathrow Airport approach ramp that Camilla realized they probably weren't going out for dinner for her birthday. At least, not to any restaurant in England.

'Now can you tell me where we're going?' whined Camilla, pulling at the sleeve of Nat's jacket as they hurried to the Swiss Air check-in desk. Nat stopped at the counter, pulling out two airline tickets. 'Happy birthday, darling,' he said. 'We're going to Megève for dinner.'

Camilla's mind momentarily ran over all the work she had to get done for a case that began on Tuesday, but she quickly shook it off. She was going to Megève! She loved the French ski resort more than anywhere else on earth, and Camilla loved skiing almost as much as work. The Balcon girls had all been forced onto the slopes from toddling age. They used to go to Gstaad then, when Oswald would abandon them on the slopes while he disappeared into the exclusive Eagle Club. So now she had found a different winter resort to frequent. Megève was like Paris on the slopes:

all chic Europeans, delicious food and laid-back rustic charm, without the St Moritz glitz she hated.

And of course it was just like Nat to whisk her off there for her birthday. He was prone to flamboyant gestures, and as a rich banker with family money he could afford them – especially when it was in the pursuit of pleasure. In the two years they had been courting, he and Camilla had exhausted not only the British social calendar but the international one as well. Countless weekends had been spent at the polo in Argentina, at the racing in Dubai or sailing in the Grenadines. On top of that, Nat had spent many more weekends with his friends partying around the jet-set circuit while Camilla was preparing for an important case on the Monday morning.

She watched him as he checked them in at the airport desk. She had to admit she'd had some fabulous times with him, but lately the hedonistic streak had been troubling her. She certainly hadn't liked the profile of him in last month's *Tatler*, which had labelled him as the English arm of the Eurotrash. But as he led her towards the executive lounge, she reminded herself that this was his birthday surprise and she tried to push any uncharitable thoughts to the back of her mind.

They arrived in Geneva at six p.m. A black four-by-four was waiting to drive them the seventy kilometres to the village. As they wound higher and higher into the mountains, they watched the architecture change from charmless concrete blocks to wooden chalets, with long icicles dripping from their eaves. As they turned into Megève, its quaint streets smudged with snow, Camilla pressed her nose against the window to watch the skiers in their bulky padded suits head to cafés for *vin chaud* and fondue after a hard day on the slopes.

Their driver turned off the main route, just before the village centre became pedestrianized, and drove up a small road that took them sharply up the mountain, stopping a few hundred metres above the village at a beautiful chalet. Its front was guarded by a thick row of hedges where clumps of snow hung in the branches like giant frozen magnolia buds, while a thousand fairy lights dripped off its carved balcony.

'We've arrived,' said Nat happily, while he waited for the driver to open the car door.

'This is so lovely,' said Camilla. An old, flustered-looking woman in a grey apron came out of the chalet, a glow of golden light escaping behind her.

'*Bonsoir, bonsoir*!' she called, removing her apron to greet them. Nat ignored her welcome, instead motioning towards the car boot, watching impatiently as the woman struggled in with their three large cases and Nat's set of skis.

'*Merci*,' smiled Camilla awkwardly, flashing an embarrassed look at Nat as he pulled her inside the chalet.

'Wow, Nat,' sighed Camilla, pulling off her parka and taking in the chalet's interior. It really was exquisite. Like a Hollywood fantasy of a ski-lodge, it was filled with wide brown sofas and fur rugs, leather cushions and cashmere throws. Chocolate-brown velvet drapes hung at the windows, scented candles lined the windowsills, a stag's head hung above a stone fireplace complete with crackling fire. There was a sauna, a heated boot-rack, and a games room with a gigantic plasma screen. Even Camilla was impressed.

'Come and see this,' said Nat, leading her to the back of the chalet where doors opened out onto a patio, a black mosaic Jacuzzi already steaming and bubbling.

'What's that?' laughed Camilla, feeling chilly at the thought of it.

'For later,' said Nat with a lazy smile.

All thoughts of work and the case files sitting on her desk at home had dissolved.

'Want to get ready for dinner?' asked Nat, pointing in the direction of the staircase. 'I'll join you in a sec.'

She nodded and went upstairs into the bedroom. It had an incredible view of the whole of Megève village, which twinkled in front of her in the blue-grey light, while the mountain made shadowy, ominous shapes behind it. It was all so wonderful, yet still Camilla felt unaccountably on edge.

Relax, woman. Enjoy yourself, she scolded herself. This is wonderful. *Can't you let yourself be happy?*

She sat down on the edge of the bed and went over it in her mind once again. At least once a week for the past few months, Camilla had been asking herself what she was really doing with Nat. Conscientious, cautious Camilla Balcon and rakish, man-about-town Nat Montague. It just didn't add up. Being far too busy working through her twenties, she had only had two real boyfriends before Nat: Jeremy Davies and Crispin Hamilton. Both Jeremy and Crispin had been barristers – dry, hard-working, more interested in their case-loads than in Camilla. So when she had met Nat at the Serpentine summer party, he'd been like a firework going off in her hand. The sex was incredible. Lovemaking with Jeremy and Crispin had been like watching paint dry compared to the passion that Nat had unleashed in her. She had never had a single orgasm before she'd met him – now she knew precisely what all the fuss was about. Then there were the exotic holidays, the mad parties and the extravagant gestures that made her feel wanted and loved. But somehow, Nat just didn't make her feel . . . oh! She just couldn't put her finger on it.

Swearing to herself, she unzipped her leather holdall, wondering what on earth Nat had packed for her. She pulled the clothes out quickly, holding each item aloft like a child rummaging through a goody bag. Two sets of her most sexy sheer underwear: you could tell a man had packed this, she smiled. Her ski suit, some socks, a couple of thick cashmere jumpers, her favourite black backless Dior cocktail dress, some five-inch satin heels and – what was this? she wondered, pulling out a tiny pair of black mesh crotchless panties. She didn't recognize *those*.

After she had taken a quick shower, she pulled on her cocktail dress and blow-dried her hair until it fell in a golden sheath onto her shoulders. Not usually one to wear much make-up, she rubbed some rouge tint onto her cheeks and dabbed some peach gloss onto her full lips. Catching her reflection in the mirror, she worried that she looked too formal for just a dinner in a chalet, even if it was her birthday. Her concern was interrupted by the sound of the housekeeper's old Peugeot 205 gunning to life and then fading away into the distance.

'All alone at last,' called Nat from the bottom of the stairs. She came down to meet him; he handed her a glass of Chateau Margaux and led her to the table by the long windows. It was set for two people with crystal glasses, linen napkins and white bone-china crockery, all shining in the saffron glow of candlelight.

'I never knew you could be so romantic,' said Camilla, only half joking, as she sat down. Their previous romantic nights had often been interrupted by at least six of Nat's society friends turning up 'unexpectedly'.

'I aim to please,' said Nat, going into the kitchen to fetch a casserole pot and two dishes of steaming vegetables.

'I feel like a bloody waiter,' he grumbled as he placed the food on the table, pushing away a lock of brown hair that had flopped over his face. 'Still, I didn't want that housekeeper hanging around too long,' he said, pulling a bottle of Krug from out of a snow-filled ice bucket. 'Happy birthday, darling.'

They sat for a few minutes, eating in silence. 'I love the pot-au-feu,' said Camilla, scooping up some of the rich stew with a forkful of buttered carrots.

'And I love you,' said Nat quietly, his head bowed slightly over his glass.

Camilla's fork froze in midair. In their eighteen months together, Nat had never once said 'I love you'. He'd skirted round the words, usually when drunk and, if she was totally honest with herself, it had never been an issue. Camilla hated the sort of women who constantly sought reassurance with declarations of love from their partners. She herself had never wanted to appear so weak, dependent or desperate.

She took a small breath, taken aback by his words. 'You love me?' she repeated, as if it was some kind of alien concept. She was smiling now, almost mocking him, but Nat ploughed on with uncharacteristic fervour.

'You're so good for me,' he said, putting down his knife and fork to look directly at her, the dimple in his chin becoming more pronounced. 'My family loves you; my colleagues love you.'

He picked up the bottle of Krug and poured himself another glass, wiping his hand across his lip nervously.

'I know I can be a bit crazy sometimes, but that's the job and the pressure . . .'

Camilla started to play with a chunk of meat nervously.

'But you calm me down. You make me want to settle down. I'm thirty-four, for Chrissake. I can't go running around like some ageing playboy for ever.'

Now it was Camilla's turn to take a huge glug of wine as her female intuition told her this conversation was going somewhere she wasn't entirely sure she wanted it to go.

'Do you know why I brought you here?' asked Nat, fixing his gaze on hers through the candlelight.

'Fondue? A few black runs?' replied Camilla, laughing nervously.

'Marry me,' he said matter-of-factly.

A thick silence rang around the room. Camilla felt her breathing become deep and uneven. She was used to thinking on her feet, arguing, debating on the hoof in court. But at this second she was utterly lost for words. She felt a little nausea in the pit of her belly.

'Marry you?' she said with a small smile, stalling for time.

Nat got up and came over to her. He didn't quite drop to one knee but perched on the edge of the chair and pulled out a claret-coloured Garrard box from his pocket. He flipped it open to reveal an enormous marquise-cut pink diamond that twinkled yellow and lilac in the soft light.

'We're good together,' he said.

She looked at him.

Was he being sincere? Did he really love her? She grimaced. *What was love anyway?*

But Nathaniel Montague was a good catch, she thought, composing herself.

Or was he? He was wild and careless, but he was rich, successful, important.

Her father liked him. Not that that mattered, she reasoned, immediately putting the thought out of her mind. And being with Nat got her noticed. It wasn't just Serena who desired the eyes of the crowd on her. She just didn't know, she agonized, digging her fingers into her thighs.

Nat picked up her left hand and, placing it on the knee of his jeans, pulled the ring out of its box and slid it onto the third finger of her left hand.

'Does it feel good?' he asked softly, lulling her with his voice.

She nodded. It did feel good. Heavy and secure.

Nat pulled her to her feet, taking her in his arms and running his hands down her bare back. God, he was sexy.

'Say yes,' he whispered into her ear.

'Yes,' she responded suddenly, willing herself to relax and be taken by the moment.

'You've made my day,' he murmured into her neck, pushing the fabric of her dress off her shoulder with a deft movement of his chin.

'Are you wearing my present?' he breathed, moving his hand down towards the cleft of her ass. For one moment, Camilla wondered what he could mean, then, remembering the crotchless panties, she started to smile, a rush of power shooting through her like a drug.

'Actually no,' she said but, feeling suddenly brave and sexy, she looked at him seductively. 'Would you like me to?'

Nat took her by the hand and led her up the stairs. The bedroom was in soft darkness, lit only by the moon in a black sky.

'Put them on,' said Nat, pointing to the skimpy underwear lying on the bed.

He sat back in a biscuit leather armchair in the corner of the room and watched as Camilla slowly peeled off her dress. She turned around, slipped her La Perla thong down her long legs and stepped into the crotchless knickers.

'Keep the shoes on,' drawled Nat, his eyes fixed on her glowing body, shining like a beautiful marble statue in the moonlight.

She slipped the five-inch Jimmy Choo heels back on and stood facing him, on the one hand feeling a little awkward about the sheer sexiness of what she was doing, on the other hand feeling a powerful sense of womanliness as she could see Nat getting visibly aroused.

'Stand up,' she purred, holding out her hand.

160

Nat stood slowly, tugging at the buttons of his shirt. Camilla pulled at his belt and popped opened his Levis, pulling them down along with his boxer shorts. Standing naked together, the same height in her towering heels, Nat took two fingers and pushed them between her legs, quickly finding the gaping hole in the mesh fabric and stroking her slowly there. Camilla groaned and arched her back. As she did so, Nat took one nipple between his lips, biting on it gently. Clasped tightly against each other, they moved towards the fireplace, Camilla taking small, backwards steps as she breathed in his ear, 'Now, please. Take me.'

Their bodies glowed in the flames from the fireplace. He lowered her onto the fur rug, kissing her all over her face, then slowly moving his mouth down her body, gripping the elastic waistband of her panties with his teeth and pulling them down with one sharp tug. Uncovering her small, tidy pubic growth, he burrowed his face into it, probing his tongue in and out of her and bringing moans of pleasure.

'Now, please,' begged Camilla as his hips hovered over her, his throbbing cock waiting to penetrate her. He slid himself slowly into her, lifting her back off the sheepskin so the two rocked together, each thrust going deeper and deeper until she saw his face crease in pleasure and felt his body spasm in release. 'Fucking incredible,' he breathed, rolling off Camilla onto the fur rug. Camilla was naked except for the huge diamond. She couldn't stop smiling as she looked at it twinkling in the firelight.

'Eight carats,' he nodded, stroking the ring. 'Do you know how expensive these pink diamonds are?' he said, looking up at her to impress the point.

'It's beautiful.'

'And it's going to be a big, beautiful year for the two of us.'

Suddenly Camilla felt the cold and pulled a cashmere throw around her to cover her body.

'A big year in more ways than one,' said Camilla, snuggling closer to Nat. 'I haven't told you yet, but I've got the Tory candidate Selection Weekend next month. You know, the thing I was telling you about? I have to go to it to get on the Central Office approved list.'

Nat turned to face her, propping his head up with his elbow.

'Baby, you're not still banging on about that MP nonsense again, are you?' he said with irritation. 'Look, sod Parliament and a crappy little salary and eighteen-hour days. This year you're going to be my wife.'

He stood up and moved over to a big armchair, his flaccid cock flopping onto the leather.

'I fancy maybe a September wedding,' he continued, reaching for the glass of wine he had brought upstairs. 'Of course, that rules out half of the good long-haul destinations for a honeymoon. Pisses it down in the Caribbean around then. But how about a month-long tour around South America? Rio. Peru. Argentina. Maybe we can even take in Mexico.'

Camilla looked at him, unconsciously pulling the cashmere throw more tightly around her body.

'Nat, this is important to me,' she said.

'Darling . . . it's silly.'

'Silly?' she felt herself bristle. 'The things I want to do, my ambitions, they're not silly.'

He sipped his wine and laughed gently at her.

'Come on. Don't get your knickers in a twist.'

With his toe he lifted up the crotchless thong, discarded on the white rug, and flipped it at her. 'Anyway, fuck all that. We'll talk about it later. Why don't you phone home? Give Venetia a ring. Old mother hen will love this bit of happy news.'

Nat sat back naked in the armchair, downing another glass of wine and Krug he had brought upstairs as if they were lemonade. She looked down at the pink dazzling ring and suddenly it felt like a vice. Before she could think further, she was startled by the sound of a loud horn beeping right outside the front door of the chalet.

'What the hell . . . ?' she said, pulling the cashmere blanket even tighter.

Nat sprang up from the chair and looked at his watch, pulling on a towelling robe as he did so. 'Fuck. Is it nine o'clock already?'

'What's going on?' asked Camilla, watching him run downstairs.

Nat stumbled with his words. 'Er, JJ and Rich, Ant and a few others are in town. I said we might go out to cele brate.'

'What?' yelled Camilla. She stood up and wrapped the blanket around her like a toga, following him. 'I'm not going anywhere! Not tonight of all nights! Nat, what are you thinking?'

There was a loud rattling of several hands on the front door.

'Come out, come out wherever you are,' sang a loud, drunken voice.

'They are not coming in,' spat Camilla, feeling the romance drain from the evening with every knock on the door.

'Jesus, Cammy, lighten up!' said Nat. 'I found out this afternoon they were in town. There's a party going on at JJ's chalet. What was I supposed to say when they rang up? Anyway,' he smiled, trying to wrap his arms around her, 'I knew we'd be celebrating . . .'

'You can never leave it alone, can you?' she hissed, pushing him away and catching a glimpse of him reflected in the window. Half naked, his glass tipped at an angle, he looked like a more glamorous version of the Dudley Moore character in *Arthur*: a rich, pampered buffoon.

'What can't I leave alone?' asked Nat, in a soothing, placating voice.

'The friends, the parties. Even on the night you bloody propose.'

Nat shook his head and flashed her a patronizing look as he reached for the door. 'Baby, you know you love me!'

Camilla ran back upstairs into the bedroom and Nat opened the door to let in five raucously drunk Sloaney men. As she sat in the dark listening to their bellowing voices, she knew in an instant that she was not going to marry him. She was Camilla Balcon, destined for Parliament, and she would let nothing and no one get in the way of her ambition.

16

Cate glanced anxiously around the impressive glass and steel atrium of PCT, London's biggest firm of accountants, feeling a little sick. Damn Nick Douglas, she muttered, stealing another glance at her watch. He was late again, and on such an important day too. She didn't need anything else to make her more nervous. Her laptop PowerPoint presentation sat in a slim case beside her, a sheaf of dummy magazines poked out of her Bottega Veneta holdall. She felt shaky enough without him being twenty minutes overdue. As David Goldman had taken great pains to tell her this morning, this was their biggest – and probably only – opportunity to raise the £2 million they needed. After all, the six venture capital firms David had approached had turned him down flat without even asking for a presentation. So David had pulled out all the stops to gather together twelve private investors who might be interested and who had agreed to assemble in the PCT boardroom this afternoon. If Cate and Nick failed to impress them with their presentation today – well, that was going to be it: dream over. David wouldn't plough any more of his time or money into an idea that was clearly going nowhere fast.

And maybe they were right, Cate grumbled to herself,

maybe it was a waste of time. Especially since that phone call yesterday, the call she would have killed for on the day she was fired. Out of the blue, the editor of *Harper's Bazaar* in New York had wanted to know if she would be interested in an editor-at-large position on the prestigious glossy. Why didn't I just say yes? She smiled grimly to herself. The easy option was never her style.

'Sorry, sorry, sorry,' said Nick, flying so fast through the glass door that his caramel overcoat flew behind him like a cape. 'Defective train in God-only-knows-where,' he spluttered, desperately trying to catch his breath. 'Brought the whole bloody tube to a standstill. Had to run all the way from Angel.'

Cate didn't try to disguise her annoyance. 'Well, maybe you should have left a bit earlier,' she said drily.

Nick ignored her, instead giving a playful wolf-whistle. 'Woo-wee! You look great,' he whistled and, despite herself, Cate smirked back, confident for once in her appearance. She'd spent ages that morning getting ready. Her russet-gold hair was pulled back into an elegant chignon, she'd teamed a black Michael Kors pencil skirt with a mint green cashmere polo neck. Her make-up – glossed lips, bronzed highlighted cheeks – was understated but elegant. She looked professional but not boring, striking but not intimidating.

'You'll knock them dead,' said Nick with a wink, walking up to the marble reception to announce their arrival.

They rode the lift to the boardroom in silence – each not needing to tell the other how vital the afternoon was. Cate and Nick had worked so hard over the last three weeks since their initial meeting with David. The dummy magazine was finished, the business plan was polished. There'd been tough negotiations with printers and reprographic houses to get the best possible deals lined up. A deal to distribute the magazine in all airports, train stations and newsagents had been hammered out. They'd even set up meetings with important advertisers such as Estée Lauder, Chanel, British Airways and Armani to canvass support should they have to move quickly for a summer launch.

The lift door hissed open and David was waiting for them. His grey eyes were serious, his mouth unsmiling: David's operator mode, thought Nick.

'Everyone's here,' said David in a hushed tone, ushering Cate and Nick down the corridor to the boardroom. 'Ten men, two women. Watch out for Nigel Hammond who's sitting at the head of the table,' he said, lowering his voice even further. 'Nigel made a billion in spread betting, will be very tough in questioning, but if we can get him, the rest will follow.' At the heavy oak door, David turned towards them, resting a hand on Cate and Nick's shoulders. 'Be confident, answer all the questions as we've discussed and leave any of the tricky ones to me. Good luck.'

He squeezed Cate's shoulder and she felt a warm, fuzzy glow. 'You'll be fantastic,' he whispered as they walked into the room.

The boardroom was so enormous, Cate felt as if she was looking at it through a fish-eye lens. A large oval walnut table dominated the centre of the room, around which sat a dozen sombre faces, each painted with differing levels of hostility, boredom, impatience or 'come-on-impress-me' arrogance. Only Lesley Abbott, an elegant-looking women in her mid-forties who had made a fortune from selling her market research agency, looked faintly welcoming. Cate decided she would be her focus point.

David Goldman stood at one end of the table and cleared his throat. He had the swagger of a car salesman and the confidence of a presidential candidate.

'We all know why we're here,' he began. 'This is a venture

that I think has great potential. It's well-researched, has a fantastic management team and, as they will explain, they have spotted a real niche in this market.'

Cate felt her stomach lurch and she realized it was her time to talk. Nick flashed her a look that was a mixture of reassurance and anxiety. She stood up and pressed the return key on her white PowerBook. A big image of *Sand* magazine appeared on the projection screen behind her.

'Ladies and gentleman, thank you for coming. I would like to take a minute to introduce myself and our travel and style magazine *Sand . . .*'

Damn, thought David Goldman watching Cate in full flow. She's incredible.

What's your marketing expenditure?
Is it enough?
Who wants to advertise?
Do you think anyone cares that much about travel?
What are the brand extension opportunities?

Questions, questions, questions. Cate and Nick expertly handled each one with passion and authority. They surprised themselves with their ability to address every objection. But it was hard. Cate had fudged a couple of the trickier points and she was sure she'd missed too many of the crucial selling points.

Cate glanced at her watch. Christ, had they only been talking for forty-five minutes? She was physically exhausted, her throat hurt, her mouth was parched and her head was pounding. She needed a large glass of wine and a lie-down.

'Can I just ask Cate, why do you think your magazine will succeed, when hundreds of magazines supported by greater investment and bigger publishing companies fold every year?'

Nigel Hammond took a sip of his Evian water, placing it

quietly in front of him. His tone was mildly sarcastic, his expression sceptical.

Nick opened his mouth to speak but Cate got there first.

'Mr Hammond,' she began calmly, 'you don't need me to tell you that there are safer, more lucrative investments out there to spend your money on.'

Nick Douglas flashed a look at David Goldman. He had gone the colour of fresh white paint.

'But this isn't a vanity publishing project,' she said, placing her palms on the surface of the table. 'It's not a Me-too magazine. This is filling a genuine niche in a lucrative market and we have the talent, the vision and the contacts to exploit it. Yes, to be brutally honest, this is a punt: magazines are very high risk. But for the person who has the balls to invest in it, they will not just be buying a potentially valuable business, but buying into a slice of publishing history. Don't you wish you could have bought *Rolling Stone* or *Wallpaper* magazines when they were started on somebody's kitchen table?'

She looked at Nigel Hammond who stared back, giving nothing away. 'Perhaps, yes,' he replied, 'but why should I be persuaded that you're the woman to make that happen, particularly when you were fired, very recently, from your last job?'

Cate swallowed, her hands clammy. She knew she had a very important choice to make. She could be apologetic or she could fight.

'I was fired in February, that's true,' she said evenly. 'But, Mr Hammond, out of the dozen very successful people sitting in this room today, I would wager that nearly every one of us has been fired at some point. Achievers often are.'

She glanced around the room and noticed Lesley Abbott smile.

Nigel Hammond looked back and scribbled some notes

on the book in front of him. Then he closed it with a thud, his face completely impassive.

'Cate. Cate! Where are you going?' Cate was fleeing the building as fast as her Manolo Blahniks would carry her and Nick, in his flat black loafers, was struggling to keep up. She stopped and turned to face him with tears in her eyes.

'I'm sorry,' she said, 'the thing about me being fired. I'm sorry – I've spoilt it for both of us. I'm going to see my father. Maybe he'll want to invest or perhaps he could call his friend Philip Watchorn who's very connected and wealthy and . . .' The words tumbled out of her mouth until they became tangled up and she just let her arms flop at her sides.

Nick just wanted to reach out and give her a hug: this beautiful, dynamic career woman who at this moment looked like a disappointed child.

'Slow down, Cate. Slow down,' he said softly. 'I thought you did brilliantly. I've been fired too, remember? It just so happens that you're better known than I am, so people have heard about it.' He put his hand on her arm but she snatched it away, pulling on her trench coat.

'I bet no one in that room had been fired,' she said miserably, fiddling with the belt.

Nick shrugged. 'You impressed *me*. I'd have given you the money.'

Cate looked at Nick and she could have sworn his cheeks had gone slightly red. 'Do you wanna go and get a drink?'

She shook her head slowly. 'I'm going into Mayfair. I'll get us the money, Nick. I will,' she said quietly, determinedly.

He watched her go down the street and gave a slow smile at the brave girl hailing a taxi. It was getting dark and the streetlights were just winking on. In his heart of hearts, Nick didn't think it had gone very well either. They had answered all the questions with passion and authority, but Cate had been right. It was a punt. If he had a million quid, would he really want to put it into a magazine run by a start-up company that might very well fold within six months? He seriously doubted it.

The Balcon Gallery was tucked away on a tiny side-street off Mount Street, a quiet, rarefied pocket of London, full of society hairdressing salons and upmarket art dealerships. Its proud red-brick frontage had a crisp white canopy, a sombre blue door and a large window full of expensive eighteenth- and nineteenth-century masterpieces. The gallery was a world away from the trendy Brit-Art spaces of London's East End, where men in mullets painted swastikas in blood to sell to millionaire admen and rock stars. The Balcon Gallery pitched itself at the other end of the art-lovers' spectrum; quiet, old-school money who preferred more traditional pieces to sit in their old-school Belgravia and Kensington homes. Known as a specialist in nineteenth-century Dutch artists, the gallery had recently begun to move with the times and branched out into late nineteenth- and early twentieth-century French bronzes and, as Cate approached, she could see a dainty Degas ballet dancer in the window.

Cate pushed open the door and a tinkling bell rang over her head. Sitting at a table at the end of the room, Mark Robertson, the gallery's office manager, was drawing up an invoice for an immaculately groomed middle-aged couple, while Oswald perched on the edge of the desk talking to them.

Oswald looked up and flashed Cate one of his most charming smiles.

'Ah, here's my daughter,' he beamed to the customers. The woman, with her honey-blonde highlighted hair, Hermès ostrich Kelly bag and Ferragamo shoes, recognized Cate from *Class* magazine and smiled a little more broadly.

'Do you want to go upstairs to the office, darling? I'll be up shortly,' Oswald said cheerily. Cate nodded and walked up the tiny spiral staircase at the end of the room. As she went, she watched her father at work. It was a shame he spent so little time at the gallery, she thought: he was a natural salesman. Even that little jovial father-greets-daughter interchange was perfectly pitched. A showman and a charlatan, she thought grimly.

The building was tall, long and thin, a perfect space for a gallery, although it meant that the office, located in the eaves, was rather cramped. The table in the middle of the room was spilling over with invoices and papers; as she sat at it, she flicked through an auction brochure detailing the sale of some rare Henry Moore sculptures.

Helping herself to a coffee from a pot on the sideboard, she sipped it slowly, her mind a maelstrom of thought. She felt just as nervous now as she had earlier in the day. But it had been a gut-wrenching, heart-pounding adrenalin rush in the PCT boardroom; sitting in the Balcon Gallery offices she felt small, apprehensive and resigned. She really hadn't wanted to come and see Oswald, but she could still see Nick's proud but disappointed expression as they had left the investment meeting. She looked at the dummy magazine sitting in her bag, its cover slightly thumbed and torn and she felt a rush of sadness. *Why was she getting sentimental about a magazine*? she scolded herself. It wasn't an abandoned puppy, it was a business – and a damn good one, if only someone would give them a helping hand. And, as she thought this, she heard the slow thud of her father coming up the spiral stairs.

He was wearing his London clothes, noted Cate, taking in his fine navy suit with a Dracula red silk lining, no doubt going on to one of his fancy St James's gentlemen's clubs afterwards.

'So to what do we owe this pleasure?' asked Oswald briskly, 'I assume you want something – something too important to be resolved with a phone call.'

He pulled a pocket watch from inside his jacket, peered at it through his half-moon reading spectacles and put it back with a tut. 'I have to be at White's at seven for dinner with Watchorn so you'd better make it snappy. Make me an Earl Grey, would you?'

Cate went over to the sideboard, switched the chrome kettle on and put two spoonfuls of tea into the bottom of Oswald's teapot. Turning back, she pulled the dummy out of the holdall and put it on the table in front of her father.

'I wondered if you'd have a look at this, Daddy?' she said as casually as she could.

Oswald picked it up and quickly thumbed through the pages.

'I'm aware of this. Your friend David Goldman sent it to a friend of mine.'

Cate should have known. It was typical that her father would know her every move. Whatever she'd done, good or bad, even when she was thousands of miles away, she'd always had the feeling that he was watching her, a disapproving look on his face. 'However, I believe you've been offered a job in New York.' Oswald pointed over to the kettle which was billowing out huge clouds of steam. Cate jumped up and began to make the tea, beginning to feel genuinely unsettled now.

'Venetia told me,' said Oswald, as if reading her thoughts. 'Frankly I feel it would be the best for everyone. You've let yourself and the family down with this sacking. And this way you can be some company for Serena. At least one of you has some sort of career.'

'Daddy, I don't want to go to New York,' she said slowly. 'I want to do *this*.'

'Ah, this.' He picked up the magazine and started flicking through the pages dismissively. 'Yes, Nigel Hammond called me to ask what I thought about it.'

Cate's heart froze. Nigel Hammond? 'You know Nigel Hammond?' she said, a tremor in her voice.

'I have a great many friends, Catherine,' said Oswald, looking at her over his glasses. 'I have done something with my life and they respect my opinion.'

'So what did you say to him?'

Oswald put the magazine down and looked at his daughter, clearly enjoying his moment of power. 'What could I tell him? Hmm? That you'd just been fired from a very similar business to the one you're asking him to invest his money in? I simply referred Nigel to William Walton at Alliance. I thought he'd be the person best placed to comment on whether you were a good risk. Nigel is a very cautious investor.'

She span round and glared at him, her eyes blazing at his betrayal. 'But you knew . . .' she hissed, 'you knew that . . .' But she could see it was pointless. The frustration she had felt over the last few weeks gushed to the surface. 'You don't want me to succeed,' she shouted, her voice thick. 'What's wrong with me? What's your problem with me? What's sodding wrong?'

Oswald smiled over sourly. 'I didn't give you a two-hundred-thousand-pound education to talk like that. Now, I think you'd better be running along. I'm going to be late for dinner.'

As she watched Oswald pull away in his Bentley she squeezed her hand into an angry fist. She knew Daddy would be difficult – obstructive even – but couldn't believe he'd put a mere acquaintance before his daughter. She took deep gulps of London air, vainly trying to stop the fat tears streaming down her cheeks. Scrabbling to pull a tissue out of her bag she noticed the luminous blue light of her mobile ringing. She took a deep breath, wiped her nose and flipped it open.

'Cate?' It was Nick.

'Hi Nick,' she replied, trying to hide the wobble in her voice with a sniff. 'I can barely hear you. Where are you?'

'I'm in the pub getting very, very drunk. Cate, you'll never believe it! We got the bloody money!'

She stopped, staggered.

'No way! But how? Nigel Hammond spoke to my dad and the bastard passed him on to William Walton.'

She could hear Nick laughing down the phone.

'I know! David told me about that. Apparently Hammond thought William Walton was a cocky American jerk. I believe "full of crap" was his phrase. Quite taken with you, though. Thought your presentation was "very spunky". I think you've found a fan. And Cate?' said Nick, his voice happy and slightly slurred, 'I think you're pretty damn great too.'

She wiped her eyes and a small grin started to form on her lips. She was beginning to feel much better.

17

'She will absolutely love this,' said Camilla, sipping a mineral water and looking around Venetia's Kensington home. The interior of one of West London's smartest houses had been transformed into an indoor rose garden. Lattice-work trellises had been erected on every wall, wound around with delicate flowers in every shade of pink. Doorways were festooned with pale cream satin ribbon, and layers of lilac tulle had been arranged on the ceiling like fabric waves. On every available surface sat enormous bowls of scented water with tiny tea-lights floating inside. At one end of the ballroom a stage, strewn with petals, had been erected, on which a jazz orchestra would play. Janey Norris, Serena's PA, was striding around with a clipboard and a headpiece, barking orders into the ether, while at least thirty catering staff scurried around dusting trays of rose martinis with gold cinnamon and arranging canapés on pink porcelain serving trays.

Venetia nodded happily. She was nothing if not inventive when it came to throwing parties. Along with Andy and Patti Wong's New Year bash and Elton John's white-tie and tiara ball, Venetia Balcon's summer party, held every August in Kensington Park Gardens was a must on the social calendar.

With such an impressive reputation as a hostess, Venetia knew she had to create something very special for Serena's leaving party. She wasn't overjoyed that her youngest sister was moving to New York – especially with a man of Michael's reputation – but the least she could do was to give her a decent send-off.

Camilla picked up one of the party invitations. 'Farewell Our English Rose,' she giggled, reading out the gold-embossed words on the front. 'But aren't roses out of season? Shouldn't it have been a Daffodil Party, or something? This must have cost a fortune.'

Venetia laughed along, shrugging off the cost of importing all the flowers in from Amsterdam. 'Mmm . . . "Farewell our English daffodil"? Serena would love that!'

The two girls moved up to Venetia's bedroom to avoid the chaos of the last-minute preparations, pilfering a chilled bottle of champagne as they went. It was now half past six. Guests were arriving at half past seven, and Serena had insisted on arriving an hour after that. Despite her experience as a hostess, Venetia was always nervous before one of her social events, and was glad of Camilla's company – particularly as her sister had just dropped the bombshell that she had finished with Nat.

'Champagne?' she said, popping the cork.

Camilla shook her head. She wasn't quite in the mood to party. Two hours earlier, she had been standing in the rain at Canary Wharf, looking into Nat's confused eyes.

'Why do you want to meet here, Cam?' Nat had asked when she had intercepted him dashing out of his Docklands office, his jacket held over his head against the rain. 'Weren't we meeting at Venetia's?'

Camilla took a deep breath and told him there wasn't

going to be a party – not for him, anyway. More importantly, there wasn't going to be a wedding. Camilla had chosen this neutral ground because it was cold, anonymous and clinical. Shivering by the Thames, surrounded by huge glass buildings sweeping into the sky, splats of rain falling on their cheeks. Telling him was hard, but the decision had been easy. When she'd returned home from Megève and seen the Tory party Selection Weekend application papers on her desk she'd known immediately what she'd wanted. She didn't just want to be an MP, she wanted to be a cabinet minister. Or, when she dared to dream, achieve an even higher position. And for that she needed the right partner: a political partner. Not someone whose glamour-model and drug-dabbling past might tarnish her own reputation. After all, Camilla had enough tarnish of her own.

'Cheer up,' said Venetia, pressing the flute of champagne into her sister's hand. 'You did the right thing.'

'Did I?' asked Camilla, suddenly unsure of herself. 'It's nice to share nights like tonight with someone.'

Camilla walked across to the long French windows looking down onto the park.

Suddenly she turned back to face Venetia. 'Jesus, though! Can you believe that Nat told Daddy about our so-called September wedding, too? Before he'd even proposed?'

'Ouch,' replied Venetia. 'I'm sure he was looking forward to having a banking scion in the Balcon family. This news is going to put him in a bad mood.'

'Bad mood. There's a change,' sneered Camilla.

'No, a *really* bad mood,' continued Venetia, her soft features suddenly looking drawn. 'He was already threatening not to come tonight.'

'Oh, he'll come,' said Camilla, absent-mindedly squirting some jasmine-scented perfume from the dressing table onto her wrists. 'Why on earth would he miss an opportunity to be the centre of attention?'

The taxi pulled up against the kerb of Kensington Park Gardens and, as Cate stepped onto the pavement she heard a string quartet strike up, 'Come Fly with Me' from inside Venetia's house. She thrust a twenty-pound note in the cabbie's hand and breathed in the early evening air. She was already in a good mood, and the addition of a Sinatra soundtrack made her feel like she was in a Doris Day movie. Of course she was sad that Serena was leaving for New York, and she was dreading seeing her father at the party, but none of that could dim the happiness she felt now that her own life was finally full of excitement and promise. Cate caught her breath and almost hugged herself as she thought about it: she was editorial director of her own publishing company! How many journalists could say that? Only that morning they'd signed a twelve-month lease on an office, a tiny space squidged between London Bridge station and Borough Market, but it was a cool address with a decent rent and a boardroom-cum-broom-cupboard that doubled as Nick's office. She'd arrived – not exactly in style yet – but she was definitely on her way there.

'Where's your date? I thought you were bringing someone?' asked Venetia, hugging Cate as she waltzed through the door in a fitted inky-blue Lanvin dress.

'Ooh, a new man,' teased Camilla, shaking off her bad mood and giving her sister a warm squeeze.

'Two men actually,' smiled Cate, taking a Martini.

'Your date is coming with another man? How *modern*!' said Venetia with a wry smirk.

'Oh, stop it,' said Cate, tapping Venetia on the arm in

mock reproach. 'One is my business partner; the other is our investment guy. No gossip I'm afraid.'

'Famous last words,' winked Camilla.

'Farewell Our English Rose!' scoffed David Goldman to Nick as he pulled his invitation out of its fuchsia tissue-paper wrapping. 'What the fuck's all that about?' he hissed, handing it to a doorman.

'Don't get us thrown out before we even get in,' muttered Nick out of the side of his mouth, making a big show of smiling at the burly security guards standing in front of Venetia's house. The front door had been roped off from eager paparazzi looking for famous guests. 'Cate must have been pissed when she invited us to this.'

'She knows what two handsome young men like ourselves can add to a gathering like tonight. We're in demand,' said David, entirely seriously, slowing down as they passed the photographers. The photographers merely scowled. Funnelled into the queue by the door, David started checking out the well-heeled, underdressed party-goers in front.

'God, everyone sounds so posh,' he whispered.

'Irritable vowel syndrome,' smiled Nick, pushing his friend through the door. 'Now just get inside.'

At that moment, the street lit up with flashbulbs as a black Mercedes pulled up to the kerb.

'S'rena. Over 'ere, darlin'' shouted the paparazzi, elbowing each other to get a shot of the bronzed beauty climbing from the car and walking elegantly across the Kensington pavement. By any standards Serena looked fantastic, her hair swept up into an elegant chignon with sexy tendrils curling onto her high cheekbones.

Momentarily annoyed that the photographers had got wind of the party, Serena nevertheless stood at the foot of the steps and slipped off her vintage Chanel mink to reveal a blush-pink gown in such fine silk jersey it seemed to slither off her body. The total effect was magnificent – the colour of the dress was so pale, the fabric so fluid, that to the casual glance she looked almost naked. She turned slightly sideways and pushed one leg forward so that the long slit in her dress revealed a hint of tanned thigh, bowing her head seductively. She knew that this would be the shot on the front of the tabloids tomorrow morning.

Reluctantly allowing herself to be ushered inside by Conrad Davies, her agent and escort for the evening, she glanced at her Piguet watch. It was eight forty-five: good. Everyone should be here, she thought. Clinging to Conrad's arm, she moved through the huge hallway, accepting a rose Martini from a waiter and stopping to kiss an assortment of London society players. It was a glittering turnout, she thought smugly, noticing Sting and Trudie Styler in one corner, Elton John and Elle Macpherson chatting on the stairs and Jade Jagger laughing with Matthew Williamson by the cocktail bar – it seemed the whole of London's fashionable elite had swung by to say their goodbyes.

'This is just darling of you,' gushed Serena, embracing Venetia and planting a half kiss on each cheek. 'Everybody's here. And all for me.'

Venetia smiled weakly. Thank goodness for Janey and her Rolodex – Venetia had had no idea who Serena's friends were. Much like Serena, she smiled.

Cate and Camilla appeared through the double doors and all four women squealed together, embracing in one huge, glamorous scrum. Ignoring the stars around them, the Balcon girls huddled together and swapped gossip like schoolgirls at a slumber party.

'Where's Michael?' asked Cate, disappointed not to see him. 'I haven't even met him yet and you're leaving us for him!'

'I am not leaving you for Michael,' Serena smiled sweetly, stroking her sister on the arm. 'I am leaving London for New York. Anyway,' she continued, helping herself to a tiny carrot shaving from a passing tray, 'Michael's on business in Cape Town. So Conrad is my date tonight, aren't you darling?' She blew a kiss over at the handsome middle-aged man wearing a crisp white shirt and a cravat.

'Our last night before we embark on our long-distance relationship,' he shouted over in a deep Richard Burton baritone.

You wish, thought Serena spitefully, knowing that as soon as there was some distance between them, she was going to fire him. Now she was moving to the US, a London agent was, frankly, surplus to her requirements. Conrad should be grateful she wasn't telling him tonight and spoiling this fabulous party.

Serena turned back to the girls. 'So, anyway, where's Daddy?' she asked.

No party's going to start properly without me, thought Oswald confidently, rolling up outside Venetia's front door in the Bentley. He glanced at his watch: nine fifteen. Good. Everybody should be there now, he thought, screwing up Venetia's handwritten note asking everyone to be at the party for Serena's arrival at eight thirty. His youngest daughter should be bloody glad he was bothering to turn up at all. He was deeply unhappy about this Sarkis fellow she had hooked up with. An American was bad enough, he reflected, but this Sarkis was half Lebanese. Why on earth should he turn up to a party to celebrate that? He was glad she'd ditched that plebeian poofter Tom, of course – father was a miner or some such, but if Venetia could find someone like Jonathon von Bismarck, surely Serena could have *anyone*. Someone of good, solid English stock. He wiped his lightly sweating brow with a handkerchief and turned to Maria

Dante in the back seat, taking her hand gently. Tonight's the night, he thought, gleefully taking in her voluptuous body as they stepped out in front of the paparazzi. Tonight's the night.

'At bloody last,' whispered Venetia urgently to Jonathon. The man of the house was craning his neck around the room, sure he'd just seen an inept waiter spill cranberry juice on the carpet. He would be taking that off the caterer's bill.

'What? What the hell's wrong with you now?' Jonathon snapped back.

'Daddy's here,' said Venetia, nodding towards the front door. 'He's only just arrived.'

'And look, he's brought Maria Dante with him,' smiled Jonathon, knowing that would impress some clients he had invited to the party. They had no idea who Robbie Williams was, but Maria Dante, now that was classy. She was wearing a vast cyan gown, her breasts spilling over the low-scooped neckline, her black hair piled up on top of her head, looking every inch the opera diva.

Oswald and Maria moved slowly through the crowd, nodding and accepting compliments graciously like a royal couple on walkabout among their subjects, finally stopping to kiss Serena. Oswald had not seen her since Christmas. It was no secret she was his favourite daughter, a chip off the old block in more ways than one, but his patience had been pushed to the limit when Cate had let slip that she was moving to New York. In Oswald's eyes, it constituted betrayal.

'You're making a big mistake going to New York,' he whispered in her ear, his muted voice dripping with superiority. Serena had not become his favourite child by being submissive. 'You're my father, not my travel agent,' parried Serena smoothly.

Noticing that several people had started to eavesdrop on

their conversation, Oswald instantly changed gear and embraced his daughter.

'So – let's party,' he boomed, lifting a gin and tonic from a passing tray. 'We've got Sinatra and Serena, both my favourites. Let's face the music and dance.'

Venetia pulled on Serena's arm to ask her to stay while Oswald drifted off into the crowd. 'What?' asked Serena.

'So, what do you think of her?' smiled Venetia, pointing in the direction of Maria.

'What is she *wearing*?' sniffed Serena indignantly. 'And that big hair! Her head looks like a petrol cloud.'

'Don't forget you're making a speech at ten, darling,' Venetia reminded her sister. 'We've put a microphone over by the grand piano, so, you know, just a few words.'

'Do I have to?' pouted Serena, secretly relishing any opportunity to be centre stage. 'In that case I'd better have some more champagne.'

Venetia began to work the room with Camilla at her side, weaving in and out of the sea of guests, occasionally bumping into one of her own friends. She had felt guilty about inviting them to Serena's party, but Venetia didn't want to feel too much of a stranger in her own house. Right now she wanted to feel popular and loved and supported, particularly when Jonathon was being so distant. He was being colder than ever towards her and never seemed to be at home, always providing excuses to her for his absence – client dinners, overseas deals. Her husband was a workaholic, but she knew the truth was that they were drifting apart. And, much as she wanted Serena to have a fabulous last night in London, the party could not have come at a worse time. That morning she had returned to Dr Rhys-Jones's clinic to get the results from the last round of tests and her worst suspicions had been confirmed. She had hardly

184

any eggs left – having children either naturally or through IVF treatment would be, within a matter of months, impossible. She'd told no one, stoically blocking it out like bad weather or a light headache. A lifetime with her father had taught her how to switch off when all she wanted to do was dissolve into a flood of tears. No, she would deal with it tomorrow, she decided, when Serena's special night was over and when she and Jonathon could sit down and sort out their future.

'Are you OK?' asked Camilla, resting a gentle hand on her sister's shoulder. 'You seem a bit, well –'

'What?' said Venetia defensively.

'I don't know. A bit sad? Don't worry, Van, she's only going to New York, you know,' said Camilla softly.

Venetia simply nodded. Let her believe she was sad about Serena. 'Come on,' she chirped with forced good humour. 'Come and Meet Diego Bono, the fabulous designer I was telling you about. Graduated from the Royal College last year. I hear that Calvin Klein and Burberry both want him, but I think I've persuaded him to come and join Venetia Balcon as our new women's-wear designer.'

'You're going into women's-wear?' asked Camilla, surprised.

'Logical brand development for us,' said Venetia, her eyes beginning to sparkle once more. 'I'm so excited about this, Cam. It's what I've always wanted to do.'

Camilla hadn't seen her sister so animated in ages: she was glowing with enthusiasm. She wanted to hear more, but suddenly they were interrupted by two handsome men brandishing flutes of champagne in front of them. 'Ladies, ladies, ladies. The drinks are on us!' said one. Cate walked over, laughing at her sisters' bemused expressions.

'Don't worry, girls. They're not intruders. Venetia, Camilla, meet my partners in crime, Nick Douglas and Dave Goldman.'

Nick immediately threw an arm around Venetia and Camilla, promising in a slightly tipsy voice to tell them 'secrets' about Cate, while David moved in close to Cate, his sharp black suit brushing up against her.

'So, what do you think?' asked Cate, unnerved by his closeness, but hiding it by gesturing at the decor.

'Is it always this floral?' asked David with a smile.

'Only for birthdays and special occasions,' answered Cate, popping a mini-strawberry tartlet into her mouth.

'You know you've made it if you live in a place like this,' said David with a hint of envy. 'But I do hear Jonathon's hedge fund is doing fantastically. Mind if we go for a snoop?'

'Where did you have in mind?' asked Cate. 'Have you seen the kitchen? It's incredible.'

'I was thinking of somewhere a little less noisy,' said David, moving close to her ear and picking up a bottle of champagne from a table. 'Let's go and explore.'

David took Cate's hand and led her through the crowds towards the back of the house. David wanted her all for himself. Cate Balcon was his kind of woman. Bright and beautiful, she also had that something special. Breeding. Polish. Whatever. And as such, she would be the final piece in his jigsaw, the ideal way to complete his transition from market-trader's son to sophisticated player. Feeling his cock harden the way it did when he was about to close a deal, he took Cate's hand and slipped through an open French door at the back of the house, pulling her into the darkness. The string quartet faded into the background along with the laughter and clinking glasses as they crunched up a garden path.

'Where are we going?' laughed Cate, feeling more nervous than she sounded.

'To explore,' said David wolfishly, heading towards the bottom of the garden. 'Let's see what's down there!'

'There's nothing down there, I can assure you,' replied Cate, her voice a whisper. 'Except maybe a few rocks we might fall over. Foxes, owls. Who knows? I think we should go back . . .'

'I'll protect you,' grinned David, pushing back a dangling branch and leading Cate towards a marble bench lit by a garden torch. David pulled a flute from each of his jacket pockets and noisily splashed champagne into them with a flourish. Suddenly it was quiet. All Cate could hear was the crackling of the garden flame and she was suddenly nervous of the intimacy between them. Cate was notoriously poor at distinguishing between when a man was being nice to her and when he was flirting, but even she could recognize this wasn't flirtation, it was full-on seduction. She took a sharp intake of breath as David's broad body moved closer towards her; she could feel the heat emanating from him. She wrapped her arms tightly around her chest, narrowing the V of her cleavage. Her hands shaking now, as David moved closer and closer.

'Cold?' purred David.

Frigid, more like, she thought, willing herself to relax.

'You're fantastic,' he whispered roughly, lifting his hand to stroke her cheek. The fine line of dark hair that ran from his fingers to his wrist tickled her skin.

'You're making me blush,' she stammered, turning her face slightly away from him. *Christ*, she thought, *I'm behaving like some sort of Jane Austen character*.

Time seemed to slow down. His fingers rested on her chin and pulled her towards him.

'What's wrong, Cate?' he asked, still stroking her face. 'Don't you want to?'

What was wrong with her? she asked herself, feeling her stomach turn in a mixture of lust, anxiety and nerves. *Christ, he was sexy*, she thought, looking at the thick lashes around his intense grey eyes and the long, firm, masculine nose. She wasn't sure what was stopping her leaning gently forward and taking his lips with hers, or running her hands through his wavy black hair.

'I'm not sure, David. I'm sorry.'

David Goldman was used to an instant surrender.

'What? You *do* like men, don't you?'

Cate looked shocked. 'Well, yes. Of course. But . . . Jesus, David. I'm grateful for everything you've done for us, but . . . Look, I'm sorry . . .'

David let his fingers fall from her face to his lap, his expression part annoyed, part disappointed.

'I guess not,' he smiled ruefully, smarting from the rejection. He stood up. 'It's getting cold. We'd better go back to the party.'

Inside the house, Maria Dante knew she was attracting attention. Having taken a long, hard look at Serena Balcon, she grudgingly admitted that Oswald's girl was as beautiful in the flesh as she looked in photographs. But that was all she was: a girl. Any man who yearned for Serena Balcon must have homosexual tendencies. Look at her – all skin and bone. No ass to speak of, tits the size of olives; she had the figure of a boy. But Maria Dante – well, Maria Dante was all woman. She could sense all the men in the room – the grown-up men, at least – appreciating her ripe breasts spilling out of the low-scooped Oscar de la Renta dress, the round curves of her buttocks pushing against the silk of its skirt. A glamorous, talented, cosmopolitan woman – exactly what the tired London scene needed; and with Serena Balcon out of the way, she was just the person to fill the gap. OK, so Oswald was an old man, she thought, looking at him with disgust. She was dreading seeing him naked. But it was a small price to pay. He was

188

rich, he was connected, he was a proper English aristo-crat with a magnificent home. And Oswald was besotted. She laughed to herself. Who would have thought it? Maria Dante, the little Italian girl from the dirt-poor Puglia village: she was going to become a Lady.

'I thought you were just sensational at the Nice Opera last month,' gushed Nicholas Charlesworth, appearing at her side to hand her a glass of champagne. 'Do you like perform-ing in Europe?'

'I adore it,' she breathed seductively. 'You must come to the Royal Opera House when I'm there next month.'

'I'd be delighted!' said Nicholas with a stammer, trans-fixed by her chocolate fondant eyes. 'And, erm, how's the music event at Huntsford shaping up? I'm afraid I've been a bit out of the loop with what's happening, although I think Oswald is planning a little pow-wow at our club, White's, next week. Just let me know if you need anything,' he smiled, tapping the side of his nose know-ingly.

'I think Oswald has all the organizational side well under control.'

'What about the creative side?'

She looked down her nose at this weaselly-faced little man. What did he know about creativity?

'I will be getting some friends on board to sing,' Maria said mysteriously. 'Myself . . . a couple of arias, maybe Bizet, Debussy, Mozart of course, maybe even some other songs in different styles – Gershwin, perhaps. I am doing a recital at Carnegie Hall in New York a few weeks before, so maybe I will do something from that.'

'Any sneak previews?' asked Nicholas hopefully.

Bored, and wanting to have a little bit of fun with all these tedious, pompous Brits, she looked at him, an idea forming in her mind. 'Sneak preview?' she smiled, flipping a coil of ebony hair away from her forehead, 'You just might be in luck.'

Serena glanced at her watch. Two minutes to ten. She smoothed the silk jersey over her thigh, and made her way to one end of the room where Venetia had placed a microphone ready for her speech. She hadn't prepared anything, but she was a good speaker, and she wanted to make sure her swansong in front of all her old London crowd was nothing short of sensational.

Just then she noticed Maria Dante turning to the small orchestra, who were partway through a version of Debussy's *Clair de Lune*. Maria raised a finger to her lips and moved in front of the microphone. Her chest started to wobble as if her lungs were being pumped full of air, then, from out of her scarlet lips, strains of her rich soprano voice began to lift around the room. Charlesworth, recognizing the Rossini *bel canto*, shut his eyes as if mesmerized by a siren's call. All heads turned to listen, Maria's high notes perfectly clear in their resonance and diction, her voice so strong and powerful that there was no need for the microphone. The crowd drifted towards her and, as the room throbbed with an emotional pulse, Oswald looked around appreciatively, basking in the reflected glory. Standing at the back by the staircase, Serena looked on furiously.

'Cate, Cate,' she hissed, waving at her sister who, like everybody else in the room, was transfixed by the performance. Cate turned around and mouthed, 'What?'

Serena grabbed Cate and pulled her behind a pillar. 'What do you mean "what?"? That woman is making an exhibition of herself.'

Cate laughed quietly. 'Serena, she's fantastic. You've got one of the world's biggest opera stars singing at your party.'

'Oh fantastic!' sneered Serena, pulling Cate so close that

190

pink fingerprints appeared on her arm. 'She is trying to steal my thunder. I'm supposed to be speaking in five minutes. Who's going to want to listen to me after hearing Fat Woman of the Opera?'

Serena's lip was quivering, her eyes had started welling up with tears. Then, seeing she was having no effect on Cate, she pushed Cate back into the room. 'Oh, just get Venetia!'

Cate found her eldest sister sitting back on a cream chaise longue.

'Serena is furious,' whispered Cate, trying to play down the drama. 'Can we get Maria off?'

'What am I supposed to do?' asked Venetia, a look of panic on her face. 'I'll get booed if I try and stop this.'

Incensed, Serena had decided to take matters into her own hands. She walked to the front of the crowd and stood in front of Maria Dante, the smile on her mouth saying, 'How delightful!', her eyes blazing and hostile. Oswald looked on from the bar, enjoying the single malt in his hand, but not as much as seeing the cat-fight brewing between his daughter and girlfriend. Oswald crept over to stand behind his daughter and whispered in her ear. 'Highlight of the evening, isn't she?'

'She's ruining my evening,' said Serena, her voice wobbling, 'Daddy, please!' she implored. 'Please do something.'

Oswald smiled, loving the drama of Serena's discomfort, feeling her misery and disappointment build as the song grew, spiralling into its triumphant crescendo.

'Please,' whispered Serena. 'Please.'

Maria's voice rose like a balloon, filling every corner of the house with light and beauty. Her voice was so strong yet so intimate, it was as if she was giving each and every guest a personal audience. Locking eyes with Serena, Maria

191

drew her hands together in front of her and brought the music to a close, her eyelids closed, her head bowed in exhausted rapture.

The crowd exploded into a rich applause, the musicians looked elated, and Maria Dante smiled triumphantly at her audience. For the briefest moment, she glanced over at Serena, who was mechanically clapping and smiling with perfect, gritted teeth.

'Get up there,' hissed Venetia to Serena, looking at her watch.

'Thank you, thank you,' purred Maria. 'Now let me introduce the real star of the evening: Serena Balcon.'

But her words were drowned out by the chatter of the crowd, who were talking excitedly about the performance and drifting towards the bar.

Serena was right, no one wanted to hear her after that performance. Fury welling up inside her, she curled her hands into such a tight fist that her nails clawed into her palm. She wanted Maria Dante out of her father's life as soon as possible, and she was going to do whatever was necessary to make that desire happen.

18

Milan still cut a glamorous dash, even in the middle of March, thought Nick Douglas as his eyes panned across the Piazza del Duomo. Although the carnival of Fashion Week had rolled out of town two weeks earlier and the city was wrapped in a grey, damp drizzle that reminded him of Manchester, it still buzzed with a sophistication and elegance that was hard to match in any other city in the world. Not even Manhattan's Upper East Side could boast so many immaculately groomed women shopping for groceries in full-length sheared mink coats and dark sunglasses. New York might be the land of opportunity, where a tie-salesman like Ralph Lauren could become a retail billionaire, he thought, but Milan was the real centre of the glamorous fashion universe, particularly when it came to glossy magazine publishing. Without impressing the city's fashion giants – Armani, Prada, Dolce & Gabbana, Versace – and securing their lucrative advertising spend, a glossy magazine launch was as good as dead in the frothy, rose-scented water.

Cate and Nick sat in a tiny café in the shadow of the enormous cathedral and celebrated a productive afternoon's work with a Bellini. Prada had made positive noises about coming in after the first couple of issues if they liked what they saw, while Giorgio Armani, who insisted on inspecting and OK-ing every magazine personally before he would green-light any advertising, had been even more positive. Not only had he committed to advertising the Armani Collezioni line in *Sand*'s debut issue, they had even talked about doing a shoot and interview with the fashion legend at his sumptuous home on the Italian island of Pantelleria.

'Have we really only known each other a month?' smiled Cate, now on her third Bellini and feeling a bit giddy. She was flipping through her pink Smythson diary to make a note to contact the Armani PR and had noticed the line 'Meet Nick Douglas in Flask' scrawled on a page in early February. 'Seems like a lifetime,' she said.

'I think you'll find it's six weeks,' corrected Nick, looking over her shoulder to peek at the diary. 'And you're too right. I feel like I've grown another head – yours.'

She kicked him playfully under the table and reached to scoop up a handful of peeled almonds from the bowl on the table.

'Want to go and get some dinner? I'm starving,' she said, peering through the café window at the sky. Pink clouds were floating over the spire of the Duomo and she couldn't stop a smile spreading across her face.

'Although I wouldn't mind changing out of the career-bitch power-clothes,' she added, looking down at her slate-grey Helmut Lang trouser suit.

'OK, come on,' said Nick, throwing a fifty-euro note into the small silver ashtray. 'Back to the hotel.'

They were staying at the sumptuous Bulgari. The hotel was well over their budget, but it was a suitably impressive address to give to the various fashion PRs. 'A lot of money just to dish out a posh fax number,' Nick had grumbled. Still. There was no denying it was gorgeous. The lobby was a riot of black marble and elegant styling. In the rooms, crisp linens lay on huge squashy beds, while the marble bathrooms were laden with white fluffy towels and expensive toiletries.

As she wasn't due down at the bar until half past seven, Cate took a swim in the gold mosaic swimming pool before returning to her suite. She ran a frothy bubble bath and, for the first time in weeks, allowed herself a long, luxurious wallow. She wiggled her big toe in the balloon-shaped tap, letting the hot water spurt out around her skin and the bubbles rise up her back until she was lying neck-deep in the suds.

God, she felt good. She'd never felt so proud and satisfied with herself, even when she'd got her first internship at *New Yorker* magazine, or when she'd won the prestigious PPA New Editor of the Year award, or even when *Class* magazine had first outsold *Vogue* on the news-stand. Doing it for yourself, under your own steam, was something else – especially when it all seemed to be coming off. She smiled to herself and wondered what Nick was doing in the adjacent bedroom. Hopefully getting ready, she thought with an eye on the time. She imagined him getting into the shower and running his soapsudsy hands over that cute crop of brown hair. She felt herself blush.

What was she thinking? She couldn't start having sexy fantasies about Nick Douglas! Annoyed with herself she climbed out of the bath, damp hair dripping down her neck, and started vigorously towelling herself down to distract herself. She padded over to the walk-in closet to choose an outfit for dinner, selecting a rust and bottle green Missoni dress with a deep scoop neck that clung to every curve. Inspecting herself in the mirror she was pleased. The colours brought out the russet strands in her thick, wavy hair, and the sky-high beige Manolo Blahnik slingbacks made her long, curvy legs look sensational. Rubbing a musky Donna Karan body cream onto her legs and clipping a sheaf of hair to one side with an antique diamanté clip, she threw her hotel key card into her clutch bag and she was ready. She paused, slightly puzzled – but ready for what?

The Bagutta restaurant was humming. Famous for its enormous Tuscan steaks, it attracted a glamorous crowd that wasn't afraid to eat.

'What do you fancy?' asked Nick, running a finger down the wine menu. 'I reckon today calls for champagne.'

'Pink champagne,' agreed Cate. 'To go with an enormous chunk of meat.'

She looked at Nick. If she wasn't very much mistaken, he had made as much effort as she had for the evening out. Instead of his usual jeans and a sweatshirt, he looked suspiciously as if he was out to impress with his tailored grey trousers and black cashmere jumper. He smiled back, his big hazel eyes crinkling at the sides.

'To us,' he said, lifting up a flute to clink against hers.

'And to our magazine,' she replied, suddenly nervous of the intimacy between them.

Nick looked at her, a twinkle in his eye.

'Glad you turned the *Harper's Bazaar* job down, then?' he asked.

Cate sat up in her chair. 'How do you know about that?' she gasped.

'Serena told me at her party. She said she was very upset you weren't joining her in New York.' He sipped his champagne slowly. 'Why didn't you tell me?'

Cate dipped a piece of bread in some olive oil and swirled it around on her plate. 'I didn't think it mattered enough to tell you. Didn't want you to think I wasn't committed.'

'I would never think that about you.'

They looked at each other. She felt uncomfortable. It was the sort of look that lovers might share.

'I'll be honest, I might have considered the job if we hadn't got the money that day,' she continued slowly. 'But I've lived and worked in New York before. It doesn't hold that mythical appeal it does for some people. And it's not like I even particularly wanted to go the first time.'

'So why did you go?'

She looked at Nick and felt for the first time she could really trust him. They had been through so much over the last few weeks, spent so much time together, she felt a desire to be honest rush over her.

'I went to get away from my father.'

Nick said nothing. He just looked at her reassuringly, encouraging her to talk.

'I guess he's always made me feel so inadequate, and when you're old enough to get away from it, you do.'

'Why, what did he do?' He touched her hand lightly. 'You have to talk about it, Cate, or you will never get it out of your system.'

She paused and took a deep breath that seemed to go on for ever. But the champagne, her good mood and their growing close friendship made it easier to discuss.

'You want to know when it started? When my mother died.' Cate began to play with the ring on her middle finger. 'My mother was wonderful. Kind, beautiful,' she said quietly. 'She was a Dior model in the sixties. She just had this way of making everything seem OK even when it wasn't, like she'd read me *The Wizard of Oz* every time I was ill and couldn't get to sleep.' She smiled softly, then paused, noticing that his gaze was directly meeting hers.

'Anyway, when I was seven, she took Camilla and me to see a musical in London. Venetia was at Pony Club camp. Serena was still a baby and at Huntsford with our nanny. We went to see *Oliver!*' She giggled at the memory of it, then the smile faded and her face clouded over.

'I remember my dad was supposed to come with us but he was busy. He was always busy. Some meeting in London – I don't know what the excuse was at the time. Anyway, we went to the theatre and then came back to our house in Chelsea where we were staying that night. I remember it was a really hot evening. I was running around in the garden in my sundress while my mum was watering the flowerbeds.'

Nick noticed her voice had started cracking, but she carried on.

'Then she collapsed right there in the garden. I just didn't know what to do. I was only seven, Nick.' Cate looked up pleadingly at him, as if she was trying to persuade him to see her side.

'I couldn't get hold of my dad. I found an address book in a drawer with all these numbers in and I tried them all, but I couldn't reach him. I called the ambulance and a neighbour who I didn't know came to stay with Camilla and me.'

She took a large gulp of wine and brushed something away from her cheek.

'The next thing I knew, it was the middle of the night. My dad came to the house and told us mum was dead – it was a clot on the brain. He said I hadn't been quick enough.' Cate looked at Nick. 'He said it was my fault.'

She exhaled deeply, and felt strangely liberated. Nick could see the guilt painted on her face, an inch thick. He wanted to come round the table and hold her tightly, but instead he stroked her fingers across the table.

'No wonder . . .' he began. 'Cate, it's –'

'It's fine,' said Cate quickly, brushing at her cheek again and looking away. 'I'm glad I told you. Now I bet they do a great tiramisu.'

Nick knew she didn't want to talk any more and distracted

her with jokes and silliness. Cate giggled. She hadn't giggled in a long time and it was fun. So much fun that she hardly noticed that the meal was over, the bill had come and the restaurant was emptying out.

'Wanna walk back or get a cab?' asked Nick as they moved from their table.

After the champagne and the earlier Bellinis, Cate felt tired but light-headed.

'Do you mind if we walk? At least some of the way. I hate going to bed with a fuzzy head.'

'OK. Let's go and get our coats.'

They joined a small queue of diners at the cloakroom. In front of them a couple laughed as they collected long over-coats from the elegant brunette holding a coat hanger. The man was tall and thickset and his hand looked huge as he stroked the curve of the small blonde woman's buttocks. The platinum blonde squealed as her companion's fingers slid down the waistband of her skirt.

'Inappropriate behaviour for such a refined establishment,' whispered Nick into Cate's ear and she laughed.

The couple turned round, and suddenly they came face to face with William Walton and Nicole Valentine. Cate's giggles immediately dried up and Walton's mouth dropped open.

'Catherine Balcon. Erm, hi . . .' Walton was stumbling over his words, his face flushing slightly.

'William. Nicole. What a surprise,' said Cate in a flat voice.

'Yes, well,' said Walton, clearing his throat. 'Out here seeing advertisers. Getting them excited about Nicole's appointment to editor and *Class*'s imminent relaunch.'

Nicole smiled smugly at Cate and cocked her head to the side. 'On a mini-break are we?' the American woman asked sugary-sweetly.

'Actually, no. We're here for the same reason you are,'

said Cate with as much confidence as she could muster. Nick touched the small of her back for encouragement. 'We're in the middle of a launch ourselves.'

'So we hear,' said William, trying to repress a smirk. 'Surprised you got the money to be honest.' His lips were drawing into a thin, sly smile.

Cate met his gaze firmly. 'Well, our investors were very impressed with both the product and the team,' she replied pointedly. 'I think we're going to do very well. Very well indeed.'

Walton's arrogance had returned. He looked at Nicole, his hand moving back to her buttocks.

'Don't go trying to poach any of your old colleagues,' he stopped to grin wolfishly. 'Not that you could afford them.'

Cate's eyes narrowed.

'Well, I'm glad to see you're getting everything you've paid for, William,' she said. 'Staff loyalty and all that.'

Nick stepped between them and handed Cate her coat.

'Goodbye, William. Goodbye, Nicole,' said Cate as they moved away, her voice refusing to falter. 'Have a good time in Milan.' She smiled as sweetly as she could. 'It certainly looks like you are already.'

William and Nicole stared back. Fuming.

'You OK?' On the street Nick put an affectionate arm around her waist. Cate let him keep it there, proud of herself that she had had the final word with Walton and Nicole, but still feeling angry and frustrated. That bitch!

'You were one cool customer,' grinned Nick.

'Well, it all makes sense now,' she replied angrily. 'Do you think she was sleeping with him before I got fired?'

'Almost certainly,' said Nick slowly. 'And he's got terrible taste in women.'

'But she's engaged!'

'Since when did that ever stop anyone having an affair?'

A monochrome lunar light lit the pavement as they ambled side by side through the quiet streets. Cate dug her hands into her pockets and tried to quicken the pace, aware of the arm still there. They turned into a little park where a line of crazy paving snaked across a stretch of grass.

'Urgh. It's all wet,' she laughed, looking down at her strappy Manolos. 'My toes'll get soggy. Let's go back to the street.'

In one movement, Nick bent down and scooped Cate into his arms, her legs dangling in the air. 'Well, we can't have soggy toes, can we, Catherine Balcon?' he said, moving forward in a stumble.

'Careful you don't give yourself a hernia,' she teased, feeling as light as a feather in his grip.

As her arm hugged the back of his neck, she felt a crackle of electricity between them. She let herself relax into the warmth of his coat, her head turning into his neck. He smelt good – of aftershave and freshly washed hair. Her lips were an inch away from his skin. His hold was surprisingly strong and she felt completely protected, a million miles away from William Walton and magazines and everything else. As she relaxed further and further into his arms, everything became suddenly clear. The reason she wanted to spend every waking hour working with him. The reason she flinched when David Goldman came on to her. She didn't want David when, in her heart of hearts, she wanted Nick.

Nick turned his head. His mouth was so close she could almost taste the trace of champagne on his lips. 'Cate,' he murmured, his eyes closing as he moved towards her.

Her eyes shut as he gave her the most gentle kiss. It was perfect.

She let her lips kiss him back and then, just as quickly,

Cate came to her senses. His girlfriend. Nick hardly discussed her, but Cate knew she existed. Rebecca. Plus Cate worked with Nick. They were business partners. It was unprofessional. It was no better than William Walton and Nicole Valentine. It was all wrong. She pulled her head away.

'Nick. You're with someone.'

She could see him flinch in the darkness.

'But Cate. You are . . . I am . . .'

Her stomach tumbled as she desperately waited to hear what he would say. But she was scared he would confirm that she was second choice.

She got in a pre-emptive strike.

'Anyway. We work together . . . It wouldn't . . . it would be . . . awkward.'

He looked so deeply into her eyes that she could see the flecks of yellow in his irises.

There was a long pause that seemed to go on for ever. 'Maybe you're right.'

He said it so softly she couldn't gauge his tone. Was it sadness? Relief? What? He placed her gently on the ground. The current of electricity between them, which seconds ago had burnt and jolted her, dispersed almost as soon as it had arrived. Cate felt nothing except a crushing sense of disappointment.

'It doesn't look wet any more,' said Nick, slowly.

'No, it looks fine.'

'Gosh, we're drunk.'

'Yes, we are.'

And they headed out of the park towards the hotel.

19

Tom Archer stood by his kitchen window looking out into his garden and began to chop the carrots for his casserole. The renovations to his property had been completed exactly two months ago, and so Tom was back living in his Cotswold mansion, having returned from Dorothy Whetton's seaside retreat. He laughed to himself at how absurd the change was from his life in London. What would I have been doing now if I was still there with Serena? he thought to himself. No doubt recovering from the Saturday night before, drinking Bloody Marys and debating whether to go round to some glamorous friend's for dinner. Perhaps reading scripts over a cocktail or just talking shop. That's what they usually did.

Things are very different now, he thought, staring out onto the lawns bursting with herds of daffodils. The birds were singing in the clear afternoon sky, there was no sound of traffic chasing through the streets and he was alone, enjoying his own company. And he was chopping carrots. He chuckled about his life now, researching and writing his script. The cricket season was beginning, too, and he had joined the local club, the Mitchenham Tennis and Cricket Club, which seemed to have caused much excitement in the village. Ah, the pressure to get in the first eleven, he smiled to himself.

He was mildly concerned at how easily he had slipped into this new routine. The turning heads and autograph hunters in the local pub had finally subsided, and now he was just Tom, one of the lads in the village who could enjoy a quiet pint and a chat about the council's plans to move the bus stop from outside the bakery. His friends in London, his agent, his publicist – they had all said this country-living lark was just a passing fad, an inevitable result of his break-up with Serena. But two months in, he was still enjoying it, loving the freedom to do whatever he wanted in his own time without the say-so of the London crowd.

That wasn't to say that he didn't get a little bit lonely. In fact, he had actually begun to look forward to the visits from Edna, his cleaning lady, who came round three times a week to spruce up the house. Maybe I'm more sociable than I thought, he smiled. Which is why he couldn't believe he hadn't thought to invite his old friend Nick Douglas over before. When Rebecca Willard, Nick's girlfriend had insisted on coming down too, Nick had suggested that they also invite Cate for the weekend.

Tom stopped chopping and put the knife down. He had very mixed feelings about Cate's imminent arrival. He looked at his watch and realized that she, Nick and Rebecca were due to arrive in forty minutes. Yes, he had always enjoyed Cate's company; the two of them would always pair off at Oswald's parties, huddled in a corner, guzzling Martinis and poking fun at the rest of the party guests. However, Tom hadn't seen her since that day she had come down to persuade him into a reconciliation with Serena. It had been a fairly clean-cut break-up with Serena; but he had a nagging feeling that he should let any ties to the Balcon family go. After all, they were her family. They were her.

What the hell, he thought quickly, putting three bottles of Dom Pérignon 1983 into the fridge and filling some wooden bowls with crisps. He flung open the French windows that led onto the garden terrace and, deciding that it was warm enough for a late-afternoon gin and tonic out there, he struggled to put up the huge cream linen umbrella over the garden table and chairs before lighting the patio heater for extra warmth. Back in the kitchen, he tossed the carrots into a bright orange Le Creuset casserole along with thick chunks of pheasant, parsnips and onions and hoped that a casserole and mashed potato would suffice for his guests. If Serena had been here, she would have demanded he bring in Le Caprice's outside catering for extravagant canapés and an elaborate five-course meal – just for a casual supper. He closed the oven with a thud. Why didn't I think of this before? He smiled.

Cate had been having misgivings about attending Tom's dinner party, too, almost from the moment she had impulsively accepted his invitation. Now that she was driving through the pretty Gloucestershire villages, getting closer and closer to his manor house, she was even less sure. Even though Tom had been a good friend over the last five years, she was still a little awkward and embarrassed about seeing him. After all, her loyalties were to her sister. She didn't even know if Tom knew about Michael.

But most of all, she was seriously anxious about spending the weekend with Nick, especially when he had his girlfriend in tow. Ever since that night in Milan when they had shared that brief kiss, her relationship with Nick had noticeably cooled. The first week back in the office was intolerable for her. Her feelings for Nick seemed to explode overnight to the point where she could hardly concentrate with him working in the next office, but it was clear that their relationship – while still close – was now purely professional and much more guarded. No more long boozy nights in the pub, ostensibly talking about the magazine, but spilling over into laughter and flirtation. No more Sunday brunches and eleven-o'clock-in-the-evening telephone calls to discuss 'ideas' and share their excitement. Gosh, she thought to herself in retrospect: what must Rebecca have thought about all that?

The Mini rattled across a lonely level crossing and past a herd of cattle peeking curiously over a hedge. Thank God she'd been so busy at work she hadn't had time to dwell on any lost love, thought Cate, turning a CD on. She was big enough to admit she missed him – his humour, his cleverness, his friendship. She banged the steering wheel with her fist. Over the years her sisters had often teased her, laughing about how useless she was at interpreting signals, but she was sure she had read the signs right with Nick. The little things he said, the way he looked at her, his willingness to spend every available second with her. The reason must be Rebecca.

In anticipation of their meeting, Cate had spent hours that afternoon deciding what to wear. Every outfit that made her feel special also made her look ridiculously overdressed for a relaxed dinner at Tom's. She had finally chosen a pair of her favourite jeans, a red, cowl-neck cashmere sweater and some high black Louboutin boots; the dark-red flash of the soles never failed to make her feel sexy. She had scooped her hair up into a high ponytail so it swished from side to side when she walked and had added a pair of large diamond earrings that had once been her mother's. In all her hurry this afternoon, she had forgotten to pick up a nice bottle of wine to bring along for the evening. Spotting an off-licence ahead, she pulled up outside and hurried in to get a last-minute gift, having to settle on a cheap Bordeaux from a poor selection.

* * *

Nick and Rebecca were already there by the time Cate drew up outside Tom's, Rebecca's silver TVR sitting triumphantly outside the house. Cate felt slightly sick as she knocked on the front door. This could be awful, she thought. Moments later, the door opened to reveal Tom carrying two gin and tonics. 'Here she is!' smiled Tom, 'the international business-woman of the year. Watch out Rupert Murdoch!' He stepped forward, kissed her on the cheek and thrust a glass into Cate's hand, instantly wiping out her butterflies. He turned and led her down the long corridor towards the light-filled kitchen.

As soon as she stepped into the room, she spotted Rebecca. Not what she was expecting, she quickly decided. She knew Rebecca would be glamorous, of course. The few times she had been to his flat, Cate had spotted Manolos on the carpet and Marni coats flung over a chair, but she hadn't been expecting her to be quite this glamorous. God knew Nick was attractive, but he was definitely punching above his weight here. Poker-straight honey-blonde hair framed a perfectly oval face. Her eyes were a startling green, her cheek-bones were high and angular, her mouth large and highly glossed. There was no getting around it, Rebecca was beau-tiful. If she hadn't been sitting in a Cotswolds manor house, you'd have said her natural habitat was in LA, draped over a Hollywood star, with her wasp-like waist, tiny hips and her large round breasts hidden by an expensive Gucci jacket. But there was definitely a hardness about her face, Cate thought, something too smooth, too polished.

Cate turned her attention to Nick. She knew him well enough by now to see that the smile on his face did not mask the anxiety in his eyes. 'Hi partner,' he smiled gently, subtly removing his arm from the back of the chair in which Rebecca was sitting. 'Did it take you hours to get here? It took us ages.'

'That's what you get for living in London,' laughed Tom, moving towards the terrace doors, 'too much time wasted in traffic jams. Talking of which, shall we go outside?' he asked. 'It's too nice to be stuck in the kitchen and the chef needs to get some air,' he grinned.

They moved out onto the enormous terrace which stood above the lawns. It was hardly a balmy evening, but for April there was a surprisingly warm and fuzzy glow to the evening. The shrill, lazy sound of birds singing high in the trees filled the garden, the cherry blossom had just burst into bloom and there was a hazy early dusk light that made the whole scene feel vaguely continental. Knocking back a big gulp of gin and tonic, Cate lifted her face to the sun, letting it warm her for the first time that year.

'So we finally meet the famous Cate,' said Rebecca, sidling up to her, sipping from a kir royale. 'Although it's amazing we've never met before, isn't it? You being in magazines, me being in PR and all that,' she added. Rebecca's voice had a knowing, confident undercurrent, over-friendly in that insincere PR-executive way that Cate had witnessed a thousand times over in her job.

'I know,' smiled Cate. 'Being editor at *Class* meant that I was pretty much chained to my desk, so I didn't get out half as much as I should have. I'm sure you must know everyone from the fashion department, though?'

'Oh yes,' said Rebecca, putting an over-familiar hand on Cate's arm, 'Lucy, Cheryl, Susie – lovely girls. Terribly sorry about what happened with you, though. Just awful. Although you must be glad that your job went to Nicole Valentine and that they didn't bring in an outsider.'

'Yes, delighted,' smiled Cate thinly, trying not to show her annoyance. She could tell it was going to be a night of backhanded compliments and endless chat about Rebecca and what Rebecca did. Nick had always been very sparing in his descriptions of Rebecca, but in the five minutes it took for Rebecca to introduce herself properly, she found out more about her than she had heard from Nick in two months. They had met in New York where Nick was in publishing and Rebecca was working for a PR company. She had returned the summer before and set up her own fashion PR company, which had become, according to Rebecca, instantly successful. After ten months they had already secured accounts for three major fashion labels including Roman LeFey and Clerc, the international jewellers, not to mention several luxury and beauty clients. She had a staff of ten at her Bond Street offices and business was going from strength to strength. Cate was surprised she hadn't offered her details about the size of her house and how wonderful her sex life was.

As if reading her thoughts, Tom appeared with a bowl of crisps; when he knew Rebecca wasn't looking, he grimaced at Cate in sympathy.

'Of course, I will do whatever I can to help your little project,' said Rebecca as Tom moved back into the house. 'Nick and I are so close, it's almost as if it's my project too. What's his is mine and all that,' she said, looking over to where Nick was sifting through a pile of CDs. 'Anyway,' she continued, flicking back a strand of hair and pouring herself a glass of Dom Pérignon from the bottle on the wrought-iron garden table, 'how was Milan?' She moved out of Nick's earshot and lowered her voice. 'I couldn't bear to come out and meet Nick there, however much he tried to insist. I spend so much time in the damn place, it would have been more torture than treat!'

Cate's stomach contracted. 'Oh, I didn't know Nick invited you to come and join him . . .'

'Oh yes,' smiled Rebecca, her jade eyes opening wide, her voice still low. 'We love going on little mini-breaks, but they had stopped since you two had been knocking heads together every weekend. But you must remember I will do anything I can to get *Sand* off the ground. Just give me a nudge. Nick never likes to ask, he's so sweet.'

Cate reached for a handful of pistachio nuts and watched Rebecca as she drifted off to join Tom and Nick, who were laughing loudly at a private joke. In a funny way Cate was almost disappointed by Rebecca. She'd met a thousand girls like her before. Pretty, yes, beautiful even, but not particularly witty or clever. Just a very self-confident PR girl who could talk and smile and fill the silences with chit-chat about herself. She looked at Nick exchanging smiles with Rebecca and wondered what she had been expecting.

Dinner was a noisy, calorie-laden and haphazard affair. Nick and Tom were both on great form. The two men had not seen each other in a while, so the gossip came thick and fast and the banter swelled between them. The food was delicious: the meat had been cooked in thick game gravy that Tom ladled over the plates. OK, so the mustard mash came ten minutes later, but Tom took it all in his stride, laughing about his lack of coordination and quaking at the thought of cooking a Christmas dinner. The champagne and red wine flowed, and Cate cringed when she saw her bottle of off-licence plonk sitting on the table next to the Château Lafite that Rebecca had brought.

After dinner it was too cold and too dark to carry on drinking outside, so they filed into Tom's enormous living room where he lit a fire and turned on the lamps around the room, which spilt a saffron glow up the walls and across the cream carpet. It's a beautiful space, thought Cate, looking around the room – old, traditional, yet sophisticated and modern. When they all stopped talking, they could hear nothing but the crackling of the embers. Cate wondered how lonely it must be for Tom when the visitors had gone, the fire had died down and the birds had stopped singing. Maybe that was why he still had a sideboard full of photographs to remind him of the life that was still out there. One large black-and-white photograph in a tawny leather frame stood out from the rest of the happy smiling shots of friends and family. It was a shot of Tom and Serena laughing on a boat. Cate felt embarrassed to be looking at them, almost as if she was intruding; she turned her head away, conscious of the fact that Serena's name had not been brought up all evening.

'Is it really corny if I go and make some egg-nog?' asked Tom, shoving a poker into the fire. 'It's a big house and it's a spooky night outside,' he said, looking at the full moon shining down through the windows. 'But we've got friends and a roaring fire; it's just crying out for some egg-nog! Hang on, what is egg-nog?' he asked, looking at Cate, his brow furrowed. 'Milk, whisky and cinnamon?'

'Don't ask me,' replied Cate, laughing. 'I'm more of a Martini girl.'

'Uh-oh, prepare for an alcoholic disaster,' smiled Nick lazily.

'Well, I lived in New York for three years,' announced Rebecca, walking towards the kitchen. 'I know how to make a *great* egg-nog. I'll come and help you.'

Cate and Nick settled into two big red armchairs at either side of the fireplace, Cate curling her feet up into the squishy cushions contentedly. 'What would you do for a place like this?' said Nick softly, looking around the room and up into the high-beamed ceiling. 'Oh sorry!' he said, teasing a little, 'I forgot: you *do* have a house like this.'

'Oh stop it,' grinned Cate, 'it's the family house – and anyway, you obviously haven't been. It's not half as cosy and delicious as this place.'

211

'Are you staying over?' he asked, immediately looking embarrassed. 'I mean, it's a great house, you just want to stay in it as long as possible,' he added quickly. 'You should see my room, it's got a bloody Jacuzzi at the bottom of the bed!'

'My room?' queried Cate. 'Sleeping solo tonight then?'

'Well, no . . .' mumbled Nick.

'Well, you'll enjoy that then,' said Cate, instantly regretting sounding as peevish as she felt. 'Make up for not being with Rebecca in Milan.'

Nick looked at her, confused. 'What are you talking about?'

'Anyway . . .' gushed Cate, suddenly nervous to be alone with him.

He looked at her as if he was examining her face and she felt her heart lurch.

'. . . at least I haven't been put in the stables,' she blustered nervously. 'I'm up in the attic, it's absolutely gorgeous – loads of beams, wooden floors, and the view is fantastic: you can see all the way over to Stow on the Wold.'

'Cate –'

Tom and Rebecca came back into the room, Tom carrying a huge terracotta pitcher of steaming drink. 'Is egg-nog supposed to be hot?' asked Tom. 'Seemed like it would be better if it was hot, anyway.'

Cate glanced up at Rebecca and noted that somewhere between the living room and the kitchen, Rebecca had lost her jacket. She was now just wearing a tiny, spaghetti-strapped vest.

'Come on, Tom, confess,' laughed Nick, who didn't seem to have noticed the change. 'How are you enjoying it out here in the wilds all on your own?'

Tom perched on the edge of Cate's armchair and lay his arm along the back of the headrest. Cate was surprised to find herself enjoying Tom's protective presence, but she also noted that Rebecca was now looking over at her with a questioning expression.

'Actually, I love it,' said Tom. 'I'd be a liar if I didn't admit that it gets a bit lonely at times, but I just love having some time to myself to do the things I want to do. Can you believe that the Women's Institute even invited me to give them a talk on creative writing?'

'Does your agent know about this?' said Rebecca in a voice so serious that nobody in the room knew whether she was joking or not.

'I suspect the fee will be in pots of gooseberry jam,' said Tom, sipping his egg-nog. 'I'm not sure my agent will be interested in a percentage of that. But no, I love it. And I don't think I'll be coming back any time soon.'

'But what about your acting career? How can you give that up?' asked Rebecca solemnly.

There was an awkward silence as Tom looked at Cate again, one eyebrow slightly raised. 'Oh, I think Hollywood will wait,' said Tom finally. 'At least until I finish this egg-nog.'

As the evening wore on, they talked and laughed and played Pictionary, after which Tom took them on a torch-lit tour of the house, telling them tales of ghosts and spirits that he'd heard from the village gossips over the past few weeks. 'Apparently there's a ghost of a one-armed servant that lives down here,' he said as they stumbled around the dusty wine cellar. 'Oh my God!' squealed Rebecca. 'Aren't you terrified?'

'Not quite sure I want to be all the way up in the attic tonight,' laughed Cate.

'Oh, don't worry,' said Tom, putting a hand on Cate's arm. 'I haven't seen anything since I've been here. The only spirits in this house are in that drink.'

* * *

213

That wasn't so painful, thought Cate, climbing into her cotton pyjamas and creeping in between the Pratesi sheets and thick down duvet – a relic from his old life with Serena, thought Cate with a smile. As long as they had not been left alone, Nick was not awkward and shy; in fact he had been totally on form. It had been great to see Tom too. She still wasn't sure whether he was genuinely happy out here in the country, or whether he was trying to convince himself that the sadness he felt was not there. It must be so hard, she thought, moving from a whirlwind life of nonstop parties and socializing – and she knew from her teenage years that Serena was a loud and domineering person to live with – to Tom's splendid isolation with just a few rumoured ghosts for company. But no, her worries about the men had been unfounded.

And she had met Rebecca and in some ways she was relieved. Now she was real at least and she could no longer just dismiss the idea of Nick having a girlfriend. After Milan she had still harboured a glimmer of hope that there was something between her and Nick, but now she had seen him as half of a couple, she knew that there was nothing there. The cocktail of gin and tonic, red wine and egg-nog was making her drowsy now. Feeling just a little scared about the ghosts, she pulled the duvet right up to her chin, tucked her head deep into the pillows so they surrounded her ears, and tried her best to fall asleep.

The Cotswold countryside is full of noises at night: barn owls hooting in the distance, leaves swooshing as the evening wind tickles their branches and the clanking of pipes and cisterns throughout the ancient brickwork. It was something Tom had learnt to sleep through. But at three o'clock in the morning, he was suddenly disturbed by a sound he didn't quite recognize: a long creak coming from the dark area over by his bedroom door. Still semi-conscious, he dismissed it, turning over and flinging the duvet away from him as he turned. Suddenly he froze. No, this time there was someone else there. The covers moved and he felt another body slip under the sheets beside him.

'What the –?'

Feeling a dart of terror shoot up his spine, he slowly turned to face the intruder. A long French-manicured finger brushed the hair from his forehead. 'Shhh,' whispered a voice. As Tom's eyes adjusted to the darkness, the shape beside him began to take on a form he recognized.

'Rebecca,' he hissed, as she pushed herself up against him and he realized in the dark-greyness that she was naked.

'Rebecca, what the hell –?'

'Shhhh . . . ' she repeated, putting her finger to his lips. Suddenly his mind leapt back to earlier in the evening when she had followed him into the kitchen to help him with the egg-nog. He remembered how she had suggestively slipped off her jacket and brushed up against him, her bare arms against his. At the time, it had seemed accidental, but now her friendliness had taken on a whole other perspective. Now, as she shifted beside him, the firm curve of her breasts and nipples were silhouetted against a shaft of moonlight coming through a crack in the curtains. Frozen in terror, his mind searching for a way to escape, he was struck by how much Rebecca's outline looked like Serena's. The long blonde hair falling onto her bare shoulders, the firm, slim, smooth body, pushing up against his. She was so warm, so soft, he thought drowsily. But no.

Desperately, springing to his senses, Tom shook his head and moved his body away from her. 'Look, Rebecca, what are you doing?' he hissed urgently. 'Don't, no, don't –'

Before he had time to object further, Rebecca's head had moved under the covers, her hair brushing against his navel as she went down. Tom groaned as he felt her ripe lips surround his cock, her whole mouth going down the shaft of his penis until its tip touched the back of her throat. Up down, up, down. For a second he moaned with pleasure: it had been over three months since he had had any physical contact with a woman – and he missed it. Suddenly he came to his senses.

'Fuck, Rebecca. Get off me. Now.'

Her head came up for air and she slid out of his bed as smoothly as she had entered it.

He turned to watch her, wretched with embarrassment, as her naked body walked away from him. Completely unaffected by what had just happened, she picked up a silk dressing gown that she had discarded on the floor seconds earlier and looked over her shoulder to smile at him.

'Any time,' she purred seductively. 'Remember, Tom, any time.'

20

Diego Bono rolled back exhausted onto the crumpled sheets, beads of sweat glistening on his firm, bronzed skin and looked across the room at his new lover. He never usually felt uncomfortable bringing the many conquests he picked up in the gay clubs of Soho back to his Camden apartment, but this one was something else. Elegant, sophisticated and obviously very, very wealthy. Now he was moving in more affluent circles, Diego was definitely going to have to sharpen up his act. He didn't want anyone to think Diego Bono was just some handsome Spanish hustler on the make. Diego Bono was going places. He propped himself up on his goose-down pillows and lit a menthol cigarette. The silhouette of his partner moved towards the window to open the curtain, letting in a thin stream of late afternoon sun. Diego blew a smoke ring as he admired his companion's taut white buttocks in the dusty light.

'May I just say,' announced Diego in his lightly accented European drawl, 'you really do have the most amazing arse.'

Jonathon von Bismarck looked over to the bed and started

to pull on his crumpled chinos. 'Yes,' he replied coolly, giving Diego a thin, arrogant smile, 'I know.'

Venetia looked at Diego Bono's sketches, which were strewn across her desk, and smiled. Gosh, this young designer straight out of the Royal College of Art was such a find, she beamed to herself. The designs were perfect for the Venetia Balcon line of women's wear she was planning to launch in September: clean, casual lines with a hint of preppiness. Cotton jackets with nipped in waists, sheath dresses with slashed necklines and lightweight cashmere sweaters in candy colours. It all added up to a classic jet-set look, Britain's answer to Michael Kors' sexy New York chic – exactly the vibe she was after.

She pinned up a drawing on the wall and looked around the office, which was on the top floor of the four-storey Georgian house in Mayfair's Bruton Street. The first two floors were retail space, selling fine textiles, beautiful crystal, bedding, curtains, soft furnishings and beautiful, handcrafted pieces she had sourced from France, the third floor was their bespoke interior design department and, while she dreamt of turning the fourth floor into the fashion floor, for the moment it was Venetia's studio.

She sat back in her leather chair and took in the creative chaos with an affectionate look. Venetia Balcon Limited was becoming quite an empire, she thought happily. Swatches of Venetia Balcon fabrics covered the sofa at one end of the room, silver paint pots containing the new Venetia Balcon paint range were piled in another corner, and fine wallpaper, curtains and piles of bedding in soft deluxe fabrics were draped across the big oak table in the centre. But it was the clothing line she was most excited about. Along with Kelly Hoppen and Nina Campbell, Venetia was fast establishing herself as one of the country's top interior designers. Ever since her days at *Vogue*, fashion had always been her passion. She admired the way Ralph Lauren and Jasper Conran had created a huge lifestyle empire out of a line of clothes. If they had gone from fashion to homeware, why couldn't she do it the other way round? She knew the yummy-mummies and bored housewives from Chelsea to Clapham were desperate for a touch of the Venetia Balcon vision of life and she was more than willing to provide it for them. At a price, she smiled.

She took a swig of strong coffee and decided that she'd been working so hard, it wouldn't hurt to clock off early for the afternoon. She casually flipped through her diary to check she was free. Damn! There was an appointment pencilled in. Jack Kidman? Who on earth was that? She picked up the phone to call her assistant, Leila.

'Leila – Jack Kidman? Remind me who he is again. Apparently I've got a meeting with him in five minutes, but I'm due for a facial in an hour.'

'You asked me to pencil in a meeting with him after Serena's party,' replied Leila anxiously. 'Friend of one of the guests, I think.'

Venetia groaned. Now she remembered. Amanda Berryman, the PR who looked after Venetia Balcon homeware had asked her to meet one of her friends, some ex-advertising guy who had bought a house in Spain and was looking for an interior designer for the renovation project. She glanced at her watch. Why on earth had she agreed to see him? It wasn't as though she particularly needed the business. Her diary was already fit to burst with international private and corporate clients, all eager for her style overhauls in their homes or offices. She had got to the stage where she would only personally look after a select handful of projects, farming the rest out to Caroline Rhodes, a young but talented interior stylist she had poached from

Kelly Hoppen. And I think Caroline will be the one heading out to Jack Kidman's holiday home, thought Venetia.

'Leila?' she asked, picking up the phone again. 'Can you see if Caroline is available to take an appointment with me?'

"Fraid not, Venetia. She left about half an hour ago on appointments. And Jack Kidman has arrived. Shall I send him up?'

Cursing to herself, she glanced in the huge Venetian glass mirror on one side of the room and settled behind her desk, resigning herself to another grinding meeting. Admen. Cocky, arrogant, swaggering buggers, most of them. Didn't know good taste if it slapped them in the face. She was certainly going to need that facial.

'Venetia Balcon?'

A tall, handsome man in his early forties, with the louche, casual air of the very successful, strode into her office.

'That's me,' she smiled, standing up and smoothing down her skirt unconsciously. For a second, she felt guilty sizing up her new client. His shoulders were broad, his salt-and-pepper hair offset by a smooth, tanned complexion and a pair of twinkling dark green eyes. Only a slightly off-centre nose – perhaps a sports injury? – tempered the good looks. She took another sip of coffee to distract herself.

Jack nodded to Venetia, but walked towards the French windows that went out onto the roof terrace.

'Nice room,' he said, 'what a great place for a studio.'

He walked back in and shook her hand, his grip strong and firm, and sat down quickly, drumming his hand on his leg and taking in the space with darting eyes.

Venetia started smiling.

'What's wrong?' said Jack, with a slightly puzzled expression.

'This is an interior designer's, not the dentist,' she smiled.

Jack Kidman held up his hands and started laughing. 'I

know. I know. Just never done this whole interior design thing before,' he smiled. 'It's a bit nerve-racking, sorry.'

'OK, so why don't we start at the beginning?' said Venetia, rising. 'Tell me why you're here. Tea? Coffee?'

'Espresso, if you have it,' said Jack as Venetia moved to a jet-black Gaggia machine behind her desk. Jack watched her busy herself with the tiny cups and decided that the crisp, cool blonde in front of him was just the woman he was looking for.

'Well, I have bought a *finca* just outside Seville,' he began, clearing his throat. 'I'm selling my business and the plan is to leave London, part time at first. After that, who knows? Might turn into my home, might not. Anyway, it's a fantastic building. Old olive press with a few stables and outbuildings, twenty acres of land. Plum trees, apple trees, everything.'

He reached into a leather holdall he had left by the chair and took out a handful of large photographs, spreading them out on Venetia's desk. They were interior and exterior shots of a crumbling stone building standing in the parched grounds of a neglected Spanish farm. The walls were white but faded, the brickwork exposed and frayed. The courtyard was a ruin except for huge patches of wild lavender. Still, Venetia nodded appreciatively, it had enormous potential. Bags of character, she thought, flipping through the photographs. I'd love a place like this, she mused, imagining the hot rays of Spanish sunshine burning down onto her bare skin . . . She coughed suddenly.

'Um, very nice ceilings,' she said, flushing slightly. 'Beams in every room, lovely.'

'Absolutely,' said Jack, bringing his head closer to hers and pointing at the photographs. 'Look at this wonderful turret, and that staircase,' he said, trailing a finger over the prints.

'Pretty run-down, though,' said Venetia, turning towards him, unwilling to step too far away.

'It is, but I have a Spanish architect and team of builders working on it now,' said Jack. 'Structurally it will be sound in a matter of weeks, so now I'm thinking about the interiors. I've never done a renovation project before.' He paused with a smile, 'You can probably tell.'

Venetia was excited despite herself. She knew she was looking at a long, expensive but fascinating job. She was sick to death of tarting up boutique hotels and chi-chi restaurants that closed down after a matter of months. This house was an organic beauty and she also knew that Jack Kidman had the money to do it justice. She had read in the *Guardian* Media section about the sale of Kidman Agency – the cutting-edge advertising agency that had ridden out the nineties' recession to become one of the industry's biggest players. Apparently Tempest Communication – the huge French media conglomerate – were rumoured to be buying it for £75 million.

She looked up and Jack's dark, laughing eyes met hers. 'Interested?' he asked her, downing his espresso in a gulp that left him with a cute moustache of brown froth.

'I just might be,' said Venetia. 'I just might be.'

Venetia rarely turned down the opportunity for a spa treatment at the Knightsbridge Mandarin Oriental, but after Jack Kidman had left her office she suddenly felt unsettled, an excited nervousness running round her body. The mood she was in, she couldn't sit still for five minutes, let alone lie back for an hour having Decleor's finest oils massaged into her face and skin. She picked up the phone, cancelled the appointment and her car, slipped off her Yves Saint Laurent slingbacks and pulled on a pair of soft Tod's driving shoes, which resided permanently under her desk in case of emergencies like this.

Despite having the luxury of a driver, Venetia liked to walk home when she wanted to clear her thoughts. Leaving the office, she weaved through the back streets of Mayfair, past the casinos, the gentlemen's clubs and society hairdressers, avoiding Mount Street where she would have had to walk dangerously close to the Balcon Gallery. Even though Oswald was rarely there, it wasn't worth the risk; she certainly wasn't in the mood to talk to him.

Hyde Park looked crisp and hazy in the late April afternoon. The grass was lush and punchy while a rash of bluebells lined the walkways, which were busy with joggers, Rollerbladers and nannies pushing pushchairs. It was surprisingly warm, and Venetia took off her jacket and let the light sun warm the sleeves of her shirt. Seeing a small crowd of children playing, she took a moment to sit on a bench and watch them. A little girl with red patent shoes chased another child, her pigtails bouncing up and down as she ran away laughing. A little boy began crying as his nanny took away an ice lolly that was melting down his anorak. Three slightly older children were comparing toys, each trying to impress the other. None of the well-groomed mothers standing nearby, Venetia noted, were watching the children, preferring to gossip with the other yummy-mummies. *Why aren't they paying attention to the children?* thought Venetia sadly. *What could be more interesting than watching them run and laugh?* A tear ran down her cheek and she quickly wiped it away. So she'd had a great day, a juicy design project with a handsome owner had just appeared from nowhere. But Venetia knew that the reason she worked so hard was no burning desire to succeed like Camilla, but to escape from her day-to-day loneliness. In a heartbeat, she would gladly swap all the high-powered meetings and the wealthy private clients for one afternoon with a child – her child – playing in the park.

* * *

She walked briskly the rest of the way home. She was angry at herself for crying, angry with Jonathon for being so insensitive over her infertility, even angry at Jack Kidman for making her think she could get away from all this misery. Slamming the front door and running up the stairs, she was surprised to find Jonathon lying on the bed in his bathrobe. His hair was wet from the shower and he smelt of musky soap.

'What are you doing back so early?'

'I could ask the same about you,' said Jonathon sharply, picking up on Venetia's mood. 'Aren't you playing tennis this evening?'

'It was the spa actually,' said Venetia testily, 'I didn't feel like it.' She pulled off her jacket and threw it on the chaise longue in the bedroom. 'Anyway, you didn't answer my question, what are you doing back so early?' It wasn't the first time she had caught him back at home when he should have been at the office and it was beginning to make her suspicious. Of what, she couldn't pinpoint.

'Am I not allowed to get home before eight now, is that it?' barked Jonathon, getting up off the bed to walk into the dressing room, still rubbing at his hair with a towel. He tossed it carelessly on the floor and began flipping through a rail of clothes before selecting a pink Charvet shirt and a pair of dark beige chinos. 'I had a dinner with a potential client who cancelled, if you must know.' He stopped in front of the enormous Venetian glass mirror, examining a couple of stray nose hairs with distaste. 'Anyway, we may as well take advantage of the reservation. Do you fancy Cipriani for some supper?'

Venetia sighed to herself, feeling the anger slowly subside. She walked up behind Jonathon and, resting her chin on the shoulder of the white towelling robe, she wrapped her arms around him and began to undo the belt. 'I thought we could stay in,' she whispered into his ear. 'It's a *good time*.'

'A good time?' said Jonathon, pulling away from her slightly, 'for what?'

'Well, I'm ripe,' she responded a little awkwardly. 'Darling, do I have to spell it out? We have to do it!'

He pushed her hands off and looked at her coldly. 'I do wish you would stop treating sex like some military bloody operation. I don't particularly want to do it on command.'

Venetia's anger instantly came flooding back. 'I didn't realize you were such a bloody romantic!' she spat, her eyes blazing. 'I don't need to remind you that we are running out of time.' Her voice started wobbling and she could feel hot wells of tears rolling down her face.

'Oh Jesus,' growled Jonathan, walking away from her.

Venetia snapped. She grabbed hold of the robe and spun him round. 'This is our child we're talking about!' she screamed. 'Which part of this don't you understand? The doctor has told me that I am going through a premature menopause. I am running out of eggs, I've got maybe three or four months at most. If we don't start trying very hard for a child this month – every month – that's it! There is no more time, there is no child!'

She was crying now, streams of tears smearing her foundation. She bit her lip to try and staunch the flow.

'So this is what we have in store for the menopausal years, is it?' Jonathan snarled cruelly. 'Violent mood swings? Tears at bedtime?'

He calmly walked back into the dressing room, giving the top of his chest a squirt of Aqua di Palma. 'So you don't want to go out for dinner then?'

Venetia just stood with her back to him, staring out onto the street, her shoulders heaving with silent tears.

'I'll assume that's a no then,' he said tartly, threading his

Asprey cufflinks through the holes in his shirt. 'That's a shame, because we do have a few business matters to discuss.'

Venetia turned to look at him, her eyes red but indignant. 'Well you can tell me here. We don't need to go to a restaurant to do business,' she said icily.

'In that case, I might as well outline my future plans,' he replied briskly, fully the businessman now he was dressed again. 'I noticed from the diary we have another Venetia Balcon board meeting on Monday afternoon.'

'That's right,' said Venetia, taking a sip of Evian to clear her throat. For the last eighteen months Jonathon had attended all board meetings for her business, including many other smaller but important meetings relating to the Venetia Balcon business. He had been the company's main commercial adviser. After all, just after their marriage he had injected two million pounds of his own money into her business – the two million pounds that had enabled her to move from a tiny shop in the Fulham Road to the beautiful Georgian Mayfair base that Venetia Balcon now occupied. After Venetia, Jonathon was the largest shareholder with forty-five per cent of the company, her finance director Geoffrey Graham holding three per cent and Caroline, her senior interior designer, with a one per cent share.

'I've decided I can't afford the time any more,' said Jonathon, combing his hair in the mirror. 'Orion Capital is looking after a five-billion-pound fund now, and if we're going to open a Geneva office by the end of the year, I can't afford any distractions whatsoever. So I won't be so involved with your business affairs any more, darling.'

Venetia felt a sense of panic. While she found it hard working with her husband – he could be a demanding, controlling perfectionist, she still valued the business perspective he brought to her company. She wouldn't have dreamt of expanding so rapidly with her women's-wear line, or opening the New York shop without Jonathan's enormous commercial input. Geoffrey was an efficient number cruncher, but he didn't hold a candle to her husband in terms of business acumen.

'But what do you expect me to do?' she stammered. 'You're part of the business, it's your investment!'

'It's hardly my primary business concern,' he laughed coldly, 'However, you're right, I do want to protect that investment, which is why I have decided to nominate someone to take my place at the board meetings to make decisions about the company on my behalf. Someone who can make rational, impartial decisions. I know you can be a little too passionate sometimes.'

'Who?' she asked, playing with the platinum band around her finger.

'Your father,' replied Jonathon coolly.

For a moment she wasn't sure whether he was mocking her or whether he was actually suggesting it seriously, until she saw the triumphant look in his eye.

'But how . . . ? What can you be thinking?' she coughed, moving towards him, rubbing her palms together. 'Jesus, Jonathon, you know how difficult he is. He's belligerent, obstructive and a downright pain in the arse at the best of times. I can't – no, make that I *won't* – work with him. You can't seriously expect me to do it!'

Mirroring Venetia, Jonathon began twirling the gold signet ring around his little finger and smiled confidently. 'As a forty-five per cent stakeholder in your company, darling, I expect you to do whatever I suggest.'

21

'Fruit juice, Earl Grey, or is it just a little early for Martinis?' said Serena, sitting down next to Roman LeFey on the terrace of Michael's impressive Upper East Side duplex.

'Just some mineral water would be great,' replied her friend, relaxing back in his Adirondack chair to let the sun shine on his face and his eyes wander to enjoy the view. From the terrace, Roman could see all the way from downtown Manhattan across Central Park and up towards the horizon where upstate New York beckoned over twenty miles away. There was probably no better spot to have lunch anywhere in the city and no more glamorous a dining companion.

He turned his critical fashion eye to Serena, whom he had not seen since their dramatic Egyptian cruise. She had certainly slipped into the role of New York power-blonde, he thought, looking at her slim-fit tailored trousers, Proenza Schouler T-shirt and ice-pick-heeled mules dangling off her crimson-painted toes. Serena had, of course, always been his most thoroughbred friend, but there were definite subtle differences he noted, taking a little sip of Pellegrino. Her make-up was a little more dramatic, her hair a paler shade of blonde. And she had certainly lost an awful lot of weight.

The slight curve of her hips had been smudged away to squeeze her into a size four. It was a glossy, expensive and highly polished look, but Roman half wondered whether, in her pursuit of the New York make-over, she hadn't lost a little of the English naturalness he had so loved about her.

A Hispanic maid bustled onto the terrace holding two big bowls of shrimp salad and a jug of iced water with floating wedges of lime. 'A light lunch,' smiled Serena, stabbing at a curl of rocket. 'Sorry we couldn't have popped down to Da Silvano or somewhere in the Village, but I'm rushed off my feet with appointments today before this damned party. I've got a manicure, pedicure and massage at Bergdorfs at two, and I've not even been for a run yet,' she said, a quiver of panic in her voice.

'But at least you have a gown for this evening,' smiled Roman proudly. 'You are going to look beyond fabulous.'

Serena nodded. She knew she was going to have to look her very best if she was going to shine at this evening's Costume Institute Gala. Held at the Metropolitan Museum, the gala was unique in attracting an A-list mix of New York society, music industry cheeses and Hollywood stars, not forgetting the glamorous fashion pack. Eight hundred of America's hottest, hippest and most fashionable were about to vie for attention in the hottest party of the year. Serena's publicist Muffy had told her that if she could make a splash tonight, not only New York but the whole of America would wake up to the charms of Serena Balcon. Of course, she had to make the right kind of splash. The gala usually had a theme and tonight's was 'A Night of Burlesque'. It was a delicate balancing act. Too often guests took it too seriously and ended up dressing like some half-clothed gothic tragedy. On the other hand, she appreciated that looking totally glamorous while also entering into the spirit of the evening would certainly get her noticed.

But trust Roman to come up with such a fabulous concoction, she thought, picturing it lying on her bed. A long, strapless gown with acres of fabric billowing out into a sumptuous train, it had been woven from strips of dark chiffon in various shades of black from charcoal to darkest ebony. A boned corset made by Mr Pearl clung to her body like molten metal. Whilst the couture confection had been a present from Roman, he wasn't doing it entirely without ulterior motives. He knew that once Serena Balcon walked up those steps, all of New York's big fashion spenders and front-row girls would want to know who had made her incredible gown. He wasn't going to sit back and let Carolina Herrera and Oscar de la Renta dress American society for ever.

'Anyway, tell me all about New York,' said Roman, nibbling daintily on a Honduran prawn.

'Oh, it's fabulous,' beamed Serena. '*Town & Country* are shooting me for their cover next month. At Michael's beach house in Southampton.'

'Holidays in the Hamptons,' grinned Roman. 'So we're a fully converted New Yorker, are we? Or still hankering after London life?'

Serena snorted. 'You've got to be kidding! I don't know why I didn't move here years ago. That whole Chelsea thing just seems so parochial now. I have met so many amazing people – artists, directors, and I mean really big directors, not just someone who's been to film school and owns a camera,' she gushed, almost knocking over her glass with excitement.

The fact that she was lonely in New York was something Serena tried to push to the back of her mind. Everyone in the city took everything so seriously and, while there was always something fabulous to go to – a party, a benefit, a gallery opening, she missed someone she was close to, to talk to, to share in her triumphs. She missed her sisters. She'd also realized too late that Michael was too much of a workaholic to be the Manhattan sidekick she craved. The vast scale of his business empire had only become clear once Serena had moved to New York – three hundred hotels under numerous divisions, two casinos, as well as a raft of prime real estate.

His life had a routine that Serena's day had to be fitted into. He worked from 7 a.m. to 7 p.m. each day. Serena was expected to meet him for dinner at the New York Sarkis hotel at 7.30 p.m. Only then – and if he wished – would they hit the social scene together. He disliked Serena going to parties without him and he made his displeasure evident. Normally Serena wouldn't have put up with such behaviour from any man: she was used to calling the shots in her relationships. But in New York she didn't have her support network of friends and family to fall back on, so for the time being she wasn't going to rock the boat. And especially not with the summer season – the Hamptons house, the weekends on his yacht – so close. At least I'm *practical*, she thought smugly to herself.

'Anyway,' continued Serena, stretching her legs out and toying with the lime floating in her drink. 'It's not as if I can go back to London now, is it?'

'Oh? How come?' asked Roman, a bemused expression on his face.

'Well,' replied Serena, tossing back her hair, a dazzling white in the midday sun. 'A few weeks ago we put the Cheyne Walk house on the market. I thought it was about time – everything's being done through the lawyers, of course. It's only been on a week and we've already had an offer over the asking price. Not surprisingly, of course, you can't put a price on it being Serena Balcon's old place, can you? The buyers want an early completion and I guess there's nothing stopping us, is there? I'm out here now and Tom's apparently enjoying being a country bumpkin.'

'But is that wise?' asked Roman, taking tiny sips of water. 'I mean, shouldn't you try to keep a base in London?'

'Whatever for?' asked Serena, appearing totally surprised, 'This is my life now. If I want to go back for a holiday, I can stay with one of my sisters – preferably Venetia, at least she has quite a nice house. But really,' she sighed, pulling the aqua-tinted sunglasses off the top of her head and peering at the fabulous view, 'I have no intention of going back any time soon.'

Freshly blow-dried, massaged, manicured, tweezered and made-up, Serena decided to blend herself a frozen margarita before attempting to squeeze herself into her Roman LeFey original. Michael was due any moment, cutting it fine as usual, she noted, looking at the clock. Dressed in nothing but a scrap of lacy underwear, a pair of sky-high Manolos and brandishing an enormous cocktail glass, Serena felt like some villainous Bond girl as she walked across Michael's living room towards the CD player. In fact, Michael's whole apartment lent itself to the high-tech assassin ambience. There was a bank of plasma televisions across one wall, a glass Christian Liagre coffee table in the centre, and cream pop-art furniture on either side of the floor-to-ceiling windows, which were hidden by curtains made from long threads of tiny pearls. The whole look was maddeningly seductive and expensive and made the Cheyne Walk town-house she shared with Tom seem, well, a little parochial.

Serena picked up a remote no larger than one of Michael's Cohiba cigars. She pressed a button and ambient jazz oozed through the room. Gulping back the rest of her margarita, she felt sexy and alive. Her eyes closed, she swayed to the music, beginning to move her arms up over her head like an exotic snake charmer hypnotizing her prey. Swinging her hips to the rhythm, she drew her fingers down from the top of her neck down over her breasts to her navel in her erotic private dance. Then she heard the lounge door close. She whirled around to find Michael standing there. He flung his copy of *Fortune* magazine on the coffee table and began loosening his tie. 'Don't let me stop you,' he smiled, looking her bronzed body up and down.

'You can't say I don't ever give you a royal welcome,' replied Serena, dancing over to him and kissing him gently on the neck. Michael growled and reached for her, but she playfully pushed him away and moved towards the dressing room.

'No time for play,' she smiled saucily. 'I have to go and beautify myself.'

Michael spread his hands in appeal and ran after her. 'Well, why don't we take a shower together then?' he called, a hungry tone in his voice.

'No, no, no!' squealed Serena, running away from him and pulling the bedroom door closed behind her. 'I'm going to get dressed,' she called. 'Just wait until you see my dress! It's perfect!'

Michael shrugged and padded to the marble and limestone bathroom, sliding his clothes off as he approached, while Serena stood gazing down at the delicate fabric of her gown before she began to pull it up and over her body, careful not to touch her hair. Orlando Pita had teased her mane into a sleek ponytail and she fastened a black orchid into the nape of her neck for effect. She turned to look at her reflection in the floor-to-ceiling mirrors and almost gasped at the elegant beauty staring back at her. 'Eat your heart out, Nicole Kidman,' she smiled, gazing at herself until she heard the sound of bare feet padding across thick carpet.

She turned around to see Michael, naked except for a small white towel, the hair all over his forearms, shoulders and chest glistening with moisture from the shower. She stood there, posing for a second, ready for Michael's gushing praise for her breathtaking beauty. 'Jesus, Serena!' he said finally.

She smiled seductively, pulling her ponytail around onto her bare shoulder like a python. 'Isn't it fabulous?' she purred. 'It's a present from Roman.'

'It's awful!' said Michael flatly.

Serena's smile disappeared as she smoothed her hands across the chiffon. 'But it's beautiful,' she said.

'Serena, it's fucking awful,' said Michael forcefully, dropping the towel to the floor. 'You look like you're going to a funeral! This is supposed to be a glamorous event tonight. Take it off!'

The cold menace in his voice slapped Serena in the face. She had never been told she was anything short of sensational. Even her father, who had been quick to call Cate fat or Venetia a string-bean, had always treated her like the family's Helen of Troy.

'What do you mean you don't like it?' she gasped. 'Just because it's shades of black doesn't mean I look like a bloody widow,' she said, biting the top layer of her lip.

Michael's response was cutting, impassive. 'Take it off,' he said.

He walked over to the mirror and started towel-drying his hair. 'Wear that red Valentino I bought you,' he sniffed without turning to face her. 'And take the funeral wreath out of your hair. Is it supposed to be sexy?'

'Fuck you!' said Serena, stalking on her heels into the bathroom where she slammed the door shut, a little strip of chiffon catching on the door as she went. She sank down onto the cold limestone floor and sat there, shocked. She had never once doubted her appearance. She had thought she looked incredible tonight. She wanted to be the girl in the beautiful Roman LeFey gown that every magazine from

W to *Vanity Fair* would photograph and run as the lead picture on their society pages.

She knew she looked fabulous, and she also knew she didn't have to listen to Michael. She could walk out of the bathroom, take his arm, turn up to the party like a stunning chiffon cloud and outshine everyone. But, for one second, she felt more scared, vulnerable and alone than she had felt in a long time. Michael's dangerous edge that she had found so enticing in Mustique kept her submissive. His constant instructions on where she could and couldn't go, his gifts of clothes and jewellery which would make her look a certain way, his jealous monopolizing of her social life, it was all slowly breaking down her resistance. Each time she let him have his way, the Serena Balcon she had been in London got a little smaller, a little more timid. And it scared her. She'd seen the same fear of displeasing her man in Venetia's eyes when Jonathon would angrily round on her at some party or dinner. Not once had Serena ever thought that she would turn into this woman, sitting on a cold floor, slumped against a door, anxious, nervous – terrified – to return to the man on the other side of it. For a fleeting second, the nagging doubt that had been building over the past weeks reappeared. Why was she living with Michael Sarkis? Away from the parties and the benefit dinners, did she really like his company?

'Jesus, pull yourself together, Serena!' she scolded herself, pulling herself up, looking at herself in the mirror. It just wasn't worth it. It wasn't worth ruining her evening and it wasn't worth upsetting Michael. After all, being with him was definitely getting her noticed in the place that counted – America. It moved her up another notch in society. And a dress wasn't worth upsetting that applecart for.

Staring at her reflection, she stroked down the silk from

the top of the strapless bodice all the way down to her legs, wondering for a moment how disappointed Roman would be if she did not wear the gown he had spent weeks creating. But only for a moment. Pulling the black orchid from her hair, she walked out of the bathroom into the bedroom, ignoring Michael's looks. She stepped out of the gown and pulled on the red slinky floor-length gown, adding a huge diamond choker that Michael had given her. Immediately she felt like a different woman. More obviously sexy, and still sophisticated, but she felt she had regained control. 'Better,' said Michael as she waited by the door for him. 'Now I think we had better go. Dinner starts at eight.'

Fifth Avenue was pandemonium by the time the car pulled up at the huge façade of the Metropolitan Museum at Eighty-Second Street. A line of black limousines snaked back up the road, each taking their turn to unload their glamorous cargo onto the red carpet before driving off into the night. The entrance was a marquee-covered tunnel where photographers from picture agencies, television companies and glossy magazines lined up behind the crash barriers to get their shot of the A-list guests as they walked inside. Seeing that J-Lo, looking spectacular in a snow-white gown, had entered only seconds before her, Serena was anxious that she would get a subdued response from the snappers. She need not have worried. The lenses raised, the shutters whirred and the paparazzi all shouted her name as she glided past them up the enormous staircase and into the building where the Great Hall had been decorated with a thousand flickering votive candles.

She took a blood-orange cocktail from a waiter and surveyed the scene. Thank goodness she'd given the burlesque theme a miss, she decided. Amber Thompson, America's hottest platinum-blonde supermodel, was wearing a lavender powder wig and a long corset dress that was laced from her shoulder blades down to her heels and exposed a cheeky flash of bronzed buttock as she walked. More Marilyn Manson than Marilyn Monroe, thought Serena with a sneer. Thankfully no one else was wearing red.

'You look stunning,' smiled Michael into her ear, biting the bottom of her lobe, stroking the palm of his hand across her bottom. She smiled at him indulgently. Basking in New York's social elite limelight, she had almost forgotten about their earlier spat. Industry and society figures drifted up to them, exchanging air-kisses, compliments and platitudes. She grabbed Michael's hand as they worked the crowd, talking to producers, senior figures from the museum, and the wives of billionaire philanthropists. It was a heady exotic mix. Rumour was right; everybody came to this party – Hollywood society, editors in chief and the world of fashion all seamlessly mingling.

As they sat down, Serena took a minute to survey her table. It was impressive. To her left was Tyler Sang, the multimillion-selling hip-hop mogul and Sahara, his raven-haired twenty-five-year-old wife. Next to them was a space where Roman LeFey and Patric, who was flying in from Paris, would sit. Petula, the fashionably odd-looking model, was sitting next to her rock-star fiancé Zachary, while to Michael's left sat Warren Johnson, the legendary Wall Street financier and his much-younger fourth wife Marissa. Roman and Patric arrived at the table just as Serena was reading the menu out loud to everybody. Roman's face was stony, shaking his head so slowly it was almost unnoticeable. As he took his seat, the determined, unsmiling line of his mouth spoke volumes.

For half an hour, Serena entertained herself talking to Sahara, whom she found amusingly vulgar. The half-Tahitian beauty was regaling her with her plans for a jewellery and make-up line for babies. It wasn't until they were halfway through the lamb shank with quail gravy that Serena realized to her horror that Sahara had been feeding her food to a tea-cup Pomeranian dog peeking out of the top of her bag. 'Poor Rococo is thirsty, aren't you baby?' cooed Sahara as she lifted a flute of champagne to the dog's mouth and let it lap up greedy gulps.

Turning away in disgust, Serena tried to catch Roman's eye, but he appeared to be locked in conversation with Petula and Zac, the model and rock star. Realizing that she had definitely upset him, she excused herself from Sahara, stood up and walked around to the back of Roman's chair, putting her hand on his shoulder. 'Please don't be cross,' she whispered into his ear, 'I had an accident with the bathroom door. The chiffon split, it was awful! I didn't want to embarrass you by wearing a less than perfect dress.'

'You ripped it?' said Roman, raising an eyebrow as if he didn't believe a word of it.

'I know!' sighed Serena dramatically. 'Not really a rip. More of a slash, actually. I'm so, so sorry, I'll make it up to you somehow, I promise.'

Roman glanced over at Michael who was leaning in to Sahara, his hand on her bare arm, sharing a private joke. He simply nodded. 'I understand, Serena,' he said coolly.

Christ, some people are so sensitive, thought Serena, walking back to her chair to pick up her clutch. She was desperate for a cigarette. Where the hell was she supposed to have a sneaky ciggie in an art gallery? It was probably smoke-alarmed up to the rafters. Not entirely sure where she was going in the throng of people and tables, she found herself back in the Great Hall, where she stood for a moment, gazing up at the soft, blurry glow from a thousand candles.

'Enjoying yourself?' asked a sarcastic voice from behind her. She turned around and her stomach lurched.

The voice, a curious combination of venom and sadness, belonged to Marlena Verboski, Michael's ex-girlfriend, from the Egyptian yacht. She was a beautiful woman, long, cocoa-brown hair falling either side of an oval face, but her buttermilk complexion was showing all the signs of sleepless nights and tears.

Serena took a confident sip of her Mandarin Martini. 'Can I help you?'

'Marlena Verboski. We met in Egypt?'

Serena swirled the liquid around in the base of her glass. 'Yes, I vaguely recall you.'

The woman sneered. 'We had breakfast together, Serena. Surely you remember? But that's not all we have in common, is it?'

'I don't follow you,' replied Serena coolly, wanting to avoid the confrontation.

'Well, let me spell it out for you, shall I?' said Marlena, her Eastern European accent making her words clipped and precise. 'Same taste in dresses.' She nodded at Serena's red Valentino gown, then ran her hands over the crimson fabric of her own strapless dress. 'The parties we like to go to,' she continued, her hand trailing in the direction of the diners. 'And of course the same taste in men. But then how could I have forgotten that?'

Serena had, of course, been aware that Marlena Verboski had moved out of Michael's duplex shortly before she had arrived in New York. But she was in no mood to apologize for the breakdown of Michael's relationship with this tramp.

'Get over it, darling. Relationships end. Things move on. Now, if you'll excuse me, I'd like to get back to the party.'

Marlena pointed a long manicured fingernail at her.

'Relationships end when some bitch comes along and steals your man from right under your nose.'

'Oh dear,' said Serena smugly, 'somebody seems to have coat-checked their manners at the door.'

Marlena moved between Serena and her exit, bringing her face up close to hers.

'Oh I'm not here to be nice to you, you arrogant bitch,' she hissed. 'I want to tell you what you have done to my life. You have destroyed it. I gave Michael six years of my life and you took it all away in one afternoon.'

'An afternoon?' laughed Serena nervously, 'I hope you're not referring to the time I met you both in Egypt. Believe me, that was all terribly harmless. I was in the middle of a break-up with my boyfriend at the time, in case you didn't read the papers.'

'You seduced him in Egypt and fucked him in Mustique,' spat her rival, moving closer, shaking with rage. 'I'm not stupid. We were taking a holiday in Palm Beach together and then he disappeared. I contacted his pilot so I know he was in Mustique. I know you were there too. He left me in Palm Beach, he left me . . .' Her voice began to crack with emotion.

'You can't blame me for what Michael told you,' replied Serena icily. 'He told me that your relationship had been winding down and that you couldn't face the reality that it was over. I see that is clearly the case.'

Marlena's laugh came out like a cackle. 'Is that what he said?' She pointed to the grape-sized diamond dangling on a chain around Serena's neck and nodded. 'See that stone? Did he tell you it was a special gift he had bought for you? That diamond was on my finger two months ago. He gave it to me for Christmas. Learn two things about Michael,' she said coldly. 'Never believe anything he says, and understand why he is so successful in business. He never wastes any money.'

Serena put a hand protectively over her necklace. 'Don't

be ridiculous: this diamond is mine. This is a piece of estate jewellery Michael bought at auction. For me. Stop acting like a jealous, crazy woman. I was beginning to feel sorry for you.'

Marlena gazed at the jewel and then trailed her eyes up to Serena's face. 'I know every facet, every shadow, every pool of colour in that stone. I loved it. I loved it enough to recognize it immediately when I saw it hanging off your neck. It has a heart-shaped flaw in the centre when you hold it up to the light, no? I can see from your face that it has . . .'

She paused and Serena could see that her eyes were glistening.

'I loved it, but I loved myself more. That's why I gave Michael everything back when I left him,' she whispered. 'Anyway. You deserve that stone. Beautiful. Hard. Flawed,' she spat.

'Gave everything back?' snorted Serena, taking a haughty sip of cocktail, 'I didn't think that would be your style.'

Marlena laughed coldly. 'Is that all you think I am? A gold-digging Russian? A model on the make? A whore? I am better than that and I am better than him. You two deserve each other.'

'Oh, for God's sake. Go home.'

Serena had had enough and moved to push past Marlena.

'No, you go to hell!' Marlena pushed back but, as she did, slipped and stepped backwards. The train of her dress swished sideways over the parade of tea-lights, instantly catching light.

'Shit! SHIT!' cried Marlena, twisting her body back and forth, trying to get away from the flames that were creeping up her back. She stumbled, twisting her heel and falling hard on one knee. A quick-thinking waiter ran over and, whipping a cloth from a table in a shower of silver and glass,

241

smothered the flames. Serena looked down at the woman sprawled on the floor of this grand party, her knee bleeding, her dress charred and torn, her body shaking as she sobbed openly. Serena turned away, not wanting to be connected with this social humiliation and, as she did, her eyes locked with Marlena's just for a second. 'You're next,' mouthed Marlena. 'You're next.'

Serena fled back through the hall. When she was far enough away, she leant against a pillar and breathed deeply, inhaling the scent of tuberose that was coming from the candles. Just then, a photographer from *W* magazine's diary pages tapped Serena on the shoulder and asked to take a picture. Gathering herself, Serena posed for the flashbulbs. 'Serena, can you tell me who your dress and necklace are by?' asked a pretty journalist with her Dictaphone poised. 'Oh, Valentino . . .' mumbled Serena distractedly, her eyes wandering into the main room where New York's finest were polishing off their symphony of desserts.

'And the necklace?' asked the journalist.

'My necklace, my necklace . . .' she started, the words bubbling in her throat. Lost in her thoughts, she walked away from the journalist who was left looking at her openmouthed. She moved purposefully back towards the dining room, weaving between the powerful players without recognizing anybody, her mind a swirl of guilt, rage, and – most of all – shock. How dare Michael Sarkis treat her, Serena Balcon, like some second-rate girlfriend you give cast-off trinkets to? She saw his face through the crowd and she felt her fingers stretch into claws. He could shove the ten-carat diamond up where the sun don't shine, she thought, stalking over in her heels. Ignoring Michael's companion, she walked up to him, bringing her eyes level with his dark orbs and growled, 'We need to talk.'

Michael laughed lightly and took a nonchalant sip of his cognac. 'Actually the person you need to talk to is this man,' he said, gesturing towards the middle-aged man in a double-breasted dinner jacket standing at his side. Serena ignored him and carried on staring at Michael, her eyes blazing with fury, until Michael spoke again. 'Serena,' he said slowly and patronizingly, 'meet Ed Charles.'

The two words got Serena's attention. Ed Charles was Broadway's most powerful producer, who had made millions from a dozen sensational musicals over the past twenty years, four of which had been made into hugely successful Hollywood movies. While he wasn't quite Steven Spielberg, Ed Charles had the power to make careers. She took a deep breath to compose herself and turned to face him.

'Mr Charles,' she smiled as broadly as she could manage, 'how wonderful to meet you.' She extended a hand towards him, conscious that it was still slightly damp. He waved a glass of port in front of her good-naturedly. 'No, the pleasure is all mine,' he smiled. 'In fact I was just telling my old friend Michael here that I would love you to come by my house next week to talk about a project I think you'll be interested in.'

Serena tried to suppress a delighted grin. Her agent had told her that Charles was producing a version of *Fin de Siècle* for adaptation into a big blockbuster. Anyone who could hold a note was rumoured to be up for a part. Greg Dyson, a hip music-video director turned major Hollywood talent was already down to direct. Serena felt her throat become clammy with excitement, her fury instantly forgotten. She stroked Ed on the arm and launched into a full charm offensive. 'I can't imagine what that could be,' she smiled, 'but you can definitely count me in.'

'I'm just off Sutton Place,' said Charles, nodding. 'I'll let you know the time and day later in the week. But it would be lovely to have a proper conversation then. Now, if you'll excuse me, I have to get back to my table for coffee.'

Serena turned to Michael, who was loosening the waistband of his trousers and grinning like a Cheshire cat. 'What's the matter with you?' she teased, forgetting how she could have been so angry. Michael wrapped a hand around the back of her waist and pulled her in towards him, licking the side of her neck with the tip of his tongue. 'Just don't say I never do anything for you,' he said.

22

The Two Thousand Guineas at Newmarket racecourse was the first classic of the English flat-racing season, and the weather honoured the occasion with a cornflower-blue sky and a beautiful morning light that made the turf gleam like emeralds. Away from the Millennium Grandstand where a glittering crowd was anticipating some of the finest racing of the season, Oswald Balcon was pacing by the saddling boxes, lecturing the trainer of his horse about tactics for the big race.

'We'd better be in for a result today, Broadbent,' rumbled Oswald, slapping the gleaming chestnut rump of Fierce Temper, his favourite toy. He kicked the heel of his brogue into the turf, barely making an impression. 'Are you sure Temper can run on this? Bit bloody firm this ground, don't you think? Too firm if you ask me. It'd better not be a waste of money adding him to the racecard.'

Barry Broadbent merely inclined his head and nodded sympathetically. He was a trainer of the old school, his crinkled sun-weathered face had seen everything the racing game had to offer, and overprotective owners were just part of the scenery. He tipped the brim of his conker-brown trilby towards Oswald and smiled.

'You know how competitive it is these days, your lordship,' he said. 'With the likes of the Coolmore and Godolphin stableyards out there we've got to pick races where we think we have a great chance. The ground could do with a bit more juice, but I think we've got a great chance today.'

Oswald snorted dismissively and looked over to their young jockey, Finbar O'Connor, a nineteen-year-old Irish boy who had recently been signed up by Barry.

'Yes, but what about him?' said Oswald. 'You know my thoughts on this. The boy is too bloody young. Where's the experience there, eh? Why can't you get someone like Kieran Fallon or Dettori locked into your yard? I'm paying you enough, I want quality!'

Broadbent shrugged, but stood his ground.

'Finbar may be young, sir, but that doesn't mean he can't be a champion jockey. Remember Walter Swinburn? He was still a teenager when he won the Derby with Shergar. You see sir, Temper is a fantastic horse,' he smiled affectionately, stroking the white blaze of the chestnut's nose, 'but you need someone who can control you, don't you boy? And Finbar has that in spades.'

'We'll see,' said Oswald, and stalked off.

For once, Oswald's ill temper hid a real nervousness about the day. Horse racing was the one thing the tenth baron had a genuine and enduring passion for. Since his days at Cambridge in the late fifties when he would skip lectures to take the short hop to Newmarket, he had dreamt of a day like today when he would stand by a winner in the paddock, a winner that actually belonged to him. Well, part-owned, anyway. The fact that he shared Fierce Temper with Nicholas Charlesworth and Philip Watchorn under the name of BWC Holdings Limited was a constant source of annoyance to Oswald; he wanted both ownership of the horse and the glory. OK, so going in with Charlesworth and Watchorn had eased the financial load of owning a world-class race-horse, but what had they brought to the party except money? He was the expert, he was the one with the vision.

Oswald had suggested the idea to Philip and Nicholas twelve months ago. Not that it was much of a hard sell: fellow gambler Charlesworth had taken little persuading, while Watchorn could easily see the corporate hospitality opportunities that came with being an important owner. As soon as the others were on board, Oswald had immediately dispatched Aidan O'Donnell, a respected Irish bloodstock agent, to find them a suitable horse. They had picked up Fierce Temper, son of Triple Crown winner Danes Hill, for a decent price, because the horse had been having a mixed season in his juvenile year and didn't show any obvious signs of becoming a champion. Aidan O'Donnell had, however, thought otherwise and, having secured the horse, he had brought in Barry Broadbent, a former Derby-winning trainer who, after a bout of prostate cancer ten years ago, had retired from the business. O'Donnell had talked him into returning to the turf and Fierce Temper had become the jewel in the crown of Barry's new small yard in Epsom. He was the most promising horse he'd seen in years; it was to be his career swansong.

Philip Watchorn had taken a hospitality marquee opposite the Millennium Grandstand from where his guests could have lunch before the race and which would give them a magnificent viewpoint of the Rowley Mile. Oswald saun-tered across the ground, revelling in the feeling of being an owner rather than just a punter. He felt like he'd won already.

'Oswald!' boomed Philip Watchorn as he walked into the marquee. Thrusting a glass of Moët into his hand, Watchorn introduced Oswald to his guests who, along with Venetia and Jonathon, were sipping champagne and talking excitedly about the bets they had placed for the earlier race, the One Thousand Guineas. Oswald curled his mouth in distaste. Didn't these people understand how important racing was? It was more than a day out and some free booze.

'Don't say you have been harassing Broadbent again,' said Philip. 'Can't you leave the poor man alone?'

'I hope we made the right decision with him,' grumbled Oswald, taking a small sip of the champagne. 'Why didn't we go to one of the big Newmarket super-yards where all the important owners keep their horses?', he continued, almost talking to himself.

'Well, correct me if I'm wrong,' chortled Philip, helping himself to a quail's egg canapé, 'but didn't you talk glowingly of Barry nine months ago? According to you he had a fantastic record and reputation before he got ill – and he's built up a great yard since we persuaded him out of retirement, hasn't he? I thought you wanted an Epsom yard – it's a damn sight nearer to where we all live. I don't know about you, but I enjoy popping down there to watch Fierce Temper train.'

Oswald secretly knew that he had been premature in dismissing Broadbent's capabilities. Since he had started looking after Fierce Temper they had won two important Group Two races and he had come third in the top juvenile race, the Dewhurst Stakes – considered to be a training ground for three-year-old champions the next season. Oswald looked around the marquee sourly and made the decision to avoid Philip's sister-in-law Elizabeth, who was here yet again and wearing her usual predatory gleam. He also had little desire for polite chit-chat with the chairman of a Japanese electronics company and his wife, no doubt invited by Philip as some sort of business sweetener. Bloody freeloading Japs, he thought sourly, they come halfway around the world and stand around in a tent grinning and bowing for no reason – makes you sick.

He moved outside where he found Venetia and Jonathon leaning on the white rails that overlooked the racecourse, sipping Pimms and studiously avoiding eye contact. Venetia, looking beautiful if a little gaunt in an Escada eau-de-nil tulle dress, was studying the racecard intently, and flinched when Oswald moved to her side.

'Oh, hello Daddy. I thought Maria would be joining us today,' said Venetia, turning around to face Oswald, shielding her eyes from the bright sun.

Oswald shook his head slightly.

'No, she's in Verona this weekend. She's an incredibly busy woman. Anyway, where's Camilla, I thought we'd extended an invitation to her? Don't tell me she has something more important to do than support Fierce Temper?'

'Actually, I think she's swotting,' said Venetia.

'Whatever for?' guffawed Oswald.

'I think she has some Conservative Party selection day this week. Not quite sure how she will swot for it, mind you,' said Venetia. 'Read a load of Anthony Trollope? Absorb Maggie Thatcher's memoirs?' She took another sip of Pimms, letting the slice of cucumber touch her lips. She noticed with some concern that her father's face looked like thunder.

'What does she want to do that for?' he growled softly. 'She's earning good money at the Bar. Paid a fortune for that girl's education and now she's wasting her time with her little games. She's just not cut out for politics.'

'So, how do you think the race is going to go?' interrupted Jonathon, unbuttoning his cream linen jacket. 'Don't really understand all this form business,' he said, waving the *Racing Post*.

Oswald stamped an angry foot on the turf. 'It's pretty firm,' he said, 'which is OK for us, although God only knows what tactics our so-called trainer is going to employ. He's a law unto himself.'

'How much have you got on the horse?' asked Jonathon, eager to steer the conversation around to money, something he did understand.

'Only a couple of grand,' said Oswald, 'but at ten to one, that should bring home a tidy sum.' Oswald stepped forward and leant both elbows of his green tweed jacket onto the railings, looking out at the enormous crowd opposite in the grandstand.

'Today's not the day, obviously,' he said without even looking at Venetia, 'but we do need to talk about business some time over the next few days.'

'Daddy, look, I really don't think it's a good idea –'

'I'm obviously looking forward to joining the board of my daughter's company,' continued Oswald, ignoring Venetia's protests, 'but I've been over the recent board minutes and accounts with that Geoffrey fellow and I have to say I'm a little concerned about expanding into New York at this point.' He took a cigar out of his top pocket and cut the top with his Dunhill guillotine, as if the subject was closed.

Venetia pulled herself upright into a taller, more deter-mined line. 'The New York expansion is non-negotiable,' she bristled, banging her palm onto the rail for emphasis. 'I already have a small concession in Bergdorf Goodman which is doing really good business. I think Manhattan is ripe for our line of interiors on a bigger scale.'

'Non-negotiable?' queried Oswald, blowing a cloud of smoke. 'I think I had better explain business to you, my dear. Any investment over one million pounds can only go ahead with the passing of a special resolution. For that, you need Jonathon's approval and, as such, under the new arrangement, you need mine.'

Venetia grabbed hold of the railing so hard that her nails

250

began to sink into the wood. 'I'm not talking about this now, Daddy,' she said, her even voice disguising the real fear she felt, 'but I will fight you all the way. You're in this to protect Jonathon's investment, not undermine it,' she snarled.

'Oh, I realize that,' he said, almost laughing. 'And I shall do whatever is best for Jonathon. You can be sure of that.'

After a generous lunch and numerous bottles of champagne, Philip and Nicholas left the marquee to wander over to watch the parade. Grudgingly, Oswald went along to join them, unable to keep from watching the beautifully groomed Fierce Temper trot around the ring. He was a magnificent horse, his muscles rippling under a shining chestnut coat. He looked alert and impatient, pawing the ground and tossing his head. Finbar sat regally in the saddle in the amber and red silks of BWC Holdings, patting Fierce Temper's neck and whispering in his ear. Oswald couldn't help but feel a rush of pride. It was his horse. Finally he was going to get a taste of the sport of kings from the owners' enclosure.

'Hey, Oswald old man,' said Nicholas, breaking the spell, 'you know I don't study the form. What do you really reckon Fierce Temper's chances are this afternoon?'

Oswald began stroking his chin in a superior manner, enjoying the knowledge he had over his friend.

'That's the one we've got to watch: Warhorse.' He pointed at an enormous ebony colt dancing nervously sideways, his flanks already darkened with sweat. 'He's big, powerful, and he's damned fast. And look at the jockey. Tiny fellow, but he controls him with an iron fist. And I reckon Eastern Promise is going to be pretty useful too,' he said, nodding at a wiry grey. 'Belongs to another bloody Arab, of course. These so called sheikhs are taking over racing, just throwing all their oil money at the turf.'

Nicholas Charlesworth slapped Oswald on the back. 'Don't

say the Arabs are bad for the sport, old boy. Look at all the Dubai races: enormous purses! Don't say you wouldn't like a piece of that action!'

'Vulgar. That's what I call that Arab circuit, and I'm not letting Fierce Temper anywhere near them.'

Fierce Temper trotted gracefully around the paddock, swishing his finely groomed tail and nodding his nose up and down in a confident fashion. Satisfied, Oswald began to amble back to the marquee in preparation for the big race. The racecourse rumbled with excitable murmurs as the thousands of fans, owners, trainers and gamblers waited for the race to begin.

Finding himself a place at the rail, Oswald pulled out his binoculars and waited for the flag. Suddenly the stalls burst open and the runners shot off down the Rowley Mile. Fierce Temper had been drawn in Gate Six on the faster side of the ground, and Oswald craned his neck, anxious to see Fierce Temper's position. The thunderous noise of hooves pounding on the turf was drowned as Philip's marquee exploded into a frenzy of excitement: Fierce Temper had edged into the lead.

'Come on! Come on!' screamed Venetia, jumping up and down in her delicate Roger Vivier stilettos, waving her crossed fingers around in the air. Philip Watchorn was going slightly red in the face, while Barry Broadbent stood silently, his mouth in a grim, determined line as he watched the action.

'Get a move on, get a move on!' growled Oswald, still peering through his binoculars, his eyebrows furrowed into a jagged crease. There were five horses now in a tightly grouped pack, including Fierce Temper, Warhorse and Eastern Promise. With a sinking feeling, Oswald trained his binoculars on Warhorse and saw the powerful ebony race-horse start edging towards the front with only three furlongs to go. The crowd roared as Warhorse and Eastern Promise moved a length clear of the pack. Oswald saw Finbar raise his whip and give his mount another swipe and then another. Oswald flashed a glance at Barry Broadbent who was staring silently out at the course. 'There's no point whipping him so much,' snarled Oswald.

As the seconds ebbed away, and the outcome of the race looked more and more clear, the buoyant and excitable mood began to leave the marquee. Finbar urged his mount for one last effort, bending down over the horse's neck in one last big push to catch up. But it was no good, Warhorse was now three lengths ahead and two horses were passing Fierce Temper as they approached the post. And then it was over.

Oswald flung his binoculars down onto a mock-gilt chair. 'Jesus Christ! Fifth?' he shouted. 'Not even a place!' he spat over at Barry Broadbent.

'Oh, but that was fast!' said Barry, shaking his head slowly. 'That was a great horse having a brilliant race.'

'Forget Warhorse!' shouted Oswald. 'What about Fierce Temper? I told you! I told you you'd cock it up with your bloody tactics!'

Philip Watchorn walked over and put an arm around his friend's shoulders. 'Come on, Oswald, fifth place in a classic isn't too bad. It's more than we'd have dreamt of twelve months ago.' Watchorn turned to the trainer for support. 'He's still young, eh Barry? Still has lots to learn, I should think?'

'I know I'm pleased,' said Broadbent.

'Well, you would be!' snarled Oswald, rounding on him. 'We're not paying you thousands in trainer's fees to make worse decisions than I can!' shouted Oswald, taking a long swig of Moët.

Barry Broadbent turned and walked out of the marquee, but Oswald stomped after him.

'You promised us results, Broadbent, but then again,' he

laughed cruelly, 'I was warned that you were past your prime.'

Barry Broadbent stopped and turned to Oswald, his face taut. 'You know as well as I do that our horse is getting better and better all the time,' he said, struggling to be as professional as possible. 'Twelve months ago he wouldn't even have been entered in a Group Three race. And now he's coming in barely a length behind Warhorse! I tell you, we will have a Group One winner by the end of the season.'

'I have every faith in my horse,' said Oswald, his voice still raised, so that people were turning around to watch. 'But I'm not so sure I have such faith in you. You're not dealing with an idiot here, so don't treat me like one. What was all that whipping? Was he trying to kill the horse?'

'You need to trust me about my jockeys,' said Barry, going a little pink in the cheeks. 'Temper is a lively, intelligent horse and not an easy one to handle.'

'Don't give me excuses,' hissed Oswald, 'I am the owner. You're only the trainer, remember that!' he added through clenched teeth, pointing a stubby finger at Barry.

Broadbent just shook his head and walked over to where Finbar was still sitting on Fierce Temper, his chin down towards his chest. 'Sorry, boss,' he said in a small voice. 'It just wasn't our day today.'

'Too sodding right it wasn't!' said Oswald. 'You shouldn't have pushed him so early. Anyone could see he couldn't sustain that level of speed for the whole mile. No wonder all the others caught up with him!'

'With all due respect, sir,' answered Finbar back, his head rising, 'this horse has speed and stamina. It just wasn't his day today.'

'So everyone keeps telling me,' he laughed out loud, taking a step towards Barry Broadbent threateningly. Slightly startled, Barry lurched back and lost his footing on the turf. He stumbled backwards, and Martin, Fierce Temper's groom, ran forward, just catching Barry before he fell headlong.

The old man drew a hand across his forehead and stared grimly at Oswald. 'You may pay our yard training fees, but that doesn't give you the right to behave like a spoilt child,' he said, lifting his cane in the air to point at Oswald.

Undeterred, Oswald swiped a hand at the wavering cane, knocking it from Barry's hand.

Suddenly Fierce Temper gave a loud snort and reared up on his hind legs, his hooves coming down just inches from Oswald's head.

'Damn you, man! Can't you control him?' he yelled at Finbar, who was struggling to stay in the saddle as the horse kicked out backwards, whinnying and rolling his eyes.

At that moment, Jennifer and Philip Watchorn arrived, along with Venetia trotting along beside them in her high heels. 'Come on now, stop all this,' said Philip Watchorn, seeming to address the horse as much as the two men.

Venetia went over to Fierce Temper and, with soft words and gentle hands, began to calm him down again. 'You did wonderfully boy, didn't you?' she cooed, lovingly stroking his nose. 'There are greater things to come for you, I'm sure.' She looked up at Finbar and smiled at the jockey, who was just grateful to be in one piece.

'Well, we're not in the winner's enclosure just yet,' smiled Philip Watchorn, timidly putting out a hand to pat the gleaming rump of his horse, 'but we soon will be, won't we lad, eh Barry?' He helped the old man to his feet and handed him his cane.

'Now come on, everyone, let's get this young man un-saddled. Then let's all go for a glass of champagne. I think we deserve it.'

'I still bloody can't believe it,' said Oswald once again as he settled back into the passenger seat of Philip Watchorn's helicopter. They were preparing to go back to the heliport in Battersea. 'I knew he'd get a race ban, that bloody jockey,' he grumbled to himself.

'Will you just stop it?' laughed Jennifer Watchorn, patting him on the knee good-naturedly as she buckled his safety belt. 'I think Fierce Temper is doing incredibly well, considering the majority of the horses belong to rich Arabs and come from the super-yards.'

'That's right,' agreed Philip, 'you know we weren't getting into this particularly seriously. We've got one horse, not three hundred. We were supposed to be doing this for friendship, for the hobby, a bit of hospitality. Remember?'

The helicopter blades chopped into life and whirled into the air, leaving Newmarket behind; a tiny black dot in the sky as it made its journey south towards London. Oswald's mood began to calm as they passed over the green belts of Cambridgeshire and Bedfordshire towards the metropolis. Oswald was staying that night at his Cadogan Garden house rather than making the two-hour journey down to Huntsford. Epsom really is so much more convenient, he thought, shaking his head as he put his key into the royal-blue front door.

He walked in and flung his jacket over a Chippendale chair and stalked into the kitchen, breathing a sigh of relief that Gretchen, the forgetful Ukrainian housekeeper, had remembered he was coming and had filled the fridge accordingly. He helped himself to some big chunks of granary bread and a thick slab of venison pâté and went to sit down in the drawing room with a bottle of claret.

The house, which was only used four or five evenings a month, felt cold and unlived-in. A little bit chilly, he thought, stoking up the fire. He put on his sheepskin-lined slippers and reclined back on the mustard damask sofa to read that day's *Racing Post*. That horse had better start earning some money, he thought, shaking his head slowly. Watchorn might not be in this seriously, Oswald mused, but he certainly was. OK, so he wasn't the Aga bloody Khan with six hundred horses, but if the one he did have was a winner, he would be up there with the best.

Even though the yard fees and training costs were split three ways, Oswald was still feeling the enormous financial burden of 'just' one world-class racehorse. It was about time they started winning some decent purses. He knew that Barry Broadbent did not like to field a runner without it having some hope of success. But sod that, he thought angrily, he would tell him to put Fierce Temper in for as many races as possible this season. After all, if you don't shoot, you don't score. So the bloody creature might be knackered by the end of the season, but a good run could make BWC Holdings upwards of half a million pounds.

Oswald was just beginning to doze off, having downed the bottle of wine and polished off at least half a pound of the pâté. He was disturbed from his light slumber by the irritating ring of his mobile phone. He picked it up and heard a soft, almost muffled voice. Was that an Irish accent, he wondered, as the caller said his name.

'Yes? Yes?' replied Oswald, 'who is this?'

There was a long silence, disturbed only by some buzzing interference on the line.

'Is there anyone there?' snapped Oswald, irritated now, rubbing one eye groggily.

'Oswald Balcon had better learn some manners,' said the voice softly but menacingly, 'Or else –'

'Or else what?' asked Oswald shortly, his voice raised to get over the crackling line.

'Or else,' said the voice quietly, 'we're going to kill you.'

23

Camilla cursed herself. What had possessed her to take the lonely B-roads on the route back to London rather than the motorway? It had seemed like a good idea to drive through the pretty Lincolnshire countryside rather than down the busy M1, but now she was exhausted; all she wanted was to get back to the flat, creep under her goose-down duvet and drift asleep. That prospect seemed a long way off as she pulled her slate-grey Audi to a stop at a lonely crossroads, craning her neck to read a signpost. Dammit, even Bedford was still forty-eight miles away.

It was getting dark, a sooty dusk had seeped over the fields that stretched flat for miles on either side of her. She let the car window purr down, giving her face a blast of cold air. What a day, she sighed, glancing at the time on the dashboard clock: 8.35 p.m. It seemed a lot later. Camilla was used to long stressful days debating in court, but this was something harder, more personal. The Selection Weekend at the Tory Party's residential centre in Melton Mowbray had been gruelling – more like a mental assault course than an away-day. Hours of interviews and psychometric testing to gauge her suitability as an approved candidate. Had she appeared ambitious or ruthless? Confident or cocksure? She had answered honestly on her views on Europe, foreign policy, education – but were they close enough to the party line? It was just the first rung on the political ladder and she really hadn't thought it'd be so rigorous. There were so many duff MPs in Parliament; how they had managed to jump through all those hoops?

Feeling tired and thirsty, she reached over for a bottle of mineral water on the passenger seat, wedging it between her knees to unscrew the top. She took a long gulp, her heavy eyelids closing for just a moment as it soothed her gravelly throat. Opening her eyes again, she saw a large van approaching fast behind her, its headlights blaring in the dark. As she quickly tried to screw the lid of the bottle back on, it slipped from her grip and tipped over on her lap. Just then, the van moved to overtake her.

Its driver had misjudged the width of the lane and it came within inches of her Audi. Instinctively, she turned the steering wheel away, trying to pull her car as close to the side of the road as she could.

As the car's wheels bounced off the verge, the water bottle rolled on her thighs, spilling cold ribbons of liquid over her Comme des Garçons trouser suit. Shit, she thought, reaching down to brush the water off the expensive fabric. Panicked and distracted, her eyes dazzled from the headlights, she noticed too late that the road was banking sharply left. Camilla slammed her feet onto the pedals, but it was too late. The car ploughed straight into a hedge.

In a split second, a decade-old memory dislodged itself from the back of Camilla's mind. Another night, another country lane, another car out of control. Traces of blood smeared on the headlights of an old Renault. Her father's face staring at her in fury. No! She screamed out loud, her body jarring against the steering wheel as the car skidded to a halt.

At first, she felt nothing. Then she was sucked back into the moment with a jolt. Physically, she was unharmed. The car had brushed the bushes aside and bounced to a halt in an open field. But she felt shattered. The memory had been unlocked, an awful truth that she realized in a flash could devastate her future. A flood of nausea seized her body as she yanked the car door open, vomiting violently on the grass. No one could ever know what happened back then, no one. She had not worked so long, so hard, to let it bring her down.

Behind her a car stopped at the side of the road and an old lady approached her battered Audi. 'Are you all right, love?' she asked cautiously, skirting around to the driver's side where Camilla was sitting, her head hung hopelessly between her knees.

She nodded weakly and wiped her mouth with a proffered tissue, breathing deeply and rubbing her eyes as if erasing an image she did not want to see. She looked at the woman, then turned away, her eyes drifting off to the horizon where the sky was turning midnight blue.

'I'll be all right,' said Camilla softly, her fingers squeezing into a tight fist. 'I'll be all right.'

24

It was simply not possible to squeeze another computer, pot plant or Post-it note into the *Sand* offices, thought Cate, looking round her new workplace with a grimace. Every inch of floor and shelf space was crammed with boxes, piles of magazines and press releases. She pushed her chair away from her desk, only moving two feet backwards before it collided with a filing cabinet. She rubbed her eyes, needing a moment or two away from the blank stare of the computer.

It was only noon but she was already exhausted. The late nights and fifteen-hour working days were catching up with her. Still, it was worth it, she thought, looking up at the magazine layouts they had pinned to every inch of wall-space. It was better than she could have dreamed, a feat made all the more remarkable by the fact that it had been put together by the nine people crammed behind the jumble of desks in front of her. To think she'd had a staff of forty at *Class* magazine – and she had thought that was difficult.

'Here's everybody's itinerary for the cover shoot,' announced Sadie Wilcox, moving around the office, putting sheets of A4 paper on desks. How strange it was being back working with her old PA, who had been fired within a month of Nicole Valentine becoming editor. Of course, Sadie wasn't her PA this time round: there were no luxuries like that at Sand Publishing. Here Sadie was junior writer/office manager and general lifesaver rolled into one rather poorly paid package. Not that Sadie seemed to mind; in fact she seemed to be thriving in the tiny office. The same seemed to be true of the entire *Sand* team, and Cate was touched on a daily basis by the hard work and commitment the whole staff was channelling into the magazine. She made a mental note to buy some pink champagne for their Friday night drinks.

The phone rang. It was Nick, calling from the luxury of his office. 'Cate, can you just pop through for a minute?' he said.

Cate smiled. Nick's workspace was only on the other side of a thin plasterboard partition, and he could just as easily banged on the wall to get her attention. Cate walked through to the office, a space no bigger than the gun room at Huntsford, where Nick sat behind a desk looking at a copy of Sadie's cover-shoot budget.

'W'sup?'

Nick pulled a face that Cate instantly recognized was about money.

'This cover shoot is costing a bloody fortune,' he said, punching a bunch of numbers into his calculator.

'Yes, well cover shoots cost money,' said Cate, 'especially when we want it to be as good as a *Vogue* cover. Agius is shooting for free; we've got the rooms at a fifty per cent discount in return for some coverage – and the rest? Well, the rest costs money, Nick. Sybil Down is one of the world's top models at the moment, and when you do something with her it has to be a big production.'

'Yes,' said Nick impatiently, 'but does she really have to go business class? I mean, the flight to Nice is only about an hour and a half. All you get in business class on those short hops is a curtain and your lunch served on a porcelain plate. I'm not paying an extra three hundred quid for that!'

Cate smiled indulgently. 'What do you expect? Do you expect Sybil to travel down on EasyJet?'

Nick waved a hand and then pressed its heel against his temple. 'OK, I get the picture. Just don't forget that our entire editorial budget for one issue is about the same as a *Class* fashion shoot, OK? Just be careful, you know?'

Cate looked at him and raised one eyebrow warily. 'It's my money, my business too, you know, Nick.'

His face softened and he smiled. 'I know, I'm just being a budget Nazi. It took so long to get this bloody money – I hate to see a penny wasted.' He took a deep breath and pushed the paper away from him. 'Anyway, fancy going for lunch in about half an hour? We could take a walk to Borough Market. They do the world's best falafel.'

She hesitated. Cate was still trying to avoid situations where the two of them would be alone, but the sun was pouring through the small window and the first issue was nearly finished. 'Just let me go and get my bag,' she said.

'Before you go, boss!' shouted *Sand*'s fashion editor Vicky Morgan, clutching a huge white floppy-brimmed hat. 'D'you wanna look at the rail of clothes for the cover shoot?'

Cate walked over and pulled a handful of skimpy fluorescent tropical-print bikinis from the pile. 'I love these Missoni and Pucci prints. Honestly, Vicky, thank you so much for sorting out this shoot with Sybil. She is such a perfect cover girl for us.'

Cate had been very lucky to get her old friend to work at *Sand*. Vicky's fashion eye was the best in the business, and her contact book of model agencies, photographic studios and top photographers was bulging. From Vicky's point of view, the flexible working week suited her; she could still freelance as a stylist to a long list of actors and pop singers, and she knew a stunning magazine idea when she saw one.

'Yeah, well, I did that Victoria's Secret campaign with Sybil six months ago,' shrugged Vicky modestly, 'and she said she really wanted to work with me again. I gave her a ring, and here we are. It's going to be fabulous!' she laughed, holding a leopardskin bikini top up to her chest and posing.

'This just came for you,' said Sadie, bustling in and passing Cate a large white bag tied up with a black ribbon.

Cate put down an espadrille and grinned at Vicky. 'We may not be *Class* magazine, but looks like you're still getting the perks of the job,' said Vicky. Cate pulled off the ribbon and peeked inside. There was a message on a compliment slip: 'For all your hard work. Good luck. Rebecca.'

'What the hell is this?' whispered Cate, pulling crumpled handfuls of white tissue paper out of the bag.

'Rebecca? Not Rebecca Willard from Mode PR?' said Vicky, reading the card.

'The very same,' said Cate, raising an eyebrow at her friend. 'And also Nick Douglas's girlfriend,' she whispered.

'You're kidding,' said Vicky, her hand over her mouth. 'I would never have put those two together in a month of Sundays. Anyway, what have you got? She's just got the account for Alexander Dupont, maybe it's something from him! Ooh, let's see!'

At first Cate could just see a flash of yellow. She pulled out the garment bit by bit, catching a flash of a huge gaudy gold button.

'Eek!' giggled Vicky, pulling a face. 'Not one of his classic pieces then.'

Cate held the jacket up. It was one of the most revolting items of clothing she had ever seen. It was vast and vulgar, with vivid gold stitching and hideous outsized buttons. And there were horribly dated patch-pockets on the front. 'I think this is the sort of stuff he aims at his Saudi customers,' said Vicky diplomatically. 'Not really you, is it?' she smiled, 'although I suppose it was nice of her to send it over.'

Like hell! thought Cate, putting the jacket over the back of Vicky's chair.

Just then Nick strode into the room, pulling a suit jacket on over his shirt and jeans. 'What you got there, Cate? A pressie?' he asked.

'Rebecca sent it over for me, actually,' said Cate, holding it up for him to see.

Nick tried to suppress a look of horror. 'Oh that's, umm, the colour is really, err, bright,' he said. 'Perfect for, well, summer I suppose.'

Vicky started giggling as Cate carefully folded the garment and put it back in the bag. 'Perfect for the bonfire . . .' she began to mutter before stopping herself. Her reaction could so easily get back to Rebecca through Nick, and she wasn't going to let her rival win this round. She knew that woman's game.

'Yes, it's really kind of her,' said Cate to Nick. 'Every woman wants an Alexander Dupont piece after all. I must phone her and thank her this afternoon.'

She caught an expression in his face that she couldn't quite work out. Was it relief or embarrassment? Or something else? She picked up her jacket and left Vicky to pack the clothes into big wheelie suitcases, ready to take to the south of France on Monday. 'So anyway, falafel?'

Nick nodded. 'Falafel.'

Borough Market on a Friday lunchtime never failed to make Cate smile. Hungry crowds filled the warehouse-like covered market, slick City workers jostling with East End housewives at the organic fruit and vegetable stalls, while a hundred

265

different exotic smells mingled in the air. Chorizo with cheese, flowers with fish, pies with pickles. It was a wonderful assault on the senses, and Cate always came back with her stomach full and her arms laden with bags of scallops, pastries and long French loaves.

'I'm really excited about the advertising,' said Cate as they queued at the Turkish food stall. As usual, she wanted to keep the conversation with Nick strictly about work. *Sand*'s tiny advertising team had managed to secure twenty-five pages of excellent, high-end advertising: vital if they were going to have a successful launch.

'Yes, considering the time we had to land them all, it's an amazing line up,' nodded Nick, as they collected their falafels. 'Pity some of the biggies like Chanel are still waiting to actually see the first few issues, but I'd say the signs are pretty good. So I think I can safely come to Monaco without the fear of bankruptcy looming over us just yet.'

Cate pulled off a piece of pitta bread and looked at him cynically. 'Good point, Mr Douglas. If you're so bothered about the cover-shoot budget, why *are* you coming down to the south of France with us?'

She noticed his cheeks go a little pink, but it could have been the sun. 'You may have noticed, Miss Balcon, that I'm paying for it myself. EasyJet to Nice.'

'Honestly,' laughed Cate, digging him gently in the ribs, 'the mere whiff of a supermodel and you're on the first budget flight there.'

'I'm a class act, I know,' he laughed. He took his thumb and wiped a dollop of hummus from Cate's chin. The simple intimacy of it startled her and she stepped back, stumbling on a barrel of apples. Collecting herself, she realized that she really didn't want him coming down to Monaco for the shoot. She had by now blocked out what had happened in Milan, and seeing Nick and Rebecca at Tom's the previous weekend had made her realize that any thoughts of a romance between them were both ill-advised and futile. The charge between them had disappeared and the chumminess they had felt before was returning, although Cate still felt as though she could not talk as freely with Nick as she could have done before Milan. While she had successfully squashed any feelings for him into the tiniest darkest recess of herself, she really didn't want to put herself into another vulnerable situation. Self-preservation, that's the name of the game, she thought to herself.

By the time they got back to the office, it was almost empty. Only Ruth Grey, the picture editor, had been left sweltering in front of her screen. It was a boiling-hot afternoon, a real scorcher considering it was still May.

Cate pulled open a window to let in some fresh air and sat down behind her desk, squirting a spray of Evian mist over her face. She looked at the magazine plan in front of her. One more week before everything was due at the printers' and it all looked in pretty good shape. The only thing really missing was the cover shoot. She hated leaving such an important thing so late, but it had been worth it to get Sybil, the glamorous New Yorker who was the biggest noise in the modelling world since Kate Moss. Cate switched her computer back on and began sorting through her backlog of emails, noticing that one from ILF model agency was flagged up as urgent. She clicked on the envelope icon with a frown. She was sure that Sadie had sent over all of the flight and hotel details to Sybil's booker earlier that week. As she read the email, Cate's blood ran cold.

Hi Cate,
    Sorry to give you this news at such short notice, but Sybil Down will be unable to attend the *Sand* magazine

shoot from Monday. As you know, she was only able to accommodate this shoot because she was going to be down at the film festival, but is now unable to attend due to illness. Please give me a ring to discuss.

Best regards,

Caroline Davis, head booker.

'Shit!' shouted Cate, almost spilling the bottle of water sitting on her desk. She never swore. But this time she couldn't help it.

Ruth, the picture editor, looked up from her light-box where she had been looking at some photos from paparazzi agencies. 'What's the matter?'

'Bloody Sybil Downs has pulled out from the shoot!' said Cate, screwing up her itinerary and throwing it towards the wastepaper basket.

'You're kidding!' said Ruth. 'How come?'

'Apparently she's too ill to get to Cannes,' said Cate, already up and beginning to pace around the room. 'But she was fine yesterday when they confirmed.'

Ruth began to sort through a huge pile of photographs on her desk. 'That's weird . . .' she murmured, moving from the prints to her computer, where she scrolled through yet more celebrity shots on her screen. '. . . I'm sure I saw . . . yes! Here it is! Come and have a look at this, Cate.'

Cate strode over to Ruth's desk and looked at the digital photographs from the previous evening's parties in Cannes. And there – walking up the steps of the Cannes Palais des Festivals in a strapless white gown – was Sybil Down, looking stunning, happy and perfectly healthy.

'Not in Cannes! That bitch!' shouted Cate, rushing back to her desk and snatching up her phone. She punched in ILF's number in New York. 'Bloody hell, she's on voicemail!'

said Cate after a moment. 'No wonder!' she added, slamming the phone down.

She had to think quickly. The magazine was due down at the printers' in ten days and they had no cover to print. 'Right, Ruth!' barked Cate across the room, 'Call up all the picture libraries and see what they have got in terms of celebrities or the really big models. On a beach, on a yacht, wandering through St Tropez, I don't care what they're doing, it just has to look really "holiday".'

Cate pulled her hair back into a tight bun as she always did when she was nervous.

Nick poked his head around the door. 'Swearing like a navvy, Cate?' he teased. 'What's up?'

'Let's go back into your office,' said Cate, pulling at his shirtsleeve

Cate quickly filled him in on what had happened.

'Bugger,' said Nick, sinking down into his chair. 'That's the cost of all those flights and hotels up the Swanee.'

'Forget the money for a minute,' said Cate irritably, 'we have no cover. Ruth is looking for an image we can buy in, but that's a last resort. If our first cover isn't an exclusive, then the industry is going to think we're amateurs, just another run-of-the-mill magazine with no pull in the world of fashion.' She paced around Nick's office, her brow furrowed.

'As soon as Vicky gets back, she can ring around all the other model agencies and see if there are any other big girls around next week. I'll call some publicist friends, although offhand I can't think of any Brits who'd be right for the cover. We need it to be *glamorous*. It's only really the Hollywood stars or the big, big models that really sell.'

'What about Serena?' asked Nick, looking up at Cate. 'Isn't she supposed to be in London and Cannes over the next week or so?'

Cate started nodding absent-mindedly, gazing out of the office's tiny window overlooking a car park. Of course she had thought about asking Serena, who was arriving in London the following day en route to Cannes, but that was the last thing she wanted to do. Everyone was expecting her to put her sister on the front cover, and Cate didn't want to be predictable. She wanted to show that – while she might be a Balcon sister – she could do things her way; edit this magazine on her own terms without resorting to family connections.

'So . . .' said Nick, 'give her a ring.'

Cate turned to face him and placed her hands on the desk. 'Look, I'd rather not,' she said. 'You can understand why I don't want my sister on the first issue.'

'Christ, Cate,' said Nick anxiously, 'we're in a fix. We don't want to put *me* on the cover, do we? We've got less than ten days! You know that.'

'Look, just give me a couple of hours,' Cate said evenly. 'First thing I need to do is get back in touch with Sybil's booker. I'm going to tell her that we're going to invoice her for all the flights and hotels and that I've seen pap shots of Sybil in Cannes. Maybe we can change their minds.'

'Here's hoping,' said Nick.

Damn the Cannes film festival, thought Cate, slamming the telephone receiver down for the dozenth time. Hardly anybody seemed to be in the office that Friday afternoon. She'd left countless messages at the film publicist's offices in Cannes, but nobody seemed to be getting back to her. Well, no wonder, she thought, calming herself a little: it was a frantic time for everyone in the business. Vicky, meanwhile, had drawn a blank with the model agencies. All the top three agencies had said in the nicest way possible that they wanted to wait to see the first issue before they would

270

commit to sending their top girls. It was still too early to ring the LA publicists, thought Cate, checking her watch – only seven in the morning over there. Anyway, she doubted she would pull off any miracles in that direction. LA shoots usually took three or four weeks to organize, and they had hours, not days. Her phone rang again and she picked it up expectantly.

'Cate, it's only Nick. D'you wanna pop through a minute? Rebecca's here.'

Cate groaned and stalked through to Nick's office. Rebecca was perched on the edge of Nick's desk in a barely-there sundress, brown leather boots and a big pair of aviator sunglasses, her glossed-up lips glistening.

'Hi darling!' she gushed, reaching over to kiss Cate on both cheeks. Cate flinched both times. 'I just called Nick,' she explained, waving her hands around in the air for dramatic effect. 'And he mentioned you were in a bit of a fix. I was only in Covent Garden, so I got a cab straight over, because I think I might be able to help you out. Either way, did you love the jacket or did you *love* the jacket I sent over?'

Cate looked at her, trying to plaster a smile onto her face. 'Yes, I really loved the jacket, thank you so much.'

'Anyway,' said Rebecca, lifting her sunglasses off and fixing them on top of her head, 'I've just heard what a witch Sybil Down's been, but I think I've got the solution. We've only just confirmed it, but we're taking on someone terribly exciting for the face of one of my clients – Flaubert jewellery – and she just so happens to be in Cannes next week, hosting the party for the client. I'm not totally sure yet, but I think I could get you two or three hours for a shoot as long as she will be wearing some Flaubert jewellery.'

Rebecca grinned triumphantly.

Cate cleared her throat. 'Sounds great, but who is it?'

'It's only Rachel Barnaby!' gushed Rebecca, turning to fix a dazzling smile on Nick. 'She'd be perfect! You know she was *Vogue*'s biggest-selling cover girl of last year, don't you?'

Cate groaned inwardly. Even though she knew this was the perfect solution to their problems, she felt her heart sink as Nick smiled up gratefully towards Rebecca. In the small confined space of Nick's office, she felt trapped by Rebecca's gloating. Cate dug a thumbnail into her palm and tried to stop feeling so uncharitable. After all, Rebecca was helping them out of a hole, wasn't she? But why did it have to be Rebecca?

Nick stood up and walked over to where Cate was standing. 'You OK, Cate?' he asked, putting a concerned hand on her shoulder. 'It's great, isn't it? Rachel Barnaby. She's good, even I know that!'

Cate smiled weakly. 'Yes great. She's perfect. And it doesn't look like we're getting very far with Sybil's people. No, she'll be perfect. Thanks, Rebecca, thank you.'

As Nick turned to sit back at his desk, Rebecca flashed a look at Cate, one eyebrow raised and the edge of her lip curled up into a slightly malevolent smile. It was the face of a child who had successfully shifted blame for their mischievousness onto a hated sibling, but it vanished as quickly as it had appeared.

Cate was instantly filled with suspicion.

Could Rebecca have planned all this? Surely she couldn't have sabotaged and then saved her cover shoot? But that would just be too . . . well, *insane*. She looked up at Rebecca smiling sweetly and pulling her bag over a shoulder ready to leave. No, she was just paranoid, how could that be?

'Well, I'll leave you two worker bees to it,' purred Rebecca as she reached the door. 'I'd better rush back and get all this sorted for you. Of course my client will be picking up Rachel's expenses so you've no worries there, but I'd better book a flight for myself. The client will definitely want me there to supervise it all. And Nick, sweetie, I can slip into your hotel room, can't I?'

Cate stared after her, mouth agape, suddenly feeling that she'd had the whole operation snatched from beneath her. And something told her that her conspiracy theory was right.

25

From seat 1a, the only seat Serena would consider when travelling by commercial airline, she had a clear view of the Home Counties. She watched the fields of Berkshire drift into view and, beyond them, the sprawling metropolis of London, today looking green and inviting, unobscured by the smoggy drizzle that often hung over the capital whenever she flew in from New York.

'Ten minutes to landing,' said an upright British voice over the PA system as Serena drained off the last of her fruit juice, popped her seat into the upright position and moved her cashmere pillow to her lap. She had mixed feelings about coming home, even if it was just a pit stop on her way to the south of France. She was mainly here for business: there was the sale of the Cheyne Walk house to complete and an important meeting to attend – her contract with Jolie Cosmetics was due to be renewed any time now, and she felt she could push up her money if she went to see the British chief executive of the company personally at his Eaton Square home.

It was all pretty tedious stuff, although if she was totally honest with herself she could do with a break from the New

York scene anyway. For the past few weeks, her days had been filled by endless trips to the salon; the evenings had been crammed with so many New York parties that they were blending into one. It wasn't easy being this glamorous. Still, the blur of canapés and air-kissing seemed to be paying off: Serena Balcon was hot again.

The meeting at Ed Charles's house had gone well, although she still couldn't believe that she had actually had to *sing* for the Broadway producer in the basement studio of his brownstone townhouse. She hadn't had to do that since when she was in the dramatic society at school. But Ed had made all the right noises about her not just getting a role in *Fin de Siècle*, but *the* role of Letitia Dupont. It was a killer part in more ways than one: Letitia was a Vegas showgirl with a murderous side, as glamorous as Nicole Kidman's character in *Moulin Rouge* and as sassy and spiky as CZJ's Oscar-winning role in *Chicago*. And, on top of that, only yesterday her agent had called to tell her she'd been asked to do a screen test for a big action thriller; a big action thriller rumoured to be starring Tom Cruise, no less.

Serena stretched her legs out and wriggled her toes around in her cashmere socks, more than satisfied with her progress. An Oscar nomination could be hers in eighteen months, she smiled smugly. Who needed Tom Archer, anyway?

'Hi darling, it's me!' cooed Serena, wafting through Cate's front door and looking around with a slightly displeased look on her face when she saw the size of Cate's mews house. 'Tell me my luggage has arrived or I will just die!'

Cate, wearing her Saturday-night uniform of Juicy Couture tracksuit and no make-up, came over to give her sister a hug.

'It's arrived, but why did you need to FedEx it over? It's only two small bags,' she asked, pointing at the two Goyard cases in the corner. 'Could you not struggle through customs with those?'

'Darling, everyone pre-sends their luggage these days,' said Serena. 'Anyway, those cases might be chic but they're a little heavy. I don't want to strain anything.'

Serena wafted past Cate into the living room. Cate's house was a slender, three-storey mews painted a pale pink and tucked away off the Portobello Road. It wasn't big, but Cate had turned it into a light, girly space full of cream carpets, neutral walls and huge vases brightening every corner, over-flowing with sweet peas and peonies.

'I'm cooking a roast, hope you're hungry,' said Cate, pouring them two big glasses of mineral water. 'I know you like to sleep rather than eat on the plane.'

'That's sweet, Cate, but I really do feel a bit icky,' said Serena, rooting through her bag to pull out a big box of face cream.

'There you go,' she said, thrusting the package into Cate's hands. 'Some sort of anti-ageing cream: thought it would be right up your street. Apparently it's the latest thing; got diamond dust in it, although why on earth anyone would want to send me products for mature skin, I don't know.'

Serena took a tiny sip of her water and followed Cate into her stylish walnut and marble kitchen.

'Are you sure you don't want any of this?' asked Cate, sticking a knife into the beef.

Serena shook her head and patted her stomach. 'I'm on a funny diet at the moment.'

'What is it?' asked Cate, arching an eyebrow. 'The Not Eating diet? You've gone so thin!'

'It's OK for you,' said Serena, looking her sister up and down, showing off her curves in her velour tracksuit. 'You don't work in fashion any more – and anyway, you've got your big, happy personality. You don't need to be a size four.'

Cate smiled and shook her head, reminding herself that, in Serena's mind, that was a compliment. There was no point in complaining anyway, as her sister had moved on to a more important subject: Serena's Fabulous Life. According to Stephen Feldman, Serena's new manager, word was that she wasn't just going to be the British and European face of Jolie Cosmetics, but was going to become the worldwide face as well. That was, she said, a deal which had to be worth in excess of four to five million. And, she added, it wouldn't do her Hollywood prospects any harm to be on every billboard and magazine in the known world, either.

As Serena gushed out the gossip, Cate began to notice that Serena hadn't mentioned Michael Sarkis once. There was the constant referral to 'we', as in 'When "we" went to the Save Venice Ball', 'When "we" were invited to Henry Kissinger's duplex', or 'When "we" were scouting real estate in the Hamptons'. But nothing about 'him' or 'them'. And she never referred to Michael by name. Cate was curious, but she knew there was no point in asking. Everything was always glittery and right on Planet Serena; she never bitched about her own Wonderful Life, only other people's. But Cate couldn't help thinking it was strange. It had been a long time since Cate herself had been in that position, but she remembered well enough that the first three months of a new relationship were so full of excitement, passion and fun, it just spilled over; you wanted to tell the world.

As if reading Cate's thoughts, Serena abruptly changed the subject.

'Anyway,' she said, kicking off her Stephane Kélian heels and stretching out on the long beige sofa, 'I want to know what's happening with you. I'm sure someone told me you had the hots for that Nick Douglas? Don't get me wrong, honey, he's very cute. God knows I fell for those rough Northern-boy charms with Tom, but Nick's really not right for you.'

Cate smiled softly. 'No, no. We're just business partners and that's all. Nick and I get on really well and we're good as a team. I know he's Tom's friend and that's bound to make you biased towards him, but honestly, Sin, he's really a good guy.'

'And Venetia?' asked Serena, checking her reflection in a gold compact she had taken from her bag. 'I can't believe she went to Spain! The first time I'm back in ages, and Venetia's swanning around in Seville, Camilla's on some management weekend – and I have to camp out here!'

'Well, I'm sorry you find my house so distressing,' said Cate, finally annoyed now. 'Perhaps you should go to Claridge's, or somewhere where they understand your special needs!'

Serena looked up from her compact mirror vaguely. 'Mmm? Sorry darling, I was miles away. What's Venetia doing again?'

Cate sighed, seeing that her rebuke had not even registered on her sister. 'Van's doing a big job renovating some guy's farmhouse in Andalusia. It sounds wonderful out there and she really needed to get away, what with all the trouble.'

'Trouble?' asked Serena, snapping her compact shut. She was faintly aware that her older sister had seemed worried and distracted at her farewell party weeks earlier, but she had thought it was just the pressure of throwing a super bash for Serena.

'Did she not tell you?' asked Cate. 'She's having a premature menopause or something. It's really weird.'

Serena looked at Cate blankly, as if once again she'd failed to absorb the information. 'Oh,' she said finally, her voice almost a whisper.

Cate frowned and looked curiously at her sister. Serena was very rarely lost for words. 'Anyway, apparently Van's ovarian reserves are so low that she has to get pregnant in the next few months, or that's it. She'll be heartbroken if she can't have children.'

The room welled up with silence. Cate looked up, waiting for some response. Serena swung her legs off the sofa and walked towards the kitchen. 'Is it all right if I get something to drink? A Diet Coke or something?' she asked distractedly over her shoulder.

'Sure,' said Cate, 'but I was just about to open a bottle of wine. There's a nice Sauvignon Blanc in the fridge.'

Serena shook her head, 'No, no. I think I'll have tea,' she said as she opened the fridge. She definitely looked shaken by Venetia's news, thought Cate. Maybe she does have a soul, after all.

'Are you OK?' she asked, following Serena into the kitchen and putting her plate on the marble worktop.

'Of course I am!' snapped Serena, slamming the fridge door shut.

'I know it's upsetting about Venetia,' said Cate, putting out a hand, 'but she'll get through it, she always does.'

Serena walked back into the lounge past Cate and curled up on the sofa, bringing her slim knees up to her chin, her arms hugging her legs. Cate walked back and sat next to her, putting a reassuring arm around her shoulders. 'Sin, is there something wrong? Tell me what it is.'

Serena fell silent for at least a minute, then exhaled sharply and buried her face in her knees. The weight of her own troubles had been building for the past few weeks; now, with this news about Venetia, she felt as if she might burst. She thought back briefly to when she was with Tom – she could always tell him anything or offload all her anxieties, however trivial, onto him. But in New York there was no one who she could talk to; not any of her fabulous new friends, certainly not Michael. And in all the career excitement of the last few weeks, this little secret had been buried inside her so tight and so deep, she had almost convinced herself it would go away.

She looked up into Cate's kind face. Her sister was so concerned, so eager to help. That's what she had missed being in New York. Her family. Serena took a deep breath.

'I think I might be pregnant,' she said, her voice husky with emotion.

It was Cate's turn to catch her breath. She put her hand on Serena's knee. 'But that's a good thing, isn't it?' she said, trying to gauge her sister's emotions.

'No, it isn't a sodding good thing!' said Serena, giving a mocking laugh. 'It certainly isn't what I want, and I doubt very much it's what Michael wants either. My career is really taking off, Cate,' her voice now was loaded with panic. 'I'm up for two really big roles and people in LA are beginning to recognize me. I just can't take time off, I just can't be off the scene.'

Cate had never seen Serena cry so bitterly before, not even the day after she'd split with Tom. She usually seemed so composed and in control. Now, even as fat tears rolled down her cheeks, Serena still had poise and elegance, but Cate could tell she was near to cracking.

'Are you sure about it?' asked Cate as gently as she could.

'It's probably fine,' said Serena briskly. 'Probably just some hormone thing.'

'But have you been to the doctor, have you done a test?'

'No, nothing,' Serena said, shaking her head.

Cate smiled to herself. It was just like Serena to bury her head in the sand. When her pet rabbit Marilyn had died when she was six, she had hidden her in a wooden box and insisted to anyone who had tried to sympathize that Marilyn had 'gone to France for the summer'.

'I've just missed a period, that's all,' said Serena. 'It might be stress, it probably is. I've been so busy . . .'

'But you're obviously worried about it. Why don't you take a test?'

'I'll go and see my OB when I'm less busy,' said Serena, climbing to her feet. 'Now please let's stop talking about it.'

'No!' said Cate, pulling her back down onto the sofa. 'Look at you, you're a nervous wreck!'

'Cate,' said Serena calmly, 'you probably don't understand what it means to be incredibly busy, but I do not have time to go to the doctor. I've got meetings in London, press in Cannes, I've got the Amfar party – and then Michael is taking the yacht to the grand prix in Monaco.'

'OK, so let's put your mind at rest,' said Cate, firmly in editor mode. 'I'll go and buy a test now from the chemist around the corner.'

Serena suddenly looked frightened. 'But what if someone knows it's me? It would be a disaster if this got out.'

Cate patted her knee. 'Don't be silly: I'm buying the test. No one around here gives a hoot about me – I'm hardly the most famous person in Notting Hill. If it makes you happier I'll wear a baseball cap!'

'God, it all sounds so cheap,' muttered Serena, fanning herself with a newspaper. 'Look, Cate, please don't bother, we're not at boarding school now. I'll go and see my gyno back in New York when I'm ready.'

But Cate had already slipped on her jacket and grabbed her car keys. 'I'm going. I'll see you in ten minutes.'

'Cate, no . . .'

As the door clicked shut, Serena put her face in her hands and let the sobs come, tears streaming down her face, plastering her six-hundred-dollar Sally Hershberger haircut to her cheeks. Finally, she blew her nose and took a deep breath. She didn't know whether to be annoyed, angry, or simply relieved that Cate had winkled the truth from her. Maybe it was for the best, she thought, wiping her eyes and sniffing. She hadn't 'just' missed her period: she was now almost four weeks late. When she had discovered it, she had been terrified and alone. Michael was the only person in New York she knew well enough to talk about it, and she could hardly tell him. How would he react? Would he be pleased or furious? Would he welcome fatherhood or, God forbid, run away from it? *What if he dumped her?* His lifestyle wasn't exactly child-friendly – and while they were happy now, the hedonistic social life they both enjoyed might not be quite so fabulous with a toddler in tow.

She shuddered and knocked over a wine glass on the floor with her foot, not noticing the stream of liquid trickling over Cate's carpet. It seemed so unfair. Why couldn't someone like Venetia be having the baby? Venetia so wanted to have a little brat, whereas it was the last thing Serena needed in her life right now. But then Serena Balcon always got what other people wanted, she thought, a slow smile appearing on her lips.

The door slammed. 'That was quick!' said Serena as Cate came back in, baseball cap pulled low over her eyes.

'Quick? I had to go all the way up to Kensal Rise in disguise. Didn't want anyone to see a Balcon girl buying a pregnancy kit – oh, the scandal!' she added with a weak laugh.

'I can't believe you talked me into this,' said Serena, taking the package and reading the back. 'I mean, it's all so primitive, weeing onto those little sticks. I have the most expensive medical care in New York, you know.'

'Well you can't put a price on peace of mind,' said Cate, going over to switch on the Dualit kettle.

'If you are pregnant,' she ventured cautiously, 'would it be Michael's or Tom's?'

'Jesus,' said Serena, choking, 'it's bad enough as it is without you trying to make me out as some sort of slut!'

'Come on, hardly,' said Cate awkwardly. 'But you did get into a relationship with Michael pretty quickly after you split with Tom, didn't you?'

Serena threw Cate a withering look, snatched up the box and stalked up the stairs to Cate's small white and wood bathroom. Perching on the side of Cate's claw-foot bath, she sat silently for a moment, gripping the box tightly. It wasn't as if she hadn't been in this situation before. She remembered crouching in the gloomy bathroom at Huntsford, cold and alone, terrified that her father would come barging in and catch her. Then the test had been negative, but in many ways she would rather it had been positive then than now. After all, there was something rather decadent and careless about a teenage pregnancy. Jade Jagger had had her children young and she now was deliciously boho with her family trailing after her from London to New York and Ibiza. But not now, not when her career was on the verge of exploding into what she had always wanted it to be. *Not now, God, please not now.*

On the other side of the door, Cate sat on the top step leading to the bathroom, waiting for her sister and trying to prepare herself for either result, not knowing which would be best. Finally, Serena crept from behind the door and sat beside her, staring straight ahead. Cate put her hand on Serena's and squeezed tightly; the superstar and the glossy magazine editor, just two confused and anxious girls sitting on the stairs. Serena slowly uncurled her fingers to reveal the white plastic stick. 'There's a line,' she whispered. Cate reached out and pulled her sister close.

'How accurate are these things?' asked Serena weakly, passing the stick to Cate.

Cate looked down at the thick pink line. 'Pretty accurate,

I think, but you never know,' she replied not too convincingly. 'It *will* be OK, you know.'

'I'll get fat,' said Serena weakly. 'Tits like balloons and everything.'

'Don't worry,' smiled Cate. 'Chanel make clothes up to a size twenty.'

They almost laughed.

'Catey, what should I do?' sighed Serena, resting her head on her sister's shoulder, all the bluster and confidence of the movie star gone now.

'Let's get an early night,' said Cate. 'We'll talk about it in the morning.'

Serena couldn't sleep. Tossing and turning on the lumpy bed in Cate's spare room, her dilemma would simply not go away. In the rare minutes she did close her eyes and fall into slumber, her dreams were full of crocodiles and helter-skelters and other things that Serena recognized from women's magazines as pure anxiety dreams.

Serena gave up. Sitting up in the bed, she lit a cigarette, then immediately stubbed it out. She had to find a way out of this mess. There was no question that now was the wrong time to have a baby: it was professional suicide. But the thought of an abortion; she didn't even want the word in her head. She was surprised how strongly she felt. She'd always regarded abortion as just another one of those handy surgical procedures that a modern woman could keep in her arsenal, just like Botox or lipo. But now . . . she shook her head. Maybe it was something to do with losing her mother so young that made the prospect of termination seem so wrong. But there was another reason.

She stroked her stomach, the taut, bronzed skin still flat, still smooth, and a smile began to form on her lips. Serena's baby was Michael's baby. As Michael had no children, that made the baby Michael's first-born and therefore heir to a billion-dollar fortune. If they had a son, it would also mean he was directly in line for the Huntsford house and title. Their baby would have wealth, position and status. So would she. So would Michael. It was a win-win situation, definitely worth taking a year off from film sets and photo-shoots. She snuggled back down in the pillows, still hugging her belly, a sleepy fog pulling her eyelids closed. There were no more anxiety dreams that night.

Jack Kidman was already in the British Airways executive lounge by the time Venetia had got to Heathrow, sipping a bottle of mineral water and flicking distractedly through his *Financial Times*. As Venetia approached, he looked up and smiled, a gesture Venetia found somehow disconcerting. She had been abroad on countless occasions on design jobs for clients: hotels in Dubai, country clubs in Florida, second homes in Tuscany; but this felt different, more intimate. Jonathon never looked so casual, so relaxed, she thought, her eyes slowly appraising Jack. In a marl-grey polo shirt, dark blue jeans, brown leather loafers, a suggestion of stubble on his jaw, he looked like a wealthy businessman about to take a holiday. Damn, he was good-looking, she thought, and going over to meet him with her small overnight bag felt illicit.

Stop it, she chided herself. This was not a dirty weekend. It was an overnight business trip. It hadn't, however, stopped her lying to Jonathon when he had quizzed her about it the previous evening.

'So who's going?' her husband had asked coolly over supper.

'Myself, the client, and Nina one of our stylists.'

Even though his interest had seemed decidedly feigned and Jonathon's question had been made without any trace of suspicion, why had she lied about Nina coming on the trip? What had possessed her? It was a harmless visit to discuss the project. She shook her head to dismiss it from her mind and strode over to say hello.

'Good morning. I see you're travelling lighter than I am,' smiled Jack, looking down to a small brown holdall by his foot.

'I've checked my four cases and my shoe trunks in already,' she deadpanned.

'Shoe trunk?'

'It's a joke.'

'Ah, the ice queen melteth,' he grinned.

'Are you saying I don't have a sense of humour?' It came out in a slightly peevish tone that Venetia instantly regretted. Jack was, after all, a client.

'I don't know you well enough. Yet . . . ' he smiled.

She could feel herself flush, just as she had ever since she was a child, when the slightest embarrassment would set off a scarlet rash that crawled from her cleavage all the way up to her neck.

'Anyway. This is all my work stuff,' she smiled, holding up a black leather case. 'I've got some things for you to look at already.'

'I look forward to it,' he grinned flirtatiously. The corners of his dark green eyes creased up, sparkling mischievously, 'but there'll be plenty of time for that later at the hotel. I've checked us into the Casa Della Flora.'

There it goes again, she thought, feeling the flush flare up once more. She twisted the band on her wedding finger nervously. She was completely on edge. She'd hardly exchanged a hundred words with the man, so why did it feel as if they were having an affair?

Seven hours later – as long as it'd take to get to New York, grumbled Venetia – the silver four-by-four that Jack had

286

hired from the airport pulled up outside his *finca* in Andalusia. A huge dilapidated farmhouse hanging on the side of a sun-blasted hill, with a small Andalusian village, nestling like tiny white cubes of sugar beneath them, Venetia hadn't seen a more splendidly isolated spot in years. The main house had old shutters creaking off arched windows, framed by clouds of wisteria vines climbing its whitewashed walls. The terracotta tiled roof rippled in the sun like tide marks on the sand, and outbuildings surrounded a vast courtyard overrun by wild lavender and lined with huge, cracked earthen-ware pots. It was breathtaking in its raw simplicity and, from Venetia's point of view, bubbling over with potential.

'So, this is it,' said Jack with undisguised pride. 'I know you're probably knackered, but did you mind coming here first, rather than to the hotel? It's just that it's four o'clock already. I wanted you to see it before the sun started to go down.'

She clambered out of the car, her Tod's loafers scuffing on the dirt track that rose up in a cloud of saffron dust. The sun beat so hard on her forehead that she had to take her neck scarf off to mop up beads of sweat.

'No. It's fine. I want to see it in as much natural light as possible,' she said, striding towards the building, her eye absorbing every detail as she proceeded. A lot of the struc-tural work had already been done, but it was still a shell. The walls were roughly plastered, the floors were just a series of boards, but the old tower, complete with ancient bell had been saved, much of the original woodwork salvaged, and the brick walls re-pointed back to old glories. Even the air smelt sweetly of jasmine.

She got out her Nikon digital camera and began snapping away, taking in the ceilings where mahogany rustic beams stretched across the soaring roof. A huge olive press loomed impressively in the atrium. Venetia walked out of a pair of unrestored French windows onto a vast terrace that over-looked the sun-scorched valley. Daunting, beautiful, timeless. Looking at that view she could have been a Spaghetti-western heroine or an Andalusian gypsy. This was the kind of place in which you could reinvent yourself, she thought, letting her imagination run wild. Jonathon would never decamp to somewhere like this, she decided suddenly, sadly. But moving to somewhere like this wasn't about money – it was about spirit, it was about adventure.

Hearing the slow advance of footsteps behind her, she turned round.

'So what do you think?'

'I love it,' she said softly, her eyes fixed on the digital camera screen.

She walked back into the house, her mind full of thoughts about how to breathe new life into this stunning house.

'Follow me.'

As they walked from room to room, Venetia's eyes focused on the building, the floor, the light; talking to Jack but not looking at him.

'How often do you intend to be here?' she asked when they reached a huge space she knew immediately should be the main reception room.

'I don't know yet. Maybe up to nine months of the year.'

'What will you do? Work, relax, entertain?'

'A bit of all three,' he smiled. 'What I really want to do eventually is open an art school where a handful of people can come and paint and enjoy the farm. An arty B&B, I guess.'

'A far cry from advertising,' she said, wondering if it had come out cynically.

'That's the plan. Always was. To work my arse off for twenty years and then retire.'

Venetia moved her hands across the walls like a sculptor,

feeling every bump and crack, tapping on the plasterwork as if she was trying to detect life.

'Married?' she said, deliberately avoiding his gaze.

'Separated. Should get the decree nisi through when we've sorted out the financials. As you can imagine, that gets complicated when you've just sold your company.'

Venetia was sure she felt a thrill pump through her body as he said the words 'separated'. She immediately tried to quash the feeling. 'So it's not amicable?'

'She ran off with her personal trainer,' he said slowly. 'The cliché.'

'Kids?'

'Three girls.'

'How old?'

'Seven, nine and twelve.' He looked at her quizzically. 'Hey, what is this, twenty questions?'

Venetia sat down on a stack of boards in the corner of the room, smoothing down her jeans as she tried to adopt the facial expression of someone completely unbothered by what they had just been told. The truth was, she had already known the answers to Jack's questions. Before the trip, she hadn't been able to resist doing a Google search on him, reading all the recent interviews in the trade press. She was embarrassed by the amount of information she had managed to accumulate, but it had certainly given her a clearer picture of the man before her. She knew his preferred public image of an ordinary bloke made good – the Mockney accent, casual clothes, the cheeky-chappie bravado – was just a façade. So he'd started his agency from nothing, but he was cut from a similar cloth to her. His father was a wealthy Shropshire landowner, he'd had a troubled childhood – been expelled from a public school for smoking cannabis and lost his mother as a teenager. He had, she guessed, been driven to succeed for similar reasons, too.

'Jack, I wouldn't normally be interested in your private life. But this is how I work,' she replied as professionally as she could. 'I need to know how you want to live in this place and I need to know your lifestyle if we are going to do the job this house deserves.'

His eyes toyed with hers. 'So the fact that I have a seven-year-old means no to glass, chrome and Jacuzzis in every room?'

She was troubled by the flirtation in his voice. 'Something like that, Jack. I'm not sure piles of glass and hard edges would work well here, anyway.'

'So what would work? Isn't that what I'm paying you for?'

Forcing herself to switch back into full-on professional mode, she turned her head to look at him. 'This place has the most incredibly understated charm.'

'A little bit like its owner?' asked Jack.

She studiously ignored him. 'The place has charm and I want to work with that.'

'Jonathon! I didn't expect you to call.' Venetia felt rattled as she picked up the phone in her hotel bedroom, while simultaneously trying to apply a slick of gloss across her lips.

'Am I now not allowed to call my wife?' He was trying to chide her, but she could hear his displeasure.

'Of course.'

'What are you doing? Off on the town?'

She laughed nervously. 'It's hardly Soho around here.' She looked at her watch, anxiously realizing she should have met Jack in the lobby more than twenty minutes ago.

'Anyway, Nina and I were just going out to get some dinner.'

Instantly she felt blood rush to her cheeks. What if he had popped into the office or seen Nina on the street?

'What I was actually ringing to tell you was that it looks as if I'm going to be in Geneva this weekend,' said Jonathon. 'I'm sorry.'

'But we're booked into Babington House.'

'Your little spa fix will have to wait,' he said coolly. 'I have to work too, you know.'

There was a knock at the door. She ignored it but it persisted. 'Look, I'm going to have to go . . .'

'Nina?'

Was he mocking her? she thought anxiously, the stab of paranoia returning.

'Yes,' she mumbled quietly into the receiver. 'I have to go. I'll be back tomorrow by the time you get home for dinner.'

Jack was standing in the frame of the doorway when she opened it. He had changed into a pair of cream trousers and a black T-shirt and, although they had only seen a couple of hours of sun that day, she could see a smattering of latte-coloured freckles across his nose. She was embarrassed to feel a stir in her groin.

'Thought you'd blown me out,' said Jack, 'now come on. You can't come to this part of the world and not have a real Andalusian night out.'

They got into the four-by-four, which Jack drove higher and higher into the hills. As the sky turned dark and the night closed in, Venetia felt a strange rush of freedom. She was having a good time; a really good time. Jack was great company; banter swelled between them, and she found herself laughing, making jokes. Conversation with Jonathon was so sombre she often doubted whether she had a sense of humour at all. But tonight she felt clever, funny and interesting; she felt worth listening to. Tonight she felt the centre of attention. She wondered if this was how Serena felt every moment of her life.

Glancing over at Jack's handsome profile as he concentrated on the twists and turns of the road, she caught herself thinking why she was not feeling a stronger sense of guilt. It was as if the deeper they went into rural Spain, the more detached she felt from her life in London. She felt free.

Finally they stopped outside a compact stone building, wrapped in the darkness of the hillside. Coloured bulbs hung in strings at the windows and at least forty cars – beaten-up trucks, old jalopies, even a tractor – were parked on a patch of land alongside it.

'Where are we?'

'The best place to see flamenco in about a hundred miles.'

Jack guided her inside confidently, his nods and smiles showing that he already knew half the locals, who were knocking back beers at the bar. They sat at a table near a small raised stage, where plates of tapas were placed in front of them: chorizo in hot pepper sauce, mushrooms swimming in garlic oil, frittatas oozing with red and green peppers.

They were just washing it all down with a big jug of Sangria when a slender man in tight trousers took to the stage with a guitar. His short black hair shone like a crown of patent leather as he watched an exotic, tawny-skinned young woman weave through the crowd towards the stage. She had thick raven hair, her ripe, wasp-waisted body was poured into a black and scarlet satin dress and she walked like a tiger. The music started slowly at first, just long, clear plucks of the guitar strings; the dancer swayed her hips to the slow, sensual beat.

'This woman is fantastic,' whispered Jack, touching the top of Venetia's knee. As the sound swelled around the room, the flamenco dancer's body began moving more dramatically

– at once balletic and graceful but almost animal-like in its power. The music was frenzied now, the dancer, as if hypnotized, gliding across the wooden floor of the stage, the curves and lines of her body captivating the entire audience.

When it was over, Venetia felt her whole body pulsate with raw energy. 'I think I need some fresh air after that,' she laughed.

Just then, an old man with a bushy white moustache approached their table to greet Jack. Not wanting to interrupt, Venetia made her way out of the smoky room. The silence of the outside air almost made her head rattle, and she walked away from the bar until she was at the outer perimeter of cars. She looked up into the sky. She had never seen it look so dark, like the pure black of printers' ink. She tried to make patterns with the constellations: a dog, a bear, Jack's face . . .

'Venetia!'

She turned round quickly just in time to see Jack jumping forward and grabbing the sleeve of her dress.

'Be careful,' he said softly. 'Watch you don't step off the edge of the cliff. I'd hate to lose you.'

Even in the dark she could see his eyes glisten. Sangria and the beat of the music still filling her head, she allowed herself to move close to him. She tried to tell herself she was just very drunk, but the sensation of her nipples ripening told her she was experiencing the very unfamiliar sensation of pure lust.

'I'll be careful.'

'Are you OK? I turned my back for a second and you were gone.'

She smiled. 'Don't panic. I'm still here.'

Her eyes looked out into the pitch-black valley as Jack moved closer to her side. 'Listen. Can you hear it?' she said. 'The silence.'

'I love the fact you can hear silence,' smiled Jack.

'It would just be fantastic to live somewhere like this. No noise, no problems. Oh dear,' she smiled. 'Listen to me rambling. I'm a bit drunk.'

'A beautifully mannered drunk,' replied Jack.

Despite the calm, she began to feel restless, disturbed by Jack's presence at her shoulder.

'I think we should go home,' said Venetia huskily.

He stared her straight in the eye. 'If that's what you really want.'

Her inner voice was warning her she was being charmed. The guy was an adman! A professional seducer. Get the interior designer out to your Spanish retreat and get all the added services thrown in for free. He took a step towards her and rested two fingers underneath her chin. 'Is this what you want?' he whispered.

But her resistance weakened to practically nothing. The air was so charged she felt sure it would light up the whole of the valley. Her eyelids instinctively closed as his lips moved towards her.

'No, I don't want to go home,' she whispered.

Jack grabbed the back of her neck and pulled her in closer, his hands weaving through her hair.

'Don't stop,' she pleaded, feeling every sexual instinct in her body being activated from its dormant state. Jack manoeuvred her gently against the bumper of a battered truck, unknowing or uncaring whether its owner was anywhere nearby. His hands slid higher and higher up her leg, under her dress, until his fingertips reached the inside of her thigh. Hearing her gasp, his thumbs flipped inside her panties, pulling at the soft cotton until they slid over her hips towards the ground.

Still vaguely aware that she should stop, Venetia nevertheless felt powerless to make herself do anything but pull him towards her. She unzipped him and, totally aroused, guided his throbbing cock towards her. Jack licked the top of his fingers before they went to stroke the soft folds inside her, but she needed no help in getting wet. After months of Jonathon's coldness, and endless sessions of perfunctory sex in the name of conception which had left her feeling empty and worthless, she finally felt like a ripe, sexual woman ready to explode.

'Please, now,' she moaned into the curve of his neck, and Jack cupped her buttocks in his firm hands and lifted her onto the bonnet of the truck. She felt a cool breeze on her exposed pubic hair as she straddled her legs, resting her feet on the bumper.

Jack relaxed the full weight of his body on top of her, inching his shaft into her warmth, so slowly, so sweetly, she had to bite her lip to stop herself screaming out. They moved together, slowly, intensely. Venetia felt the bonnet of the car creak gently under the rhythmic thrust of their bodies. She felt the beginnings of spasms deep inside her as Jack quickened his pace. Every sensation was heightened: her stomach knotted, her skin prickled, her clitoris felt so swelled with pleasure, she thought she'd pass out.

She came powerfully as Jack exploded inside her, collapsing immediately on the warm metal of the bonnet as his hot juice trickled down the inside of her thigh. They said nothing. Jack rested his head on the mound of her breasts as she waited for the guilt to rush over her. It never came.

'Bloody hell, you're up early. It's only half past seven,' grumbled Cate, sloping into the kitchen with bed-head hair and a sleepy scowl. Serena was sitting at the breakfast bar, sipping a glass of grapefruit juice and nibbling on a toasted bagel slathered in honey. Dressed in tailored black Dolce trousers, a crisp white shirt and ballet flats, it was a look that Cate had rarely seen on Serena. Any traces of the soft side of Serena that she had seen last night were gone; now she looked as if she meant business. Serena fished around in her tan Birkin bag and pulled out a notebook in which she scribbled a series of numbers.

'This is where I'll be over the next few days,' she said officiously. 'The studio have got me booked in at the Du Cap but I'll probably be at Michael's villa. You can try both.'

She glanced at her watch and discarded the bagel. 'Now my car ought to be here any moment,' she said, wandering over to the window and peeking through the blinds. 'Not sure where Farnborough Airfield is, but my friend Elmore said he'd give me a lift to Nice in his jet if I get to him by nine o'clock. He has a house out there.'

Cate poured herself a coffee from the cafetiere and rubbed her sleepy eyes.

'I thought you weren't due in Cannes until Wednesday?'

'Silly,' sighed Serena. 'In case you've forgotten last night's revelations, I have a few things to sort out. No point hanging around in London shopping.'

'But what about your meetings . . . ?'

'Everything else can wait,' she snapped with a brusque, 'let's-get-on-with-it' efficiency that Cate didn't recognize. 'I'll let you know how it goes.'

'But Serena . . .'

'Ah, the car's here,' she chirped, already at the door. 'Now let's go and sort out my life.'

Elmore Bryant, ageing rock star, screaming queen, and Serena's New Best Friend after relations with Roman LeFey had soured, was humorous, distracting company for the eighty-minute journey to Nice. His in-flight menu was luxurious, but a hazard for a pregnant woman, thought Serena, declining the shrimp puffs and steady flow of Cosmopolitans from the beautiful, chiselled male steward. Besides, with the ripples of nausea she was feeling, particularly once they were airborne, the last thing she felt like was snacking.

Generous to a fault, Elmore had arranged for a white Bentley to pick her up from the runway and take her to wherever she wanted to go on the Côte d'Azur. Flipping down his diamond-encrusted sunglasses when they reached the terminal, Elmore gave her a penetrating look as he said his goodbyes.

'Short but sweet, my love, but always a pleasure to see you. Now remember,' he added ominously, 'if anything happens and you need somewhere to stay while you're out here . . . Someone to talk to?'

Serena wondered if telepathy was one of Elmore's many talents. She kissed him on both cheeks and got in the car. 'I'll bear it in mind.'

The traffic was foul and they moved at a snail's pace down the busy coastal road towards Cannes. Above her head, the helicopters doing the Nice–Cannes shuttle buzzed about like red wasps. She sank back in the cream leather seat and wondered how to break the news to Michael. There was no easy way to tell him; she just had to come straight out with it. To her surprise, she found her mind wandering to wedding dresses. Caroline Herrera could concoct something wonderful: elegant, timeless, beautiful. Then again, John Galliano had the magician's touch. She wouldn't have had the pink flourishes on the wedding gown he'd made for Gwen Stefani, but still, a wonderful Dior fantasy in tulle and duchess silk could be the dress of the decade . . .

Cannes was absolutely heaving, observed Serena, pressing her nose against the smoked glass of the window. Crash barriers lined the Croisette, nosy tourists poked their cameras at every crowd of people, and the entrances to all the major hotels – the Carlton, Majestic, Martinez – were guarded by burly security guards, their sole task to prevent the riffraff from infiltrating their glamorous lobbies. Thank God she was staying somewhere more civilized, thought Serena, giving her driver the directions to Michael's villa.

The harbour, by Cannes Old Town, was also busier than she had ever seen it, packed with luxurious yachts, row after row of cream and walnut hulls glinting in the strong sun. Driving past, she wondered whether Michael would be on board his hundred-foot cruiser, *Pandora*. She checked the time: 11.45. No, too early. He usually made it on board around one-ish, to take lunch, have the odd business meeting and watch the Croisette circus from the safety of the sea. So the car wound up the steep hills that backed Cannes town, the streets getting quieter and quieter as they went.

For once the villa they were approaching wasn't actually Michael's: he was merely renting it for the season. The Sarkis real-estate empire hadn't yet got as far as the Côte d'Azur, although that was one of the reasons he was having an extended stay in the area. Yes, Michael loved the glitz, glamour and parties of both the film festival and the grand prix meeting, due to take place the following weekend in Monaco, but Michael was really here on business. To make money. He had heard that a vast *belle-époque* villa belonging to some grand old dame was up for sale after her recent – and, it was whispered, suspicious – death, and Michael wanted it. He wanted a Côte d'Azur Sarkis hotel to rival the south of France legends the Du Cap and the Grand Cap Ferrat. And by the end of that fortnight, he had boasted to Serena, it was going to be his.

Big wrought-iron gates and a three-metre wall covered in climbing bougainvillea surrounded Michael's temporary home. Serena had been given the security code, a gesture that Serena had been touched by, and she punched the number into the panel on the gate. Wanting to make an entrance, she waved off the Bentley and walked through the gates, past the line of palm trees and towards the house, admiring its huge sloping terracotta roof, pink Mediterranean brickwork and balconies filled with tubs of pretty flowers. She felt a small flurry of excitement. The front door was ajar. An old man with a weather-beaten face and messy grey hair was silently sweeping the entrance hall, brushing the dust out into the warm air. He glanced casually at Serena and carried on with his chores as if in a trance. Her heels tapped against the marble as she strode in, dropping her case on the floor with a thud. The whole house had the quiet, abandoned air of the morning after.

'Michael! I'm here!' she shouted up the stairs, unbuttoning her shirt and kicking off her shoes. Nothing. Just the hum of a Hoover somewhere at the back of the house. A maid popped her head over the banister and simply nodded, as if she was used to strange women wandering around Michael's villa. 'I – am – looking – for . . .' spelt out Serena in slow, deliberate English, but the woman was gone.

Serena slowly climbed the stairs, craning her neck for any hint of life. She breathed in deeply and, despite the balmy, summer air, she was sure she could smell the pungent whiff of smoke and stale alcohol. Intuitively she felt something was wrong. She padded down one long corridor towards the back of the house and, hearing muffled noise coming from behind a large oak door, pushed it gently, craning her neck to see into the dark room.

It was a huge bedroom. Despite being midday, the long shutters were still closed, a narrow crack of sunlight cutting down the centre of the floor, but there was enough light to make Serena catch her breath. In front of her was a huge round bed with three bodies writhing around on the crumpled silk sheets.

Michael's body was naked except for a thin sheen of sweat. His lips were clamped around the right nipple of a slim redhead, whose firm breasts were pushed into his face. Astride him, a curvy blonde bent over his cock, her mouth going down hungrily over his wide shaft while Michael's fingers played with her clitoris. It was a tangle of limbs, a mass of tanned flesh, the moans were feverish and passionate – but Serena's gasp was still audible. Suddenly the blonde sat up, her head spinning round with a swoosh of hair. Michael looked up and his mouth dropped open. There was a moment when his eyes locked with Serena's across the walnut floor, before he began to smirk, instantly composed again.

She felt a thud of sickness, her brain light-headed. 'You disgusting, you cheating . . .' Serena's voice was thick with rage as she took slow steps towards the bed.

Michael lay back on the stack of pillows, one leg flung over the chocolate silk sheets, his hairy brown hand still lazily stroking up and down the leg of the blonde. His face was now a mask of sheer arrogance.

'Serena. Perfect timing. Why don't you come and join us?' he grinned.

The redhead, buck-naked except for a nipple ring, smiled seductively, stroking her own breasts as she beckoned Serena over. 'Three's company.'

'And four's an orgy,' hissed Serena, her lips curling into a snarl. 'Now, if you filthy sluts will get the hell out of my boyfriend's bed . . .'

Michael was still casually reclined, as if this scene was routine to him.

'Come on, darling. It's Cannes. Party time.'

She shook her head slowly. 'Well, why don't you all carry on having a wonderful time then?'

She turned to the door, shooting Michael with a pitiful gaze as she went. He began to get off the bed, walking towards her with his still hard cock leading the way like a knight's lance.

'Serena, please. It's just a bit of fun,' he said, his hand stretching out in a placatory gesture.

She turned and pointed a finger at him viciously. 'Save it for your whores!' she spat.

And she slammed the door shut.

26

'Look at it this way,' said Elmore Bryant, hoisting up his bottle-green Vilebrequin floral shorts and lowering himself into his pool. 'It was only a threesome. Some of these really rich business types are into all sorts of kinky shit so it could have been worse. A lot worse.'

'Elmore, you're not helping,' replied Serena, helping herself from the fruit bowl on the terrace of her friend's Cap Ferrat mansion.

'Of course, billionaires can't keep their dicks in their pants, full stop,' continued her friend, waving a bejewelled hand around in the air. 'It surprises me, naturally; I'm sure they all have tiny ones. What do you think drives them to make so much money in the first place? *Was* it small?' asked Elmore, starting to splash in the water. 'Are we talking chipolata or acorn?'

Serena dug her French manicured nails into the peach she was holding, imagining for just one moment that it was Michael's testicles as her nails pierced the flesh.

'If you don't mind, I would rather *not* talk about the size of Michael's penis,' said Serena indignantly.

'As you wish,' smiled Elmore playfully, beckoning over to the pool-boy. 'Earl Grey?'

Serena stretched herself out on the sun-lounger facing south on the terrace of Elmore's mansion. The house overlooked the bay of St-Jean-Cap-Ferrat and had one of the best views in the south of France.

'I'd kill for something stronger,' she sighed, adjusting the straps of her tiny turquoise bikini.

'Well, not in your condition, young lady,' said Elmore, nodding his head sagely so that the diamanté around his sunglasses winked in the late-afternoon sun.

Elmore, of course, knew everything. He knew that Serena had found Michael Sarkis having a threesome with two silicone-enhanced hookers. He knew that Serena had stormed out of Sarkis's Cannes villa and that, as she'd left, she'd pushed a heavy terracotta plant pot from the balcony, smashing through the windscreen of her now ex-boyfriend's flame-red Ferrari. He also knew that Serena was carrying Sarkis's child.

She'd had no choice but to tell him. Turning up at Elmore's villa only hours after she'd left him in such a buoyant mood at Cannes airport, Elmore had naturally insisted on knowing the source of her sudden hysteria. At first Serena hadn't wanted to tell him anything, but she was feeling vulnerable, alone and emotional. As she had left Michael's villa she had felt an overwhelming feeling of something she hadn't felt in a long time: loneliness. She was a beautiful, famous woman, desired the world over, and she had literally nowhere to go.

She had immediately phoned her PA, Janey Norris, demanding she get her on a flight home as soon as possible. But it was the middle of the Cannes Film Festival, and not even Janey's fearsome efficiency could get Serena out of there before nine that evening. She was also not going to use her reservation at the Du Cap – the place would be like a fish-bowl – so Serena had called her nearest lifeline, the driver of Elmore Bryant's Bentley. He had still been crawling through the traffic on La Croisette and rushed back to take her to the sanctuary of Elmore's villa. In tears, she had been seated by Elmore under an elaborate pagoda overlooking the Mediterranean Sea, and the words and secrets had spilled out.

Elmore was obviously delighted with the drama of it all but, while he was an inveterate gossip, he also had a heart as big as the moon. He had assured her she could stay with him as long as she wanted, shooing her to a guest suite overlooking the dazzling sweep of Cap Ferrat. The villa was a fabulous place in which to curl up and retreat from the world; somehow creeping between the crisp Irish linens on the huge Louis XV bed in the guestroom, her brain comfortably numb, Serena had felt just a little better. But now, almost twenty-four hours later, her shock and hysteria – and, if she was brutally honest with herself, hurt and betrayal – had now evolved into something more potent: rage. Just as she thought that things couldn't get any worse, her publicist in New York, Muffy Beagle, called Serena to say that the *Sun* and *Mirror* tabloids were both planning to run stories about her the next morning. The *Sun* was going with an interview with the two French hookers who had mysteriously managed to employ the services of Charlie Nolan, the ruthless kiss-and-tell PR who had been brokering lurid tabloid tales of this kind for the last twenty years. And the *Mirror* had managed to find out about something even more damaging. Her pregnancy.

'I just don't know how they found out about the baby,' moaned Serena, throwing the peach onto the floor of the terrace with a soft thud.

'It's my stupid fucking sister, isn't it?' she said, 'God, do you think Cate actually went to the press?' She looked up at Elmore in horror, considering the thought for just a second before catching Elmore's disapproving face.

'No. I suppose not. But she was stupid enough to go and buy that pregnancy test. She is so naïve and selfish. She goes running off to the chemist without any consideration for the impact it might have on me. It's *got* to have been someone from that chemist. They must be on the lookout for celebrities all the time.' She paused her frantic train of thought for a moment, thinking of all the possibilities.

'Or maybe some reporters went rooting through her bins. Or maybe they tapped my phone! I don't know. How do the press get hold of these things? They're like bloody Mossad!'

Elmore pulled up a sun-lounger alongside her and plumped up the white padded cushions to lower himself into a more comfortable position. 'Darling, it's happened, there's no point in worrying about it. What you've got to think about now is how you can minimize the damage.'

Serena had already had that particular conversation with her manager, Stephen Feldman; she had contacted him in New York as soon as she found out that the papers knew about her pregnancy. Feldman had pulled no punches. Abortion was now totally out of the question, he had told her. She had bitterly denied even entertaining the thought, feeling her face flush with shame as she did. The night before, curled up in Elmore's guest bedroom, she'd kept herself awake for hours, convincing herself of the benefits of terminating her pregnancy. She was realistic enough to know that Michael could, and probably would, wash his hands of her and the child. And where was she without Sarkis *and* her career? Did she really want to be a single parent at the expense of everything else? But, as Feldman had pointed out in his brutally matter-of-fact way, abortion was the preferred route if news of her pregnancy had not

305

yet leaked, but now that it had . . . Well, to have an abortion now would be career suicide. In Middle America, having an abortion was tantamount to being a serial killer. Worse, in fact. The American public – any public she was trying to seduce – just wouldn't have it.

Serena lay back, sinking deeper into her lounger and pulling the white fluffy towel wrapped around her up to her chin like a comforter. Equal parts wounded and glamorous, she looked like a cross between a Bond girl and a lonely little girl.

'You could always take him back,' offered Elmore, pausing to take a sip of his Cristal. 'Women have forgiven men for far, far worse crimes. And people *do* go a little crazy in Cannes.'

Serena shook her head violently. She knew that what she was experiencing was not heartbreak. It felt too detached, not numb enough for that. She knew it was fifty per cent fury, fifty per cent the torment that came with betrayal, and it was the betrayal she could not handle. Serena's ego would never let her forgive anybody who had been unfaithful. She was simply too vain to accept that someone would choose another woman – especially a hooker – over her, no matter how beneficial it could be to her in the long run.

'I don't want to get back with him, I want to chop his balls off,' she said flatly.

Elmore took a sideways glance towards her and smiled. 'There's more than one way to skin a rat, my darling. Hit him where it hurts. In the wallet.'

'I don't want that bastard's money. I don't want anything from him, except maybe his head on a platter.'

'Don't be pig-headed.'

'I mean it. I don't want a penny of his money.'

'Pride comes before a fall, darling,' her host said sagely.

'Keep your cod philosophy, Elmore dear. I don't want anything from him. Michael Sarkis can rot in hell.'

27

Serena stayed at Elmore's villa until the end of the week. Elmore had deliberately banned any papers coming into the house and, when her sisters had all frantically called to see how she was, she had purposely told them not to tell her about the full impact of the story. That pleasure was left to her publicist, Muffy Beagle, who had however insisted on filling her in. All the UK tabloids had gone heavy on the story for two days. It was only the emergence of pictures of a supermodel smoking a crack pipe and an affair between two cabinet ministers that had relegated the story to page eleven by day three.

It had helped that the hookers had had very little to say for themselves. One of them had embellished the incident of Serena dropping the plant pot onto Michael's Ferrari by claiming she had slashed its tyres, but as Muffy had pointed out, Fleet Street would have stayed on the story a lot longer if Michael had been both British and as famous as, say, Tom Archer. The news of her pregnancy had actually attracted lots of sympathetic column inches for Serena, with countless cynical columnists waxing lyrical about the difficulties faced by single mothers, no matter how rich or famous. To

Serena, however, the sympathy was worse than the hookers. She hated to think of herself as a victim in any way, but as Stephen Feldman had said, this was exactly the way they had to play the game in the press. Stephen was well aware that she had a glamorous if difficult persona in her home country, and he was convinced that this whole episode could soften her image considerably. She could make a few choice chat-show appearances on both sides of the pond, he decided. After this, Oprah and *Vanity Fair* might be interested.

However tempting it was to stay at Elmore's villa indefinitely, the practical and ambitious side of Serena knew that she had to get back to London to get her life back on track. London first, then New York, she corrected herself, not wanting to venture back onto Michael's territory quite yet. Anyway, there were a few pressing things that needed sorting out immediately: namely, the renewal of her contract with Jolie Cosmetics. Her agent was quite happy to wade in with negotiations, but Serena still felt it was a good idea to pay a visit to the London-based CEO Sidney Parker personally, reasoning she should tell her side of events face to face and charm him into another lucrative deal.

'Well, you *look* good,' said Venetia, reaching out to give Serena a hug. Serena had just fast-tracked through customs after Elmore's jet had landed her on a small strip of runway at Luton Airport. Her older sister had insisted on picking her up and Serena was quite happy to let herself continue to be mothered.

'I can assure you I don't feel it,' said Serena, embracing Venetia and giving a dramatic shudder to emphasize the point.

'I knew there was something about that man I didn't like in Mustique,' said Venetia, linking her arm through Serena's and leading her towards the BMW four-by-four that was parked just outside the small terminal building.

Serena arched one eyebrow. 'You could have fooled me,' she said. Venetia let the comment go as they settled into the cream leather seats.

'Men with too much money, Sin, you have to wonder if they are worth the bother,' she said in a quiet voice.

Serena gave her sister a sidelong glance. She rarely let the mundane nuances of other people's relationships affect her, but it had been plain even to Serena that all had not been well between Venetia and her husband for some time. Her sister's vibrancy had visibly diminished since her wedding nearly two years ago. Venetia had never been very confident, but it was clear that life with Jonathon, no matter how rich and connected he might be, had not had a positive effect on her sister's self-esteem. But now there was something different here. She stole a glance at Venetia's profile and noticed that her skin was slightly more flushed and sun-kissed than usual and her eyes had a sparkle she had not seen in a long time.

'I have to say that *you* look rather well too,' said Serena, probing for information. 'You've been in Spain, haven't you?' Venetia had turned the keys in the ignition and her eyes were focused forward through the windscreen, but Serena saw the pink flush rising up her sister's cheeks. She simply nodded.

Serena could see that this wasn't something Venetia wanted to talk about; while she was a gossip junkie, she wasn't in the mood to work too hard for it. Instead she began to rummage around in her Chloé bag, hunting for her Blackberry. She had a barrage of messages and emails. She switched it off as quickly as she turned it on. It was enough of a distraction to switch Serena's attention back to herself.

'So I assume I'm staying at yours, then?' said Serena, playing with the air-conditioning buttons on the walnut dashboard like a distracted child.

'As long as that's OK,' smiled Venetia.

'I don't want any crappy rooms, darling. I like the one with the walk-in wardrobe. Now come on, step on it, let's get back to London.'

Despite being a native of Chicago, Sidney Parker, CEO of Jolie Cosmetics, lived for nine months of the year in a vast, six-floor stucco-fronted Eaton Square house, on account of his much younger English wife Lysette. Mrs Parker was a bottle-blonde former cocktail waitress from southeast London, who had chased the better life with single-minded determination from a very young age.

In another life, Lysette would have been a politician or a gangster. Her finely balanced mixture of ruthless ambition and her chameleon-like ability to charm important people had landed her the prize of Sidney Parker, but Lysette hadn't stopped there, quickly establishing herself as a feared and fêted society player whose opinion and patronage was highly valued. If Lysette Parker didn't come to your charity fundraiser or RSVP your party invite, then you were dead in London society.

Happily for Serena, Lysette had always admired the beautiful Balcon sisters. Throughout her campaign to ensnare a rich husband, Lysette had devoured *Tatler* magazine, becoming intimate with the society movers and shakers and grand aristo families contained within its pages. Serena was everything Lysette had wanted to be when she was growing up in Lewisham two decades earlier, and it had been Lysette who had persuaded her husband to make Serena the European face of Jolie Cosmetics. Polished, privileged and ridiculously beautiful, she knew that Serena embodied that English rose fantasy so many British girls secretly harboured.

Sidney would have much preferred to go with a supermodel as the Jolie Cosmetics girl three years earlier, but he respected his wife's streetwise outlook on the business and, as it had turned out, Lysette's hunch had proved correct. Within six months of Serena becoming the face of Jolie, profits across the board were up sixty-three per cent and the perception of the brand was transformed from a fusty traditional European cosmetics house into something much more fresh, modern and glamorous. In a bid to get a sultry Serena pout, women from fifteen to fifty were clamouring for Jolie's plum and peach lip-glosses, while sales of their line of skincare products tripled as customers sought to replicate Serena's flawless complexion. She didn't know it, but Serena owed more to the Parker family than she realized.

With a wave, Venetia dropped Serena at the small flight of steps that led up to the enormous midnight-blue door of Sidney and Lysette Parker's home. Rarely nervous, Serena still felt a little bout of butterflies in her stomach as she rang the bell. She usually relished meetings like this, but it had only been six days since the scandal had broken in the newspapers about her pregnancy and Michael Sarkis, and it was impossible to tell how Sidney would take it. Mindful of this, she had dressed to impress. Virgin glamour, she smiled: cream billowy Chloé dress, gold ballet flats, a smudge of Jolie blush swept across her cheek.

She knew it was the right decision to come and see Sidney so quickly. She would rather he heard things from the horse's mouth than from the tabloids. And anyway, the contract had to get resolved as soon as possible: with her Cheyne Walk home sold and her going back to New York temporarily out of the question, Serena had to find somewhere new to live quickly, and she needed to assess the size of the contract before she made any decisions on that.

A Filipino maid in a grey dress opened the door and beckoned Serena in. A tall, sturdy man of about sixty, dressed in a razor-sharp navy suit, came to greet her in the hallway. Clearly once a very handsome man, Sidney had lined skin that somehow looked more brushed and polished because of its light mahogany colour. Grey hair swept back off his forehead and a pair of thin, gold-framed glasses perched on a long firm nose completed the cosmopolitan look.

'Sidney, how are you?' said Serena, grabbing his hand and kissing him on both cheeks.

'Fine. And you look wonderful,' he replied, smiling benevolently. 'Let's go through to the study. Oh Joyce?' he said, addressing the maid, 'Could you get us some tea?'

They walked in silence through to an ornate library. It was a formal room, decked out in rich flock wallpaper, walnut panelling and shelves of colour-coordinated books. The room reminded Serena a little of her father's study at Huntsford, except this place was more airbrushed, like a Ralph Lauren fantasy of an English gentleman's library. The old-money feel was further undermined by huge framed photographs of beautiful women on the walls: portraits of all the Jolie spokeswomen. Serena was next to Kelly Sanders, a stunning, red-haired Texan model-turned-TV-presenter, who was the North American Jolie spokeswoman, and next to them was Bay Ling, the up-and-coming Chinese model who was the face of the burgeoning Far Eastern cosmetics market.

Sidney sat down behind his huge desk and sank back into his chair, playing with a gold Mont Blanc pen as Joyce silently entered and placed a silver tea tray on the desk. Serena took a moment to glance around the room. She had never been in the study before; usually when she met

Sydney they would take drinks in the drawing room. Perhaps Lysette was entertaining elsewhere in the house.

'I'm glad you came to see me so quickly,' said Sidney, handing Serena a bone-china cup. He still had a slight American twang, although he had purposely tried to rub it away in favour of clipped English tones.

'Well, I know we have plenty to talk about,' smiled Serena, folding one long tanned leg over the other. 'As you know, I've hardly been in London lately, living in New York and all that,' she gushed, making her voice as pretty and singsong as possible.

'What do you think of Bay Ling?' said Sidney suddenly, waving a hand in the direction of the girl's picture. Serena looked up to inspect her. She was certainly the most Western-looking Oriental girl she had ever seen. Her skin was slightly tanned rather than sallow, the hair cut into the severe bob that was currently all the rage in Manhattan. In fact, there was hardly a trace of the Chinese about her. Her bone structure was perfect, the delicate face oval rather than round, her lips pale and plump.

'She's stunning, isn't she?' prompted Sidney. 'China's first supermodel.'

'Yes. Well, the press call anyone with long legs a super-model these days,' laughed Serena lightly.

She noticed a muscle in Sidney's temple twitch.

'But . . . she *is* extremely beautiful,' she continued quickly.

'We've moved a quarter of a million units of China Rose lip-gloss already,' he said, nodding his head slowly. Serena found herself echoing the gesture.

'Have you ever been to Beijing?' he asked. It was the sort of question that veered towards an offer. Serena felt her anxiety diminish. 'No, I haven't,' she said earnestly, 'but I did stay at the Amanpuri in Phuket last winter,' she said seriously.

'A Thai holiday resort is hardly the new global commercial headquarters,' replied Sidney, a disapproving tone in his voice.

Serena's back stiffened.

'Unbelievable city,' he said suddenly, stroking the side of his face and continuing in a more benevolent tone, 'when Bay Ling and I opened the Beijing store three months ago, I swear the queue was as long as the Great Wall of China!' He guffawed lightly to himself. 'It makes the opening up of Russia as a commercial territory insignificant. China is the future.'

Serena had to suppress a bored sigh. She was not in the mood for a lecture on global economics. 'Well, perhaps you could arrange a visit for me. I'd love to see it all,' she smiled, taking a delicate sip of tea. 'It's probably about time all the Jolie spokeswomen met up anyway,' she said generously.

Sidney laughed, a little forced.

'Anyway,' said Sidney more brusquely, 'I suppose we're here to talk about your contract?'

Serena smiled and recrossed her legs. 'Just the broad strokes,' she smiled playfully, 'the rest we can leave to my agent. That's what I pay him fifteen per cent for.' Inwardly, Serena shuddered at the thought of that figure. If she was about to be made Jolie spokesperson for North America as well as Europe, that was a deal in excess of $5 million a year. Fifteen per cent of that was . . . she couldn't do the maths, but it was certainly a lot of money, she thought, suddenly feeling a little cross.

Sidney paused, moving his swivel chair from side to side. 'Lysette and I have been giving the renewal of your contract a lot of thought in the last few days.'

'How is Lysette?' asked Serena, smiling broadly.

Sidney nodded. 'Very well, very well indeed. As you know, I have enormous faith and trust in her opinions about the direction of this company.'

'She is a very astute woman,' nodded Serena sagely.

'She is indeed,' agreed Sidney, rubbing his chin. 'Not only is she my wife, she is my line of communication to the general public. She was right about signing you up three years ago, and I trust her instincts about your position now. Having moved to New York and taken up with Michael Sarkis –'

Serena jumped in eagerly. 'I know!' she gushed. 'Moving out there is the best thing I have done in years. It has raised my profile Stateside enormously. I can understand why you were initially hesitant to make me the face of North America as well as Europe but now, yes, things are much different.' She smiled.

'I didn't mean that,' said Sidney without emotion.

'Oh . . .' said Serena. 'Then I'm not sure I . . .'

Sidney leant forward on the desk, shuffling up the sleeves of his dark navy jacket. 'Your relationship with Michael Sarkis has been damaging to the brand.'

The smile fell off Serena's face.

'Well, as you are no doubt aware,' said Serena quickly, trying to sound confident and in control, 'I found my ex-boyfriend in a compromising situation in Cannes and I terminated the relationship immediately. I felt that was the responsible thing to do.'

'And you're pregnant,' said Sidney matter-of-factly.

'Yes,' answered Serena with a little annoyance. 'Men and women in a relationship often conceive a child.'

Sidney leant back in his chair as far as it would go, seemingly anxious to put as much distance between them as possible. 'You are a very, very beautiful woman,' said Sidney, with the hint of a smile. 'But we took you on because you represented certain things. Elegance. Class. Tradition. They are the cornerstone values of Jolie Cosmetics.'

'And I remain all those things,' said Serena indignantly.

Sidney let the silence hang in the air for a few moments. 'Lysette feels, and I agree with her, that the revelations of this week have changed things considerably. It looks messy, Serena.'

'Don't be ridiculous,' said Serena haughtily. 'So Michael revealed himself as a playboy. I did the decent thing and got rid of him. I'm having a child. This is the twenty-first century. Plenty of children are conceived out of wedlock.'

'We are a traditional company,' said Sidney slowly, emphasizing every word. 'You know how Midwest America is a conservative market. It is vital for our company to be seen to be projecting the correct values.' He cleared his throat. 'This, er, threesome, the prostitutes . . .'

'Does this mean I'm not going to get North America?' said Serena, visibly flustered. 'But we discussed –'

Sidney appeared to ignore her. 'As you are aware, your European contract is up for renewal, and we feel that at this time it is not appropriate to renew it.'

Serena began to feel a rage swell up inside her. 'If this is because I am pregnant, you do realize there are laws against this sort of thing?'

'Your contract is at an end and it is entirely up to our company whether we renew it. Or not,' he added. 'In any event, Bay Ling has been so successful for us in China we feel it may be the appropriate time to increase her profile in the west. We think that will drive even more sales out in the Far East.'

Serena stared at him. 'You're going to replace me with *her*?' she screamed, her voice a quivering, shrill sound. 'You sell in this country and all over Europe because of my English Rose image! It's successful! Why replace me with someone who looks like, who looks like . . . they work in a chip shop?' she ranted.

'We've made our decision,' interrupted Sidney calmly. 'It

really has been a pleasure working with you over the years. Lysette and I would like to give you this as a small token of our appreciation.' He reached into his top drawer and pulled out a Jolie powder compact that, from the way he lifted it, looked as if it might have been made from solid gold.

'Please, give it to Bay Ling,' said Serena, mustering up as much dignity as she could. 'It looks like she needs it. I'll see myself out.'

Sidney simply nodded as Serena rose. He flipped open the compact and looked at his reflection in the mirror, rubbing a tea-stain off his teeth with his finger. Then he snapped it shut.

28

It was a perfect day for polo. Possibly not for the players: the sun was quite ferocious for a late May afternoon but, sitting in the shelter of the big marquee at Staplehurst Polo Club, Camilla sipped her Pimms and thought there could be few better ways to spend a Sunday. Watching a few chukkas, eating a good lunch and being seen at one of the most high-profile social events of the season: it wasn't too taxing. She didn't particularly enjoy exhausting the social calendar in the way Serena did, but having just been accepted onto the Conservative Party's approved list of candidates, Camilla knew she had to step up her profile. Potential politicians didn't just have to be seen and heard, they had to be seen at the right places, and Staplehurst's Annual Charity Day seemed as good a place as any to start. Especially when she was here at the special request of club owner Josh Jackson, bass guitarist of legendary rock band Phoenix.

'So then, where is he?' asked Cate, straining her neck to look around the tent, where everyone from actors to the local aristocracy were knocking back champagne and pretending they knew about polo. Although *Sand* magazine was two days away from going to press, Cate couldn't refuse Camilla's offer to join her at the Staplehurst Charity Day at the invitation of the great Josh Jackson. Not only was Phoenix's music one of her guilty pleasures – she'd revised for her A-levels listening to their multi-platinum album *Albatross*, but their bass guitarist was gorgeous and she couldn't resist the chance of an introduction.

Camilla pointed to a lone figure on horseback, cantering across the emerald-green polo pitch and swinging a wooden mallet with a muscular, bronzed arm. 'There he is,' she said. 'He's playing in the game after lunch so I'm not even sure he'll be eating.'

'That's a shame,' smirked Cate. 'You mean we've come all this way and I don't even get to say hello.'

They were sitting on a table with eight other guests, so Camilla turned her head to be out of earshot. 'I've only come to be polite,' said Camilla, lowering her voice so no one could hear. 'You know I've never been one for polo but, when a client invites you, you have to make an effort.'

'Oh yes,' said Cate with a sceptical smile. 'And why did Josh invite you again?'

'I acted for him in a case recently. His accountant had siphoned off over three million pounds from his various bank accounts. A clear instance of fraud. We won. I guess today is a thank you.'

'No, I mean, why did he *really* invite you?' smiled Cate as a starter of asparagus in lemon butter arrived in front of her.

Camilla's face clouded. 'I don't know what you mean.'

'Well, is the instructing solicitor here, or is it just Josh's favourite gorgeous lady barrister?' probed Cate playfully.

Camilla tried to look shocked. 'OK, his solicitor isn't here, but don't go reading anything into it, OK? I won the case, he's grateful. Case closed.'

Although Cate had never passed judgement on any of her sisters' boyfriends – she had never once mentioned to Camilla that she considered Nat Montague to be a boorish, philandering waster – she'd have been delighted to see her hooked up with one of rock's most eligible bachelors. With his upright sinewy body, dark skin and intelligent grey eyes, it was impossible to believe that Josh Jackson was in his late forties. Twenty years earlier he'd traded LSD for yoga, drink for detox and had spent his songwriting royalties buying a three-hundred-year-old Jacobean manor, attaching a four-pitch polo club and taking up the sport with such gusto he gave a whole new meaning to rock royalty.

'Now we are going to start the bidding for some of this afternoon's fabulous prizes.'

With lunch over, rock singer and legendary lothario Rich Clark stood up to begin his stint as auctioneer. 'Be generous. You know why we're all here. Dig deep. We're not starting any game of polo before we've got at least two hundred thousand quid in the kitty. For the first lot we have a week for two at the One&Only resort, Le Saint Géran, which has been kindly donated by Exit Travel. Can we start the bidding at two thousand pounds?'

An excited buzz rumbled around the marquee as the bidding climbed to four, ten, then twenty thousand pounds, fuelled by sun, champagne and social competitiveness. A home-cooked dinner prepared by Gordon Ramsay went for £10,000, a fortnight at the Amanpuri fetched £30,000, five nights at the Copacabana Hotel in Rio was a bargain at £8,000. Camilla looked around the marquee, spotting the minister for sport and culture, four well-known benefactors of the Tory Party and two newspaper editors and decided that it would be a wasted journey if she didn't make herself and her philanthropy known. No one here would know she had already joined a committee to fund a battered wives' shelter in Notting Hill, or signed up for three 15-kilometre 'fun' runs in the name of charity. She was here to impress, and if you were going to do that today, you had to put your hand in your pocket.

'A weekend in New York staying in a loft suite at the Mercer,' said Rich Clark. 'Do I have five thousand pounds?'

Camilla felt her hand go gingerly into the air as it was quickly countered with a bid for six thousand.

She nodded towards the auctioneer again as Cate tugged at her arm playfully. 'What do you want to go to New York again for?' she whispered.

'Eight thousand from the lovely Camilla Balcon!' said the rock auctioneer, recognizing her. 'Who'll give me nine?'

With the room ever more drunk, bidding spiralled towards £15,000 as Camilla bowed out, satisfied she had been seen to take part.

When the auctioneer motioned to the rear of the tent and the gavel came down at £20,000, Camilla breathed an internal sigh of relief that it hadn't been an unnecessarily expensive afternoon.

'That was a close one,' smiled Cate as diners began to wander outside to watch the start of the polo. 'I know you probably want to treat yourself after you got on the approved list, but there are cheaper ways of getting to New York,' she laughed.

Camilla smiled knowingly. Cate wasn't aware that she had already treated herself, having a spree at Yves Saint Laurent and buying one pair of shoes, one shirt and one jacket that would perfectly complement Camilla's precisely coordinated wardrobe, an exercise in restrained but elegant dressing.

'Bloody hell, don't look now, but guess who's coming over.'

Josh Jackson was striding towards the sidelines in white, skin-tight jodhpurs, tall black boots, knee guards, and polo shirt in the Jackson Team's navy-and-white colours. The sun had brought out a flame of freckles across the bridge of his Roman nose and the lines of his face wrinkled as he smiled in the bright light.

'Ladies. Good of you to come. I've got to shoot in a minute, but I thought I'd come and say hello.'

Cate smiled, trying to think of something humorous or interesting to say, but gave up when she saw that his gaze was fixed entirely on Camilla.

'Well. It's a great day for it,' stumbled Cate. 'I'm not going to drink too many Pimms, though, or I'll be stumbling over the divots.'

Neither Josh nor Camilla seemed to be aware of Cate or anyone else. Feeling uncomfortably as if she were intruding on some personal moment, Cate mumbled an excuse and moved off towards the bar. As she left, Josh pressed his fingers on Camilla's forearm.

'I appreciate you coming,' he smiled.

Camilla stared at him, then, as if coming out of a trance, took a small step back, so that his hand fell away from her skin. 'Yes, it's a nice day out.'

'You didn't have to come. So I thought I'd make it worth your while.'

She smiled, trying not to be playful. 'How do you mean?'

'I saw you bidding for the New York weekend.'

Camilla felt a jolt through her stomach which she fought to suppress. 'Oh. I thought you were practising. I didn't see you at the lunch.'

'I had to go to the auction,' he smiled. 'Rich Clark was there, God knows what he might say.'

'Yes, well. The bidding got a little too hot for me,' stuttered Camilla. 'Anyway, I was only in New York before

Christmas, so it doesn't matter. I'll make a donation to the charity, though.'

'Well that's a shame.'

'What? Why?'

'Because I got the winning bid.'

'Oh, it was you!'

'And it's a shame because I won it for you.'

Camilla felt her throat dry. 'I don't understand.'

'You bid, so I figured you wanted to go to New York.'

'Josh. You didn't have to . . . I couldn't accept it.'

'You could accept it. Especially if you invite me along . . .'

Cate returned with two glasses of kir as the klaxon sounded for the first chukka to commence.

'Josh Jackson is hot,' she smiled to Camilla, watching him mount a polo pony.

'He won the bid for the New York weekend and he's given it to me.'

'You're kidding!'

'And he wants me to take him too.'

Cate watched her sister's face, so intently fixed on the polo pitch. She glanced at the field herself to see Josh astride a shiny bronze polo pony. He thundered down the boards to hit the ball up the field with his mallet.

'You like him, don't you?' smiled Cate.

'I do not.'

'Please tell me you're going to take the trip. Tell me you're going to take him with you.'

'I didn't finish with Nat to start dating a rock star,' said Camilla, turning to face her sister. 'I just don't need any distractions at the moment.'

'But Cam, he's gorgeous, not to mention very nice and very, very loaded!'

Camilla simply turned back to watch the match. For her,

the conversation was clearly over. She had just rejected one of the country's most eligible bachelors without a backward glance. Cate stared at Camilla and shook her head slowly. The discipline of her sister almost scared her.

29

Cate balanced on the toilet seat in *Sand*'s tiny office bathroom, attempting to pull on a black Pierre Hardy heel, apply her lip-gloss, and rub some bronzing cream into her legs all at the same time.

'Cate? Are you still in there?' said an impatient voice, followed by a bang on the door. 'Come on, the taxi's here!'

'Give me two minutes, Nick,' she muttered, swearing to herself as she dropped a huge dollop of bronzer onto the floor. She took a deep breath. 'Ready?' she sighed as she looked in the mirror, but was surprised to find that she was pleased with what she saw. She had poured herself into a cream Donna Karan cocktail dress. She knew it wasn't the most forgiving colour, but if you forgot about the slight wobble around her thighs, she really looked quite pretty. Her hair fell loose and glossy between her shoulder blades and her eyes, lined with lashings of kohl and mascara, looked wide, sparkling and alert. She pulled a blue velvet box from her bag and opened it. Sitting on a little satin cushion was a pair of large diamond drop studs. Her mother's. She hadn't worn them for years, always waiting for a special occasion. No night had ever felt special enough. Well, if there was ever an occasion to wear them, it was tonight, for *Sand* magazine's launch party. She threaded them through her lobes and smiled. 'Ready.'

As she stepped out of the bathroom into the office, Nick was waiting for her, dressed in a one-button charcoal suit with a crisp pale-blue shirt, his sandy-brown hair swept back from his face. She caught her breath, wishing Nick wasn't looking quite so handsome, and slid her clutch bag under her arm. She felt his eyes brush over her, but he said nothing about her appearance; the compliments had stopped long ago, but the smile on his face revealed his approval.

Quickly flicking his eyes away, Nick nodded to a pile of boxes by the door. 'How many magazines should we take down then?' he said.

'I don't know,' said Cate. 'About fifty?'

'Cheapskate,' teased Nick, 'I thought I was the one with the tight fist!'

'I'm just worried that this launch party is getting expensive,' replied Cate.

'Well, that may be so, but until we're selling one hundred and fifty thousand copies a month, we've got to become experts in the art of illusion,' smiled Nick.

'How do you mean?'

'I know I've been a bit tight on budgets, but we have to know when to save and when to spend. And tonight, the last thing we want to do is look cheap, especially with all the top-notch advertisers there. We might be a little magazine operating out of a room next door to a Moroccan takeaway, but we don't want to look it,' he grinned.

Despite herself, Cate was impressed. Because they'd both been on the same journey in launching *Sand*, climbing the same learning curve, making the same mistakes, she'd always seen Nick as someone who was making it up as he went along, someone who was playing the same game as she was.

326

But right now, here in front of her, she saw him for what he was – a talented businessman with drive and vision, a sharp entrepreneur whom she could trust to make her magazine a success.

'Hmm, "Image is everything"?' she said with a wry smile. 'You must have got that from me.'

He bent down to open a carton and took out a box-fresh copy of the first issue of *Sand* magazine, holding it out in front of him with both arms extended.

It was hard for them not to feel a rush of pride as they looked at it, touched it. On its cover, a sumptuous, sexy image of Rachel Barnaby in a gold swimsuit, smiling seductively in front of a Cote d'Azur palm tree. Inside, pages of glossy images of gorgeous people and glamorous places which made you want to jump into the rich, expensive wonderland they had created for the reader.

'Who'd have thought it?' she grinned. 'Brought to you straight out of Borough Market rather than some trillionaire's yacht?'

'Pretty good,' said Nick.

'Pretty good,' admitted Cate with a shy smile. 'Although ask me again in three months' time when we've got a run of sales figures.'

'You are so miserable sometimes,' smiled Nick, shaking his head. 'Now let's get these magazines to this party and show everyone just how good you are!'

'How good *we* are,' said Cate.

Nothing had quite prepared Venetia for how guilty and exhausted having an affair would make her feel. She had read all the features on infidelity that the women's magazines could provide; she had devoured virtually every bodice-ripping glamour novel in the airport bookshop. She had even listened wide-eyed to the stories from her most indiscreet and philandering friends over the years. But she had never, for a moment, ever considered that those experiences would relate to her life.

Taking a shower in the top-floor suite of One Aldwych Hotel, letting the warm jets of water flood over her skin, she felt the full weight of it, the full burden of the guilt and the exhaustion of living the lie. After Seville, she had resisted Jack's calls for a full week. Every instinct in her body had urged her to stop the one-night stand in its tracks. But that perfect moment under the stars in Spain had reawakened some life-force inside her and she had found it impossible to stay away from Jack Kidman.

When he had daringly called her at home, she had finally agreed to meet him, telling herself it was only to persuade him to stop calling. They had ended up having sensational sex at the Mandarin Oriental, two bodies entwined perfectly on a tapestry rug. It was the beginning of a series of snatched, sexually charged moments in hotel rooms, at his Westbourne Grove apartment or, on one particularly risqué occasion, in the fabric store-cupboard at the Venetia Balcon shop. Over the past three weeks, they had met up at least a dozen times: before work, after work, between appointments – and as the lies to Jonathon increased and her workload doubled, she wondered daily whether it was worth it. But it was worth it, despite everything. For the first time in years, she felt alive.

Jack was lounging on the bed, wrapped in a tumble of white sheets and finishing off a room-service club sandwich as she walked back into the room from the shower.

'There's some fruit salad here. Do you want some?'

Venetia shook her head. 'I'm half an hour late for the party as it is.'

'I don't know why I can't come along. I could pretend not to know you.'

Venetia looked at him mournfully and shook her head adamantly. 'Because I'm meeting Jonathon. Anyway, it wouldn't feel right. I can't lie to my sisters.'

She began towelling herself down vigorously, trying to rub out the smell of sex and guilt before the party.

'I guess you're right. I might not be able to keep my hands off you. Then we'd be in all sorts of trouble.' He smiled wolfishly.

Venetia looked at him intently, taking in the firm tanned body and the open smile. She knew she had to ask a question that had haunted her since that first night in Seville.

'Jack, what do you see in me?'

He started laughing softly and reached out his hands to gesture her onto the bed. 'What do I see in you?' he paused with a faux-puzzled expression. 'You have a nice nose, I suppose.'

She immediately looked wounded.

'I'm joking, I'm joking! Although yes, you do have a nice nose. Come here,' he laughed.

She sat on the edge of the bed and lay back in his arms. He fed her a strawberry, letting his fingers rest on the inside of her bottom lip.

'Van, you are sexy, you are beautiful, you are talented. You are going to take over the world with your business and I'm going to keep kicking you up that pert, sexy little bum to help you do it.'

Venetia stayed silent for a while. This was all so wrong, but there was something about Jack Kidman that made her feel powerless to stop it. He made her laugh, he made her feel clever, he made her feel interesting. He was creative, clever, spontaneous: the type of man she'd been looking for all her life. But she had simply met him too late. She closed her eyes and willed herself to think of Jonathon. But it was no good, she couldn't even picture his face. Jack Kidman had got right under her skin and her morals had crumbled. Pandora's box had been opened.

The party was being held in the penthouse suite of the brand new Monument Hotel in the City, rumoured to be the biggest penthouse suite in London. As it had only been open a week, they had managed to get the use of it for free, in return for some publicity in the magazine. The press officer had been salivating over the proposed guest list: after all, it never did any new establishment any harm to host a glamorous party in the first few days of opening. Cate would have preferred a West End location for the party, but with such a tiny budget, she knew that beggars couldn't be choosers.

'Bloody hell, this is nice,' said Nick, as the lift doors hissed open onto the atrium of the penthouse, where Pete Miller, the art director, had erected a twelve-foot-high blow-up of *Sand*'s first cover. In fact, the whole place looked really impressive. Handsome members of hotel staff in black Armani suits were floating around the rooms adding the final touches to the party: lighting candles, straightening ashtrays, making sure the two bars were fully stocked.

Cate and Nick wandered from room to room, taking in its luxury. It was striking, if masculine, in design. The walls were lined with Japanese cherry-wood, long black leather sofas filled the huge lounge area, which had floor-to-ceiling windows leading onto an enormous terrace that overlooked the entire city. It was a fabulous entertaining suite, no doubt squarely aimed at male CEOs visiting London on big business.

Nick opened the glass doors and the pair of them slipped out onto the terrace, grinning at each other like kids. The warm June evening air hit their faces as they stepped out. The city stretched out in front of them, lit up like a miniature New York skyline. You could see the strange 'Gherkin' building with its impressive lattice of lights, you could even make out the circular shape of the London Eye in the distance, and the shape of Tower Bridge, like two bishop chess pieces facing each other across the Thames.

A middle-aged man in a black suit came bustling over and introduced himself as Willem, the general manager of the hotel. 'We are so pleased to be accommodating you tonight,' he gushed in a light Eastern European accent. 'Just let me know if you need anything. You will find me on extension two-two-five-three. Will your sister Serena be attending tonight?' he asked Cate expectantly.

'She will be attending, yes,' said Cate with a smirk at Willem's triumphant look before he hurried off to straighten some more ashtrays.

'So Serena's coming?' asked Nick, helping himself to a glass of champagne.

'Of course she's coming,' replied Cate. 'She's my sister.'

'But so's Tom.'

Cate looked back at him with a start.

'Well, of course he's coming,' said Nick, mimicking her, 'he's my best friend. Not to mention an investor. Actually, he's staying here in the hotel tonight. We thought Serena might be coming so I said I'd ring down to him in his suite when she's gone.'

'God, this is all so childish,' muttered Cate. 'I can't believe they haven't even seen each other yet.'

'They will in time,' said Nick. 'But I guess tonight isn't quite the right time for a reconciliation, in full view of one hundred and fifty people and the gentlemen of the press.'

'I can't tell her he's coming,' said Cate, playing distractedly with her earrings. 'She's stressed enough at the minute. She'll just refuse.'

'Oh Cate, you look fantastic!' said Vicky, *Sand*'s fashion

editor, who had rushed over and was running her fingers over the fabric of Cate's Donna Karan dress. Nick mumbled his excuses and moved away to check on the guest list as the first arrivals were starting to trickle into the suite.

'How many people have you seen?' asked Cate anxiously. 'Have any of the VIPs arrived?' She was secretly worrying again that the City venue might have been a mistake, no matter how economical it had been to stage the party here.

Vicky pulled a face and handed Cate a glass of Moët. 'It's an awful lot of champagne to take back to the office if people don't show.'

There was no need to worry. By eight o'clock, the penthouse was heaving with glamorous bodies. Senior representatives of all the major advertisers had come and were thumbing eagerly through the copies of *Sand* displayed around the suite. The soft jazz background music had to be turned up to full volume to be heard above the laughing crowd and Cate, a few drinks more relaxed, allowed herself to bask in the attention she was receiving from all quarters.

'I am so proud of you,' said Lucy, her old friend from *Class* magazine, kissing her on both cheeks. 'You are going to whip the arse off *Class*,' she smiled, 'and I hope you do. That Nicole Valentine has become a big old bitch.'

'Become?'

They both giggled.

Meanwhile, Camilla and Venetia had arrived, looking stunning in Marni and Prada respectively, and were doing a sterling job helping Cate circulate around the advertisers and showering them with attention. The ad people didn't seem to mind that the sisters were not actively involved with *Sand* magazine – they were just happy to talk to one of the Balcon sisters – while a photographer from the *Evening*

332

Standard snapped away gleefully at the great, the good and the gorgeous.

All the magazine's investors were out in force, drinking champagne and all looking very pleased with themselves, lapping up the reflected glory. David Goldman had been very clever to know that evenings like this, rubbing shoulders with celebrities in a penthouse suite, was actually what they were investing in, not the magazine itself.

Cate took a minute to stand back in a corner and survey the scene. She had never felt more confident, more alive, more in charge than at this very moment. Across the room she could see Nick standing talking to a group of PRs, with Rebecca hovering by his shoulder. He had undone the button of his jacket and looked handsome and casual. She felt a glimmer of sadness, but immediately pushed it to one side. She and Nick might not be a couple, but they were certainly a great business partnership, and it was definitely time to move on from thinking it could be anything more. At that moment, she caught a glimpse of David Goldman, who was talking to one of the investors. After a few moments, Cate became aware that, as he spoke, his eyes kept wandering in her direction, accompanied by a flirtatious smile. After three glasses of champagne, she certainly had to acknowledge that he was attractive. His hair had grown a little longer since the last time they'd met, and his steel-grey suit matched his twinkling eyes, she thought, giggling to herself and beginning to wish that he would come over to say hello.

'Catherine, what a charming evening.'

Cate looked up in surprise to see her father. So he had come. A big part of her really didn't want him here. She was still furious at his meddling with Nigel Hammond, the investor whom he had sent in the direction of William Walton for a reference, almost strangling their investment process at birth.

On the other hand, she hadn't quite been able to bring herself to snub him entirely, being a little fearful at the ramifications of not asking him. Daddy was a man who held a grudge. So she simply sent an invitation to the gallery and put it out of her mind, hoping he simply wouldn't bother.

'I was just telling this young lady here,' said Oswald, pulling her towards an eager-looking journalist busily scribbling away on a notepad, 'how I introduced you to your first big investor and got this whole ball rolling.' The journalist looked up bright-eyed, her pen poised to take down more of the story. 'Yes, Cate, you must be very grateful for all your father's support.'

She stifled an angry snort.

'Even though I lost my wife many years ago,' continued Oswald, turning to the journalist with a grave look, 'I have always done my very best to ensure that the girls have had everything they wanted and were given every opportunity to follow their dreams.'

'Has Serena arrived yet?' said the journalist, her eyes searching the room. 'What would be fabulous is a family photo. All the sisters with their father?'

'She's due any time,' said Cate, wondering where she had got to.

To avoid the paparazzi clamouring outside the front of the Monument, Serena had arranged to be smuggled into the hotel through the kitchens. A kind-faced concierge accompanied her to the penthouse suite via a service lift. When Cate had begged her to come to the party, she had promised her there was only going to be one photographer there, yet the crowd of snappers on the street was as big as a rugby scrum. She knew she looked sensational in a chocolate-brown jersey minidress that stopped provocatively mid-thigh, but for the first time she could remember, the presence of the photographers had brought on a sense of dread so strong she could feel her skin become clammy. The lift door hissed open at the top floor and, for a moment, Serena stood watching the party. By the window she could see Cate surrounded by people, laughing, while her father was hovering by the bar.

'Have a good night, Miss Balcon,' smiled the concierge, waiting for her to step out into the party.

Serena turned to answer him and an unfamiliar emotion gripped her. Panic. Suddenly her heart was pounding so violently that she had to clasp her chest, her breath coming in little pants and her hands starting to tremble. She slammed the button of the lift door for it to close before anyone had the chance to see she'd arrived.

She inhaled sharply to calm herself and turned to face the concierge.

'I'm not quite ready yet,' she smiled, rubbing her damp palms together nervously. 'I, I . . . think I'd like to check into the hotel, first. Discreetly, of course,' she said, resting her hand on his arm to make the point. 'Now, this suite is obviously taken. Which suite would you recommend after this?'

The concierge straightened his jacket and coughed to clear his suddenly dry throat. 'I would normally recommend the Fenchurch Suite on the floor below, but I believe it is occupied tonight. There is a wonderful junior suite just next door to it, however. I can take you there now and we can do the formal checking-in later.'

'Excellent,' said Serena with false composure. 'Let's go.'

The Threadneedle Suite was small compared to the penthouse, but it had a huge emperor-sized bed that was plumped up with a white duvet, black leather throw and cream-coloured mongoose cushions. It was surprisingly cosy. And it felt safe. 'I'll take it,' she said.

When the concierge had gone, Serena kicked off her heels, sat back on the mattress and pulled her knees up to her chin like a vulnerable child. It felt better now, alone, unobserved. She pressed her hand to her forehead as if she were dealing with a particularly stubborn headache, but it was not enough to stop big droplets of tears spilling down her cheeks. She angrily wiped them away, but felt powerless to stop the sobs that creased her shoulders. She thought about what it would be like to go into the party, where every pair of cold, prying eyes would be on her, judging her every thought. Serena was a woman born to bask in people's attention, but tonight her armour wasn't strong enough. After all that had happened, she wasn't ready for it. Cate should have known she wasn't ready for it.

A searing charge of jealousy ripped through her body as she thought about her sister upstairs, circulating like a frantic butterfly, basking in the glow of compliments. Cate was never the successful one, she thought angrily, raising her eyes to the ceiling where the sound of jazz could just be heard. Serena was the one who was supposed to be fêted and adored. And she *was*, she reminded herself – but it really didn't feel like that right now.

She hugged her knees in tighter when she thought about the events of the last few days. She could get over her contract with Jolie Cosmetics not being renewed; it was a stupid, stuffy company, anyway: hardly Estée Lauder. But *To Catch a Thief* was bombing at the box office, not even making the top ten of releases in its opening weekend after the critics had slated it unanimously. *'For Serena Balcon to take on the famous Grace Kelly role was not just ill advised, it was imbecilic,'* one particularly vicious review had pronounced. Her agent had delivered even more painful news. Ed Charles, the producer of *Fin de Siècle* had called him up at the weekend to say that they had decided to go with someone else for the role of Letitia DuPont. A smaller role in the production had not been mentioned; in fact, no part was offered at all.

'It's because I'm pregnant, isn't it?' she had screamed to her agent down the phone. 'How dare they? How *dare* they? We have to leak this information everywhere, it's just so unfair!'

Her agent pointed out that no contract for the role had ever been signed, that she was merely being considered. But that role had been *hers*, thought Serena, uselessly punching her fist against her shin. She knew her meeting with Ed Charles had gone well and that her screen test had had a very positive reaction in LA. It was Michael. Michael Sarkis had ruined her life.

The tears were coming out in huge sobs now, as she stroked her arms, like a mother trying to calm her child. For a second, her mind wandered to thoughts of Tom Archer. Four months' distance had mellowed her feelings towards him. She thought back to a time last summer when they had been at the casino in Monte Carlo. Standing at the roulette table, her number immediately came up the moment Tom moved to her side. 'I'm your good luck charm,' he had whispered in her ear. Maybe he was right, thinking about how everything had gone wrong since they'd split up. Maybe Tom Archer *was* her lucky charm.

She suddenly sat bolt upright and rubbed the tears from her face. This was no way to think, she told herself. She jumped to her feet and switched on the room sound system to drown out the noise of the party upstairs, then strode into the bathroom and splashed water onto her face, looking at herself in the mirror with a determined look. It was time to move forwards, not back.

'What's that scent you're wearing tonight?' asked

Jonathon, sniffing the hollow of Venetia's neck in a half-hearted fashion. She flinched slightly away from him. It was the same perfume as she always used but, having sprayed it on liberally to mask any trace of Jack Kidman or the hotel room, she had drawn attention to it.

'Chanel Number Five. Same as ever,' she smiled at him, not quite catching his eye. 'You don't usually notice.'

But Jonathon's attention had already been distracted away from her.

'I have to say she's done quite well,' he said, scanning the room critically.

'Who?'

'Cate. When she mentioned she was trying to raise money for a magazine, I didn't think she had a cat in hell's chance. I wouldn't put a penny of my cash into it, of course. It'll almost certainly go tits up by Christmas, but you have to commend her on this evening.'

'Well, it's a bloody good turnout if you ask me,' replied Venetia defensively. 'Oh look. There's Diego. Let's go and say hello.'

Diego de Bono, Venetia's head of women's-wear design was standing on the terrace in a pair of black sunglasses, even though the light was steadily darkening over the London skyline. Venetia looked at his whippet-thin frame and jet-black crop of hair and thought he looked like some French heroin addict.

'Actually, I think I'll go and get some drinks in,' said Jonathon, steering himself away from the direction in which she was pulling them.

'Don't be silly. You're a partner in the business. Come and say hello to the man who's going to make the company more money.'

Venetia felt the resistance in his arm and pulled back, annoyed by yet another sign of casual disregard for her life,

338

her day and her business. She shot him a furious glance and pulled on his arm again.

She greeted Diego with an embrace and kissed him on both cheeks.

'Diego. What a surprise. I didn't know you were coming.'

'I met a friend for dinner who insisted on taking me to a magazine party. I didn't know it was your sister's.'

'We get around,' laughed Venetia. 'Diego. You've met my husband, haven't you?'

The two men's eyes locked. 'Yes, I think so,' smiled Diego at Jonathon. Venetia caught his gaze wandering around the room.

'Anyway, good opportunity to work a room,' Diego added with a languid smile. '*The Times* and *Guardian* fashion editors are both here, so I'm going to go and spread the word of Venetia Balcon.'

He nodded and left them while Venetia rounded on Jonathon.

'You're so bloody rude. I know designers aren't quite your cup of tea, but there's no need to look so patently bored.'

'I just hate shop-talk,' replied Jonathon. 'Even if it is my shop.' Venetia sighed and shook his hand away as he tried to take her by the arm.

'I don't know why we bother . . .'

'Darling, I'm sorry. Let me get you a champagne.'

She felt his behaviour do an about-turn as the curve of his mouth softened and he stroked her forearm with his finger-tips. His old trick. Testing her, baiting her, infuriating her and then reeling her in at the last moment with a burst of controlled charm.

Relenting, she felt her body soften against him. 'I just wish you'd make more of an effort with my friends, my colleagues.'

He slid his arm around the back of her neck and pulled

her into him, planting a dry kiss on her forehead. 'Sorry, darling, I've been a bit distracted. Work is hard. The Geneva office . . . but that's no excuse.' He pulled his hand up against her face and trailed his fingers down her cheek. 'Why don't we blow the party, check into a suite and not come out until the morning.'

The gesture took her by complete surprise. She recoiled inside, but tried not to stiffen in his grip. Not so long ago she would have given anything for Jonathon to inject some passion, spontaneity into their life, but now it all seemed too little too late. And she was certain that she could not face two hotel suites in the space of one day.

'I think I have a headache coming on. I haven't been feeling too well all day.'

Jonathon stared down at her with his piercing blue eyes and steered her away to the exit. Trying hard to rub out all thoughts of Jack Kidman, she looked up at him – her husband – and allowed him to take her hand.

'A headache?' said Jonathon with relish. 'In that case, why don't we say our goodbyes and go home?'

Cate retreated to the tiny third bedroom of the penthouse and tried to call Serena's mobile. The party was buzzing with journalists, with a mob of paparazzi outside. Serena's presence at the party would be great publicity for the magazine, but she had to admit that it was probably not a good idea for her to come after all. There was no answer. Where *was* she? Cate left her a message, when she heard the door of the room slide open and she turned to see David Goldman standing there. He looked razor sharp in a tailored iron-grey suit and a stark white shirt that showcased his tan.

'Sorry,' she laughed nervously, 'I just came in here to take a couple of minutes' time out. I'll get back to the rampant socializing in a moment.'

340

'Well, if you want to be alone, you really should shut the door,' said David wolfishly, clicking the latch shut behind him. 'Mind if I join you?'

'Shouldn't you be out there being all man about town?' smiled Cate, accepting a flute of pink champagne from him. David shrugged. 'The investors seem to be looking after themselves and Nick is off with Rebecca.' Cate felt her heart sink momentarily.

'So, the only other person I know here is you,' he said, perching himself on the edge of the huge mahogany bed.

Her five-inch heels were killing her, so Cate shrugged and sat down next to David. He immediately moved up against her, the sleeve of his jacket lingering against her bare arm. She felt a rush of giddiness; she wasn't quite sure whether it was down to the success of the party, the champagne or David's proximity.

'You really have done such a fantastic job. I've just been telling everyone what an impressive woman you are.' He paused. 'One of the most impressive women I've ever met in my life.'

Cate felt nerves jangle around her body. She had expected him to pounce as soon as he had locked the bedroom door, and suddenly she found herself thinking that that wasn't such an unwelcome prospect after all.

'Oh, I'm sure you make a habit of meeting impressive women,' said Cate playfully, draining the last of her champagne and placing the flute on the carpet.

'Are you making fun of me?' smiled David, finally moving one hand to rest on Cate's knee.

Cate's head was starting to spin now, and she did not move away as he pushed a thick strand of hair off her shoulder, even though she could feel his clichéd seduction manipulating her senses.

'How about a celebratory kiss?' he whispered. His lips

came down on hers. Although a warning bell shrieked on in some distant part of her brain, she found herself responding.

David threaded his hand through her hair, gently pushing her back on the bed. Part of her wanted to resist; the other part just wanted him to kiss her more deeply. They fell back on the fluffy cream duvet, David's fingers lowering themselves down her neck to touch one of her nipples through the thin fluid fabric of the dress. She gasped and cupped his face with both hands pulling him into a deeper and deeper kiss.

'What are we doing?' she said, finally pulling herself up for air.

His hand slipped up the cream folds of her dress, and crept up to the top of her thigh. 'Finally having some fun.'

'At last!' laughed Nick, throwing an arm around Tom Archer's shoulders. Tom smiled back. He felt grateful to be with his old friend, enjoying the London social scene once more. It had been a long time since he had ventured into the city for a night out and he wanted to make the most of it. So, he hadn't enjoyed waiting downstairs in the Fenchurch Suite, especially when someone in the next room had started playing music at enormous volume. But when Nick had called to say that it looked as if Serena wasn't coming, he felt ready to join the fun, even if a small part of him had been looking forward to seeing her. He grabbed a drink and downed it in one.

'So is it my turn to spend some time with the man of the moment?' teased Tom.

'I can't help it if suddenly everyone wants to talk to me,' said Nick with a broad smile. 'Anyway, it's taken thirty-five years for anyone to notice me, so let me enjoy my moment.'

'So where's Cate?' asked Tom.

'Dunno,' said Nick, looking around the packed room once again. 'I've hardly seen her in the last hour. It's about time we shared a celebratory drink.'

'Oh yes?' said Tom playfully.

Nick prodded him in the ribs. 'No, nothing like that.'

Tom wasn't entirely convinced as Nick's eyes continued to dart around the room looking for Cate.

'Actually, I thought I should mention something,' said Tom, taking his friend's elbow and steering him to a corner where they wouldn't be overheard. 'I was talking to Marion Doherty; you know, she owns ILF model agency. I'm not sure tonight's the right time to bring this up, but she told me something I think both you and Cate should hear.'

Nick looked at Tom, watching him shift uncomfortably and loosen his tie a little. 'The woman was totally coked off her head, so I'm not sure how much to believe, but . . .'

Nick took a smoked-salmon roulade off a passing tray and waved it at his friend. 'Go on,' he urged.

'Well, she obviously didn't know that we were friends or that I was an investor in *Sand*, so there was probably no reason for her to lie.' Tom paused and took a nervous sip of his second drink, finally looking Nick in the eye. 'Look, I think you should have a word with your girlfriend,' he said seriously.

Nick stuffed the canapé into his gaping mouth. 'What do you mean? What's happened?'

Tom looked away.

'Go on, what? Tell me!'

'According to Marion, you were supposed to be having Sybil Down – you know, the supermodel? – as your first cover. She's one of Marion's girls, right?'

'Yes, that's right, she pulled out at the last minute. That's why Rebecca had to draft in Rachel Barnaby. All worked out for the best, as it happened.'

Tom looked at his friend awkwardly. 'According to Marion, Rebecca phoned her, telling her that Sybil shouldn't be working for *Sand*. Said that you were a tinpot organization and that you were going to fold as quickly as you launched. Made some veiled threat that, if Sybil did the job, she wouldn't get an important job with one of her clients. Apparently now Marion's seen the first issue, she thinks *Sand* is wonderful, but for a few weeks there, you were *persona non grata* at ILF, mate.'

Nick looked at Tom incredulously. 'Why the hell would Rebecca do that?'

He let his eyes drift out towards the London skyline. It didn't make sense. Why would Rebecca sabotage the *Sand* cover, only to dig it out of a hole immediately afterwards? Cate had set up the Sybil Down shoot and had been distraught when it all fell through. Suddenly he remembered ignoring a remark from Cate, a remark he had thought uncharitable at the time, telling him she had felt awkward about Rebecca drafting in Rachel Barnaby and saving *Sand*'s first cover shoot.

'She just wants to undermine Cate,' said Nick quietly to Tom, as if he was thinking it for the first time.

'Cate and Rebecca not get on then?' said Tom, raising one eyebrow quizzically.

'Fucking Rebecca,' muttered Nick under his breath. He caught sight of her platinum-blonde hair in the corner of the room and left Tom's side, moving towards her.

'Rebecca.'

Rebecca spun round and flung her arm around Nick's neck, pressing her plunging neckline against his chest. She looked stunning, her curves poured into a backless metallic-coloured dress, cut to mid-thigh. Her breath smelt of whisky, her eyes were wide from cocaine. The longer he looked at her the less he could see a beautiful woman and the more he realized she had an ugly soul. Had Rebecca always been this way or had it taken him this long to wise up to it? He was an idiot.

'Fabulous party,' she breathed into his neck. 'Although I took two goody-bags and there isn't anything decent in any of them.'

He pushed her away forcefully. 'I know what you said to Marion Doherty.'

'About what, darling?' she giggled, dragging him onto the terrace.

'Advising her that Sybil Down shouldn't do our cover.' He stopped to look at her contemptuously. 'How fucking dare you?'

Rebecca threaded her hands behind his neck and tried to pull him close to her. 'Who's been telling porky-pies? I haven't done anything of the sort,' she slurred, brushing her lips around the curve of his neck.

'Someone I trust,' Nick replied impassively, shaking her arms away from him. 'Someone I trust more than you.'

'Nick, I haven't said anything,' she replied, pouting.

'Really?' he said sarcastically.

Knowing she'd been caught out, she stepped back away from him and rested her hands on her slim hips. 'It all worked out for the best though, didn't it?' she hissed defensively. 'When you leave things to me rather than Cate Balcon, things get done. *Properly*.'

'Leave Cate out of this,' snapped Nick. 'Anyway, she had everything under control. You might have made things right, Rebecca, but you created the fucking problem in the first place.'

'Listen to you,' she sneered, tossing her hair back. 'You're pathetic. Always defending her. Go on. Surprise me. Tell me you're sleeping with her. You are, aren't you?'

'No, I'm not.'

'You're fucking sleeping with her,' she screamed, pointing a long finger against his chest.

'This isn't about Cate, Rebecca. It's about you. Why did you do it? Are you really that insecure?

He looked at her, her face twisted with such venom it negated her beauty.

'No, don't insult me with an answer. I'm out of here,' he whispered.

'Go on,' she shouted, downing a shot of vodka as he walked off the terrace. 'Go and find your lapdog. And don't bother coming home tonight.'

His fists clenched in fury as he walked away from her, feeling ridiculous that he had wasted so much of his time with her; foolish that he'd allowed himself to be taken in by her shallow good looks and mistaken her love of good times for being simply good fun. Still, Rebecca was right about one thing. He wanted to find Cate.

Scanning the room once again, he caught movement as the small bedroom door opened slightly and Cate looked around nervously. He sighed with relief and found himself beginning to smile as she began to walk out of the room. He had to get to her, tell her about Rebecca, Marion, Sybil. But the crowd was thick now. He pushed past a group of guests, knocking a glass of champagne from someone's hand. He looked down, mumbling an apology, and when he looked up again, he froze. David Goldman was coming out of the room, inches behind Cate, his hand proprietorially around her waist. They were heading in the direction of the lift. They were leaving. Together. Nick inhaled sharply through his nostrils, grabbing a cocktail from a passing waiter. He downed it in one, and slammed the glass back onto the tray.

30

Compared to his Mustique villa, his New York duplex and his Hamptons beach house, Michael Sarkis's London base was a smaller, more discreet pied-à-terre tucked away in a quiet pocket of Mayfair. However, it was still a sumptuous place. A white stucco façade, a marble atrium, a sweep of stairs leading to a mezzanine floor.

Serena parked her Aston Martin outside and looked around for paparazzi, knowing full well that they'd love this story. *Serena arrives at Sarkis's hideaway to talk cash!* Well, for once they'd be right, she thought. Almost right. She still wasn't sure *what* she wanted from Michael, and had spent a sleepless night before today's meeting thinking about it. She'd asked for the meeting, having avoided his calls since Cannes. While a part of her still didn't want that bastard's money, if she was brutally honest, she needed it. The Jolie Cosmetics contract had gone, her agent wasn't exactly coming up with the goods work-wise (he would definitely have to go), and without Tom or Michael around to pick up the tab for her day-to-day things, she couldn't quite believe how expensive life was, having to fend for herself. It was outrageous! Well, she wasn't going to start penny-pinching now. A new house, nanny, Portland hospital bills, couture: it all cost. And she was going to make Michael pay.

'Serena.'

She walked into the reception room and put her clutch bag on the table.

Michael was sitting on a black leather and chrome sofa in a pair of jeans, Hermès belt and a red shirt open at the neck. Serena looked at him and felt an electric shiver fire up her spine. She'd spent hours going over in her mind what she'd first say to him, but hadn't factored in the helpless lust she felt as she saw him in his den of luxury. Just by walking into the room, her defences weakened, and she knew she was already on the back foot. She tried to gather her thoughts, but she couldn't take her eyes off him and an unbidden thought crept into her head, a thought she had been trying to quash the last week. Had she been too hasty in cutting him dead? Maybe she should just let him squirm for a few more days and then take him back. Take all *this* back, she thought, looking at the expensive furnishings in the apartment.

For two individuals who defined confidence, the tension between them was so strong you could almost see it. Michael's enormous presence seemed to surround her and she immediately regretted agreeing to meet him on his turf. Thank God she had chosen to wear skintight McQueen.

'Can I get you a drink?' he asked, walking over to a small bar in the corner of the room. 'I'm having a Bloody Mary. Do you want a Virgin?'

She raised an eyebrow then shook her head, watching him pour tomato juice into a glass. He relaxed back into the sofa and fixed her with his gaze.

'I wish I'd found out from you about the baby rather than the papers,' he said.

Serena crossed her legs, smoothing her long tanned legs with her fingers. 'You didn't give me the chance.'

They stared at each other in silence and Serena felt her nipples swell as his coal-black eyes penetrated hers. She remembered the last time they were in this room. After Mustique. Naked on the thick carpet. Michael sliding on top of her, grabbing her hair and thrusting into her. Exploding passion. Togetherness.

With each passing second, Serena felt her anger ebb away, to be replaced by another potent emotion. Longing. She wondered if he was thinking the same, then fought to stay angry, controlled, in charge of her conflicting emotions as Michael continued to watch her.

'Michael, I just wanted to say . . .'

Sarkis lifted one finger. 'Just a moment. We're waiting for one more, then we can begin.'

'Begin what?' asked Serena, bemused.

A buzzer sounded and Michael pressed the intercom beside him. In walked a short, squat man in a dark suit carrying a leather attaché case.

'Who's this?' asked Serena, suddenly feeling edgy.

'This is Jim Berger, my attorney, who you'll be dealing with after today.'

'What the hell is this?' spluttered Serena. 'Michael! Tell me what's going on?'

'It's very simple. I want a paternity test,' replied Michael flatly.

'What!' screamed Serena. 'You humiliate me with those hookers and now you ask for a *paternity* test?'

He looked at her coolly, relaxed on his sofa, a smirk on his mouth, every inch the ruthless businessman. 'If it is my child we can talk an allowance and you can thrash that out through Jim. But if it isn't? Well, of course, I know why you're here, Serena, and let me assure you, you won't be seeing a penny.'

31

It was one of the hottest June weeks on record. The grass had reached its apex of green and each blade had begun to wilt lazily in the heat. The trees surrounding the grounds looked wild, lush and almost tropical, and the lake in the middle of the grounds was beginning to dry up leaving a pale brown rim, as if dirty bathwater had just swirled away.

Oswald sat in the shade on the terrace at Huntsford, having just taken some light lunch. Curls of Parma ham, chunks of lime-coloured avocado, and rocket drizzled with his favourite balsamic vinegar, which he had specially imported from a tiny village outside Modena. He washed it down with a large gin and tonic that had become a little warm in the balmy air. Feeling suddenly tired, he glanced at his watch, deciding to wrap up his lunch meeting as quickly as he could to go and sleep off the draining heat of the day.

'So, Mr Loftus,' he said to the man sitting on the other side of the table. 'If you can leave the samples of your work with me, I can read them and maybe we can talk again early next week. You must appreciate, however, that I am talking to other writers as well.'

David Loftus, a brooding man in his early forties, reached into his bag and slipped a small pile of books and magazines in front of Oswald, which he studiously ignored.

'I'll give you my card as well, so call me if you need to know anything else.' The man peered earnestly at Oswald. 'I've been waiting twenty years to assist with memoirs like yours.'

Oswald smiled thinly. Despite David's fawning performance over lunch, he had already made up his mind he was going to use Loftus to ghost-write his memoirs. He came highly recommended by his agent, his credentials were decent: Oxbridge, several historical biographies under his belt, a couple of well-received crime novels under a pseudonym. More importantly, he lived locally, plus he was quick – and Oswald needed to strike while the iron was hot.

Oswald had had lukewarm interest from publishers in the past about his memoirs, but, after the recent Serena revelations, there had been a frenzy of interest in the man behind the UK's most glamorous siblings. His publisher wanted the book completed as quickly as possible, and while Oswald considered himself an eloquent writer, more than capable of penning it himself (not to mention the fact that he'd been looking forward to the opportunity of reclaiming the limelight from his daughters), writing a book was hard work. He needed a mug like Loftus who'd take a small cut of the advance and no royalties in return for doing the bulk of the work.

'I'll be in touch,' said Oswald, looking at David's business card and waving him off.

'I look forward to it,' replied Loftus. 'This could be good for both of us.'

As Loftus left, the French doors to the terrace opened and

in bustled Zoë Cartwright. Oswald had hired the young woman to be the production coordinator for the Huntsford musical event and she seemed in a dreadful hurry, clutching a pile of brown files to her chest like a mother suckling an infant. Oswald groaned. He had initially got her on board a couple of months ago to make his life easier: he was willing to admit that he hadn't fully appreciated the workload involved in planning an event on the scale he envisaged. Zoë had an excellent track record, having planned two huge events in Richmond Park the previous summer, and in the early days she had been indispensable. She had just got on with it and let Oswald occupy his time with other, more important things: polo, wooing Maria Dante, taking the cars for a spin.

But now, as the day drew closer, with the Musical Evening only four days away on Saturday, Zoë was like an albatross around his neck. She had moved operations from her flat in Chelsea to the Blue Room at Huntsford, arguing that it was time- and cost-effective to be based close to the site. While Oswald had seen the sense of it, Zoë was now pestering him on an hourly basis, demanding lengthy daily debriefs and annoying him constantly for decisions on the minutiae of the event. She wasn't even a pleasure to have around. A young, mousy Sloane, Oswald found her girl-guide owlishness infuriating. It wasn't even as if she was attractive. She reminded him of the friends Cate used to bring home from school: pasty-faced virgins with personalities to match. Not like Serena's friends, he thought, suddenly becoming excited at the memory: a parade of foxy sixteen-year-olds with their too-short skirts and rebellious low-cut tops. Oswald smirked as he drained the last of his gin and tonic.

Zoë took a seat, preparing herself for a fight. For her part, she had long had cause to regret the day she had agreed to organize the Huntsford Musical Evening. Yes, she was ambitious, yes it was a terrific coup for her fledgling events company, but she hadn't been treated like this since school. Lord Oswald Balcon was a mean, self-important bully who had been frightful as an employer. She had been waiting over two hours for him to run through the latest costings and spreadsheets, only to be told by Collins that Oswald intended to have a sleep after luncheon. Sleep! Zoë could only dream about it. For the last six weeks, she'd been working eighteen-hour days to make the Musical Evening a success, while Oswald's penny-pinching and aversion to publicity threatened to undermine all her hard work. She'd met his type before: desperate for social glory but too lazy and arrogant actually to make it happen.

'Your lordship,' she said with some trepidation, 'I hope you don't mind the intrusion, but I think it's vital that we have a meeting. The event is in four days' time and I have various concerns we need to discuss.'

'Very well,' said Oswald, wiping the corners of his mouth with a linen napkin and looking at the girl disapprovingly. 'Let's make this quick.'

Silently she opened her files and began to spread out various charts and projections on top of the wrought-iron table, while Oswald beckoned Collins to remove the remnants of lunch.

'When's the circus rolling in then?' said Oswald. 'I thought I'd have been disturbed by the cavalcade of equipment by now. Aren't they leaving it a little late to erect the stage?'

Zoë cleared her throat and shook her head. 'No, you'll remember that we discussed this. We are charged per day for all that equipment and you were adamant that it should come as late as possible to avoid any extra charges. It is coming tomorrow, but I'm assured it shouldn't take longer than a day to erect, weather permitting, of course.'

She looked at Oswald over her glasses and drew a deep breath, knowing he wasn't going to like the next item on her agenda. 'I'm not particularly worried about the stage,' she began carefully, 'what I am concerned about is that Johnny Benjamin, the guy doing our finances for the event, has just emailed me a projected profit-and-loss spread-sheet. Unless ticket sales dramatically improve,' she hesitated, 'it looks as if the event could make a substantial loss.'

The corner of Oswald's lip curled up into a snarl. 'We're in this to make money, not lose it.' His voice was low, controlled and forbidding. It made Zoë more nervous than if he had laid into her with a torrent of abuse.

Zoë pushed her glasses further up the bridge of her nose, trying to compose herself. 'With all due respect, your lord-ship, I ran every single expense past you.'

Zoë ran a finger down the spreadsheet, wincing at the figures. She knew Oswald was going to make her feel as if it was her who had let the evening go careering out of control, but it was Oswald's approach to event management that was threatening its success. While he was prepared to cut corners on necessities, such as the stage, he wanted the best of all the trimmings to give the illusion of grandeur. If Glyndebourne had two on-site restaurants, then, reasoned Oswald, so should Huntsford. Zoë had managed a compro-mise, making one food outlet a hog-roast, which she had thought would be fun and cost-effective, yet Oswald had insisted that the main restaurant should be housed in a top-of-the-range marquee that had set the event back a hundred thousand on its own, not to mention getting Mark Tennant, the executive chef of San Paulo, in to oversee all the cater-ing. Zoë had tried to point out that Glyndebourne was a slightly different proposition: a long-established, dazzling fixture in the social calendar which attracted the highest level of corporate sponsorship, and thus was able to support the staging of full production operas such as *Figaro* or *Madame Butterfly*. She'd always seen the Huntsford Musical Evening as a much more casual event, along the lines of the summer evenings at Kenwood House in north London, where an orchestra and various artists would do short sets to entertain the picnicking crowd. She didn't see the need for black tie, full restaurant facilities, and state-of-the-art Portaloos, especially when he wanted to skimp on staffing and marketing.

Oswald let his gaze sink to the bottom of the spreadsheet and began to splutter. 'Now that figure can't be right!' he shouted.

'I'm afraid it is,' said Zoë confidently. 'And obviously we have committed to most of it by now.'

Oswald could hardly believe his ears. Was this Sloaney pipsqueak patronizing him? He snatched up the spreadsheet, absorbing the figures with a great deal more attention than at any time before.

'I have always maintained that the staffing levels for this thing have bordered on the ridiculous,' he said coldly, reeling off the various salary costs. 'Stage manager, lighting engineer, box-office manager, head of catering! I mean, the list is bloody endless!'

'We are running on a skeleton staff for this size of event,' replied Zoë patiently. 'Without any of these people, the event just wouldn't function properly. You always wanted the Huntsford Musical Evening to have size and prestige. It's not a local am-dram production.'

Oswald took a moment to take stock at Zoë's words, still staring at the ominous figures on the spreadsheet. Begrudgingly he admitted that she was right. Not that he was going to let her see that. Oswald had dispensed with Venetia's involvement months ago because she had argued that the Huntsford Musical Evening should be on a much smaller scale. But Oswald's vanity wouldn't allow that. He had seen the way the Christie family had nurtured Glyndebourne from a small outdoor event held in their family grounds in the forties, into a huge international brand enjoyed by millions. He wanted a piece of that action and he wasn't prepared to wait sixty years for it.

How hard could it be to organize a rival to the big opera festivals? he had reasoned to himself. It had been easy raising a substantial loan from the bank to cover upfront costs, and his social circle had embraced the idea enthusiastically. Now clouds of worry were beginning to bank up in his mind. He had already been a little concerned that the roster of artists Maria had mobilized were a little – how could he put it? – a little *patchy*. Yes, there were some good international names on the bill, but none of the *real* greats: no one of the stature of Pavarotti, Dame Kiri. Then there was the thorny issue of Maria's considerable fee. She had argued that the event was pulling her away from a big-money job in Dubai. But that small point paled into insignificance when he mulled over the thought of having a financial disaster on his hands. The loan was huge, the interest high; this whole thing could ruin him.

'There is a solution,' said Zoë slowly, taking a sip of the tea that Collins had brought over.

'Continue,' said Oswald coolly.

'Ticket sales are – shall we say – a little slow.'

'Ridiculous,' spat Oswald, staring at the wrought iron of the table. 'A fabulous event like this should have people jamming the phones desperate to get returns.'

'I did impress upon you several weeks ago, your lordship, that we should allocate more resources to the marketing and publicity side of the event,' said Zoë.

'Nonsense!' he barked. 'This evening is a talking point with everyone I know!'

Zoë knew she had to tread carefully. 'Possibly in your circle of friends, yes. But with the Great British Public it doesn't quite have the profile of a Glyndebourne.'

This was exactly where it had all gone wrong, she thought to herself miserably. She remembered their conversation all those weeks ago when Oswald had dismissed her pleas to hire a PR agency as 'vulgar'. He had also vetoed the idea of them hiring a ticket agency to handle the box office – Oswald had been vehemently against paying an agency ten per cent of the ticket proceeds. Instead, ticket sales were being dealt with by a student in the Blue Room manning a single telephone.

The sun had drifted around the side of Huntsford so that it threw long rays of heat onto the terrace, making Oswald feel even more uncomfortable. 'So what's the big idea, missy?'

'We need to sell another two thousand tickets to minimize losses. If more people know about it, the crowds will come and we can rely on ticket sales on the day. However, to reach those people, we have to make a big publicity splash.'

Oswald looked at his young employee in a new light. 'And how do you propose we create this "splash"?' he asked sceptically.

'Your daughter,' said Zoë. 'Serena. She hasn't made a single public appearance since the tabloid revelations three weeks ago.'

Oswald shifted in his chair. He would rather not think about his youngest daughter's disgraceful behaviour at this moment in time. While Serena could rarely do anything wrong in Oswald's eyes, he had taken a very dim view of her pregnancy by Michael Sarkis. It wouldn't have been so bad if she had still been in a relationship with the American

357

– he might be a tacky colonial, but Oswald could appreciate his immense wealth. But the last thing the Balcon family needed was a bastard child tarnishing their reputation. However, with the thought of incurring debts over the Huntsford Musical Evening uppermost in his mind, he was prepared to hear Zoë's idea.

'Nobody is expecting Serena to attend on Saturday,' Zoë said, picking up the pace of her words. 'After all, there was that story in the paper about you two feuding over her pregnancy.' Oswald bristled. He had yet to get to the bottom of how the bloody tabloids had got wind of his and Serena's argument only ten days earlier.

'If you could persuade Serena to perhaps compere the evening, or at least introduce Maria Dante, that would generate oodles of pre-publicity.'

Oswald felt his anger cool before he started to raise objections. 'Yes, but how will a few random stories in those grubby rags sell tickets to the calibre of guests that will come to Huntsford?'

'You'd be surprised,' replied Zoë, raising one eyebrow above the tortoiseshell rims of her glasses. 'We just need some media hype. I've worked in marketing, I guarantee you we'll be at full capacity if we can give the public a first glimpse of Serena. Perhaps we could even arrange for her to do a little sympathetic interview with the *Telegraph* on Friday. You know she hasn't breathed a word to the press since her recent troubles.'

Zoë sensed she had struck a chord.

'When needs must, I suppose,' said Oswald tartly, looking away from Zoë, his eyes lingering on the lake glittering silver in front of him. He had to admit it was a good idea. He had no idea how Serena would respond to the suggestion, though. She was her father's daughter and she would probably still be hostile towards him, volatile at the very least. Well aware that they could both manipulate each other, he decided it was worth the risk, especially as it was either that or face financial ruin.

He dismissed Zoë Cartwright to her spreadsheets and reached for the phone.

32

A stocky man in a pair of dirty jeans stopped Serena's driver at the gates of Huntsford by slapping a meaty hand on the windscreen of the Mercedes. The driver calmly leaned out of his window and politely enquired what the problem was.

'Gotta wristband?' asked the gorilla, waving a clipboard.

Serena pressed a button and allowed her electric window to purr down. 'This is my *home*,' she said sternly, too tired to flash the man her movie-star smile. Immediately recognizing Serena, the security guard gruffly apologized and let the car proceed on its way.

'How ridiculous,' she hissed, looking back at the bothersome man over her shoulder. As she turned back, her mouth dropped open at the transformation of Huntsford before her. Even half a mile away from the main house, she gasped at the size of the operation. On the horizon she could make out an enormous, dome-shaped stage held up by a web of scaffolding. The driveway was lined with iron railings, topless men in jeans were erecting signs pointing to toilets, car park and restaurant, while at the far side of the lake was a parade of vans, lorries, generators and trailers. At least sixty people milled around, lugging cables, striding across the lawns with clipboards or carrying huge tureens into the catering tents. It was vast – impressive, she thought, a smile curling up on her full lips.

She had driven a hard bargain with her father when he had called her two days earlier to persuade her to attend. Her instincts were completely against it. She still felt raw and betrayed, especially after her meeting with Michael, and certainly didn't feel ready to venture out into the public eye quite yet. After news of her pregnancy had broken, some of the knives had really come out. The suggestion that she was yesterday's news, or lacked the exotic, world-wide appeal in a new, more cosmopolitan age had particularly hurt. If she was going to thrust herself back into the limelight willingly, she reasoned, then it was going to have to be worth her while. So she had demanded a cut of the action. She had told her father that she wanted seven per cent of the box-office takings, which Oswald had ruth-lessly negotiated down to three per cent. Not ideal, she thought to herself, but well worth the drive into the country-side. It was sure to impact positively on her profile, too; the dutiful daughter helping out at her father's musical event: even the detractors would love that one.

'Something of a transformation, wouldn't you say?' said Oswald to his daughter as she pulled up to the double doors, helping her from the car and giving her a cautious embrace.

'Yes, it's quite a change,' smiled Serena, pulling her microshorts further down her legs to look a little more respectable. 'It looks just like Glastonbury.'

Oswald recoiled in horror. 'That dreadful hippy festival? I don't think so,' he replied curtly.

Serena swung her Mulberry bag off her arm and saun-tered inside. 'Only joking, Daddy. I can see it's going to be fabulous.' She let a silence pass between them, waiting to

361

see if he would bring up their argument of a few weeks earlier. But Oswald seemed content to let that incident – and the bigger subject of her pregnancy – pass without comment.

'Maria is arriving at the house at five,' he informed her casually. 'I assume you'll be joining us for dinner? Perhaps you could make a little more effort to get to know her better.'

Yes, right, she thought darkly. She hadn't spoken to the woman since her leaving party back in April, and had zero intention of offering an olive branch now. She had hoped that the pushy Italian would have been a passing fancy for her father, just like all the other women in his life over the past fifteen years: the divorcées, flight attendants, ageing models and middle-aged society women had all lasted about as long as his shampoo. But it disturbed her that this liaison seemed to be growing a little more serious. They had been seen out and about together at all sorts of social events over the past three months; Richard Kay's *Mail* column had even begun to refer to Dante as Oswald's partner. It irked her, but she couldn't put her finger on why.

Hot and sticky, she decided to go up to her room to change, quickly selecting a tiny Sass & Bide denim miniskirt, a vest top and a glittery pair of Gina flip-flops. Pregnancy had yet to make an iota of difference to her slender figure, she thought happily, admiring her reflection in the mirror by the window. Of all the sisters, Serena had by far the best-appointed room in the house, with two huge bay windows overlooking the lake, giving a view that was more breath-taking than if she had been overlooking the New York Cityscape or the Thames. It was special, natural, stunning.

She felt a sense of belonging as she opened the windows and let the balmy breeze kiss her face. It was the family seat, so she would always feel a special bond with the place, but today she felt even more intrinsically tied to its stonework, grounds and atmosphere. An ultrasound scan the previous day had discovered that her unborn foetus was a boy. She was going to have to investigate the title of Huntsford as a matter of priority, hoping there weren't any bothersome laws barring children of an unmarried couple from inheriting the title. Surely not: this was the twenty-first century. She smiled as she thought about her child as the eleventh baron of Huntsford. That would give her a powerful grip over the estate that lay in front of her. There was so much she could do with it: not like Daddy, who had let vanity and greed cloud his judgement. With Serena in charge, Huntsford could become one of the great English estates to rival Longleat. She had every faith that her career would resurrect itself, but she was realistic enough to know that fame was transient and that she would not be able to rely on her looks for ever. Plus she had already consulted a lawyer about getting a huge child-maintenance payment off that bastard Sarkis. She was going to take him for every penny she could.

Feeling energized by all these thoughts of money, Serena decided to go and explore the circus outside. Making some attempt at a disguise, she put on a large pair of Chanel sunglasses and fixed her long hair back with a navy-and-white Breton headscarf. As she now had a vested interest in the success of the event, she didn't want all the male workers now beavering about to have any distractions. As she walked out into the sunshine, Serena had to admit that the young events manager, that poor, plain-looking girl Zoë Cartwright, had done an excellent job. The Lady Penelope Carvery, the main restaurant festooned with cream layered voile and named after Oswald's beloved 1922 Rolls-Royce, was as spectacular as any marquee she had been in, while Zoë had told her that huge tropical flower arrangements were due to arrive the following morning to give the place the feeling of a botanical hothouse.

As she walked around the impressive site, Serena ran over the short speech she had prepared to deliver the next afternoon to open the event. She was going to enjoy that, she thought. What she was going to wear, however, presented more of a challenge. Her travel trunk was packed full of delicious gowns that Serena knew would make an impact – but which one should she choose? For the first time ever, she found herself favouring something simple. An Armani gown in molten brown with a stunning topaz clasp at the bottom of the deep V of the back. Far less revealing than the sheer, diaphanous black gown she had also brought along, and less showy than the white Grecian Versace number in which she knew she looked fabulous. But it was stunning and appropriate, nevertheless, and it was a gown that said she was a successful, powerful woman who wanted to be taken seriously.

'Preparing for tomorrow?' asked a voice behind her. Serena turned to find herself eyeballing a very attractive man in a pair of pale jeans and a white short-sleeved shirt unbuttoned to reveal a laminated identity card dangling over a ripple of taut, bronzed six-pack. His hair was sexily dishevelled, his deep blue eyes flashed at her, wanting to play.

'Do I know you?' asked Serena haughtily, caught off guard by the effect that this man was having on her.

'Miles Roberts,' he replied, tucking a hardback book under his arm and extending a hand to shake.

'And what do you do, Miles?' asked Serena, unable to stop the teasing tone.

'I'm the artist liaison manager.'

Serena pulled off her glasses and smiled broadly at him. 'And what does that mean?' she asked.

'Oh, I'd have thought a woman in your line of work would know all about it,' said Miles with a small smile.

'So you'll have the pleasure of tending to the every whim of Maria Dante tomorrow?'

'Something like that,' said Miles.

'I hope you're getting paid handsomely,' she smiled tartly.

'Mind if I walk with you?' replied Miles, dropping into step with her. 'I only started a couple of days ago and I haven't quite got used to the grounds. They're huge, aren't they?'

Serena smiled. 'You get used to it,' she laughed, feeling her powers of flirtation come back to her. After Michael Sarkis, Serena had sworn she was giving up men for at least the summer, but great-looking men were always worth toying with. He was only some festival worker, after all, but he was model-grade handsome, she thought, sneaking a look at his profile. She could allow herself a few minutes of fun, she thought, pulling her sunglasses back onto her face. Besides, it was better that she walked around with a staff member. She was well aware that anybody could be hiding a camera to take snaps to sell to the tabloids, and the last thing she wanted to do was spoil this philanthropic gesture of appearing at Huntsford by being pictured tripping over cables or arguing with security.

'So where are you walking to?' asked Miles hopefully.

'Walk with me to the stage,' she said, her hand brushing his ever so lightly, 'I need to go and check it out and look at the view.'

'Why?' asked Miles. 'Are you really hosting the evening? I did hear a rumour.'

'Not entirely hosting, *introducing*,' she said with a coquettish smile. 'Subtle difference. I intend to be in bed by nine o'clock. Opera festivals really aren't my scene.'

'Oh yes, I suppose you must be getting tired, what with

the . . .' Miles had a sudden stricken look on his face, realizing he'd made a faux pas. He couldn't help staring at Serena's firm bronzed midriff poking out from under a little bit of cotton vest top.

'So you've been pregnant, then?' She laughed, 'Yes, I'm in that stage commonly known as "knackered all the time", darling.'

'Well I don't fancy your chances of getting a good night's sleep tomorrow night,' he smiled. 'Not unless your bedroom is a soundproofed nuclear bunker.'

'Oh, so you know about the nuclear bunker?' laughed Serena.

Miles looked confused. 'My father built a nuclear bunker in the eighties. Out behind the rose garden, of all places. Can you believe the paranoia, not to mention the waste of money? But you're right, I can't imagine it will be the best night's sleep I ever had. Maybe I should go back to London . . .' She trailed off.

'Oh, but I thought you were staying here for a while,' said Miles, disappointment in his voice. He stopped, once again embarrassed at knowing details about Serena's life. 'Well, that's what the crew have all been saying anyway,' he shrugged. 'It's caused quite a bit of excitement.'

'Oh yes?' she flirted. 'How much?'

'A *great* deal.'

'That's good,' she grinned. 'I was hoping to make a splash.'

'Oh you will,' said Miles. 'You will.'

The last thing Maria wanted to be doing at that precise moment was preparing for the tinpot festival at Huntsford. Oswald had been in a terrible mood ever since her arrival three hours earlier, solidly grumbling and moaning about the soaring costs of the evening. There had been a dramatic surge in ticket enquiries since the papers had reported that

Serena was going to make a public appearance, but she doubted it would be enough to balance Oswald's gluttonous outlay on the event. And the torrential rain forecast for the following day would surely keep the crowds away on the day. Not that she wanted him to lose money; what use was he to her then? But mostly she was furious that all the attention had shifted away from herself to Serena.

When Oswald had told her that his youngest daughter was going to be involved in the Musical Evening a few days earlier, Maria had been incandescent. Maria had been sure that the talentless little tramp was out of the picture for the time being. Her scandal-filled lifestyle had made Oswald purple with rage at the reflected shame it brought on the family name, yet now he was prepared not only to let Serena lead the event and become the star attraction, but also to *pay* her for the privilege. Maria almost admired Serena's gall for her ruthless bartering with her father, were it not for the clear indication of the influence she had over him. Well, that was going to stop. As long as Serena could manipulate her father, she controlled Huntsford, and Maria was not going to stand for that. She wanted to snuff out Serena's influence once and for all.

She crunched her heels into the grass as she stalked angrily towards the trailer she would be using tomorrow. The sun had sunk behind a line of forest-green trees, so the evening was lit like a partial eclipse, the birds still singing in the eerie greyness. Maria glanced at her watch: 7.40 p.m. She cursed again. Dinner was due to be served at the house at eight and it would take fifteen minutes to walk back there. Her trailer was a standard issue twenty-five-foot Portakabin with a long seat and table at one end and a row of chairs and mirrors at the other. In between was stuffed with rails of clothes, hairpieces and vases of flowers. She knew better than to turn on the huge mirrors that were circled with

Hollywood-style bulbs, and instead flipped on a little overhead light that gave the cabin a soft glow. There was a man sitting at the long table smoking a cigarette. 'Oh, you're here,' snapped Maria, looking at her watch again. 'On time, well done.'

'We'd better keep this quick,' said the man. 'There're about fifty people still milling around the stage. We're not going to stop until midnight.' He pushed an envelope over the table like a poker player folding his cards. Maria picked it up and began counting the crisp fifty-pound notes inside with her long fingertips. The feel of large amounts of money still never failed to give her a sexual thrill, and the poor girl from Puglia in her wanted to feel every last note. She felt the cool gaze of the man at the table and stopped herself, stashing the envelope in her black velvet clutch bag.

'OK, listen,' she said. 'We'll be starting dinner in fifteen minutes. Oswald never allows a dinner to be finished in less than two hours. He likes to luxuriate over every course and insists his guests do too. There are only three staff in the whole house, so it will be easy for you to avoid them.' She tossed a plain brown envelope onto the table with a thud. 'Here is the key to the back door. Her room is straight up the main stairway, the third door along the large corridor at the front of the house. I'm sure you'll find everything you need in there.'

'You're sure?' asked the man.

'The girl takes cocaine. I saw it with my own eyes at her party in March. She'll almost certainly have some on her. It wouldn't surprise me if she wasn't drinking spirits and taking pills too. She's such an irresponsible little bitch.' In Maria's Italian accent the word came out 'beach'. The man smiled in the darkness. He could feel himself becoming turned on as he imagined the glorious shirt-tearing catfight

368

that would be had between these gorgeous, dominant women.

'Well, we'd better find what we're looking for,' he said finally, dropping his cigarette into a plastic cup, where it fizzled out with a hiss in the dregs. 'The newspaper is paying a lot of money for this.'

'Oh, you'll get what you want,' said Maria Dante, nodding so vigorously that a strand of hair fell across her dark brown eyes. 'Serena Balcon never fails to disappoint.'

Oswald Balcon sat at the head of the Louis XV table in the Red Drawing Room with Maria and Serena flanked on either side of him like two concubines, each gently picking at their asparagus spears.

'Oswald Balcon,' chided Maria lightly, looking up at him with glossy chocolate eyes, 'I think this is the smallest dinner I have ever attended at Huntsford. What happened to the other girls? I thought it was going to be a family affair tonight.'

Oswald placed down his silver knife and fork pointedly, looking more than a little disgruntled. 'Neither Cate and Camilla nor Venetia and Jonathon will be attending until tomorrow,' he said, pursing his lips with disapproval. 'As you are well aware, I can never rely on family support for anything.'

The comment echoed around the room, which was indeed empty, being large enough to seat twenty. The situation was not helped by the frosty atmosphere between the two women, who were pointedly not looking at each other except when passing condiments. A rumble of thunder could be heard far away, like a growl coming from the core of the earth. The sound brought an anxious look across Oswald's face; he immediately tried to disguise it.

Collins came through the door pushing a silver trolley

laden with cloches. He placed Serena's dinner in front of her, pulling off the silver dome with a flourish. A seared tuna steak was accompanied by a plateful of potatoes and vegetables.

'What's this?' snapped Serena, looking up at Collins, throwing her napkin down angrily. 'Look at it! It's practically raw!'

'But that's how you always like your steaks, Miss Serena,' said Collins, looking a little flushed in the face.

'That was *before* I became pregnant,' sighed Serena, not hiding her irritation.

'Serena! Stop making such a fuss!' said Oswald, banging his hand on the table. 'It's been such a hot day, I asked Collins to serve something light.'

'Well, obviously you've never been pregnant either,' said Serena, flashing him an icy stare and pushing her chair out from under the table. She was tired and bad-tempered. Exhausted in fact. She felt as if she would melt into the floor at any moment. All she could think of was her room and getting some sleep. She certainly couldn't stand another two hours being bored to death by her father and Maria cooing at each other.

'No, neither of you will understand how I am feeling,' said Serena, standing up now and placing her napkin beside her plate, 'but I can tell you, it's pretty awful.' She fixed her gaze on her father. 'If I'm going to be in any fit state to do a decent job tomorrow, I need to get some sleep. Now, if you'll excuse me.'

Knowing the wisdom of having Serena as her fresh dazzling self the next day, Oswald nodded and gave the familiar wave of his hand to let her know she had been dismissed.

Maria glanced at the grandfather clock behind her: 8.45 p.m. She stood up suddenly.

'Serena, please,' said Maria, giving her the most sincere smile she could, 'I would feel so offended if you went to bed now.' She opened her arms like a Madonna. 'Please stay. We need to get to know each other so much more now. Collins can cook you a nice, well-done steak, can't you Collins? Then you can stay and relax at the table.'

'As I said,' smiled Serena, trying her best to look gracious, 'I really don't think you understand how tired a woman in her third month of pregnancy can get. Daddy, maybe we can meet in the morning so we can go over my introductory speech?'

By now, Serena had crossed the room's Oriental carpet and was moving to the lounge. Maria sprang up from her seat to go after her, almost running through the doorway to catch up with Serena. 'Serena,' she said quietly, 'your father told me earlier how important this dinner is to him – and how we get along.'

Serena span on her heel. 'He'll get over it,' she spat. 'And in future, I suggest that you make a little more effort with the lady of the house.'

Maria stood and anxiously watched Serena ascend the enormous flight of stairs, as she sulkily stepped up them one by one. 'Stupid Italian cow,' said Serena under her breath, already pulling off her shoes to walk up the thick red corridor carpet barefoot.

On the first floor of the house there was a spooky quiet. Most of the lights were turned off. She had seen Collins go around, methodically switching off lamps earlier, no doubt in a desperate attempt to economize. Saving a few pennies on electricity wasn't exactly going to refill the Huntsford coffers, she thought with irritation. Passing a window that overlooked the lake, she flinched as the lights were switched on over the domed stage, drowning the grounds in crisp, sterile light. Thank goodness she had drawn the curtains in her room, she thought. She didn't want her bed being lit up like a football stadium.

371

She pushed down the gilt handle of her bedroom door and stepped inside. Immediately she knew that something was wrong. A presence. Instinctively she clutched the Jimmy Choo shoe with its four-inch heel in her hand like an axe. With her other hand she felt around on the wall for the light switch. There was definitely someone in the room: she could sense it. Finally she found the switch and flipped it on. Her first reaction was to scream, but the sound in her voice transformed into a shout as she immediately recognized the intruder. 'MILES! What the *hell* are you . . . ?'

He was carrying a small torch in one hand while the other was rifling through her overnight bag.

'You won't find anything in there,' she said slowly, almost riveted to the spot with disbelief.

'Serena, I, look . . .'

Realizing he'd been caught out, he darted for the door. Serena reacted too slowly to stop him, waving the heel of the Jimmy Choo above her head in frustration.

The spell broken, she screamed but, sensing its piercing blast had too far to travel before anyone would hear, she ran out into the corridor, shouting as loudly as she could. Between screams she could hear the sound of frantic footsteps taking the stairs of the grand staircase in bounds, followed quickly afterwards by the roar of a motorcycle engine revving up quickly outside the front door. Oswald stormed into the hallway as Serena looked down from above.

'What the Dickens is going on?' he yelled up at her. 'You decided to leave your dinner, now at least leave us to enjoy ours in peace!'

'An intruder! There was an intruder in the house!' shouted Serena.

Oswald ran to the door to see the red taillight of the

motorbike disappear as Serena sank slowly to the floor. Putting her head against the banister, she began sobbing.

Camilla walked into the Royal Suite at Claridge's to find Serena upside down on the floor, her body bent into an inverted V.

'What on earth are you doing?' she asked, cocking her head to look at her sister.

'The downward dog, what does it look like?' sighed Serena, uncoiling herself. 'My life-coach is in Capri, my shrink has gone AWOL and my agent is fucking useless. Yoga is about the only thing keeping me sane at the minute.'

'Is there anything I can get you?' asked Camilla helpfully, sitting down on the sofa.

'How about a revolver?' said Serena, pursing her lips.

Serena had gone missing for twenty-four hours after the intruder had been found at Huntsford. Disappeared. Missing from the Musical Evening without a word or message to anyone. It was only when Camilla received a text from Serena the morning after the event that the mystery of her whereabouts was solved. Claridge's Royal Suite was one of Serena's favourite bolt holes when the world was closing in: deliciously chintzy, totally private, it even contained Gilbert and Sullivan's old piano. Not that she could play.

'Do you want to tell me what happened?' asked Camilla, helping herself to a grape from the fruit bowl.

The strain was unmistakable in Serena's face. Camilla was shocked: her sister never looked anything less than gorgeous, confident and totally in control.

'I put up with a lot of things you know,' she said fiercely. 'Paparazzi calling me bitch in the street. Reporters going through my bins. Having my phones tapped. But to find someone in my house. My room.'

She rubbed her temples and her voice softened dramatically.

'I came here because I wanted to hide. It was awful, Cammy. It really was.'

Bending her knees, she sank down onto the carpet of Claridge's luxurious suite.

Camilla paused, used to her sister's dramatics, before noticing that real tears were rolling down Serena's cheeks. She came over to throw her arm around her shoulder.

'It's OK. Come on, this stress isn't good for the baby,' she whispered. 'You're safe. The intruder didn't hurt you or take anything.'

'It's not OK though, is it?' replied Serena, blotting the corner of her eye with her fingertip. 'I heard the evening was a bit of a disaster. How bad was it?'

'Pretty bad,' said Camilla with a grimace. In fact, 'pretty bad' was an understatement. The previous night had been an unmitigated disaster, which had no doubt cost her father thousands.

'The main thing was the weather,' said Camilla. 'It was so foul yesterday that it kept a lot of the crowds away. Then the PA shorted for about twenty minutes and, to be honest, it was an absolute mud bath. People were still queuing to get out at four in the morning.'

'What about the introduction? Who opened it?' she asked, feeling guilty that it should have been her role.

'Who do you think? Daddy. He droned on for so long he was booed. They'd have started throwing bottles if they hadn't all been holding umbrellas.'

'Oh great,' said Serena, rolling her eyes. 'I suppose that's my fault as well. Blame it on the bad guy – everyone else does,' said Serena. She fell back into the ruby-red sofa and drew her knees up to her chin.

'How do you mean?' asked Camilla.

'Look at the papers. Haven't you seen them this morning?'

Camilla picked up a stack of Sunday papers that were sitting on top of the suite's grand piano. *The Sunday Reporter* had a splash: *Serena deserts family for lover*.

'Go on, read it,' sighed Serena. 'According to them, *I'm* the reason the evening was a disaster. Apparently I was supposed to be the star attraction and left Daddy in the lurch.'

Camilla traced the newspaper text with her fingertip. *'Pregnant Serena flouted her family duty when she skipped the event for a booze-fuelled rendezvous with her lover.'* Camilla looked up. 'What lover?'

'Precisely, but I can take that,' replied Serena, her mouth setting in a thin determined line.

'What I don't like is the stuff about my family. I don't like the implication that I don't care.' Her voice trailed off until it was small and fragile.

Camilla looked at her sister, slumped like a glorious film-noir heroine on the sofa. Framed by the glorious backdrop of the Royal Suite, she couldn't help but think how misery suited Serena. But while she managed to carry off her gloom with style, her obvious upset was completely out of character. Serena's hide tended to be bulletproof, but Camilla suspected that the run of recent events was beginning to grind her down. Tom, Michael, the tabloid frenzy, the pregnancy, the intruder. How much could one person take in just a few months; even Serena?

'There's another thing,' said Serena, her face darkening. She stretched over to a suitcase that was lying on the floor, ribbons of clothes and shoes tumbling out of it, and pulled out a seal-able bag the size of a matchbox. She placed it on the table.

Camilla touched it with her fingertips, feeling the white powder inside the bag. 'Shit, Sin. Cocaine?' she said, looking up in surprise.

Her sister nodded slowly.

'Yours?' offered Camilla gingerly, knowing her sister had dabbled in the past.

'No! Not mine!' snapped Serena, grabbing back the bag. 'I'm pregnant, remember?'

'So whose is it?'

'I don't bloody know. I found it in my overnight bag,' said Serena, her voice regaining its fire. 'And if that intruder who'd been rooting through my stuff had been there a second longer, he'd have found it.'

'So what are you saying?' asked Camilla, sensing more of her sister's theatrics. 'That he put it there?'

Serena shook her head vigorously. 'No, I don't think *he* planted it there. I think Maria did; in fact I feel sure of it. That intruder, Miles, I'm certain he was a reporter. Maria tipped him off because she wanted him to find the drugs.'

Camilla couldn't suppress an incredulous laugh, wondering whether it *was* Serena's cocaine and it had made her paranoid.

'Come on, Sin . . .'

'I know how it sounds, but Miles wasn't on Zoë Cartwright's list of employees for the event: I asked her. And the way he called himself the artist liaison manager, the way he knew exactly where Maria's trailer was and knew all about her movements that day . . .'

'Supposing you're right, why on earth would Maria do it?' asked Camilla, still not convinced.

'Because she's a total bitch, Cam. She wants to discredit me. God, this is all so stressful.' She pulled a mirror out of her bag and started inspecting her face, fingers frantically moving over her smooth skin. 'I look bloody awful. Do you think I should get a botox shot?'

Camilla looked at her wryly. 'So you won't take coke but you'll have botox?'

'It's not funny,' said Serena, flopping onto a cushion. 'I tell you, Maria Dante is bad news for this family.'

'Well then, you know what?' replied Camilla. 'I think she and Daddy really deserve each other.'

33

Venetia's summer flew by. Work, Jack, work – with a two-week interlude at the Hotel Cala Di Volpe in Sardinia with Camilla, who had insisted Venetia needed the break. Venetia had spent the entire fortnight miserable, missing Jack so terribly she had forced herself to see a shrink on her return. Her discussion with eminent pyschotherapist Dr Margaret MacKenzie in her Marylebone practice had thrown up all sorts of thorny personal issues she would rather have pushed under the carpet, including her teenage abortion and subsequent sexual relationships. But it hadn't been the quick fix Venetia had wanted. Dr MacKenzie explained that it was not her job to give Venetia any answers, only to guide her towards finding those answers herself.

'How would you describe your sex life with your husband?' Dr MacKenzie had asked Venetia from the comfort of her B&B Italia sofa.

'Laughable,' Venetia had answered, before telling her that over the past eighteen months she had constantly faked orgasms with Jonathon in the name of carnal duty.

'And why do you think that is?' the doctor had replied.

'I got pregnant at seventeen. My father forced me to have

it terminated, and for a long time I thought sex was dirty, guilty, wrong.'

'Is that how you feel now?'

Venetia squirmed when she thought of her guilt over Jack Kidman. 'Guilty, yes.'

'Guilty about the act of sex?' asked Dr MacKenzie after Venetia had told her about the affair.

'Guilty about how I feel,' said Venetia.

And that was at the heart of it, she thought as she walked away from the practice. It wasn't just raw passion any more with Jack Kidman; it was a deeper, more spiritual connection than that. Infidelity was supposed to be something illicit, dangerous and destructive, wasn't it? It wasn't supposed to feel like this: something secure, protected and meaningful. Venetia didn't need Margaret MacKenzie's expensive services to tell her that her relationship with Jack was heading towards something more serious.

Ten days later Venetia lay in her lover's bed, a shaft of morning light pouring through the window over their naked bodies.

'What are you thinking about?' asked Jack in a gentle, amused voice, his fingers removing a piece of stray hair from her face.

Venetia shifted her body against his. 'I was just thinking I should get to work. It's the show in ten days and I've so much to do.'

'You should have stayed here last night. I thought Jonathon was away on business.'

'I know,' said Venetia, 'But . . .'

She still did not feel that brave yet. What if Jonathon had phoned the house late at night? What would her housekeeper Christina have thought coming down to make breakfast to find nobody in the house? What if, what if, what if? It was all simply too risky.

'Can I see you tonight?' teased Jack, pulling her closer with his arm. 'You're starving me of attention.'

Thinking about Jonathon's return from Geneva that afternoon, she suddenly found herself becoming very cross, angered by the injustice of the whole situation.

'You're so bloody selfish,' she snapped, twisting her long body towards him.

'Selfish?' asked Jack, surprised.

'It's OK for you. You're *retired*, you don't have a job, you don't live with anybody, you're separated from your wife. You can come and go as you please. I wish it was like that for me too, but it's not. Things are different in my world. I can't afford to be so bloody selfish.'

She swung her legs out of the bed and pulled on a silk kimono, stalking into the en-suite bathroom to splash her face with water. Jack let her irritation wash over him and sat back in the bed to watch her, furiously flossing her teeth in front of the mirror. She padded across Jack's huge Westbourne Grove apartment and into the high-tech stainless steel kitchen, opening the fridge to pour a glass of ice-cold milk into a crystal tumbler. Leaning her elbows on the marble top of the breakfast bar, she let the cool liquid slide down her throat. She heard his footsteps behind her and felt a pair of strong arms wrap themselves around her waist. For one moment, she didn't look back, enjoying the sensation of his fingers touching her skin through the silk of the kimono. She could tell he was naked, too, feeling the shape of his penis push in against her back.

'So leave him,' whispered Jack.

Venetia spun around, stunned. 'I can't leave Jonathon,' she said flatly.

'Why not? You've told me you don't like the way he makes you feel; you don't have any kids. Do you even love him?'

She angrily pushed the hair back off her face and put the glass down on the marble, unfathomably finding herself wanting to defend her marriage. 'Love hasn't got anything to do with it. Jonathon is my husband.'

'Love has got everything to do with it, Venetia.' He looked at her, shaking his head, uncharacteristically losing his temper. 'You've serious fucking issues.'

'Meaning?'

'Meaning that you make excuses for people, stay loyal to people, no matter how badly they treat you, because that's how you expect to be treated – badly. You will never be happy until you learn to say no, learn to walk away or learn to just be a little more selfish.'

His words were so raw and truthful and brutal, that she physically ached. 'If you'd had my father, you'd understand,' she said softly, too pained to respond with any anger.

Jack came and held her chin between his fingers. 'You deserve to get whatever you want, Venetia. Don't let your father make you think you're not worth it. Because you are.'

She nodded.

'I love you,' he said quietly.

Venetia went to take a breath, but nothing seemed to happen. Her throat felt clamped in a vice with a sense of rising panic. He loved her. It seemed about two minutes ago, that night under the stars in Seville when they'd first kissed. Now he was suggesting breaking up the fabric of her life as she knew it.

She pressed her fingers against his back, pulling him as close as she could. She knew what she wanted. She wanted Jack Kidman. But she didn't know if she was strong enough to have him.

It was half past twelve by the time Venetia got back to her

shop. Brix Sanderson was waiting for her on the roof terrace, sipping a cup of Earl Grey tea – no milk, but a thick wedge of lemon. Brix was London's top fashion PR and one of the capital's most fabulous dykes. She had a long mane of auburn curls, an eighties nose-job and the urgent manner of someone who always got things done.

'Nice spread,' said Brix with a wicked smile as Venetia strode onto the terrace.

'Sorry?' said Venetia.

'This!' said Brix, motioning towards the table. 'You've got such sodding good taste!'

Even a cup of tea at Venetia Balcon's shop was an event. The wrought-iron table was covered with an ebony-coloured linen tablecloth. The china was sparkling white, Art Deco in design. Sachets of tea sat colour-coded in another circular china bowl, while napkins, starched white and stiff, were folded like Origami figures on the table.

'Thanks for coming to the store,' said Venetia, pulling up a chair. 'And sorry I had to cancel lunch, I'm too busy to even think about going anywhere other than here or home,' she said, feeling slightly guilty that she'd had enough time to spend the entire morning in bed with her lover.

She knew that Brix would have been equally busy in the throes of Fashion Week. Her agency, Blue Monday, did the PR for many fashion labels not dealt with in-house, plus numerous other premium brands such as a large champagne house and a luxury make of car. Venetia was delighted to have secured Brix's services for the launch of the Venetia Balcon women's-wear range. Hovering around the age of fifty, Brix had three decades' experience of the fashion world under her belt. It also did no harm that she lived with Ginger Foxton, the country's most influential fashion writer.

Venetia poured herself a cup of tea from the pot, letting the tobacco-coloured leaves whirl through a silver strainer.

'So what did you think of New York?' she asked Brix, knowing that she had arrived back in London from Manhattan that morning where one of her clients was showing at New York Fashion Week.

'Really gorgeous,' she gushed, throwing a clump of dark red curls over one shoulder. 'I usually get much more excited about Fall collections, but this year – well, put it this way, you're right on the money.'

'What do you mean?' asked Venetia, puzzled.

'Well, from what I've seen over there, next summer is going to be all about little tea dresses, crisp tailoring and lovely sorbet colours.'

Venetia thought nervously about the collection she was preparing to show on the following Wednesday in London. Tennis whites, sheer cashmere, butter-soft accessories, long pale palazzo pants and vintage-feel camisole tops.

'Oh, that sounds rather like where I'm coming from,' she said, her voice betraying her disappointment.

'Don't worry darling,' Brix laughed at Venetia's fashion naivety. 'It's cool to be thinking along the same lines as the other big names. You don't want to be channelling military if Marc Jacobs has decided it's going to be all about boho this year. It's good commercial sense that you're in the same ballpark as all the other big designers, although the Venetia Balcon range does have its own unique twist, which is great. Anyway,' said Brix excitedly, pulling off her Fendi leather jacket and flinging it over the back of the chair, 'guess who's coming to your show?'

'Who?'

'Only Miranda Seymour!' beamed Brix, putting her cup down with a rattle.

'No! Christ, that would be such a coup!'

Miranda was America's most influential glossy magazine editor. Feared and admired in equal measure, she had the power to make or break any designer. Certainly she had the clout to pull a struggling novice from obscurity and make them the next Donna Karan. Despite the fact that Miranda was English, she very rarely made an appearance in her native city for Fashion Week, choosing to go straight from the New York shows to Milan a week later. Her thinking was that London just wasn't a significant enough fashion capital for her to deign it with her presence.

'But why on earth is she coming to my show?' said Venetia, still in shock.

'I knew you'd be pleased,' laughed Brix, clearly delighted. 'She doesn't usually bother with London, but she's collecting some gong from some university or other. Her assistant called me and asked for a ticket for the Venetia Balcon show while she was in town. If you ask me, the woman is just obsessed with the whole English upper-class thing. I mean, you do tick all the right boxes, don'cha?' said Brix, her south London accent becoming deliberately more pronounced. 'You're an aristo, you're Serena Balcon's sister, and you live this glamorous life with the hedge-fund husband. No doubt she saw your house in American *Vogue*. Put on a good show, young lady, and mark my words, she will champion you.'

Brix pulled a large brown lizard-skin notebook from her Mulberry bag and began running through her notes with Venetia. 'As you know, your ten a.m. show slot is considered something of a graveyard,' she began.

Venetia was aware of this, but she'd had to pull every contact she had with the British Fashion Council just to show her debut collection in the first place. Such an unknown was lucky to be part of the shows at all.

'However, the response is just phenomenal,' said Brix. 'Every UK glossy magazine editor is coming. All of the key fashion writers, plus the usual celebrities that turn up to these things. I take it Serena is coming?'

Venetia nodded.

'*The Times* want to run an interview with you, the Saturday *Telegraph* magazine want to do Diego: that's if we can get him photographed this week.'

'I'll give him a ring now,' said Venetia, picking up her mobile.

Leila Barnes, Venetia's assistant, walked onto the terrace with a rather unsettled look on her face. 'Venetia, can I talk to you one second?' she asked. Venetia immediately picked up on the anxiety in her voice and excused herself from Brix, moving through the French doors that led back into the building.

'The police are here to see you.'

Venetia's first thought was for her Range Rover, which she had parked on a meter outside the shop. Surely that hadn't expired yet? She walked into her office where two police officers – one male, one female – were sitting down, looking very uncomfortable, on the upright leather chairs.

'Mrs von Bismarck?' asked the female officer as she stood up.

'Yes, that's me,' said Venetia as calmly as she could. 'Please, sit down. Now what can I do for you?'

The policewoman was around thirty, with an intelligent face and pale brown hair tidied neatly behind her head. She introduced herself as Sergeant Gillian Finch, cleared her throat, and waited as Venetia sat down behind her desk.

'I'm afraid it's bad news,' she said softly, cutting straight to the chase. 'It seems there has been an accident – a fire at Diego de Bono's apartment in North London.'

Venetia felt her blood run cold. 'He's all right, isn't he?' she barked, the words almost jumping out of her throat. 'I mean, when was this? Where is he? What's happened?'

The two officers looked at each other briefly before Sergeant Finch continued. 'I'm afraid Mr de Bono was killed

385

in the fire . . .' She paused hesitantly as the shock registered on Venetia's face, her hand flying to her mouth.

'But that's not exactly why we're here, Mrs von Bismarck.'

'I don't understand,' she replied, her voice quavering with anxiety.

'We have reason to believe that your husband was also in the house at the time of the fire.'

Finch stopped, allowing the full gravity of the situation to sink in. 'We have found a body we believe to be that of your husband, and we would like you to come with us to identify the body.'

She was hysterical now. 'Jonathon is dead? That's what you're telling me? At Diego's house?' said Venetia, her fingers clutching at her breast. 'It's ridiculous. My husband hardly knows Diego. What would he be doing at his flat? What makes you say such things?'

'The body is partially burned,' said the other policeman, not meeting her gaze, 'but there was identification in the clothing. Credit cards, and so on. They all have your husband's name on them.'

'No, it's not right, it can't be.' She started to shake her head slowly.

'I think you had better come with us, madam,' said Sergeant Finch. 'So we can get this cleared up as soon as possible. I think it's best if we drive you,' she added kindly, putting a hand on Venetia's shaking shoulder.

Venetia waved a hand in front of her face. 'Yes, yes, um, I'll come, yes, I just need to . . . I need to tell my colleague.'

She took slow deliberate steps towards the terrace, her head down, pressing her fingertips against her temples.

'What's wrong?' said Brix, standing up immediately. Venetia took a deep breath, trying to think rationally. She put one hand on the black tablecloth, trying to steady herself as she looked up at Brix, her face pale.

386

'There's been a fire,' she stuttered, her eyes dazed. 'Diego has been killed.'

She could see Brix's mouth open in horror, like a movie in slow motion.

'Jesus, oh my God, oh my God,' said Brix after a few moments.

'And maybe Jonathon too,' said Venetia, her voice a cracked whisper. 'They say Jonathon was in his flat too.' She looked up at Brix, trying to make sense of it all. 'But I don't see how that can be . . . They hardly know each other . . .'

As she looked up at Brix, she saw a flicker of something dart across her face. Knowledge . . . embarrassment? Brix would not meet Venetia's gaze. Despite her shock, she did not miss it.

'Brix, what is it?'

Brix sat back down and stared intently at her tea cup, dipping a silver spoon into the liquid and watching it go round and round in spirals.

'Brix, tell me! You know something, I can see it!' said Venetia, her voice stern.

'No, I don't know . . .' said Brix quietly.

'Tell me! Is it about Diego and Jonathon?'

Brix looked up, her eyes meeting Venetia's. 'Jonathon and Diego did know each other. They were . . . friends. I've seen them around town together over the summer.'

Brix had paused slightly on the word 'together' and Venetia hadn't missed it. An ugly thought rolled to the front of her mind that she tried to bat away. Together? Did she mean *together*?

She knew in her heart that Jonathan had had affairs in the time that she had known him. Mysterious receipts for florists and hotels, female callers putting down the phone as soon as she answered, the rumours he'd been seen at one of those high-class sex parties where the rich and decadent explored the darker side of desire. But she had become an expert at ignoring anything in Jonathon's life that she did not see with her own eyes. She knew that Brix knew more, but at that moment she didn't want to know.

'I'm going with the police,' she said softly.

Brix nodded. 'Do you want me to do anything? Do you want me to come with you?'

Venetia shook her head and turned to follow Sergeant Finch. Her Range Rover was outside, but she could not drive, her hands shaking like a blender on low speed. She sat in the back seat of the police car – isolated, vulnerable, looking straight ahead, seeing nothing. On autopilot, she punched Camilla's number into her mobile phone and waited for it to ring. Cool, calm Camilla. She needed her.

'Hello, Camilla Balcon.'

'It's me.'

'Venetia? Are you OK?'

'Not really, I . . . I . . .' The voice down the line was soft and cracked. 'Listen, Camilla, where are you?'

'Working from home.'

'Cam, I need your help.'

Her voice was beginning to wobble now, the tears beginning to come.

'Van, where are you? What's going on?'

There was silence. 'Look, tell me where you are,' said Camilla urgently. 'I'm coming to get you.'

Venetia had never been to a mortuary before. Her mother's death had been the only death she had experienced, and she'd been ten years old then. The nearest she had come to the body was seeing the walnut casket at the funeral from the front row of the church, festooned with lilies and roses the size of saucers. But she had seen enough crime dramas on Sunday-night television to know what to expect. A sterile, fluorescent-lit building, like a long, deserted school.

Venetia and Sergeant Finch were greeted by a mortician who led them silently into a cold, plain room. Her shoulders clenched with tension as the mortician led her to a slim table, on which a long shape was covered in a sheet.

'It was the smoke inhalation that was fatal,' said Sergeant Finch, trying to sound reassuring. 'The face largely escaped burns.'

Her clammy palms gripped the leather straps of her handbag as Gillian Finch pulled back the sheet covering the top of the body. Instinctively Venetia flinched and looked away. Cursing herself, she forced herself to look at the face of the body. The eyes were shut, leaving two dark crescents beneath the forehead, but she would recognize the shape of Jonathon's face anywhere: the high cheekbones, the continental nose, the stern lip. She resisted the urge to choke.

'It's him,' she said, turning to look at the policewoman. The mortician slid the sheet back over his face, silently closing a chapter in Venetia's life.

Camilla was sitting on the grey plastic chair in the reception area. As she saw Venetia, she stood up and walked slowly towards her, stilettos tapping on the bare floor.

'I am so sorry, Van,' said Camilla, hugging her. 'Come on, I'm taking you to my house.'

Camilla looked at Sergeant Finch. 'Is there anything else?'

The policewoman looked at Venetia sympathetically. 'No, I have Mrs von Bismarck's number and your address. I will have to come and speak to you later today or tomorrow to ask some more questions.'

Venetia looked at her. 'What else is there? What more do you know? Please tell me,' she croaked.

'Early word from the fire investigation officer is that it

was probably started by a cigarette down the back of the sofa. There were several wine bottles near where the fire had started. I think the two men had been drinking.'

'Where were they found?'

Sergeant Finch avoided her gaze.

'Where were they found?' Venetia repeated, her voice trembling. She knew the answer. She predicted the words that were to come out of the policewoman's lips before she had time to say them.

'In bed,' said Gillian Finch softly. 'I'm sorry.'

Venetia clasped her sister's arm as they walked across the car park towards Camilla's Audi. It was drizzling, the lunchtime sunshine having given way to iron-grey clouds. They sat in the front seat of the car. The only sound was the tap-tapping of rain on the windscreen as the inside of the car steamed up. Venetia stared down at her lap, examining a piece of thread on the seam of her trousers, trying to remember the last thing Jonathon had said to her. She couldn't remember. She laughed. It came out cruelly, like a bully's laugh.

'We were both having affairs, did you know that, Camilla?' said Venetia. 'Both with other men, as it turns out.'

Camilla remained silent.

'I know things weren't perfect between Jonathon and me, far from it. But what did I do that was so wrong? Why was he seeing Diego? A *man*?' She gulped for breath and her composure crumbled, her head slumping to her chest as she sobbed. 'What did I do?'

Camilla reached over and took her trembling hand. 'It's not your fault. It's not your fault,' she repeated quietly.

Venetia inhaled deeply and struggled to pull herself together, staring in front of her and trying to count the splats of rain falling on the glass. 'It doesn't matter now. I won't be seeing Jack Kidman again.'

Camilla knew exactly what her sister was trying to do. Punish herself for Jonathon, punish herself for trying to find affection outside a loveless marriage. 'Van, you don't have to . . .'

'I've got to cancel the show as well,' said Venetia coolly.

'Are you sure?' asked her sister. 'But you've worked so hard.'

'I have to,' said Venetia quietly, pulling at the loose thread until it came unravelled completely. 'I have to do it for Diego.'

Camilla looked at her, not understanding her loyalties. 'But he was seeing your husband.' She stopped herself.

Venetia laughed sadly. 'Doesn't make sense, does it? Nothing makes sense.'

The show did go on. Oswald insisted on it.

'Until Jonathon's estate has cleared, I still have forty-five per cent voting rights in this company,' he had told her, grinding down her best intentions until, ultimately, she was too weak to resist.

The timing of her debut collection couldn't have been worse: the day after her husband's funeral. Her world, once so calm, ordered and simple, was shifting beneath her feet like sand.

Venetia couldn't spend a second at rest or her head would become a hive of guilt, doubt and pain. It wasn't the grief that was unbearable, it was the betrayal. Had her husband really burnt to death? Was he really having an affair with another man – her own designer? Was it all her fault, some twisted retribution for her own infidelity with Jack? And Jack: she couldn't allow him to creep into her thoughts. Not now.

As the show approached, Venetia's legendary poise vanished. Her skin was sallow and dull, her hair untidy and her clothes creased. She was running on empty, and only the thought of bad reviews for the collection kept her going. Model castings, the fittings, all the frantic preparations for the debut collection were conducted in a fog of numbness and desperate energy. She couldn't let herself fail at this, not when she had made a mess of everything else.

In the event, the tent at London Fashion Week was packed. Diego's death was the best possible publicity for the show. The fashion rumour mill went into overdrive about how he died, and Venetia felt a fool. Brix Sanderson scotched much of the scandal, telling everyone that Jonathon and Diego had been together to discuss business. If the truth had got out, that the two men had been meeting for sex, Brix knew that Venetia would completely retreat from the world – and she was not going to let that happen to her friend.

At the start of the catwalk, Flower Productions' elaborate waterfall effect had been replaced by a huge black-and-white portrait of Diego. Venetia simply nodded when she had seen it, managing to swallow the bile she had felt rising in her throat. But, as the show's production manager had pointed out, they needed impact. And it worked. Half the people in the front row were crying as the models stalked the catwalk in the beautiful selection of clothes. The show got a standing ovation.

Backstage, Venetia couldn't move for the number of people piling towards her to offer their words of both condolence and congratulations. Miranda Seymour shuffled backstage in a fitted grey cashmere jacket with a huge silver fox fur collar and kissed her twice on the cheek. 'If you can continue that vision, you're ready for New York next season. Call me,' she added, and disappeared.

Front of house, Oswald held court on the front row, basking in the attention and clear delight of the fashion royalty, whom he didn't really understand but wanted to. Behind the scenes, hiding behind a huge rack of clothes, Venetia listened to the laughter, the applause and the sounds of delight. She'd never felt more desperate.

34

'To Fierce Temper!' said Philip Watchorn, raising yet another flute of 1975 Dom Pérignon. Sitting in the presidential suite of the Hôtel de Crillon, six other men, all flushed pink from the effects of all-day drinking, tipped their glasses towards him. Fierce Temper's trainer, Barry Broadbent, unaccustomed to such luxury, sat back and drained all the liquid in his glass in one large gulp. Reclining back on the silk chaise longue like some feudal lord, jockey Finbar O'Connor, looking too small to hold such copious amounts of alcohol, nodded contentedly at the scene while Philip and Nicholas Charlesworth chatted happily, congratulating each other on a splendid day. Only Oswald seemed more sober, surveying the scene from the doorway, stroking his glass thoughtfully as he reflected on the events of the weekend.

It had indeed been quite a day. He still couldn't believe that his horse had won the premier flat-racing prize in Europe. Not long ago he had been calling the Arab thoroughbred a donkey. Maybe he had been a little hard on Barry Broadbent after the fifth place at the Newbury Races back in April. Damn, that seemed so long ago! Six months later Fierce Temper had won the Prix de l'Arc de Triomphe at

Longchamp. That made three Group One wins in a row, two runners-up positions and almost a million pounds in prize money. What a season!

The thrill of seeing Fierce Temper's long neck pass the finishing post in first place today had been like the kick of a drug. The only black spot was the malevolent little presence of Declan O'Connor, Finbar's brother and 'agent', who had been tagging along all day. Evil-faced little pikey, he thought, watching him sit protectively on the chaise loungue next to Finbar, drinking all their champagne. He had hardly spoken all day, except to talk obliquely about 'bonuses' for Finbar. When Oswald had pointed out that BWC Holdings more than generously compensated their jockey, he had smiled his twisted smile. 'Just looking after my little brother,' he'd said.

Just looking after my little brother. It was the sly, loaded way he'd said it. And there was something very familiar about his voice. He'd heard it before somewhere. Oswald's brain made a slow connection: could it have been the voice that had threatened him on the phone on the day of the Two Thousand Guineas? Could that have been Declan? But why would that foul little man care about him? He shook off his suspicions as Nicholas Charlesworth tapped his glass to call the men to order on the other side of the room. 'What we need now, gentlemen,' he announced, 'is to get out of this hotel and enjoy Paris. Dinner is booked at the George V and then I know a marvellous little club in the sixth, which will stay open for us as long as we want. The car is right outside to take us, so get your coats, chaps!'

A strong sense of *déjà vu* coursed through Oswald's body. It was just like the sixties again. Here they were, all powerful, successful men with the prospect of more power and success just in front of them for the taking. Back then Oswald would have been the first one to join the group touring the clubs of Mayfair or Paris, but not tonight. He picked up his camel jacket, slipping his arm into the red silk lining. 'I'm afraid it's all been a little too exciting for me tonight, gentlemen. If you don't mind, I think I'm going to retire. It's been a long weekend.'

'What's got into you?' said Philip, clapping his friend on the shoulder in a chummy manner, 'Still, if you are going to be a killjoy, make sure you are up and ready in the morning. The car is coming for us at eight o'clock. Be ready, eh?'

Oswald offered a small smile to his friends, backed out of the door, and walked down the corridors until he reached his suite on the floor below. After several bad-tempered attempts to force his credit-card key into the door, Oswald finally managed to open it and strode in without turning on the light. His suite was small, but the views were spectacular across the Place de la Concorde. He felt surrounded by darkness; the blank shape of the unlit room behind him with the whole of night-time Paris in front of him, only peppered by saffron streetlights blurred in a damp autumnal Parisian drizzle.

Standing high above the cityscape he felt like the master of some black universe. A thin smile cracked his lips. He was still feeling high on the rush of winning and, although the alcohol had furred his instincts, the future suddenly seemed clear. They were sitting on a gold mine. That fool Watchorn could spout on about the 'sport of kings' all he liked – and yes, there had been a definite thrill in seeing Fierce Temper scoop one of racing's top prizes. But racing wasn't about the race any more; it was about the marketing. He'd learnt that from the Huntsford Musical Evening debacle and he wouldn't make the mistake again. The real profits these days lay in the making and marketing of prize stallions for stud. The great yards around the world had been doing it for years: champion horses, horses like Fierce Temper, could charge fifty, a hundred thousand pounds a time to sire a mare. They stood to earn stud fees that would run into millions, making the purses they had won this season look like pocket money.

The almost sexual thrill of expectation coursing through Oswald's body was delicious. He couldn't rely on his daughters to maintain the Balcon legacy in the appropriate manner; he knew it was going to be down to him and how shrewdly he played the game. He looked out greedily onto the city below. In the streetlights he could just make out Nicholas Charlesworth, Finbar and Declan disappearing into a Bentley for their frivolous night on the town. They all thought they were so clever, but of course it was Oswald who had all the big ideas around here. And he was having one now. An idea popped into his head that made his body twitch and made him feel sick with anticipation. Yes, it was good. This was going to work. And this was going to be his year.

35

Elmore Bryant's white Bentley weaved through the Oxfordshire countryside, along a labyrinth of thin, twisty-turny rural lanes barely wide enough for the big motor to pass through. It was a gorgeous afternoon for a wedding. Considering it was October, the weather had been much kinder than it ought to have been.

Elmore turned to Serena and squeezed her hand, which was resting on the leather seat alongside him. 'Can I just tell you again what a darling you are for stepping in as my gorgeous escort for today?' he smiled, pursing his lips up into a faux-kiss. 'I can't believe Horatio blew me out at the last minute. Serves me right for involving myself with fly-by-night Brazilians, I suppose.'

Serena smiled. 'Well he *is* awfully handsome,' she said. 'You have to make some concessions for that.'

'Anyway, we'll have more fun,' said Elmore, waggling the crisp white invitation in his hand. 'It's going to be a right old mix of people there, so it's going to be fabulous for people-watching.'

They were en route to witness the nuptials of Elmore's friend Melissa D to her banker boyfriend. Melissa D, the

Canadian MAW – model-actress-whatever – and resident of Notting Hill had become firm friends with Elmore Bryant, having met him two years earlier at the Water Meadows Clinic. She had been recovering from a cocaine addiction, leaked to the press as 'exhaustion', while Elmore was in there to try and kick a nasty Roederer Cristal habit. Melissa was fairly well known in the British party pages, but like many MAWs, she had very little real steady income of her own, and had decided to tread the well-worn path of pretty It-girls before her and marry well.

She had managed to bag Robert Charles Baker, Old Etonian and successful merchant banker, whom she had met at The Cow gastro-pub in Westbourne Grove twelve months earlier. Robert Charles Baker had led a very grey life up until the point he had met Melissa, and was more than happy to acquiesce to her desire for *Hello!* to cover the wedding. The couple had been even more delighted when Elmore had told them he was bringing Serena Balcon as his guest, which would substantially increase the celebrity quota of the wedding, and hopefully the money Melissa could demand from the magazine. Serena, on the other hand, had failed to share their enthusiasm when Elmore had first invited her, initially refusing to go on the grounds that celebrity magazine weddings were just tacky.

She hadn't taken that much persuading, however. All summer, with the exception of the catastrophe that had been the Huntsford Musical Evening, Serena had deliberately kept a low profile. Not only had she enjoyed retreating into her shell to lick her wounds, but her absence from the scene had had the welcome effect of making people more desperate for gossip, pictures and information about her life. But it was now October and, as the weeks had rolled on, media interest had waned. Even more alarmingly, a new batch of girls were being discussed in the press. She had instructed her publicist to turn down so many requests for cover interviews that the magazines had simply stopped calling.

In a strange, twisted way, Serena missed having her mobile phone clogged up with random callers from the tabloids and the long-lens snappers camping outside her home. Serena Balcon would never be forgotten, but there was just the slightest chill of worry blowing through her life right now. Yes, it had been her decision to take a little time out, but she was well aware how this game was played, and the last thing she wanted was her next appearance in the press to be a paparazzi shot of her all pregnant and big-breasted. She wanted to retreat and then emerge, butterfly-like, in January, once she had delivered the baby. But perhaps a little show-stopping publicity wouldn't hurt in the meantime.

Almost as if reading her thoughts, Elmore gave her a sly sideways glance and grinned. 'You know, Melissa is a beautiful girl, but I think she may be in danger of being upstaged by you this afternoon. You look utterly ravishing. Even if a tad naughty for wearing white.'

Serena looked down at her wonderful silk dress, so fine you could see a suggestion of her La Perla underwear underneath. Its neckline was deeply scooped, with tiny pearl buttons running all the way down the front, the bottom half of which Serena had left half undone to show a length of creamy leg. Her figure had filled out a little, the curve of her bump evident, so her form filled the dress like a delicious Greek urn, the fabric draping over it. Finishing the look with a pair of bronze high-heeled sandals with straps that wound all the way up her calves, and a thick gold bangle on her wrist, she looked like a ripe Grecian goddess.

'Anyway, I'm not wearing white, I'm wearing *blush*.'

'You're terrible,' smiled Elmore. And they both laughed.

* * *

The Chateau d'Or was one of the hottest destination restaurant/hotels in England, its marble mantelpiece straining under the weight of the many culinary awards it had scooped in the two years since its revamp. Once a grand old stately home modelled on one of the great Loire Valley chateaux, it had recently been transformed into a deluxe Michelin-starred restaurant. But the chateau's popularity was as much to do with the sexy, sumptuous suites that peppered the grounds. It was the number one venue for romantic weekenders from all over Europe, and the Melissa and Robert nuptials had taken over the whole place for the day. Lime trees flanked the long gravel drive, while the dove-grey stone chateau had four dreamy turrets pointing into the strong blue autumn sky. The ceremony itself was due to take place in the vast conservatory at the back of the building, which had been decked out with tropical flowers and melting ice sculptures shaped into the initials of the bride and groom.

It was not difficult to work out which side was the bride's and which was the groom's, one half being awash with Roberto Cavalli, Dolce & Gabanna leopardskin, plumed Philip Treacy hats and the exotic smell of bespoke scent; the other half traditionally British and sombre, packed with a collection of morning suits in various shades of grey, kilts and old school ties. The *Hello!* photographers sprang into action when Serena walked through the door, their motors whirring frantically as she expertly posed for the shots. Despite not being a real acquaintance, let alone a close relative, Serena was ushered to the second row where all eyes were upon her, greedily inspecting what she was wearing.

Desperate to have a good look around the room to see who else was there, but knowing she shouldn't appear too eager, Serena stared at her order of service until the music announced the entrance of the bride. From the corner of her eye, Serena examined Robert Charles Baker with a critical eye. A young, early thirties' face made older by a serious expression and a country solicitor's haircut, he had watery eyes and a weak chin. His rugby-player's physique had run to seed, thanks to too many hours behind a desk. He must have thought his luck was in with Melissa, she smiled to herself. It was a classic case of the W11 compromise, where coltish models with a bog-standard background and no real talent would give good genes to the plain, whey-faced upper-middle classes – men whose public-school-bred arrogance made them believe they deserved gorgeous girls rather than the cosy, Alice-banded Sloanes they were far more suited to. Finally all heads turned as the strains of Paul Weller's 'You Do Something To Me' filled the glass room and Melissa floated down the makeshift aisle.

'What's she wearing? What's she wearing?' hissed Elmore, straining to look. 'She told me she was going "boho bride".' Melissa's dress was loose and billowy; yards of snow-white organza falling from a high, Empire-line waistband, the sleeves voluminous and trumpet-shaped in the sheerest voile, like some medieval princess's robe. Her dark chestnut hair hung loose, parted in the centre and falling in long, Pre-Raphaelite waves down either side of her face, cascading onto her shoulders. Instead of a tiara, she was wearing a fine gold headband. 'All very Ali McGraw,' whispered Elmore, his head turned almost 180 degrees.

'Ali Baba more like,' giggled Serena, turning to look towards the front again. 'What on earth is that gold headband all about? Has she come as Flash Gordon?'

Satisfied that she was by far the most beautiful and well-dressed woman in the room, Serena settled back to enjoy the ceremony. Of course, it wasn't her idea of a dream wedding: she found the notion of getting married in what was essentially a hotel more than a little common. Despite having no religious convictions whatsoever, she still thought

402

that floating down a cathedral aisle with a train the length of an Olympic-sized swimming pool was the way to do it. But even Serena found it hard to remain cynical for very long. She'd tried to snort when the couple recited their home-made vows, but she had secretly felt quite touched when Robert and Melissa had kissed for the first time as man and wife and a warm roar of applause had rippled around the room.

As Robert and Melissa walked hand in hand up the aisle and the crowds filed out of the conservatory amid a swell of good-natured banter, Serena's hands unconsciously began to stroke the curve of her pregnant belly. Just for a second she felt the hollow of loneliness. Shaking her head, she grabbed Elmore's hand.

'Let's get out of here,' she whispered, aware that people were beginning to look at her. 'I haven't had a drink in about three months, but right now I could murder one.'

'Hello, sister-in-law! Well. Prospective sister-in-law.'

Serena, sitting at her table in the banqueting hall, turned to see David Goldman standing in front of her, holding a glass of champagne, wearing the expression of someone for whom sobriety was soon to be a distant memory. Smiling, she stood, matching him in height in her four-inch Grecian sandals.

'Sister in law?' she replied. 'I know I haven't seen Cate much recently, but is there something you want to tell me?'

David laughed. 'Merely a term of endearment,' he said, taking a long sip of pink Moët.

'Let me guess,' said Serena, allowing a passing waiter to half-fill her flute, 'friend of the groom?'

'Ouch!' winced David. 'Below the belt, Miss Balcon. I am not, you should know, a traditional member of the financial community.'

403

Taking a moment to look him up and down, Serena had to agree with him. His midnight-blue suit was sharp and tailored, the brightness of his white shirt set off his golden tan, his jet-black hair was fashionably tousled, and his eyes – she noticed for the first time – were a rather startling steel grey, like a stormy night sky. In fact David Goldman had enough glamour to belong to the bride's side of the room. Not that she was going to tell him that.

'So where's Cate?

Cate and David must have been together almost four months now, thought Serena, ever since the night of the *Sand* launch party. While she had only met David once or twice over the whole summer, she knew the couple didn't see much of each other. Cate seemed to be constantly working, David doing whatever he did in the City. Still, she was rather surprised not to see her sister with her new boyfriend at this wedding.

'Ah, you know what she's like,' sighed David, 'always doing something or other with that bloody magazine. This weekend she's in LA doing a cover shoot. Anyway,' he smiled slowly, 'as I'm dateless this evening, I would be delighted to spend it with another beautiful Balcon sister.' He gave a mock bow.

She smiled, admiring his chutzpah. Serena often found that men were intimidated by women like her.

'I hope you're not implying that I'm second best? I never play second fiddle.' Serena was conscious that her voice had a hint of flirtation in it.

'I don't doubt it,' replied David with a smirk. 'Now, can I tempt you with a dance?'

Despite herself, Serena was enjoying herself. Elmore had abandoned her, having disappeared to do a set on the piano, his gift to the happy couple. Thrown into the company of

404

David Goldman, she found she rather liked his style. He was happy to gossip about misguided wedding outfits and to deflect the attentions of drunken investment bankers keen to talk to Serena; he also laughed in all the right places when she spoke, and swirled her around the dance floor making her feel as light as a fairy instead of six months pregnant. He wasn't her type, of course. David Goldman wasn't a star like Tom Archer or a billionaire businessman like Michael Sarkis, but she was beginning to see what Cate saw in him. David had eyes that looked as if they were constantly thinking up mischief, and a charm that made flirting seem like an art form. She began to wonder what David Goldman saw in her sister. So Cate was sweet, clever and pretty in her own way, but Serena knew David's type: men that were turned on by beauty, glamour and women with a profile they could parade like a trophy. Men like that just weren't turned on by women like Cate.

The party was winding down. A handful of guests were now flailing around on the dance floor to cheesy seventies disco music, while across the room, empty wine glasses stood in herds on claret-stained linen. The bride, minus her headband and shoes, and groom, minus his jacket and tie, left waving and giggling for the Honeymoon Suite on the first floor of the chateau. Elmore had last been seen disappearing with the DJ's assistant, a young, swarthy man with a bottom as firm as an iceberg lettuce. In one corner, Melissa's bridesmaid, a singer in a fading girl band, was passionately snogging an accountant in a grey suit. Looking around, David picked up a bottle of Moët and, disappointed to find that it was empty, declared that the party was over.

'Had too much to drink anyway,' he said, rubbing his temples. 'So, where are you staying tonight, Miss Balcon? With Elmore? Or can I walk you somewhere?'

'I believe I'm in somewhere called the Dovecote,' said Serena. 'I'm not entirely sure where it is.'

'At the bottom of the herb garden, if I remember rightly. I'm not far from there,' said David, standing to pull Serena's chair back for her.

'Just as well,' replied Serena, 'I may need an arm to steady me. I haven't had a drink in ages and three glasses of champagne have pushed me right over my limit.' She felt wobbly in her heels, but when they stepped out into the night, the cold air on her face woke her up with a start. Hurricane lanterns hanging from the trees released a gentle glow like fireflies, so she could just make out the shapes of other couples crossing the lawns on their way back to their suites. Her heels were sinking into the grass. She bent down to unlace her sandals, hanging onto David's arm for support until she was barefoot on the wet lawn, which was strewn with autumn leaves and confetti. She didn't let go of him as they walked to the Dovecote and, when they arrived at the door, David didn't need to ask to come up to her suite. A duplex building, like a giant wooden beehive, they ascended a stone flight of steps to the first floor. A bluey-silver moonlight flooded through the windows, so that the enormous four-poster bed sccmed lit up by a spotlight.

'It's such a beautiful room, isn't it?' she said, her voice soft and nervous.

'Yes, beautiful,' said David, unable to tear his gaze away from her. Her dress had gone almost totally sheer in the strange lunar light, giving her an unearthly shimmering glow.

Only feet from her, David reached his hand out to touch her fingertips. 'What would you do now if I tried to kiss you?'

She paused for several seconds until David took a step closer towards her, touching her cheek with his fingers.

'I'd let you,' she faltered, drawing his head closer until

she could feel his warm breath on her neck. As his soft lips touched her skin, she felt a fire of longing. It was too long since she had felt someone's touch.

His fingers expertly moved up to the scoop of her neckline and began slowly, deliberately undoing the tiny pearl buttons one by one, until the fine fabric just slipped off her shoulders and onto the floor like a feather. He unclipped her coffee-coloured lace bra, his head swooping down to take a hard, brown nipple between his lips. Unable to stop herself, her fingers played with the buckle of his belt, uncoiling it from the loops of his trousers like a snake springing into action. A fleeting picture of Cate flashed before her eyes, but she squeezed them shut. Cate wasn't serious about David, she thought, they hardly saw each other, pushing the image of her sister back like a genie into its bottle.

David pulled Serena's tiny thong down over her thighs and she pushed him backwards. Not wanting him on top of her with her protruding bump, they fell back into the goose-down folds of the duvet.

'Like this,' she whispered.

Totally naked, except for a condom straining over his massive erection, Goldman lay back and Serena straddled him, her firm thighs pressing against his submissive body. She took his cock and tipped the end into her wetness, stroking her clitoris, then sliding him in so slowly that he groaned out, his hands reaching up greedily to play with her breasts. Rocking, then grinding her hips into him, her pelvic muscles squeezing his shaft tightly inside her, she watched his face crease with pleasure, his eyes closed, an ecstatic moan escaping from his lips. Completely in control now, and enjoying the sense of power, she lifted her body upwards so she almost slipped off him before thrusting back down on him again, her free hand cupping his balls.

'Fuck, fuck, incredible,' he moaned. His body arched

towards her before caving back on the mattress while Serena felt her own intense orgasm. Looking down to see his exhausted, handsome face, his lips tilted upwards, she felt another wave of pleasure rush through her. She smiled, satisfied and reassured. Serena Balcon had not lost her touch.

At half past twelve on Sunday morning, David Goldman rapped noisily on the door of Nick Douglas's Highgate flat, hoping that his friend would be up and functioning. He needed help. He had slipped out of Serena's bed hours earlier, hastily checking out of the Chateau d'Or before he bumped into anyone, and no doubt clocking up several speeding tickets on his frantic 120-mile journey back to London, while torturing himself with the question of what to do next. Did he regret having slept with Serena Balcon? Honestly? No. Serena was the conquest he had been waiting twenty years for. Christ, she was sexy, beautiful, *horny*; he had never slept with a pregnant woman before and, OK, at first the swell of her stomach was a little strange, but my God, the woman had been insatiable until the early hours of the morning. David Goldman had slept with many women, but the glamour models, the bit-part actresses, the fluffy-blonde bits about London: all of them were now instantly forgettable next to Serena Balcon. Except her sister Cate, of course.

He felt suddenly anxious once more. Cate Balcon. Pretty, yes, but not the best-looking woman he'd ever been out with. The body a little bit too curvy for his liking, but she was funny, clever, privileged. And with that sweet, trusting innocence he found lacking in so many women, she had managed to get right under his skin. David Goldman had never seriously considered settling down before, but increasingly he thought that adorable Cate Balcon might just be the woman to . . . well, not *tame* him exactly, but at least make him want to settle in one place for a little longer than usual. Which was why, standing outside Nick Douglas's front door, he felt absolutely terrible. He didn't want to think about last night any more, but he had to. The champagne, the Pimms, the whisky: it was all still swilling around his bloodstream making his body feel like jelly and his head like cotton wool. He knew that he had two options: to tell Cate what had happened, or to keep quiet. Of course the latter choice was by far the more appealing option, but was Serena the sort to confess to her older sister? In which case it would be far worse than if he tried to undertake some damage limitation himself. He decided to turn to the one person who knew Cate the best: Nick.

The intercom buzzed and he walked in to find Nick lying prostrate on the sofa, surrounded by Sunday newspapers and a plate showing the remains of a full English breakfast: coagulated rivers of egg, bacon rinds and the leftovers of tomato skins. David felt even more sick.

'Enjoying yourself?' said David, flipping a pile of magazines off a chair to sit down.

'Like a pig in shit,' smiled Nick. 'Do not underestimate man's love of pottering about on a Sunday morning. It's a great British tradition.'

'Lucky for some,' said David, resting a foot on the coffee table. 'I've just bombed it back from Oxfordshire.'

'Oh yes?' said Nick, getting up and moving towards the kitchen. 'Weren't you at some wedding or something? Tea?'

'Coffee. Strong.'

'Coming right up. There's some football starting in a bit if you feel like hanging around this afternoon. Cate's not back until tonight, is she?'

'No, not back until tonight . . .' repeated David distractedly.

He shifted himself in his chair until he was perched on the edge, his hands nervously running through his hair.

He took a deep breath, for a second wishing he hadn't come round to Nick's. Seeing his old friend's flat, once a pristine designer apartment when he had shared it with Rebecca Willard, now an untidy bachelor pad spilling over with books, CDs, even a pizza box from last night, he realized how much he had grown apart from Nick over the past few months. Suddenly he wasn't at all sure where Nick's loyalties would lie. The plain facts were that Nick had spent far more time with Cate recently, and was probably actually closer to her than to David. But David had to bet that their friendship of fifteen years was strong enough. Besides, men had to stick together on these things, didn't they?

'I haven't come for football or for some morning-after TLC, but thanks for the coffee,' said David, lifting the steaming mug Nick had placed in front of him. He paused.

'What's up?' asked Nick.

David took a deep breath. 'I've done something I shouldn't.'

'Jesus, what is it?' asked Nick, suddenly concerned by David's grave manner. 'Has there been an accident?'

'No, nothing like that,' said David, reaching up and pulling his collar away from his neck as if it was strangling him. 'As you know, I was at my friend Robert's wedding last night. I didn't really know anybody there.'

'Not like you,' smiled Nick cynically.

'Well . . . Serena was there.'

David let the silence hang between them, waiting for Nick to take the bait and stop him from having to say the words himself.

'And?'

David just looked at the floor.

'Tell me you didn't . . .' said Nick, his eyes wide.

'She was there, I was drunk,' said David, his voice getting a little high-pitched. 'You know what she's like, she was giving me this whole, "Oh look after me, I don't know anybody here" thing. She took advantage of me.'

Nick's voice was deadpan. 'I find *that* hard to believe.'

David began to relax a little. He could tell Nick was furious, but at least he wasn't going to punch him or throw him out of the window.

'You're a bloody idiot!' said Nick quietly, trying to contain his anger. 'What is Cate going to think? What's she going to feel? Don't for a second think you can trade one sister in for another! I'll tell you this now: Serena won't give a shit about you. She probably won't even remember your name this morning – you're hardly *Hollywood Reporter* fodder, are you?'

'She's not that bad,' said David quietly.

'Anyway,' said Nick, putting his cup down in disgust, 'this isn't about Serena, this is about Cate.'

'That's why I'm here,' said David, getting a little irritated now. 'You know her best, what shall I do?'

'You should have thought about that before you put your . . . God! The woman's six months pregnant!'

'Look,' said David, 'I know you're pissed off with me and that you're close to Cate, but that's why I came here, to ask your opinion. Do you think I should tell her?'

'Oh, and what's the other option?' said Nick tartly. 'Brush it under the carpet and hope it goes away?'

David looked a little helpless, much less like a powerful City player, more like a confused little boy. 'You never know,' said David, shrugging his shoulders. 'Serena's not likely to tell Cate, is she? And if I don't tell her . . .'

'Knowing you, I bet you slunk off with your arms around Serena in full view of everyone yesterday. And wasn't the place crawling with journalists from *Hello!*?'

411

'They'd all gone home,' said David petulantly.

Nick struggled to keep some level of composure in his voice. 'Look mate, you've got to tell her. And you have to take the consequences. You've made your bed, so to speak.'

David sat back in his chair and exhaled loudly, as if a weight were being lifted from his chest. Suddenly resigned to his fate, he felt a little less lost, a little more like his old self. 'Well, I'll think about it,' he said grumpily.

Nick kicked a pile of newspapers under the sofa. 'You're a real wanker, aren't you?' he said, shaking his head. 'She really doesn't deserve you.'

David stood to go, snatching up his car keys from the arm of the chair. 'That's a matter of opinion, Nick,' he said, his confidence almost fully restored. 'Thanks for the coffee.' And he sauntered out the door.

Cate was jet-lagged, but otherwise was in a good mood. Having breakfast at the swish Wolseley on Piccadilly with Nick and Jenny Tyson, her favourite PR, a lively no-nonsense sort of woman who loved to spill industry gossip, she was feeling tired but happy. And hungry – Cate quickly polished off her American waffles covered with streams of maple syrup, accompanied by a cup of Earl Grey tea. Jenny had nibbled at a bagel, but was in a hurry to dash.

'Big kiss to you both,' she said, puckering up at the air over both of Cate's cheeks. 'I have to be back at the office by ten, otherwise nobody will do a thing.'

'I know the feeling,' said Cate. 'I'm just going to finish my juice,' she said, pointing to her glass, 'then we're off too.'

As Jenny disappeared through the revolving doors, Nick picked up a brochure for a Maldives island retreat that Jenny had left for them. 'Well, that was pretty useful,' he said. 'I can't believe I've been so hard on PRs in the past. What she was saying is that this hotel will let us take a celebrity out to the Maldives, spend a week shooting them, and they're going to pay for it all?'

'Something like that, yes,' said Cate, amused. 'Music to your ears, eh Mr Scrooge?'

Cate took a gulp of orange juice and kicked back in the banquette, stretching herself in an effort to wake up a little more. 'But I tell you, that is the last weekend I am working for the rest of the month. These trips to LA just kill you for the next few days. I think it's about time I started reclaiming a little bit of my life back from the magazine. What did you do this weekend?'

'Nothing much,' shrugged Nick, beginning to feel a little uncomfortable. 'Just mooched around, read the papers, watched a video. A quiet one.'

Cate nodded. 'I was supposed to go to some wedding with David this weekend, but I had to knock that on the head. That model, Melissa D? Not too keen on her, but I wouldn't have minded going to the Chateau d'Or: it sounds gorgeous. Maybe David will take me one weekend,' smiled Cate, reaching to pull on her jacket. 'I hope it wasn't too unbearable being on his own, but he's so sociable, isn't he? Have you spoken to him?'

'No. Yes. Er, no,' said Nick, reaching down to pick up his bag from the floor. 'Have you?'

'Well, have you spoken to him – yes or no?' said Cate, amused.

He looked over at the revolving door, pretending not to have heard her. 'Shall we go?'

Cate's instincts, although muted by jet lag, could still pick up on the atmosphere. 'Nick, what's wrong? Have you spoken to David?' she asked, more seriously this time.

'No,' said Nick crossly, 'now let's go. I've got a meeting at eleven.'

413

Cate smelt a rat. It wasn't like Nick. During the meeting he had been ebullient and chatty as usual but, as soon as the conversation had switched to David, he had become like a Trappist monk.

'Nick Douglas,' said Cate again sharply, 'is there something you're not telling me?'

'No!' said Nick.

'Well you're a crap liar,' said Cate, who put her bag back on the table with a thump. 'Have you seen David?'

'OK. Yes, actually, very briefly yesterday afternoon.'

'And?'

'And nothing.'

Cate narrowed her eyes at him. 'Come on, Nick, what am I missing here?'

'Look, I'm sure David will tell you all about the wedding himself,' said Nick, suddenly regretting having said anything.

'And is there anything to tell?' asked Cate again. She knew intuitively that something was wrong. The prospect of David attending a wedding that had no doubt been packed with glamorous young things was not one to fill her with confidence. She was not a fool. Things had been going well between them, but she was not deluded: she knew that David had an eye for the pretty girls and, while she'd never seen any evidence of it during the four months they'd been seeing each other, what better place to test his faithfulness than at a wedding like that?

'Is there something I should know about David at the wedding?' said Cate, trying to catch Nick's eye. Nick simply shook his head.

She grunted. 'I could just ask David, but who knows whether you'll get the truth from any man?' she said pointedly. 'I think I'll ask Serena to ask her friend Elmore. I know he was at the wedding.'

'Well, why not ask Serena directly?' said Nick. 'She was there too.'

'Well I will!' said Cate, collecting her things.

Nick grimaced, cursing himself for letting his mouth run off again. He had been sure David Goldman would have talked to Cate already. 'Leave it Cate,' said Nick, trying to sound more casual, 'there's nothing to tell. You're just over-reacting.'

'Well, forgive me if you've made me paranoid, Nick,' she said sarcastically.

'Let's just get back to the office,' said Nick, putting a re-assuring hand on her shoulder. 'You're just jet-lagged.'

Cate shrugged him off and turned for the door. 'We'll see, won't we?'

Back at her desk, Cate was restless. She didn't see David more than two or three times a week, but they spoke frequently and it was unusual that, during the twelve hours she had been back, she hadn't heard a peep from him. Nick had definitely been on edge about something at breakfast that morning. He was a terrible liar. Very soon after they'd met back in February, she'd noticed how his eyes shone when he was trying to get something past her.

Unable to concentrate, she picked up her jacket and walked out of the building to hail a cab, giving the driver Serena's address in Chelsea. The weather was on the turn: blobs of rain started to bounce off the window where she lightly rested her head, watching London slip by in a daze. Suddenly her mobile rang. She picked it up and looked at the number. It was Nick. She put it back in her bag. The second time it rang she ignored it, and the third time she simply switched it off.

Her first thought had been to confront David, but some-how she knew that he'd be able to outmanoeuvre her. It would be easier to wheedle it out of Serena if she had seen something or heard something. If her sister was one thing, it was a terrible gossip.

Serena had the top two floors in a striking white Palladian-fronted house in The Boltons. Cate rang the intercom buzzer three times before a sleepy voice answered and she was buzzed inside. Cate wondered frantically how to play it. Bluff, she thought. Pretend she knew more than she did. That was the way to do it. Serena answered the door still yawning in a white cotton gown, her long blonde hair tousled like a surf girl's, an embroidered silk sleep-mask on top of her head.

'Cate. What do you want?' she mumbled. 'It's my day off.'

'From what?' asked Cate, unable to help herself.

Serena tutted and glanced down at her watch. 'Well, you've got about half an hour. The Moonstone Club are coming round at three.'

'The Moonstone Club?'

'Elmore's found this incredible psychic who's got a PhD and everything. She chairs these meetings where we all talk about spirituality and stuff. There's about ten of us and it's just *amazing*. It's like the, the new . . . book club.'

Cate couldn't believe Serena had ever attended a book group.

She took a moment to look around Serena's new flat, which she had just moved into after a two-month stay at Claridge's. It had not been carefully interior-designed, just like Serena and Tom's Cheyne Walk house, but there was a pretty insouciance about it, a blank white canvas with polished walnut floors, full of beautiful, glamorous things for a beautiful, glamorous person. Overlooking St Mary's Church, it must have been costing her a fortune.

'How did you find this place?' asked Cate curiously.

'Remember Sheikh Kolum, who I used to see *all* the time when I used to go down to L'Equipe Anglais?'

Before Tom, Serena had gone through a phase when she was never out of London's Eurotrash nightclubs. 'Vaguely,' she lied.

'Well, it's his London pad. He's hardly ever here; always in Paris these days, so he says I can have it until at least New Year. Anyway, can I get you anything?' she yawned, waving her hand in front of her casually as if she had no intention whatsoever of going to get anything for her. Cate knew she could spend half an hour making small talk until the Moonstone Club arrived, or get straight to the point, her curiosity about David still gnawing away at her.

'How was the wedding?'

'OK, nothing special,' replied Serena casually.

There. Cate could see it. She knew her sister so well that she could distinguish her arrogant indifference from evading an issue.

'I want to know what happened,' said Cate quickly. 'And you might as well tell me everything because Nick's already told me.'

Serena seemed to twitch awake as if she'd been given an adrenalin shot. 'Oh, and what's Nick told you?' she said haughtily.

'He told me about David.'

'Oh, what does Nick Douglas know about anything?' said Serena, tying her cotton gown around her more protectively. Serena was an actress. She was a good liar: convincing, manipulative, natural. But Cate could see a look of pure guilt painted on her face. Not obvious, more soft and subtle like a watercolour, but it was there nonetheless.

'David went to see Nick yesterday after the wedding. He told him,' said Cate with false knowingness in her voice.

Serena gazed down at her fingers stretched out in front of her. For a few moments the room fell totally silent.

'He came on to *me*, you know,' she said, looking up suddenly, her eyes blazing defiantly.

The enormity of what had just been said spun around the room. Cate's breath quickened. Five simple words: 'He came on to me.' Me. Serena. Her sister. She felt as if she had been kicked in the chest.

'It was you?' she whispered.

Serena's face was pallid with guilt. 'Cate, seriously. Nothing happened,' she said quickly, trying to sound casual.

'I don't believe it!' said Cate, the words starting like a whisper, building in ferocity until she was screaming. 'You slept with him, didn't you?' she spat, jumping up off the sofa.

Serena took a step backwards, beginning to edge out of the room. 'Cate, I didn't. I promise,' she stammered.

'At least have the guts not to lie to me,' Cate yelled, struggling to catch her breath. She looked at Serena's pale face and wanted to summon up a barrage of hate in her voice, but it wouldn't come. Instead she turned her back away from her sister and started pacing the room, blinking tears back furiously. She felt every muscle in her body crumple.

'Catey, I'm sorry. I really am.' She moved forward to touch Cate who recoiled back so quickly she almost stumbled.

'Get away from me,' she started sobbing. 'Get away.'

She sank back into the sofa, her body like a rag doll.

'Why? Serena, why did you do it?'

'Cate. I feel so terrible. I was drunk. You know I haven't been drinking. I didn't think –'

'I don't care if you were drunk,' she said ferociously. 'I don't care if you were so drunk you screwed every man in the room. What I care about . . .' Cate could feel her voice crack. 'Is why him . . . ? When you could have had anybody, why did you have to pick him?'

Serena sat on the edge of a chair, her hands falling in her lap. 'Because he wanted me,' she said softly. Her voice was low, calm and controlled. Cate couldn't tell whether it was with guilt or arrogance.

'You bitch,' whispered Cate, feeling her fingernails dig into her palms. 'You selfish, spoilt, self-obsessed little bitch.'

'It didn't mean anything,' faltered Serena.

'It didn't *mean* anything?' Cate replied incredulously. She swiped her hand in frustration through the air. 'Well, it means something to me,' she croaked. She put her head down and, biting her lip to keep controlled, picked her bag up and headed for the door.

'Cate, don't go. Please, let's talk about it . . .'

Cate looked back, her eyes simply sad. 'There's nothing to talk about,' she said, opening the door.

'Cate, wait. No . . .'

But Cate had gone, running down the stairs and onto the street, feeling as if her whole world had exploded and was raining down around her in a cloud of thick, dark, choking ash.

36

Sitting in the high-back leather chair in the offices of Mayfair's most prestigious accountants, Oswald's blood began to boil. He was beginning to harbour grave reservations about whether the young man in front of him could manage to find his backside with both hands, let alone manage his business affairs.

Six months ago, Lionel Davenport, Oswald's accountant since the sixties and senior partner in the firm of Davenport Davis, had retired and handed over the reins of the company to Peter Cable, whom Davenport had pitched to Oswald as 'the firm's dynamic future'. Since then, Oswald had heard nothing but doom and gloom about his financial situation, and today, it seemed, was no exception.

'So what can we do then?' challenged Oswald, his irritation mounting. 'Lionel said you were creative, so come on. I need to raise about two and a half million by the end of the year. A forty-five per cent share in my daughter's business is up for sale. Her husband died in that terrible fire, didn't you hear?' a hint of a smirk appearing on his lips. 'And I need liquid funds to buy them.'

'Well, that might take some time,' said Cable hesitantly, peering at the figures in front of him.

'Time? There isn't any time,' snorted Oswald. 'My daughter is talking about expanding into America and I don't doubt the share valuation will increase if she does. So I have to find the money quickly. How are we going to do it?'

Peter Cable shuffled a pile of papers in front of him uncomfortably, and rested his elbows on the leather-topped desk. He was struggling to find the right words to break the news to his client.

'I have to advise you, your lordship, that you shouldn't be raising money to expand your business interests at this particular time. Instead, I would strongly recommend that we shore up the Balcon family accounts and even think of a contingency plan.'

'What do you mean "contingency plan"?' scoffed Oswald, leaning back in his chair. 'The Balcon estate has flourished for the last three hundred years, and I certainly don't envisage that financial situation changing any time soon.'

Peter Cable, normally an efficient and composed man, had to stop himself exhaling loudly in front of his client. He'd been warned that old Oswald Balcon was the firm's most difficult client but, even for Davenport Davis, he was prestigious business. It was worth putting up with his mood swings to have a client as connected as Lord Balcon. It was better to keep the man sweet, however bloody-minded he became.

'Financially, it has been a poor eighteen months,' said Cable. 'And I think we need to look at some damage limitation by the end of the financial year. Paying last year's tax bill, which is due very soon – well, we can probably just manage. But next year's bill: frankly it could be catastrophic for the whole estate.'

Oswald sighed loudly and deliberately. 'I pay you a great

deal in professional fees to sort out this kind of thing. I assume you are able to do something, or perhaps I should take my business elsewhere?'

'Lord Balcon, I can only work with what I have,' said Cable, beginning to get exasperated. He leafed through a sheaf of spreadsheets, raising his eyebrows like a cartoon character.

'Frankly, every pillar of your potential income is crumbling at the moment. Huntsford is costing a fortune to maintain and the gallery is also suffering. I don't know a great deal about the art world but, looking at the figures, I really don't think your investments are bringing you the returns you need there.'

Oswald averted his gaze to prevent Peter Cable seeing the flicker of anxiety there. He was finally beginning to see what his gallery manager, Mark Robertson, had been trying to tell him for months: that Oswald's decision to invest in eighteenth-century Dutch bronzes had seemed like bad timing. They were beautiful, true. And at the moment, they were very cheap, but only because that market had temporarily fallen away. They had been buying art that nobody wanted.

'On top of that, the trust fund is low. That's the culmination of twenty years of business investments that perhaps haven't been – shall we say? – terribly successful,' added Peter, trying to be as diplomatic as possible since he could see his client beginning to flush around the cheeks. In an instant, Oswald was reminded of the *Daily Telegraph* piece months before, where they'd described his business interests as 'harebrained schemes' and 'badly-planned ventures'. How dare they! He thought again now. All he had ever tried to do was speculate to accumulate. He was a good capitalist, and how did they repay him?

'What bothers me the most,' said Peter, wondering if the seriousness of the situation was finally beginning to sink in with Oswald, 'is the loan agreement you signed to raise money for the Huntsford Musical Evening.' He pulled another stack of papers out of a file. 'Now, although Davenport Davis didn't do the accounts for that event, I have been forwarded the financials from it and – well, it is clear it did make a considerable loss.'

'It was a new business in its first year!' huffed Oswald, waving a hand in front of his face to dismiss the idea. 'Any entrepreneur will tell you that you need to take an initial hit if you are to raise the scale and profit the following year. It's basic business practice.'

'Oh, so you plan to have another one next year?' said Peter, genuinely surprised.

Oswald ignored him and continued to gaze around the room like a child whose attention span was waning.

'Anyway,' continued Cable delicately, 'there was a proviso in the loan conditions that your home is at risk should you default on payments.'

'Huntsford is in trust,' said Oswald arrogantly, 'we're safe.'

'Not exactly, no,' said Cable slowly. 'And I believe you have already defaulted on one payment?'

Oswald sighed loudly. 'One payment, they're not exactly going to put the noose around my neck quite yet, are they?'

Peter glanced at his wristwatch. He had been with Oswald for two hours and was keen to keep a lunch appointment with his new girlfriend. He leant forward and steepled his fingers.

'Quite simply, Oswald, we need to increase the monies coming into the estate – and quickly, otherwise we're in danger of being forced to reconsider our options.' He paused. 'Can you get any additional funds from your daughters? I believe they are quite successful?'

'I am not taking any charity from anyone, least of all them,' he replied loftily, clearly angered.

Cable decided to try another tack.

'What we *could* do – and let me point out that this is what other estate owners in your position have done when they had debts to pay – is to lease Huntsford for a duration of say, fifty years. There are at least a dozen hotel and leisure companies that would kill to occupy such a magnificent property. They would lease it for commercial use – conferences, for example – and Huntsford would still officially belong to the Balcon estate. You could even live on the grounds in a separate cottage. In fact, only last week, we were approached by a representative of the Sarkis Group, a very large hotel conglomerate, and the figures they mentioned were really quite impressive.'

Oswald had gone quite pink. 'Sarkis?' he shouted. 'Leasing Huntsford? How dare you even suggest these things as viable solutions?'

'Well, we have to think of something,' said Peter, flustered by the severity of Oswald's reaction.

'Quite right,' said Oswald, picking up his case and standing. 'And if you're not prepared to think creatively, then it's quite obvious that it's down to me.' He stormed out of the room without another word, slamming the door shut behind him.

37

Cate gazed around the cocktail reception of the British Society of Magazine Awards, held every year at Park Lane's Grosvenor House Hotel, and couldn't help but wonder once again how she had managed to be up for a gong. *Sand* was such a tiny magazine compared to the industry players walking around the room; there were five hundred representatives from right across the spectrum, from *Vogue* to *GQ* via *Golf World* and *Country Life*. From issue one, sales of *Sand* had been surprisingly strong. A magazine packed with gorgeous clothes and exotic locations had struck a chord with the general public over a long hot summer, and the high-paying, high-end fashion and cosmetic advertising had just started trickling in. But editing and publishing her own magazine still felt something of a hobby, so to have been nominated for Launch Editor of the Year had stunned her. Looking around the reception, Cate felt slightly fraudulent and undeserving to be there, like a child who had wandered from the playpen to the grown-ups' room and was about to get found out any second.

'So, who do you know? Who are the big names here?' asked *Sand*'s art director, Pete Miller, who looked awkward in a rented dinner suit and dirty trainers as he guzzled a buck's fizz. Cate was grateful that, despite the huge cost of a table, Nick had insisted the whole team should come. She craned her neck to look at the sea of black tie and cocktail dresses. 'A few people. And there are a few people I'd rather avoid, so if I give you a nudge, hide me.'

She wasn't sure what was making her feel more nauseous: butterflies at the prospect of winning an award, or anxiety at the thought of bumping into William Walton. Although she had long recovered from her dismissal from *Class* magazine, which seemed another lifetime away, the recent fight with Serena had dredged up all her feelings of rejection, shame and inadequacy. She had spent the last three weeks throwing herself into work and long hours, trying to distract herself from the absolute pain of betrayal that Serena had inflicted. She had surprised herself by feeling nothing for David's fecklessness. In fact he had been simple enough to jettison from her life, despite all the deliveries of expensive flowers. But Serena: that was a different matter. Cate still felt so fragile and bruised, she would rather have skipped the entire award ceremony in favour of another solitary night alone with a bottle of wine, where no one could touch her or hurt her.

Cate excused herself from Pete, who had begun a ham-fisted attempt to chat up Ruth the picture editor, and went to freshen up in the ladies' room. She reapplied her lip-gloss and took a moment to check her reflection in the mirror. An emerald-green Matthew Williamson silk evening dress floated over her curves, her long hair was brushed over her shoulders, sweeps of blush made her cheekbones look high and round: at least she looked good. She went into a cubicle, locked the door and took a few deep breaths. Gradually she was aware of voices in the adjoining stall. 'Apparently she is a shoo-in for the Launch Editor award,' said the first voice, followed by the gentle snorting sound of white powder disappearing up a nostril.

Another voice responded tartly. 'I mean, we would all win awards and prizes if Daddy bankrolled us with a magazine to play with, just because we'd been fired.'

Cate tipped down the toilet-seat lid and perched on the edge of the cold plastic, not daring to breathe and wishing that she could tap together the heels of her Jimmy Choo sandals and be whisked off home. The dinner had yet to start. Maybe she could slip out unnoticed and be home for eight. It wasn't as if she was going to win anything anyway.

'Someone looks miserable, considering she's about to collect an award,' smiled Nick Douglas, catching her coming out of the ladies' room.

'Where have you been?' she asked, pasting on a smile. 'You're supposed to be here supporting me on the eve of victory.'

'I've been checking out the table plan with Vicky and Marie.'

Cate felt a ridiculous stab of jealousy. Nick was perfectly entitled to socialize with members of the staff – even the prettiest members, she thought. She remembered the way all the *Sand* girls had been flirting with him over drinks at the office. While her feelings for Nick had petered out, or possibly been suppressed over the last few months with David on the scene, now she was back on her own, she had once again felt that familiar stir of emotion when she walked into the office. She still found herself spending a little extra time getting ready every morning so she would look her very best. It annoyed her, but she couldn't stop herself.

'You'll be delighted to know we're on table ten,' said Nick. 'Not that far from the stage, which I'm taking as a good sign.'

'Hmmm,' she said distractedly.

'Are you OK?'

She forced herself to perk up. 'Yes. Just nervous, I guess.'

'I know you're going to win it,' said Nick, moving a fraction closer to her, so the space between them seemed to exclude everyone else. 'You're the best in the business and you've proved it with this magazine.' He smiled, his hazel eyes warm and encouraging and she felt her mood lift a little. She had been used to her father telling her she was an also-ran, a master in the art of the mediocre; so to hear such unabashed confidence in her abilities coming from a male voice lit a light inside her.

'Come on, let's go and win some awards.'

Forty miles away, in the heart of Surrey, Camilla Balcon was also trying to impress, but she had no glossy magazine covers to hide behind. The task at hand was to convince the members of the Esher Conservative Association that her track record, her ideology, her passion were enough for her to be chosen as their next prospective parliamentary candidate. Looking out onto a sea of faces in this chilly hall, expressions running the spectrum from bored to challenging, she tried to compose herself. Camilla was never this nervous in court, but then in court she was shielded by the law. Whether she won or lost was down to her agility in manipulating the law to best serve her client. She had rules and precedents to lean on and she was good: the best. But tonight, she felt far more exposed. People were judging her on her ability to be the constituency's next MP, not on her ability to present a set of facts.

Still, she had thought her speech addressing the association's committee members had gone well. Camilla was, after all, a natural public speaker, and she had surprised even herself with the force of her views and the depth of her beliefs. She was opinionated yes, but political? That had been the challenge. Living at Huntsford for eighteen years and being force-fed her father's bludgeoning views had taught her how to fight her corner, but she had never been particularly political, despite the endless sniping debates over the dinner table. And her lack of political allegiance was the one thing that had worried her over the last few weeks as she had swotted up on party policies: would her views come over as passionate, genuine and committed?

Standing in front of the party in the Esher Conservative Association headquarters, a grand hall that was like an overgrown gentlemen's club, she wondered if she had done enough to clinch it. Having survived a twenty-minute barrage of questioning from the floor on everything from the euro to education, she took a final look at the party members who would decide her fate, fixing them with a farewell smile that she hoped struck the right balance between authority, competence and graciousness.

Gillian McDonald, chairwoman of the association, and wife of Charles, Camilla's boss, stood up to thank Camilla and make the final address before the members went off to vote.

'We won't be long,' she whispered to Camilla as a ripple of applause rang around the room.

Camilla walked off the stage and into a dimly lit corridor where her two rivals, Gerald Lawrence and Adam Berry, were sitting with their wives on a row of chairs propped against the wall.

She smiled weakly at them, realizing at once how badly she wanted the opportunity, and wondering which of the three of them would be chosen. They had already done well to get this far, having been whittled down from a list of sixty-five applicants approved by Tory Central Office. She looked at the man nearest to her. Gerald Lawrence was a local solicitor, balding, stooped, fifty-ish. Not only were his views firmly right wing – always a winner with the large number of over-fifties in the audience – but he had also lived in Esher all his life and had served as a local councillor for five years. That was one thing Camilla knew she couldn't compete with; she knew that a fair percentage of the crowd would welcome a local representative rather than someone they perceived had been drafted in from London.

The second candidate was even more dangerous competition. Local businessman Adam Berry had made a million in retailing. He was a self-made Tory dream who was also handsome, under forty years old, snappily dressed, and had a sheen of Thatcherite charm that had no doubt helped him make his money. He didn't have Camilla's considered, intelligent manner – she had seen him speak and thought his views a little shaky and vague – but of the three of them, Berry probably ticked the most boxes. He had the classic Tory image and strong local support.

'This is it then,' said Berry as they were beckoned back into the main hall.

The three candidates stood next to each other at the front of the stage. Camilla held her hands clasped in front of her, nervous sweat gluing them together as Gillian McDonald stood to speak.

'We have been honoured to have three such fine individuals willing to represent us as Esher's PPC,' she began. 'However, we can only invite one person to fight for the constituency seat in the next general election.' Gillian paused. For Camilla it was agonizing.

'And on this occasion the committee has decided it would like to invite Camilla Balcon to be the candidate to fight for us.'

Camilla's brain froze as she heard the announcement, not quite able to grasp the meaning. Was it her? Had she got it? Momentarily confused, she looked over to Gillian, who

430

was smiling warmly at her. The crowd erupted into cheers as Gerald and Adam reached across to shake her hand charitably. In a second, she was surrounded by party members wanting to shake her hand and congratulate her.

'It will be fantastic to have a strong young woman representing Esher,' beamed one elderly woman, shaking her hand warmly.

'It was because I admire your modernist views,' said another. 'The party has to fight the central ground.'

A man of around sixty with a craggy face and fine silver hair walked straight up to Camilla and touched his hand lightly on her shoulder.

'Congratulations, Miss Balcon. You got my vote. Not that you needed it,' he said with a wink.

She grinned back at him, grateful she was getting support from all quarters: young, old, traditionalists and activists, who saw in her a more liberal future for their party.

'I knew your father from his political days,' said the silver-haired man, and Camilla's happy smile evaporated at the mention of Oswald's name.

'Is that why you voted for me?' she queried, hoping her triumph wasn't about to be undermined by the shadow of Oswald doling out favours. She knew that if her father got wind of the fact that even one person had voted for her because of his time in the Lords, he would never allow her to forget it. Even if Camilla became prime minister on her own merits, Oswald would still believe it was all his doing.

The old man shook his head, the hint of a smile on his lips.

'I voted for you *in spite* of your father, not because of him,' he replied, before drifting off into the crowd.

Camilla tried to stop him, desperate to know who he was and what he knew about her father, but he was gone. She

431

spent the next thirty minutes gratefully receiving praise and flattery from everyone in the room. But no compliment was sweeter that night than the one from the old man with the silver hair.

Cate and Nick filed through into the Great Hall for dinner. The ceiling had been draped with folds of black cloth and tiny white fairy lights, like a sea of stars. The room was filled with the noisy buzz of backslapping and the sound of competitive boasting. Determined to enjoy herself, Cate was still so nervous that she hardly touched her rack of lamb and instead downed almost a bottle of New Zealand Sauvignon Blanc. By the time Simon Patterson, the ribald TV presenter and master of ceremonies for the awards' presentation had taken the stage, Cate was feeling a little dazed and tired.

'And now we come to the category of Launch Editor of the Year,' said Patterson after a ten-minute volley of industry in-jokes. Half a dozen magazine covers flashed up on the screen behind him, forcing Cate awake with a start. As each cover flashed up, the magazines published by big companies were supported by a huge roar. When the *Sand* cover appeared, the ten people on Cate's table made as much noise as possible, including Pete Miller banging on the table with an empty bottle of wine, but their cheer sounded tiny in the huge hall. From behind her, there were encouraging shouts of support, and Cate inwardly thanked them for their kindness, whoever they were.

'I'd like to invite Hugo McElvoy, the chairman of Alliance Magazines and sponsor of the Launch Editor of the Year category to come up to make the award,' said Simon Patterson as a robust, grey-haired man in his sixties made his slow way to the stage.

'Oh no,' groaned Cate, 'my old boss. The sweet irony.'

432

Reaching the podium and adjusting the waistband of his trousers, he read out the nominations from the card in front of him.

'This year, the competition was so fierce, we have also decided to award a highly commended prize,' said McElvoy, looking out to the crowd, which had fallen still. 'This award goes to a glossy new launch that has really revamped its market, and found a clear niche in a competitive market.'

Cate felt Nick's hand clasp hers. Could this be us? Could this be us? thought Cate, fiddling with the stem of her glass.

'And the highly commended award goes to . . . Greg Davies, editor of *Men's Style Weekly*!'

Cate felt her shoulders sink as a ripple of applause swelled up around her.

'Who wants to come second anyway?' said Nick, leaning over and squeezing her shoulder.

'The winner of this category,' continued Hugo McElvoy, fighting with the microphone which had started producing a horrible squeaky feedback, 'is a publication that has made an enormous impact in a very short space of time. The judges described the magazine as fresh, sexy, and a breath of fresh air in the industry, and its editor as a talented, driven, risk-taker. The award for Launch Editor of the Year goes to . . . Cate Balcon for *Sand* magazine!'

There was a loud roar of applause. As she stood up to go to the stage, Nick grabbed her and hugged her so tightly she could feel the warmth of his fingertips through the thin fabric of her dress.

After the awards, Cate had had to fend off the crowds of well-wishers who were gathering around her table. Cate's old friend Laura Warren, features editor on *Class*, gave her a kiss on both cheeks and wished her well. 'You must be feeling pretty pleased with yourself,' Laura smiled.

'Thank you so much,' said Cate. 'What a funny old year, hey?' she added, laughing.

'Isn't revenge sweet?' said Laura, waving a flute and wobbling visibly on her heels.

'How do you mean?' said Cate, pouring herself some hot black coffee in a vain attempt to sober herself up.

'Haven't you heard?' said Laura. 'William Walton and Nicole Valentine were fired on Monday. It was sooo embarrassing,' she gushed, excited to be able to impart the hot gossip. 'Nicole refused to leave her – your – office. She practically had to be carried out by security, and then it turned out that ten grand's worth of stuff had gone missing from the fashion cupboard. *Obviously* she nicked it.'

'Nicole was sacked for theft?' said Cate, her hand over her mouth in disbelief.

'No, silly!' laughed Laura, having to sit down. 'They were both fired by the top brass. Hugo McElvoy himself, I think, for the relaunch they "masterminded" three issues ago. Have you not seen the circulation figures? Down by about fifty per cent. Apparently it was so bad, McElvoy insisted that they both had to go. It was such an ill-conceived vision: the advertisers just hated it. It was madness to try and make *Class* like *Glamour*.'

'Oh dear,' laughed Cate, glowing.

'*Apparently*,' continued Laura, enjoying the wealth of gossip at her disposal, 'it didn't help that Hugo was on the judging panel for these awards and he wanted to know why the editor of *Sand* wasn't working for his company. When he found out Walton had fired you . . . well, that was the last straw.'

Cate sat there, stroking her Perspex trophy, and grinned. She wasn't a vengeful person, but this evening was starting to taste sweet.

'Don't be surprised if you get a call pretty soon to go back to *Class*. That's the word on the street.'

Cate shook her head good-naturedly, 'I do miss you all,' she said, pouring Laura a cup of coffee. 'But why would I go back when they fired me at the beginning of the year?'

Laura rubbed her thumb and forefinger together. 'Money, my love. Ask for double your old salary and I'm sure you'll get it.'

Feeling drained, emotional and more than a little drunk, Cate decided to go home while she was on a high. She craned her neck over the crowd to find Nick, who was standing several tables away talking to a dark-haired man in his fifties who was peering at him intently through half-moon spectacles. Catching his eye, Nick made his excuses and came over to Cate, weaving through the bodies and chairs, carrying a bottle of champagne.

'Here she is, the proud winner,' he said, grabbing a glass and filling it with Moët.

'You'll never believe it.'

'Hey, you'll never guess what!'

They both said it at the same time and stood there grinning.

'OK, you go first,' said Nick.

'William Walton and Nicole Valentine were fired!'

'Old news,' laughed Nick. 'The hot gossip, Miss Balcon, is that not one, but two MDs have approached me in the last twenty minutes, wanting a meeting to discuss buying our company. And one of them is Alliance Magazines. Hugo McElvoy said – and I quote – "It would be a pleasure to get Cate Balcon back on board in a senior editorial capacity". I'd be publishing director and *Sand* would be brought into their women's magazine portfolio. They love us!'

Cate started to giggle, building in her throat, until it came out as a deep belly laugh. It was difficult to believe she had felt so miserable only a couple of hours earlier.

'What's the matter?' said Nick.

'Oh, it's just been such a funny night. I think I've had too much champagne.' She continued to giggle, only stopping when they turned into hiccups.

'So what shall we say to the suits?' asked Nick after she'd gained control.

A buyer for *Sand* was being offered to them on a plate. They each owned twenty-five per cent of the company. That would rake in a lot of money.

'I say "Bollocks to them"!' said Cate defiantly, clinking her glass against Nick's bottle.

'So do I, Cate Balcon,' he smiled, throwing an arm around her bare shoulder, 'so do I. It's me and you together on this one. *Sand* is our baby and I think we should look after it just a little while longer.'

38

Camilla sat on the bumper of the midnight-blue Land Rover used to transport everyone to the shoot and watched her father raise his Holland and Holland shotgun into the air. A deep bang rattled around the watery grey sky, followed by the flutter of a bird falling to the earth. Oswald turned and beamed at the party watching: Philip Watchorn, Nicholas Charlesworth, Maria Dante and three Japanese businessmen who Watchorn had brought along to sweeten a deal. Decked out in a dark-brown Huntsford tweed jacket, long tweed plus twos, a canary yellow jumper and a flat cap tipped at a slight angle, Oswald looked like an eighteenth-century poacher.

Her father was in his element during the shooting season, thought Camilla, keeping her distance from the party. More than anything, she wanted to go back to the house. She wasn't particularly against shooting, unlike Cate and Venetia. She quite enjoyed the smell of cordite pinching at her nostrils, and the feeling of being warmed up by lashings of Earl Grey tea, whisky and thick-buttered scones that were always served at the post-shoot tea. But today she was tired and irritable, and the sight of Maria Dante in a pristine waxy

Barbour and thick make-up, pawing at her father, made her feel uncomfortable. A herd of spaniels leapt and barked, scampering off to retrieve the birds.

'Bloody hurt my shoulder,' said Oswald, pacing over to his daughter, rubbing it with a stout hand. Despite his protestations, Camilla could tell he was having the time of his life. Oswald caught sight of Camilla's long expression.

'What's the matter with you? You've been miserable all afternoon. Either join in or go back to the house. You just look bloody ungrateful, sulking here by the car.'

'We won't be too long though, will we?' said Camilla, standing up to meet him eyeball to eyeball.

'We'll go when the shoot's finished,' replied Oswald curtly, 'and not when you have reached your boredom threshold.'

Oswald turned to look across the long expanse of grassland to the edge of Huntsford Wood where the dogs were dashing around looking for pheasants. He folded his gun over his left arm and began to stamp some mud off his boots.

'I'm disappointed you've failed to persuade Catherine to come down tonight,' he said, not meeting Camilla's gaze. 'I did request that the whole family come home this evening, but clearly nobody pays a blind bit of notice to what I say.'

'You know the situation there,' said Camilla, zipping up her camel coat so the collar came above her chin. 'Cate and Serena just don't want to see one another.'

'Pathetic!' snapped Oswald, petulantly snapping his gun to fully cocked. 'This isn't still that argument over some boy, is it? You know I haven't cared for some of Serena's behaviour this year, but after the time she has had, Cate should allow her sister some happiness. When it comes to the opposite sex, Cate really can't expect to compete with Serena, can she?'

Not wanting to get embroiled in that particular discussion, Camilla thought that the best course of action was to remain silent, hoping that her father would move on. Maria Dante had monopolized her father's attention all day, so it was the first snatched five minutes she had shared with him. It was the first time they had spoken face to face since she had won the nomination to be Esher's prospective parliamentary candidate. She had yet to bring it up with him; Camilla's political ambitions still seemed to raise a prickliness in her father, so she had kept quiet in the hope that he would raise the issue or offer some crumb of congratulation. So far, nothing. At first she had thought that the news had somehow escaped him, despite the acres of local news and broadsheet coverage that her nomination had garnered but, as the silence rang between them, she realized that no acknowledgement of her achievement, no matter how small, would be forthcoming. She wondered why. She felt a knot of tension in her stomach as she thought of one reason, and quickly tried to rid it from her thoughts.

Sitting in Serena's bedroom at Huntsford, Venetia looked out of the window and stared at the watercolour sky turning purple like a bruise. 'They're having a tea up at the shoot when it's finished. Didn't you want to go? You know how Daddy gets if we don't make any effort.'

Serena lay back in her enormous four-poster bed, propped up by some pillows. She motioned her head towards the walnut bedside cabinet, on which sat a china teacup and a scone with a tiny bite taken out of it.

'Don't want to. Had some,' said Serena sulkily, rubbing the sides of her bump with her hands. 'Anyway, I'm with child.'

She motioned to a newspaper folded at the end of the bed. 'Have you read that?'

'No,' said Venetia.

'Tom has been nominated for a Golden Globe.'

Venetia wasn't sure how to respond. 'That's good news, isn't it?'

Serena looked crestfallen. She hadn't needed a newspaper to tell her about Tom's nomination. At least five people had called her to tell her as soon as nominations were announced, and every conversation had torn her up with a peculiar emotion she was unable to recognize. But she wasn't going to let Venetia know that.

'Of course it's good news in a year that my own movie has bombed and I have had to put my entire career on hold,' she said, trying to sound sarcastic. But her voice just came out in a small squeak.

Venetia was sure that Serena was going to cry. She looked at her sister with uncharacteristic concern, glad to distract herself from the weight of her own problems. In twenty-seven years, Venetia had never once been worried about Serena. Not seriously worried, anyway. Yes, as a child Serena had been a constant headache after their mother's death, and Venetia had adopted the mother role in the family. She'd been concerned when Serena had stayed out late at night, when she got expelled from school, when she was caught stealing sweets from the local village store. But Venetia always had this innate feeling that Serena was going to be just fine, no matter what life threw at her or what she brought on herself. Her youngest sister didn't have the inner strength of, say, Camilla, but she did have a sort of golden protective glow, as if some angel was watching over her to give her a blessed existence.

But this afternoon Camilla was less sure. Serena's skin was still perfect, like the curve of an alabaster sculpture, but there was no light coming from her: neither the famous pregnancy glow nor the legendary star quality that she usually radiated. She was sulky, truculent, quiet. She looked beautiful, but it was a 'so-fragile-she-might-break' beauty. She looked thin, her collarbone sticking out, and her bump protruded awkwardly, as if it did not belong to her body. Venetia was sure her sister was depressed. During the time that Venetia had desperately wanted a baby herself, when she had wondered frantically what was wrong with her body, Venetia had read thousands of words in books and on the Internet about pregnancy and considered herself quite an expert. Prenatal depression was much rarer than postnatal depression, but she was convinced that her youngest sister had it.

'What's wrong?' asked Serena petulantly, looking at her sister's concerned expression.

'The truth? I think you're depressed,' said Venetia flatly.

'I'm not depressed,' sighed Serena wearily. 'I'm just very tired.'

Venetia wasn't convinced. 'You know what you need to do?' she persisted.

'What?' replied Serena angrily.

'Make up with Cate.'

Serena lifted herself up against the headboard, deliberately avoiding her gaze. 'Can you pass me the tea?' She took a sip and turned back to her sister.

'Who do you think Tom is going to take to the Globes?'

It was a Balcon tradition that, on the Saturday night of the shoot, Oswald would hold a black-tie supper to feast on the game they had bagged, starting with drinks in the Great Hall, gathered around the staircase. The gentlemen, welcoming the opportunity to change out of damp, scratchy tweeds, put on DJs and patent-leather opera shoes, while for the ladies it was a perfect chance to slip into a fine cocktail dress, which always looked good against the grand backdrop of Huntsford.

Even though she didn't feel like socializing, Serena had made an effort to outshine everybody, particularly with Maria in situ. A silver-grey sheer vintage Ossie Clark kaftan hid all traces of pregnancy, and her hair was swept up into a chic ballerina's bun. She knew she looked like a beautiful society hostess from another age. In fact, as the girls had descended the stairs and gathered in the Great Hall, Camilla had remarked how much Serena resembled her mother, Margaret Balcon, at the height of her beauty. But the compliment dissolved almost instantly as they watched Maria Dante sweep down the staircase, looking for all the world as if she owned the place. Serena thought she looked like a pantomime dame taking centre stage for the big finale. Yes, she was a beautiful woman, she thought begrudgingly, but it was a dated, overblown beauty, her scarlet velvet gown too long and heavy, her raven hair scraped back too severely.

Serena had always assumed that her father would one day find another partner, but she had never for one moment believed that another woman would replace her in Oswald's affections quite as much as Maria had. She wondered whether it was any coincidence that her own relationship with her father had cooled ever since Maria had come on the scene. He was undoubtedly disappointed with her pregnancy, but over the last twenty-seven years, Oswald had allowed Serena to get away with anything: being expelled, dating the sheikh, becoming an actress – he never turned a hair. Serena had always been spared the fierce disapproval, the crushing rejection, the patent indifference her sisters had had to endure – until now. She could almost taste the rejection on her tongue, like metal. She hated it. She didn't want it. She wouldn't stand for it.

Collecting a Campari and soda from Collins's silver tray, Venetia was biding her time. It was never a good time to broach anything difficult with her father, but post-shoot and in polite company, his mood slightly brightened by whisky, it was as good a time as any. She caught him off-guard, just as he was breaking off conversation with Nicholas Charlesworth and was looking around for Collins to bring him another aperitif.

'How's your shoulder?' said Venetia. 'Camilla said you hurt it on the shoot.'

'Oh, nothing to worry about,' scoffed Oswald, waving a hand in the air. 'Anyway, why weren't you at the shoot? I know you have a ridiculous objection to shooting, but you could have come along for the tea.'

'I'm trying to have a relatively quiet weekend,' said Venetia. 'I'm getting back to London early tomorrow morning. I've got lots of work to get out of the way because, as you know, I'm flying to New York at the end of the week.'

'No, I did not know,' said Oswald coldly, the good mood seeming to seep from his features. 'Why are you going? To spend more of Jonathon's legacy, I assume?'

She smarted. 'You know why I'm going to New York. I've told you at least half a dozen times.'

He swilled his drink around his crystal tumbler. 'This defiance is really getting you nowhere. There will be no expansion into New York; not without the board's approval. Your ridiculous desire to keep pursuing this is exactly the reason why Jonathon gave me power of attorney in the first place – to protect his interests.'

Aware that she had to keep her voice down, Venetia's words came out in a stern whisper. 'I just can't understand your objections to the New York expansion. We have found a fantastic retail site, our orders at the Bergdorf concession have never been higher and, after the US *Vogue* profile, our office has been flooded with enquiries –'

'As I explained fully in the board meeting last week,' interrupted Oswald, 'the company needs a special resolution to get your New York plans through and I am going to use my voting power to stop it. I am not being difficult. I simply believe the business needs to expand slowly. American expansion will cost more than the business can currently afford.'

Venetia shook her head vehemently. She had been through the financials with a fine-tooth comb and the business could indeed afford it. She was convinced her father had another agenda, and that no amount of reasoning or pleading was going to change his mind. So in desperation she had tried to take matters into her own hands and acquire Jonathon's share-holdings herself. She'd been devastated weeks earlier when Jonathon's will had been read and she'd discovered that, while he had left the house and a considerable amount of money to his wife, his forty-five per cent shareholding in Venetia Balcon Ltd had gone to his brother Stefan in Austria.

Jonathon had been a difficult bastard, and now he was trying to stifle her from beyond the grave. Giving his shares to Stefan was the worst thing Jonathon could have done; he knew that Venetia and Stefan von Bismarck did not get on. In Venetia's mind he was a callow misogynist who had none of Jonathon's work ethic, but all of his expectant arrogance. So when she'd flown to Vienna to try to persuade him to sell the shares to her, it wasn't with much hope. As she had expected, Stefan had revelled in her desperation; he had spent their entire meeting dangling a carrot in front of her that she knew she would never be able to reach.

'I could sell them to you for a good price,' he had told her in his stern Teutonic tones from the family's *schloss* just outside the Austrian capital. 'But that would not be in accordance with Jonathon's wishes.'

She returned home with nothing except a body tense with anger and a bag of stollen she'd picked up at the airport that she had no intention of ever eating. Now, without Oswald's cooperation, the company was in stalemate and her father was clearly in no mood to find a compromise tonight.

Oswald drifted off and Venetia listened absently to the chatter in the Great Hall. The Japanese party had now left, so Philip Watchorn was in a more relaxed mood. While Collins began to move through the crowd, topping up their champagne flutes with the pale yellow nectar, there was a sudden tinging sound as Oswald tapped on his crystal glass with a spoon.

'I'd like to make a little announcement before dinner,' he said, his voice cutting through the buzz of conversation. He was standing on the second step of the great staircase, and Maria Dante now moved to join him at his side, hanging onto his arm possessively.

'I am delighted to tell you all, my family and closest friends, that I have asked Maria to marry me and I am amazed to say that she has accepted.'

There was a round of applause, even a loud cheer from Philip.

Portia Charlesworth put a hand on Serena's shoulder. 'You must be so delighted!' she purred.

Serena was so staggered, she could barely draw breath.

'Delighted is not the word,' she managed after a second, smiling glassily, her teeth bared.

She darted across the hallway to Venetia, whose mouth was still gaping.

'So we have finally acquired a wicked stepmother. What a fairy-tale ending to the story.'

Venetia shook her head, trying to force a smile.

'If it keeps him out of our hair, then it can only be a good thing.' She wasn't even convincing herself.

'Are you not going to congratulate your father, then?' said Oswald, appearing at their side and stretching out a maroon velvet arm.

Serena didn't proffer a cheek and instead grabbed his arm awkwardly. 'So when's the happy day going to be?'

'As soon in the New Year as we can make it,' Oswald replied. 'The reception will be at the house, of course, and we will marry in the church in the village.'

Both girls thought the same thing: the very same church in the grounds of which their mother was buried.

'Congratulations, Daddy,' said Venetia coolly, pressing the side of her cheek to his. 'It's something of a surprise, but we're obviously all pleased. Now if you'll excuse me, I must go and say the same to Maria.'

Maria was still at the bottom of the stairs, smoothing the collar of her dress like a peacock. As she saw Venetia approach, she took several steps towards her, coming so close that Venetia felt off balance, as if Maria was invading her personal space. She could see the large pores on Maria's nose and the fine red veins in the whites of her eyes.

'Welcome to the family,' said Venetia, trying to sound genuine.

'Oh, it means so much to me to hear you say that,' smiled Maria, kissing her on both cheeks and squeezing the tops of her arms tightly.

Suddenly, Maria's voice acquired the most subtle edge. 'It must be such a relief for you. You have been the lady of the house for so long now without actually being Lady Balcon. You must feel rather liberated.'

'I wouldn't exactly say that,' said Venetia, immediately putting up her guard.

'Well, I would like to say thank you,' said Maria, grabbing Venetia's hands with her red-tipped fingers. 'You have done an excellent job of feathering the nest for me. There's so much to do to the house, of course,' she whispered conspiratorially. 'I have persuaded Oswald of the need to renovate the whole place. I have a friend in Paris, one of Europe's top interior designers, who just can't wait to get started.' The curve of Maria's smile was superior. 'Perhaps we could all get together to have lunch. I'm sure you'll have lots in common.'

Venetia felt shell-shocked. She had spent the last ten years trying to persuade her father that Huntsford needed a sympathetic overhaul and surely she was the person to do it. She had such an intimate knowledge of the house and its history and her whole design style was exactly right for this sort of project. She felt like she'd been kicked.

'I think it's important I take full charge of the project though, don't you? Stamp my taste on the place,' continued Maria in a stage-like whisper. 'After all, I am considerably younger than Oswald.'

At first, Venetia couldn't quite understand what she was implying, but Maria was quick to fill in the blanks. 'The day will come when it will just be me rattling around this place, so I need it *exactly* how I want it.'

'Just you?' queried Venetia.

'As Lady Balcon, I'll have a life tenancy of Huntsford in the event of my husband's death. In fact, Oswald is already making provisions in his will to that effect.' Her voice dripped with superiority and she exhaled dramatically. 'Of course, I hardly want to think about life without Oswald, but you have to be practical and I need to love living here. It is a little, well, fusty at the moment.'

Venetia was frozen to the spot, unable to process all this information.

'It's a family home,' stressed Venetia, still feeling dazed. 'I'm not sure Huntsford should be redesigned in one person's vision.'

Maria snorted. 'That's a little naïve, isn't it, darling?' she cooed. 'I'm hardly going to call a family meeting every time I want to choose new curtains.'

Collins approached and offered Venetia a top-up of champagne. She nodded and gulped it down. The status quo of her family, her home, her roots – everything she had known for nearly forty years – was about to change violently. And she felt absolutely powerless to stop it.

39

Cate felt lousy. Not even the strings of tinsel festooned around the room or the steady flow of Christmas presents that had started to come in from the fashion houses could begin to cheer her up. Her head was pounding, her nose streaming, and she hadn't been able to eat a thing all day. As everyone was out of the office at lunch she took a big gulp of water and lowered her head on the desk with a groan. If only she just could have a little sleep, she thought, letting her eyelids drop just for one moment. She sprang back upright in her chair when she heard footsteps. Nick Douglas came into the room, dropped a brown paper bag on the desk in front of her and folded his arms, regarding her with a mock-serious expression. 'Don't think I can't hear you sniffing and coughing and wheezing from my office. You sound like an old man.'

'You make me sound so glamorous,' she muttered sarcastically, reaching for another tissue. '. . . Actually, I do feel pretty crappy.'

Nick pulled up a chair next to her desk.

'That might have something to do with the fact that you haven't had a day off in about four months.' His voice teased her, but he was clearly concerned. 'Anyway, I've booked a cab for you. It should arrive any minute and everything you need should be in that brown bag. Now go on, clear off. You look crap. If we'd wanted Rudolph the Red-Nosed Reindeer to make a guest appearance in the office, we'd have spoken to Santa.'

Cate snapped open the compact sitting on her desk and looked at her face. He was right: she looked awful. Ill, with watery eyes and a bright red, flaky nose from too much blowing. Then she peered into the bag. There was a box of Lemsip, two brownies crumbling with chocolate, a wedge of gossip magazines and a bumper package of Kleenex.

'Your survival kit,' said Nick. 'Now will you please go?'

Back at home, curled up on the sofa under a rose-pink cashmere blanket, sipping a big mug of Horlicks, Cate still felt guilty. She also felt a little uneasy. This was an unfamiliar universe that existed outside of her sixty-hour working week. The streets of Notting Hill she'd passed in the car were full of glam mothers with buggies, high heels and freshly highlighted hair. The television was crammed with food programmes, black-and-white movies and cosy chat shows, not the crime shows and post-watershed dramas she was used to when she got home from the office.

Groaning at her aching muscles, she wondered whether it was time yet for another Lemsip. Could you have them every two hours, or was it four? she thought, wishing she hadn't thrown the box away. She gave up and opened a copy of *Heat*. She smiled and settled into her pillow. Despite herself, she couldn't resist reading about who was sleeping with whom, all the latest Hollywood gossip and the paparazzi shots of soap stars stumbling out of nightclubs. Devouring it, she moved onto *OK!* and *Hello!*, before pulling out *Splash*, the naughtiest, most scurrilous of the UK celebrity magazines. Leafing through the pictures of celebrity cellulite and teeny-tiny red-carpet dresses, she reached their Christmas feature special: 'Winners and Losers of the Year'. Turning the page, she jumped, her mug jerking up so a few drops of Horlicks dripped on her blanket. In the centre spread of the magazine they announced, 'The Number One Loser of the Year': Serena Balcon.

The fluorescent pink headline was accompanied by a montage of unflattering paparazzi photographs, the sort Cate recognized as the out-takes, snapped when the celebrity was sneezing or blinking or their hair had been caught in a gust of wind. The papers didn't usually want these, but they were perfect when it came to illustrate somebody in the throes of personal turmoil. Cate knew her sister too well – Serena would never cry in the street or get drunk at a very public party, but these misleading photographs told another story. The accompanying text catalogued Serena's break-up with Tom, her relationship with Michael Sarkis, the pregnancy and the hookers in the south of France. Also detailed were her missing out on big parts in Hollywood, being dropped from prestigious modelling contracts and the intruder at Huntsford. Worse, they also implied drink, drugs and mental problems. Only a year previously, this very magazine had devoted an eight-page section to 'The Style of Serena', and now she was a car-crash, a deranged, vain, fame-seeking lunatic on the verge of a complete breakdown.

Cate's first reaction was fury. It ignited every protective instinct she had and she was overwhelmed by a sudden desire to see her sister. She had no idea whether Serena read magazines like *Splash*, but she knew that, if Serena did see it, it would crucify her. Not that Serena couldn't do with being brought down a few notches – Cate still couldn't forget the flippancy of her 'he wanted me' comment when she had confronted her about David Goldman. But from what Venetia had said about their youngest sister at the shooting weekend, it wasn't her ego but her spirit that was being slowly eroded away by the events of the last ten months. Before she had a chance to think about it any more, she had flung down the magazine, grabbed a jacket and her car keys and run for the door, heading for Chelsea.

The Boltons, where Serena lived, was essentially a circus of huge multimillion-pound properties circling an oval of communal gardens and the grounds of an old church. She parked her Mini opposite Serena's flat and slammed the car door, picking up the brown paper bag from the passenger seat. She rang a dozen times on the bell. Nothing. She tried the mobile, which went straight to message. Concerned, Cate wondered where she could be. Serena wasn't likely to have gone very far at eight months pregnant. Standing in the cold, Cate wrapped her scarf twice around her neck and peered up to the windows to see if there was a light on.

'Where the bloody hell is she?' she muttered, walking back to the car. She leant on the roof of the Mini and tried the mobile again. There was a flutter of anxiety in the pit of Cate's belly. For a second, she wondered if she should call the police, then dismissed the thought as ridiculous. To her left, she watched an elegant elderly woman with two cocker spaniels on a lead walk into the garden square; her eyes followed the woman distractedly as she listened to Serena's message again. She was just about to get back in the car when she spotted a thin blonde woman sitting alone on a bench in the square. She went over to the railings and peered over into the gardens. It definitely looked like Serena, she thought, moving closer, her eyes narrowing.

Cate found an unlocked gate and went inside, her shoes scuffing through the carpet of copper leaves on the path. Serena did not look up as Cate approached, sitting stiffly on the bench, her eyes focusing on some distant point, a huge marl-grey poncho pulled tight around her body. She looked pale, her eyes shadowed and her hair . . . Cate was momentarily stopped in her tracks. What had happened to her hair? It was sticking up in short ragged clumps as if it had been attacked by a pair of shears. She felt a rush of guilt and foolishness as she approached her sister. She should have been there for Serena. Yes, Serena had hurt her, but the anger had faded, so over the last few weeks it was only stubbornness that had stopped her picking up the phone.

Cate said nothing as she sat down next to her on the cold bench and Serena remained statue-still. The pair of them watched the two cocker spaniels that were jumping around after a thrown stick.

'I thought you might like one of these,' said Cate softly after a few moments. She put her hand into the brown paper bag and pulled out a chocolate brownie, placing it gently on Serena's leg. Serena picked it up, broke a piece off and threw it towards a group of pigeons crowding around the paving stones. Finally she turned to face Cate.

'I hope you haven't come to lecture me,' she said.

'I've come to give you a brownie,' smiled Cate hopefully. Cate watched the edges of Serena's lips slowly begin to twitch upwards.

'Shouldn't you be at work?'

'I'm ill.'

'Your nose is all red,' said Serena, reaching out to touch it with her fingertip.

Another silence grew between them, the only sound the distant yelps of the dogs.

'So,' started Cate, 'what do you think about Maria joining the family?'

'Obviously *delighted* at the news.' The warmth and biting humour – the old Serena – was beginning to creep back into her voice.

'So does that mean you'll be coming to the Huntsford Ball next week?'

'Are you?' Serena replied hesitantly.

Cate nodded.

'I've missed you,' said Serena quietly after another pause.

'Me too.' It came out detached, a little too insincere, like responding to an 'I love you' with a 'Me too'.

'I'm sorry, Cate, I'm so sorry,' said Serena, looking up at her sister with wide eyes.

'It's OK, it doesn't matter now.'

'It does matter. I didn't set out to seduce David, you know. It just happened.'

Cate stared out in front of her, reminded of the brutal pain of their last meeting. She turned to look at her sister and noticed that her eyes were glistening. Cate felt a lump in her throat.

'I was lonely,' continued Serena. Cate wondered if her speech was rehearsed. She had thought so many times about what *she* was going to say to Serena. But now none of it seemed right.

'There was a moment when I could have stopped. But I didn't stop . . .' The words came out like a croak as she remembered the night at the Chateau d'Or. 'I was jealous of you, Cate. I thought about you at your launch party. With a business, a handsome man on your arm, all those people saying how fabulous and successful you were. I was so jealous I wanted to take a little piece of that away.'

Cate was knocked back by her honesty and her self-awareness.

'You were jealous of me?' she said, slowly shaking her head, almost laughing. 'Sin, you have everything. You're beautiful, you're famous, you're successful. Look around. You're surrounded by success, you're in the thick of it.'

Serena turned her head to look at the huge white

houses, some as big as embassies, that circled them. 'Oh yes?' said Serena blankly. 'The guy who owns my house, the guy who's letting me stay here? He's probably expecting to sleep with me.'

Drops of tears were now falling down Serena's cheeks; she wiped them away with the corner of her poncho. Cate moved closer towards her and put an arm around her shoulder and the anger, the betrayal, evaporated like water on warm skin. 'Come on, don't think like that.'

'I deserve it, Catey. I'm a bitch. You were right. A spoilt, self-obsessed bitch. I've thrown everything away this year: friends, career, love.'

Cate squeezed her shoulder. 'That's not true.'

'Roman sent me some flowers,' she said slowly, smiling softly as if with a chink of acceptance.

Cate looked surprised – she knew Serena and her old friend the designer hadn't talked in some months.

'Well, not flowers. A plant really,' said Serena. 'A beautiful poinsettia with a lovely card for Christmas.' Her mouth was fixed with shame. 'I don't deserve it.'

'It's not too late to start making things right,' Cate said firmly. 'Call Roman, call your agent.' She paused. 'Call Tom.'

'Maybe,' Serena said softly, not meeting her sister's gaze.

Cate pulled the side of her sister's head towards hers. As she stroked Serena's hair, she could see it had been cut, badly, crudely. She retracted her hand as if she'd been shocked. 'Sin, what happened?'

'I cut it.'

Cate could feel herself welling up as she looked at her sister, looking so vulnerable and sad on a park bench, her beautiful face framed by hacked hair, a big bump protruding from her skinny little body.

'Catey, I cut it all wrong.'

Serena's voice started out strong, then began wobbling

until she could no longer stop a flood of sobs. Cate pulled her in tight. 'It's OK. It's OK.' She shushed.

The tears were gushing out now. 'I hate it, Cate. I hate it.'

Cate let Serena's head rest on her shoulder and squeezed her arm through the thick wool of her poncho.

'The first thing we're going to do is go inside and get a nice cup of tea to go with these brownies,' she smiled, feeling Serena laugh into the fabric of her coat. 'And then we're going to sort out this hair. Surely we can get John Frieda to squeeze Serena Balcon in for an appointment before Christmas Eve?'

Serena blew her nose, looked up and shrugged with a wonky smile. 'If I can't, who can?'

40

New York was having a cold snap. It was trying to snow, the sun was unable to penetrate a blanket of thick, white cloud and the biting wind was the type that froze you to the core. It was just the weather for balaclavas, not that the Upper East Side New Yorkers seemed to notice too much. The collars on their thick coats were pulled up just a little higher, the pace of their walk was just a little bit brisker. Venetia had spent the entire day tucked up at her hotel, the St Regis, making full use of her room, the Christian Dior Suite – ordering room service, drinking hot chocolate and just pottering about the exquisite dove-grey space, too cosy even to think about going outside to shop.

There were plenty of things she wanted to buy, of course; Christmas was coming. She wanted to pick up scented candles from Henri Bendel, trinkets from Tiffany, toys for her friend's children from FAO Schwarz, but it would all have to wait until tomorrow. Today there was only one thing on her agenda other than keeping warm: getting her New York expansion moving forward. An image of her father, scoffing at her ideas, wanting to undermine all her hard work, popped into her mind. She wouldn't let him paralyse her, she thought, her mouth set in a thin, determined line. She was here to make things happen.

At half past three on the dot, Venetia took a cab to Fifty-Seventh Street. It stopped outside a tall brownstone building with a bronze plaque at the top of its stoop, which announced that she had reached the offices of Katz, Lloyd and Bellamy.

Christopher Bellamy, Cambridge graduate, City high-flyer and brother of one of Venetia's schoolfriends had emigrated to New York five years earlier, having married well into a prominent Connecticut family. He had taken his American Bar exams, joined a New York practice and was now a partner in a flourishing real-estate law firm in Midtown.

'Venetia,' said Christopher, standing up from behind a wide desk to welcome her. 'An awfully long way to come for a meeting, but it's always a pleasure to see you.'

In his late thirties, but looking ten years older, Bellamy's hair was thinning, the eyes tired from too many sixteen-hour days; but it was an open, honest face, brimming with an integrity that Venetia trusted. She took off her grey cashmere overcoat, folded it over the back of a leather chair and sat down opposite Christopher while he opened a sky-blue cardboard file, a few pages of correspondence fluttering out.

'So, I see there's been no movement in your father allowing the board to approve the lease on the Madison property?' said Christopher briskly.

'Chris, it's so frustrating,' said Venetia, twiddling her fingers on her lap. She was not nervous, just agitated.

'Well, I've had another letter from Zuckerman Real Estate this morning, enquiring when we propose to exchange on the lease,' said Christopher, taking a swig of coffee. 'I don't need to tell you, Venetia, that if the company isn't authorized to release the funds to do this transaction, then we're going to have to pull out.'

'But I need more time,' said Venetia imploringly. 'The site is so perfect for us, I just don't want to lose it.'

'You may have to,' said Christopher, kindly but firmly. 'We can always look again in the New Year if your father becomes a little more, compliant, shall we say?'

Venetia pulled a face. 'Will it help if I personally pay the premium on the lease?'

She did not have an enormous amount of liquid capital at her disposal, although she knew that as soon as probate on Jonathon's assets came through, any week now, she would be a very wealthy woman indeed. Although he had left the shares in the company to his brother, the Kensington Park Gardens home, £5 million in cash and a small collection of modern art had been gifted to her.

'I know how desperate you are to have this site,' said Christopher, looking sympathetically at her, 'but I'm here to advise you in the best way I can. For a start, I'm not entirely sure that the freeholders will lease the premises to an individual. Most companies want a commercial outfit as a lessee.'

Venetia had been thinking strategy for the last fortnight.

'But then I could sub-let it to the company for an amount that doesn't need a special resolution to be released from the company account, couldn't I?'

'Hmm, sub-letting is rarely allowed in most standard commercial leases,' said Christopher, admiring her lateral thinking, 'but I've set up a meeting with a representative from Zuckerman tomorrow, so we can go down and see if we can thrash this out. At the very least, hopefully we can buy a little more time. In the meantime, your husband's probate may be through and the new owner of those shares – his brother, I believe – can use his voting rights to allow the New York transaction to go ahead.'

Venetia shook her head. 'No. Stefan has already told me

that when he gets Jonathon's shares in the Venetia Balcon company, he's going to continue to allow my father to have the power of attorney until he decides what to do with them. Basically, Stefan can't be bothered with the company shares, but he certainly doesn't want me to have them.'

'That is a worry,' said Christopher slowly.

'I do have another idea, though,' said Venetia, resting her hands on the top of the desk.

'Go on,' said Christopher.

'Stefan refuses to sell the shares to me, but what if a third party acquired them? A consortium or a wealthy individual that was perhaps in favour of my vision for the Stateside expansion?'

'Jesus, Venetia,' laughed Christopher, 'I never knew you had such a devious streak.'

'I'm desperate,' said Venetia flatly, 'I know this is the right thing to do for the company.'

'Well, I can see a few holes in that scheme. For one, it will take too long – you said probate has yet to come through on Jonathon's estate? And it really is – how shall I put this? – skirting around the boundaries of the law, shall we say?'

Venetia found herself blushing slightly as Christopher pushed on. 'If your father really isn't willing to cooperate, then you have got to hope that he somehow gets off the scene. I hear he's getting married? Perhaps he'll lose interest in business. On the other hand – worst-case scenario – he may be interested in buying Jonathon's shareholding himself. Then we're in trouble.'

'I doubt he could afford it,' said Venetia, shaking her head, 'I don't think his finances are very healthy at the moment.'

'Well, you've got to think of something. And if you don't want the lease on the Madison Avenue property to slip through your fingers, I suggest you think it up pretty quickly.'

* * *

460

When the heels of her Gucci boots hit the pavement outside Christopher's offices, Venetia just kept on walking. Block after block slipped by as she meandered her way uptown. Every now and then she would pause to look in the shop windows of all her favourite stores. She admired the jewels on velvet cushions in Bulgari, the feathered tweed jackets in Chanel. It was growing dark, and that was when New York started to look its best, The Plaza festooned with fairy lights like a glorious wedding cake, laughing couples, well wrapped up, riding in the hansom cabs that trotted by towards Central Park. It was a cold, crisp, romantic scene that made Venetia think about Jack. She hadn't been able to shake him out of her consciousness ever since she had cut short their affair after Jonathon's death. Sheer force of will usually kept him at the back of her mind, but moments like these only made a picture of his face, the sensation of his body, so sharp and real it was as if he was by her side.

She stopped herself. Suddenly feeling the cold, she curled her hands up tighter in her brown leather gloves and strode on purposefully.

After forty-five minutes of walking, she reached her destination. A small store on Madison between Seventy-Eighth and Seventy-Ninth Street. *Her* store. Although it was a stone's throw from various Upper East Side favourites: Vera Wang, Cartier, Gucci, it looked a little unloved. White spray-canned writing in the front window announced that its final closing day had only been last week, but already it looked cold and abandoned. To Venetia, however, it glowed with potential as it had done the first time she had set her eyes on the shop two months earlier. The location was perfect, the brownstone building small but with bags of char-acter, with long elegant windows and a white awning that sloped onto the street.

She rested her fingers against the glass and a cloud of

chilled breath escaped from her lips, misting up the window-pane. She stayed there a few minutes, trying to peer in, but her eyes would not focus, such was her anger at her father. Let's see what the meeting at Zuckerman holds in store, she told herself. It was not over yet.

Taking a step backwards from the store she could see the reflection of a man in the glass, watching her. Venetia span around and froze as she looked into his face.

'Luke . . . Luke? Is that you?' she stuttered. It was him, it *was*.

The past flooded back like a tsunami, memories swelling over her so quickly she could hardly catch her breath. Luke Bainbridge had been the love of her life; or so she had thought at the time. They had split three years ago, shortly before she had met and married Jonathon. They were the odd couple – she the polished aristocrat, Luke the gung-ho photographer – but it had been a match that worked. For the two-year duration of their relationship they had enjoyed each other, complemented each other, understood one another. He'd slowly knocked down Venetia's defences, helped her trust men again, enjoy sex, helped her build her business up from the ground. Above all, he had taught her not to take life so seriously. She would have married him in a shot, and she'd been confident he was on the brink of proposing, when the phone call came out of the blue, telling her that he had met somebody else. She had never felt pain so brutal. Her heart ached so badly it eventually went completely numb. Standing in front of her now, Luke looked embarrassed and a little shell-shocked, as if he had instantly regretted stopping at the shop window.

'I thought it was you,' he said slowly, 'I could only see the side of your face.' He touched his chin as if he were telling her that he could recognize her from a tiny part of her body. She felt a flutter in the pit of her belly. The slightest movement or gesture could still ignite something inside her. Physically he was still the same – his light brown hair was now a little longer, his skin a shade more tanned, he was still incredibly sexy – but his clothes had changed beyond all recognition. Jeans, shirt, expensive loafers, a very polished look, not like the louche scruff that had been his trademark around London. And she couldn't help but notice the gleam of a gold ring on his wedding finger, so shiny it was almost certainly new.

'New York suits you,' she said finally.

He nodded imperceptibly. 'So what are you doing here?'

'I'm here on business,' she replied casually, 'I leave tomorrow night. And you?'

The atmosphere was thick and taut like a cello string.

'I live here now,' he said haltingly, casting his eyes up and down the pavement. 'Have done for a while.'

'The photography, I take it?'

'Kind of,' said Luke. He now had a slight mid-Atlantic accent. 'Actually, I've got a studio. Two, in fact. One in Chelsea, one in the Meatpacking district.'

Finally he smiled and it reminded Venetia of Jack's smile, crooked and confident but with a slight hint of awkwardness. They stood awkwardly on the pavement together, seconds seeming like minutes. Venetia just wanted to let him walk away. She certainly had the feeling that Luke was ready to run down Madison screaming. But there was too much unresolved business to let him go. And she didn't want New York to be an entirely wasted journey.

'Do you fancy going for a drink?'

Luke's expression froze, then melted. 'OK. The Carlyle is just around the corner.'

She smiled to herself. The Carlyle Hotel was chic, its bar a fragrant watering hole for ladies who lunched. Not Luke's usual style at all. In the old days it had been a running joke that Luke had been Venetia's 'bit of rough'. The charming, lovable photographer who could drag her into dive bars and make her stay out late at parties. She was still the same person back then – elegant and poised Venetia, but he brought out another side in her, a more relaxed and casual woman. They turned back towards East Seventy-Sixth street and slipped into the Carlyle's bar. A cosy, intimate space with an expensive Art-Deco feel, it had the understated intimacy of the rest of the hotel. It didn't surprise Venetia that many assignations had occurred here: rumour had it that Marilyn Monroe used to meet JFK here for secret trysts.

She felt as if she was having one of her own.

'Want to share a bottle of red?' he asked as they slipped onto a chocolate-brown banquette. Ah, just like old times, she thought sadly. 'OK.'

Luke summoned the waiter, visibly loosening up as he took off his overcoat.

'Nice tan,' smiled Venetia. 'Not a New York tan.'

'Mauritius, actually,' he said, shrugging. 'I've just got back.'

'Oh yes,' asked Venetia, 'a job?'

He looked down, fiddling with the button of his coat. 'Honeymoon, actually.'

It was not the punch in the stomach she had been expecting, more like a slight sting. She had, after all, seen the thick gold band on his finger.

'Congratulations. Who is she?'

He was silent for a moment, staring intently at the rim of his wine glass.

'Fernanda,' he said quietly, 'she's South American. She's nice, you'd like her.'

Great, thought Venetia, she could picture it now. A twenty-three-year-old model stalking down the Upper East Side with legs as long as ladders and chestnut hair swaying in the wind.

'A model?' she asked, knowing the inevitability of the answer.

'Sometimes. Her family lives in New York. She does a bit for the family business, marketing and so on.'

'Oh yes? What sort of business?'

Luke cleared his throat. 'They have a few, actually. Paper, timber, jewellery: they own Lempika's.'

Venetia nearly choked on her wine. The ridiculously wealthy Brazilian DeSantos family. Fernanda was an heiress. Luke had hit the jackpot.

She sat back in her seat and listened to the bar's piano. They talked a little about their lives. She told him about her ideas for the New York store, omitting her father's objections; talked about what her sisters were doing, even about Jonathon's death three months ago, at which Luke looked genuinely saddened and shaken.

Life looked rosier for Luke. Newly married to Fernanda, living in the townhouse on Eighty-Fourth Street – her money – while the two studios he owned downtown were not just any old studios, but the Banana Studios, two of the most prestigious photographic studios in New York, where swanky ad campaigns were shot and supermodels posed for the covers of the biggest, glossiest magazines. How the hell had he managed that? she thought suddenly. In London he had been just a jobbing photographer.

Luke topped up her glass and told her another story. Anecdotes and reminiscences slipped by as easily as the wine went down. He was still fun to talk to, she thought: that was what she'd always loved about him. But there was one topic that remained unaddressed and, as the minutes ticked by, it became more and more obvious. She had to ask the question. She had to know. She was here in New York to confront issues, to get things moving again, and she wasn't going to let this one slip by.

465

'Did you leave me for Fernanda?' she said as the last dribbles of the Merlot were poured into her glass.

Luke met her gaze, then stared back down at the table.

'I didn't leave you for anybody, Venetia,' he said softly after a few moments.

She looked at him, puzzled. 'But that's what you told me. That day you called it all off.'

He wiped his mouth with the back of his hand and cleared his throat.

'I'm sorry how it all happened,' he said, his voice quieter now. 'I'm not proud of it, but what happened, how I did it, at the time I thought it was for the best.'

She found herself snorting. 'For the best? It was like one of those urban myths: movie stars terminating their marriages by fax.'

It still hurt, damn him. Two years of absolute happiness had dissolved into nothing in the space of one phone call when he'd told her he had met somebody else on a job in Paris. She had cried solidly for forty-eight hours, but when the tears had stopped she had driven around to his flat, having decided not to let Luke Bainbridge go without a fight. But nobody came to the door. His home phone had been cut off, his mobile number changed. Neighbours said they hadn't seen him in a week. He had disappeared out of her life like a ghost.

There was another long pause before Luke spoke again. 'Four years ago, if you had asked me if I would ever let your father come between us, I would have said no way. Not ever in a million years.'

Venetia felt suddenly nauseous. That word again. *Father*.

Luke continued in a rush. 'About a week before it happened' – Venetia did not need the 'it' to be qualified – 'do you remember? We went for one of your father's dinners at Huntsford?'

She nodded vaguely. She didn't really remember, but let him continue.

'It was late; you'd gone to bed. I remember thinking how I should stay up and try to make an effort with your father – you know, drink, try and have a laugh with him.'

He sighed, his cheeks puffing out noisily.

'Anyway, it turns out he had a similar idea. He took me to one side and asked me where our relationship was going. I told him how much I loved you, respected you. I thought that's what you're supposed to say to fathers.'

His voice lowered a few tones. 'Of course it was true, anyway. I did love you.' Luke's eyes met hers for a fraction of a second then darted away.

'I told him we were going to move in together that month. Do you remember how we'd planned it all out? It seems weird now that after two years together we weren't already shacked up. But we were busy, I guess, weren't we?'

By 'we', Venetia knew he meant her. She had resisted his attempts to buy a place together, fobbed him off with excuses about work and hectic schedules, wanting to wait until she was absolutely sure.

'I thought he would have been pleased,' said Luke, looking at Venetia imploringly, searching her face for some register of emotion, but it remained blank, impassive. Luke took a slow, deliberate breath before dropping the bombshell. 'Your father told me he didn't want me in your life. That I wasn't good enough for you. He said we all knew it, especially you . . .'

Luke looked searchingly at Venetia again before continuing. 'He asked me to think about why you'd been dragging your feet about us moving in together. Of course it had been something I'd been thinking about . . . He said that you'd told him you saw no future in the relationship. That you didn't see me as "husband material".'

'That's not true!' exploded Venetia.

'What was I supposed to think?' asked Luke, his face pinched.

'Then what?' asked Venetia, not wanting to know any more but being drawn towards the morbid truth.

'I told him to go fuck himself. Part of me didn't want to believe it. Then . . .' Another long pause. ' . . . he threatened me. My flat was ransacked two days later. I never told you, because I knew he was behind it. All my camera equipment, thousands of pounds worth of the stuff, just smashed up and broken. Then I started to notice these nasty-looking blokes following me everywhere, just loitering near me, staring at me. I was scared and I went to see him at the gallery. He said he could make life hell for me, for you. For both of us. I didn't want us to look forward to a future like that.'

'So you finished it, just like that? Without even telling me the truth . . . ?' Venetia's voice was almost a whisper.

Luke's face flushed with shame. 'He offered me money to disappear. A *lot* of money. I took it and came to New York. I thought it would be best for everyone.' He dropped his chin to his chest and rubbed his forehead with his palm.

'How much did I cost?'

Luke could hear the rage in her voice. 'Van, it wasn't like that,' he said, trying to grab her hand across the table.

'Well, what the hell was it like?' said Venetia, forcing herself to speak loudly, firmly at him.

'It was enough for me to get out of your life.' She looked up and saw him turn away, putting a fingertip to the corner of his eye.

'Oh yes,' she spat. 'Enough for you to open a studio downtown and for you to become the king of New York.' The shiny gold ring on his wedding finger winked cruelly at her once again. Unconsciously she looked down at her own bare hand. She had taken her ring off a few weeks after Jonathon's death, put it in a box and kept it there.

'I thought we were happy, I thought we were in love,' she said finally, slowly. 'We could have been happy together.'

'Oswald wouldn't have let us be happy,' he said simply. 'Can't you see that? He didn't want you to be with someone like me, and who can blame him? A jobbing photographer with no real money or kudos who could bring nothing to the Balcon stable. He made me see that I could never give you what you deserved in life. I read that you married Jonathon von Bismarck. You needed someone like him. *Oswald* needed someone like Jonathon.'

She shut her eyes, remembering. Her father had introduced her to Jonathon shortly after Luke's departure. Lonely, depressed and hurt, she had let herself be steamrollered into a relationship that should never have got as far as second base, let alone the altar. And now, here she was, a widow, childless, frustrated in her business and hampered by her father. With or without Luke, he had still managed to make her unhappy. She felt defeated, too weak to be angry.

'I'm sorry, Van.'

Venetia stared blankly at him. She was not in love with Luke Bainbridge any more. He was a coward, an opportunist, who had sold her down the river, and now he had the wife, the house, the business, the gilded life. Luke had the life she should have had. She felt cheated, robbed, manipulated. But one emotion above all others was growing second by second like a virus. It was hate. She hated Oswald for meddling with her life and packaging it up into boxes he approved of. She loathed him, despised him. She knew now that she had to escape his web at all costs. And she would: she just needed some time.

41

Huntsford Castle looked spectacular, a bright twinkling light in the black winter sky. Flaming torches lined the drive, the long windows of the house glowed amber like jack-o'-lanterns and tea-lights floated gently around the moat like an angelic collar. It was eight o'clock on Christmas Eve. Guests were still streaming in, some carrying extravagantly wrapped presents, others just an air of privilege and sophistication. Even though it was always held on Christmas Eve, everybody always made the effort to go to Lord Balcon's Huntsford Ball. Ex-Cabinet ministers, Mayfair players, locals from the estate, socialites, artists, even a smattering of Maria's opera crowd: anybody who'd been sent a ticket made the effort to come, however foul Oswald's behaviour had been throughout the rest of the year. And they were all rewarded by a spectacle the moment they stepped through the door. The fire roared in the Great Hall, jazz flowed through air that smelt of spices and pine trees, the staircase was polished so brightly it shone like a conker, the muskets on the oak-panelled walls gleamed. Huntsford was on parade, and it had never looked so good.

Upstairs, in her old bedroom, Venetia was not in the party

spirit. The sound of laughter, music and conversation floated up the stairs, but it wasn't nearly enough to get her in the mood. Since she'd returned from New York she'd been eaten up by rage, made worse by not knowing what to do about it.

The easiest thing to do would be to cut Oswald out of her life completely. Not turn up to the ball. Not come running every time he picked up the phone. Not pretend that his bullying was acceptable behaviour. But it was not as simple as all that, was it? Now he was part of her business, she couldn't just block out his existence. Some sort of confrontation was necessary, inevitable. So she'd turned up to the ball without any exact plan of action about what she was going to say or do, just a resolve that she had to do *something*.

Her eyes moved to a stack of presents peeping out from her Mulberry leather holdall on the bed. Gifts for Cate, Serena, Camilla, Mr and Mrs Collins. But nothing for Oswald. It was a small mark of her defiance, but a step forward. She had never fought with her father before, but the prospect of confrontation filled her with a strangely perverse power. Staring at herself in the long mirror of her dressing table, she decided to have a last-minute change of outfit, swapping her elegant cream organza shift-dress for an altogether much stronger look. She took it off and squeezed herself into a fitted, pewter-grey Prada cocktail dress, adding her highest thin pointed heels. Her hair was pulled back into a chignon, a diamond tennis bracelet dangled confidently on her wrist. She felt armour-plated, strong, in control. She exhaled slowly, looking at the reflection. For a moment she half expected to see Jonathon behind her, sitting on the bed, adjusting his cuffs or pulling on a brogue with a shoehorn. Closing her eyes, she listened to her breathing for a moment, then turned out the light and went to join the party.

* * *

471

'There you are,' said Cate, appearing on the landing just outside Venetia's room. 'I was just coming to find you. The party's beginning to fill up and Daddy's been asking where we all are.'

A look of slight embarrassment flashed across Cate's face. 'And there's one other thing,' she said hesitantly.

'What?' said Venetia, walking towards the top of the staircase.

Cate took a moment before answering. 'I hope you're not going to be angry with me, but –' there was a guilty pause – 'I've invited Jack Kidman.'

Cate saw her sister's face light up at the mention of Jack's name, then turn suddenly angry and flustered. 'You've done *what*?'

Venetia felt her pulse race. She hadn't seen Jack since Jonathon's death. No matter how much she had wanted to see him over the past three months, to be held in his arms, to be reassured and encouraged by him, she couldn't bring herself to contact him, constantly reminding herself of the promise she'd made when she had seen Jonathon's burnt, lifeless body in the mortuary. Jonathon might not have been the love of her life, but she had still mourned, and she knew she could not cope with the guilt of continuing the affair with Jack on top of those feelings of grief and loneliness. She had lost Luke, Jonathon, the chance to have a baby, and then she had lost Jack too. All at once, the year flashed in front of her, unfolding like a macabre slideshow. It had one overriding theme: it was all about loss. She didn't want to see Jack and be reminded.

'How dare you?' said Venetia, almost choking on her words. The two women moved back into the shadows of the west wing so that they could not be seen and their raised voices could not be heard by the rest of the party.

Cate shrugged apologetically. 'I'm sorry, but . . .'

Actually, Cate wasn't sorry. She knew her sister needed

something to stop the guilt that was slowly beginning to crush her. She grabbed her by her shoulders and glared at her. 'Van, will you stop being such a martyr and see him? You need him.'

'I don't *need* anyone, Cate. I certainly don't need your interfering.'

'Just see him.'

Venetia turned away, shaking her head, already realizing that she was excited at the prospect of Jack Kidman being just downstairs.

'Where is he then?' she said icily.

'He's outside. I don't think he'll come in unless you invite him in yourself. Go on, go.'

Venetia nodded her head so gently that it was barely a movement. She made her way down the staircase, her delicate hand gripping the polished banister so tightly her knuckles went pale.

People were still filing in through the vast front doors, handing their invitations to black-tied security guards and accepting a flute of champagne from one of the many white-tailed serving staff. As she weaved through the crowd, people called out to greet her, some kissing her on the cheek, others offering awkward condolences. The chilly night air hit her as she looked out into the darkness; the line of blazing torches stretched off down the drive, fading to specks of orange light. The heels of her peacock-blue-satin shoes crunched along the gravel and she lost her footing, turning her ankle slightly. She wobbled slightly again on the loose stones, holding her champagne flute aloft, and looked around. Flanking both sides of the house were long lines of expensive cars that had brought the guests here. Rolls-Royces, Bentleys, BMWs, Range Rovers. Nearest to the house, she could see a familiar shape propped up against the bumper of Oswald's 1922 Rolls-Royce, the man's face lit up by the glow from one of the guttering torches. Her heart flipped as she realized it was Jack. He was in a black tailored dinner jacket, his hair had been cut slightly. His chin was lowered, but his eyes looked up, sexy and twinkling in the light of the flame. She took a quick sip of champagne to steady herself. She had come here tonight to be strong, not to be weak. Jack Kidman represented weakness.

'Happy Christmas, Van,' he said softly, his voice almost getting lost in the hum of noise in the background. She remained motionless, trying to stare coolly at him.

'I nearly didn't come,' he continued.

'So did I,' said Venetia.

Silence. They could hear the crackle of the torch at Jack's side.

'What are you doing here, Jack?' asked Venetia finally.

'Cate invited me.'

'No, what are you really doing here?'

He laughed softly to himself. 'This really isn't my usual style,' he said, trying to lighten the atmosphere between them. 'If I'm told to stay away, I usually get the message.'

'Well, why haven't you then?' she said curtly. *What was her problem? She missed him*. She might have told him not to contact her any more, but a part of her had been desperate for him to turn up on her doorstep.

'Sometimes I can't help myself,' he said quietly.

She looked at his face. It was earnest, hopeful. 'I've spent the last three months trying to work out how we ended up like this,' he added.

She must be strong. But her aristocratic stiff upper lip didn't feel particularly stiff right now. She bit it so hard she could feel a rush of blood to the skin.

'What isn't clear, Jack?' asked Venetia, straightening her back. 'We were having an affair, I betrayed my husband.

He's dead now. Maybe you can't work out how that changed things, but for me it's patently obvious.'

'Van, why are you doing this to yourself?' asked Jack suddenly, looking her directly in the eye. 'You're miserable, you feel guilty, OK, I give you that. But why can't you let yourself be happy?'

'Don't come here to judge me,' she snapped, jerking her hand for emphasis and spilling her champagne.

'Listen to yourself! That's not you!' said Jack, pushing himself upright. 'You're behaving like the person I first met back in Seville. Angry, suppressed, wound up like a little toy, not letting yourself be the real you. You're not that person, Van. Let yourself out!'

Deep down, she knew he was right, but she couldn't accept it – not now, not when she had steeled herself to be so strong with her father. Crippled with bitterness, she wasn't going to let herself be talked into anything or be manipulated by any man ever again.

'Let me say it again, Jack,' she said coolly. 'My husband died. That changed things. That changed everything. I'm not the same person.'

'You never really loved him.' Jack's voice was quiet, daring, unsure of whether he had pushed one boundary too many.

'I never, ever, said I didn't love him,' said Venetia, her voice trembling, loose teardrops beginning to fall onto her cold cheek.

Jack took a moment to watch her standing there, champagne dripping out of her angled flute, like a fragile, broken Hitchcock blonde. He began to move towards her, his arms still by his sides, walking slowly, cautiously, like a man venturing out into the sea to rescue a bobbing dinghy. Venetia didn't move, just staring at some unfocused point, letting the teardrops fall. When he was inches away, his hands reached out, pulling her in gently towards his body. As if she were floating, Venetia allowed herself to drift towards him. His grip tightened around her slender body and she let the weight of her head fall on his shoulder. She was sobbing now, leaving a dampness on the black fabric of his jacket shoulder.

'I love you, I miss you, I want to be with you. Let it go, let everything go,' he said, whispering into the paleness of her hair.

'I'm sorry,' said Venetia, pulling her head back so she could look into his eyes. 'I don't want to feel like this, I don't want to be like this, but he's made me like this.'

'Who? Jonathon?' asked Jack.

'My father. My *father*.'

Jack's eyes narrowed in anger.

'He's trying to ruin my business, control me, manipulate me. He wants to take everything I want away.' She was crying hard now, in big, gulping sobs.

'Tell me what's happened,' said Jack softly, leading her back to the bonnet of the car. Sitting huddled in the warm crook of Jack's arm, Venetia told him what she had found out in New York. How Oswald had betrayed her, paid Luke to stay away from her.

'I have to find out why,' said Venetia, spinning around to look at him, suddenly ready to confront her father again. 'I have to ask him; I have to find out the truth.'

'What good is the truth if it's only going to make you more miserable?' replied Jack slowly. 'We're going to go into the party, we're going to have a great time, and tomorrow I'm going to take you back to London and we're going to make ourselves happy.'

'But I have to,' said Venetia softly.

'You don't have to do anything,' said Jack, pulling her close, 'except kiss me.'

* * *

Even at eight months pregnant, Serena was still beautiful. Towering over most guests, her billowing scarlet dress flowed from her ample breasts in an Empire line. A huge aquamarine cocktail ring sat on her middle finger like a duck's egg, twinkling in the low light. Even her chopped hair had been sorted out with a few subtle extensions, so it now framed her face beautifully, flowing past her shoulders like shiny drapes of gold. She took a deep breath as she swept down the staircase above the Great Hall, realizing it was the first time in five years that she had been at the party alone. She rubbed her tummy wistfully – no, she wasn't on her own.

'Serena. There you are.'

Serena took a breath as she saw the tall figure of Roman LeFey standing in the hallway smiling awkwardly at his old friend.

'Roman. You came,' she replied, her megawatt smile lighting up her face.

She walked towards him, feeling a conflicting sense of relief and embarrassment. She hadn't seen him since the Met Gala, when she had not worn the gown he had specially made for her and their friendship had deteriorated because of it. At the time she'd dismissed him. A queen having a hissy-fit, she remembered telling Michael. But when she'd received the scarlet poinsettia from him, it was another reminder of how she had let pettiness come in between her and the things that mattered. Cate had been right that afternoon in the square of The Boltons. It was never too late to make things right. She had reciprocated Roman's gift with a huge holly wreath sent to his atelier in Rue Cambon, along with an invitation to the Balcon Christmas Ball.

'Of course I came,' grinned Roman. 'Patric and I were going to spend Christmas in London anyway. And Patric was dying to see Huntsford.'

Roman looked her up and down appreciatively. 'Still not wearing one of my dresses.'

For a second she winced with embarrassment until she realized her friend was joking. 'Well, I didn't know you made maternity wear. Hardly anything fits any more. I'm a whale.'

'Hardly,' said Roman. 'When is it due?'

'Officially in three weeks' time. Elected C-section. Too posh to push, you know me.'

'But it could come at any time!' he said, in mock horror. 'We'll have to airlift you to the Portland!'

'Don't say that.'

They laughed and hugged, the friendship coming back to life with each gesture, sentence, expression.

'I'm sorry. I was stupid,' said Serena softly.

Roman took her hand and shook his head, smiling slowly. 'You don't need to say it.'

In the ballroom, where the Tempest Jazz Band were halfway through a Cole Porter medley, Cate Balcon floated happily around the dance floor, unaware that she looked as if she'd been lit from within. Her pale pink Chloé dress skimmed off her curves and the large scoop neck showed off her round cleavage. Her hair had been fastened back, tendrils falling around her face, lips dabbed with a rouge gloss on a smile that was as wide as the Thames. She was thoroughly enjoying being on the arm of Nick Douglas, who had been charming and lovely and attentive all evening.

It was the first time that Cate had ever brought anyone to one of her father's balls. Cate being single at Christmas was her own cruel and personal standing joke, as she thought back to the number of times she'd been dumped in December. Her mind skipped back to the dull conversations she'd had at this annual ordeal, talking trade deficits with the men or society gossip with the women, when actually she was aching with loneliness and resolving to get somebody by her side the following Christmas Eve. No wonder the Huntsford Ball had always seemed like a chore that had to be suffered.

But tonight was different. For once she was not jealous that Nick was attracting a lot of attention; she was simply proud that they all saw him with her. At the back of her mind was the cautious expectation that something might happen between them tonight. They were friends, yes, and that friendship was wonderful, but surely not every friendship was like this, she'd asked herself time and time again. They didn't kiss, make love, wake up in each other's arms; but the past few weeks they'd felt too close, too intimate, as if their friendship had become so swollen and full that it had spilled over. But into what?

She looked up at him, holding onto her arms and trying to keep up with the fast beat of the music. It was love, she thought suddenly, the idea popping into her head like a light bulb coming on. Away from the hard work, the worry and the stress of running a business, away from all that, wrapped in a bubble of happiness on the dance floor, she could admit it to herself now. She loved him. The song ended. Nick took two drinks from a passing waiter and they both collapsed onto a chaise longue on one side of the room.

'I haven't seen Venetia and Jack come in yet,' said Nick, looking through the ballroom doors into the hallway, which was crowded with people.

'Hmm, I hope I haven't goofed up there,' said Cate, looking worried and brushing a strand of hair back from her cheek.

'Oh, you're just spreading a bit of Christmas love,' laughed Nick. 'Don't worry, you did the right thing, definitely.' He grabbed a sun-dried tomato sitting on a disc of bruschetta and popped it in his mouth. 'I don't know why you were so dreading coming. This is such a great party. I thought your old man was skint.'

'I thought so too,' mumbled Cate. She had to admit however that tonight's party was bigger and better than ever, and that wasn't just to do with her buoyant mood. She picked up a spiky green holly leaf, part of a wreath decorating a small table, and pricked Nick playfully. 'Anyway, you,' she said, looking at him sipping a Diet Coke while she drank her flute of Krug, 'why are you not drinking?'

'I'm driving,' said Nick, looking surprised. 'I thought you knew that.'

Cate was feeling a little brave tonight. 'But I said you could stay,' she said, feeling her cheeks flush lightly, hoping that it was camouflaged by the peach blush. 'No one comes to the Huntsford Christmas Ball and doesn't drink.'

'So what are all these people going to do?' asked Nick, looking around the room. 'It's Christmas Day tomorrow. Everyone's going to want to get back to London or wherever after the party, aren't they?'

'Darling,' said Cate, making her voice as plummy as she could, 'simply everyone here has a driver.'

'Ah, of course!' smiled Nick.

'Go on, what are you going to do?' pressed Cate. 'We have seventeen bedrooms. I'm sure there's room for one more person.'

Shit, had she sounded too pushy? She was sick of being so crap with men, sick of waiting to be seduced when *she* could do something about it. Suddenly she thought back to their night in Milan and winced.

'Are you sure?' asked Nick. Cate breathed a sigh of relief. No rejection just yet. 'I mean, wouldn't your dad be pretty furious to find me here on Christmas morning?'

'Oh yes, I forgot,' said Cate good-naturedly. 'He'd probably skin you alive with the turkey carving knife.'

'Well, in that case, I'll stay, so long as I can make a quick getaway in the morning.'

Cate felt a little arrow of hope shoot into her heart. 'Brilliant! Well, I'd better go and get us two glasses of champagne to celebrate.'

'You have no idea, have you?' scolded Oswald, waving his finger at the head waiter, who was visibly trembling. 'At this rate we're going to be out of champagne by ten o'clock. You'll have noticed that my guests are like gannets when it comes to alcohol, so you need to show a little initiative.'

Oswald looked at the dark-haired, middle-aged man standing awkwardly in the middle of the kitchens, sweating in his black tails, and stabbed a finger at the twenty white boxes stacked up at the end of the room labelled 'Cava'. 'I want you to fill up those empty bottles of Moët with that stuff there. Everybody will be too pissed to notice anyway. Put them in the flutes on the trays, too. Go on, man, what are you waiting for?' he shouted.

All of the serving staff looked at Oswald nervously and upped their work-rate by fifty per cent. Oswald turned to leave the kitchen, tugging down his white silk waistcoat and allowing himself a self-satisfied smile. What a night, what a party, he thought to himself, what a turnout! Two High Court judges, twelve members of the House of Lords, a handful of important American buyers from the art world; he hoped Mark Robertson was charming them sufficiently. No doubt he would have to intervene at some point: he couldn't trust anybody to do anything properly, certainly not Robertson. Still, it was quite a night.

As he strode out into the corridor, he collided with Venetia coming the other way. Venetia panicked. She'd been studiously avoiding her father all evening, especially since she had come back into the party with Jack. She had only

481

ventured down into the kitchens to see if she could find Mrs Collins to let her know that she had a present for her and Mr Collins. And now here he was, face to face with her.

'Come down to help the staff?' asked Oswald sarcastically.

'No,' replied Venetia coolly, trying to back away from him. She had left Jack in the ballroom talking to Cate, Nick and Camilla, and wished she had him by her side to strengthen her resolve.

'So who's your little friend?' asked her father mockingly. 'Didn't take you very long, did it?'

'What do you mean, "Didn't take you very long"?'

'Well, Jonathon's hardly cold in the ground, is he?' said Oswald callously. 'And you've clearly got the next one lined up. What is he this time? Writer? Waiter? Wastrel?'

Venetia could feel something snap inside her like a rubber band wound too tight. 'Why?' asked Venetia, taking a deep breath, 'are you going to try to pay him off, too?'

A cloud drifted across Oswald's face. 'Pay him? Why? Is he an escort? That wouldn't surprise me either.'

'I was actually referring to Luke Bainbridge,' said Venetia, trying to sound as composed as possible.

'What are you talking about?' said Oswald arrogantly.

'You know exactly what I'm talking about,' hissed Venetia. 'I met Luke in New York and he told me everything.'

For a second, Oswald actually looked flustered.

'I know everything, Daddy,' she hissed, willing herself to be strong and resolute. 'I know you paid him to stay away from me. I know you – or someone you paid – ransacked his flat, that you threatened him, that you lied to him and said that I didn't think he was good enough for me.'

Oswald grabbed her by the arm and then dropped it

contemptuously, as if he had had some sudden change of heart. 'And you choose to believe him?' he sneered. 'Your stupidity and gullibility surprises even me sometimes.'

'Not so stupid that I won't be manipulated by you one last time, Daddy,' she spat. 'You're pathetic. You want to control everybody just to make yourself feel better.'

She could tell Oswald did not know which emotion to feel first: anger or shock. It was the first time Venetia had ever raised her voice to him, let alone spoken back to him in that manner.

'Whatever did I do to deserve you?' said Oswald, shaking his head, hands on hips. 'You really are so ungrateful, aren't you? Always taking and giving me nothing. Fine, you're quite right, I got rid of Bainbridge. Because I had met Jonathon and thought he was far more suitable for you.'

Venetia spluttered. Yes, she'd been introduced to her husband by her father, but she hadn't, for one second, thought it had been so calculated.

'You would never have amounted to anything if I hadn't helped you,' continued Oswald scornfully. 'I introduce you to someone decent and what does that make me? An ogre?'

'No, a pimp,' replied Venetia under her breath.

He looked down on her condescendingly. 'What's it like to always make the wrong choices, Venetia? Why can't you ever get anything right? You really had an opportunity with Jonathon, but you wasted it, didn't you? Was anybody really surprised he ended up having to sleep with men to fill his life with a little excitement?'

She felt herself tremble with rage. Instinctively she drew her arm back and the glass in her hand tipped back, spilling champagne onto the Persian carpet behind her.

'What's going on?' Jack ran up behind Venetia and grabbed her arm just in time.

'Is everything OK, Van?' he asked, gently pulling her

hand down to her side. He stared coldly at Oswald. 'Why don't you just give your daughter a break?' he said sternly.

'Oh calm down, young man,' laughed Oswald, looking back to see that several waiters had begun to crane their necks around the door to see what the commotion was. 'Not in front of the servants.'

'Well,' said Jack, drawing himself up to his full height, 'does that mean you'd like to step outside to sort this out?' He motioned to the stable door at the back of the kitchen.

Oswald snorted at him and looked down patronizingly. 'I doubt a duel is quite your speed is it, young man? Besides, I haven't brought my rapier.'

There was a thud as Venetia let the flute fall to the floor, as if she was simply too exhausted to hold it any more.

'Are you proud of yourself?' snarled Jack, looking at Oswald. 'Are you proud that you've made your daughter like this?'

'What? Proud of a daughter that's just tried to assault her own father? *Very* proud,' he mocked.

'She's her own worst enemy, Venetia. You'll find that out soon enough,' Oswald added with a callous laugh.

'I don't need you to tell me anything about her,' said Jack.

'No, I imagine you're right, young man,' said Oswald, straightening his jacket, 'I imagine you've seen it all already.'

Now it was Venetia's turn to get between Jack and Oswald, reaching out to grab his wrist before he could form a fist. 'Jack. Don't. He's not worth it.'

'How dare you try and abuse me in my own house?' said Oswald coolly, smoothing down his dinner jacket. 'I don't know who you are or where you came from, but I do know where I want you to go: out there,' he said, pointing through the kitchen to the door. 'Go on. Get out.'

Jack stared coldly back at him and began gently to pull Venetia away. 'Come on, let's go,' he said.

But Venetia simply squeezed his hand, then turned the other way and ran. She ran off down the corridor, away from them both. She turned around, glared at Oswald, and ran up the stairs towards her room.

'Miss Balcon. Can I have a word?'

Serena looked round to see one of the doormen motioning towards the door. 'We have someone outside without a ticket,' he whispered. 'I can't let him in without your say-so.'

'Who is it?' asked Serena impatiently, wondering if Elmore had decided to come after all.

'Says his name is Michael Sarkis.'

If she'd been wearing high heels, Serena felt sure she would have fallen over. 'Are you sure?' She felt a muddle of emotion: apprehension, excitement, outrage. How dare he come to Huntsford? On this night of all nights? On the other hand, she thought, feeling a thrill shoot down her spine, what did he want with her on Christmas Eve?

Part of her wanted to leave him in the cold for at least an hour – all night, preferably. But her curiosity was too much. She hadn't seen him since the summer. There'd been the odd terse phone call, but mainly they'd been communicating through lawyers trying to wring out a mutually acceptable level of maintenance payments for the baby. They'd finally approached a level of money Serena considered almost generous, but she wanted to screw him for every penny she could get. Over the last few months, Michael Sarkis had become a folk devil in her mind, the reason for all her failures and problems – the break-up with Tom, her career in freefall. She'd blame him for stubbing her toe, given half the chance.

'Let him in,' said Serena. 'Tell him to come to the study.'

She wanted to keep him out of view of her father who

would freak if he saw him here. While Oswald had been furious to find out that Serena had been 'stupid enough' to get herself pregnant, the main vent of his wrath had been directed at Sarkis. He'd never been able to attack the man's success – Serena was convinced that Michael's immense wealth irked Oswald as much as the pregnancy – but he'd taken every other swipe he could: *flash wop, robber baron, whore lover*.

Serena took a seat in the study, pretending to study a weighty text, and waited for him to arrive, desperately trying to summon up all the clever put-downs she'd been composing over the past months. The knock on the door was timorous. Having only had a few minutes to prepare herself to meet him, she was taken aback at how quickly her icy composure disappeared once he stood in the doorway. Bloody hell, he looked good, she thought, taking in the way his midnight-blue Armani tux strained over powerful shoulders. His hair was shorter, steel grey at the sides, but it suited him. He had a tan that suggested he'd been in places other than New York. Compared to Oswald's throng of upright, elegantly English party guests, Sarkis was like a slick cosmopolitan shot of sex appeal. She fixed him with an icy stare.

'Hello Serena.'

'Michael,' she nodded.

He sat down on a leather sofa opposite her, playing with a silver bracelet around his wrist.

There was a silence as their eyes locked, electricity bouncing off the ceiling.

'I was in London . . .' he said finally.

'No you weren't,' she replied curtly. 'What do you want?'

'How are you?'

'Cut the crap, Michael. Why are you here?'

'Serena, come on. Let's at least be civil.'

She stared at him silently. 'Drink?' she said finally, taking the crystal stopper from a decanter of brandy.

He nodded. 'Jim Berger said you turned down my last offer of money for the baby?'

Serena could feel his eyes greedily appraising her, his eyes focusing on her deep cleavage. 'Frankly it was an insult,' she said tartly.

'Insult?' replied Michael, furrowing his brow. 'I'd have thought it was enough to live in luxury. Even for you.'

'It depends on your idea of luxury, Michael,' said Serena, angry at herself for feeling attracted to him.

'Anyway. I don't think it's necessary . . . The money, that is,' he said slowly.

That threw her. 'What do you mean?' she asked cautiously.

'I mean I have been a fool.'

'You could say that . . .'

Michael let his hands fall between his legs. 'I was a fool to let all this get out of control, Serena. After what happened in Cannes, I should have tried harder to stop what we had falling apart.'

She took a breath, wrong-footed. 'But you did. You asked for a *paternity test*. How was I supposed to feel? Flattered?'

'You wouldn't take my calls, you wouldn't see me . . .'

'I was livid! You were a shit, Michael. A total shit.'

Michael downed the brandy in one. 'How do you think I felt when I found out about the baby from the *National Enquirer*? I thought, fuck you.' His dark eyes flashed arrogantly and then immediately softened.

'Well, I'm so sorry I hurt your feelings,' she said sarcastically. She could sense a grovelling apology and was determined to enjoy it.

'Help me out here, Serena. I'm here to say sorry. To say I've been a grade-A jerk. I want to make it up to you.'

Her eyes opened dramatically, incredulously. 'You haven't

487

so much as picked up the phone to me in months, we've been conversing through your lawyer, and now you want to "make it up to me" . . . ?'

'My mother died three weeks ago.'

She stopped herself spitting more hostility in his direction. 'I'm sorry.' She knew they were close.

'Lung cancer. Diagnosed in September, dead by December. I thought, at least she saw her son become a success. At least she could be proud of me. And you know what she told me?' Serena shook her head. 'She told me to get my arse into gear. Sort my life out. I couldn't believe it.' He dropped his chin mournfully into his chest.

'She said "Where's your base?",' he continued, his voice cracking. '"Where's your anchor? What do you come home to?"'

Serena was tempted to reply *your whores*, but bit her lip just in time.

'Michael, where is this going?' She wasn't sure what to think: whether he deserved her sympathy or whether it was just another piece of brilliant showmanship designed to win her over.

'I can have a family,' he said softly. 'It's right here. That's our child,' he said, standing up to move towards her, pointing a finger at her belly.

Serena took a step away from him. 'No, Michael it is not your child. You gave up that right when you fucked those whores and then cut me out of your life.'

'Please, Serena, I know what I've done. I know it was wrong. My mom's death showed me that. I just want to be back in your life. Our child's life. Give me a chance.'

'What do you want me to say?' she asked quietly.

'Say you'll be my wife.'

He delved a hand into his pocket and pulled out a ring box, flipping open the lid to reveal an enormous emerald-cut diamond – at least ten carats, thought Serena appreciatively – flanked by two smaller stones. She reached out with her finger to touch it. She longed to slip it on and see the stone dance and twinkle in the soft light of the study. She was mesmerized. It wasn't just the jewel – she'd worn many beautiful pieces before, it was everything that was attached to it. He was offering her her old life back: private jets, beautiful homes, billions in the bank, a legacy for her child. There were so many reasons to jump at his offer, and so many more to run screaming away from it. She looked at him and her groin ached, her mind thinking about the incredible sex they once had. Then an uncomfortable thought stopped her. Is that what it was all about: sex and money? Didn't that make her little more than those women in Cannes? She didn't want to consider it.

'I need to think about this, Michael. You could say you've caught me a little by surprise.'

'Of course. But please, do think about it.'

She nodded slowly. 'I should get back to the party.'

Michael Sarkis wasn't used to giving up that easily. 'I have the plane at Farnborough Airfield. We could fly to my hotel in Vegas. We should do it on New Year's Eve. I can fly your sisters over. Your father –'

'Michael. Slow down.'

'Can I see you tomorrow?'

'Michael. Please.'

'When?' he urged.

'I'll call when I'm ready.'

Oswald stepped outside to get some fresh air, feeling a little bloated from the mix of brandy, champagne and attention that had been lavished on him from grateful party guests. He pulled on his Cohiba and exhaled a ring of dove-grey smoke into the chilly night air, glad to have just a couple of minutes alone to re-energize.

'I saw that little scene down in the kitchen before.' A voice came out from a shadow and a face lit up in the glow of a cigarette.

'Declan O'Connor,' said Oswald, recognizing his jockey's brother. 'I don't recall inviting you.'

'I came with Finbar, didn't I? Of course you *did* invite Fierce Temper's prize-winning jockey?'

'I suppose so,' said Oswald, angry to be caught out by this foul man. 'But you could have made an effort,' he continued, looking at Declan's scruffy linen jacket and black jeans. 'This is a ball, not a hoedown. Anyway, what are you talking about? What little scene in the kitchen?'

'Being so rude to your poor staff who are working so hard.' Declan pulled on the cigarette cupped in his hand. 'Oswald Balcon really should learn some manners.'

Rage gripped Oswald's throat as he thought back to the death threat he'd received on the night of the races at Newmarket.

'It *was* you,' he growled, recognizing quite clearly the mysterious caller's voice. 'You little shit, you phoned me up and threatened me.'

Declan threw the half-spent cigarette onto the soil and started to laugh. 'Don't be so sensitive,' he scoffed. 'Just a bit of fun and games. You shouldn't have bollocked Finbar that afternoon, should you? Put the wind up you, did we?'

Oswald couldn't believe the gall of the man, who seemed no more than twenty-five years old.

'Not only could I have you arrested, I could have you ruined,' he said haughtily, trying to regain the upper hand.

'Don't be like that, Oswald,' smiled Declan insincerely. 'You know me and you have a lot in common . . .'

'Not bloody likely.'

490

'You'd be surprised. See, I don't usually come to parties. Not my scene. But I wanted to talk to you about a little business idea.'

'Not interested, O'Connor,' said Oswald, turning to go back into the house.

'A way we could both make quite a bit of money.'

With party guests starting to mill around them, Declan lowered his voice to tell Oswald his plan.

The older man laughed superiorly when he had finished. 'Get out of my sight, O'Connor,' said Oswald. 'I wouldn't get my hands dirty with any of your grubby little schemes – not that you've a hope in hell with that one.'

He threw his cigar on the floor and deliberately ground it out with his heel. 'And anyway, when it comes to making money, I have plenty of plans of my own.'

'Are you all right?'

Camilla had floated through the double doors of the study looking like Helen of Troy. Her hair was swept back from her face and held in place by two Art-Deco clips; her dress, long and floaty and pale lilac, slid off her body so seamlessly it seemed as if the fabric hardly touched her skin. Her turquoise eyes instantly narrowed, however, as she saw Serena sitting on a chair, staring out of the window into the darkness.

'Serena?'

'Michael Sarkis has just paid me a visit.'

'What? At the party?' said Camilla incredulously. 'Well, I hope you got him kicked out.'

'He asked me to marry him,' she said slowly, still looking out of the window.

Camilla nearly coughed up her cocktail. 'Bloody hell. That's a bit out of the blue! What did you say?' she asked cautiously.

'I didn't say anything. I'm not sure how he thinks he can just turn up after months of being an arsehole and expect me to jump at his marriage proposal. After the way he's *treated* me.'

Camilla looked at her sister, searching her face. Over the last few months, Serena had changed, mellowed, her hard edges softened: everyone could see that. But she was still the same woman, and a part of her sister would be drawn by the powerful magnet of his wealth and power. Sarkis's proposal would still be attractive to her, so Camilla knew she had to be careful. Everyone had been glad to see the back of Sarkis – men like that were selfish and damaging – but she knew Serena. The more you joined in with the bad-mouthing of her boyfriends, the more she became drawn to them.

'So you're not seriously considering it?'

Serena's face twinkled enigmatically. 'But you should have seen the ring.'

'Has your father given any indication of when the wedding of the year is going to be?' asked Jennifer.

Jennifer Watchorn had sidled up to Camilla and Serena as soon as they had re-entered the ballroom. She gestured in the direction of Maria Dante, who was parading territorially around the party.

'I'm not sure it's any of our business,' replied Serena, wanting to add that she didn't really care. She did care, though. She cared a great deal. She had been surprised to learn that the happy couple were due to bring their wedding forward to as soon as February. She really couldn't think what all the hurry was for, which peeved her more than she cared to admit. Surely it couldn't be to do with children?

'How are the two lovely Balcon sisters then?' said Philip

Watchorn good-naturedly, taking the opportunity to kiss both girls on the cheek. 'I didn't have much chance to talk to you at the shooting party last week, Camilla, but we're all very excited about your selection for Esher.'

Philip was a well-known contributor to the Conservative Party coffers and skirted around the edges of politics himself, using his powerful contacts to help further his business empire. Camilla had heard her father talk dismissively about Philip's connections with the party, saying he was only angling for a life peerage.

'You must arrange a meeting with my assistant if you would like to discuss your campaign,' said Philip kindly. Camilla perked up. She could do with having powerful people on her side, particularly with talk of a general election looming within the next eighteen months.

'I am afraid money talks, young lady,' he said, patting her on the back. 'If I were you, I would talk to your father as soon as possible about arranging a fundraiser at Huntsford. I know he lost his seat in the Lords,' he adopted a wincing expression, 'but you need to have the family name visibly rallying around – and who wouldn't want to come to a party here?' He gestured around the ballroom and downed half a balloon of whisky in one gulp.

'Yes, actually that is something I've been meaning to bring up with Daddy,' said Camilla. She didn't know why, but she had a slightly sick feeling in her stomach just talking about it.

Jennifer glanced down at her diamond-encrusted Cartier watch. 'Don't forget the fireworks in fifteen minutes,' she cooed excitedly. 'Are you going out on the drive or up onto the ramparts to watch them?'

'Either way, I think I'm going to go and fetch a wrap,' smiled Camilla. 'The night is cold and the dress is thin!'

She excused herself and walked up the stairs to her

bedroom, where she picked up a fine cream pashmina to put around her shoulders. She was almost back to the door when she heard the distinctive voice of Maria Dante from just outside her room in the corridor. She seemed to be talking to one of her opera friends. Something stopped Camilla from opening the slightly ajar door; instead she stood by the crack to listen to them for a second. 'Of course the whole place needs gutting,' said Maria in her singsong Italian accent. Camilla could hear a tapping on her bedroom wall, as if Maria was checking for rot. 'The English, they do not have the style, *n'est-ce pas*?' said a male voice with a French lilt. 'I think most of the horrible furniture in this house needs to burn with the fireworks.'

'Obviously, I can't change everything immediately,' said Maria, her voice a conspiratorial whisper now, so that Camilla had to lean right up against the door to hear.

'However, I have a lifetime in which to do what I want with this house,' she said with a low, gravelly laugh. 'And this house has got to begin to pay for itself. We could make a fortune hiring it out for these sort of events. Not that Oswald will hear of it at the moment,' she said, sighing.

'Why is that?' asked the Frenchman.

'He's so stubborn: it clouds his judgement. The Musical Evening didn't line his pockets, so now he won't hear of doing anything commercial with Huntsford.'

'So how are you going to do it?'

She laughed. It rose in the air as a cackle. 'I have my ways, *cara*. I have my ways.'

'We'd better get going then,' said Cate to Nick, pulling lightly at the sleeve of his dinner jacket, too afraid to be presumptuous and grab his hand.

'Where are we going?' asked Nick, looking around the room. The party didn't look over.

'Fireworks at midnight, silly,' said Cate. 'Family tradition. Best place to watch them is up on the ramparts of the castle. You might actually enjoy it.'

'Actually we have a bit of a family tradition,' said Nick smiling back at her. 'Not that I go home much, but it's a tradition I like to keep.'

'What is it?'

'Well, we give each other a present on the stroke of midnight on Christmas Eve. I've got yours here,' he said, tapping his pocket.

Cate turned to him in surprise. She hadn't imagined Nick to be the sort to dish out presents, though she based this solely on how careful he was with the company's money, but she was glad now that she had bought him something. She'd gone late-night shopping the week before and, while she had wanted to buy him something special he'd love like a beautiful Dunhill lighter or a sharp Savile Row suit, she had restrained herself. Extravagant present-giving meant exposing yourself, and there was no way she could open herself to that when he'd barely registered a flicker of inter-est. Instead she had plumped for a book she knew he'd enjoy: a hardback biography of David Niven, one of his favourite actors. She was pleased with it – she thought she had hit just the right note: a decent gift and yet nothing too personal that might hint at deeper feelings towards him.

'So do you want me to go and get my present to you?' she asked, motioning towards the staircase.

'Well, that's if you've got me anything,' he said teasingly.

Cate nodded and darted upstairs to fetch the gift, aware that people were starting to move out of the front door or to the stairwell that led up to the ramparts. She quickly grabbed the present, which was wrapped in silver foil paper with a big black bow, tucked it under her arm and went back to Nick.

'OK, shall we go?'

'The fireworks? Yes, but let's go somewhere quieter, just for a few minutes,' said Nick, shaking his head and guiding her away from the crowds.

Quieter? Cate gulped to herself, what did that mean? Strangely she found herself becoming anxious. She wished she had made a few adjustments in the mirror when she had been in her room. She was sure her hair was probably looking like a scarecrow's by now.

'What about the Orangery?' said Cate. 'It's not far, and Daddy usually closes it off for the party. It's all glass, too, so we'll be able to see the fireworks without getting pneumonia.'

They weaved through long hallways until they reached the eastern limit of the house. Finally Cate opened two old double doors with a key she found under a Chinese urn. It wasn't big, but it had one wall and a ceiling of glass that looked out onto total darkness. In the summer, Cate explained, it was full of plants and climbing vines, but now it looked a little neglected. To the left was some large exotic tropical plant, yellow-edged and drooping, and on the other side was a small indoor pond surrounded by a few empty tubs.

'So . . .' said Cate, aware of her growing nervousness.

'So, it's five to twelve,' smiled Nick. 'Present time!'

'I suppose I'd better go first,' said Cate, pulling the package from under her arm. 'I hope you haven't got it already,' she started gabbling. 'I know you like him . . .'

'Don't give the game away,' said Nick, who was still tugging at the silver wrapping paper. Nick's face burst into a genuine smile when he saw the book; he started to leaf through the pages. Cate was glad she had resisted the urge to write some schmaltzy message on the opening page.

'That's fantastic, thanks,' he smiled, tapping the book's cover. 'Now for Cate's present,' he grinned.

Nick's hand disappeared into his pocket and he pulled out a box. She was convinced she saw Nick's face cloud over with anxiety and embarrassment as he passed it over. It was remarkably well wrapped for a gift from a man, she thought as she pulled at the red ribbon and the present winked at her from under the crisp white paper. She was left holding an old copy of *The Wonderful Wizard of Oz*, its spine slightly cracked, its cover a beautiful black-and-white line drawing. It was a first edition.

'I remembered you loved it. You told me your mum used to read it to you –'

She stopped him, feeling too emotional. 'I know,' she said, her voice cracking. 'I'm embarrassed,' she continued, looking down at the cheap hardback she had bought him.

He grinned. 'Don't be. You deserve it.'

Cate looked up at Nick's face; there was definitely a look there that she did not recognize. His easy confidence seemed to have evaporated into a shy awkwardness. He stepped forward, another foot closer.

'Cate, I . . .'

Cate felt a desire to deflect the tension that had suddenly grown between them. She began to babble inanely as if to diffuse it. Stop it, woman, she cursed herself. Stop it. Isn't this what you wanted?

Finally she took a deep breath and smiled broadly at Nick. 'What would this year have been like if we hadn't met?' she said slowly, aware that his body was only inches from hers now.

'Dull,' replied Nick quietly. Suddenly they were not like two friends exchanging gifts on Christmas Eve, but almost two strangers, unaware of what to say to the other. Slowly, Nick put his hand up to her cheek. He was so close now that Cate could feel the heat exuding off his skin. She could see how long his brown eyelashes were, his dark hazel eyes locked on hers, and suddenly she wanted to kiss his eyelids, his neck, his cheek, the soft curve of his lips.

Then the door clattered open and they turned to see Serena framed in the Orangery entrance.

Nick jumped back suddenly at the interruption and Cate almost tripped on her four-inch heels in her haste to get some distance between them.

'There you are, you two! I've been looking for you every-where! Daddy wants us all together on the ramparts. Oh, sorry! Is this a bad time?' Serena smiled, suddenly aware of what she had done. 'I'll see you two upstairs in a minute, then?'

Serena closed the door behind her as quickly as she had opened it. She felt cross with herself. She was desperate to ask Cate what she thought about Michael's proposal, but was also hoping she hadn't ruined it for Cate. She stopped, surprised at herself. She wanted her sister to be happy, and she really did like Nick Douglas, even though he irritatingly reminded her of Tom. Tom's voice had been honed by three years at RADA, but the underlying accent was still the same, as was the boisterous, slightly silly sense of humour. Dammit. Michael had just asked her to marry him, so why was she thinking about Tom? Already she could hear the sound of the first firework being sent up, howling like a banshee, and she hurried onwards.

Huntsford was a labyrinth of corridors and passages; it even had a secret tunnel dating from Edwardian times to allow the servants to move silently from one end of the house to the other. Serena and her sisters knew every inch of this house, having often used the passageways to hide from their father, or move about without triggering his anger. She headed towards the library, where she knew there was a door behind a bookcase that led straight up to the ramparts.

'Serena. I hope you're heading up to the ramparts now?' Maria Dante had appeared in the corridor ahead of her.

Serena was taken aback to see her there. 'Not with Daddy?' she asked with a hint of accusation. There was still something that unsettled her about Maria Dante.

'We are not quite joined at the hip,' she smiled.

'Well, I'm going this way, would you like to come?' said Serena, consciously making a gesture of goodwill. Serena reached out and touched a gold handle just beneath a pile of books and a door sprang open.

'A secret passageway,' said Maria sarcastically. 'How cloak and dagger!'

'It's hardly Agatha Christie,' said Serena, mildly irritated. 'Basically there's only one corridor that connects the kitchen to the front bedrooms. Apparently my great-great-grandfather installed it to stop the servants from having to talk to the master of the house.'

'Oh, you quaint English,' said Maria, following Serena into the thin passageway.

It was hardly a catacomb. Serena had never got over her disappointment as a child to find out that the secret passages in Huntsford weren't at all like a cave in a Famous Five story; they were simply another corridor, albeit out of sight. Still, it was dimly lit and silent, and the darkness was made all the more oppressive by a row of dark family portraits hung on the stone wall. The pale faces of various Balcon ancestors peered down at Maria and Serena like ghouls. Maria was walking behind Serena, the long velvet of her dress swooshing as she walked.

'You do know how much I'm looking forward to spending Christmas with the family, don't you?' said Maria.

Serena couldn't put up with the pretence any longer. 'Really? And what are you going to do at this family gathering? Put more drugs in my suitcase and prowlers in my bedroom? Or are you going to go for something a bit more subtle. Bombs in the bathrooms? Rattlesnakes in the beds, perhaps?'

'What on earth are you talking about?' said Maria, looking startled.

'Don't pretend you don't remember the Huntsford Musical Evening. Your artist liaison manager, Miles, snooping around my bedroom.'

'Serena, don't be so stupid. We were not security conscious and there was an intruder. How can you think such a thing about a member of your own family?'

'Not quite yet, Maria,' Serena huffed.

'Well, I will be soon,' continued Maria smugly. 'Although by this time next year Oswald and I may have a family of our own. Not that you girls wouldn't still be family as well, of course,' she added, as if that was the last thing she believed.

Serena stopped and turned to face her future stepmother. She was smiling in the dark, so all Serena could see were the shadows of her face and the whiteness of her teeth.

'Really?' said Serena cattily, unable to stop herself. 'You *are* still able to have children then?'

'I am only just forty, *mia cara*,' said Maria with more than a trace of sarcasm. 'I know that may seem ancient to you, but we have plenty of time to conceive.'

Serena felt herself unable to respond – unable to breathe, in fact.

'Are you all right?' said Maria smugly. 'You must understand that Oswald wants to try for a son. A son he's always wanted.'

'Of course,' said Serena quietly.

'You can't imagine he would want his bastard grandson to inherit Huntsford now, can you?'

Serena felt her back arch like a cat about to spit. 'I'm sorry?' hissed Serena.

'Your illegitimate child. I am merely pointing out the obvious,' smiled Maria sweetly. 'A bastard child shall not – cannot – inherit Huntsford. Our child, Oswald's and mine, will be the heir to the title, the house – everything.'

Oswald looked up to the skies, his arms folded in front of his chest, his feet wide apart, looking like an English bulldog protecting his territory. Ribbons of light were shooting up into the sky and exploding in vast clusters of thin, spidery flames like amber dandelions. Camilla pulled her pashmina tighter around her shoulders. As she walked up to her father, a red bolt screamed into the sky and opened out into fans of red, green and blue light above them.

'Very impressive this year, Daddy,' said Camilla, noticing that he did not turn to look at her.

'Maria has paid for the display,' he said, smiling slightly. 'It's her gift to the family for Christmas.'

'How generous,' said Camilla coolly.

About seventy people had collected on the ramparts, over a hundred feet up above the grounds of Huntsford. All necks craned to watch the spectacle.

'I think it's gone extremely well tonight,' continued Camilla as Oswald grunted back at her dismissively.

'Of course it has,' he scoffed, still not meeting her gaze. 'It's always been one of the highlights of the social calendar. Look around you: everyone's having a marvellous time.'

'I was wondering . . .' began Camilla, pausing to consider tactics one last time. She knew she was not adept at manipulating her father in the way Serena was, but she knew the trick was to make it look as if she was not really asking for his assistance, rather to flatter him so he would feel powerful and indispensable. '. . . I was wondering, as you're so fantastic at arranging things like this, if you could help me with a fundraising event I'm doing early next year?'

A smug smile curled at Oswald's mouth. 'Fundraising for what exactly?' he asked.

She took a deep breath. 'You'll be aware that I have just been selected for Esher. I'm their prospective parliamentary candidate.' She was careful to say it in a way that suggested he might not have heard about it. 'I need to raise funds for the campaign. I thought it might be a good idea to have a little fundraiser here; what do you think?'

Oswald did not answer, instead extending his head further back to watch the fireworks. 'The Huntsford Ball is not a fundraiser, Camilla,' he said finally. 'You must appreciate that, after the Musical Evening, I am a little less inclined to invite complete strangers into my house for any enterprise – commercial, charitable or otherwise.'

Camilla could tell this was going to be an uphill battle. 'But I'm not a stranger, I'm your daughter.'

'Yes, when it suits you.'

'What's that supposed to mean?' asked Camilla. 'I thought you would have been supportive in my attempts to get into politics. To be honest, I'm bloody surprised that you haven't mentioned it before now. I've had congratulations from everybody else except my own father.'

A rocket screamed into the sky and exploded into a star-burst. Oswald finally turned his head to look at her. 'I have neglected to discuss your foray into the political arena, not because I didn't hear about your little "triumph" –' he said the word sarcastically – 'but because it is yet another of this family's misguided enterprises.'

'But you were in politics for years,' replied Camilla. 'You loved it. Why would it be any different for me? Why is it suddenly "misguided"?'

Oswald turned his head so that he just stared out into the blackness in front of him. 'The fact is, Camilla dearest, you are not suited to life in Parliament.'

Camilla rounded on him angrily. 'How can you possibly justify that remark? I have every credential you need –'

'Oh yes? Really?' smiled her father malevolently. 'Including the odd skeleton in your closet?'

Camilla froze. She tightened her arms protectively around her body and stared at the ramparts in front of her, not looking in front of her, but back in time.

Oswald gave a little chuckle. It was cruel and callous and dark. 'Yes, too many politicians have dark little secrets, don't they? Except yours is perhaps a little darker than most.'

'That was a long time ago,' she said coolly, willing herself to mask the dread that was coursing around her blood.

Oswald tipped his chin back and flared his nostrils arrogantly. 'Just because it was a long time ago, doesn't mean it didn't happen. Luckily I'm the only person who knows about it. At the moment, anyway.'

'Daddy. That was all in the past. Please, let's keep it there,' said Camilla, trying to control her voice.

'The past has a habit of coming out,' said Oswald, his eyes fixed on a burst of flames in the black sky. 'Now I suggest you stop all these silly fantasies and withdraw yourself from the candidacy.'

A switch in Camilla's mind clicked as she realized the root of his objections.

'You're jealous, aren't you?' she said, spinning her body towards him to challenge him. 'Jealous that I could be the one in the family with the political career. Most fathers would be glad that their children were trying to achieve something. But not you. Nobody can be better than you, can they?' she said scornfully.

The look on his face told her she'd hit on the truth. 'Jealous? Of you?' He looked at his daughter standing contemptuously in the darkness.

'You are,' she replied defiantly. 'You lost your Lords seat

and, because of that, I have to give up *my* chance of a career in politics. My dream. My ambition. Well I really want it and I am not going to give up the opportunity because of you.'

'Won't you?' smiled Oswald cruelly.

Camilla's voice softened, knowing the steel wills of father and daughter were locking forcibly together. 'I think I'd be good,' she said quietly, meeting his gaze so firmly that she could make out the image in his pupils of a firework exploding. 'I think I can be a really good politician. If I become an MP, think of it as a house-win.'

'Until you become one of this country's opinion formers, which, in view of what we both know, isn't going to happen, I really don't care what you think, my dear.'

Camilla could feel her face blanch as she understood the power he held over her.

'Withdraw your candidacy,' he replied flatly.

'I will not,' said Camilla, her feline eyes narrowing towards her father.

'Oh yes, you will,' smiled Oswald as another rocket exploded across the sky. 'And you'll do it straight after the New Year, unless you want the whole world to know about your dirty little secret.'

42

Cate wasn't sure whether it was a bright light creeping through the long crack in the velvet curtains that had woken her, or the throbbing head that came with a rotten hangover. Whatever it was, she was awake and she groaned as she sank her head back into the downy pillow. It might be Christmas Day, but she needed another half-hour's sleep before she would feel vaguely human again. But then she froze. She was sure she had heard the quiet squeak of the floorboard, the sound of someone's breath on the air. Feeling a little apprehensive, she rolled over to face the door.

'Cate, it's only me,' whispered a voice, croaky with sleep and the effect of drink. Her eyes struggled open until she could see Nick standing there, trying to tiptoe across the floor. His white dinner shirt from last night was open at the neck and not tucked into the waistband of his trousers. There was the suggestion of stubble on his chin and a pink-tinged bleariness about his eyes.

A feeling of love, lust and hopelessness whirled in the pit of her stomach as she looked at him. She remembered the events of the previous night and cringed. What was she doing inviting him to stay over? Linking her arm with his

505

as they watched the fireworks? *Flirting* with him. Yes, she had definitely flirted. So there had been that moment in the Orangery. She could have sworn he was about to kiss her before Serena had barged through the door. But nothing had happened then, or during the rest of the evening. She had made a promise to herself that if she and Nick didn't get together at the ball, she wouldn't waste another minute thinking about what might happen, regardless of the first-edition fairy tales or the teasing near kisses. The Nick Douglas book was now closed. Finally. But what was he doing here now?

Nick edged closer to the bed and Cate pulled her white cotton sheet further up towards her chin.

'Thought I'd better be off,' he said, smiling gently. 'I can hear noises already coming from downstairs.'

'Already? People will have been cleaning downstairs since straight after the party. Daddy hates coming down and finding it looks like Hiroshima,' she grinned. 'Anyway, I hope you had a good time last night.'

'I had a great time.' Nick edged nearer to the bed before sitting stiffly on the edge of the mattress.

'I did, too. Thanks for coming.'

Somehow Cate could sense that he didn't want to go.

'So,' he said hesitantly, 'will I see you before New Year? When are you coming back to London?'

She felt a flutter. Did he *want* to see her before New Year?

'I usually stay here for Boxing Day,' she said guardedly. 'If you wanted to meet up, maybe give me a ring after then.'

'I will.'

'Goodbye then.'

'Bye.'

He leaned forward, stretching out over her body, his lips directed towards her cheek.

Cate stretched up to kiss him on the cheek and, as she

did so, the sheet fell from her chin, the thin strap of her nightdress slipping off her shoulder to expose a square of creamy flesh. At that moment, Nick seemed to change direction. His eyes locked with hers, the target of his mouth swerving from her cheek to her lips. She was stunned, but the softness of his lips drew her in like a tractor beam and she reciprocated hungrily.

'I wanted to do that all last night,' he smiled, his voice soft and underpinned with embarrassment.

'So why didn't you?' she grinned, thinking her Christmas presents had all come at once.

Nick's finger stroked her cheek. 'Well –'

Suddenly a scream pierced the air. A bloodcurdling, guttural scream that at first sounded hollow, then rose and curdled as it filled with terror.

Nick scrambled up with a jolt. 'Jesus, what the hell was that?' he said, running over to the window.

Cate leapt out of bed, grabbing her dressing gown. 'It sounded as if it was coming from behind the house,' she said anxiously, instantly forgetting the moment they had just shared.

They both ran out into the hall. Camilla emerged from her room opposite them, for a second looking both surprised and amused to see them tumble out from Cate's room half dressed.

'Did you hear that?' asked Camilla.

'Couldn't miss it,' said Cate, still struggling to pull on her slippers.

Another bedroom door opened and Venetia joined them to see what was happening. By the time they had reached the top of the stairs, the front door had swung open, letting in a cold, frosty draught. Standing there, framed by the stark white of the day outside, was Serena, her face pale, one hand on her chest, trying to control her breathing.

'Christ, what's the matter?' called Camilla from the top of the stairs, taking them two by two until she reached her sister. As she got closer, Camilla could see that Serena's top lip was quivering, little diamond-shaped tears escaping from her eyes onto her cheeks.

'Call an ambulance,' she said between shallow gasps. 'It's Daddy. His body. It's in the moat. He isn't moving.'

The moat, only partly excavated, ran around the back of the house. Everyone ran outside, bare feet freezing cold on the light layer of snow that had fallen in the night.

Lying face down in the black icy water was a body. Only the back of its head was visible, but it was definitely Oswald.

'Nick,' screamed Camilla, running to the edge of the water. 'Help me, quickly.'

'Damn,' he murmured under his breath, knowing he was going to have to get in. Glancing momentarily at Cate, he jumped into the moat, the thick, oppressive coldness hugging his body. Weed clung to his jacket; ice water stung his eyes.

He grabbed Oswald's arm and his body turned sluggishly, sodden and saturated with the freezing water. Suddenly the body rolled back from the water, only inches away from Nick as he pulled him to the edge.

'Shit,' he gasped, as Oswald's purple, frozen face stared back at him, grotesque eyes and mouth open.

'You'd better go and get Maria,' said Cate to Venetia, and together they tried to haul the body onto the grassy verge.

'Did anyone phone for the doctor? The ambulance. Quickly.'

Cate helped pull Nick out of the moat. No one needed to take a pulse to confirm what they were all thinking.

'Too late for an ambulance,' grimaced Nick as he hunched over the lifeless body. He looked up with a stony face towards the sisters. 'He's dead.'

* * *

The local police in Huntsford village rarely saw any action at any time of year, let alone a high-profile death on Christmas Day. With the last big seasonal incident in the village being the theft of a goose three years earlier, the most that Sergeant Danner could hope for over the Yuletide season was being called to a minor disturbance at the village pub or a small house fire caused by the overcooking of a chipolata. Frankly, the constabulary were expecting to spend Christmas with their feet up, so Danner was not at all amused to have to climb into the station's only squad car and head over to the castle to inspect a body. At least his colleague PC Browning was looking forward to seeing Serena Balcon; after all, her picture was pinned up in his locker.

'Looks like one for the CID in Lewes, this,' said Sergeant Danner, scrunching up his thin, weasely features as he walked to the edge of the moat where Venetia had put a blanket over her father's body.

'CID?' asked Serena, concerned.

'Procedure,' he said tersely. 'Accidental death. Suicide. Impossible to tell at this point. We'll have to get the boys in. Have you called the doctor?'

'Yes, Dr Tavistock,' replied Camilla. 'Should be here any minute.'

Camilla wrapped her dressing gown around her tightly and looked at him suspiciously. Police college was such a distant memory for Sergeant Danner that she doubted he'd have a clue what procedure was in cases like this.

When he finally arrived, Dr William Tavistock, also miffed that he'd been disturbed from his Christmas family breakfast, revealed that he thought Oswald had drowned, which, as Nick pointed out, any of them could have diagnosed without the benefit of twenty-five years of medical experience. 'Can't be sure though until an autopsy,' he added dismissively.

It was only with the arrival of Detective Chief Inspector Paul Cranbrook an hour later that the sisters began to think that the death of their father was finally in the hands of someone competent.

Altogether more impressive than the members of the local force, Cranbrook had been fast-tracked to Inspector after police college and could have been no more than thirty-five years old. His girlfriend read the celebrity magazines voraciously, so while he could have done without trekking out to Huntsford on Christmas Day, it was worth it to have a nosy around Huntsford Castle and meet the famous Balcon girls.

Inside the house, the atmosphere was as deathly as the body now being photographed by the forensic team. Everyone else had gathered in the drawing room. Cate was staring out of the window, her face expressionless, while Nick perched on the arm of her chair, gently rubbing her back. Collins hovered around the door, unsure of what to say or do, while his wife wept in the corner. Serena was occasionally emitting a loud sniff while Camilla and Venetia were both sitting upright on a velvet sofa, as if they were in a doctor's waiting room. The loudest noise in the room came from the direction of Maria Dante, who was weeping into a tapestry cushion. '*Mio caro, mio caro,*' she moaned over and over again, her voice totally muffled by the fabric.

Aware that no one had spoken to her in twenty minutes, Cate went over to sit beside her. 'Come on, Maria. It's OK,' she said softly, placing a compassionate hand on the woman's knee.

'OK?' spat Maria, suddenly rounding on Cate with a fury. 'The death of your father might be OK for *you*, but it is certainly not all right for me.'

The sisters turned round to look at Maria, shocked by the strength of her venom. 'Cate didn't mean it like that,' replied

Camilla, firmly springing to her defence. 'She was only trying to be sympathetic.'

Maria was in no mood to be pacified. 'Go ahead. Defend her. You girls always stick together. It was you against your father. Now it is you against me.'

Although Maria clearly had a grip on the girls' dysfunctional relationship with Oswald, Camilla felt suddenly protective of the father–daughter bond. 'How dare you!' she snapped, also angered by the implication that Maria had somehow replaced him in the dynamics of the family.

Cate held a hand in the air to try and diffuse the atmosphere. 'Hang on a minute, everyone. Maria is just upset. We all are.'

'Really?' accused Maria.

Now even Cate was furious. 'Maria, you're in our home. Don't insult us.'

'*Your* home? Oswald was my fiancé.'

Camilla and Venetia looked at each other. What was she implying?

Serena glared over from the window, her general dislike and suspicion of Maria bubbling over into open hostility. 'Yes, Maria. Our home. Not yours. *Ours*.'

The air crackling with resentment and the conflict between Maria and the girls, Nick shifted awkwardly on the arm of the chair. 'I think I'm going to get off,' he said, looking across to DCI Cranbrook, 'unless you want me here? I just think it's a time that the family should be together alone right now.'

Cate nodded without even looking at him. 'Yes, you'd better go.'

'I'm sorry,' he said, stooping down to give her hand a squeeze. 'Call me if you need anything.'

'If you're going to London, I want you to take me, Nicholas,' snapped Maria, standing up suddenly.

'That's probably for the best,' said Serena sharply.

Nick looked uncomfortable, but after a few seconds he nodded.

Cranbrook stopped him at the door. 'Before you two go, I'll need an address and telephone number for you both for follow-up enquiries. We need to take statements from everyone here.'

'Why? Why do you persecute me?' wailed Maria. 'My fiancé is dead and you make me feel like a criminal.'

Cranbrook stifled a sigh. 'Just procedure, madam.'

'Procedure? Have you no heart, no soul? I need time to grieve, to mourn, not to be interrogated.'

'Yes, yes, of course,' Nick said to Cranbrook, taking a card out of his wallet and scribbling on the back.

'I'll be back in a few days,' sniffed Maria. 'I need some time alone.'

After they'd gone, Cranbrook turned to the sisters.

'So, what happens now?' said Venetia, exhaling slowly.

'I'm afraid I need statements from you ladies as well. I know you had a party last night. We'll have to get the names and addresses of all the guests and any catering staff. It's important I speak to as many people as possible. Detective Constable Lane here will help – he's part of my team.'

Venetia motioned towards the grounds where some more policemen were climbing out of a van. 'How long will all this take?'

'I'm afraid we'll have to wait until the pathologist comes down from London. He's on his way, so it shouldn't be too long, and it looks as if the SOCOs have arrived too.'

'SOCOs?' asked Venetia.

'Scene-of-crime officers. They take prints, samples. Help us build up a picture. Bloody snow hasn't helped us, though,' he said, looking at the thin carpet of white outside. 'They'll have difficulty getting what they want in this weather.'

'Can we get on with these interviews, please?' asked Venetia, suddenly unsettled by the talk of pathologists and fingerprints. She led Cranbrook through to the library, switching on a couple of lamps to make the room look a little less forbidding, then sat on a leather Chesterfield sofa, ready for his questions. Cranbrook flipped open his notebook. He was used to dealing with the dregs of society – criminals, junkies, thugs; he had to admit he was slightly unnerved to be sitting in the luxury of Huntsford Castle facing this refined, but quite fragile-looking woman.

'So,' began Venetia anxiously, 'do you have any idea what happened yet?'

Cranbrook almost smiled. 'That, I'm afraid, is a slightly premature question. First of all, my team need to find out as much about last night as possible: your father's movements, the last time he was seen alive. Then the autopsy, which should be done tomorrow or the day after, will give us a clearer picture of what we're investigating.'

'In what way?'

'Our aim is to find out what happened. It will help if we can determine whether we're dealing with accidental death, suicide or foul play. I take it you haven't found a note?'

'To be honest, Chief Inspector, we haven't really looked,' replied Venetia, rather taken aback. 'We all assumed it was an accident. That's why I'm a little shocked with all this talk of statements and scene-of-crime officers. You don't think this is in any way suspicious?'

Aware that he was talking to a grieving daughter, Cranbrook tried to be as sympathetic and patient as possible.

'Everything we're doing is standard procedure when we're dealing with a sudden or violent death.' He didn't like to add that this was bound to be a high-profile case, possibly a career-maker, and that he was determined to do things by the book.

'Anyway, I imagine you're fairly familiar with the process?'

'I'm sorry? What do you mean?' asked Venetia, looking a little startled.

'Your husband, Miss Balcon. He died in a fire a few months ago, didn't he? I'm sure the procedure was similar then.'

Cranbrook noticed that Venetia's face had gone even more ashen. He hoped he hadn't sounded too accusatory: he didn't want to upset the Balcon sisters and have them running to one of Daddy's friends high up in the force. Besides, he had to handle this one especially carefully, he thought. He'd read that the inquest into Jonathon von Bismarck's death had returned a verdict of accidental death, but part of him couldn't help but think that Venetia had suffered almost *too* much bad luck in the space of a few months. It could be a coincidence, but no smoke without fire, and all that. He had to suppress a smirk at his unconscious pun. In front of him, Venetia simply nodded and brushed something away from her knee.

'However, we have discovered one unusual thing already,' said Cranbrook slowly. 'The door leading up to the ramparts was locked from the *inside* of the house, which makes me wonder how on earth your father could have accessed the area he fell from.'

'There's no mystery there,' replied Venetia. 'It's usually locked after the firework display. You know, so drunken people don't go up there alone and fall off . . .' She stopped herself, aware of the irony.

'However, there is another way up; a servants' corridor weaves up through the house and you can bypass the door that way. My father would have known that way up.'

'Who else would have known?'

'The family; the house staff.'

Cranbrook made a brief note in his book. 'And when was the last time you saw your father?'

'I saw him on the ramparts at midnight, watching the fireworks with everyone else. I think he was standing with my sister Camilla. After that, everyone filtered back down into the house. I must have last seen him at about one in the morning, talking to Maria. Then I went to bed. The next thing I knew was this morning when Serena had found his body in the moat.'

'Was your father drinking heavily last night? Acting unusually? Did he argue with anyone?

Venetia was certain she should not tell him about her quarrel with Oswald by the kitchen. 'My father was a difficult, argumentative man, Inspector Cranbrook. He liked everything to be just so at his social events and there would almost certainly have been cross words with members of staff at some point. But that was his way. I'm not aware of anything out of the ordinary. And yes, he was almost certainly drunk. The drink flows freely at a Huntsford party.'

Venetia looked up and noticed that Cranbrook was gazing at her intently.

'Was he depressed?'

'Absolutely not,' she replied flatly. 'Far from it, in fact. He had recently become engaged to Maria; Maria Dante, the opera singer.'

'And how do you and your sisters feel about Miss Dante joining the family?'

'Fairly ambivalent to be honest,' she answered cautiously. 'As you can imagine, no one can replace our mother, but if Maria makes him happy . . .'

'I read recently that your father may have had financial problems,' said Cranbrook, still writing in his notebook. 'Is it true?'

Venetia nodded slowly, thinking about the musical evening.

'There were some cash flow problems yes, but surely you can't be suggesting he committed suicide?'

'Right now, I'm not entirely sure how your father died. In the meantime please do not leave the house without telling me, Miss Balcon.'

Christmas Day disappeared in a flurry of snow, tears and strange activity. Scene-of-crime officers tramped round the ramparts and the moat in their white overalls collecting soil samples, looking like spacemen against the snow. Cranbrook completed his questioning. A black mortuary van came to take Oswald's body away. The phone had been ringing off the hook with journalists. Cate switched on the television for two minutes to see that her father's death had been promoted to the third lead story on News at Six. A sombre-looking reporter was interviewing a local who claimed to have been at last night's party.

'Why, oh why?' grumbled Serena, pressing the remote control with a manicured finger. 'You'd think the Pope had died or something.'

'Christmas Day: slow news day,' replied Cate.

'I want to go home,' moaned Serena, sitting on the window seat in the drawing room. 'All this stress can't be good for me.'

Cate looked sympathetically at her sister. 'I'm sure it isn't, Sin, but I think we should all stay put until we hear back from the police.'

Mrs Collins entered the room. 'Miss Cate, there's a call for you. Do you want to take it, or should I take another message?'

'Who is it?'

'David Loftus. He says it's important.'

Cate frowned. 'I've never heard of him.'

'He comes round sometimes,' said Mrs Collins. '*Came* round,' she tailed off. 'He came to see your father.'

Cate wandered out to the hallway, rather bemused. She pressed the old-fashioned receiver to her ear.

'Hello, Cate Balcon speaking.'

'It's David Loftus. A friend of your father's. Firstly, I'd like to pass on my sincere condolences.'

'Thank you.'

'Secondly, I wanted to arrange a time when I could come and see you. All of you.'

'As you can imagine, Mr Loftus, this is a difficult time for all of us,' said Cate firmly but politely. 'For the moment we are spending time alone, as a family.'

'I really think we should meet.'

She cleared her throat, irritated. 'It really isn't very –'

'Don't brush me off, Miss Balcon. I thought you might want to know why I need to see you.'

Cate was beginning to feel a little freaked out. There was something rather creepy in his voice. 'OK. So what do you want to meet us for?'

'To talk to you about your father's death,' said Loftus coolly. 'As you might know, I've been writing his memoirs for the last few months. I think I know why he's dead.'

She felt her heart leap. Her palms began to sweat as she gripped the telephone tightly and spoke quietly into it. 'In that case, Mr Loftus, you'd better come round.'

PART TWO

PART TWO

43

David Loftus had been a man down on his luck until the day his agent had arranged a meeting with Oswald Balcon. Ever since he'd been name-checked in *Granta* magazine in his early twenties as a promising young talent, David Loftus had expected great things from his career, but when the predicted success had not materialized, it had served to make him angry and bitter – with an almost pathological dislike of anyone with anything resembling success, wealth or privilege. By rights, Oswald Balcon should have been the kind of person David Loftus hated but, the more time he had spent with the irascible Lord Balcon, the more he had used the relationship to his advantage. It soon became clear that Oswald was lonely living on the estate by himself and, as the months had passed, he had come to rely on Loftus for day-to-day friendship and conversation, as well as for his writing duties. Loftus had jumped at Oswald's offer to move into one of the estate cottages a month earlier, and now the man was dead . . . well, Loftus was beginning to see the true benefits of their professional bond – power and knowledge.

And now, here he was, sitting in front of Oswald's four beautiful daughters in their beautiful home, Huntsford. It gave him a hard-on just looking at them. And now he had their full attention and he was going to make it last.

'You ladies *do* know that a lot of people wanted your father dead?' Loftus told the sisters as he took a long glug of his whisky.

'He could be a bit difficult, if that's what you mean, Mr Loftus,' responded Cate tartly. 'But it's hardly the same thing.'

'Difficult.' He snorted loudly. 'Is that what you call it?'

'This is quite enough,' said Venetia, her voice starting to bristle. 'I think it's time you left.'

Loftus ignored her.

'Your father was despised by half the people who knew him,' said Loftus, knowing that he had the girls gripped with his narrative. 'And I'll go further. Despite what the police are saying, I don't think your father threw himself or fell from the rooftop.'

He paused, noticing how nervous Camilla looked, twisting the topaz ring round and round on her finger.

'I believe he was pushed. Deliberately.' He paused to look each sister directly in the eyes. 'I think your father was murdered.'

The fire was spitting and crackling in the background as the sisters looked at him, not daring to speak.

'And I think that one of Daddy's little girls killed him.'

Serena rounded on him like a wildcat. 'How dare you come into our house and make suggestions like that?'

He sat back in his chair to watch her, the trace of a smile on his lips. He looked like a man with all the cards in his hand.

Camilla had had enough. 'My sister asked you a question, Mr Loftus,' she pressed him. 'What brings you to make such rash claims? What do you know that we don't?'

Loftus wasn't about to be deflected so easily. He looked confident, relaxed. 'You'll be aware that I know your father.

522

I've been helping him with his memoirs. Oswald was not a man blessed with the reserve of the upper classes. He spoke rather freely about his past. This family's past. Funny what was thrown up. Very funny.'

'Don't try to threaten us, Mr Loftus,' said Camilla, her voice cool. 'A few of my father's ribald anecdotes hardly make a motive for murder.'

'You sound confident.'

'I am.'

'Hmm. Well, I wonder what the police will make of it?' There was a smugness in his voice that riled everyone.

'So you *are* threatening us.' Serena's voice was angry.

David Loftus smiled again, happy to get a reaction. 'It's not a threat, Miss Balcon. I just know things I'm sure you'd rather I didn't.'

'He's bluffing,' said Venetia blankly.

He laughed harshly. 'Really, Venetia. Your relationship with your father really hasn't been ideal for the last twelve months, has it? Not that it ever really has been.'

Her face went pale. Loftus stood and started pacing in front of the desk. 'Oswald told me all about your business. I'm not big into furniture myself, but apparently it's a nice little earner. He's a director, isn't he?'

'I doubt you'd understand interior design,' replied Venetia calmly.

'Yes, a director,' continued Loftus, ignoring her, 'a director using his voting rights to stop your expansion into the American market; a director about to buy your ex-husband's shareholding in the company. Yes, he told me you were *very* pissed off about that.'

'You're suggesting that's my motive?' said Venetia, a hint of amusement in her voice.

'You disagree?' he smiled arrogantly. 'Life would be so much easier for you with him out of the way, wouldn't it?'

'Forgive me,' asked Serena sarcastically, fixing him with her coolest gaze. 'Did we not ask you to leave?'

'Getting nervous?'

'Not of you, no.'

'You always were the feisty one, weren't you, Serena? Feisty enough to push him off the top of his castle in a rage, perhaps. After all, you were the only one Oswald had any time at all for. The castle is not attached to the title and you are the one he would leave Huntsford to in his will as things stood. I don't suppose you were that happy to find out that Oswald and Maria were going to try for a baby. Now, how does it work . . . ?' He pretended to concentrate, steepling his fingers in front of his mouth. ' . . . If Oswald were to produce a male heir before he died, then you would get nothing. Possibly worth pushing someone off the top of a castle for . . . yes, no?'

By now, Cate was acutely aware that his whole pantomime was going somewhere. David Loftus wasn't just a nasty piece of work; she had a feeling he was an opportunistic one as well.

'What do you want, Mr Loftus?' she said simply.

'Ah, Cate Balcon, the clever one. Good girl. I don't suppose you want me to continue, do you? To remind you how Oswald almost sabotaged your magazine business? How he blamed you for your mother's death? That sort of thing can affect the mind of a seven-year-old quite considerably.'

He turned to Camilla. 'Or Camilla. So proud to have got your parliamentary selection, aren't you? I'd vote for you,' he sneered. 'Or would I? Oswald said you have a secret. That's why he controls you isn't it, Camilla? I'm sure the police would be very interested. Maybe I can point them in the right direction.'

'What do you want?' repeated Cate, matching his stare, her voice controlled.

Loftus sat back on the edge of the desk and looked at her. 'I think it's what we *both* want, Miss Balcon. You don't want the police to know what I know. I want it to be worth my while.'

'Bastard,' breathed Serena.

'Possibly. Pragmatic, certainly,' he countered.

'It's not what he wants; it's how much he wants. Isn't that true, Mr Loftus?' said Camilla.

He looked her up and down approvingly. 'I heard you were a clever young lady as well.'

Venetia got up off her chair and marched to the door. 'Get out now, or I'm calling the police,' she said.

'My point exactly,' said Loftus, laughing.

He looked at each sister, his face impassive. 'One million pounds and this whole matter can go away.'

'One million,' scoffed Serena.

'Oswald was – shall we say – my financial lifeline. Now he is dead, the memoirs unfinished, I have to recoup that income from somewhere.'

'Well, you're not getting it from here,' said Camilla. 'And do I have to point out that blackmail is a criminal offence?'

'Only enforceable if you report it, though, Miss Balcon. Which you're not going to do,' said Loftus, his voice dripping with superiority.

'Get out,' repeated Venetia.

'I know you're all a little emotional at the moment,' he smiled, standing and brushing himself down. 'It's only natural, so I'll give you some time to think about it.'

'When?' asked Serena, her face pale.

'They won't do an inquest over the holidays, so how about I come back on New Year's Day? Bring in the New Year together. I'll be in touch.'

He stood at the door, a smug smile all over his face.

'And ladies? Happy Christmas.'

44

'Call the police,' said Cate after she heard the front door bang shut.

'And you think that's a good idea?' said Serena.

'We've got nothing to hide, so why even think about allowing ourselves to be blackmailed? As Camilla said, it's a criminal offence.'

Serena looked anxious, distracted. 'Look, this is the last thing I need. This year my name has been dragged through the mud. Papers, scandal, muck-slinging . . .' Her mouth twisted at the thought. 'I . . . my career . . . I can't take much more of it, to be honest.'

Cate couldn't believe what she was hearing. She moved over to Serena who was stroking her stomach and grimacing. 'I appreciate you've been through a lot, Sin, but you're prepared to pay a million to an opportunistic fantasist who has no evidence against us whatsoever?'

'I realise that,' said Serena, her voice beginning to wobble. 'But I can't bear my life being pulled through the wringer again – by the police, the press . . . You don't know what it's like. I don't know if I could cope with much more.'

She started to sob quietly. Venetia went over to put her

arm around her shoulder, but Cate pressed on. 'Sin, do you know something?'

'No!' Serena shouted, the sobs becoming louder. 'What are you bloody suggesting? That I killed Daddy, like he said? I didn't, I didn't.'

She was gulping her breaths, tracks of mascara streaking down her cheeks.

Cate moved closer. 'No one's saying that, Sin,' she said quietly.

'I just want everything to be OK again,' sobbed Serena. 'But he's right, it does all look suspicious. Suspicious as regards me.'

'You and me both,' said Venetia. 'Last night I nearly smashed a glass over Daddy's head. Jack had to stop me. Half the staff would have seen it.'

Serena looked at each of her sisters and shrugged. 'Let's be honest, we all look a little bit guilty.'

'But we're not,' said Venetia firmly, stroking Serena's hair. 'No one killed Daddy. It was just a horrible accident.'

Cate had been staring out of the long French windows, watching the snow settle like lace on the frames. 'What if it wasn't?' she said softly, her fingers running down the soft, red velvet of the curtain. 'What if someone did kill him?'

'Hang on, can we just calm down for one moment?' said Camilla abruptly. 'If Loftus is right about one thing, we're all just a bit emotional. The police don't seem to think this is anything suspicious.'

'We'll have to wait for the inquest,' said Venetia.

Mrs Collins put her head around the corner of the door. 'Is everything all right? How about I make a pot of tea? There's some Christmas cake left as well . . .'

Venetia smiled. Mrs Collins' solution to everything: tea and cake.

'Thanks Mrs C., that would be lovely.'

'When will the inquest be?' asked Cate, hoping Venetia had all the answers to the grisly procedural side of her father's death.

'Straight after the New Year, I should imagine. We should start thinking about the funeral, too. I've no idea how many people would like to come. I suppose Daddy would want something on the grander side of things.'

'We'd better phone Aunt Sarah,' said Camilla, flipping aimlessly through a heavy album of photographs. 'I wonder if she knows he's dead yet. She'll want to come.'

Aunt Sarah, their mother's sister, was their only living close relative, although she had played no part in the girls' lives for over twenty years. There had been the odd birthday and Christmas card stuffed with a couple of ten-pound notes. The girls had thought it was because she lived in Singapore, then Riyadh, then Paris – it was hard to keep in contact when you were always on the move – but the older they had become, the more flimsy that excuse had seemed to be. They were sure it was something to do with Oswald; there was certainly no love lost between Sarah and her brother-in-law.

'Who's going to call her?'

Everyone looked at Cate. 'What? Now? What should I say?'

'An invite to the funeral should cover it,' smiled Venetia.

Her number was in an old diary. Cate went to the telephone on the walnut side table in the hall. The phone rang in a low, hollow rasp.

'*Bonjour*,' said a quiet, elegant voice.

'*Bonjour, c'est* Cate Balcon.'

The accent changed from perfect French to Queen's English. 'Oh Cate. What a surprise.' She paused. 'I'm sorry about Oswald's death. I heard about it on the World Service.'

528

'So you know,' said Cate quietly. 'It's all a bit hard to take in at the minute.'

'Do you know what happened?' asked Sarah. 'I checked the news on cable and it's a big story. There seems to be a suggestion that it's somehow suspicious.'

Cate was surprised. She'd hardly turned on the television or radio, and had no idea how the media were treating it. 'We don't know much ourselves. There has to be an inquest, then the body can be released and we can have the funeral. We will of course be in touch to let you know when.'

'It would be lovely to see you,' her aunt said softly, although Cate got the feeling that she would not want to come to Oswald's funeral.

There was a long pause.

'I was going to call you actually,' said Sarah quietly. 'About the death. About the reporters saying it's suspicious . . .'

'Go on,' replied Cate, curious.

'No, not on the telephone. Face to face is probably best.'

'But you're in Paris, aren't you?' replied Cate, a little mystified.

'Could you come?'

'When?'

'When can you get here?'

It was ridiculous: why would she up sticks and go all the way to Paris at a time like this? But Cate found herself nodding. 'Not today. Tomorrow there should be trains . . .'

'Good. Let me know when you're arriving.'

Cate stared silently out of the window as Sarah said her goodbyes, suddenly sure that, whatever her aunt wanted to talk to her about, she wasn't going to like it.

45

It was a twenty-minute taxi ride from the Gare du Nord to Paris's leafy seventh arrondissement. Past the Opéra Garnier, past the Hôtel de Crillon and the majesty of Place de la Concorde, over the Pont de l'Alma and the waters of the Seine turning inky in the dusk, and on towards the Eiffel Tower, lit up for Christmas on the Left Bank of the city. It was a smart part of town, thought Cate as the taxi pulled to a halt in a little street off the Parc du Champ de Mars. Black spiky trees lined the road, tiny dogs trotted behind chic owners, joggers pounded past the tall cream porticoed buildings on their way to the green open spaces.

Cate checked the address scribbled in her diary and waved the taxi off. Weary from the Eurostar, she drew a deep breath and pressed the buzzer next to a tiny bronze plaque that read 'Holden-Jones'. The door clicked open and she entered the tiny lift with its old-fashioned pulley door and small velvet stool parked in the corner. *Let's hope I'm not wasting my time*, she thought as the lift jerked upwards through the spiral of stairs to the top of the building.

The heavy wooden door to Aunt Sarah's apartment was slightly ajar by the time Cate reached it. She pushed it open and edged into a hallway that smelt of lilies.

'*Bonjour*,' she shouted. 'It's Cate.'

'I'm in the salon,' said a small voice. 'Keep walking through.'

Sitting by the long sash window that overlooked the twinkling lights of Paris sat Sarah Holden-Jones, a cream and copper King Charles Spaniel lying at her feet. Cate's only memory of her aunt was of a terribly chic dark-haired lady who constantly smoked, her long, pianist's fingers covered in diamond rings. She'd changed, of course. Cate thought she must be over seventy years old. The hair was now completely white, pulled back with a tortoiseshell clip into a tight chignon, while the chic Parisian chiffon shirts Cate remembered had been replaced by loose cashmere knits and flat soft leather slippers. Sarah's face cracked into a delighted smile when she saw her niece. She pulled herself out of her Louis XV armchair using her cane.

'No, no, sit back down,' said Cate, rushing to the window. 'Don't get up because of me.'

The old lady eased herself back down, and gestured to the chair opposite her. 'Well, come and join me over here then,' she smiled, stroking the dog's head. 'Catherine, say hello to Charlie.'

The dog trotted over to where Cate was standing and began to lick the top of her boot. 'Friendly,' smiled Cate.

'A good companion.'

There was a long pause. What do you say to a relative you have only met twice and who had shown practically no interest in getting to know you, thought Cate uncomfortably.

'You must be tired,' said Sarah, beginning to pour two glasses of Bordeaux from a bottle on the table. 'Might a drink help?'

Cate nodded and took a sip.

531

'I'm really sorry about your father,' said Sarah after another pause.

Cate raised a brow. 'Really?'

'Nobody wishes death on anybody.'

Her niece shrugged. 'Well, I know he wasn't your favourite person. Otherwise we might have seen more of you,' said Cate.

'It became difficult,' said Sarah, looking out of the window and running a craggy finger over the rim of the glass. 'I didn't want to see him after your mother died. I just felt bitter that he'd made her life so miserable, and I felt that if I saw him again . . .' She trailed off. 'Well, let's just say I felt I would be betraying Maggie somehow.'

'I understand,' said Cate, noticing for the first time how much Sarah looked like old photographs of Cate's grandmother. 'Although you could have tried to see us when we left home . . .'

Sarah tapped Charlie's fur with her cane so he scampered across the room. She slowly got up and walked over to a walnut bureau, shaking her head as she did so.

'The beauty of living in Paris, my dear, is that this has become my world. It is so close to what I know, yet so far away. I feel connected to my old life, but at the same time I can forget.' She turned to look Cate directly in the eye. 'There's been so many times I've wanted to fly over to London to see all you girls,' she said sadly. 'I still can't get used to that Eurostar – a train under the Channel? *Non, non,*' she smiled, her eyes twinkling mischievously.

She turned her back to stoop over the desk and, as she did so, pulled out a stack of papers and envelopes from the drawer. Returning slowly to her chair, she began putting the contents into a neat pile on the table. 'Just because I don't see my nieces doesn't mean I don't know what you've been up to.'

She looked proudly at Cate and passed her a pile of newspaper and magazine cuttings. There were pictures from *Paris Match* of the girls at glamorous parties, reviews from *The Times* of Serena's films and Venetia's design books, and pages torn from Cate's magazines with her by-line or picture, each one neatly, lovingly trimmed around the edges. Cate put them back on the table and looked at her aunt.

'Don't ever think I don't care, Cate,' she said softly.

Cate wanted to give her a hug but, feeling awkward, just touched her lightly on the back of the hand. 'It's good to see you,' she said.

Sarah smiled and reached out her arms, pulling Cate down into an embrace. Disarmed by the gesture, Cate spoke softly into her aunt's shoulder. 'We're in trouble. I don't know what to do.'

Sarah looked at her knowingly and nodded.

'We are being blackmailed.'

'Go on,' said Sarah.

'You know that my father is dead. His body was found in the moat . . .' Cate stopped, not wanting to think about it all over again. 'That was all distressing enough, of course, until a friend of my father's, a writer called David Loftus, appeared at the house to tell us that he thinks that Oswald was murdered.'

'And how does he know this, if the police don't think so?' asked Sarah, her intelligent eyes bright.

Cate looked down and began shaking her head. 'Loftus had been ghostwriting Dad's memoirs and he's been reading between the lines. Somehow thinks we all had a motive. He says he's going to the police with his information if we don't pay him *a lot* of money.'

'I see. But that would only be a problem if you had something to hide,' Sarah observed.

'But we don't!' shouted Cate, suddenly. She began to

flush slightly, embarrassed by her reaction. She glanced at Sarah's open, enquiring face and took a deep breath.

'Did we all have a difficult relationship with our father? Yes. Do his diaries probably suggest that? Quite possibly.' Cate stopped. 'But kill him, absolutely not. I did not, and I trust that my sisters did not.'

Sarah noticed that her niece's hands were slightly shaking and she reached out to steady them.

'It's never quite as simple as having nothing to hide, is it?' said Cate after a pause. 'Of course everyone is innocent until proven guilty, but even the slightest whiff of scandal and, well, it isn't going to do any of us any good. We have careers. High-profile lives . . .' She tailed off, a tear for the first time appearing on her eyelash.

Sarah patted her niece's shoulder reassuringly. 'Don't worry, my dear,' she said. 'It appears that the bulk of what this Loftus is saying is clearly opportunistic conjecture. *However* . . .' She took Cate by the arm and led her through long double doors into her bedroom. Cate wished it were her own. Tiny Chanel jackets hung off cream padded coat hangers; surfaces were covered with silver photo frames and big glass perfume atomizers. The walls were lined with dove-grey silk and a huge cream and gilt sleigh-bed sat in the centre of the room.

'Forgive the mess,' said Sarah absently, motioning at a pile of beautiful, delicate clothes draped over the back of a chair. 'I'm just going to find something.'

Cate sat down on the eiderdown so that her feet just dangled over the edge of the bed, and watched as her aunt began rummaging at the back of her wardrobe, finally pulling out a big cream wooden box. She put it on the bed next to Cate and sighed.

'I knew this would all come out sooner or later,' she murmured, wiping a layer of dust from the top of the box and opening it. 'This is what I wanted to talk to you about.'

Cate kept quiet, waiting for her to continue.

'We were close, your mother and I. She was the beautiful one. I was the sensible one, the typical elder sister, always nosing around to see if she was behaving herself.' She laughed, enjoying the memory. 'But in the days when you were all little girls, your mother and I hardly saw each other. As you know, Marcus, my husband, was in the diplomatic corps, and he got posted all over the world – which meant that I had to go with him.'

By now she was flipping her fingers through bundles of letters in a rainbow of coloured papers.

'But Maggie, your mother, she loved writing letters. Wherever I was – Singapore, Honduras, Lagos – at least twice a month I would get something through the post. I'd always know it was her,' she smiled. 'Maggie never wrote on white paper. She said to do so was boring.' She chuckled again as she started reading snippets, her eyes darting from letter to letter. Sarah finally reached a faded lilac envelope and placed it in her lap.

'At first, Maggie and Oswald's marriage was good. He could be terribly charming when he wanted to be. However, after Venetia was born, the relationship deteriorated rapidly. Their jet-set life together was over. No rushing off to Marrakech at a moment's notice – not for Maggie, anyway. Your mother found it hard to lose the weight from pregnancy – it was difficult in those days when mothers didn't breast-feed – and your father belittled and teased her. Oswald loved the high life; I think he felt bitter that a family and the responsibilities were tying him down. He started drinking heavily and then gambling in all those smart clubs in Mayfair. Far too tempting for a weak and willing man like Oswald.'

Sarah's voice dripped with contempt. 'He would stay in

London all week, going out with that group of friends – Philip Watchorn, Nicholas Charlesworth, Jimmy Jenkins. The newspapers thought they were such a glamorous bunch, and I suppose it was glamorous if you were young, free and single. But your father wasn't single and, all those exciting things he should have been doing with your mother, he started doing them with his friends. He completely neglected her and his children.'

Sarah unfolded the letter from its envelope and passed it to Cate, who drew the tips of her fingers across the navy-blue ink and the distinctive, swirly handwriting of her mother.

'It was a very lonely time for your mother,' continued Sarah. 'Oswald wasn't around for days on end, I was out of the country, and our parents were dead by that point. At Huntsford, friends were thin on the ground.'

Cate looked up. 'So Mum had an affair?'

Sarah was nodding slowly. 'A few, I'm afraid. One gentleman was a friend of your father's. Alistair Craigdale. Oswald, your mother and their friends were always up at Craigdale Castle, his home. It was a wonderful place for shooting, fishing, parties. I suppose one thing led to another. Alistair was terribly charming . . .'

Cate let out a bitter laugh. 'The Craigdale Killer? Oh, Christ.'

She sat back to let it all sink in for a minute. Although the murder of Gordy Spencer, a groom at Craigdale Castle, occurred before Cate was born, it was a slice of criminal history that had always fascinated her. Only the Lord Lucan episode eclipsed it as *the* scandal in the upper classes during the seventies. The story went that Alistair Craigdale, the Earl of Loch Lay, had shot and killed his groom at point-blank range after having suspected him of having an affair with his wife. That Oswald and Maggie were two of the guests at

Craigdale that weekend had only added to its intrigue for Cate: not that either of her parents would ever refer to that weekend, except in the vaguest of terms.

'Such a ghastly time,' said Sarah softly, taking another sip of wine.

'My mother had an affair with Craigdale?' repeated Cate, slowly mulling over the facts. 'But Alistair was in love with his wife, wasn't he? Certainly enough to kill a man for it.'

Sarah shuffled off into the kitchen and fetched a white china plate piled high with pale green, pink and chocolate sugary discs.

'Macaroon?'

Cate shook her head, decidedly unhungry. Sarah settled down and continued her story.

'Everybody thought Alistair killed Gordy Spencer for having an affair with Laura, his wife. He didn't. It was because he found him with Maggie.' She paused, struggling with the next words. 'I believe he found them *in flagrante*.'

The glass of claret in Cate's hand trembled slightly, spilling a tiny droplet of wine, like a spot of blood onto the grey silk eiderdown.

Sarah was now pulling more letters out of the white box and handing them to Cate.

Up at Craigdale again this week. Each weekend there seems to get better and better. The groom there is quite charming and terribly handsome. I am afraid I'm having another crush.

She reached for another dated one month before the shooting:

I am calling it off with Alistair. Each time the men are out shooting I go to the stables with Gordy. I know it's wrong, dear Sarah, don't judge me, but I can't help myself. Gordon is so kind and good, he makes me feel alive.

Cate was shaking her head. Forget the Swinging Sixties;

537

her parents' group of friends were obviously all in and out of bed with one another all the time!

'Enough, please stop.' The thought of an affair tarring the sacred memory of her mother was bad enough, but two affairs? 'Did my father know?' Cate asked nervously.

'About Alistair? Yes, shortly before the shooting. Maggie called me, hysterical. Oswald had found out. He'd pushed her down the stairs, and had apparently threatened Alistair quite violently,' she said quietly. 'He could be *vicious*.' Cate saw the old woman bare her teeth.

Cate climbed off the bed and paced to the window, pressing her palms against the glass. She looked out onto the skyline, vaguely focusing on the outline of the Eiffel Tower. While it was all shocking and perversely fascinating, she doubted its relevance to the death of her father.

'You're wondering why I got you here?' said Sarah behind her.

Cate turned and shrugged. 'Well, I thought it was to do with Dad's death. What happened at Craigdale – I can't really see how it's significant because it was so long ago. My mother is dead, Alistair is dead . . .'

'Is he?' asked Sarah gently.

Cate looked back, puzzled. 'But I've heard the story a hundred times over,' she said. 'After Alistair shot Gordon Spencer, he disappeared. His car went missing and was found days later by Loch Ness. Everyone assumed he'd done the honourable thing and drowned himself.'

'The loch was dredged. They found nothing,' said Sarah.

'But the loch is over fifteen hundred feet deep. They've never found Nessie with all their million-dollar equipment,' Cate countered feebly.

'That's probably because Nessie isn't in there either.'

Cate flopped into the chair by the window, confused and tired. Sarah joined her and continued her story. 'A couple of months after the Gordon Spencer killing, your Uncle Marcus and I arrived in London for a couple of days. We'd been living in Singapore at that time and were on the way to Marcus's new posting in Honduras. As you might imagine, I was desperate to see Maggie. I knew what a rough time it had been for her. Gordon dead, now Alistair too.'

Cate looked at Sarah intently, sensing a development in the tale.

'Maggie came to my hotel room when Marcus was out. She seemed jumpy, on edge. And I finally got it out of her.'

'Got what out of her?'

'Something that she would never tell me in a letter.'

Cate kept staring at her.

'Maggie had received a letter from Alistair. From Belize. *After* his disappearance. It was short, coded, but it basically said he was alive and well, but that for obvious reasons he couldn't and wouldn't contact her again.'

Cate stared at her aunt, trying to make sense of it all.

'So Craigdale *didn't* kill himself?'

Sarah shook her head. 'Which means that he is quite possibly alive today.'

Cate bit her lip. Suddenly they had a suspect.

46

Cate rested her elbow on the windowsill next to her first-class Eurostar seat. They were shooting through the tunnel now and she watched almost hypnotized as the blackness flashed in front of her eyes. Her body felt numb, her eyes drained of tears. She had spent the night at Aunt Sarah's, lying back in the antique sleigh-bed, listening to the sound of Parisian traffic, the car horns fading to a silence in the winter's night. She hadn't had a moment's sleep. Her mind was too full.

She blinked as the train came out of the Channel tunnel and the greyness of the English countryside came into view. Immediately her mobile began ringing, lost at the bottom of her bag.

'Cate? It's Nick.'

She mumbled a hello, unable to muster any enthusiasm, even for him.

'I was just ringing to see how you were . . .'

She was tempted simply to ring off, but instead she told him, 'I've been in Paris just sorting a few things out.'

'Paris? What's happened?' asked Nick, instantly recognizing that something was badly amiss. 'Are you all right?'

She wanted to lie to him, but she could feel hot tears begin to well in her eyes. She looked around: thankfully the carriage was empty and no one could see the droplets spill down her cheeks.

'It's OK,' she said, suddenly wanting to tell somebody. 'I can't really speak now. I'll call you when I'm back home,' she said softly.

'When does the train get in?' asked Nick anxiously.

'In about forty minutes. Look, I'll call you later.'

'You know who I don't like,' said Camilla, kicking a clump of frosted grass with her riding boot. 'Michael Sarkis.'

'What have you got against ageing himbos?' smiled Venetia, pushing her hands deeper into the pockets of her Barbour. The two sisters had taken a walk around the Huntsford grounds to clear their heads, but it was so cold it had only succeeded in freezing their fingers.

'You know he's asked Serena to marry him?' said Camilla.

Venetia stared back at her, wide-eyed. 'No! When? Hell, why didn't she tell me?'

'It only happened on Christmas Eve. He turned up in his limo with a massive rock and asked her to go to Vegas. *Classy*,' she said sarcastically. 'I guess after what's happened, Serena's just kept it quiet.'

'I can't believe it,' said Venetia slowly.

'I can,' said Camilla, lifting a brow.

'Why?'

'If Sarkis marries Serena before the baby is born, their child will be the heir to Huntsford.' She swept an arm around them, gesturing towards the house and the hundreds of acres of picture-postcard England stretched out in front of them. 'All this.'

'Only if Daddy and Maria don't have a son,' replied Venetia absently.

Camilla looked at her sister. 'Well, that's not going to happen now, is it?'

Venetia shrugged, still not used to talking about her father in the past tense. 'So what are you saying?'

'Think about it,' said Camilla, her sharp brain whirling. 'Sarkis kills Daddy, marries Serena, and he effectively gets control of Huntsford. I read somewhere that he was looking to expand in Britain and this place would be the perfect English country hotel. He was at Huntsford that night. He had motive *and* opportunity.'

Venetia gave a hollow laugh. 'Cam, are you off your rocker? Michael's many things – he's ruthless, certainly – but he's not a murderer.'

Camilla turned to look at her. 'How do we know?'

'Cam, you should really read the diary pages of our national newspapers before you start lining up the suspects.'

'How do you mean?'

'Michael Sarkis is in today's *Daily Mail*. A big picture of him at some fancy London party on Christmas Eve. I don't know how long he was here wooing Serena, but by the early hours of the morning, he was living it up in Mayfair. How can he have killed Daddy when he was strutting his stuff for the cameras ninety miles away?'

Camilla stamped a foot on the frosty grass. 'Shame,' she said sardonically. 'I really wanted it to be him.'

Nick was already waiting at the end of the platform as the train hissed into the station. Wrapped in a brown tweed coat and wearing a sad smile, he stood there and waited for Cate to walk up to him. He gave her a hug, wrapping her up in the fabric of his coat. He picked up her small overnight bag and handed her a takeaway coffee as they walked in silence to the car park. Nick had an old British racing green MG. The seats were low and cramped and their legs almost touched as they sat back in the black leather seats. As Nick sipped his cappuccino, Cate simply told him what had happened with David Loftus and what she had learned in Paris.

'What do you want to do now?' he asked, wiping a white frothy moustache from his lip.

'I want to go home. Will you come?'

Serena had always fancied playing a glamorous detective in some blockbuster Hollywood movie, and now here she was, being given the chance to star in her very own murder mystery. There were less fanciful reasons for her poking around her in father's study, of course. She needed another suspect. David Loftus might be a snake and a profiteer, but Serena had to accept that she did not exactly look innocent in the recent chain of events. The police would be well aware that over half of all murders were committed by a family member. There had to be something here that shifted suspicion away from herself and her sisters.

It didn't look promising, however. There was nothing much in his desk drawers: pens, paper, art auction catalogues, a file of correspondence relating to the Huntsford Musical Evening, an old black-and-white photograph of Oswald and their mother on a yacht, curled up at the edges and spotted with blue ink. Serena touched it and wondered about her parents' relationship. She had always supposed it to be cold and loveless, but the happy, intimate photograph looked loved and well handled. She shrugged; the ins and outs, the ups and downs, the hot and cold of Oswald and Maggie Balcon's marriage was something she would now never know about.

Serena looked around the rest of the study. The only place she had not looked was in the walnut trunk by the window. She lifted the heavy lid and coughed as a puff of dust lifted into the air. It was very old stuff in here: yellowing note-books, deeds, letters. She rifled through, sorting them into piles, but none of it looked at all interesting. But then, near the bottom, she came upon a stained, crumpled envelope with a handwritten address, incongruous among all these official documents. Serena straightened herself and pulled the letter out. She only needed to read a few lines to know that she had found something important. Her heart started beating faster and she whistled through her teeth.

Holy shit! This guy really hated her father, she thought, turning the page to see who the letter was from. She squinted to decipher the scrawled signature and stopped dead. It was from Alistair Craigdale. It was from the Craigdale Killer.

The journey to Huntsford took a couple of hours. The roads were quiet and, inside the car, Cate and Nick were even quieter. The snow had stopped, but telltale patches of ice were sprinkled at the side of the road like broken mirrors. As they turned off the A-road and down the narrow lane into the centre of Huntsford village, Cate's eyes were drawn to the long spire of the church stretching up into a steely sky soiled with dark clouds.

Cate tapped Nick's knee. 'Do you mind if we pull over?' she asked.

The MG purred to the side of the lane and she pointed to the graveyard. 'My mum's buried here, you know. Can we . . . ?'

They buttoned up their coats as they walked slowly through the grounds, crunching on the frosty grass. Cate stopped at a gravestone, in front of which was a tiny posy of yellow roses, still fresh. Cate wondered who had been down so recently. She bent down and touched the petals, ashamed that she had not brought any flowers to her mother's grave herself. She pressed her hand against the cold stone.

'He gave you a horrible life. I understand,' she whispered. 'It wasn't your fault.'

Nick put a hand on her shoulder and Cate exhaled sharply, her cheeks puffed out like two pink golf balls. They walked on to the perimeter wall of the churchyard and sat down on a bench, Cate feeling the cold stone even through her thick coat.

In the distance there was the sound of a heavy door closing. In the church entrance stood an old woman in a red coat, carrying a long bristle brush. As the figure moved closer, Cate recognized who it was.

'I thought it was you,' said the old woman as she approached the bench. She was about seventy-five; her hair was almost blue and swept up into two clumsy clips, her old face kind but heavily lined. 'How strange,' the old woman continued, 'I was just going to come and see you. I'm sorry about your father.'

Cate turned to Nick. 'This is Mrs Graham,' she said. 'Her husband was the gamekeeper at Huntsford for many years.' She looked at Mrs Graham. 'You weren't at the Christmas party, were you? I expected to see you both there.'

A cloud of sadness came upon Mrs Graham's face. 'Leonard died. Over a year ago now.'

'Oh, I am sorry,' said Cate.

Mrs Graham gestured towards the church. 'I miss him, but I keep busy. I clean here.'

They smiled politely, sensing that conversation was quickly running out. Nevertheless Mrs Graham pressed on. 'I was going to drop by the house, but if you can come to me, it would be better. I think you should.'

Cate glanced at Nick, wondering what the old woman was talking about.

'I have something I must give you,' said Mrs Graham vaguely. 'Do come, my house is only over there.'

Cate was apprehensive. 'What is it?'

'Come to the house, I'll tell you when we're all there. I'm sure we could all do with a nice cup of tea,' she smiled.

Silently, they walked to the house, a grey cottage with three windows and a highly polished blue front door in a row of almost identical grey cottages. Inside, it was small and homely. A ginger cat came over to Mrs Graham, stroking its furry head against the brown nylon of her tights.

The room was half filled by a Christmas tree decked out with gold baubles. There were at least fifty Christmas cards strung up on ribbon around the room.

'Can I get you a drink?' asked the old woman, taking off her coat and hanging it on a wooden peg.

'No it's fine,' said Cate, keen now to hear what the woman had to say. Mrs Graham was not to be rushed. She bustled into the kitchen to make herself a cup of tea before sitting in front of them in a wicker chair. Cate noticed she had a small envelope on her lap.

'I don't know what this is,' she said, shaking her head. 'Although I've nearly opened it a hundred times, I can tell you.' Mrs Graham smiled thinly at Cate and leaned forward to pass her the envelope.

'Leonard was ill for quite a while before he left us,' said Mrs Graham quietly. 'About a week before he died, he gave me this and told me to look after it until a time when both he and Oswald Balcon were dead. Then I was to give it to one of his daughters.' Mrs Graham smiled. 'I wanted to give it to you, Cate. You were always my favourite,' she said kindly.

Cate made small talk for a few minutes, then excused herself, Mrs Graham insisting she take some homemade jam with her.

'Things just get stranger,' said Cate, as she and Nick stepped into the lane. It was beginning to get dark; the sky had a cast of dark blue and the trees stood out in silhouette.

In Nick's MG, Cate ripped open the envelope and unfolded the letter inside; it was dated fourteen months earlier. As each word unfolded, her blue eyes grew wider in confusion and shock.

If somebody is reading this letter it means that both I and Lord Oswald Balcon are now dead. Please forgive my cowardice in leaving it until now to reveal this information – perhaps I am a coward – but it is something I have to say. It just feels safer revealing it now I am no longer around. At least in death, I can unburden myself.

Eleven years ago, I buried a body. My employer, Oswald Balcon, asked me to do it. His daughter, Camilla Balcon, had knocked over a man with her car and the man was killed. The victim was an old vagrant who sometimes passed through the village. Oswald said his life did not matter and that we should hide the body to protect the life of his daughter. I was scared of Oswald so I agreed to help him. It's not something I am proud of. I regret what I have done more than anything in my life.

Oswald's words have weighed heavily on me all these years. No life is worth nothing. Every life means a great deal whether you are rich or poor. However, Oswald has been good to me and my family ever since that night. For this I am grateful, and that is why I did not want to tell anyone until Lord Balcon had also died. But as my own death approaches, I must tell someone about it. You may choose to do with this information what you wish. Be merciful on Camilla Balcon. She was young, it was an accident, and her father insisted that they should cover it up. Camilla was desperate to go to the police, but Oswald forced her into silence. What could she do? What could any of us do? It has been a terrible secret I will carry with me to the grave. But please believe that what I am saying is the truth. I hope people can understand what I have done.

Yours faithfully,
Leonard Graham

The paper trembled in Cate's hand as she passed it over to Nick to read.

'My God,' he said quietly, whistling through his teeth.

Cate folded up the letter and put it in her pocket. 'I think we'd better show Camilla.'

47

Camilla was sitting at the mahogany desk in the big bay window in her bedroom, the half-light of late afternoon bathing her in shadow. There was a bundle of files in front of her, along with an open notebook, and she was holding a pen poised to write. As she heard the door open, she turned to smile at Cate.

'Look at me, trying to work,' she said, slightly embarrassed.

'Workaholic,' smiled Cate weakly.

Camilla put down her pen and span around in the chair to face Cate. 'So what happened in Paris?' she said. 'I thought you were going to call. Shall we get Serena and Venetia up?'

Cate stood awkwardly at the door and shook her head, unsure of whether to proceed any further into the room. 'No,' she said softly, 'let's just talk.'

Camilla frowned as she saw a look of unmistakable anxiety on her sister's face.

'What's wrong?' she asked.

Driving back from the village, Cate's confusion had turned to anger. When she had first read the letter, panic had gripped her. But, looking at it more closely, the idea that Camilla was behind it all seemed simply ridiculous. Surely it was more likely Leonard Graham had run over the poor man himself and now he just wanted to blame somebody else, deflecting a decade of guilt onto some poor innocent. But why Camilla? Why choose her? And *did* she know something about it?

Cate edged into the room and sat on the bed. She wanted Nick to be at her side to help her, but she knew she had to do this alone. She looked at Camilla sitting at the desk, composed and refined even in jeans and a T-shirt, and suddenly her faith in her sister wavered. Camilla had star quality all right. Not in the obvious 'look-at-me' way of Serena, but a cool, calculated, powerful presence that was totally suited to a respectable career like politics or the law: exactly the sort of career that would crumble with just a whiff of scandal. In a rush, the doubts poured in. Perhaps that's why Camilla had been keen to hush up Loftus. She hadn't exactly volunteered to pay him off but, looking back, neither had she stood up to him and told him to shove his blackmailing scheme. Cate felt sick.

'Cam, I think you'd better read this.'

She leaned over and handed Camilla the old envelope.

'What is it?' Camilla unfolded the letter and began to read.

'We met Mrs Graham,' Cate said hastily, suddenly wanting to explain it all away. 'She gave me the letter. I'm sure it's all lies, Cam. I don't know what Leonard Graham had against us, but I thought you'd better see it.'

As she watched her sister read, she saw the colour and confidence drain from Camilla's face. Cate's heart dropped like lead. 'Oh Cam. You didn't . . .'

Camilla folded up the letter and carefully placed it on the writing desk. She stared at the floor, concentrating on the red swirl of the carpet. It was a couple of minutes before she spoke.

'One Friday night I was driving back from Oxford,' she began slowly. 'You were in the States at the time. Venetia had moved to London and Serena was still at school. Daddy had summoned me home, for some reason. One of his little soirées that he wanted one of his not-so-precious daughters to attend, probably. I remember it was the last day of Michaelmas term. I'd wanted to stay in college, but Daddy had insisted I return home.' She stopped and glanced out of the window. 'I hadn't got far out of Oxford when it started to rain heavily. It became really bad – a horrible night. It was dark and I was hurrying because I was running late.'

Camilla's eyes were beginning to well up with tears, her poise dissolving. 'I had almost got to Huntsford when it happened. I remember that the windscreen wipers weren't working too well, and were leaving a horrible smear on the glass. The light was bad, I guess I was tired too . . . The next thing I knew, I heard a thud.'

She turned to Cate, her eyes pleading. 'I honestly hadn't seen him, Cate, I hadn't. I got out of the car. I had swerved up a bank right near the back of the grounds, you know, on Greenbank Lane. It was that man, that tramp we some-times saw around the village. Old Tom, we called him.' Cate nodded, recalling him. An old man in a dirty coat who was always drunk and who seemed to delight in scaring the chil-dren.

'He was on the ground at the side of the road. I knew he was dead.' Camilla's voice was really trembling now. 'There was blood on the headlight and a little trickle coming out of his ear.' Camilla fluttered a hand up to her face as if to demonstrate. Cate noticed that her fingers were trembling violently.

'I didn't know what to do,' she said, sobbing now, all composure gone. 'I called the house from the phone box at the end of the lane. Daddy's guests hadn't arrived, and he came down twenty minutes later with Mr Graham – he was still the gamekeeper back then. Daddy told me to get into the car and drive home at once and that he would sort it out.'

'You didn't call the police?' asked Cate, knowing the answer already.

'I asked Daddy that when he came back to the house about an hour later. He said that he would make the situation disappear.'

'So you didn't call them?'

Camilla's chin sank into her chest, as if her whole body was consumed with guilt. 'I wanted to, I wanted to so badly. But I was so scared, Cate. Scared of everything. Scared of Daddy. He said I had the family to think about, that I would ruin things for everyone. And I wanted to believe him, I wanted to believe that it would all be OK if I kept quiet,' she finished softly, tears streaming down her cheeks.

Cate went over and gave her a brittle hug. The gesture made her feel guilty, but she had never once seen Camilla cry before.

'What are you going to do?' asked Camilla, looking up, her eyes searching Cate's.

'Don't worry,' whispered Cate, 'we'll sort it out.'

Camilla suddenly straightened her back, her eyes alert as she realized the wider implication of her confession. 'Oh Cate, I know how this looks, but I did not kill Daddy.'

'I know,' replied Cate, trying desperately not to think about how culpable it made her sister seem.

Seeing Cate's doubt, Camilla grabbed her by the arm. 'Cate, you must believe me,' she said urgently. 'This thing crucifies me every single bloody day and somehow I've kept it a secret. But I would never kill anyone to keep it that way. I wouldn't kill my father. I swear it.'

Cate believed her; wanted to believe her. For a second she

thought about what she might have done in Camilla's situation, a scared and confused teenager who in one careless moment had shattered the promise of her life, and who had been offered an escape if only she was prepared to keep quiet. It was a moral dilemma that Cate did not even want to think about. Finally she pulled her sister into a tight embrace.

'I look so guilty, Cate, I look so guilty,' she sobbed.

'Don't worry,' said Cate, surprised by the defiance in her own voice. 'We're going to get to the bottom of this, we really are.'

48

'I hope this isn't a *total* waste of time,' yawned Camilla, following her finger along a road map. 'Hang on. I think we should have taken the left about two miles back.'

'You're navigating, I'm trusting you,' snapped Venetia from behind the wheel of her navy-blue four-by-four. They were both feeling irritable, having been up and on the road by seven a.m. to make the long drive to Derbyshire. The bleak beauty of the Peak District suited their mood, with its olive green hillsides, barren fields, stone walls etched with frost, snow settling on distant peaks like a catholic veil.

After Camilla's confession and Serena's breathless revelations about Alistair Craigdale's letter, Cate had called a council of war among the four sisters to examine the evidence. Not only was Craigdale still possibly alive, the letter Serena had found seemed to suggest that the missing earl had an almost murderous hatred for Oswald. Written in a shaky hand and full of threats and ugly promises, Craigdale's letter confirmed what Aunt Sarah had told Cate in Paris: that Oswald had discovered that Maggie and Craigdale were having an affair and had confronted Alistair about it, warning him to stay away from his wife. By the threatening tone of the letter, Craigdale didn't like it one bit. It was postmarked shortly before the Craigdale Killing. Cate wondered if Alistair's love for Maggie and jealousy had pushed him over the edge even then.

After some debate, the girls decided that they needed to know more about the Craigdale case, even if it was only to deflect the finger of suspicion from them. They swung into a frenzy of desperate activity. Camilla suggested that speaking to the person who'd been investigating officer in the case would be a good place to start. Nick had a friend on the *Sunday Times* newsdesk, and within two hours they had a name – Inspector Jim Dalgleish – now retired to Great Asquith in Derbyshire. By ten p.m. they had made the call to the retired police inspector; he sounded irritated to be roused, until he found out the caller was a Balcon sister and that they wanted to talk about Craigdale. He had invited them up at once.

'This must be it,' said Camilla, pointing at the sign as Venetia's four-by-four purred around a tight bend. Great Asquith was little more than a street of cottages, and Jim Dalgleish's house was at the end of the terrace. The house was made from honey-coloured stone, a holly wreath was nailed to the fire-engine-red front door, and a spiral of smoke escaped the chimney into the pewter sky. Retired Inspector Jim Dalgleish answered the door. He must have been about the same age as Oswald, but had weathered considerably less well. Faded tweed trousers hung off a rake-thin frame, brown socks bagged around checked slippers. A small mongrel dog snapped happily at the new visitors as he beckoned them in.

He switched off the television and offered the girls a seat on a worn sofa.

'We were surprised to find you this far south,' said Venetia, grateful that the drive had been only four hours rather than ten. 'We assumed you must live in Scotland.'

Dalgleish smiled. 'The name? No, I came from these parts originally. My wife is from here too. It made sense to return when I retired. Tea?'

The girls shook their heads. They'd had enough tea recently. Dalgleish sat back in his chair officiously, his eyes still bright and watchful.

'So,' he began briskly. 'You want to know about Craigdale? I suppose your father will have told you the story over the years. I'm sorry, by the way,' he said, pointing at the blank television screen, 'I saw it on the news. They never seem to talk about anything else at the moment.'

'Thank you. And yes, we know a little about Craigdale,' said Camilla carefully. 'We just wanted to know what you thought.'

'Why do you want to know about Craigdale now?' The old man was still sharp.

Camilla glanced at Venetia, both girls unsure of how much to tell to a stranger. Dalgleish was a retired copper, but he would no doubt still have connections in the force.

'We just wanted to find out everything about our father's past,' said Venetia, knowing it sounded lame. Dalgleish seemed to understand that she was holding something back, but let it go.

'I don't know how much you know already,' he said, his eyes beginning to sparkle as if he was relishing telling the story once more. He took a sip of his tea and wiped his top lip.

'Lord Alistair Craigdale was one of Scotland's most glamorous aristocrats. He went missing after Gordon Spencer was murdered in the grounds of his home, Craigdale Castle – gosh, almost thirty years ago to the day,' he recalled, looking both women in the eyes. 'Craigdale was a great entertainer. That weekend, all of his crowd, including the wives, were up for a shooting party. That afternoon, the men were wrapping up the shoot and making their way back to the house, but Craigdale had gone on ahead of the party. The stable girl had seen Alistair and Gordon rowing; then, about thirty minutes later, Spencer was found dead in the stables with a bullet straight through his chest. The bullet was an exact match with the one from Craigdale's hunting rifle. It was fairly cut and dried that Craigdale did it. Spencer was having an affair with his wife, Laura. Driven mad by jealousy, Craigdale killed Gordon. It was all pretty straightforward.'

Venetia gave Camilla a sideways glance. So far, Dalgleish had not told them anything new: his story matched everything that had been written about the case in the media.

'Then the case got murkier,' continued Dalgleish more quietly. 'Craigdale went missing almost immediately after the shooting. Before anyone had time to – or should I say, *got round to* – calling the police.'

'What do you mean, "got round to"?' asked Camilla.

'The question was never really about who killed Gordon Spencer – that was fairly open and shut,' said Dalgleish. 'The question was, what happened next? Craigdale's car was found on the northern shores of Loch Ness days later. The waters were swept, of course, but nothing was ever found. It's over a thousand feet deep down there, did you know that? People assumed he had committed suicide.'

'And what did you think?' asked Camilla, knowing he thought otherwise.

'I never had anything to back up what I'm about to tell you – nothing except a policeman's hunch,' he said with a wry smile. 'But I always got the feeling that his friends knew far more than they were letting on when we interviewed them. The police were called so late, there *had* to have been some sort of cover-up. I believe his friends spirited him away and harboured him for many years afterwards. Possibly they still are doing.'

'What gave you that impression?' asked Venetia, curiously.

'As I said, a policeman's hunch. I took their statements, but I always felt that they were not as upset as they should have been if a close friend had just committed suicide. At first I thought it was just the upper classes keeping a stiff upper lip, but it just nagged at me. Then I found out that some of Craigdale's friends owed him a great deal; possibly enough to risk their own reputations to help him.'

'Like what?' asked Venetia.

'Did you know that Philip Watchorn and Craigdale were friends at Oxford? Watchorn didn't come from the wealthy background he pretends to, and Craigdale put him up rent-free when they moved out of college after their first year. He was almost like a benefactor to Watchorn, and you could tell that Watchorn was terribly, terribly grateful. Craigdale was also one of the first investors in Nicholas Charlesworth's club at a time when gambling was considered a risky venture, and he bailed Jimmy Jenkins's business out when it was on the verge of bankruptcy. At the time Craigdale went missing, all three men were powerful, rich, successful and connected. They were all in a strong position to get him out of the country. For me, it felt like it was payback time for Craigdale.'

Camilla and Venetia couldn't help but notice their father had yet to be mentioned, despite being at the heart of Craigdale's social group.

'And our father?' asked Camilla, wondering what he could possibly have owed Alistair Craigdale. Oswald Balcon behaved as if he didn't owe anybody anything.

'Oswald? I'm not sure,' said Dalgleish thoughtfully. 'I got

the impression that he was not as close to Craigdale as the others. Or, more accurately, he had less reason to be in debt to him.'

Venetia had to bite her tongue to prevent herself from telling him that Maggie Balcon had been having an affair with Craigdale.

'Do you think any of this has any bearing on what happened to our father?' she asked.

'Ah, so that's why you're here,' smiled Dalgleish. 'No, I haven't given it a second's thought, to be honest. Didn't your father just slip and fall from your rooftop?'

'He did,' said Camilla briskly. 'It was a terrible accident.'

But Venetia wanted to probe him more. 'Do you think the Craigdale Killing might have *any* relevance today?'

'Relevance?' repeated Dalgleish, frowning. 'Well, it all happened so long ago I'm not sure whether "relevant" is quite the right word to use, my dear. The only impact I think it might have would be on Craigdale's friends. If they really did spirit him away, and if they were ever found out . . . Well, men that rich, that important, they don't want ghosts that big to come back and haunt them.'

The shrill ring of her mobile roused Serena from a light afternoon sleep.

'Yes?' she asked sleepily, pulling back the cashmere throw she was curled under.

'It's Michael,' said the voice.

Serena sighed softly. She'd been trying to blot out his dramatic reappearance at the party, knowing she should turn him down flat, but not being quite able to deal with it at the present moment.

'What do you want?' She didn't mean it to sound rude, but she was not in the mood.

'A car is going to arrive at Huntsford in about twenty

minutes. I want you to get in it and come and meet me.'

'Michael, please. I am eight months pregnant. I'm exhausted . . .'

'Come on, Serena, I think you'll like it.'

She opened her eyes, curiosity jolting her awake. 'What's the *it*?'

'Just get in the car and I'll show you.'

They were heading to London, that much was clear, although the driver of the Mercedes had been unwilling to tell her precisely where she was to meet Michael. Serena sat back in the supple leather seat, smoothing the lines of her dark jersey dress. She had dressed with a nod to a funeral dress code, in case she was spotted by paparazzi. Ebony sheared mink shrug, charcoal Chanel quilt bag, black pearl earrings in her lobes, hair scooped up and held in a mother-of-pearl clip. She looked good, but she still felt tired. Daylight was draining from the sky and rose-pink clouds hovered above. Then motorway became surburb as they turned along the banks of the Thames.

'Almost there now, Miss,' said the driver.

Where are we going? thought Serena, looking out of the smoke-tinted window.

The car parked outside an expensive-looking apartment block overlooking Chelsea Harbour, the front made almost totally out of glass. Serena had been vaguely aware of the prestigious development while it was being built. Discreet, secure, exclusive, it was now home to numerous celebrities and London's super-rich. The driver punched a security code into the door and motioned her inside.

'Top floor,' he told her.

Not one to waste words, smiled Serena to herself as she got into the silver lift. The door hissed open onto a large lobby with chocolate-leather-lined walls. A door at the far side of the lobby was slightly ajar, and Serena pushed it gently, walking into a huge living space. It was a shell – devoid of furniture – but what a shell! Thick oyster-coloured carpets, big walnut doors, a vast open-plan kitchen in cream and chrome, and a bank of floor-to-ceiling windows that gave a splendid view of the river and the skyline of Chelsea. Hearing footsteps behind her, she turned to see Michael in a dark grey suit holding two flutes of champagne.

'Do you like it?'

'It's fantastic,' said Serena, still looking around to take in every detail. The apartment occupied the entire width of the building and, from the look of the spiral stairs in the corner, it was a duplex.

'It's yours,' said Michael.

Serena's pulse quickened. 'Mine?'

'Well,' replied Michael, putting down the flutes on the kitchen top and striding over to embrace her. 'It's yours if you marry me.'

Serena caught her breath. She should have guessed. Michael was used to getting whatever he wanted in business and in life. She hadn't said yes to his marriage proposal at the party, and this was his way of upping his offer.

'Michael,' she said softly, shaking her head. 'You can't bribe me into marrying you. It's a massive decision and we have to do the best thing for our baby.'

'This is not a bribe, it's a wedding present,' said Michael, sweeping his arms expansively round the apartment. 'I know you weren't really happy in New York, so I thought we could live here for part of the year. I want to expand my European operations anyway. Serena, we can make it work.' He brought his arms back around her, his hands skimming over the curves of her body, sending shocks of desire through her.

Although she had tried to ignore the thought of Michael's

561

proposal over the last few days, it was an idea that refused to be suppressed. It had been a foul year for her, and for months she had blamed it all on Michael. But she was nothing if not practical, and she knew that if Michael had been the reason for all her problems – splitting with Tom, the unplanned pregnancy, the failing career, he could also be the solution. The roaring anger she had felt after Cannes had slowly dimmed and been replaced by something else: fear. The thought that her life could continue on the same downwards trajectory terrified her. Serena wanted to be someone, not a no one. She could not face living in the cold.

Michael pulled her head into his shoulder. He smelt good: like lime and musk.

'Come on, Serena. The chopper is at Battersea heliport. We can take the jet out to Vegas. Let's do it now,' he said, squeezing her hands.

'Michael, my father has just died,' said Serena, gently pulling away to look into his dark eyes. 'The funeral is in a week. And, anyway, I still need to think about it.'

'Let's just do it,' he repeated. 'Oswald is dead, but don't let that stop you living life.'

'Michael, please.'

'Serena, I want you. For ever.' His voice was soft, but had an edge of steel. He was making her an offer she couldn't refuse.

A montage of the images from the past ten months flashed through her mind: Loss, grief, betrayal. She stroked her stomach. *New life*.

'Say yes, Serena.'

She took a deep breath. 'Yes,' she whispered.

Tom Archer picked up the phone again. For the last fifteen minutes he had been hovering by it, picking up the receiver, staring at the dial, then putting it back onto its cradle, unable actually to make the call. He swore under his breath and steeled himself. 'Come on, Tom, come on,' he muttered. He snatched up the telephone and quickly punched in the numbers for Huntsford Castle. He had already tried Serena's mobile, which it seemed was no longer in use. 'Why am I doing this? Why?' he asked himself out loud. Maybe it was Nick's constant badgering at him to call Serena, or maybe Christmas was actually making him soft. Either way, there were a thousand reasons never to make contact with Serena again, and only one reason to do so: because he wanted to hear her voice.

Despite himself, he had followed the story of Oswald's death fanatically since the story broke. The media had gone crazy for the story, chasing their tails with wild theories about suicide, murder and drunken decadence, and Tom wondered how his ex-girlfriend was coping with one more trauma to deal with. Oswald had been a difficult bastard, but Serena had loved him, he knew that much. He paced up and down, the phone to his ear, his stomach flipping as he listened impatiently to the rings. Finally he heard a voice. Mrs Collins.

'Oh, hello there. Is it possible to speak to Serena?'

Mrs Collins' voice was guarded, having spent the last three days fielding calls from the press. 'It's not a good time at the moment. Who is it that's calling?'

'It's Tom. Tom Archer. Hello, Mrs C.'

'Oh Tom. Of course,' said Mrs Collins, delighted to speak to the star again. 'I'm afraid Miss Serena has just left. Some car came to pick her up. You've missed her by a minute.'

'Oh. Do you know when she'll be back?'

'No idea, I'm afraid. But I can leave a message to say you called and I'm sure she'll call back when she can.'

'No. No message,' Tom said. 'But Merry Christmas

anyway.' Tom put the phone down carefully, wondering where and with whom she'd gone, wondering if she would ever bother to return the call. Wondering if he had left it all too late.

The Mercedes snaked back along Cheyne Walk, past the long line of red-brick townhouses, moving at a snail's pace. They'd already detoured via Serena's flat to pick up her passport and a small holdall of things, and Michael was getting impatient.

'Serena, please hurry!' Michael had snapped impatiently as Serena had rifled through her wardrobe. 'We can buy you whatever clothes you want when we get to Vegas.'

Back on the riverfront, the road was unusually busy and it had begun to rain. Michael balled his fist in frustration as the car became caught up in a long queue of traffic. 'Come on, move it,' he snarled.

Serena tilted her head against the window, looking through the spots of rain, and saw with surprise that they had stopped right outside her old Cheyne Walk house. There was light glowing from the front bay, the outline of a Christmas tree, a bushy holly wreath on the front door. It looked warm, lived in, a happy house. *And that's what it had been when she had lived there too*, she thought, a wave of regret suddenly overwhelming her. *Tom Archer*.

From this distance, she could see how things had soured between her and Tom towards the end, how complacent they had become. They'd both taken each other for granted and neglected to keep the fire of their relationship burning. But there had been plenty of good times in that house: reading scripts in bed, croissant crumbs and jam messing the sheets, or just lying together at night, entwined, watching Albert Bridge twinkle. And then there were those legendary cocktail parties, with Tom's terrible margaritas and even worse karaoke. She smiled and wondered where he was now. And with whom. That thought made her nauseous.

The driver swung the car around and began to thread through the traffic, expertly finding a route through the gridlock; ten minutes later they were turning into the heliport. Michael took her arm and led her through a small terminal building and out onto the concrete helipad, where the rotors of the midnight-blue Sarkis Corporation helicopter were already spinning. Michael ran ahead, ducking his head to avoid the down-draught of the blades, and opened the door of the helicopter to speak to the pilot. Serena hesitated and hung back.

'Serena! Come on!' Michael shouted back to her, 'it's time to go!'

'Michael, I . . .'

Sarkis turned back to her, a confident smile on his face. 'Come on, when we get back to New York, we're going to throw a big party,' he said, his voice shouting to be heard above the whirling blast of the blades. 'You're going to love it!'

She stared at his shape against the night sky. His cashmere overcoat flapping in the turbulence, his arm beckoning her over.

'Can we just make terrible margaritas and sing karaoke?' she yelled back, clutching her hands to her head to stop her hair whipping around in the wind.

Michael looked back at her, totally perplexed. 'What? What the hell do you want to do that for?'

'Do you like watching Albert Bridge twinkle?' she yelled, smiling now, a thought of enormous clarity dawning on her.

'Serena, I don't understand you.'

She shook her head, laughing. 'No, I know. You never did, Michael.'

Michael opened the helicopter door. 'Do you just want to get inside?'

'No,' she shouted, moving away from him and pulling her shrug as tightly around her body as she could. 'No, I don't, and I don't think I ever will. Goodbye, Michael.'

And she turned back and ran into the terminal.

While Camilla and Venetia were in Derbyshire, Cate was restless. She was tired from her trip to Paris, but she still wanted to feel useful, to do something – anything – that would help sort out the mess. She did what she always did in times of crisis: work. Recruiting Nick as her research assistant, she drove into London to St Pancras and the modernist monolith of the British Library, convinced that somewhere in its vaults there would be information about the case that would give them a clue on where to go next.

After three hours of searching through books, papers and magazines, however, Cate felt they were going nowhere fast. There had been very little in all the thousands of words written about the Craigdale Killing that they didn't already know.

'There's nothing, is there?' said Nick, rubbing his eyes, blurry from staring at the microfiche screen. 'Want to get lunch?'

'I suppose so.'

Cate felt her mobile vibrate in her pocket and held up a finger to Nick. 'One minute,' she mouthed, realizing that mobile-phone conversations probably wouldn't go down too well in the British Library.

'Hi Van,' she said, moving into the foyer to talk. 'How's Derbyshire?'

'Interesting,' said Venetia down the line. 'Jim Dalgleish, the policeman who was in charge of the case, doesn't believe Alistair Craigdale killed himself at all. He thinks his friends helped him escape out of the country and that they have been hiding him ever since.'

'Who would hide him all this time?' said Cate incredulously.

'Philip Watchorn, Nicholas Charlesworth, Jimmy Jenkins. Maybe even Daddy. If Dalgleish is right and Craigdale is still alive, he could easily have killed Daddy and disappeared again!'

Cate wasn't so sure. The theory of Alistair coming back from the dead had been buzzing around her head since she'd visited Aunt Sarah's apartment. But why would he come back after thirty years?

Because he missed England, thought Cate suddenly.

Random pieces of thought started slotting together. Obviously Craigdale's exile would have suited Lord Balcon, but why would Craigdale stay away for so long? His home, his family were here. After all this time, he could easily have returned to the UK and lived quietly among friends. But only if those friends cooperated. Oswald would have known if Craigdale was back. He hated Craigdale: it would be just like him to hold a lifelong grudge. He could have caused all sorts of trouble. Looking at it that way, Oswald was the only man standing between Craigdale and a return to his life in England.

Cate hung up from Venetia and found Nick waiting for her.

'Ready for lunch?' he said, pulling on his coat. 'I'm starving.'

'No, come on, we're going back inside,' said Cate, pulling his sleeve. She steered him into a small alcove.

'Where are you taking me?' said Nick with an amused smile.

'Inspector Dalgleish thinks that Craigdale was put into hiding by his friends.' She had an earnest, concentrated expression that made Nick smile. 'That tallies with what Aunt Sarah was saying about my mother getting a letter from Craigdale from Belize.'

'Go on,' said Nick.

'It was just that . . .' she paused, unsure of herself now. ' . . . It's just something Jennifer Watchorn said to me earlier this year. I was talking about doing a fashion shoot in Costa Rica and Jennifer was raving about how beautiful Central America was. It was as if she'd been there. I'm sure I read something in an old magazine years ago . . .' She trailed off, shaking her head, and started to pull Nick up the staircase.

'Philip and Jennifer got married about thirty-five years ago. Let's go and check out all the society mags from the time. I bet they were interviewed. I know I've read something about it,' she muttered.

'So what magazines are we looking for, then?' called Nick, trotting to keep up as Cate strode off.

'*Tatler*; it was called *The Tatler* then. *Debutante, Talk*, all those. Don't you know anything about magazines?' she smiled.

'But what are we looking for?' he whispered as they found a corner in the research room.

'See if you can find anything at all about Philip or Jennifer Watchorn: profiles, news pieces, interviews. I know it's in here somewhere. I just know it.'

Her fingers stopped at page eighty-four in an ancient *Talk* magazine. It was only a single-page interview, but that figured: Philip Watchorn was just a London mover and shaker in those days, not the international player he was to become. Jennifer Watchorn smiled out of the picture in a taffeta gown, blonde hair swept up into a tall beehive. She was terribly beautiful in her day, thought Cate, considering Jennifer's tight, face-lifted appearance now.

The interview was short, but boastful and indiscreet. Here was someone who could not believe her luck at having made the jump from air stewardess to society wife in twelve months: she was bursting to tell the world about it. Cate's finger ran down the text as she read on. The interview was all about Jennifer's forthcoming marriage to 'handsome financier' Philip Watchorn. The dress by Ossie Clark, the reception at the Savoy, the honeymoon travelling around Central America. She read the quote, her hand running slowly under each word. 'We are spending a week at the lodge my fiancé has recently bought in Belize. It's remote and wild and beautiful.'

'Bingo!' whispered Cate.

49

Philip Watchorn's New Year's Eve party was like the city leg of Oswald's Christmas ball. Held at Philip's enormous mansion on the edge of Hampstead Heath, the party attracted a similar crowd: country aristos and slick corporate players along with his wife's society crowd, foreign princesses, middle-aged former models and charity-circuit veterans. The house was vast, white and Georgian, the heath stretching out behind like a thick black carpet; its windows glowed amber as Serena's Aston Martin pulled up at the black double gates. The front of the house was a hive of activity, with tumblers and fire-eaters dancing around a huge fir tree on the front lawn, while valet parkers rushed to spirit away a procession of expensive prestige cars and to help their plump owners in through the doors.

'Tell me again why we're not just phoning up Philip Watchorn and asking him what he knows?' asked Serena, adjusting the straps of her silk dress. The theme of this year's party was white, and Serena had taken the opportunity to make sure she looked like a snow queen, complete with long ivory gown and polar white fur shrug.

'Oh, yes,' said Cate cynically. 'Let's just call him up and

ask if he smuggled Craigdale to Central America thirty years ago. Oh, and by the way, have you seen him recently? Perhaps killing our father? Yes, *surely* he'll say "yes".'

The truth was, Cate wasn't exactly sure what had compelled her to come to the party or what it would achieve. It was less to do with what Dalgleish had called his 'policeman's hunch', and more to do with a desire to feel that at least they were doing something. She'd cooked up plenty of theories, but she still didn't even know for sure whether the Craigdale Killing was related to Oswald's death. However, it certainly felt like an avenue that had to be explored, especially with their meeting with David Loftus scheduled for the next day.

Two security guards on the door instantly recognized Serena, and the two sisters were ushered inside, where crowds were circling a vast champagne fountain made from hundreds of bowls of champagne and waiters in white tails topped up everyone's glasses with Krug.

'So, now we're here, what do you suggest we do?' asked Serena like an impatient child. 'If you ask me, we're wasting our time. Bloody Maria is the person we should be talking to. Don't you think it's strange we haven't heard a peep from her? Not the actions of a grieving widow, I'm telling you.'

'Look,' said Cate flatly, a little tired with Serena's obssession with Maria. 'We probably are wasting our time here, but let's have a little look around, shall we? I don't know what for. Maybe we'll know when we see it.'

'Ah, so we're here to snoop? I love a snoop,' smiled Serena. 'And who's going to suspect a pregnant woman on the prowl?'

Most of the rooms were open to guests, and everywhere glamorous people dressed in white were milling around, eating canapés, laughing and chatting to the sound of clinking glasses.

'Talking of which, the pregnant woman needs the bathroom. Again,' said Serena, as they wandered into the ballroom where a swing band was playing.

'I'll see you back here,' said Cate, her eyes scanning the room.

A few people recognized her and stopped to offer their condolences. She picked up a cocktail, a White Russian she thought, tasting its creaminess, and moved to a set of doors opening onto a terrace.

'Catherine Balcon, is that you? What a pleasant surprise.'

Cate turned to see Jennifer Watchorn dressed in the palest silver taffeta gown, enormous diamonds dangling from her ear lobes. She embraced Cate and kissed her on both cheeks as Cate inhaled the smell of heavy foundation and a rose scent.

'I'm so sorry about everything,' said Jennifer sadly, 'I really didn't think you'd be able to make it.'

Cate smiled weakly, thinking how odd their attendance must look.

Jennifer waved her hands around at the party. 'I insisted we carry on and have the party tonight,' said Jennifer, looking a little guilty and embarrassed. 'Philip was against it, naturally, Oswald being one of his closest friends and all, but I really thought the show must go on.'

'I'm sure that's what my father would have wanted,' said Cate politely.

Jennifer led Cate out onto the terrace, where red berry fairy lights cast a scarlet glow onto the stones. Jennifer linked one arm through Cate's and, with the other, lifted her glass to take a sip of Krug.

'You must tell me if you need *anything* at all. I'm here to help you.'

Cate knew it was time to strike.

'Well, I'm just trying to keep busy,' she said. 'Work and

572

so on. After the funeral, I'll be going on a photo-shoot,' she lied. 'We're going to Belize to shoot the cover. Haven't you been there?'

Jennifer looked distracted as her eyes scanned the party guests. 'Where? Oh. Yes, dear. Years ago, though. Before you were even born, I think. Philip had a lodge there, but he sold it years back. I never actually went there, Philip said it was far too isolated. Anyway, I much prefer the scene in Mexico.'

'But when you were in Belize –'

Jennifer grabbed her suddenly by the arm, her mind racing off on another train of thought. 'Now I don't know who you're here with,' said Jennifer conspiratorially, 'but you'll never guess who's come tonight as a guest of my dear friends Dickie and Ann Browning.'

'Who?' asked Cate, disappointed at the lack of information Jennifer had revealed.

'Tom Archer!' she said, smiling triumphantly. 'Why don't you go and find him? We have a whole mini-fairground out there.' And she was gone.

Camilla pulled her Audi up outside Maria Dante's Onslow Square home and peered up at the arched windows for any signs of life. She knew she should have called before descending unannounced, but she had come here on impulse, having driven through the square on her way to Venetia's house.

She looked at the windows again and conceded that this wasn't the only route to Venetia's. She had wanted to see Maria. James Willoughby, the family solicitor, had called Camilla up earlier in the day to beg her to stop Maria hassling him on the phone, asking to know about Oswald's will. 'She's called me three times demanding to know when the will is going to be read,' said the lawyer, trying to be polite but clearly annoyed at being interrupted on his Christmas

break. 'I tried to explain to her that I would inform all bene-
ficiaries after the funeral, but she wouldn't hear of it. I think
someone should have a word.'

When Camilla turned off the car engine, Onslow Square
was in silence. Through glowing windows around the square,
she could make out people raising glasses and throwing their
heads back with laughter. *Happy New Year*, she thought.
quietly wondering what the New Year had in store for her.
She shuddered, despite the warmth of her cream cashmere
coat, and ran up the small flight of stairs to Maria's door,
knocking on it sharply. Camilla had always felt ambivalent
about Maria Dante, not really caring how or with whom
her father found happiness. But hearing about Maria snooping around her father's will, Camilla had been surprised just
how protective she had suddenly felt towards the family –
even her father.

The door creaked open and a tall, slim man of about forty-
five, with a grey crop of hair and a sombre, pinched
expression, answered the door. Camilla looked down to see
bare hairy legs poking out from a knee-length silk dressing
gown.

'Can I help you?'

For a second Camilla wondered if she had the right address.
'I'm looking for Maria Dante,' she said, craning her head to
look into the hall.

She saw a figure coming down the stairs, unfolding into
view like a concertina. First the feet, knees, black curtains
of hair falling onto shoulders, a face . . . Maria Dante.

'Jean-Paul? Who's there? Camilla!'

Camilla took a step into the house. 'Maria, I'm sorry, I . . .'

As she walked forward, she saw that Maria was standing
in a short red kimono that barely covered her thighs. She
looked pallid. Washed out. For a second, Camilla thought it
was the face of grief, until she realized she was simply not

wearing her heavy make-up. It was the face of someone who had just got out of bed, the flush of her cheeks against her pale skin a telltale sign of sex.

'Who's this Maria – housekeeping?' said Camilla, jabbing a finger at Jean-Paul, who inched away from her, backing up the stairs.

'What are you suggesting?' snapped Maria, looking flustered. 'Jean-Paul is a friend from Paris. My new interior designer now that Venetia is so busy with her fashion.'

Her arrogance lit Camilla's fuse. She stepped closer to Maria, glaring ferociously, daring her to continue the pretence.

Realizing she'd been found out, Maria exhaled dramatically, her wounded expression changing instantly into something more aggressive. 'I suppose you're loving this, Camilla. Seeing me and Jean-Paul,' she hissed. 'Well, I'm sorry. I'm sorry you've found me like this, but life goes on. Oswald is dead.'

'My father, your fiancé, has *just died*! How can you sleep with your decorator when your fiancé has just died?'

'He'd have done the same,' whispered Maria, her jet-black eyes blazing at Camilla. 'You and your sisters, you've been dying to catch me out for something from the second we met. I loved your father, but all you wanted to do was to sabotage our relationship from the start.'

Camilla felt a burst of anger.

'Let's talk sabotage, shall we?' spat Camilla, moving closer towards Maria. 'The huge fee you conned my father into paying you for the Musical Evening. The cocaine you planted in Serena's suitcase. The reporter you sent snooping in her room. And, while we're talking subterfuge, how long have you been sleeping with Jean-Paul? I'd say weeks, months, rather than days, wouldn't you? You didn't love Oswald, Maria. You loved what you thought he had.'

Maria had a tough hide, but she was not prepared for the ferocity of Camilla's attack. She clutched her arms defensively around herself. 'Do you blame me?' She lifted an eyebrow to challenge her. 'You know what he was like.'

'Yes, I do,' said Camilla more calmly. 'I know exactly what he was like.'

She fixed the woman who was so nearly her stepmother with a look of pure contempt. 'And now I know just what you're like. You're a devious, manipulating, power-hungry bitch who's betrayed my father and betrayed my family. I know I speak for my sisters when I say that we don't ever want to see or hear from you again.'

'Finished?' asked Maria coldly, not meeting the younger woman's gaze.

'No,' replied Camilla, trying to catch her eye. 'Tonight I actually came to talk to you about the will, but I won't bother. Because if you even *think* about trying to take my family for every penny you mistakenly think is owed to you, I swear that I will ruin you. I will drag you so long and so hard through the courts that you won't be able to afford a paintbrush, let alone the services of Jean-Paul.'

And with a look of pity directed towards the man in the dressing gown, Camilla turned on her kitten heel and walked back into the square. As the door slammed shut, she was sure she heard a scream.

Philip Watchorn's house really was spectacular, thought Serena, wandering away from the main thoroughfare of the house. Personally, she wouldn't have thought of living in Hampstead; it was too far north of the Thames for her. But this house really was as chic and grand as some old embassy from a fifties film. It was less stuffy than Huntsford, more cosmopolitan, more her. She licked her lips at the prospect of owning a house this large, tasting the watermelon gloss which she had slicked on during her visit to the bathroom. While she was in this wing of the house, she might as well look for a library or a study or something, she thought, taking a left down a quiet corridor.

Not all of the rooms at this end of the house were open. Serena tried two door handles: one was locked, one led to a dining room. With the lights switched off, the mahogany furniture cast spooky shadows in the darkness. She closed the door quietly and wandered further and further, her heels tip-tapping on the black-and-white marble floor. She turned a corner and saw a single door on her left. As it creaked open, she could see the walls were lined from floor to ceiling with heavy leather-bound books. The library. Looking up and down the corridor to check no one was around, she crept inside, shutting the door behind her.

Not having a clue what she was looking for, she tiptoed towards a big black leather-topped desk. It was ordered and tidy. There was a gold clock: Asprey, she noted. A crystal paperweight, a silver letter-opener, sheets of paper and a pile of post, some opened. The heavy Lalique desk lamp was asking to be flipped on, but she decided it was better to stay in the darkness and use the chink of light coming through the crack in the door to see. She felt like a member of the Famous Five.

Serena flipped her fingers through the post, bending low to read a few lines. Grateful letters to Philip from charities, correspondence from Coutts bank, other letters from banks in the Cayman Islands, Geneva and Jersey. She scanned them all, but there was nothing too interesting. In fact there was little she really understood. Pulling at the desk drawers, she found one locked, the others full of more papers and a pile of envelopes. Suddenly she stopped as she recognized a postmark on a large envelope: Huntsford. The handwriting was unmistakable: exaggerated initials, long loops in black ink. It was her father's.

It wouldn't hurt to look, Serena thought, pulling out a sheaf of papers. It was a contract, only three or four sheets long, unsigned and undated, between Oswald Balcon, Nicholas Charlesworth and Philip Watchorn, collectively acting as BWC Holdings, but, beyond that, it was all Greek to her. Serena scanned the words but kept getting lost: why did they insist on using such archaic language? She wished Camilla was here: her legal brain would decipher this in a second. Apparently, it was a 'transfer document' and, as far as she could tell, BWC were transferring something to Oswald. She re-read it more slowly, working it out like a puzzle. Daddy, it seemed, wanted Nicholas and Philip to transfer their shareholdings in Fierce Temper to him for the sum of one pound. She held the papers up, her eyes trying to focus in the dim light. She knew enough about contracts from her dealings with agents to know that one pound was the nominal amount needed to make a contract valid, but she was still puzzled. If she was right, Philip and Nicholas were giving Fierce Temper away to Daddy for nothing – but that couldn't be: the horse had had a brilliant season. She didn't know much about racing, but even she realized that, having won four major races in a season, Fierce Temper must be worth a fortune. So why give him away? Why? Because they *had* to, was all she could reason. Was Oswald *making* them? Was that it?

Suddenly she felt on edge, standing here in the dark, holding something she felt sure was significant. She had to get out, to show it to Cate. The contract wouldn't fit in her tiny clutch bag, so she stuffed it under her arm then glanced at her watch. Shit! Cate must be wondering what had happened to her. Making for the door, Serena froze. She could hear two low voices chatting as they walked into the room. Instinctively she ducked down behind the desk. Her belly was too big to fit into the kneehole between the drawers so she sat down awkwardly on the floor. She could hear Philip Watchorn and Nicholas Charlesworth quite clearly now.

'You must try this excellent cognac,' said Philip to Nicholas, 'it's an eighteen seventy-three. I bought it at auction a couple of years ago. I reckon we ought to toast ourselves, don't you?'

She could hear the clink of crystal tumblers.

'I'd prefer that eighteen forty-seven claret I know you've got in the cellar,' said Nicholas.

Serena didn't need to see the two men to know they were in high spirits. They were pacing around the study now and she could feel her hands becoming moist. Her legs were beginning to cramp as she crouched down on the floor, praying that they would not come near the desk.

'Did you see that Serena and Cate Balcon are here?' said Nicholas, his voice piqued and anxious.

'I know,' said Philip, clearly not pleased to see them either. 'I certainly don't remember inviting them.'

'So why the hell are they here?' snapped Nicholas. 'Shouldn't they be mourning rather than partying? You don't think they know something, do you?'

'Relax. Serena loves a party, whatever the weather.'

Serena could almost see the smirk on Philip's face. Nicholas was not to be placated, however. 'But Cate's more canny. If Cate is here, maybe they suspect something,' he said.

'Suspect what?' said Philip, his voice lowering considerably. 'Poor Oswald's just had a nasty little accident. What's that to do with us?'

'Yes, I suppose . . .' said Nicholas, sounding much less confident than his friend. 'Have the police spoken to you yet?'

'Yes, yes,' replied Philip dismissively. 'I simply told them everything we'd agreed. I can assure you the police are merely going through the motions. There really is nothing to make them believe that this is anything other than Oswald getting pie-eyed and falling from the rooftop. Anyway, the snow would have contaminated any evidence. God bless the bumbling bobby and God bless the English weather.' He sneered.

Underneath the desk, Serena's mouth had dropped open. Nicholas did not need to spell it out. *They* had pushed Oswald from the ramparts. They had killed her father. Feeling the Fierce Temper contract under her arm, she suddenly thought of David Loftus. Was it blackmail? Was Oswald blackmailing Philip and Nicholas? Finally, she heard the tumblers being put down and footsteps walking across the room towards the door. Thank God, thank God. Her leg had gone numb with cramp under the weight of her pregnant body. She tried to shift it slightly and, as she did so, the heel of her shoe slipped, sending her foot to the floor with a muffled thump.

'What was that?' asked Philip. Hearing footsteps move back into the room, Serena twisted her body until her bottom was on the floor, hanging her head between her knees. She didn't need to look up to know that the two figures were looming over her.

'Serena Balcon! What on earth are you doing?' growled Philip. His mouth was smiling, but his eyes were deadly serious. Nicholas grabbed her arm and pulled her to her feet. She slumped down in the leather chair behind the desk, Nicholas's hand lingering on her arm, squeezing the flesh a little too hard.

'What are you doing here?' he demanded, his eyes wild.

Serena tried to smile confidently, even though her hands were as clammy as glue. 'Oh, you know what it's like, being pregnant and all,' she stammered. 'I really shouldn't have come partying. I felt terrible, so I came to find somewhere dark and quiet to sit down for a moment.'

Philip simply nodded. 'On the floor. Behind a desk.'

'Serena, what are you doing here?' said Nicholas, shaking her arm. There was a flutter as the contract dropped to the floor. Philip stooped to pick it up and showed it to his friend, exchanging a cold, knowing look.

Serena tried to rise to her feet, but was suddenly aware of a taut pain on either side of her abdomen. She sat down again. Putting her head between her knees, she closed her eyes for a second. Suddenly the situation seemed crystal clear to her. She lifted her head and looked up at the two men, then at the contract, and the pieces suddenly slotted together. Craigdale had been harboured at Watchorn's Central American house. Oswald knew about it, perhaps even helped. Oswald now needed money. He was blackmailing them. Oswald was offering his silence in return for Fierce Temper. Clearly Philip and Nicholas weren't in the mood just to hand over a multimillion-dollar horse, so they had killed him. They had killed Daddy.

Venetia looked around the library of her Kensington Park Gardens home, sinking back into her favourite leather club chair, and decided that, however fabulous the property was, it just had to be put on the market. To her, the house had the same atmosphere as Huntsford: it was cold, empty and lonely, just more expensively decorated. In the New Year, she was definitely going to downsize. Her home, her life, her ambitions. She was going to expect less because what had this year shown her? That disappointment and betrayal lurked everywhere. From her husband, her father, her body – which had denied her the right to have children; even from a man she had once loved: Luke. Everything she'd had, wanted or needed had been taken away.

And then there was Jack. She'd been the architect of that failure herself, she accepted, but it didn't make her feel any less mournful. She poured herself a vodka from the bottle beside her. After Oswald had virtually evicted Jack from the ball, she had run away, unable to handle the conflict between the two men. She had felt as if she was being asked to choose between her lover or her family, and she had let Jack leave. By the time she had rejoined the party, Jack had gone, and with it, she thought, his part in her life once more. She took a slug of vodka; fate had obviously decided that their relationship was not to be.

And now, what did the New Year hold? First, they would have to deal with David Loftus. She groaned. They were due to meet him again tomorrow and she had no idea where that conversation would lead. Camilla was due any minute; she hoped that she had some bright ideas although, after the revelations of Leonard Graham's letter, Camilla had even bigger worries herself.

In the distance she could hear a tapping on the front door. She looked at her watch and cursed. She'd invited Camilla for supper and the monkfish fillets were still in their Harrod's Food Hall packaging.

'Hang on, Cam. I'm coming,' she called as she opened the door. Standing in the cold was a figure that made Venetia's heart leap.

'Jack!'

Although she was afraid, Serena was defiant. She knew she was in a dangerous situation, but rage had quickly overcome her fear and she looked up ferociously at Philip and Nicholas.

'It wasn't an accident, was it?' she hissed, thinking of her father's body lying sodden and lifeless in the Huntsford moat. 'It's the horse,' she said, her voice trembling. 'It's all about the bloody horse, isn't it? It's all about money!' she spat.

Philip grabbed her face. His grip was tight, menacing. His lips parted to speak, but Nicholas spoke first.

'Your father was always so bloody arrogant!' he said, 'but so spineless with it. Rather than face up to his debts and dig himself out of his hole, he chose to try and extort what was rightfully ours.'

Philip touched Nicholas on the arm to stop him, but Charlesworth was in full flow, as if a vent had been ripped in his chilly armour.

'When it suited him, he was happy to have us on side. *Oh yes*, happy to let us take Alistair out of the country so he could keep his hands clean. See? Spineless,' he laughed cruelly. 'And then, he takes the high ground and threatens to tell Scotland Yard unless we give him Fierce Temper. Well, we weren't going to do that, were we?'

'Where's Alistair Craigdale now?' whispered Serena.

Nicholas shook his head in a small, deliberate gesture.

'Craigdale died years ago. Just as well,' he smiled callously. 'He was becoming a terrible drain. With dear Alistair dead and Jimmy Jenkins on the way, your father was the only one who knew what happened. Now we can put it all behind us.'

'But how *could* you?' said Serena, her voice low and quiet. 'You were friends . . .'

Philip, who had been silent until this moment, finally spoke. 'It was an accident,' he said resolutely. He put his hand on Serena's shoulder and began pressing it gently into the arm of the leather chair. 'We were up on the ramparts discussing the transaction. Somewhere quiet, where we could think,' he said, as if explaining something obvious to a child.

'Don't talk rubbish!' spat Serena. 'Why take him up on the ramparts to talk?'

'Believe what you wish,' said Philip dismissively, 'it doesn't make any difference to us what you think. Oswald was

583

drunk. I'm sure the toxicology reports will confirm that. He simply slipped. No one need know anything different.'

'You liar,' said Serena, trying to stop her voice from quavering. She tried to lift herself up from the chair, but Philip applied more pressure to keep her sitting where she was. 'Let me go!' she hissed.

Philip and Nicholas exchanged a look. It was only for a second, but Serena saw it was loaded with danger. She struggled again, terrified now. They had killed one man at least, and maybe they had done away with Craigdale, too, when he had become too much of an inconvenience to them. Who knew what they might do to her? She tried hard to pull herself free, but Philip was a big man and his clutch was like a vice. With his free hand, Philip reached into the pocket of his white dinner jacket and pulled out a mobile phone.

'Dimitri?' said Philip into the telephone, 'I need you in the study as soon as possible.'

Serena felt her heart drop. She had a feeling she was in a lot of trouble.

The view from the terrace was exquisite. There was a huge gazebo-shaped marquee, and surrounding it were vast lawns that twinkled with candy-coloured lights. She could make out several fairground rides with clowns handing out popcorn, hot dogs and toffee-apples. Standing under an outside heater, she could also make out a familiar figure. Tom Archer. He was talking to a group of affluent-looking forty-somethings, but looking a little bored. She tapped the shoulder of his white Armani tuxedo and he turned to give her a surprised smile.

'Cate! What on earth are you doing here?' he said, stepping forward and embracing her warmly. 'Your father . . . I'm so sorry. Did you get the flowers I sent? I've been wanting to call you.'

'Sorry, it's all been so busy, I haven't really been able to take much in,' she said, rather embarrassed that she hadn't had time to read any of the many cards, letters of condolence and flowers that had been sent after her father's death.

Tom looked concerned. 'Shouldn't you be at home?'

'I needed to get out of the house. Anyway,' she said, quickly changing the subject, 'who are you here with?' she asked, nodding towards the group.

'Dickie Browning and his wife.'

Browning was one of Britain's most respected producers, owning the prestigious movie company, Limelight Pictures.

'Remember that script I was writing in Dorset? Well, Dickie's producing and I'm directing it. They insisted I needed a night out,' said Tom with a wry smile. He excused himself from the group and the pair of them walked to a vending trolley lined with light bulbs. A pretty, raven-haired girl dressed as Snow White handed them two cones of popcorn.

'So, who are you here with then?' asked Tom, crunching on a few chunks of fluffy corn.

'Actually,' said Cate slowly, 'Serena . . .'

Tom nodded silently, but she was convinced she could see the hint of a smile. She was sure there was no new woman in Tom's life. If there had been, surely she would have read about it in the gossip columns? There was still hope, thought Cate.

Tom smiled awkwardly. 'I tried to call Serena the other day at Huntsford. She wasn't there.'

'Well, let's go and find her now,' said Cate, looking at her watch. 'She went to the bathroom about half an hour ago.'

'That's Serena,' said Tom, looking visibly more relaxed. 'Come on, lead the way.'

* * *

The man Serena assumed was Dimitri walked into Philip's study minutes later. He had a neck as thick as a tree stump and muscles straining beneath his black suit.

'Who's this?' spat Serena. 'Security?'

'Something like that,' said Philip.

Serena felt her skin prickling with fear. She tried not to look intimidated – there had to be some way she could talk her way out of this situation.

'Look, Philip, Nicholas. I'm sure it was an accident,' she said quickly. 'It's incredibly dangerous up on those ramparts at night. And it was icy.'

'I tell you what, Serena,' said Philip. He slid his arm around her shoulder and moved so close she could smell the sour scent of cognac on his breath. 'Let's not spoil the party with all this talk about Oswald's accident. You go with Dimitri to cool off and we can discuss this another time.'

'I'm not going anywhere with Dimitri,' said Serena, wriggling from Philip's grasp. 'I want to go back to the party.'

'Don't make this difficult,' said Philip. He nodded to Dimitri who grabbed Serena's arm.

'Let me go!'

Dimitri pressed his body against hers and suddenly she could feel a cold, blunt cylinder pressing into her side. Looking down she could see the dull blue-black casing of a gun nuzzled against the white silk of her dress; she felt bile collecting in her throat. She took a breath but the room felt airless.

'Go that way,' said Philip to Dimitri, motioning his head towards the French doors.

'You and Dimitri are going to go for a drive but, as the car is parked on the other side of our little fairground outside, you're going to have to be very good,' said Philip.

Dimitri rammed the barrel of the gun harder into her side and forced Serena to move.

'I'm not going anywhere,' she howled, her eyes blazing at Nicholas.

'But you are,' replied Philip flatly. 'You're going to walk across the fairground without a peep and, if you get a little feisty, then we will find Cate and get her to join our little party too.'

'You do that and I'll kill you,' she snarled, arching her back away from him.

'Start walking,' said Dimitri.

Cate wondered if she should tell Tom the real reason why they were at the party, but decided it was better to leave him totally out of this. As soon as they had found Serena, she would go and have a look around herself. It was only ten o'clock, after all: there was still plenty of time.

Pretty girls – and older women trying to look like pretty girls – stood in the long queues for the many bathrooms scattered around Philip's mansion. But none of them was Serena.

'Where the hell is she?' grumbled Cate, beginning to get a little anxious now.

'She's probably gone home,' laughed Tom. 'She has this terrible habit of sneaking off from parties. Being eight months pregnant can't be much fun, can it? Or maybe she just saw me and decided to scarper.'

Cate looked up at his face, and for one moment her anxiety softened as she realized Tom was quite excited at the prospect of seeing her sister.

The house was vast, with huge rooms and long corridors bookended, Cate noticed, by CCTV cameras. *The security-conscious rich*, thought Cate grimly, wondering who was watching them. As they walked further from the party, they found themselves alone. The rooms were dark and the tap of their heels against the marble floors sent an eerie echo around then.

'Well, she's not going to be down here, is she?' said Tom turning back.

Cate hesitated, then nodded. 'OK. Let's go back outside. I'm sure she'll come to find me,' she said, feeling a mounting sense of unease.

The French doors led into pitch-blackness. Serena wiped the sweat from her palms onto the fabric of her dress as she stepped into the night. They picked up a path that snaked round the side of the house, the noise of the party growing in the background, louder and louder, until they turned the corner and in a burst of light the fairground appeared in front of her. Hordes of people talking, laughing, drinking, dancing. Serena hadn't seen this side of the party yet: the vast back lawns of the house had been transformed into a fairground, an orgy of light and sound. Clowns holding armfuls of balloons added bursts of colour to the stark white of the evening's theme. Despite the night's chill, half the guests were now packed into this open space, making Dimitri's closeness to Serena's body not unusual. People glanced at Serena as she walked by, eager to get a look at the glamorous party-goer, completely unaware that she was being marched through the fairground with a gun in her back. 'Keep smiling,' whispered Dimitri, as passersby did their double-takes.

She pasted a rigid smile on her face, her muscles taut with fear, her eyes frantically scanned the crowds for Cate. Her throat felt blocked when she tried to swallow. She wondered desperately what would happen if she just tried to make a run for it but, feeling the cold circle of metal against the curve of her back, knew she could not outrun a bullet.

'Please, Dimitri. What do you want? Money? Do you know who I am? I'm rich. I can give you however much you want if you let me go,' she whispered, hardly daring to turn her head.

Dimitri pressed his head against the side of hers, so close that she could feel the slight wetness of his lips on her ear lobe.

'Maybe you can give me something later,' he laughed quietly. A shiver of dread crawled over her skin as she felt his hardness push right up against her.

Suddenly she felt a sharp pain in her abdomen. For a second she thought she might have been shot, until she realized that the pain was an internal ache from her womb. She stopped and clutched her side, tears finally welling up behind her eyes.

'Please. My baby.'

Dimitri remained silent, increasing the pressure of the gun on her skin as a reminder of her situation, and pulled her forward.

'Cate, what's wrong? You look a bit pale,' smiled Tom, helping himself to a crab claw from a tray. 'Serena is a grown woman – she's quite able to look after herself at a party.'

Cate knew she had to tell him why her sister had to be found right now. 'We came here for a reason, Tom,' said Cate, stepping out onto the terrace. 'Philip and Nicholas are involved in something . . . Look, it's too long a story to tell you right now, but it would be just like Serena to confront them about it and I think that would be a very, very bad idea.'

'Mixed up in what?' he replied, perplexed.

From the other side of the fairground, Cate could make out a familiar sheet of blonde hair weaving through the crowds. 'There she is,' she said, relieved.

'I told you she'd be all right,' smiled Tom, also spotting the back of Serena's head. His heart felt leaden as his line of vision edged sideways and he saw the tall figure of a man walking so intimately behind her that they had to be lovers.

'Looks like she has company,' he said, turning to Cate with a shrug.

Seeing that they were getting close to the edge of the fair-ground, with Philip's row of cars edging into view, Serena knew that time was running out to do something. Anything. To cry out for help seemed so simple, but the barrel of the gun had locked her into an airtight bubble. She turned her head back as far as she dared to scan the crowd. Light, colour and faces blurred in surreal slow motion as she passed them, until her eyes locked with someone safe and familiar. Tom.

Cate didn't recognize the bulky man pressed up against Serena and immediately sensed something was wrong. Serena had obviously seen Tom and she watched as her sister's eyes flickered along until they locked into her own gaze. Even from a distance, she could see her jaw was tense, her skin pale, her eyes and the small crease of her brow registering one thing – fear.

'Tom, get to her,' said Cate suddenly, pushing him forward.

'What's wrong?'

'Just do it.'

Tom tried to push his way through, but the crowd was thick, and a mass of balloons clouded his line of vision in a sea of pink, yellow and red.

Serena could see Tom moving towards her and she felt a surge of power, her instincts telling her that now was the final second in which she could act. She screamed loudly, the noise shattering and silencing the crowds. She struggled from Dimitri's grasp and pushed against him with all her strength. Thrown off-balance, he grabbed for her, pulling her to the ground as Tom frantically pushed through the solid press of panicking people to reach her. Serena's knees buckled, there was a harsh crack of a firing gun, and then everything went still.

50

'How are you feeling?' said Venetia, stroking Serena's hand as she lay propped up in her hospital bed. As she was also injured as well as in labour, rather than being taken to the Portland where she'd been due to give birth, she'd been taken to the Royal Free Hospital.

'Serena, he's so beautiful,' said Venetia. She gazed warmly at the tiny baby held in her arms, with his shock of brown hair and cross, crumpled pink face. Serena looked down and smiled, the warm, proud, protective smile of a new mother. Her face was tired, exhausted, but still beautiful. She looked so tiny and fragile, not the big movie star, thought Venetia.

Venetia had hardly been able to grasp the situation when Cate had called just before midnight to say that, in the space of only a few short hours, Serena had been kidnapped at gunpoint, and had gone into labour. She had left home immediately and raced across London, a feeling of dread in the pit of her stomach. She had no idea what injuries, if any, Serena had sustained from the ordeal. All she could think about was that she did not want to lose her sister as well as her father, her husband and her lover. Please God, she had prayed, give me this one.

Venetia turned when she heard the sound of soft foot-steps entering Serena's private room. Tom was at the doorway, clutching drinks and magazines from the hospital shop. What a difference a day makes, Venetia thought to herself, as she saw Serena and Tom's eyes lock across the room.

'I'll leave you to it,' she smiled, getting up and giving Tom's arm a squeeze as she passed. Tom smiled at her, grateful for the gesture. Even while he had raced with Cate over to the hospital, following the ambulance's flashing light as it hurtled through the darkness, he had felt an overwhelming sense of awkwardness. After all, what was he in Serena's life any more? Not direct family, not her partner – not even a friend, he thought sadly. But he felt so right being there next to her.

'You're awake,' he smiled softly.

Serena's lips were cracked and dry, but she still managed a wry smile. 'Labour was bloody hard work: don't do it.'

'How's the rest of you?'

'Just a sprained ankle where I fell. It's fine.'

Tom perched awkwardly on the edge of the bed and looked over at the baby. 'Any names yet?'

'I want to see his personality first. I quite like Toby,' smiled Serena, gazing at the cot.

'No showbiz names,' said Tom in a mock-severe tone.

'Elmore will be terribly disappointed,' grinned Serena.

Tom could not believe that this was the same woman he had last seen on the Nile cruiser in February. It was barely a year ago, but she seemed a completely different person. Her body was thin, not the rounded curves of most of the new mums he had seen on his walkabout through the hospital. Although she had clearly been through an ordeal, there was a softness, a fragility about her. It had been a year of hard knocks for Serena and it was starting to show, thought Tom, feeling a powerful desire to try and make things right.

Serena felt his eyes on her. 'You're thinking I look shit, aren't you?' she said, a tremble of panic in her voice. Tom lightly touched her hand. 'Actually I was thinking how it suited you,' he smiled.

'Motherhood suits me? Ewww!' said Serena, a spark of her old self briefly igniting. 'Don't believe everything you read in the papers: I'm not a complete wreck, you know. It hasn't been the best year for me in many ways –' she glanced back to the cot – 'although in many ways it has. And next year I'm going to get everything back on track.'

'But first enjoy your baby, eh?' said Tom softly, feeling his fingers unconsciously stroke hers.

Serena looked up at him. She didn't want to seem tired and useless, not in front of him. 'I can do both,' she insisted. 'Lots of people combine motherhood and a successful career. Look at Catherine Zeta Jones or Julia Roberts.'

Tom grinned at the familiar feistiness that had fired up in her eyes.

'Funny you should say that,' said Tom slowly. 'Since I last saw you, I've been working on a script. It's been green-lighted. Dickie Browning is producing, can you believe it?' he grinned. 'I think there may be a good part for you in it.'

Serena felt her body twitch on the bed. 'Don't feel sorry for me, Tom,' she said, pulling her hand away.

'Ahh, I don't feel sorry for you, Sin. I admire you,' he said matter-of-factly.

Serena felt a pain coming from somewhere in her body. Not a post-natal pain, or one from having a gun barrel forced into her flesh, but the dull ache of her heart. She stared at him sitting by her bedside, so handsome, so concerned, so decent. He wasn't here to judge her or condemn her, to gloat or feel sorry for her. He was here because he cared.

The year seemed to rewind in slow motion as she thought about her time with Michael Sarkis, even her night with David Goldman. Neither of them was half the man Tom was, but she'd rejected him for those milksops – yet all Tom did now was *admire* her. She looked over to the cot where her son was sleeping and she couldn't help but wish it was the three of them sitting in their own home, a family. Tom followed her eyes. 'He's a fine little man,' he said.

'I know,' said Serena weakly, her voice all small and cracked.

Their eyes met and his hand gripped hers a little more firmly. Did he think the same? Could he want the same?

'I won't let you down again,' whispered Tom, his eyes drifting from Serena's face to the baby's thin body. 'I won't let either of you down.'

Cate had spent so long with the police, giving statements and being interviewed, that she had almost missed the birth of her nephew. Camilla had come down to the station and demanded that Cate be released, quoting all sorts of confusing legislation and police charters. Cate suspected that Camilla had been making it up as she went along, but it had worked, and now she was sitting in the hospital's cafeteria on a plastic chair, sipping black coffee, her eyelids feeling like lead.

She hadn't had any sleep in over twenty-four hours, she realized as she looked at her reflection in the glass. She was still wearing her white Ungaro gown from the night before. Sleep, sleep, she needed sleep. As she allowed her eyelids to rest closed for just a few moments, the previous night's events came flooding back. After the shot had rung out, the police had been called immediately. Dimitri had tried to escape in one of Philip's Bentleys, but he had been picked up on the A1 thirty minutes later, bleeding heavily from a gunshot wound in his arm.

Philip and Nicholas had denied everything, but with Serena screaming her accusations about her kidnap and Oswald's murder, they'd been taken down to the police station for questioning. Cate had no idea how seriously the allegations about her father's death were being taken, however. They had to be realistic: short of a confession, murder would be very difficult to prove. Besides, Philip had not exactly confessed to killing Oswald, had he? He had been very careful to insist, 'It was an accident.' Cate snorted. She doubted it. But men like Nicholas and Philip, who were connected, powerful, and rich enough to get the very best lawyers, they were almost certain to slip the noose.

She felt a stab of guilt when she thought once more about Oswald's body lying motionless in the moat. Somehow, after everything that had happened in the last forty-eight hours, his death had slipped from her mind and she felt guilty that she didn't feel a deeper sense of grief. She wasn't sure whether the grief had been delayed by other events, or whether the numbness she felt about Oswald's death inside was a detachment that came from not caring. She did care. Daddy was a bully, he was difficult, he had made her life hell. But he *was* her father. As Cate had cradled Serena's baby in her arms last night, welcoming in a new generation of Balcons, she had realized that family was everything. Despite all they had been through, the four girls still had each other. Nothing – not the secrets, the heartbreak, the tragedy; not even Daddy – could break their bond. That was all that mattered. Cate scrunched the polystyrene coffee cup in her fist and stood up, her creased gown still shimmering in the fluorescent light. It was time to go home.

Jack Kidman was waiting for Venetia outside Serena's room, his eyes like a lifeline across the cold linoleum. When he had turned up at her home the night before, her whole body had melted into a puddle of relief. As they lay together on her bed, he had told her he had understood her actions at the Christmas ball. He hadn't expected her to leave the family party; he had just wanted to go somewhere and cool off. He told her he wanted to be there for her, but that did not necessarily mean being at her side the whole time. Now, in the hospital corridor, he stretched out his hand and pulled her towards him. 'Want to go home?' he asked.

Venetia nodded.

'Kensington or Westbourne Grove?'

Her heart gave a little skip, wondering if she had read too much into the words. 'Do you mean my place or yours?'

The corridor was silent except for the sound of a distant trolley being rattled away by a nurse. 'This year, I think there should be an "ours",' said Jack softly.

Venetia's heart was beginning to race now. 'Ours?'

Jack held her face in his warm hands.

'When you're ready,' he said. 'I know you've just lost your father and your husband, and you have responsibilities to your family, not to mention the business.' He looked awkward and embarrassed as he continued slowly. 'But I wondered, well, I think it's something you should consider . . .'

'What is it, Jack?' she said, a smile pulling at her face.

'Well, as you know the house in Seville is finished, and I was wondering if you'd like to come out there with me?' He searched her face, looking for a flicker of emotion.

'I don't want to move there full time,' he added, 'not yet, anyway. I just thought I would go for the summer this year. Jade, my oldest child, is going to come out to spend her summer holiday there, and I want you to be there, too. I know it's a long way off, but if we plan now . . .'

She looked at him as he babbled nervously, her eyes welling up with tears. Suddenly a new life was unfolding in front of her. She had worked so hard with her business, and she would always feel proud of those achievements, but love, children and companionship was all she really craved, and it was all here in front of her now. Jack's eyes, soft and chocolate brown like a puppy dog's, crinkled up, willing her to say yes. She knew where her priorities lay. The life Jack had always outlined for himself out in Seville was her idea of Utopia: turning the house into an art school, spending the days being creative, cooking with tomatoes or oranges fresh from the garden, running around with Jack's three children. After all, she could still have a family, just a different type of family unit.

'Is that a yes, then?' he asked hopefully.

She pulled him forward to kiss him, a kiss full of hope, promise and passion. And she sighed. 'Oh, it's definitely a yes.'

Camilla's Audi sped down the dual carriageway, past grassy banks and signposts to places she would never visit. Clouds were thick, the sky grey, slowly turning to the dull blue of dusk. Streetlights like big orange orbs passed above her head, drawing a straight line down the road like arrows pointing her to her fate. Driving down the A23 she knew that in about twenty minutes she would be there: her meeting with Inspector Cranbrook. Twice she had turned off the road, prevaricating, torn between a lie and her conscience. But each time her resolve had returned and she had curled back onto the main road to continue her journey. It was time to be strong, to face up to what she had done.

Camilla had always thought that ambition was her driving force, but over the last few days she had realized an even more powerful emotion had taken over. Guilt, morality, a sense of decency – whatever it was, it was even stronger than her will to succeed. Now she was heading south to tell

Cranbrook about the hit-and-run incident eleven years earlier. She knew it would be career suicide. With Oswald and Leonard Graham both dead, the hit-and-run could have died with them. No body, no witnesses, just Leonard Graham's letter. But her sisters and Nick Douglas had read it: how could she let them carry that burden? It wasn't fair to make them shield her for something she had done. She owed it to them, to herself, to confess.

She sighed. This time last year she'd had everything: a career, a rich boyfriend, a beautiful house, money and respect. This time next year she could have nothing. Would she go to prison? Even if she dodged that bullet, she would almost certainly lose her livelihood. The Bar, politics, would all run through her fingers like sand once this information became known. Voices in her head tried one last time to persuade her to turn around to head back to London. But she couldn't. Her car pulled into a car park behind the Sussex Police HQ. She walked to reception and looked nervously at a young blonde female officer behind the desk. The policewoman lifted a telephone beside her and stared impassively back at Camilla.

'Inspector Cranbrook will see you now,' the woman said flatly.

Camilla's eyes were fixed forward, her mouth a deter-mined line, as she walked down the cold, pale corridor. Her hand tightened around Leonard Graham's letter, folded in her pocket. It was time to put things right.

Cate couldn't sleep. Not the plump feather duvet, not the cashmere jogging bottoms, or the stillness of the deserted New Year's Day streets could lull Cate off into a slumber. She might have been physically exhausted, but mentally she couldn't stop processing all the revelations that had unfolded in the last five days. She glanced at the little silver clock on her bedside cabinet: it was 8.10 p.m. Probably not a good idea to try and sleep before she had eaten anything: she remembered that she had only had a cup of coffee all day. She forced herself off the thick mattress and ran downstairs to the kitchen, switching on the Christmas tree lights as she passed through the lounge; they sparkled like pomegranate seeds against the forest green of the fir tree.

As she walked into the kitchen, she kicked off her slippers to treat the soles of her feet to the warmth coming up from the underfloor heating beneath the limestone tiles. She opened the big steel fridge with a gentle pop. Oh dear, she thought: out-of-date chicken, wilted spinach, a box of organic vegetables that looked as if they were about to return to the earth. There wasn't even any milk for a cup of tea. Tutting, she closed the door and went back through to the lounge. She perched on the edge of her brown leather sofa, staring at the Christmas tree lights and baubles, wondering if she could muster up the energy to find a shop that was open.

There was a gentle knock at the door and she got up, pulling her dressing gown around her. Perhaps it would be Camilla. She had urged her sister to go and tell the police about the body, the whole story. She had offered to go with her, but Camilla had refused. It would not have surprised her one bit if Camilla had bottled out of going. She attached the chain to the door and opened it a few inches so she could see the visitor standing on the little cobbled mews street in front of her house.

'Nick!' she said, surprised, opening the door. He stood at the doorway in a pair of dark blue jeans, a black sweater, his long camel overcoat and a blue scarf flipped over one shoulder like a college boy. Under his arms were two large bags that appeared to be stuffed full of groceries.

'If you tell me that's food, I'll kiss you,' grinned Cate, showing him into the lounge.

'You do know your mobile is switched off?' said Nick, pulling off his coat and dumping the bags on the sofa. He looked at her with a mixture of pleasure and concern. 'I couldn't get in touch with you,' he said softly. 'In the end I spoke to Tom. He's at the hospital with Serena, you know?'

Cate smiled back warmly, 'Yes, I know, I'm really pleased about that.'

'Anyway, he told me you had left, so I assumed you had come home. You look knackered.'

'Thanks,' smiled Cate, 'you know how to charm the ladies, don't you?'

'But you are OK?' he said, his eyes deep with concern. 'I wish I had been there with you last night.'

'Don't worry,' she grinned. 'I had Tom with me, the last action hero. I did feel as if I was in *Die Hard* or something.'

She instantly regretted her flippancy, wondering if Nick would think she preferred to be at Tom's side. But Nick was thinking about her, not himself.

'Have you slept?'

She sighed. 'No, not yet.'

He stood and took her by her arm. 'You go upstairs and have a hot bath or a lie-down, whatever. I'm going to cook you the best meal you've ever had,' he grinned.

'Really?' she said, trying to peek into the two grocery bags he had left on the floor. 'What have you managed to rustle up from the corner shop?'

'Mmm, well, you might be surprised, Miss Balcon,' he said teasingly. 'Now go upstairs, I'll give you a shout in about an hour.'

Upstairs, Cate sank back into the cloud-like confines of her duvet, covered her eyes with an arm and groaned softly. Friendship. That's why he was here. Or did he feel *sorry* for her? It all felt so right, she thought sadly: Nick beavering away over a steaming stove, Christmas lights twinkling, Cate

601

pottering about the house. Easy, intimate comfort. It was as if they belonged together, but their kiss on Christmas morning now seemed so long ago. Yes, they had spent hours in each other's company since then, but there had not been a glimmer of anything romantic between them. Far from it. Nick had been a helpful and supportive friend – no more, no less. She thought about them on the brink of a New Year and suddenly she felt sad. They might be spending New Year's Day together this year, albeit out of sympathy on Nick's part, but in twelve months' time it would probably be different. No doubt Nick would find another girlfriend and their closeness would become eroded. She wondered if she should make one last attempt to tell him how she felt, but it all felt hopeless somehow. She had tried so hard at the Christmas Eve party to be charming, seductive, to present herself as a more glamorous sexual thing in front of Nick, but whatever frisson there had been between them had been extinguished the next day as soon as it had ignited. As delicious smells spiralled up the stairs from the kitchen into her bedroom, her eyes fixed sadly on the ceiling. It wasn't fair, it wasn't fair, she thought to herself, as she finally drifted off to sleep.

'It's ready!' shouted Nick, rousing her. Cate took off her dressing gown and pulled on a sheer caramel sweater, shaking her hair loose from its ponytail. *I might as well make some sort of effort*, she thought, checking herself in the mirror.

As she stepped through into the lounge, she found that the whole room was glowing. Her dining table had been exquistitely set with holly, napkins, crystal goblets, and a parade of candles that was casting a glorious warm glow around the room. Nick was standing there with two glasses of champagne, the sleeves of his jumper pushed up to his elbows, a smudge of flour across his cheek. 'What's all this?'

said Cate, not quite believing the transformation, 'I thought you were doing a microwave pizza.'

Nick clinked his glass with Cate's and turned to press play on the stereo, cueing the gentle strains of her favourite Sinatra song.

'I wanted to do this properly,' he mumbled, wiping his cheek so that the flour grains fell off like tiny snowflakes. He suddenly looked awkward and the air between them charged. 'I wasn't sure tonight was the right time, after all you've been through, but . . .' he paused, looking awkward. '. . . But Cate, I couldn't wait any longer.' He moved towards her. 'I wanted to finish what I tried to start on Christmas morning.'

Cate's heart lurched. 'What are you talking about? The right time for what?' she whispered.

'Time to stop being just friends,' he said, pulling her close and planting a soft lingering kiss on her lips. It was familiar but exciting, tender but passionate. She had never tasted a sweeter kiss.

'We should have done that days ago,' she whispered.

Nick's fingers stroked hers. 'No. We should have done that months ago,' he said. 'But after all you told me in Milan –'

'What?' said Cate, jolting her head up in surprise.

'You told me that nothing should happen between us because we worked together.'

'I never said that!' said Cate indignantly. 'If I remember rightly, you said you had a girlfriend, which you did.'

'No, you said . . .' began Nick, a smile breaking out on his face. 'You said . . .' and they both began laughing.

Nick put his hands on her shoulders and looked her directly in the eyes. 'I would have given up Rebecca for you in a second,' he said, stroking her cheek with his thumb. 'You're my best friend, my partner in crime . . .' He stopped and took a small breath. 'You're the woman I love.'

Cate felt a tear trickling down her cheek. 'I love you, too,' she said, looking into his deep hazel eyes.

'Marry me Cate,' he said, his lips coming down onto hers once more, so she could taste the slight fizz of champagne. Sinatra sang in the background, the smell of roast chicken swirled around the room, candlelight crackled. Belonging. Home.

She moved her lips away from his, just enough so she could speak. 'Marry you, Nick Douglas? But we've only just kissed,' she said, her mouth moving into a slow smile.

Nick grabbed her hand and looked at her watch. 'Workaholic, when are we due back in the office?' he teased.

'Not until Monday,' she said, putting her hands around the back of his neck. Nick squeezed her tight, as if he would never let her go.

'Hmm, three days. You know what I call that?' he asked, running his fingers through her hair.

'No,' smiled Cate into his shoulder.

'Plenty of time.'

EPILOGUE

Two hundred people crammed into Huntsford village church for Oswald's funeral. Any passers-by eavesdropping on conversation and condolences about the deceased might have thought they were talking about a saint. Maria and the sisters sat on opposite sides of the church. Serena did the eulogy, dressed in black Chanel, and reduced half the congregation to tears with her poignant melancholy. It was the performance of her life.

The Crown Prosecution Service did not consider there was enough evidence to prosecute Philip Watchorn and Nicholas Charlesworth for the murder of Oswald Balcon. Their footprints were found in the secret tunnel leading to the ramparts, along with Serena's and Maria Dante's, but the rest of the evidence was circumstantial and hearsay. It was simply not strong enough to warrant a long and expensive trial, much to the intense disappointment of the sisters. Watchorn and Charlesworth were, however, found guilty of the kidnap of Serena Balcon; Dimitri Vlodanov testified against them. The CCTV cameras in Philip's home also provided incriminating footage against their owner, the grainy image of whom was seen instructing Dimitri to take Serena away. They both received a twelve-month sentence in an open prison. Stock in Philip's company plummeted, over £100 million being wiped off the share price in a week. The society smart set stopped going to Nicholas's club, which was finally sold to a Saudi Arabian businessman for a bargain-basement price.

Fierce Temper was bought by a wealthy American oil tycoon and, after another successful season, was retired to stud in Ireland. As Oswald predicted, he was in hot and costly demand to sire mares from around the globe. Declan O'Connor was investigated by the Jockey Club for allegations of horse-doping, race-fixing, and links to Hong Kong criminals. Finbar, meanwhile, went on to win the Derby.

Cate had become fixated with the disappearance of Alistair Craigdale, and sent an investigative journalist to Central America to find out what had happened to him. Locals in the Belize village where Watchorn had kept a lodge remembered a man who looked remarkably similar to a photograph of Craigdale. He had a beard, his hair was a different colour, and he went by the name of Andrew McKinney, but everyone was sure it was the same man. The man had disappeared, presumed drowned, fifteen years earlier, when his fishing boat was wrecked in a storm. His body, however, was never found. With the extra evidence, Cate pressed for the Craigdale case to be reopened by the Metropolitan Police and an investigation into the involvement of Philip and Nicholas is still pending. They could yet be charged with further crimes.

Oswald had not made a new will to accommodate Maria and she received nothing. She moved to Paris, where she spent the summer on the arm of a wealthy, twice-married, sixty-nine-year-old comte, who has a vast vineyard in the

Champagne district and a passionate thirst for opera. The French society press are predicting marriage. They call her *La Croqueuse de diamants*.

Venetia returned to Seville with Jack after Cate's wedding, where she spent a perfect summer at the *finca*, painting, swimming and riding horses with Jack's eleven-year-old daughter, Jade. Jack bought Jonathon's shares in Venetia's company from Stefan von Bismarck, for an inflated price. Her New York store opens soon.

Oswald's will bequeathed Huntsford to Serena, who in turn transferred it to Venetia.

'You love that house,' she had told her over lunch at Le Caprice. 'You will do it far more justice than I ever could.' Venetia had wept over her Caesar salad.

Venetia's renovation of Huntsford was stunning, bringing the old house back to life. When they are not in Seville, Jack and Venetia live there. Jack's daughters come on weekends and on holidays. It's open to the public when the couple are in Spain.

Camilla withdrew herself as candidate for Esher amid a flurry of controversy, and took a leave of absence from chambers. For the hit-and-run eleven years earlier, she was charged with, and pleaded guilty to, failure to stop after an accident, and failure to report an accident. The police decided not to proceed with the more serious offence of death by dangerous driving. She received a sentence of one hundred hours of community service. She considers herself lucky. Her life is taking another direction, but everyone who has witnessed her strength, courage and talent knows that, whatever she decides to do next, Camilla Balcon will succeed at it.

Nat Montague married a Scandinavian swimwear model, whom he divorced ten months later.

Camilla reported David Loftus's threats to Inspector Cranbrook during her interview. On police instructions, Cate and Venetia met up with Loftus at Huntsford following New Year's Day. Unaware of the investigation into Watchorn and Charlesworth's involvement in Oswald's murder, Loftus repeated his demands. The library had been wired up, his threats were caught on tape. He was charged with, and pleaded guilty to, attempted blackmail, suffering a nervous breakdown during a twelve-month prison sentence. The book of Oswald's memoirs remains unfinished.

Serena phoned Michael Sarkis on New Year's Day to tell him about the birth of their son and that she was, if he had been in any doubt at Battersea heliport, turning down his offer of marriage. 'Now the kid's been born, the offer's retracted anyway. I only wanted Huntsford,' he had replied spitefully. He did send a hundred-thousand-dollar cheque for their child's christening, which was immediately returned.

Serena's attempted kidnapping hit the headlines everywhere. Her agent and manager in New York, who had gone suspiciously quiet during her pregnancy, were never off the phone. Tom's film, *Campbell*, was a smash hit. Serena got rave reviews, Hollywood finally wanted her and she snagged her US *Vogue* cover – twice. But until Toby, her son, is in school, she has limited herself to two or three projects a year. She is determined to be a good mum and, second time round, a better girlfriend for Tom.

Sand won Magazine of the Year. The Sand Publishing Group

are launching a new glossy women's magazine backed by major City finance. William Walton is still unemployed.

And one hot July day that summer, Cate and Nick got married. The couple insisted on keeping the day as intimate and low-key as possible, with the exception of the £4 million pounds-worth of diamonds that Serena had loaned on the bride's behalf. Not that Cate needed any help to dazzle on her big day as she floated down the aisle of Huntsford village church, stunning in a long, strapless Valentino column of vanilla silk. Venetia gave her away to an emotional Nick Douglas waiting at the altar. Oswald's 1922 Rolls-Royce, open-topped and decked out in white ribbon, took the newly-weds back to Huntsford, where the wedding party enjoyed a sit-down meal of vichyssoise, rack of lamb and sticky-toffee pudding in the Orangery. Everyone spilled out onto the terrace for Pimms and a hog-roast afterwards. Elmore Bryant played a one-hour set on Huntsford's grand piano. Everyone said it was the wedding of the year. David Goldman was not invited.

The title to the barony of Huntsford is held in abeyance pending the production of a legitimate male heir to the estate.

'How do you fancy being the father of a lord?' asked Cate on honeymoon, turning to her new husband on the terrace of their hotel suite in Portofino.

'I'm just a poor boy from Sheffield,' smiled Nick, sipping his Bellini and taking Cate in his arms as they watched a lazy, golden sun slip beneath the horizon.

'You'd better get used to the idea,' grinned Cate, patting the flat stomach that would not remain that way for much longer.

'You're kidding!' He looked at his wife, glowing in the

dusty light, and knew he had never loved her more than at this moment right now.

'Lord Balcon,' she smiled, laying her head on Nick's shoulder. And she knew that everything was going to be all right.

Innocence

Kathleen Tessaro

Love. The greatest temptation of all.

It's a long way from Eden, Ohio to London. Eighteen-year-old Evie leaves her hometown for the first time to come to England and follow her dream of being an actress. With fellow students Imogene and Robbie, she studies drama – and life. Her friendship with the bohemian, outrageous Robbie illuminates her new world. Together, anything is possible.

But then life, and love – in the shape of struggling rock musician Jake Albery – intervene, and everything changes.

Fifteen years later, Evie is a single mother, teaching drama and living with the eccentric Bunny in her house of artistic lodgers. Robbie's gone. And Evie is trying to forget the past and dreams they once shared.

Then an old friendship comes to haunt her – literally. And suddenly everything is possible again …

'This is the 30-plus equivalent of the coming-of-age novel: a coming-awake novel for women who have wasted their 20s on cheap men and rough wine.' *Guardian*

'A warm tale of love, friendship and following your dreams.' *Cosmopolitan*

ISBN 0 00 715145 4

The Devil Wears Prada

Lauren Weisberger

When Andrea first sets foot in the plush Manhattan offices of *Runway* she knows nothing.

She's never heard of the world's most fashionable magazine, or its feared and fawned-over editor, Miranda Priestly. But she's going to be Miranda's assistant, a job millions of girls would die for.

A year later, she knows altogether too much:

That it's a sacking offence to wear anything lower than a three-inch heel to work. But that there's always a fresh pair of Manolos for you in the accessories cupboard.

That Miranda believes Hermés scarves are disposable, and you must keep a life-time supply on hand at all times.

That eight stone is fat.

That you can charge cars, manicures, anything at all to the *Runway* account, but you must never, ever, leave your desk, or let Miranda's coffee get cold.

And that at 3 a.m. on a Sunday, when your boyfriend's dumping you because you're always at work, and your best friend's just been arrested, if Miranda phones, you jump.

Most of all, Andrea knows that Miranda is a monster who makes Cruella de Vil look like a fluffy bunny. But also that this is her big break, and it's going to be worth it in the end. Isn't it?

'Sassy, insightful and sooo *Sex and The City*, you'll be rushing to the bookshop for your copy like it's a half price Prada sale.'

Company

ISBN 0 00 715610 3